Drifting in a Broken Dream

Drifting in a Broken Dream

Elana Rose

JEREZMIN

All the characters in this novel are entirely fictitious.
Any resemblance to actual persons, living or dead,
is entirely coincidental and unintentional.

ISBN 978-0-9563607-0-0

Printed in Great Britain by the
MPG Books Group, Bodmin and King's Lynn

First published in the UK in 2009 by

Jerezmin
9 Hillfoot Road, Romford, Essex RM5 3LP

In loving memory of my parents,
Jack and Nora,
and my beloved son,
Ian,
who passed away well before his time.
God bless you all.

AUTHOR'S NOTE

Whilst mention is made of real bands and performers, in the interest of nostalgia and authenticity, all the characters in this novel are entirely fictitious. Any resemblance to actual persons, living or dead, is entirely coincidental and unintentional.

Chapter One

September 1968
'Let's hear it for Rusty and co!' shouted Reg Bennett. He was a very happy landlord. He'd only had the pub for five months and it had been a brilliant five months. The summer of love had been the previous year but the hippies in this area seemed to be clinging to it. They headed here on Sunday nights to watch their favourite bands and dance to the music. The crowd applauded and the band swung into its first number as Reg went behind the bar. Tonight, Rusty had brought his brother, Ed, and Paddy, his drummer, with him. Ed and Paddy were backup for the Shelltones pop group on their UK tour. This made Reg very happy. Ed was the best way to get an introduction to the band as he was also best friends with the lusty Romany. Romany was well known for his reputation as a stud, and girls flocked to get close to him. Reg gave a broad grin as the hippies made for the bar; he'd employed extra staff tonight and the takings were up already.

At forty-five, Reg felt that the sixties was the best era ever. He pushed his long brown hair out of his eyes and began to serve the public. His deep-set brown eyes scanned Rusty and Ed; they were like chalk and cheese. Rusty was a plump man of about five foot eight with long brown hair that he wore in a pony tail. Ed was a lot younger, and at twenty-three was as blonde as his brother was dark. He wore his hair loose and it reached his shoulders; everyone likened him to a younger version of Tommy Steele.

The girls loved him which made Reg even more delighted as he knew it was only a matter of time before the pub would be heaving with love-struck females.

On stage, Ed surveyed the crowd. Most were decked out in very colourful kaftans while he was wearing pale blue which suited his lean frame. The smell of pot filled the air and Ed was getting quite high just singing on stage. The pub doors opened and he spotted his friend June accompanied by two other people. Hal Perkins was being a gentleman and holding the door open for June and her friend. Hal was a much loved comedian, and just a look at him made you want to burst out laughing. He was short with a round face and a girth to match. He'd been a boxer years ago and had broken his nose which had never mended properly, and his eyes were full of fun.

Ed gazed at June and she waved at him. She was some lady; she'd shared his bed many times and performed with all the experience of her years. She was petite and bubbly with shoulder-length blonde hair, green eyes, full lips and a small nose. She was very slim and her long legs went on forever. Dressed as a flamenco dancer tonight she was turning several heads, including Ed's, until his gaze came to rest on her friend. His mouth went dry and his insides began to churn. He was getting turned on by this newcomer; many girls had had this effect before but never so quickly or intensely. She was clad in the garb of a gypsy girl with tresses of gold that almost reached her waist. Her full red skirt revealed many frothy petticoats, the off-the-shoulder white gypsy top was embroidered and the whole ensemble was completed by a wide black belt that showed off a very slim waist. Ed was fascinated; he had to meet this lady.

After getting some drinks and finding a vacant table, the trio made their way to the dance floor and got jostled to the front of the stage by the heaving throng of dancers. Ed caught the girl's eye and smiled but she didn't return it and carried on dancing. Twenty minutes later she was still dancing, while Hal and June, who had vacated ten minutes earlier, returned as Ed swung into a Small Faces medley. He was transfixed and focused on the girl's face; blue eyes, high cheekbones, a straight nose, classical neck, firm jaw and a full bottom lip that was driving him crazy.

During the intermission, he called June over. 'Who's your friend? She's making me very horny. Do you think I'm in with a chance?' he asked.

'That's Cathy, she's the speciality act this week, she's lovely,' replied June. 'Why not get a pint for our birthday boy and join us? Faint heart never won fair lady.'

Ed grinned, his heart was racing. Moments later he presented Hal with a pint and wished him a happy birthday. He seated himself beside Cathy and his leg brushed against hers. There was no response, but undeterred, Ed said, 'there's a party tomorrow night and June will be pleased to know that the love of her life will be there, amongst the rest of the idiots, and you're all invited.'

June was beaming like the cat that got the cream, and Hal was elated. 'I love parties!' he cried.

June threw her arms around Ed's neck and was all over him like a rash. 'I can't wait to see Mick again,' she said 'my agent had work for me here and I drove him nuts to get this gig on this date. I'm on cloud nine. When my agent mentioned my work schedule here, I smiled and told him that this venue had to be top of my list, so he very kindly cancelled Swansea and gave it to me.'

Ed disentangled himself from June's grasp. 'Cool it, babe,' he said. 'Anyone got a piece of paper so I can write down the address for the party?' June opened her handbag and removed a notebook which she offered to him. He scribbled down the address and gave it back to a radiant June. 'How about some more drinks to celebrate Hal's birthday?'

'A pint,' said Hal.

'Gin and orange,' cried June.

Ed turned to Cathy and gazed at her. 'And how about you, beautiful?' he asked.

Cathy was embarrassed; on stage she'd liked him but sitting beside him she was disturbed. He was arousing feelings in her that had lain dormant for so long. She wished that he'd move away from her, and stammered, 'Er… orange juice.'

Ed got to his feet and walked to the bar with Hal. June was getting over-excited. 'Can't wait till tomorrow,' she sighed. The boys returned minutes later with the drinks, and June sat on Hal's lap singing 'Happy Birthday' to him.

'My life's getting harder now; I think rigor mortis is setting in,' said an inebriated Hal.

Ed took Cathy's hand in his. 'What music do you like?' he asked.

Cathy felt worse now she could feel his eyes boring into her. 'Small Faces, Elvis, Stones, and Dylan,' she answered, trying to maintain her composure.

Rusty shouted from the stage, 'Eden, put those women down and get your arse back up here.'

Ed got to his feet, leaned over Cathy and kissed her on her cheek. 'This next set's for you,' he said.

Returning to the stage he winked at his brother, saying, 'I'm on fire, she's coming home with me tonight.'

'Who?' asked Rusty, adjusting his microphone.

'The gypsy girl, I want her.'

Rusty frowned, how many times had he heard this? As soon as his baby brother had been old enough to talk he'd mastered 'I want' and 'got'. After Rusty had been born his mother had suffered one miscarriage after another, and her health was deteriorating but she continued in her quest for another baby. Once she knew she was pregnant again and that the baby seemed okay she'd been in another world, and ten years after Rusty's birth she was ecstatic to give birth to Ed. He was idolised and spoilt and knew exactly how to get his own way. Rusty took a back seat, as did his father; Ed was the golden child and his mother built her life around him. She'd even given him a special name, Eden, as she told everyone that he was her world and that she would die for him. She said the Garden of Eden was paradise, and that after his birth she was in paradise.

Eden, however, hated his name and insisted that everyone call him Ed. Rusty still called him Eden though, and so did the rest of his family. Rusty's name was Russell but he'd changed it to Rusty because his wife liked it. He was angry though that Ed went through life using the 'I want' with everything. He recalled the time when his mother had bought him a bike for his birthday, and Ed had wanted one too but his mother had told him he'd have to wait. So, Ed had waited until Rusty had gone to school and smashed the bike up. Another time he was given a puppy and Ed had tormented it until it bit him. He'd screamed to his mother and she'd got rid of it. He'd flushed Rusty's goldfish down the toilet too, but Ed was his mother's golden boy so he got away with it. The list was endless. Rusty felt sorry for the gypsy girl; she looked as if she was having fun and not in need of Ed's attention at all. Ed brought him down to earth, saying, 'we're doing mainly Dylan and Small Faces.'

'Why?' asked Rusty.

'She likes 'em and I want her,' replied Ed.

Cathy noticed there was a lot of activity around the stage where Rusty had erected a sign saying 'Tarot readings in the snug'.

A tall young man with a gypsy-like appearance and bulging biceps was now on stage with a small drum. A beautiful girl was also on stage. She was slim, pretty, and looked stoned, and in her hand she held a tambourine. Her waist-long, wavy brown hair went well with her scarlet kaftan and she was covered with bangles and beads. Rusty had a mouth organ. Ed strode to the front of the stage and up to the microphone. 'Okay people,' he said. 'Now it's really a family affair. On the drum is my cousin Eli, and on tambourine is his lovely wife Sky. Fawn and Summer are in the snug with the tarot cards, and if you want to keep my little neices happy, buy something from them. Their smiles alone are worth it. He indicated two little girls with red hair sitting by the stage, both loaded with baskets full of bangles and other baubles. 'Also,' he added, 'we have a birthday boy here tonight, my good friend Hal Perkins, one of our best comedians. I won't tell you how old he is, even though I know. The lovely June may give us a warble or two and there's also the lovely gypsy girl who is something else. She's the speciality act this week and they're all at the cabaret club, so get down there.' He glanced around the room and added, 'any requests, see Rusty.' He then launched into Bob Dylan's *I Don't Believe You*.

Later on, June did sing. She struck a deal with Ed that she would sing two songs if he would duet with her straight after them. He agreed and left the stage making a beeline for Cathy who was still dancing with Hal. Hal turned her around and straight into Ed's arms. 'Thank God,' he said, 'she's killing me.'

Ed held her close, very close. 'Do you want some fresh air?' he asked.

'No' replied Cathy. 'I want to dance.'

'Okay,' said Ed. He was on fire. 'How about later?'

'I'm going to bed,' said Cathy. 'I've travelled up from London today and I'm very tired, but it's Hal's birthday so June and I felt that we had to come out. She's tired too.'

'Tired!' Ed laughed. 'Do you know if I offered to run her to Mick tonight she'd be wide awake.'

'Well why don't you?'

'Can't, he's with someone else tonight. No, she'll be happy at the party tomorrow, then he'll stick with her for the rest of the week till she goes home.'

'She talks about him a lot; I think she's in love with him.'

'Do you believe in love at first sight?'

Cathy giggled. 'No,' she replied, snuggling into his shoulder.

'Neither did I till tonight.'

Cathy sighed, how many times had she heard this? Men

viewed her as on the road and available, but she wasn't. True her life at home was unhappy but she loved her daughter Sandy and missed her so much when she was away. She'd never played around before and wasn't going to start now. Her body was betraying her, however, as she moved with Ed. He was holding her very tightly. He broke her reverie, 'I mean it,' he said, 'I've never felt this way before.'

Cathy laughed. 'You don't even know me.'

'But I want to get to know you,' he said. 'I really do.'

June looked down from the stage; she could sense the heat between these two on the dance floor and smiled. There'd be some heat tomorrow between Mick and her. She concluded her song to a huge round of applause. 'Now,' she said, 'for all you lovers out there, this is for you. It's called *Light My Fire*.' Ed pulled Cathy even closer.

'I can't breathe,' she protested.

'Neither can I,' said Ed, 'what you're doing to me, coupled with all this pot; it's knocking me out. Won't you take pity on me and come outside for some fresh air?'

Cathy shook her head, 'No.'

'Ok,' said Ed, 'I guess it's Romany you want. I can arrange it if you're nice to me.'

Cathy lifted her head and gazed into his eyes. 'I do not,' she said in disgust, 'I can't think of anything worse.'

Ed laughed. 'You don't like him then?'

'Yuck! Can't stand him, too full of himself.'

'He's my best mate, all the girls love him.'

'Well I don't love him, and neither does June.'

Ed was stunned; this was a first. 'What about me then?' he asked.

'That's for me to know and you to find out,' she laughed.

She was feeling very warm and happy. When she looked into Ed's eyes she could see desire but there was something else too, like tenderness. He reminded her a bit of a young Tommy Steele.

He was very hypnotic and tried to kiss her but she averted his face and snuggled back into his shoulder. He was getting to her big time; she was practically orgasmic but she wasn't going to let him know that.

'Eden,' Rusty's voice boomed into the mic.

'Cathy!' cried June, 'you're supposed to light his fire not set light to him.' Ed released Cathy. They hadn't realised that the music had stopped, and had continued dancing.

'Little lady,' chuckled Rusty, 'I don't know what you've done to my brother but I need him up here.'

The whole room cheered and as Ed returned to the stage, an ageing hippy slapped him on the back and uttered, 'well done, man, you've got a beauty there.' His friends all laughed, nudging and winking at each other. Cathy flushed scarlet as Ed joined June in a rendering of Dylan's *It Aint Me Babe*. She headed for Hal; he was surrounded by hippy girls.

'I never knew it would be like this at my time of life,' he said, 'I think it must be something to do with the badge.' June had given him a badge with 'I am fifty and filthy rich' written on it.

Cathy took his hand. 'C'mon,' she said, 'let's dance.' When he stood up she realised he wasn't wearing any trousers. 'What happened?' she asked.

'Dunno,' said Hal, 'one minute they were on and the next minute they were off. I spilt my drink down them and a young lady helped me out of them, haven't seen them since.' They took to the dance floor, causing June to forget her words; she couldn't sing for laughing. Cathy stepped out of one of her petticoats and Hal put it on.

'Hose me down, she might run out of skirts,' shouted Ed from the stage. June was still laughing, the sight of Hal in his Y-fronts imprinted on her mind. The song over, June came off stage. Still laughing, she asked, 'what happened?'

'Ask Hal,' replied Cathy, focusing on Ed who was delivering Dylan's *I Want You* directly at her.

The evening wound down and the tills were overflowing. It had been the best Sunday night yet. The little girls had sold all their trinkets, Hal had found his trousers, June was getting excited thinking about tomorrow, and Cathy was getting tired.

She headed for the ladies', passing June and Ed who were deep in conversation. Most of the hippies were still drinking, and Reg wasn't in a hurry to call time. At the side of the stage were three young attractive girls trying to get Ed's attention. He wasn't really interested, but told them to wait behind and he'd see them later. As Cathy emerged from the ladies,' Ed was waiting. He took her hand and kissed it. 'I'll pick you up tomorrow,' he said, unless you want to wait for me tonight. We can go to the party together.'

Cathy shook her head. 'I don't party,' she said, 'I work, make money, and go home.'

Ed was taken aback 'What?' he said, 'you never party?'

'No, and I don't sleep around either. Tonight was great; I loved your vocals and thank you for including so many Dylan songs. We all had a laugh, but now I'm going back to the club where I'll work all week, go to bed early, and then go back to London.'

'But I was hoping to get to know you,' said Ed, 'We could have a laugh and do whatever you wanted. You would love the party tomorrow; June and Hal are going. I'd look after you.'

Cathy didn't trust him; or herself for that matter, so she declined the offer.

Ed frowned. 'Well, don't I even get a kiss goodbye then?' he asked. Cathy pecked him on the cheek. 'No, you can do better than that,' he said and pulled her in close, forcing his mouth on hers. The room spun, her pulse raced and she struggled with all of her emotions. She was trying to pull away but was locked in his embrace. How she wanted to give in to him but she wasn't going to. She was weakening and found herself kissing him back. Ed released his hold but wasn't prepared for what happened next.

Cathy stepped back and slapped him hard around the face. That hurt and shocked him; it had never ever happened before. He followed at a distance as she headed towards Hal and June. They waved and left for the car park. Suddenly Ed's two nieces came running towards him. They ran to Cathy, offering her an assortment of bangles.

'These are for you,' said the smallest girl. 'Eden picked out all the best ones for you.' Cathy bent down and kissed both of them.

'Thank you,' she said. The girls giggled and hugged her.

An angry Ed, having regained his composure, appeared in the doorway of the pub. 'C'mon girls,' he said, 'your mother and Summer have finished in the snug and they're waiting for you.' The girls ran back inside.

Ed strode over to the car and shook Hal's hand. 'I hope you've had a good night,' he said.

'Yes,' said Hal, 'best birthday I've had in years.'

Ed then turned to June and kissed her. 'See you tomorrow,' he said, then turned to Cathy, kissed her on the cheek and added, 'as for you, my beautiful gypsy, I'll pick you up tomorrow; Romany will be there so just remember that you're with me.' Cathy was stunned. Didn't he listen to her, or did he like getting slapped?

'Romany,' groaned June and Hal in unison. 'Oh no.'

June pulled a face. 'Well I'm keeping away from him.'

'So am I,' said Hal. 'I'm wearing a kilt tomorrow night. I'm going to put my sporran under lock and key.' Cathy collapsed in a fit of giggles. Hal never failed to make her laugh. They got in the car and drove off.

Ed went back inside the pub and started to help Rusty pack away his equipment. The girls hovered nearby, but Ed had forgotten all about them. Paddy drew his attention to them so Ed beckoned them over.

'Romany will be at the Cabaret club tomorrow,' he said, 'meet me outside there about eight thirty. I'll introduce you and you can go to the party with him.' He turned away and helped Paddy with the microphones.

One of the twins tapped him on the shoulder and he turned around. She smiled and said, 'my sister thinks it would be nice if we were to come home with you tonight.'

Ed smiled. 'Well that would be really nice, honey,' he said, 'but I promised my little nieces that I would read them a bedtime story.'

Amused, Paddy held his breath as he watched the disappointed girl walk back to her sister. 'Ed, man, do you realise what you've just done?' he asked.

'Yep, I just turned down twins.'

Rusty laughed out loud. 'So my baby brother is growing up at last.'

The little girls were jumping with glee. 'Will you really read us a bedtime story?' asked the older girl.

'Sure, honey, that's what I said, didn't I?' Ed replied.

'Eden loves the gypsy girl,' the smaller girl giggled.

Ed picked her up and swung her around. 'Little monkey,' he said, but inwardly thought she was probably right. He really had never felt like this before, and when he'd held Cathy in his arms the feelings had been mind blowing, not just sexual but something much deeper. Ed sighed; he really needed to feel that sensation again and he would, no matter how much she'd try to put him off. 'Roll on tomorrow,' he said. 'Now come on you two, let's get paid and go home.'

'Sounds good to me,' said Rusty, and carried on packing the gear away.

When Hal awoke at the Cabaret Club the following morning, he was covered up. A flamenco dress covered part of him and a gypsy skirt the other. The fringes on the flamenco dress were tickling his nose and he realised that there were bodies still inside these dresses.

The trio of June, Cathy, and Hal had only intended to doze and had slept right through. Hal sat up. 'I've had a threesome with clothes on,' he said.

June opened one eye. 'What time is it?'

'Ten o'clock,' replied Hal, eyeing the clock on the wall.

June shook Cathy. 'Wake up,' she said, 'it's late.'

'I feel like a sandwich,' said Hal, scratching his head.

June yawned and stretched. 'Okay,' she said, 'I'll go down and see what's in the fridge.'

'No,' said Hal, 'I mean I've been sandwiched between two blondes all night. I think I'll put that in my act tonight just to see old Romany's face.'

June unzipped the flamenco dress and it fell to the floor. 'Hope it's not too creased, Cathy,' she said, 'I didn't mean to sleep in it, sorry.'

'That's okay,' Cathy said, 'look at the state of my gypsy one.' She stripped out of her costume, and Hal covered his eyes.

'Will you two cover up,' he cried, 'this is more than I can take.' The girls began to laugh, especially when he put his hands to his chest crying, 'I think I've been stabbed.' Closer inspection revealed that his birthday badge had stuck in him. Relieved, he headed for the shower while Cathy pulled on a kaftan and went downstairs to make coffee.

Once on the ground floor she went through the bar and into the kitchen. It had seen better days; the ceiling was brown, tiles were cracked, and the cooker, though clean, was very old. Nearby a young woman was on her knees scrubbing the floor. She raised her head and nodded to Cathy. She looked very tired and older than her years. She wore no make-up and looked unhappy. Her dark brown hair was dragged back in a ponytail, but many tendrils had straggled free. Her eyes were lustreless and her body was so thin that she looked like a puff of wind would blow her away. 'You're too late for breakfast,' she said in a strong Welsh accent, 'but you're welcome to as much tea, coffee, or cereal as you like. If you want a cooked breakfast, you have to be here before ten. Dinner is at six.'

Cathy thanked her, and after making the coffee took it back upstairs. From the shower, June could be heard singing and she set the tray down on the table. 'Kitchen's closed,' she said, 'and dinner's at six.'

June emerged from the shower, towelling her hair. 'I'm too excited to eat,' she said. 'I can't wait to see Mick again.'

'Well my stomach thinks that my throat's been cut,' added Hal. 'I think we should find somewhere to eat and then hit the shops for anything we might need. We're in a very isolated position, and God knows where we might end up after that party tonight. I went to one once and ended up in the next county overnight.'

'Glad I'm not going,' said Cathy, heading for the bathroom.

'Wouldn't bet on it,' said June. 'I've never seen Ed so besotted, and he always gets his own way.'

'Not this time,' replied Cathy, and she closed the bathroom door. June winked at Hal. 'I still wouldn't bet on it.'

A little later, they headed for town which seemed to take ages. Wherever you looked there were mountains and farms, and after eating a hearty breakfast they went shopping. Cathy bought some items for her daughter, June bought a new dress, and Hal found a joke shop and came out laden with a carrier bag full of books. After a bit of souvenir hunting, and getting some emergency provisions, they headed back to the club. The girls took an afternoon nap while Hal read one of his books. 'Wake us up for dinner,' said June.

'Will do,' replied Hal. Cathy said nothing as she was fast asleep already.

Dinner consisted of steak, chips and various vegetables, and then it was time for the band call. Hal was done quickly, he didn't need music. Cathy handed her music over to the bandleader. She had a selection of music as she danced to so many styles; tonight it was the hula hula, tomorrow flamenco, belly dance the next, and other specialities for the rest of the week.

The trio had a drink at the bar and went back upstairs for the evening show. Then it was panic stations; the girls got in each other's way, and June couldn't find her hair rollers. Cathy was flustered, and June managed to stick her mascara brush in her eye. The only one that was calm was Hal. June took off her faded dressing gown and stepped into her new dress. 'What do you think?' she asked.

Hal wolf-whistled. 'Mick will love it,' he reassured her. June smiled, her reflection in the mirror telling her that Hal was right. Cathy was now adorned in her grass skirt, and Hal whistled again. She giggled; in show business you could walk around naked and no one noticed. Dressing rooms were usually mixed, and male artists were used to it. Hal had seen it all; he loved life and tonight was dressed as a Scotsman. 'Like the kilt, girls?' he said, spinning round. They had to steady him as he staggered towards the door. 'God,' he exclaimed, 'I need a drink, the room's spinning.' He disappeared and returned a few minutes later with drinks for all. 'Guess who's out front?' he asked.

'Dunno,' replied June, 'I just want to get this show over with and party.'

'Well, Ed's out there with three stunners,' replied Hal. Cathy felt that she could relax; three girls would keep him busy. 'My kilt got lifted,' said Hal, 'someone was trying to see what was underneath.'

The girls fell about laughing, 'Romany!' they said in unison.

'I didn't hang around,' said Hal, 'we're in Wales and I feel sorry for the sheep. If you dropped something, you wouldn't want to bend down in front of him.' Cathy was laughing so much that she had difficulty doing her bra up. 'Don't laugh,' said Hal, 'if he's got a box of matches with him, your skirt will go up in seconds.' He started doing the can-can and spun so fast that he knocked both girls over and landed face down on the floor with his kilt over his head. Undaunted he got up and started singing *I Belong to Glasgow*. He paused at the door saying, 'I'm compering tonight and I haven't a clue what to say.'

June patted him on the back as they trouped downstairs. 'You'll manage,' she said, 'you have before.'

The band was tuning up, and soon Hal strode out front to loud cheers. He began to do the Highland fling. 'Anyone got any swords?' he asked. 'I've got to do this dance right or the girls upstairs will tie me to the bed and do awful things to me.'

'I'll take your place,' shouted Romany. The audience roared with laughter.

Hal placed his hands on his hips and glared at Romany. 'You,' he said, 'last time I saw you, you were promising to be mine and now you're flaunting your women under my nose. I'm broken hearted and those girls I share with are worse. Last night, I had a threesome with clothes on. It was my birthday and the three of us went out to celebrate, and guess what, my mate Ed was performing. What a night I had. June was singing, Gypsy had taken to the dance floor and steam was coming out of Ed's ears. To top it all I lost my trousers, still haven't found them yet, that's why I'm wearing the kilt.'

He wandered over to Ed and sat on his lap. 'God, is that a gun you've got in your pocket, or are you just pleased to see me?' he said. 'Oh no, it's her upstairs you want, isn't it? Lucky cow, this is one you won't get Romany. He really wants this one; you've just lost. No I shouldn't mock, not at my time of life. These girls are wearing me out; we're sharing just about everything and they're both lusting after my body. You know I must be doing something wrong.' He spun around and attempted to dance again. 'Oh it's no good,' he said, 'I'll have to find some swords, but while I do I'll get one of my girls to entertain you.'

'Bring her on!' shouted Romany. Hal strode over to Romany and glared at him. 'I've already told you not to speak to me; you've deserted me. Even the sheep have hidden all the welly boots; they're shaking with fear. Someone told them that Romany the Ram was in town so they're all in hiding. Romany, Romany, the man that makes every female shake in fear and desire. Well maybe not all females; this next one can't stand you. She's busting out all over, put your hands together for the lovely June Maclaine. I'm off to get my swords.'

June stepped out and sang for about twenty minutes, mainly Shirley Bassey numbers. After her spot, Hal came back with some cardboard swords and attempted to dance again. He did stand-up comedy for about thirty minutes then turned to Romany and said, 'my next girl doesn't fancy you either; she's my other bed-mate. Put your hands together for Gypsy.'

The band struck up her music and Cathy glided out onto the dance floor. Romany took one look at her and shouted, 'Oh baby, come to Daddy!' Cathy moved around the dance floor in her grass skirt, completely in a world of her own. She stared at Romany; he was everything she'd seen on the television but more menacing. He had longish jet black hair and looked moody and overpowering with brown, glittery eyes. He was mesmerizing, dressed totally in black and about five foot nine. He stared at her, his eyes spelling out a clear message; 'I want you and I am going to get you, no matter what you or Ed think.'

Cathy's first thought was that this man was dangerous. He moved closer to her, striding across the floor and gazed at her under his black, long-fringed lashes. He was very slim and Cathy could sense the sensual power that he had. He was really close now and, leering at her, said, 'baby, if you only knew what I'd like to do to you.' He started to ape her movements but she ignored him and carried on dancing. The manager watched from the other side of the room; he'd had trouble with Romany two years ago. He only had to touch Cathy once and he'd be out.

Romany was so close now that Cathy could feel his breath. 'What's up with you?' he asked. 'Are you a lesbian?'

'No,' she replied, 'just fussy.' Romany was incensed and made his way to the bar. After getting a round in, he put a loaded tray on the table and went back to Cathy. Still she ignored him so, annoyed, he went back to his seat. Cathy drew level with Ed and smiled. The girls he was with were certainly stunners. One was a redhead with a very large bust, dressed all in white. She had a snub nose, a wide mouth, and very full lips. The other girls were identical twins. They had bright blue eyes and wore matching green dresses; they also had slim figures. Cathy thought they looked very young, and guessed that they were for Romany, and the redhead for Ed. As she passed Romany, he stood up and threw his drink at her. She sidestepped, and Ed got the lot. The manager moved in, and Romany was asked to leave. Ed was soaked. The girls followed Romany out, much to Cathy's dismay, as it was now obvious that Ed had come for her. She stared at him and, despite being soaked, he was not bothered and was laughing.

Cathy finished her act and headed for the stairs with Ed right behind her. He tapped her on the shoulder and once more she gazed into those blue eyes that seemed to bore right into her. She was immediately embarrassed and looked down at the floor. Ed took her hand and kissed it. 'Can we start again please?' he asked. 'I'm Ed, and you are the beautiful lady who has captivated my heart and soul; would you like a drink?'

Cathy withdrew her hand. 'No thank you,' she said, 'I'm very sleepy.'

Ed took her hand again and kissed it once more. 'Yeah, I know what it's like on the road, so if you want to go to bed straight away that's okay with me, just show me the way to your room.' Cathy flushed crimson which Ed found very amusing. 'It's OK,' he soothed. 'I didn't mean to embarrass you but you should see your face. I can see that you're not used to being chatted up, but it makes a change and I like it.' She broke away and turned to the door again, but Ed got in front of her and barred her way. 'Look,' he said, 'we're having a party tonight, won't you join us? The rest of the cabaret is going too.'

Cathy shook her head and tried to push past him. 'Come on baby,' said Ed, 'you'll soon lose your tiredness once we get there. Surely you don't want to stay here on your own? This place is miles from anywhere.'

'Come on,' said June, appearing as if by magic through the door. 'Lighten up, girl. Go with Ed, you'll enjoy yourself.'

'Well, I will,' said Hal, following her. 'It's party time and at my time of life I can't wait around.' Cathy once again felt Ed's eyes tear into her.

She looked away and said, 'No, I really do want to be alone.'

Ed cupped her chin with his hand, forcing her to look at him. He looked deep into her eyes. 'Please come with me to the party,' he said. That word stuck in his throat as if he wasn't used to saying it very often. He was beginning to feel more than attraction for this lady. He wanted her but not just for a one night stand. He loved 'em and left 'em, telling himself that was the way to be. He was furious when she broke away, and went through the door, slamming it in his face. How dare she. Didn't she know what she was missing? If she thought she was going to get away that easily she was mistaken.

Cathy went upstairs; she'd never felt this tired before. She stripped out of her grass skirt, put on a loose fitting blouse and floral skirt and flopped down on the bed fully clothed. She wasn't going to undress for bed just in case he followed her upstairs. She closed her eyes and dozed, but it wasn't for long as she was suddenly aware of another presence. There, sitting on a chair, was Ed. She sat bolt upright. 'Are you stupid or something?' she asked angrily. 'Don't you understand English? What the hell do you want?'

Ed laughed out loud and walked over to her. 'Is that a serious question, honey?' he asked. 'What do you think I want?'

Angrily, Cathy got to her feet, and Ed guessed there was probably another slap coming. 'I've had enough of you,' she said. 'I said no and I meant no. I don't want you trying to force yourself on me.'

'You're beautiful when you're angry, aren't you,' pressed Ed. 'Now you listen to me, lady. I haven't forced anything on you. Not yet anyway. I mean, you're well put together, but I guess I'm stronger and of course it wouldn't be difficult. Everyone's gone to the party so there's no one in the building.'

Cathy backed away. 'I'll scream,' she threatened.

Ed shrugged his shoulders. 'OK, but like I said there's nobody here but us.'

It was then that Cathy noticed his shirt was off. 'Pretty sure of yourself, aren't you?' she said. 'You're half undressed already.'

'Well,' Ed retorted, 'if you remember, Romany soaked my jacket, and my shirt got a bit wet too but I suppose you've got a point. Yes I'm sure of myself, why shouldn't I be? When I kissed you last night, you kissed me back. I felt it and I think I've been with enough girls to identify that.'

'I didn't,' lied Cathy, 'you imagined it.'

'OK, let's try again, and if you can convince me you're telling the truth, I'll go, but I can't imagine why you'd want to stay here alone; the place is creepy.'

'I like my own company.'

'Don't change the subject,' said Ed, 'just one kiss.'

Cathy raised her hand to slap him but he grasped her wrist, smiled, and took her in his arms. Now that he'd got her where he wanted her, he was trembling with desire, and what made it worse was that the more she protested, the more he wanted her. Suddenly he let her go and she fell back across the bed, staring up at him in terror as he towered above her. He checked himself as he saw a tear trickle from her eye.

'Please go away,' she cried as more tears ran down her cheeks. All at once, Ed felt shamed and, sitting down beside her on the bed, he took a tendril of her hair and wound it around his finger, lightly brushing her cheek with his lips.

'I'm sorry, lady, I just wanted us to have a little fun,' he said. He was shaking. What was the matter with him? Why did he feel this way? Why should he suddenly concern himself with her feelings; she lay there powerless, beaten, and he wasn't going to take her like that? 'Don't cry, Cathy, please don't cry,' he said. He checked himself again. Did he really say please? He leaned over her and, getting no resistance, kissed her on the lips; he wasn't going to rush her.

Cathy felt the tiredness leave her as he began to kiss her neck again and began to caress her. A voice in her head screamed stop, but her body was giving out the green light. She felt unable to offer up any resistance as Ed kissed her and tried to force his tongue inside her mouth. Unable to do this he returned to her neck again, content that although she wasn't very responsive, she wasn't fighting either. He fiddled with a button on her blouse and felt her stiffen slightly. 'I love you,' he whispered, wondering why he'd said it. Meeting with a little more resistance, he returned to her mouth and felt her relax again. 'I love you,' he murmured again. Damn, he'd said it again, what on earth was happening to him? He reached inside her blouse and met with very strong resistance. She pushed him off violently but he grasped her wrists saying, 'Well, darling, the choice is yours, if we stay here, I might lose control and we might both regret it.' Pulling her to him, he forced his tongue inside her mouth then released her so that she fell flat on her back again. He fiddled with the buckle on his belt, laughing wickedly and adding, 'of course we could always go to the party. We wouldn't be alone there, would we, honey?'

Cathy got to her feet. 'All right,' she conceded, 'I'll go.' She knew that she was now defeated.

Arriving at the party, Ed rang the doorbell and was greeted by Romany. 'Christ I didn't think you were coming,' he said, 'but then, maybe you already have, eh?' Ed scowled and led Cathy into a very packed room. June was indeed with Mick Fraser and they were not aware of anyone but each other. Cathy felt her stomach knot up; she adored Mick and remembered seeing him in magazines but had never expected to see him in the flesh. She'd had many a fantasy about him and wondered how she'd react if he spoke to her.

Hal was drunk already and was having problems staying upright. A group of flower children held out flowers to anyone that passed their way. Cathy was suddenly aware of a flower being shoved under her nose. 'Peace, love,' said a rather old flower-child.

Cathy moved in June's direction but Ed guided her away. 'Otherwise engaged,' he said. She suddenly noticed that June's bikini briefs were dangling from one ankle, and that Mick had his hand inside her blouse; they both appeared stoned.

Romany sidled over to Cathy, 'what's your, poison?' he asked.

'Nothing,' she replied, wondering what sort of party this was.

'Coffee,' replied Ed, and nudged Cathy, pointing to a sofa in the corner of the room. 'Over here,' he half-ordered. From the small kitchen, Romany could be heard singing *Knees up Mother Brown*. Ed led her to the sofa and from there she got an even better view of Mick as she sat down. Mick sat up and shouted, 'shut up Romany, you never could sing, I've heard better sounds when the sink empties out.' His eyes rested on Cathy. She flushed and hoped that he had not noticed. Five minutes later, Romany was back with a cup of hot coffee in his hand. Bowing to her he said, 'this is a gorgeous cup of coffee, such as you have never had before.' He winked at Ed who was looking the other way and missed it. He was engrossed in watching Mick's manager snorting coke. Finally he turned back to Cathy who had just accepted the coffee and shouted, 'hey Romany, where's mine? You've forgotten me.' Romany was stunned and his jaw dropped.

'You want coffee, not booze?' he asked. Ed nodded and Romany shrugged his shoulders. Ed rested his hand on Cathy's thigh and she removed it, making Romany hoot with laughter. As he passed June and Mick, he purposely pulled them off the settee and roared with laughter as they ended up on the floor in a heap.

June hurled all kinds of abuse at him and then, catching sight of Cathy, shouted, 'glad you decided to join us.' Mick brushed himself down and made his way over to Ed. Cathy was glad that she was sitting down; her head was spinning as her fantasy grew closer. The idol of millions was now standing in front of her, and she felt quite faint as he sat down beside her. His brown eyes gazed into hers, the long black hair was tousled, his nose slightly on the large side and his lips full and inviting. Her pulse was racing as he leaned over and took her hand in his. He liked what he could see and wondered if it was worth chatting her up but guessed that she was with Ed. He decided to wait until Ed had finished with her and then move in.

She had a very kissable mouth and very good legs; he could imagine those legs wrapped around him right now and could feel himself begin to stand to attention. 'If you want anything, just let me know,' he said. Cathy flashed him a smile revealing perfect white teeth. Mick sighed. She had a beautiful smile and as for her mouth, well, he could think of a perfect use for it. He adored fellatio and thought that he could get a perfect sixty-nine out of this lady. Romany was now offering a cup of coffee to Ed who in turn was sending out warning signals to Mick. He could read his mind and wasn't going to have him moving in on his lady.

'Do you want this or not?' asked Romany.

Ed took the coffee, sipped it, and then snapped, 'what the hell is in this?' as he handed the cup back to Romany, who grinned at Cathy. 'Yours okay?' he asked.

Cathy nodded, and Romany laughed out loud. 'Should be,' he said, 'yours is special, really special.'

Mick stared at him. 'You haven't?' he demanded angrily.

'Course I have, I was trying to help, Ed, and freak her out a bit.' Mick raised his fist and then lowered it, knowing that it wasn't going to help.

'Stupid bastard,' muttered Mick. 'You'd best take her upstairs, Ed. I doubt she's ever tripped before; she looks too innocent.'

Ed nodded and got to his feet, cursing Romany. He helped a bewildered Cathy to her feet and steered her towards the stairs. 'Come with me,' he said. 'I'll look after you.'

'I don't understand,' cried Cathy, 'is this another one of your games or do you intend to seduce me once we're up there?'

He shook his head. 'Nothing to do with me, honey; it's a bit more serious than that. Romany's laced your coffee.' He kissed her on her forehead and, seeing the confusion in her eyes, said, 'you'll be fine, I'll stay with you until you're over it.' Knowing nothing about any drugs except aspirin, she obeyed as he told her to lie down saying, 'Just think beautiful. I'm sorry, Cathy. I knew nothing about it. I wouldn't hurt you, not ever, just rest. Come to think of it you may even enjoy it. I've got to say that I've had good trips and bad.'

Cathy was scared and starting to feel very strange; she was very floaty as she heard Ed say, 'think beautiful.' Time appeared to stop and then suddenly she sat bolt upright. Ed immediately had her in his arms. 'It's okay, darling, I'm here,' he soothed. 'I've got you, everything is fine; it's all beautiful and so are you.' Cathy was shivering as objects on the wall began to move, the furniture was moving, huge spiders crawled on the wall and at the bottom of the bed a serpent raised its head and hissed. The patterns on the wallpaper began to change and Ed's features constantly changed to other people's. Someone was screaming, and the compulsion to fly became overwhelming. Ed had seen it all before. He knew that Cathy wanted to fly away from all of this torment, and honestly believed that she could fly.

She struggled desperately with him. 'Let me go!' she cried, and Ed had to summon up all of his strength to hold her down, yet still she struggled. His face was now horrific to her, his flesh was disintegrating and in her eyes he was a skeleton. She screamed louder, and Mick, hearing the commotion, rushed into the room. Cathy was still convinced that she could fly and it took both men to hold her down and prevent her from reaching the window. She seemed to be possessed with superhuman strength and this nightmare seemed to last for ages. The whole time, Mick and Ed told her that she was beautiful and then suddenly she ceased to struggle. She was seeing colours, beautiful colours and they were shining. A glazed and happy expression came into her eyes. Everything had taken on a new dimension. 'Beautiful,' she said over and over again, and placing her arms around Ed's neck began to caress him.

Ed was now fighting with his conscience and Cathy's amorous advances. Mick laughed. 'Crisis over,' he said, 'if I were you, I'd just lie back and enjoy it.' He left the room as Ed pleaded with her to stop. He was in agony; any other girl he would have taken without a second thought. He didn't understand himself any more, he wanted to love her. No, that wasn't right, was it? He was as free as a bird. Love? No way. She was just another body, and he'd feel different once he'd had her. Anyway, he was just being a gentleman. She was on a trip, but his willpower was at breaking point. The girl was trying to kiss him all over.

'Wait till you've had a good night's sleep, you know that you're tired.'

Cathy wasn't listening and continued to kiss and stroke him. 'I love everyone!' she cried, and then put Ed out of his misery by falling asleep.

Chapter Two

When Cathy awoke it was daylight. She looked around her. Ed was feeling great; he was lying beside her, fully clothed and priding himself on his willpower. She sat up. 'What happened?' she asked.

'You had a trip,' replied Ed, as casually as if he was talking about a cold. 'I said I'd look after you and I did.' Cathy rubbed her eyes which were full of sleep. Ed gazed into her eyes, 'C'mon, baby, you need some fresh air, bathroom's to your left.'

Cathy got off the bed and made her way to the bathroom to freshen up. When she returned to the room, Ed had changed into a blue denim shirt and faded jeans. She opened her handbag and rummaged around for her comb to try and get the tangles out of her hair. She could hear Ed singing from the bathroom and wondered how he could be so chirpy first thing in the morning. He returned looking much more human, and together they went downstairs. Romany was asleep on the sofa, and she resisted the temptation to kick his head in. There were bodies draped all around the room, and clothes strewn everywhere.

Closing the door, they went outside and headed for Ed's car. Ed opened the car door for Cathy and she got in. They drove for about thirty minutes and then came to a bend in the road next to a field.

Ed pulled up. 'C'mon,' he said, 'there are some people I want you to meet.' In the field was a large caravan. It was bright pink with flowers on it, and as he helped her over the style she could hear singing. It was a beautiful, young girl. She had jet black, waist-length hair, a long green skirt, white gypsy top, and many bangles and beads. In her hair she wore flowers. She was very slim and held a baby who looked about nine months old. As they neared the caravan, the door opened and Rusty emerged.

'Eden,' he shouted, 'come and have some breakfast.' A woman walked from behind the caravan with a spatula in her hand; she was obviously cooking. She was a plump lady but wore a loose fitting kaftan which helped to hide it. Her red hair was streaked with grey and she had a lovely smile. Suddenly, Cathy was aware of the two little girls from the previous night. They both offered her flowers, and Cathy bent down.

'Thank you,' she said. The girls both hugged her.

'Peace, love,' they said. The girl with the baby stopped singing and wandered over. She kissed Ed on his cheek and did the same to a bewildered Cathy.

'Hi,' she said, 'I'm Summer.'

The lady who had been cooking introduced herself. 'I'm Fawn; Rusty's my husband. Summer you've just met, and the girls are Amber and Amethyst.' Fawn gave Cathy a hug and invited both her and Ed to share their breakfast.

'This is Cathy,' announced Ed proudly as Cathy was swamped in a group hug.

The girls noted the guitar on Ed's back. 'Play for us!' they cried.

'In a moment,' replied Ed, gazing at Cathy and wondering what she made of the scene.

Rusty went back inside the caravan and returned with a guitar. 'Let's make music,' he said, 'the girls can do the cooking.' The two men went over to a nearby tree and sat cross-legged on the ground, striking up the opening bars to *Mr Tambourine Man*. The little girls ran over to them and began to dance.

After the song was over, they began to make daisy chains. Fawn saw that Cathy was overwhelmed and explained their situation. 'We live off the land,' she said, 'we pay rent to the farmer who owns this field and when the time is right we move on. Last year was the summer of love and it was beautiful, but we'd been travelling for two years previously. We'd got fed up with our lives, so we took all our money out of the bank, quit our jobs and hit the road. We work when we can, and the reward is freedom. Rusty gets gigs now and again, and Summer and I tell fortunes. Since we've been here we've been doing work for the farmer too, and he pays us in food. We're free, Cathy, and it's a wonderful way to live.'

Cathy was overcome with emotion, and could picture herself and her daughter living the same idyllic lifestyle. She envied Fawn; her eyes were wide open now.

Ed stared at the scene before him. It was 1968, and hippies were still hanging on to flower power, free love, and freedom. He was sick of it. Since leaving school, he'd gigged around England, toured the Med and then met Billy and Paddy. They'd formed a band and done pretty well, and they were now supporting the Shelltones as their warm-up act. It was his best friend Romany who'd fixed that up as he and Ed went back a long way. Still, the tour would be ending this week and so once more he had to rethink his life. It would be back to playing pubs and bingo halls and God knows what else. Working alongside Romany had certainly helped in the female department. If the girls wanted to go to him, they approached Ed first but lately that meant nothing too. He could see himself on the road with a woman that truly loved him; it was his dream.

'Come on, you guys,' shouted Fawn, beginning to serve up breakfast. Rusty and Ed wandered over and everyone tucked in to scrambled eggs and beans. Amber whispered to her mother who replied, 'ask Cathy.'

The child turned to Cathy and asked with a very straight face, 'have you got a baby in your tummy?'

She wasn't prepared for that and flushed crimson. The child was no more than four and she laughed. 'Am I fat?' she said.

Amber shook her head. ‘No,’ she replied, ‘but Eden says that when he meets the right girl he will come and live with us and be happy, so we could have a new baby and baby Blue could play with it.’

Amethyst wrinkled up her nose. ‘There are lots, must be about twenty babies on the commune,’ she said, ‘but we want one of our own. We all love each other, and if Eden loves Cathy, and I know he does, he could put a baby in her tummy and read us more bedtime stories like he did last night.’

Amber clambered onto Ed’s lap and snuggled into his shoulder. ‘Please Eden,’ she said, ‘you do love her because you were kissing last night, I saw you. We would love a new baby, and Cathy could be our new sister.’ Cathy was astounded, the child obviously observed everyone as a brother or sister; it was like a huge extended family. She wondered if the child had seen the slap that followed the kiss, but doubted it as she thought that would have come into the conversation too.

Rusty apologised. ‘Sorry,’ he said, ‘the girls can be a little bit outspoken at times.’

Everyone laughed and Ed kissed the little girl on her forehead, ‘I’ll see what I can do,’ he said. The idea fascinated him.

After breakfast, Ed and Cathy bid the family farewell and headed back onto the road. Ed drove further up the road until they reached a desolate spot. Helping her out of his car he had the urge to kiss her but decided to hold on just a little bit longer. Coming to another field they started to cross it, and Cathy was feeling so liberated that she started to run. ‘Race you to that tree,’ she cried. She ran off, with Ed in hot pursuit, and she fell in a heap under the shade of the tree. ‘I won,’ she gasped.

Ed fell down beside her. ‘That’s cheating,’ he said, ‘you didn’t have a guitar on your back or a transistor radio in your hand.’

Cathy laughed, saying, ‘you’re just a bad loser.’

Ed turned to her and, grinning, said, ‘lady, I never lose; when I set my mind on something, I always get it.’ He began to strum his guitar and played a Dylan medley. Cathy sang along with him and then got to her feet and began dancing. Ed looked on in admiration; he was transfixed. She was beautiful and very sensual, but with a fragile, childlike quality making him want her more than he'd ever wanted any woman. She was probably inexperienced but that would be a nice change. He knew that he was falling in love and he hadn't even touched her yet. He stopped playing and switched on his radio.

It was a slow number and Ed got to his feet and took her in his arms. They danced slowly with Cathy's head on his shoulder. She was relaxed, she liked him and he seemed to like her; he made her feel safe but then she could feel him growing against her and pulled away.

'Play some more,' she said. Ed was feeling hot and horny but complied with her wishes and began to reel off some more Dylan. Cathy sat beside him and closed her eyes as she listened in ecstasy. Dylan was her God, and Ed watched her with a growing excitement. He thought that he was being the perfect gent but knew that it was now only a matter of time before lust took him over. Several songs later he stopped singing and switched the radio on again. The sun shone on both of them and he closed his eyes. Cathy dozed with her head on his chest and he pulled her closer. Half asleep, she sighed.

The radio was on when Ed awoke a bit later and he looked at his watch. He needed to get her back to the cabaret club soon; they both had shows to do that night and the venues were quite a way apart. He shook the sleeping girl and she opened her eyes. She stared at Ed in silence, not sure where she was and then it came back to her. 'I need to go,' she cried.

'I know,' said Ed, 'so do I.' Cathy gazed at him, feeling aroused. She felt scared as it was obvious that he felt the same. Ed was drowning in her eyes, and he just couldn't hold off any longer. He pulled her to him, saying, 'come on, honey, what are we playing at?' and covering her in kisses. He pulled her closer.

'I love you, lady,' he murmured. 'I didn't believe it could happen to me but it has at long last.'

Cathy pushed him away. 'There's something you should know before you think of getting involved with me,' she said.

'Honey, I am involved,' said Ed, pulling her in close again. 'Tell me after, but right now I'm going crazy for you.' He nuzzled into her neck and Cathy could feel something inside start to stir.

She pushed him away for the second time. 'I can't,' she whispered.

Ed wasn't listening, and kissed her passionately. 'I had to fight you off last night,' he said. 'I kept my word to you while you were on that bloody trip, and now I'm claiming what's mine.'

'Yours?' said Cathy indignantly, 'I'm not yours.'

'I don't care what hang-ups you've got,' said Ed, 'but from now on you're mine.'

'Not possible,' cried Cathy.

'I want you,' Ed declared, 'I've always made my own rules and always will, and I'm telling you you're mine. You can have anything you want as long as you realise that.' Reaching inside her blouse, he fondled her breast.

Cathy slapped his wrist. 'Stop it! I can't.'

Ed had no intention of stopping. He removed his hand from her breast and took her head between his hands. He kissed her again and forced his tongue between her teeth. Feeling the tension in her, he returned to her breasts again; he'd had a lot of experience with women and decided that all this one needed was a little more time.

'Oh Cathy, I love you,' he said. He could feel the tension begin to leave her body and noticed the flush stain her cheeks.

She got to her feet and gazed at him. He pulled her down beside him again but she struggled to her feet.

'Leave me alone!' she shouted and attempted to run, but Ed was too fast for her. He ran after her and pulled her to the ground once more.

'So where are you running to?' he asked. 'We're miles from anywhere. Stop fighting me and chill out.'

'Just take me back to the club,' begged Cathy, 'please.'

'No way,' said Ed passionately, 'I want you, and you want me but you're too stubborn to admit it. I've fallen in love with you and I want you.'

'Supposing I don't want you?' cried Cathy.

'You do,' said Ed. 'Let me show you.' He held her to him until she couldn't breathe, then relaxing his hold began to caress her again. 'Just relax,' he soothed and she could feel the fight going out of her and relaxed.

Ed got to his feet and led Cathy back to where they'd been sitting before. Once back on the grass he began to unbutton her blouse, and then her relaxed state vanished. 'No Ed, I can't, I really can't,' she cried, 'there's someone else.'

Ed had got her left breast exposed by now and was sucking on her nipple. He raised his head and, smiling, said, 'forget him, I want you.'

Cathy was experiencing a high of newly found emotions. 'I can't,' she sobbed. Ed wasn't listening and his hands were now finding their way beneath her skirt. 'I've got a daughter,' whispered Cathy as her body began to betray her.

'I'll help you raise her, I need you.'

Cathy's head lolled back against the trunk of the tree. 'I'm married, Ed,' she cried, 'please stop it.'

Ed was far too fired up to stop, and removed her bikini briefs. 'Divorce him; I know you want this as much as I do.' He buried his head into her lap and after raising her skirt found the spot that he'd been seeking.

'Stop it!' cried Cathy, losing her balance and ending up flat on her back. She knew it was too late to stop now and her body shook with desire. Ed had increased his efforts, finally slipping his tongue inside her body which was already going through a series of convulsions. She was writhing and twisting, her pulse racing and head bursting as waves of guilty pleasure engulfed her. She raced towards orgasm; the kind that she thought only existed in romantic novels.

Ed continued until he felt her body relax, and then straightened up and raised her to a sitting position, holding her close as she burst into tears. 'It's okay, honey, everything's fine,' Ed reassured her. 'I love you, don't get upset.'

He began to caress her until she felt the same feelings begin to well up once more. Cathy was lost and now needed him very badly. Ed felt in his pocket for a condom and then decided against it; he was going to make her his personal property so there was no need for one, and for the first time in his life visualised the prospect of becoming a father. Also, the thought of going bareback excited him. He removed his clothes and entered her. He could feel the sweet surrender, and whispered softly, 'Come on, honey, just let it happen, no hang-ups, just let yourself go.' Cathy felt him take her, gently at first, but becoming very passionate and scaring her. She soon found herself responding with a powerful passion that equalled his. The transistor radio blasted out *Itchycoo Park*, and as Steve Marriot belted out *It's All Too Beautiful*, Cathy arched towards her lover in total agreement.

Ed was overwhelmed, his lady under him like his very own star-crossed lover. He resolved that this was his very own lady and that no one else would get close to her. He was in love for the first time in his life and was loving every single minute of it. He held her close and said gently, 'you are wonderful and I want to spend the rest of my life with you. I know that we've only just met, baby, but this is the real thing. I want you to come and live with me, and once you're divorced, marry me.'

Cathy was shocked. She couldn't believe what she'd just done but had to admit to herself that she did have feelings for Ed. He stroked her hair, knowing that he could never let her go. Ed got to his feet and picked up his guitar and radio, gazing at Cathy who was now on her feet and brushing herself down. She put her briefs back on and stared at Ed, and he looked back at her with so much love in his eyes that she thought all of her birthdays and Christmases had come at once. Nothing made sense, Ed was well known for being a womaniser so why did he talk of marriage? Maybe it was just talk and once she was back at the club that would be the end of their little scene. She guessed that it was, after all he'd managed to get his own way, so there was no reason for him to hang around any more. She thought that it was probably for the best as she knew her husband wouldn't give her up easily and she adored her daughter.

The drive back to the club was a long one as Ed repeatedly told her how much he loved her and that his roving days were over. He also said that he couldn't wait to meet her daughter, and looked forward to a family life.

'We can fulfil our work commitments,' he said, 'and then we can settle down like Fawn and Rusty. Maybe one day I'll get lucky like Romany did, and then my darling, I'll lay the world at your feet. If we get a camper van, I'll still be able to work and you can stay at home with your daughter. I bet she looks a lot like you; what's her name?'

'Sandy,' replied Cathy who was getting swept along in all of this. She checked herself. It wasn't going to happen; he was sweet-talking her. She dismissed the whole thing and was quite happy when the club came into sight.

'Got to go,' he said to her as she got out of the car, 'but I'll be back later and then we can go out.' Cathy sighed, thinking that he wouldn't return.

'Hey Cathy,' he shouted after her.

'What?' she replied, turning around.

Ed had got out of the car and was holding out his arms. 'You forgot something,' he said and ran over, seizing her in a fervent embrace and kissing her passionately. 'You forgot me,' Ed laughed, 'see you later.'

Cathy entered the club and went upstairs to find June. 'Just in time for dinner,' said June. 'I was getting a bit worried; are you okay?' Cathy nodded. 'Tell me, how are you and Ed getting on? He's really smitten with you, and in your position I'd leave that miserable old git you've got at home.'

'Smitten?' snorted Cathy. 'That's why he made love to me today and didn't use protection? I call that not caring for me at all. What if he's given me some nasty disease after all these girls he's been with?'

'Well then he must consider that you two are an item,' said June. 'He always uses protection. Oops, sorry I shouldn't have said that.'

'Don't apologise,' said Cathy, 'you knew him before I did. Anyway I don't care who he sleeps with, we definitely are not an item.'

All Cathy wanted was to get the show over with and go back to bed. The trouble was that she did love Ed and ached to see him again, but she'd written him off and sighed with relief when it was her turn to perform. She started to dance in an almost trance-like state. It was flamenco tonight so she took her aggression out by stamping extra hard throughout. Suddenly, out of the corner of her eye, she saw him at the bar. When she finished the dance the audience cheered; it was always one of her best dances. Ed crossed the floor, went down on one knee and kissed her hand, then smiling he said, 'hola Senorita, Te quiero.' Cathy smiled and hurried upstairs with Ed right behind her.

'Not an item?' June teased from her bed. Cathy laughed and stripped out of her costume. 'And where are you two going tonight?' asked June.

'That would be telling,' replied Ed.

'Well, wherever it is don't wake me up when you come in,' yawned June. 'I'm having an early night.' Cathy changed rapidly, went downstairs with Ed and soon they were driving down the country lanes.

'We're going to see the boys in action,' said Ed. On arrival at the venue they made their way to the stage door and once inside headed for the stage. The band was halfway through its set, and Romany looked over at Ed, grinning. Ed sighed. 'What a band, I wish I could front one like that.' About twenty five minutes later they trouped off the stage. The crowd was still cheering so they had to go back and give an encore of their latest single. Mick came off dripping with sweat.

'I'll kill myself, slogging myself to death while those lazy bastards take all the credit,' he said to Cathy. 'Romany ballsed it up again. It's like a bloody circus; you should sit in on our rehearsal sometime.' She spied Romany leering at her again and shivered.

He ambled over and grinned, knowing he was making her nervous. He fixed his gaze on her, eyes glittering. 'Come to Daddy,' he said. Cathy recalled that he'd said the same thing at the cabaret club.

'So,' said Mick, 'would you like to watch us rehearse, Cathy?'

'Love to.'

'She's too busy,' grunted Ed. 'Come on babe, we're leaving.' Already he was guiding her away from Mick; he could sense his interest in Cathy and he wasn't about to let him anywhere near her. He ushered her outside the theatre, opened his car door for her and then got in himself, driving off at top speed. He switched his car radio on and Dylan's voice filled the air.

'Love him,' sighed Cathy.

'So do I. Do you love me?'

'Of course I do, but I can't leave my daughter.'

'No one's asking you too, I told you that I'd help you raise her.' Ed was getting frustrated now; he wanted the answer to his question in more depth. He pulled over by the roadside and stared at Cathy; then taking her in his arms he kissed her. 'I love you Cathy, and I need you with me. I'll do anything that you ask me to but I need to know that you feel the same,' he said.

'I love you but I wish I were dead. Take me home; you're

confusing me. I need to sort my head out,' she cried, exasperated. She was weeping now; everything was too much, her loyalty evenly divided.

Ed stroked her hair and kissed her on her forehead. 'Okay,' he said, and starting up the engine they continued their journey to the cabaret club.

On their arrival, Cathy reached for the door handle to get out but Ed stopped her and enfolded her in his arms once more. 'Can I come up?' he asked, 'or do you really want to sleep alone? I could help you forget your dilemma for a while and we could at least make plans. I know that there's an answer and I'll find a solution. Shall I go or stay?' He ran his fingers through her hair and smiled at her.

'You'd better go, it won't make things any easier,' replied Cathy. 'Just drive away and forget me.'

'I can't forget you, I'll see you tomorrow. I'll sleep on it and work something out, you'll see.'

'It's impossible,' she said, disengaging herself from his arms. He pulled her back, embracing her so passionately that it made her head spin, awakening a strong current of desire in her. If she stayed any longer, she'd be lost. She wrenched herself away from him, gasping, 'goodnight.'

Opening the car door, she rushed towards the club and ran upstairs to her room. She undressed quietly, noticing that June was fast asleep, and got into bed, her mind racing. She tried to get a mental picture of herself, Tony, and Sandy, but unfortunately all she could see was Ed making love to her. Feeling even more confused, she fell asleep.

Chapter Three

The following morning, Ed arrived and hooted the car horn. June awoke and threw the alarm clock at him from the open window which missed him by inches. 'Oh,' she cried, 'he's completely off his rocker. Get up Cathy and show yourself before I throw something heavier at him.' She got back into bed and pulled the covers over her head.

Cathy arose and went to the window. She waved, and Ed blew her a kiss. After a quick shower she made her way downstairs and surveyed him; he was combing his hair and preening himself in front of an old cracked hand mirror. She got into his car and smiled. Ed put down the mirror, plonked a kiss on her cheek and drove off as *Tin Soldier* blared out from his radio. 'We're having a foursome later,' Ed told her, 'a picnic with Mick and June.'

'Strange how I never get told about these things,' sighed Cathy. 'June doesn't know either, and when was all this planned?'

'Last night, Mick and I decided on it.'

Cathy gazed out of the window at the scenic landscape. 'Maybe she won't want to go.'

'At her age, she can't be too choosey; she was singing in the clubs when Mick and I were still at school. She's thirty-eight if she's a day and she idolises Mick; she's got four kids and one of them is on the cabaret circuit already.'

'Then why doesn't she leave her husband if she's that hung up on Mick?'

'Not that easy, is it? If it was, you wouldn't have this massive hang-up that you've got now. I guess June does still have feelings for her husband after having four kids with him, and anyway, Mick wouldn't want her around all the time. She'd get in the way of all of these kids and groupies that hang around him.'

'That's cruel, he's using her.'

'Correction, they're using each other. He's a pop idol which does wonders for her ego, and she knows that she can pull him while some of the younger girls can't. Then after they've had their little scene together she goes home to her comfortable old man in her cosy little house and Mick pulls everything in sight until he sees her again.' Ed laughed; he found the whole thing very amusing.

Cathy on the other hand did not, and said uncomfortably, 'it's awful, terrible.'

'Rubbish, what do you think I was doing before I met you? Last night was the first time that I've slept alone for ages. Mick thought I'd flipped but I told him that I'd met the love of my life and I wanted to marry you.'

'Ed, we've already been through this one.'

'Sure, and I said that I'd sleep on it and I have. I'll tell you about it later but I'm not letting you slip away that easily.'

Cathy traced a pattern on the car window; obviously her words yesterday had fallen on stony ground. She yawned. 'Where are we going now, or do I have to wait until we get there before I find out?'

'We're going to get some breakfast, darling, and then I have a rehearsal to attend and I'd like you present.'

Cathy erased the patterns on the window, thinking that sometimes silence was golden, and this appeared to be appropriate.

Arriving at a small, brightly painted cafe, they went inside and Ed ordered breakfast. Cathy gazed around her; the place was spotless and the gingham blue curtains gave the place real country charm. Ed was thrusting something into her hand; it was a small box. 'For you, sweet lady,' he said. She opened the box and found inside an engagement ring, the diamond glinting in the sunlight that streamed through the windows.

'Didn't you understand me yesterday?' she cried. 'I'm married, I can't accept this any more than I can leave my daughter.'

Ed wasn't listening. He reached across the table, and taking the ring placed it on her finger. It was a perfect fit. From his pocket he retrieved one of her stage rings that she'd lost on her first night at the club and had searched frantically for. Obviously Ed had found it and been able to get the engagement ring properly sized.

She attempted to remove it from her finger, but Ed took her hand firmly in his, saying, 'That's where it stays, you're mine now, you can forget your husband. If you really want your child so badly, we'll deal with it later legally but from now on you're mine, one hundred per cent.'

Cathy put her head in her hands; she felt defeated. 'Why is it that nobody listens to me?' she asked exasperated. 'You're crazy; everyone seems to think they know what's best for me. Why do I never get a say in the matter?' Ed didn't answer and sat back as the waitress brought their breakfast to the table.

He grinned at her. 'We're engaged,' he said proudly.

The waitress eyed him with disinterest and, setting the plates on the table, said, 'great.'

'Miserable cow,' retorted Ed when she'd left, picking up his knife and fork. 'I bet she's frustrated. Maybe I'll tell Mick about her. She looks forty plus and a virgin to boot. Yes, I'll send Mick round here, doubt if he's ever had one.'

Cathy flushed crimson and looked down. 'Do you always talk like that?' she asked.

'Why? Does it bother you?'

'I'm not used to that kind of talk; it embarrasses me. It makes me feel like I want the ground to swallow me up.'

'Sorry, I'll try to remember that.' Ed tucked into his breakfast and soon had it finished before Cathy was halfway through hers.

They finished their meal in silence and then headed for the rehearsal hall which was about four miles away. 'Tell me,' she said, 'why is it that everyone seems to know what's best for me? Don't my feelings count at all?'

Ed rummaged around in his glove compartment with his free hand looking for some cigarettes. 'Can't speak for anyone else, Cathy; you were born with a brain and you know what's best for you. All I can do is speak for myself; I love you very much and I want you to be happy, really happy.'

Cathy wound the car window down and the sudden draught caught her hair, blowing it into a tousled mess all over her head. She pushed the tangled mane out of her eyes and said, 'then why don't you listen to me? Every time I say something, you turn around and make as if you didn't hear me.'

Ed gazed at her, feeling desire flooding his body. On stage he was convinced that she was the loveliest thing that he'd ever seen. On the drug trip he'd marvelled at her wildness, and later whilst making love to her, had felt as if she'd lifted his soul right out of his body to unite it with hers. It had been as if they were twin souls and now, looking at her all wild, tousled, and yet childlike at the same time, he was convinced that not only was she the best thing that he'd ever seen but that she was also the best thing that had happened to him. 'I love you Cathy, that's why,' he said. 'I don't want to think of your family. I want us completely reborn, and I get the feeling that you'd sacrifice your own happiness for the sake of your child, and a man who you don't love any more.'

Keeping one hand on the steering wheel he took her hand in his. Cathy felt the same shock waves hit her as before; it was electric. She blushed, and a very pleased Ed noted it. He was sure that all she needed was a bit more time. She'd soon realise that he was her soul mate in life. Later in the day he was going to split from Mick and June and get Cathy on her own in some secluded spot. From his conversation the night before, Mick had mentioned that if Ed got bored with her he should throw her in his direction, as he was more than interested. Ed had no reason to doubt him either; he'd seen that look in Mick's eyes before. He was choosey, but once interested he pursued a female until she succumbed. This time, however, he would be left out in the cold as far as Ed was concerned. Cathy was his, totally his, and his stomach was doing somersaults. He wanted her right now, and his insides were raging with testosterone. Later he would have her and his lust would be satiated. He gazed at her and once more his stomach churned at the thought of it, but he concentrated on his driving and soon they were outside the rehearsal hall.

Once inside, Ed introduced Cathy to Billy. Billy had olive skin and dark brown hair with kind, hazel eyes. He was very good looking, while Paddy the drummer was practically bald and short. There were a few patches of sandy hair and he had a round jolly face. Cathy was very impressed with Billy's playing; he seemed every bit as good as Romany, and maybe even better. She enjoyed every moment of the rehearsal, and was very surprised to be invited to their show that night. 'I think you should,' he said, 'because it must be you that made him miss our rehearsal yesterday.'

'Yes,' explained Cathy, 'we went to a party and Romany laced my coffee. I was still shaky in the morning, so Ed stayed with me.'

'Right,' said Billy. 'Romany's bad but I think you owe us a visit, and I think Ed would sing better if you were there.' Cathy had her eyes on the floor and blushed. 'Blushes pretty, doesn't she, Ed?' asked Billy. 'So that's fixed. We'll see you tonight.'

Cathy nodded, and Ed gave her an affectionate squeeze. 'Time to leave,' he said, 'we've got a date with Mick and June.'

'The mind boggles,' said Billy. 'Where are you going?'

'Somewhere quiet for a picnic,' said Ed.

Billy laughed and started to pack away his equipment. 'I've heard it called some things,' he said, 'but that's a new one on me.' Ed chuckled and packed away his microphone. He was determined to get Cathy on her own at some point in the afternoon and remove any doubts that she had about leaving him.

When Ed and Cathy arrived back at the cabaret club, June was making sandwiches, and Mick was sprawled on the bed looking extremely ruffled. It was obvious that they'd just made love, by the state of the bed, plus he was half dressed and June's blouse was gaping open. Mick surveyed Cathy and wondered if she'd accept him but dismissed the thought when he spied the ring on her finger. He decided that he didn't want a bad scene with Ed, but still he couldn't help looking at her, and Ed couldn't blame him for that. She seemed different from Ed's usual girls; her face had that untouched look about it.

Mick stared at Ed and wondered what the hell had come over him. Usually he was a lover of one-night stands and hell-raising like Mick, but now he'd changed and Mick wasn't sure if it was for the best. He'd been stunned the day before when Ed had asked him for a loan. He lent it to him, as Ed always paid his debts with interest, but he was stunned at his reason as to why he needed the money. Apparently he wanted to buy a ring for Cathy, and intended to marry her even though she was already married.

Cathy and June chatted away as the sun streamed through the windows. 'I hope you girls have got your bikinis,' said Mick. 'You might as well get the sun to your bodies while you can. The weather's always changing and knowing our luck it'll rain soon anyway so make the most of it.'

June agreed and started rummaging in the chest of drawers for hers while Cathy was engrossed in packing sandwiches into bags. Mick zipped up his flies as he'd just realised that they were undone.

'We're going downstairs to make some coffee,' said June, 'and while we're gone, you two can wash yourselves. I've never seen such scruffy looking guys in my life. Come on, Cathy, let's leave them to it.' The two girls went downstairs and Mick picked up his shirt from the floor.

'Good is she?' he asked Ed. 'Very good?' Ed stared into space. 'Hey, Ed, I just asked you a question.'

'I heard you,' said Ed, 'but I can't tell you. It's between me and her.'

'Christ, I didn't know you'd got it that bad,' snorted Mick. 'I'd hoped we might switch around a bit this afternoon.'

'Not a chance,' said Ed, walking over to the wash basin and turning on the taps. 'I'm through with all of that. All I want now is the chance to make her happy, plus the chance to get famous so I can give her everything.'

Mick buttoned up his shirt and ran a comb through his hair. 'I've told you before, Ed,' he said. 'One day you will be famous. Probably by then I'll be burnt out. It happened too soon for me; I was seventeen when I was making it. I'm twenty-four now and I can't hold on much longer. It's 1968; soon it'll be the seventies and I doubt I'll still be around then. Romany will never be out of work though; he's a lead guitarist and a good one at that. The music scene always needs good leads, but in my case I only strum and sing, and there's too many singers out there and too many out of work. Even if you don't make it until the early seventies you'll still be in with a better chance than me. You'll be a new face by then and you'll have a new decade stretching out in front of you and a new generation to follow you. By then I'll be reduced to voice-over commercials and other things. In fact, maybe not even that.' Fiddling with his top button, he added, 'I might even be dead by then. The way I live can't do my health any good; that's why I live my life to the full now, because I know my time is limited.'

Ed was dreaming of fame and family life; he felt really good. He loved Cathy and hoped she loved him. Life was good, very good. 'You'll be great, buddy,' Mick reassured him, 'really great.' Ed wasn't sure about that but he had his girl and that was all he wanted. Mick was a great guy, and he'd taken all he said on board but he thought that his career was far from over.

Ed began to lather up the soap as he washed himself. 'I'm not afraid of hard work,' he said, 'but in this business it's not what you do, is it? It's who you know.'

Mick nodded, remembering his early days when he'd trudged around from agent to agent after leaving school. He'd had no luck at all, and originally he just wanted to be part of a band. He'd wanted to be a guitarist with a few vocals in gigs, but unable to find a vocalist he had taken on the position himself. He formed many bands, all of which had come to nothing, and in his opinion were as good as the one he now fronted. He'd slogged on for ages getting nowhere, until one night a man called Doug offered him a card saying that he had great potential. Mick had been delighted, at last it had happened, all that slogging away had been worth it. The downside though was the man only wanted him and dismissed the rest of the band as poor amateurs. As far as Mick was concerned they were the best band that he'd formed but when he protested, Doug told him that he'd best stay on the pub circuit if his loyalty was that strong. He added that if Mick changed his mind, he should turn up at his office the next day, where he would find a ready-made band waiting, and a contract in which the agency would finance him in the costly process of making him a star. The new band would all be about his age and would be the best around.

That day, Mick lost a lot of friends and began to make his boss very rich indeed. It was the typical rags-to-riches tale which made Mick the number one singer in the eyes of the public; making him wealthy, but costing him his friends and his girlfriend, Mary. Doug removed her very quickly; she was bad for Mick's image. She had to go and, like a fool, Mick had let them send her away. Doug then introduced him to all the right people who were in fact, all the wrong people. There were groupies and hangers-on, and at first it revolted Mick but after a while he actually began to like the attention of all of these freaks. It was about that time that he discovered his liking for older women and met June, who brought a whole new dimension to sex. Women were now a pushover to attract but he never forgot his sweet Mary and often wondered what had happened to her.

Ed broke his reverie. 'Weather's holding pretty good for September,' he said, drying his face on a towel.

Mick agreed, his mind still on Mary, and turned to Ed asking, 'how many times have you laid the love of your life?'

'Once,' replied Ed, hanging up the face towel and picking up his comb. Mick was shocked. Ed was the most randy thing on two legs; was he cracking up? The conversation ended as June and Cathy returned with two flasks of coffee.

'You lazy devil, Mick, you haven't even attempted to get ready.'

'My dear, we were talking man talk,' replied Mick.

June swore and retrieved her bikini from the floor. 'You're still not properly dressed,' she yelled.

Mick rummaged under the bed, feeling for his shoes. He couldn't find them but found a pair of white bikini briefs and waved them in the air. 'You say that I'm not properly dressed, but you've got no drawers on,' he chuckled.

June didn't bat an eyelid; she took the briefs and stepped into them. 'I've been looking everywhere for those buggers,' she said. 'Hurry up Mick or the sun will go in.'

Cathy searched for her bikini and, finding it, asked June if they should change now. She agreed. 'It'll save changing when we get there,' she said.

Mick found his shoes and put them on. 'I'm all for that,' he said, 'give us a show, girls.'

June said angrily, 'dirty sod, we'll strip when you two are downstairs packing the lunch in the car.'

Cathy had flushed crimson once more and, noting her getting flustered, Mick tidied himself up quickly and headed for the door armed with flasks and food. Ed blew her a kiss and followed Mick downstairs. The next step was for Cathy to decide what she should wear.

'You'd look great in anything,' said June. 'I wish I had your looks. I was pretty when I was young but not like you. You're really lovely; you should come out of yourself more. You walk around as if you've got no right to be on this earth at all, when you should actually be full of confidence and hold your head up.' Reaching inside the wardrobe she saw something that caught her eye. 'This one,' she said retrieving a dress, 'it's beautiful.' The dress was scarlet, with braiding around the hem and a mandarin collar. Bells and roses were scattered all over it, and it zipped up at the front. At the collar, a larger bell was attached which gave out a tinkling sound as it moved.

Cathy was donning her bikini and looked up. 'I was going to throw it away,' she said, 'but I decided to give it one last airing before it went to the jumble sale.'

'But it's beautiful; the essence of flower power.'

'Exactly, I bought it when flower power started, but Tony said that I looked ridiculous in it so it hasn't had much use.'

'Bastard!' June exclaimed. 'That's what I like about men; they woo you, wed you, and then the next move is to make you feel like a drudge – cooking, shopping, ironing, having sex just when they feel like it. Sod your feelings; even the odd box of chocolates or flowers is beyond them, and as for compliments, forget it. Then if someone else starts paying you attention, they're hurt. The ignorant fools forget that we're human. All they do is make the kids, they haven't got to walk the floor at night when the kids are teething. All we ask for is a bit of attention but that's beyond them. They're always too tired for us but they still have the energy to go to the pub with their mates. To most men, their wife is a second class citizen.'

'June, you sound so bitter.' Cathy turned around so that she could do up her bikini top.

'I am bitter. I've no problem with committing adultery; I'm getting what I can out of life.' Cathy dressed hurriedly, pulling on the dress that June had enthused over. 'Ed's eyes will pop out of his head when he sees you, but there's no point in me dressing up as Mick and I will screw later so I don't want my clothes messed up. You look beautiful, and take my advice; don't ditch Ed, he's head over heels for you.' She dragged a comb through her hair and began to apply new make-up.

Cathy brushed her hair but she wasn't going to bother with make-up. 'Come on,' she said, 'they're waiting.'

Downstairs, Ed's eyes lit up when he saw Cathy and he began to sing, 'If you're going to San Francisco, wear some flowers in your hair.' He picked a flower and placed it in her hair. 'Come on guys,' he said, 'I feel a love-in coming on.'

A little later they arrived at a very pretty spot, and spread the food out on a table cloth on the ground. June poured the coffee out and the men drank lager. The girls stripped down to their bikinis while Mick and Ed removed their shirts. Mick stared over at Cathy. 'This sun is making me horny,' he said. He was sending out a signal and hoping that it might be picked up and returned. Cathy might be with Ed, but all is fair in love and war.

Ed had wandered over to the car. 'Fuck,' he said. 'I must have left it at your place; I could do with a joint.' Cathy was baffled; the only joint she knew of was the one that she cooked on Sundays. The foursome pigged out on the huge spread that June had prepared and then stretched out in the sunshine.

'I'm going to take a nap,' said June. Mick smiled to himself; he had other ideas. Cathy closed her eyes thinking that if she pretended to sleep, Ed might just leave her alone. Ed's testosterone was scaling alarming heights but he stretched out beside Cathy and cuddled up to her. They both dozed until June started to make some sounds of pleasure.

Ed whispered into Cathy's ear. 'Let's move off a little way, I'm sure you don't want to listen to that.' She agreed and, getting to her feet, picked up her dress and took Ed's hand. He smiled at her; he was having difficulty controlling himself but he felt that he should get a medal for his gentlemanly behaviour. The sun was beating down and it was unusually hot for September.

They walked on until suddenly Ed turned to face Cathy and seized her, holding her so closely that she couldn't get her breath. She broke free and ran off sobbing. Suddenly, she stopped dead in her tracks, and stared straight ahead of her. Ed caught up with her, wondering what it was that had stalled her. It was a waterfall that Cathy gazed at wide-eyed before running towards it. Like a child she giggled and held her hands under the water. Ed stared at her, his heart pounding, her hair shining like spun gold in the sunlight as she stepped under the waterfall and let the water run over her body. He followed her and took her in his arms again 'I love you Cathy,' he gasped over and over again. He kissed her and got no response. She appeared to be in a trance until Ed tried to remove her bikini top and then she awoke.

'No Ed, I don't want to,' she cried, 'someone might see us.'

Realising that this was just another excuse, Ed stroked her hair and said, 'relax, honey, nobody will see us, this place is far too remote.'

'No, I don't want to and I'm not very good at this sort of thing.'

'Just relax,' soothed Ed as he was getting soaked.

'No, I'm Tony's wife, and sex just doesn't turn me on like it does you.'

Ed ran his hands up and down her body. 'It's not true, any of it,' he said. 'Once you're divorced, you'll be my wife. You belong with me so don't make excuses.' He tugged on the hook of her bikini top, and added, 'as for saying that you're not very good at it, that's rubbish. You were great when we made love, and it's my job to make you good. I turned you on, I know I did, so saying that sex doesn't turn you on is crazy. You're a terrific girl and your only problem is that nobody has ever bothered to turn you on. Just relax and come to me.'

Tears were running down Cathy's cheeks and mixed with the water. Her struggling became half-hearted as Ed coaxed her and soothed her. Placing one hand under her chin, he forced her to look him in the eyes. She tried to avert her gaze but each time Ed managed to prevent this. 'Now tell me this is wrong,' he said, 'if you can.' Cathy's body was racked with sobs; she couldn't and he knew it. 'Okay, cry it out,' he added, 'because I don't intend to let you look away.' He was soaked by now, and Cathy felt him draw her to him. He had this magnetic power and she felt her willpower drain from her. Something inside her had snapped and she kissed him, clawed at him, and shook with a raging passion. They were indeed made for each other. Ed knew that somehow taking a shower would never be the same again.

Afterwards they dried off as best they could. It was pretty straight forward for Cathy as all she had to do was remove her wet bikini and step into her dry dress which was lying on the grass. Ed had a bit more of a problem; he'd been under that waterfall for ages with his trousers on, and he'd had enough trouble getting them off. Now came the ordeal of trying to get the soaking wet things back on again. He finally managed it after a struggle, and the couple made their way back to Mick and June. Mick was swigging down a bottle of lager. June was asleep, and Mick eyed Cathy up and down. 'Been swimming?' he asked.

'We found a waterfall,' replied Cathy, 'only a small one but it was very pretty.'

Mick surveyed Ed who was stripping out of his wet things. Cathy hung her wet bikini on the branch of a nearby tree.

'Perfect setting,' laughed Ed, crossing to the car and rummaging around for a towel. He found two and threw one over to Cathy who immediately began to dry her hair.

'Well I suppose you had reasons for getting under the waterfall,' said Mick, 'but normally I would take my clothes off for that.' Ed grinned but wished he'd brought a spare pair of trousers with him. As if reading his thoughts, Mick rummaged inside his car and removed a pair of jeans. He tossed them over to Ed saying, 'borrow these, can't have you catching pneumonia.'

Ed caught them. 'Thanks, pal,' he said, 'you're great.'

'Sure I am,' agreed Mick. He nudged June who protested violently at being woken.

'Can't I get five minutes sleep?' she demanded.

'We're going waterfall hunting,' replied Mick.

'You flipped or something? What waterfall?'

'Cathy and Ed found one,' answered Mick, 'and by the look of them I would say it was some waterfall. Aren't you just a little bit curious?'

June looked at Cathy, who really glowed. She looked so different, so alive, so much better. 'Sure,' she replied and got up. Hand in hand with Mick, she walked away.

After drying herself, Cathy stretched out in the sun. At last she felt that she now knew what life was all about. Tony had been her first lover. She'd always had a hot nature and Tony had chided her for it many times. If she made the first move, he'd call her a whore and also made her feel very guilty if she reached orgasm. 'I'm dominant and you're passive,' he used to say, making her feel very guilty about enjoying sex at all.

Now Ed had come into her life, however, and things were different. He'd made her realise that sexual enjoyment was not one way. As she'd soared toward her climax, he'd satisfied her fully before considering himself, and as for oral sex, by contrast Tony would have had a fit. She wanted to be with Ed but felt guilty about her daughter Sandy, although the child was growing up without her anyway, and a steady procession of Tony's girlfriends passed through the house while she was touring, so the child was never short of female company.

Ed threw a blanket over her and then snuggled under it with her. He kissed her on the cheek and then moved to the rest of her body. Already his head was going down, and Cathy shivered as Ed began to rekindle the flame that he'd lit earlier. She was soon in the throes of orgasm, and a short while later passed over the threshold of ecstasy. Ed still held her tightly and soon she could feel the same feelings rise up once more. Four times in all she cried out to him at the peak of her climax, and then he would whisper, 'are you ready?' Cathy nodded; she could take this as long as he wanted her to. Murmuring endearments into her ear, he braced himself until he felt her body convulse beneath him and then he let himself go as together they reached the height of sexual fulfilment. For Cathy, time stood still. Ed was her night, her day, and her sky. Locked together they sank and lay still in silence. There was no need for words; everything had been said in the language of love.

About five minutes later, Mick and June returned. Mick seemed rather disgruntled.

'What happened?' asked a curious Ed.

'She wouldn't go under,' grunted Mick.

'I should think not,' retorted June, 'there was a man walking his dog.'

'Yeah,' said Mick, 'a bloody sightseer.'

Ed threw back his head and laughed. 'Hope he wasn't there earlier, he would have got a real eyeful.'

June screwed up her face and sat on the grass. 'Stop moaning, there's always later,' she mumbled.

Mick stood with his hands on his hips. 'Sure, we'll put the waterfall in a paper bag and take it home.' He gazed at Cathy and the happy, love-struck Ed; how he envied his friend. He looked at his watch and voiced his feelings about leaving; time was marching on. A very contented Cathy yawned and wriggled back into her bikini bottoms which Ed had thrown over at her. They were still damp so she removed them again and decided to go home knicker-less. Ed's trousers were still wet so Mick suggested that he keep the jeans until later. They picked up their belongings and all headed back to the cabaret club.

It was getting quite late in the day, so Cathy picked up several items that she would need for the evening ahead. There was make-up, hair rollers, various items of jewellery, and of course her costume for the night's performance. Mick decided to stay with June for a little bit longer as she had to remain behind for the show. Cathy wondered if she'd be back in time for her spot but realised that Ed had everything under control and so left with him to return to his digs. 'Follow you later,' said Mick, his hands all over June once more, 'I won't be late.'

Back at Ed's digs, Romany wandered around cracking jokes. Ed told him to shut up but he persisted, so he and Cathy went to go upstairs for a nap. 'Miserable bastards,' snapped Romany, but they ignored him and Cathy felt that she should rest.

She soon dozed off but awoke after a short while in the middle of a bad nightmare. She, Ed, and Tony were standing on a sheet of ice in the ocean. Tony held Sandy in his arms. Suddenly the ice splintered into three pieces and Cathy found herself alone on the middle section. Ed held out his arms to her while the gaps between the ice blocks grew larger. Sandy screamed to her mother and finally Cathy jumped onto Ed's section while Sandy and Tony floated away. The whole thing ended with her jumping into the icy water crying that she'd made a mistake. She awoke screaming, waking Ed who held her to him, soothing her. She gazed around her realising that it was just a nightmare, and felt safe in Ed's embrace, but the dream lingered and unsettled her. She decided to remain awake as she was scared of drifting back into the nightmare.

Later that evening, Cathy arrived at Ed's venue and changed into her costume, placing her coat over the top of it. Romany leered; for the first time Ed wasn't sharing and he didn't like it. He wished that Cathy would go away, far away, so that things could go back to normal. Sidling over to her, he said, 'Ed's band is no good, we're the stars. How about you and I split; I can give you a better time than he can.'

'No thank you,' replied Cathy. 'I like the band; I watched them earlier.'

'Yeah, well I admire your loyalty, but they're rubbish,' said Romany, walking behind and pushing himself up against her. 'Ed screw you real good, did he?' He slid his hand under Cathy's coat muttering, 'once you've had me, you won't give Ed a second look.'

'Stop it,' cried Cathy, 'some best friend you are.'

She pushed his hands away but Romany just laughed at her and groped her some more. She elbowed him in his ribs and he let go of her. 'Well, are you his best friend or not, you pervert?' she demanded.

'Sure,' replied Romany, 'but we usually share things and he's being greedy with you.' Cathy faced him, eyes blazing with fury, but undaunted he leered back, his eyes glinting with lust. 'We could make great music,' he added. Inwardly Cathy trembled; Romany scared her. It wasn't the kind of fear that made her want to run, it was the kind that made her want to stay; he drew her to him. Sexually he was very magnetic, and although she was giving him the brush off she was intrigued. The most frightening thing about it was that she could see he could read her thoughts. Cathy was pleased when Mick put in an appearance.

'Go check your guitar,' he said, 'one of the strings looks a bit grotty.' Romany shuffled off, grumbling. 'Giving you trouble?' enquired Mick.

'No,' replied Cathy, 'I can handle him.'

'Stick close to Ed before Romany gets his magic working.'

'I'm unaffected, honestly.'

'Of course,' said Mick, noticing the sudden colour stain her cheeks.

His attention was drawn to the stage. The audience were restless as they wanted Mick not Ed. There were cries of 'Sod off'; 'We want Ed off, and Mick on', and, 'Get some real musicians up there.' Cathy was amazed; Ed had been so confident at the pub and during rehearsal but now he was singing to his feet. Things went from bad to worse as the next three numbers got the slow hand clap, and then a coke can hit the stage. Cathy buried her head in Mick's shoulder.

'Why don't they listen? They're not that bad.' She looked over at the performers with pity. 'They're only warm-up,' she added. Mick held the girl to him. She was warming him up too but she didn't realise this. From the stage, Billy announced, 'Ed wrote this next one, how about a big hand for him.'

'Yeah,' shouted a leather-clad youth at the front, 'a big hand; a fist right in the mush.'

The crowd at the front roared with laughter. Another heckler shouted, ''ere Ed, why are you staring at your boots, you lost a quid?'

His girlfriend shrieked with hysteria, saying, 'This bunch couldn't earn a quid.'

The whole group were doubled up laughing, and then the chant of, 'we want Mick,' began. Mick felt dreadful; he hadn't a clue what to do about the fracas on stage. However, if Cathy let him take her to a vacant room he'd attempt to put her out of her misery, and it would put him out of his misery too. If his trousers got much tighter, they would split. Then another can hit the stage and the bouncers just stood there yawning; people they bounced, cans they did not. If Mick had been getting this treatment, the trouble-makers would have been ejected, but Ed, well he was nothing. Mick gazed at Cathy and then it hit him. She was dressed to go on stage, not this one but it didn't make much difference, and something had to be done quickly.

'You can dance to Ed's music, can't you?' asked Mick.

Cathy recalled the rehearsal and knew that Ed had sung *Green Tambourine* that morning. She beckoned Billy over and said, 'play *Green Tambourine* twice, and I'll dance; Ed can do his new song later.'

A couple more cans hit the stage, followed by a bottle. Billy flinched and then said into the microphone, 'and now for something completely different.' Cathy stripped off her coat and stood in front of Mick; now he felt worse. The garb of a belly dancer covered very little and his trousers were strangling him. The band struck up the opening bars of the song and Cathy shimmied out onto the stage.

The leather-clad youth was just about to add another clever remark when his jaw dropped at the sight of the new member of the band. 'Like it,' he called out, 'like it a lot.'

'We want Mick!' shouted his companion.

'Shut up, you stupid cow,' retorted the youth, 'I like this lot now.' Ed began to sing as Cathy moved to the music, which in turn infected Paddy who'd nearly fallen asleep at the drums. Ed's eyes were out on stalks again as he'd not seen this outfit before and it left very little to the imagination. Once the song was over, the crowd went wild and cries of more followed Cathy's departure. She looked around for Mick. He wasn't there but a little while later emerged with a very dishevelled girl from a room. Cathy sighed, these singers seemed to do nothing but have sex with any girl they fancied. This was confirmed when Ed came hurtling off stage and dragged her into a dressing room.

Romany went into hysterics. 'Need any help?' he asked. Ed slammed the door in his face, and outside Romany felt only envy. He knew that before the night was out, he'd have more than his fair share of girls but it was because Cathy was unavailable that made her all the more desirable. He heard the girl give out a broken cry minutes later and he moved away from the door which was just as well as seconds later the couple charged out of the room as if they were in some kind of a race.

Back at the club, Cathy went through her act and then left with Ed to visit Rusty. They were warmly greeted by the family. Several hippies were singing, accompanied by two guitarists, and Eli was pounding out the rhythm on his drum. A sudden squeal made Cathy turn around. Amber and her sister had been playing with several children nearby, but on seeing them arrive had come running over. 'Eden,' cried Amber, 'will you come and live with us soon? You could share our caravan now you've got Cathy.'

Ed picked her up. 'Soon maybe, but I've got a secret.'

Amethyst jumped up and down with excitement. 'Tell us,' she cried.

'Well,' said Ed, 'if we do come and live with you, you will have a playmate.'

Amber stared at Cathy and gave her a really sunny smile. 'Baby,' she said.

'No,' Ed corrected her. 'Cathy's got a little girl called Sandy, and she's only three.'

Amber clapped her hands delightedly, and as Ed put her down she ran over to her mother crying, 'Sandy, Sandy, my new sister, I love her.'

Fawn wandered over to embrace Cathy and, spying the ring on her finger, said, 'welcome to the family, you two are obviously an item now.' Ed wandered over to the hippy group and she burst into tears. Fawn put her arm around her. 'What's the matter?' she asked softly.

'I'm so happy,' replied Cathy, 'but I feel so guilty.'

'Why feel guilty?' asked Fawn. 'You're what Eden really needs. All his past girls have meant nothing and, as for his best friend Romany, well he's just evil and jealous. You're probably top of his wish list now.'

'But Fawn, what about my daughter? I can't take her away from her father.'

'Then don't. Start afresh with Eden.'

'I don't know if I can do this,' sobbed Cathy, drying her eyes on a tissue.

'You can,' replied Fawn. 'Listen to one who knows. I was very unhappy in my marriage to Summer's father and then I met Rusty. We fell in love and decided to live together but Summer adored her father and I decided that she was better off with him so I left. I kept in touch with her and then, hey presto, one day she decided to come and live with us and she's a very happy girl. Then she completed our family when she had Blue, and as for our two little girls, well, you couldn't find two happier children. Follow your heart, Cathy, Eden loves you and he's come alive.' She hugged her and added, 'come on, I'll introduce you to some of our friends that you haven't met.' Cathy smiled, and hand in hand they headed for the hippy group.

After a very entertaining night, Ed and Cathy returned to the club and went to bed. 'Where do you want to go tomorrow?' asked Ed.

'Don't know,' replied Cathy. 'I've never been to Wales before.'

'Really? We'll fix that. Tomorrow I'll give you a guided tour. We're in Mid Glamorgan, and Wales is a beautiful place.' Cathy looked over at June's bed and it was empty. Obviously she'd decided to pay Mick a surprise visit. From the next room, Hal could be heard snoring. They laughed, made love, and then slept.

Chapter Four

The following morning they had breakfast at the club, and then left to explore the beauty of Wales. They went to Llynfi valley which stretched from Bridgend and Tondu. It was broad bottomed and leafy. Measteg wasn't too far from the club; only about two miles away. Coity Castle was near Bridgend. Ed said that Bridgend's Welsh name was 'Penybont Ar Ogwr'. 'It guards the entrance to three valleys,' he told her.

They visited Oldcastle, Ewenny, Priory, and Porthcawl. Cathy quite liked Porthcawl and they held hands as they walked along the seafront. She also liked Kenfig fishing port where there were gulls, ringed plovers, redshanks, and oystercatchers. Cowbridge Green was another visit, and Llangeinor Medieval Church another.

In Llantrisant, Ed told Cathy about a very famous person, Dr William Price. He was born in 1800 and died in 1893. He dressed in druid's outfits and had strong views regarding free love, vegetarianism, and anti-smoking. He also hated socks, saying that they were unhealthy.

'You know a lot about him,' said Cathy.

Ed nodded, adding, 'he cremated his dead baby son in a service on Llantrisant Common in 1884. He burnt the child in an oil drum and was arrested and sent to Cardiff for trial. He was later acquitted because cremation became legal in the UK.'

Cathy frowned, and then she laughed. 'Didn't know that I was going out with such a brainbox.'

'Oh well, I'm not just a pretty face,' said Ed, 'and did you know that the Royal Mint was moved here last year?'

'No,' replied Cathy, fascinated. She guessed that Ed must have been good at history in school. They explored new areas daily, and Cathy loved Cardiff and Swansea. 'Wales is all too beautiful,' she sighed.

'Back to the Small Faces again,' said Ed. 'Do you remember what you were doing the last time you heard that on my radio?' Cathy flushed. She certainly did.

Ed had a problem in that he was experiencing so many emotions. The intensity of his feelings for his beloved Cathy was overwhelming him. He couldn't resist touching her, gazing into her eyes and stroking her hair, but the feeling to possess, to control, to make her bend to his will was overpowering. The problem was that he wanted her dependent on him, and he was becoming co-dependent.

He hated leaving her to go to work as he was in a different area and, as soon as he'd finished his show, would drive all the way back to the club no matter how far it was. If anyone paid her too much attention he'd get jealous. He couldn't get enough of her, and his sexual demands were never ending. In his mind, if he gave her total satisfaction, she'd never leave him. Every time he took her in his arms he felt safe, loved and warm, but away from her he was in a blind panic.

The couple were together all the time, delighting in each other's company and behaving like children when out in the countryside. They'd play hide and seek, and Ed would give Cathy piggybacks and roll around on the grass in total abandon. Ed, however, was still terrified that Cathy would leave him.

Meanwhile, Rusty was becoming very concerned over his brother's possessiveness.

'He's suffocating her,' he told Fawn one evening. 'The girl is a free spirit; the hippy way is free love, peace, and freedom, and she has no freedom.'

Fawn hugged him and reassured him. 'Give him time, he loves her.' Rusty shrugged his shoulders and walked away feeling uneasy.

Saturday night was the final night of the Shelltones UK tour. After finishing their acts, Cathy, June, and Hal made for the venue to watch the final show. Hal drove as it made sense; it saved Ed having to pick Cathy up, and as Hal said, 'the final party is always the best.'

They were greeted by a very anxious Ed who took Cathy in his arms as soon as she arrived. June sighed. 'Why doesn't this ever happen to me? Mick never greets me like that,' she said.

'Doesn't happen to me either,' groaned Hal, faking tears. They all made their way to the wings and watched the band which was well into its set.

Cathy leaned up against Ed in total contentment. He kissed the back of her neck and whispered, 'I'm so lucky to have found my soul mate.' The band played brilliantly, and Cathy could still hero worship Mick who fronted the band with a mesmerising performance. She wondered what would have happened if she hadn't met Ed. If Mick had come onto her, she would have had difficulty holding him off.

The applause was deafening and the band had to give two encores. Off stage, Mick and Romany were still enemies; they almost came to blows until their manager split them up. Romany turned to a young groupie. 'Fancy coming to a party with me?' he asked. The starry eyed girl nodded vigorously and took his arm.

At the party, Romany made straight for the bar, followed by his date. June was already upstairs and congratulated Cathy. 'I'm so glad that you've made the right decision,' she said. 'Ed really is madly in love with you.' Cathy brushed her hair and did her make-up as Romany swaggered into the room.

'Mick's looking for you,' he said to June, knocking back his drink in one gulp.

June retouched her make-up and got up to leave the room. ‘See you later, Cathy,’ she said.

Romany sat on the bed beside Cathy. ‘Hi, babe,’ he said. ‘I wondered when I’d get you on your own.’

Cathy moved away from him and continued to do her make-up. ‘I love Ed,’ she said, touching up her eye shadow.

‘Sure,’ said Romany, ‘but I can’t help envying him sometimes, like now for instance.’ He grabbed her wrist hard, pulling her down beside him on the bed. She struggled but he was far too strong for her and she couldn’t break free. ‘You know what I mean, don’t you, baby,’ said Romany, gazing at her from under his very long eyelashes.

Cathy recalled that Fawn had said, ‘you’re probably top of his wish list.’

He kissed her full on her lips, saying, ‘easy, baby.’ His hand was now running over her thigh and he had her pinned down. She screamed several times but Romany laughed, ‘no one can hear you above that din down there and your struggling is only making me more determined.’ Cathy bit his arm and he yelped and back-handed her, saying, ‘just relax and enjoy yourself.’ She prayed that someone would come in but no one seemed to be missing her.

‘Ed will be looking for me,’ cried Cathy.

‘Do you think I care?’ sneered Romany. He could feel her body move toward him; she was still fighting him but not as much. No woman could resist him.

Downstairs, Mick was concerned. Ed was conversing with a reporter, but it was Romany’s absence that bothered him. His date was sitting on her own and had been for a good five minutes.

June had said that she’d seen him upstairs so he decided to check this out as he had a gut feeling something bad might happen, and there was no sign of Cathy. He didn’t trust Romany at all, and he didn’t want his lead guitarist getting involved in a punch up with Ed. The band had a continental tour to start on Wednesday.

He ascended the stairs and made for the bedroom. The sight that met his eyes was not a pretty one. Romany had Cathy completely pinned down by the weight of his body, and she was crying. 'What the fuck are you doing?' bellowed Mick, trying to pull Romany off the terrified girl.

'Get off me,' snarled Romany. 'Hold her still and I'll do the same for you after if you want.'

'Filthy bastard,' snapped Mick, 'and you call yourself Ed's best mate? You're completely evil.' He grabbed Romany again and managed to knock him to the floor. Cathy rushed to the bathroom to tidy her hair and make-up, and wash away her tears.

Romany got to his feet, grinning broadly. 'Ed would never believe you if you told him,' he said. 'He'd blame her.' Mick took a deep breath; he knew that Romany was right. He waited until Cathy had cleaned herself up and then escorted her downstairs. Romany laughed, but he didn't know why, he was feeling cheated. He knew that he could have had the girl if Mick hadn't turned up. Furious, he threw himself onto the bed and fisted the pillows.

Downstairs, Ed was now in deep conversation with June. The Stones were on the turntable. 'Any requests?' shouted the DJ.

'Yes,' said June, 'Amen Corner and Small Faces.' In a corner, Doug, who was Mick's manager, was snorting coke, and couples were smooching on the dance floor as the DJ slowed the music down. Hal wandered over to Doug and challenged him to a Highland fling contest. Romany had wasted no time. He'd only just come downstairs but already he'd pounced on his date and had his hand up her skirt.

Cathy was feeling sleepy; she'd had several drinks before she'd left the club and a couple at Ed's venue, and the alcohol was really hitting her now. Ed took her hand and led her to the dance floor. They clung together as *Love Is All Around* by the Troggs began to play. Cathy felt dizzy and Ed was holding her so tightly, she could hardly breathe. She could feel him getting harder by the second. There was a sudden crash as Doug spun too fast and landed on his back knocking several couples over in the process. Cathy was aware that Ed was steering her away from the floor and towards a leopard print sofa where she sat down and wondered if her drink had been spiked. Alcohol didn't usually make her go under this quickly. Ed was conversing with the DJ, and nearby Romany was having intercourse with his date. Many people were watching but he was unfazed, he just banged away. Ed was back again and offering her a joint, but she refused and felt him lift her legs up onto the sofa. From the record decks, Dylan's voice burst forth. Cathy let the music sweep over her, and Ed noted the ecstatic expression on her face.

'Got a fixation on Dylan?' he asked.

Cathy smiled, 'I love him,' she replied.

Ed dragged on his joint and inhaled. 'Remind me not to introduce you to him,' he laughed. 'I can't compete with him, or Steve Marriot for that matter.'

Cathy smiled and opened her eyes. 'No one can compete with Steve Marriot's vocals, but as for Dylan; well he's my God apart from you.'

Ed offered the joint to her again and this time she accepted and shared it with him. He gazed at his very drunk, very stoned lady. He got up and left the room, returning with a blanket. After getting back onto the sofa he threw the blanket over them both. Moans of pleasure echoed from almost every corner of the room, and Cathy's voice joined the throng. The DJ sighed; he wondered why everyone got a woman when all he got was a pile of records. The sensations that Cathy was experiencing seemed to be magnified, and it was strange but incredibly beautiful. She seemed to climax several times in a row, taking her breath away. Everything seemed so unreal and she was relieved when Ed suggested leaving. She felt fantastic but weird; it was a great experience but not one that she felt she'd want to repeat.

Arriving back at the cabaret club, Cathy let them in and made some coffee then took it upstairs. Flopping down on the bed she found it difficult to undress herself as she'd had far too much alcohol. She gave up fiddling with the buttons on her dress, and Ed handed her the coffee. 'I'm pissed and exhausted,' she said.

'Hope not,' said Ed with a smile, 'I've got other plans.'

'What, again?'

Ed nodded, 'I'm not planning on going to sleep yet, I want you.' Cathy was getting a bit fed up with the 'I want,' bit. Rusty had mentioned that if Ed said 'I want,' he always 'got.' In fact, Ed himself had told her just before they'd made love for the first time that if he set his mind to getting something he always got it. It was irritating. What about other people's feelings?

Having drunk his coffee, Ed was already unbuttoning her dress. 'I love you,' he murmured, nuzzling into her neck and moving down to cover her breasts in kisses. This gave way to deep tongue to tongue kissing, as he sucked her bottom lip, explored her mouth, and then began to explore her body. Cathy felt faint with pleasure as his tongue sucked and probed at her.

She gave herself up time and time again, and when Ed did finally bear down on her she nearly passed out. Several times that night she dozed off only to be awoken by Ed, who seemed intent on total satisfaction. At one point she cried out, 'I can't take any more!'

She was silenced by her lover who assured her, 'honey, you're just warming up.' It was daylight before either of them slept, and they huddled together in a contented slumber.

Sunday morning arrived and it was Cathy's last day. She had a lunchtime show to do that the manager had put in at the last moment. She was awoken by a kiss, and Ed offering her a tray with a cooked breakfast on it. She gazed at it, and though she wasn't sure if she could eat with such a massive hangover, she managed to get it down and felt better afterwards.

June arrived with Mick and looked hungover too. 'I'm knackered,' she said. 'Still, it is the last show and as soon as it's over I'm going back with Mick to spend our last few hours together. He's off to the continent on Wednesday so God knows when we'll meet up again.'

Mick looked hungover too. 'God, that was some party last night, wasn't it, Ed?'

'Dunno,' said Ed, 'we left before it finished. We're off to Bristol tomorrow.'

'We?' asked Mick, puzzled.

'Yep,' said Ed. 'Cathy's coming with me.'

'I'm going downstairs to phone my daughter,' said Cathy, putting on a dressing gown. 'The last time I spoke to her was last Sunday when I arrived here, and since then I've not been able to get through.'

'All right, babe,' said Ed, 'that's okay.'

June frowned. What did he mean 'okay?' Did she have to get his permission to use the phone? Ed was bothering her; he wasn't as outgoing as he had been, and he seemed to panic if Cathy was away from him no matter how short the time lapse. If this continued he'd end up driving her away.

'So she's coming with you,' said Mick. 'What about all that mess at home that needs addressing? She should go home and sort that out first and then rejoin you later.'

Ed rounded on Mick. 'Don't tell me what to do,' he snapped. 'That's what she wants to do but I'm not having it. She stays with me. I want her.'

June flinched; there it was again. How many times had she heard this before: 'I want.'

Mick whistled. 'I still think it's wrong.'

'Why?' demanded Ed, 'because you want to get your paws on her? I'll fucking kill you if you try.'

'Ed,' cried June, 'how can you even think such a thing?'

Mick was visibly hurt. 'I'll just pretend I didn't hear that,' he said. 'Maybe you should look a bit closer at your best friend; he's the one with his tongue hanging out.'

'You're a liar,' said Ed, 'and anyway I'm marrying her today.'

June sighed, 'you can't; she's already married.'

Mick scratched his head. 'Could be a problem,' he said.

Ed shrugged. 'It's a hippy wedding, and my cousin Seth is doing it.'

'Seth?' cried June. 'He's the one that's into the occult. Are you nuts? Why couldn't you have got someone else?'

'Seth used to be a preacher,' said Ed. 'He does all the hippy weddings.'

June wasn't happy. She crossed to the window and looked out. 'What does Cathy think about this?' she asked.

Ed threw back his head and laughed. 'She doesn't know,' he said. 'It's all set up; she thinks we're going to one of Rusty's gigs. It'll be a nice surprise.'

June shook her head. 'It's not the surprise I'd want.' She collapsed on the bed. 'I still think you're out of order. God, how am I supposed to sing? My eyes are so sore. I'm going to make some coffee, hopefully that might help. Anyone else want one?'

'Yes,' said Ed, and Mick just nodded. He thought the whole thing was crazy. He waited until June had staggered to the door and left the room, and then turned to Ed.

'What's up with you, man?' he demanded. 'You only met a week ago. Exchange phone numbers, let her go home, have a breather, and meet up at a later date when things are sorted, or when you've had time to rethink. Romany's pissed off with you; you didn't even say goodbye last night. Paddy and Billy say you've only done one rehearsal all week, and you've stopped going to parties; you're cracking up.'

'But all I want is her. Haven't you ever felt like that?'

'Yes, for about forty-eight hours, and then I've woken up.'

'But that's the difference. When I hold Cathy, I'm complete.'

'You're not giving each other any space; you're not letting her breathe,' Mick retorted, getting more and more wound up. He was about to add more when the girls arrived with the coffee.

'Still can't get through,' said Cathy, looking dejected. 'I'll try again later.'

June groaned, 'where did this bloody lunchtime show come from? It wasn't in my contract; I only heard about it yesterday. I've got to do two spots.'

'We all have,' said Cathy, 'which means two changes of costume.'

Ed pulled her onto his knee and started nuzzling her neck. He stared at Mick. 'Beautiful, isn't she?' he said.

Cathy stood up and crossed to the table. 'I need this coffee badly,' she said. 'I've got a show to do.'

About ten minutes later, Hal arrived. 'Got lost,' he said. 'Think the locals were taking the piss. Three people directed me so I'd headed for Maesteg and ended in a forest, and then I ended up driving in a circle so I came back. It's easy to get lost around here.' Cathy walked over to the wardrobe and took her Gypsy and belly dancer costumes out. She hung them on the wardrobe door. Meanwhile, June was looking for her hair rollers, Hal was wondering which outfits to wear, and Mick was falling asleep.

Ed grabbed Cathy as she walked past. 'C'mon, babe,' he said, 'we've got time. I've got to disappear soon to see Rusty for tonight's gig.'

'No, we haven't got time,' said Cathy. Ed was angry and picked her up. She struggled, but to no avail and he carried her into the bedroom and closed the door. Through the wall, Cathy could be heard protesting and then it went silent. Mick looked at June and shook his head.

Hal broke the silence. 'I need a shower,' he said. 'How about you, June?'

'No,' replied June. 'I had one at Mick's.'

Mick left the table and sprawled on the bed. This British tour had left him drained. He was finally going home tomorrow after a long tour and many rows with Romany. He never argued with the rest of the band but he clashed with Romany over everything.

He'd had a laugh with the vocal duo that also supported the band; they sang mainly folk songs but they were very popular. He'd really gelled with Ed, Paddy, and Billy, but now Ed was freaking him out and he thought the best thing that Cathy could do was to run. Ed seemed unbalanced. Still there was nothing he could do about it. By next week he would be in France with the rest of the band. A continental tour, more rows with Romany, more girls, more drugs, more booze; it was like a carousel that you couldn't get off. He closed his eyes, hearing Cathy in the throes of orgasm above the noise of the shower, and then he dozed. June busied herself getting ready for the lunchtime show, and a short while later, a very dishevelled Cathy emerged from the bedroom. She was agitated, saying, 'now I've got to shower again.'

'Well at least I've got my bedroom back,' grunted Hal, glaring at Ed.

'Sorry,' said Ed, 'but I can't keep my hands off her, and I could hardly perform out here in the girls' room, could I?' He thought it was rather funny, but no one else saw the joke. Annoyed, Ed added, 'Well I didn't think you'd want to watch.' From the bathroom, the shower could be heard running and Ed was still trying to put his point across. 'Look, the girls' room is also the living room; what could I do?'

'You could have waited until tonight,' said June, exasperated.

Ed was losing his temper. 'Don't you start telling me what I can and can't do. If I want her, I'll take her.'

'I see,' said June, 'so her feelings don't count. She didn't seem too keen to go into Hal's bedroom since you had to carry her in there.'

'You're getting old and miserable,' said Ed. Then he grinned and followed Cathy into the shower.

'Ed, leave her alone,' pleaded June, but her pleas fell on deaf ears.

June could hear Cathy pleading, 'Ed, leave me alone, stop it.'

The room went very quiet apart from the noise of the shower until there was a terrific scream of ecstasy.

Mick sat bolt upright. 'What the hell?' he shouted, and June pointed to the bathroom door.

'Ed and Cathy,' she said.

Mick flopped back onto the bed and banged his head on the brass headboard. Now he had a headache. 'But they were in the bedroom,' he said, confused.

'Yes,' said June, 'but she went to shower and he followed her in there.' Mick was open-mouthed as Ed emerged with a towel around him, grinning from ear to ear. Cathy followed him out, and began looking for a hairdryer.

'I've got to rush now,' she said.

Hal opened the bedroom door and looked around. 'What happened?' he asked, 'I thought someone was being murdered.'

'Blame Ed,' muttered June, putting on her make-up.

Hal glared at Ed. 'So, you're the culprit,' he said. 'You're getting as bad as Romany. There's too much testosterone around here; it's not good for me at my time of life.' He was dressed as a cowboy this time, complete with Stetson, chaps, and spurs, and he had two guns in his holsters. Ed dived into Hal's bedroom to tidy up and get dressed. 'God, he's after me now,' said Hal. 'I'm coming out here.'

Minutes later, Ed came out fully dressed and approached Mick. 'I guess I'd better say goodbye now,' he said, 'in case I miss you tomorrow morning. I guess that when June finishes her act, you'll take off for the rest of the day and I've got to go and see Rusty now. So all the best, buddy, good luck with your tour, and hopefully I'll see you soon.'

The two men hugged, and Mick slapped Ed on the back. 'Good luck,' he said. 'Look after yourself and Cathy, you're very lucky.'

'I will,' said Ed, and walked to the dressing table where Cathy was drying her hair. 'See you later, Cathy,' he said.

'Okay,' she said, staring into the mirror, 'see you later.' Ed repeated his farewell, and Cathy, reaching for her hair brush, said again, 'yes okay, see you soon.' She was unprepared for what happened next. He grabbed her wrist and swung her around so she faced him.

'I said, see you later, Cathy.'

'Okay,' she said, 'bye,' and kissed him on his cheek. By now Ed was really angry. It seemed as if she was ignoring him when all she really wanted to do was to get ready for the show. He pulled her to him and kissed her lips passionately. Mick, June, and Hal watched, uneasy, but felt that they couldn't intervene.

Ed released her. 'That's better. Bye Mick, bye June, bye Hal, got to go.' Then turning to Cathy said, 'I'll be back about seven. Be ready, gypsy girl.'

Cathy was rummaging in her make-up bag, and responded, 'I will, see you.'

It wasn't long before it was show time. Hal went out to introduce June, and with a big beaming smile she strode out, even though her head was throbbing. Mick was upstairs asleep.

When her act finished, she went upstairs and Hal took centre stage again. He swaggered up to the microphone looking butch and then struck a pose with his hands on his hips. In a high pitched drawl he said, 'Ooee, cowboys.' Then he drew a gun from its holster and fired. It made a loud noise, and he dropped his gun and ran behind the curtains.

Cathy chose that moment to come downstairs and he collided with her, landing on top of her and knocking over a box of footballs which scattered out onto the dance floor. 'Oh balls,' shouted Hal, knocking another one over in his confusion. 'Help,' he shouted, 'I've just landed on a gypsy and she's giving me the evil eye.' He fired his other gun. 'Oh, she got me,' he cried, and staggered back in front of the curtain, holding his chest. 'I'm dying,' he cried, 'I'm going stiff; it's that bloody gypsy.' The audience were in fits of laughter. 'Don't mock,' he said, 'I'm the fastest gunslinger in the west.' The band struck up *The Good, the Bad, and the Ugly*. They'd all donned Indian headdresses. 'Now,' shouted Hal, 'where are my guns?'

A young, tubby little red-haired boy with masses of freckles handed him the gun he'd dropped before. 'Thanks pardner,' said Hal, 'and what's your name?'

'Roy,' replied the child.

'Ooh,' said Hal, 'it's Roy Rogers.' He shook the child's hand. 'How's Trigger?' he asked.

'Fine.'

'Well, take a bow, Roy.' He patted the child on the head and added, 'go back to your seat and I'll get you a lemonade.'

The child bowed and went back to his mother.

Behind the curtain, Cathy was laughing, and she laughed even more when the bandleader started playing *The Good, the Bad, and the Ugly* again as one of the band rushed out with a tomahawk and started chasing Hal around the room. He was shouting, 'help!' at the top of his voice as he ran round and round until the band member went back to his position in the band. He then attempted to dance to the music and kicked a few footballs about in the process. At the bar, the manager fell about laughing and the audience cheered at Hal's antics.

Cathy's mind was confused; she loved show business and she was always at ease with her fellow acts. She was happy, truly happy. She missed Sandy though and wondered why she hadn't been able to get through on the telephone. It was probably just unlucky, and maybe Tony had gone to his mother's. Yes that was it, he'd probably gone there. Everything was fine but she still felt unsettled. She'd try again later.

Ten minutes later, Hal was winding down his act and peered around the curtain. 'That gypsy's still there,' he said. 'She's looking in her crystal ball but, well, without further delay, put your hands together for the lovely gypsy.' The band struck up her music and out she went, dancing, spinning, and clapping, completely lost in her own little world. Fifteen minutes later she finished her act to a huge round of applause and went back upstairs, just as Hal went out again firing his guns at the audience.

Upstairs, June was dressed in a beautiful red sequinned dress. Mick looked on disinterestedly as Cathy swept into the room. 'Crikey,' said June, adjusting her straps, 'I've got to go. Hal's only doing a short spot now to build me up.'

Mick got to his feet; he'd been sprawled on the bed since he'd woken up. 'Think I'll get a drink,' he said. 'Would you like me to bring you one up, Cathy?'

'Yes please,' she replied, parched, 'orange juice.'

'Okay,' said Mick, brushing himself down and following June through the door. About five minutes later he was back. Cathy was lying on the bed resting. Mick sat on the bed beside her and handed her the orange juice. 'So,' he said, 'tell me about yourself. I haven't been able to really talk to you since we met. Ed's been monopolising you.'

Cathy laughed, 'Not really much to tell, I'm pretty boring actually.'

Mick disagreed and stretched out beside her. 'You can't be. Ed doesn't do boring.'

Cathy swigged the orange juice down in three gulps. 'Okay,' she started, 'I'm twenty-three; I have a small daughter and a forty-three-year-old husband who won't work. I've been a dancer for as long as I can remember, and I just work, get paid, go to bed and sleep. That's it really, like I said, pretty boring.'

'So now that's about to change,' said Mick, 'with my mate, Ed.'

Cathy shrugged. 'Don't know, with Ed you never know when he's being serious.'

'Oh, he's serious,' said Mick, running his eyes over her body. 'Romany's furious.'

Cathy laughed. 'Yes, he was pretty furious last night when you dragged him off me.'

'He's a bad lot, but Ed can't see it. I even got accused of being interested in you earlier, but Romany's squeaky clean.'

Cathy propped herself up on one elbow. 'Why did he say that?'

'Because I said that you should go home and sort out your domestic problems by yourself and then rejoin him later after you've got the wheels in motion,' said Mick. 'And then I got accused of trying to get my hands on you.'

Cathy was stunned. 'Why accuse you of that when you're with June? He knows that I've never played around before. Doesn't he trust us? I thought he loved me.'

'Oh he does,' said Mick, 'but he's so bloody insecure that he's terrified of losing you.'

'That's terrible,' said Cathy. The conversation ended as Hal came into the room.

'I've got to turn myself into a pop star now,' he said, and noticing Mick beside Cathy, added, 'don't let Ed catch you two together, I can't stand the sight of blood.'

Cathy flinched. 'It sounds as if Hal's noticed Ed's insecurity too,' she said.

Hal disappeared into the bedroom singing, *All Shook Up*. Mick downed his lager and, setting his glass on the bedside table, fiddled with her hair. 'So what chance would I have had if I wasn't with June, and Ed hadn't swept you off your feet?'

'I have to say, I don't know,' said Cathy staring into his eyes. 'I don't like the band, never have, but when I used to watch them on television I was drawn to you so I guess I would have found it pretty hard to resist. Then again I don't know because I never intended having sex with Ed. All I intended to do the night we met was have a laugh on Hal's birthday and he pursued me straight away. I even slapped him the first night. Then he made me go to the party, because when he visited the club, he followed me upstairs and made it pretty obvious what would happen if I didn't. The day after that we visited Rusty's place and we went into another field where he said he wanted to practise his songs. I did like him, Mick, really I did, but unfortunately I fell asleep and when I awoke I was disorientated and he started kissing me. I fought him off several times but he's stronger than me and when I tried to run, he said that we were miles from anywhere so I gave in. I had to get back to the club. I'm not saying that I didn't enjoy it because I did, but I'd never been unfaithful before, and at the back of my mind I thought that he'd treat me like all the others and just leave. I thought that by the end of the week we'd go our separate ways. He's talking marriage, being on the road together, getting Sandy and countless other things. What about work? I have to work, and we need to be working the same area and that's virtually impossible.'

Mick cuddled her to him. 'Honey, he wants you to stop working,' he said gently.

'Well, he hasn't told me that,' said Cathy, 'but he did say that after Bristol he'd take me back to Essex to face Tony and see a solicitor to arrange custody of Sandy.'

Mick sighed deeply. 'And what happens when Bristol finishes, and all of a sudden he's gigging somewhere else? He won't have the time to get to Essex, and the same thing will happen the next week, and the next. When will you see your daughter? How long will you suffer that? He wants you all to himself and he doesn't care who gets hurt.'

Cathy pulled away and sat up, tears filling her eyes. 'He wouldn't do that to me,' she cried, 'he loves me.'

'Don't fool yourself. Go home tomorrow, whatever he says, and if he really loves you, he'll wait.' Cathy flopped back onto the bed again, and Mick held her to him once more.

'Anyway,' said Cathy, 'like I said you never know what's going on in his mind. He still might be playing with me. He might come over to you in the morning, pick up his clothes and hit the road without me.' Mick reached over to the bedside table and finished his drink.

'That won't happen,' he said. 'Ed wants to settle down, but I'd be careful. He's used to getting his own way. He lives by his own rules and nobody else's. He expects everyone to bend to them too. Don't let him control you, babe, I'd hate to see that happen and so would June.' He kissed her gently on the lips, and then added, 'if you do come to your senses and go home, take my number and call me. You can meet up with me on tour at some stage. No strings though.'

Cathy couldn't believe her ears. Now Mick was slating Ed and asking her to join him on tour for obvious reasons, plus her friend was having an off-and-on affair with him. She could have imagined that Romany, once he'd spotted her, would have phoned Ed straight away. The result would not have been a pretty picture, besides she loved Ed and valued her friendship with June. They'd been friends for ages and she wasn't going to spoil that for anyone. She smiled at Mick; he certainly was attractive. She'd loved him on the television and now she was lying in his arms.

Cathy shook her head. 'I couldn't do that to June; she's my friend.' It was crazy; the lead singer with the most popular band in the UK, even suggesting it. She wondered how many other girls would have turned this down. He kissed her again and Cathy felt herself begin to get aroused.

'I've been waiting to do this since I first met you,' he said. Cathy pulled away and Mick smiled. He knew that he'd got some kind of response.

Hal entered the room. 'Stop it,' he said, 'there will be bloodshed. Stop it for my sake if no one else's.' Cathy collapsed in a fit of the giggles. Hal did look funny; he had on an Elvis wig, complete with sideburns, huge sunglasses, a rhinestone jacket and tights plus blue suede shoes. 'Do I look like Elvis?' he asked.

'More like Max Wall,' said Cathy. 'Elvis never wore tights.'

Mick laughed. 'He might have done,' he said. 'You don't know what goes on behind closed doors.'

'Oh well,' said Hal, 'I'd better find something else.'

He retreated to the bedroom and Mick stood up. He took a card from his pocket and scribbled something on the back of it. 'There you are,' he said. 'That's my number, in case you change your mind. Now let's have a goodbye hug.' He opened his arms to her and embraced her in a friendly hug. 'Look after yourself, Cathy,' he said, 'and remember what I told you. Call me before Wednesday. I hope to see you around.'

'Okay,' said Cathy. 'June's waiting.' Mick released her and headed for the door.

'Bye love,' he called back. Cathy stared at the card and put it in her bag although she knew she wouldn't use it. June was her friend, and she loved Ed, but some of the things Mick had said disturbed her.

Hal came to the door. 'Where's my hug?' he asked.

'Next time,' said Mick, and left, chuckling away to himself.

'Does this look better?' asked Hal. He now had on a pair of leather trousers.

'Are you a mod or a rocker?' asked Cathy.

'I'm a mocker, will I do?'

'Hal, you're great.'

'Well, let's hope the crowd think so.'

'Think what?' asked June, breezing in through the door.

'Ask Cathy,' said Hal, 'I'm late; I didn't realise you'd finished.' He rushed down the stairs and Cathy began to change. It wasn't long before she faced her audience again. Her mind was even more confused now after her chat with Mick. Ed had talked her into staying with him but was her choice the correct one?

Going downstairs, she heard Hal announce her and began to move as if on autopilot. In the space of a week her whole life had turned around. She moved around the dance floor, not really seeing anyone. Hearing the music begin to reach a crescendo, she went with it, finishing her act to loud applause. Then she curtseyed to the audience and headed back upstairs as Hal faced the crowd again.

She changed her clothes and then went back downstairs to await the manager and get paid. Dai Jones was already seated at the bar; he'd seen acts come and go and had managed the club for ten years. In that time he had gone through three marriages too. That was now a thing of the past. Girlfriends were okay, but wives? No way. He was tall and slim, with a ruddy complexion, ginger hair, and a moustache. Hal and Cathy joined him and he got them a drink. He praised their acts and said that he hoped to see them again in the future. 'I thought that bit with the footballs was great,' he said.

'But that wasn't even in the act; it was an accident. I collided with Cathy and all hell broke loose,' replied Hal.

'Well, everyone loved it,' said Dai, and handed over their pay packets. 'There's a bit extra in there too,' he added. Hal asked who was at the club the following week. 'No one,' said Dai, 'we're being refurbished. That's why I put this extra lunchtime show in. Well, I have to go; my mother's paid me an unexpected visit.' He shook their hands and left.

'Right,' said Hal, 'it's you and me, kid. It's three o'clock and dinner's at six, so we've got time for a nap.' Cathy agreed and together they ascended the stairs.

Ed arrived at about seven. He was buoyant and asked Cathy if she had a white dress with her. 'I've got this one,' she said, extracting a white, gypsy-style dress with lace overlay from the wardrobe. The lace was in three tiers and it had a red corsage on the bodice with a red belt.

'Perfect,' said Ed, 'put that on.' Cathy did as she was told, and the dress met with Ed's approval.

'You look like a bride,' said Hal, gazing at her.

Ed was happy and said, 'come on, honey, Rusty's waiting at the venue.'

Hal picked up his book and yawned; he hoped that Ed would make Cathy happy, but his possessive streak bothered him. 'Early night for me,' he said. 'Long drive home tomorrow.'

The couple said goodbye, and a little while later were driving along winding country roads. Cathy recalled Mick's warning and voiced her fears about the mess at home. 'It'll sort itself out,' said Ed. 'You're staying with me; it can be dealt with later.'

'I can't just cut and run, I need to go home and get things moving.'

Ed pulled over. 'If we do it your way, Tony will talk you into staying and I'll never see you again.'

'You're being silly,' said Cathy. 'Of course I'll come back. I've told you that I'm prepared to give up my home for you and get custody of Sandy later. Then there's the divorce to sort out.'

Ed grasped her wrists, his nails digging into her flesh. 'No,' he shouted, 'and as for work, I want you to stop so that won't be a problem. Everything else can be sorted out by phone. You're not leaving me. We'll go to Essex after Bristol or the next venue. You're not going.'

'Ed, you're hurting me, let go,' cried Cathy.

Ed let go of her wrists, screaming, 'you're not leaving. You can't!' Cathy remembered Mick's words. So he did want her to stop working, and be with him all the time. He was desperately trying to get his own way. Mick said not to let him control her and so far it looked as if he was hell bent on doing so. Ed started the car up again, and instead of going to a venue they ended up at Rusty's field. Cathy noted that the place was all lit up. There were so many people there.

'Looks like a party,' she said.

'It is,' said Ed, laughing. 'Our engagement party.'

'Why didn't you tell me?' asked Cathy. Her question was answered as Amber and Amethyst came running over to her.

'Surprise!' squealed Amber. There were folding tables set out with plenty of food, fruit, and nibbles. Nearby was a table where there was an abundance of drink.

'How lovely,' said Cathy. 'I didn't expect this.'

'Well,' said Fawn, appearing with a tray of food, 'you're one of the family now. We had to move fast seeing as you two are back on the road again tomorrow. A group of hippies moved towards them and formed a circle. In turn they all embraced Cathy. There were a lot of people wanting a hug.

'This is your new sister,' said Ed proudly. A man took Ed to one side. Cathy didn't like the look of him and shrank back. He was a large man with curly black hair, a long nose, and a long beard. He sported an eye patch as he'd lost an eye three years previously in a fight. He wore long claret robes and looked quite menacing.

'It's okay,' said Fawn, 'that's Seth. He's going to marry you; he used to be a preacher. He won't bite.'

'Marry us?' exclaimed Cathy. 'But I'm already married.'

'It's a hippy wedding,' said Fawn. 'When you get divorced, you can do it again.' Cathy couldn't hear what Seth was saying but sensed it was to do with something other than a wedding and it filled her with fear.

Rusty wasn't happy either and scowled, voicing his feelings to Fawn. 'Eden wants a second ceremony with Seth in private. This is a peaceful commune and I don't hold with these rituals that Seth does.'

Fawn hugged her husband. 'You worry too much. Eden wouldn't let any harm come to her. He loves her.'

'Not knowingly, maybe,' said Rusty, 'but what concerns me is that Eden wants to take her over completely. He's so terrified that she'll leave him, I think he'd let Seth do anything.'

'Rusty, don't worry, Eden won't do anything silly,' Fawn reassured him.

Cathy, meanwhile, had wandered off with the two little girls, so heard nothing of any of this. Amber brought her battery operated, record player out and set it up on the table. 'I'm the DJ,' she said. 'We can do "Simon Says".' Eli had already started a sing-off, and several men joined him by the caravan.

Amber excitedly showed Cathy her bridesmaid dress. We wore them to Sky's wedding,' she said. 'It's nice to wear them again.'

Amethyst took a bag from the cupboard. 'We made this for you,' she said. It was a headdress made from white flowers and a veil. She put it on Cathy's head and adjusted the veil. Then she stood back to admire her handiwork. 'You look like a princess now.' Opening a drawer she handed Cathy two necklaces. 'This is so you don't forget us,' she said. Cathy gazed at the pendants; one had a piece of Amber on it, and one a piece of Amethyst.

Cathy held the girls to her. 'What beautiful gifts. I could never forget you two lovely girls, not ever.'

A young girl of about eighteen approached them. 'Hi,' she said to Cathy. 'I'm Cherry, and the family bought this for you.' She reminded her of Audrey Hepburn but with long hair. She handed her a lovely shawl in pure white with a lace overlay. Cathy thanked the girl and hugged her, then she placed the shawl around her shoulders. She turned around to see Rusty and Fawn waiting.

'Come on, girls,' said Fawn, 'time to get ready. You do look lovely, Cathy. She looks just like a bride, doesn't she, Rusty?' Rusty nodded but secretly he thought more like a lamb to the slaughter. He hated this whispering between Seth and Ed. Fawn donned a cerise kaftan, and Summer put in an appearance clad in an emerald maxi dress. The girls giggled as they changed, and Rusty changed his shirt; it was purple with a paisley design. Fawn then tended to the flowers. They were all dried flowers but were colourful anyway. The girls were getting really excited. Fawn dressed Cathy's hair with many flowers after removing the veiled headdress.

Amber started crying. 'But Mummy,' she said, 'Cathy's got to wear the veil.'

'I know,' said Fawn, 'she will, but I have to put the flowers in first and then when I've finished, you can put the veil back on.' Amber stopped crying; she had stayed up late the night before with her sister and Summer making the headdress, and the thought of Cathy not wearing it was too much for a little girl of four. Several young girls converged on the caravan, armed with an array of bangles and other adornments. Cathy ended up covered in them, so much so that she felt like a Christmas tree. 'Are we ready?' asked Fawn.

'Yes!' cheered the girls. Cathy was starting to wonder what she'd got herself into and really wished that she was back home, but she couldn't hurt all these people after all the hard work and kindness that had been put into everything.

'Yes' she replied, forcing a smile. The entourage left the caravan, and Rusty went off to find Ed.

'Wait here,' he said, 'I won't be long.' Minutes later he returned and Fawn gave him her wedding ring. Rusty took Cathy's arm and they wandered over to the makeshift altar. Summer gave her a bouquet and, kissing her on the cheek, wished her good luck.

Rusty, who was giving Cathy away, thought to himself that she would need it. Amber and Amethyst skipped along in their pretty bridesmaid dresses and clutched their posies excitedly.

Cathy stared at the altar and her mind went back to her wedding to Tony. She had been in her teens and was pregnant at the time. It had been a registry office wedding with two witnesses that had been dragged in from the street. She always remembered that occasion because as soon as they were wed, Tony had seemed to lose all interest in her, and he had given up his job the following day. Her dress had been white with a green pattern running through it.

Today, Rusty was doubling as best man, as well as giving Cathy away, owing to Ed's oversight that he needed a best man. He walked over to his brother and handed Cathy over to him. Fawn got her camera out. 'What do you think?' she asked.

Ed smiled. 'Beautiful,' he said. He was decked out in a long white kaftan that almost reached his ankles. The hippies had made the altar. It was a table covered in white fabric, flowers, and candles. Seth appeared to be bored but looked forward to what Ed had discussed with him earlier. He was deep into the occult now and practised many rituals. He still did weddings for the hippies as they were his friends and family, but he'd moved out of the commune and rented a cottage with his girlfriend and a few of his followers. The hippies were singing happily in the background as Seth began the ceremony.

It was conducted in exactly the same way as a normal wedding, and Cathy was wondering just how binding this was. The service progressed with Ed placing Fawn's ring on her finger, and shortly after that, Seth told Ed he could kiss the bride. He lifted the veil and kissed her to much applause. There were congratulations from everyone, and Cathy had never been embraced by so many people. As one moved away, another took their place. The drink flowed freely, there was singing and dancing and the girls managed to get everyone playing 'Simon says'. The food was never ending; Fawn had excelled herself. Several hippies were sparked out or making love. Cathy returned her ring and Fawn expressed her thoughts that she'd never seen Ed so happy. She lit up a joint and handed it to him. He dragged on it and then handed it to Cathy.

Normally she would have refused, but now she was ready to try anything; she was feeling so liberated and loved. All thoughts of her talk with Mick had gone. Tomorrow a new world was opening up to her, and Ed was right, they could get Sandy later. She lay in Ed's arms on a blanket for what seemed an eternity. She never wanted it to stop. Another cigarette appeared, and as one was gone, another took its place. She felt as if she were in a trance. Nearby, Fawn was singing with a small group.

In the end she dozed in the arms of her lover and, when she awoke, she was staring up at the stars. They twinkled away, the heavens so vast. She felt at peace with the world; everyone was happy and they were still singing. Everything was in slow motion; she was drifting, floating, and so happy. It was late, but the party showed no signs of abating.

Amber and Amethyst came over and laid a blanket over Ed and Cathy. 'We're going to bed now,' said Amber. 'Goodnight, Eden, goodnight, Cathy.' They both embraced the girls.

'Come and see us soon,' said Amethyst. 'Don't forget us.' She frowned and asked, 'but Eden, what do we call Cathy now?'

Ed looked down and kissed the top of Cathy's head. 'Angel,' he said, 'she's Angel.'

The girls jumped up and down in delight and ran off giggling. 'Angel and Sandy; our new sisters.'

Cathy snuggled up against Ed and fell asleep. When she awoke everyone seemed to be gone. She was suddenly aware of Seth who must have joined Ed while she was sleeping. Cathy tried to stand but fell down. Her head was swimming. 'I didn't say goodbye to Rusty and Fawn,' she said, 'I feel terrible.'

'They're in bed now,' said Ed. 'They did come over and say goodbye to us and wished us well, but you were asleep and they didn't want to wake you.'

'Oh,' said Cathy, 'but I still feel bad about it after all they've done for me tonight.' She stood up again and staggered. She nearly fell but held on to the trunk of the tree that they'd been sitting under.

'We're going for a night cap at Seth's,' said Ed. Cathy was reluctant to go but what could she do? She hadn't a clue where they were.

They drove behind Seth's car and turned into a dark alley way. It was pitch black, and once inside the cottage it wasn't much better. The interior was dark and foreboding; the whole room was empty except for a sofa and an altar, with an assortment of carved wooden dolls and the head of a goat on a wall. A goatskin lay across the back of the sofa.

Cathy was scared and asked, 'can we go?' Her arms felt all goosefleshy, and she shivered.

'Just one drink, and then we'll go,' said Ed. 'I owe it to him for marrying us, and I haven't seen him in ages.'

'Okay, but we should go soon; we've got a long journey tomorrow.'

Ed looked at his watch. 'It's today,' he said, 'just you and me babe.' Seth emerged with three drinks, and Ed shot him an enquiring look.

Seth gave them a glass each and raised his own, announcing, 'let's have a toast. To Eden and the lovely Cathy.' Cathy sipped her drink. It seemed all right and she guessed that she was probably overreacting. Seth was probably just eccentric and harmless. Her glass was soon empty, and Seth refilled it. It was quite a nice drink and she was about to ask him what it was when Ed's voice became distant and she found herself viewing him through a fog. She was feeling very sleepy. Ed's image began to get distorted. She knew she'd had too much drink, too much pot, and too much of this concoction that Seth had given her.

The last thing she remembered was Ed moving over to her and cuddling her, and also the fact that the men hadn't touched their drinks. After that there was nothing until she awoke in the car park of the cabaret club with Ed asking her for the key. She handed him her bag and he rummaged around until he found it. He opened the door and let them both in. Cathy was swaying, but Ed managed to get her inside and sat her on the floor against the wall. Then, after locking the car door, he carried her upstairs.

After laying her on the bed, he went down again to make coffee. He looked down at the dazed girl. 'Come on, drink this,' he said.

Cathy attempted to sit up but felt so dizzy and sick that she fell back down again. Ed propped her up and put the cup to her mouth. Still dazed, she drank it. 'I've got a horrible taste in my mouth,' she said.

Ed was beginning to feel guilty and wondered how much she had remembered. Seth said that her memory probably wouldn't come back for at least twenty-four hours, if at all. He'd patted Ed on the back after the ritual, saying, 'She's all yours now, buddy. Forever, even death won't release her. The deceased will wander the earth until its soul is reunited with the survivor.'

Ed was elated. 'All mine,' he said.

Seth laughed and added, 'you can split up, but you'll always reunite, no matter how long the split is. It can't be reversed. So stay healthy because you've inherited a death sentence too.'

As Ed had driven away, Seth had gone back into his cottage where his girlfriend was cleaning up. 'There was a lot of blood this time. What happens now?'

Seth had folded his arms and stared at Megan, a woman of slight build. 'If they split, I'll know. If they reunite, I'll know. When one of them dies, I'll know,' he said. 'It's just a game to me, and when they're apart he'll be in purgatory.'

'And the girl?'

'She won't suffer as much because she didn't ask for this,' said Seth. 'But she'll sense something's wrong and will never forget him, being always compelled to reunite with him.'

'But he's your cousin. Didn't you tell him about the downside of all this? Why do it at all?'

'Because I hate the bastard, and always have done,' said Seth. 'And as for the girl, I don't know her. She's nothing to me. Eden won't be crying, "I want", any more, it'll be "I need her", because now his ability to lead a normal life will be impaired. People should be careful what they wish for. This works, I've seen it done. They're like twins now, incestuous twins.' He threw back his head and laughed loudly.

Megan pushed her long brown hair out of her eyes and screwed up her elfish features. 'You shouldn't play God,' she said.

Seth had backhanded her to the floor. 'And you should learn to keep your mouth shut. Clean this mess up.'

Chapter Five

Back at the club, Cathy was vomiting profusely. She looked down the toilet and saw that the vomit was loaded with blood. Horrified, she cried, 'what's that?'

'You got drunk,' said Ed, 'and you smoked lots of dope. You've been trying to clear your system and strained yourself. Probably ruptured a small blood vessel.'

Cathy vomited again and again, until she couldn't any more. She staggered to her feet and went back into her bedroom where she fell on the bed and passed out. Ed looked on anxiously. What had he done? How could he have done this to her? He'd sunk so low. He looked at his watch; three thirty and time for bed. After washing, and cleaning his teeth, he got into bed and snuggled up to her.

About five o'clock, Ed awoke. Cathy was out of bed, and she returned a short while later with a glass of water in her hand. 'That's good,' he said, 'the more fluid you get into you, the better.'

Cathy stared at her bandaged arm. 'What happened?' she asked. 'I don't remember cutting myself.'

'You were drunk and stoned,' said Ed. 'We went to Seth's house late last night and you fell over outside and cut yourself on some broken glass. As I helped you up, you fell again and pulled me over, so I got cut too.'

'Oh,' said Cathy, 'Seth, he did our wedding ceremony.' Her mind was racing, but she couldn't remember a thing. 'I remember taking a drink from him and that was it. How rude of me, I wish I could apologise.'

'Forget it,' said Ed, 'he understood. We've all been there. I've been stoned and drunk more times than I care to remember. We're a proper couple now, so come back to bed and consummate this marriage.' Cathy got in beside him and within seconds they were in the throes of making love.

Cathy gazed into Ed's eyes. 'I love you,' she said. 'I really do.' Ed was relieved; she hadn't remembered the ritual at all. They made love over and over again until they were both satisfied and, exhausted, they slept.

A few hours later, Ed woke Cathy with scrambled eggs on toast. She didn't think she could eat, but surprised herself and cleared her plate. The door opened, and there stood June. 'Christ,' she said, 'breakfast in bed. You've struck gold there, Cathy. Oh well, I go back to my old sod and four kids today. This gig's flown by; any spare coffee, Ed?'

'Think so,' said Ed, 'help yourself.'

June poured herself a cup from the pot, and then asked them what time they were leaving. 'In a couple of hours,' said Ed. 'But I've got to drive over to Mick's first as I've left a few bits and bobs over there.'

Cathy tried to stand up but she felt black and blue and her head hurt. She found walking an ordeal too. Ed gave her an affectionate squeeze. 'Tell you what,' he said. 'I can see that you're wiped out. You stay here with June and I'll pick you up when I've collected my belongings.' He headed for the door, and Cathy followed him downstairs after throwing on her dressing gown. Once outside in the car park, Ed took her in his arms and kissed her. She leaned up against him in utter contentment until he broke free and said, 'the sooner I go, the sooner I get back. I love you.' Cathy gazed into his eyes which were full of love and adoration.

'I'll love you till I die,' she cried.

Ed hugged her. ‘I know, darling, I feel the same,’ he replied. ‘Now go upstairs and rest.’

From nowhere, June materialised. She smiled at the embracing couple before interrupting. ‘Telephone, Cathy; probably your agent.’ Ed released her and she waved, blew him a kiss, and went back inside the building. She walked to the phone and picked up the receiver.

Tony was on the other end of the line and in his usual slow drawl said, ‘What time will you be home? Sandy’s had an accident and she’s in hospital asking for you. Get here as soon as you can; maybe you can get a lift.’

Cathy was shaking with fear. ‘I’m on my way,’ she said, and replaced the receiver. She began to sob, all thoughts of a new life with Ed gone. Sandy had had an accident. What was it in the bible about the sins of the parent being visited on the child? Well she’d sinned and Sandy had paid the price.

Walking back upstairs, she encountered Hal. ‘You live near London, don’t you?’ she asked desperately. ‘My daughter’s had an accident and I have to get home as soon as possible.’ Hal nodded. He was concerned and said that he would be pleased to give her a lift. Cathy stripped out of her dressing gown, and it was then that June noticed her arm.

‘What happened? Let me look,’ she said. She took the bandage off Cathy’s arm and surveyed the cut.

‘I fell on some glass,’ she said.

June observed the cut more closely. ‘Looks like it’s been cut.’

‘We went to Seth’s for a nightcap. He’d just given us a hippy wedding, and Ed was cut too when he helped me up. I fell, but I was stoned and pulled him over. It hurts a lot.’

‘Seth? Ed’s cousin?’ asked June. She’d gone very cold, and felt scared for Cathy.

‘I don’t recall falling over; I must have been really stoned, mustn’t I?’ June hugged her friend; surely Ed hadn’t put Cathy through some kind of witchcraft? Seth was well known for his interest in the occult. Cathy pulled away. 'Hal, have I got enough time to shower?' she asked.

'Yes,' said Hal, 'but we do need to move pretty sharpish if I'm to get to my gig on time tonight.' She headed for the bathroom and June started to pack her costumes into her case. She had intended trying to talk Cathy into staying and waiting for Ed to come back, but realised that if she had a similar situation at home, she too would have flown to the side of her daughter, and Sandy was just a baby after all. Anyway, she wanted a few words with Ed herself, and they wouldn't be nice ones. Cathy had obviously been in some sort of ritual; she'd given that away unwittingly by saying that Ed was cut too.

When she emerged from the shower, June bandaged her arm again. 'Looks nasty,' she said. 'That needs medical attention so make sure you see a doctor when you get home.'

'I will,' said Cathy, 'but Sandy's my main priority.' She dressed hurriedly and packed the last remaining articles that June had left out. She removed the ring from her finger. 'Shortest engagement on record,' she laughed, feeling like she wanted to cry.

'Well you can meet up again when you sort things out, so you might as well keep it.'

'No, just in case I don't get back.'

'You will,' said June. 'He does some stupid things at times but he does love you, he really does. He can't stand to be away from you, but your love will have to stand the test. If he really loves you the way he appears to, he'll wait.'

'Well, I've got a northern tour coming up the week after next so we'll probably meet up there. It'll be nice to meet up again, June. We always have a lot of laughs, don't we?'

June nodded and said, 'I'm going north too, so I'm sure we will meet up, but I still think you should keep the ring.'

Cathy shook her head and handed the ring to June. 'No, he can give it back to me the next time I see him; that's if he still wants to see me after I leave him.'

Hal appeared and took Cathy's cases from her. 'I hate to cut in, but we really do need to go now or I'll miss my gig. Ed will be knocking on the door.'

Cathy tried to hold back the tears, but in vain, as one managed to trickle from her eye. 'I'm ready,' she said. She walked from the room and turned back at the top of the stairs before leaving. 'Bye June, tell him I love him.'

Travelling along the roads with Hal, Cathy tried to make conversation but failed miserably and began to feel drowsy before nodding off. Hal looked over at her. He felt sorry for her; he knew that she was madly in love with Ed, but was doing what any mother would do and that was to put her daughter first. He doubted that the accident was a bad one as he knew that Tony made mountains out of mole hills, but he also knew that Cathy would want to see for herself. She slept for the whole journey and was woken by Hal shaking her at Marble Arch. She was shocked that she'd slept for the entire journey, and after she had thanked Hal, she got out of his car and headed for the tube.

Arriving home, she found Tony still in bed. The room reeked of perfume, and on the floor was a solitary earring. Clothes were strewn all over the floor and there was a collection of dirty cups on the bedside table. She threw open the windows to let some fresh air in.

'Which hospital is Sandy in, and how is she?' she asked.

Tony lit up a cigarette and reached for the ashtray. 'You're crazy, what are you on about?'

Furiously, Cathy rounded on him, 'you rang me and told me that Sandy had had an accident, and that she was in hospital,' she reminded him.

Tony wrinkled his brow as if searching for an answer, 'keeping her in for observation, she got out while I wasn't looking and a car hit her. Don't worry too much, she'll be home tomorrow.'

Cathy was stunned; he was discussing this as if it was a trivial matter. She clenched her fists. 'You are talking about our daughter, not an each way bet or an odds on, hot favourite. Which hospital is she in?'

Suddenly Tony began to laugh out loud, which confused Cathy until she realised that she'd been the victim of a very sick joke. 'Try her bedroom, then,' he laughed, 'she's asleep; she never had an accident.' He flicked his cigarette ash into the ashtray that Cathy noted was full up. Many of the cigarette ends had several shades of lipstick on them. She felt like an idiot and she wanted to kill him; how could he put her through all this torment? Tony got out of bed. 'I must say, Cathy,' he said, 'you look very upset. Was Wales really that good? Maybe you're missing someone? How's Hal and June? I bet you had some laughs while you were away. You always do; June's a lot of fun. Shame she's such a whore.'

'She's my friend,' retorted Cathy, hurt.

'But still a whore.' Cathy felt defeated and wanted to burst into tears. How could he do this? She'd been at her wits end thinking that Sandy could have been on life support or worse, only to discover it was just a joke. Worse still, using Sandy made the whole episode even sicker.

'Why?' she screamed. 'How could you do this to me?'

Tony continued to laugh and pushed her away, knocking her to the floor. 'What does it matter, why? You're home aren't you? It worked.' Cathy felt completely helpless.

'Why?' she repeated, 'I can see that it's amusing you, but to me it's just sick.'

Tony sat down and viewed his wife who sat on the floor in a sorry heap. 'Since you really want to know, all day yesterday and the day before, Sandy wanted to speak to her Mummy and do you know, my lovely wife, we could never find you. We tried in the morning, afternoon, and we tried later. Eventually we got the manager and he said you weren't there. So we tried even later and somehow you'd managed to get back to the club and disappear again. I think you're in the wrong type of entertainment, you should become a magician; you'd be great. Anyway I asked if there was another number I could call and got one. When I rang this number I got a very noisy party. The guy that I spoke to was very helpful; Billy, I think his name was. I didn't say who I was so he can't be blamed for the information that he gave me. "She's with Ed," he said. "They're a couple of lovebirds." Then he added that you were going to get married and that he was going to be best man. By now, sweet Cathy, I was very interested. It seemed that he must have thought that you were a single girl.'

Cathy felt as if someone had just sunk a carving knife into her side, and she was bleeding internally; she knew she was. Tony yanked on her hair. 'You listening?' he yelled and pulled harder, forcing her head back so she was staring up at him.

Cathy winced with the pain and attempted to nod. 'I'm listening, you sadistic bastard,' she cried.

Tony was enjoying himself immensely and grinned at her as he said, 'when I rang back later, I got someone called Ronan or something like that; he was even more helpful than the other guy I'd rung earlier. This bloke was drunk and pretty incoherent but he did confirm the story. He went into more detail, rather uncouth type of fellow I should think. He said that you were taking his best mate away from him. He seemed annoyed about it. He rattled on and on, and at times I couldn't understand everything he said. Make sense, Cathy?'

'I tried to ring you all week,' said Cathy. 'You never answered the phone.'

'Why should I?' asked Tony. 'I've got a life you know, anyway to get back to this guy. He was still rattling on about you getting married so I asked if I could speak to you. He said no because you and Ed were indulging at the time. Pretty picture, eh? Anyways, then he just couldn't make any sense at all; he was garbled with what he was saying so I hung up. So you see Cathy,

I had to get you back, didn't I? I don't know if there's any truth in any of it, and I don't care, but you're not leaving me and Sandy.'

He let go of her hair and she slumped forwards weeping. Tony got to his feet and stood over his wife. 'You see, my lovely, wonderful, trustworthy, dedicated, and ever-faithful wife, I've got you back. I don't care who you screw when you're away, I'm not interested, but we're married and that's the way it'll stay. I'm very happy with our arrangement.'

'Well I'm not, I want you to work so that I can stay at home and look after Sandy. I hate touring.'

'You're crazy, Cathy,' said Tony, lighting up a cigarette. 'You make twice the salary that I could. It's much more practical this way. Anyway, you'll probably meet this guy again on the road. You can both do what you like with my permission, but I won't divorce you. We're an item and that's the way it stays.' He placed the cigarette in the ashtray and dressed himself. 'Your agent rang earlier; he's got you some work up north, then it's some gig in the West country before a Continental tour. Great, eh Cathy?'

She got to her feet feeling as if her heart was breaking, and Sandy's voice pierced the air. She crossed to the child's bedroom and took her in her arms. How she ached to feel Ed's arms around her, to tell her that everything would be all right, but she knew that it would never happen again. Sandy gave her a slobbery kiss and snuggled into her mother's shoulder. The sensation was overwhelming, making Cathy certain that her choice had been the right one.

She carried the child downstairs into the kitchen where Tony was boiling the kettle for tea. Tony gazed at his wife. 'Great to have you back,' he said.

Cathy sighed. Tony stank of cheap perfume, but she could hardly protest. It was only hours ago that she'd lain in her lover's arms. The main thing was that Sandy was all right. She had a cup of tea and then took the child back upstairs. 'Let's see what Mummy's got for you,' she said.

Downstairs, Tony sighed with relief. While he had Sandy, he had Cathy, and she was a real little goldmine. When Cathy came downstairs again, he announced that he was going out. 'Okay,' she said, relieved when he left. She ascended the stairs and lay down beside her daughter, unable to sleep in her own room because of the stench of cheap perfume, even though the windows were wide open. She cuddled up to Sandy and very soon, her eyes grew heavy and she slept fully clothed.

The following day, she took Sandy to London with her and visited her agent. Once inside the office, Sandy busied herself with a box of toys. The box had a permanent place in the office, its sole purpose being a source of amusement for tiny fingers. Cathy handed the old man his commission. He in turn began to leaf through a pile of contracts.

He was a kindly old man, known to all his friends as Noddy, as he had a habit of nodding off during social gatherings. He was rather portly and he always wore a huge grin. Nothing bothered him. He used to say that he'd seen everything that he possibly could, and that if he died the next day he couldn't have packed any more into his life. He dressed in baggy sweaters and trousers that were always too large for him, giving a rather untidy appearance. His looks were nothing like those of a typical theatrical agent; he looked more like someone's lovely old granddad. His hair, once jet black, had faded to grey and then nearly disappeared completely.

Despite all this he knew his job better than his rivals, and fought for his acts as if they were his own children. Leaning over his desk, he tweaked Cathy's hair, then with a twinkle in his eye asked, 'what's all this mystery, what have you been up to?'

'Nothing,' Cathy lied, 'I don't know what you mean.'

Mr Todd sighed. 'Look love,' he said. 'I don't want to intrude into your private life, but all I've had since yesterday is phone call after phone call from a singer that you met in Glamorgan. I keep putting him off but I need to know your take on this so I can deal with the matter.'

Cathy flushed. 'It was a fling,' she said, averting her eyes, 'it was fun.'

Mr Todd frowned. 'Don't think that's the way he sees it,' he said. 'He seemed to think that you were leaving Tony and setting up home with him. He also thought that Sandy had had an accident too, but I must say she looks healthy enough to me.'

'Tony's sick sense of humour,' said Cathy in explanation. 'But how could I run off with some singer? I'm married and I've got no intention of leaving Sandy.'

'Don't know,' replied Mr Todd, 'but you couldn't be much worse off, could you? I mean you never see Sandy anyway.' He passed the contracts across the desk to her and she signed them. Noddy continued, 'I'll stall him, but I get the feeling that he'll find you in the end. He's madly in love with you and he's completely distraught. I can tell him that you're doing a long Continental tour but he's left a contact number and an address. Shall I tell him that you'll contact him when you get back?'

'No,' said Cathy.

'But he genuinely seems to care,' said Mr Todd, taking back the contracts.

Cathy could feel the tears begin to fill her eyes. 'That's the trouble,' she said. 'He does, and so do I.' The old man nodded and walked around to the other side of his desk.

'I knew it all the time,' he said. 'You're not the kind to indulge in an affair unless it meant something. Are you in love, Cathy? He certainly is.'

'Love,' said Sandy, clambering up onto her mother's knee.

'It hurts to be apart from him,' Cathy said, 'but I love Sandy more. She's just a little girl. I can never allow myself to see him again. I owe it to Sandy to be a mother to her, and she loves her father. No, if he rings again, tell him I said goodbye. Sometimes you have to be cruel to be kind, don't you?'

'And sometimes it hurts in the process,' said Mr Todd. 'Still if that's what you want, that's what I'll do.'

Cathy removed Sandy from her knee and said, 'come on, time to go home.' She kissed the old man on his cheek and left with Sandy chattering away.

When Ed had arrived back at the club, all hell had broken loose. He raved and punched the wall, crying. June had tried to break the news as gently as possible, and told him that Cathy would contact him as soon as she got sorted out. 'Really?' screamed Ed, 'then why did she give you the ring back? Why? Why did you let her go?'

'Sandy had an accident,' replied June. She'd never seen him like this before; he never failed to amaze her lately. 'She had to go.'

Ed kicked over a table, shouting, 'then why didn't she wait for me? We could have gone together.'

'She probably didn't want you and Tony in the same room,' said June getting more uneasy by the minute. Ed was scaring her. He broke down in a rage, sobbing uncontrollably. 'Look,' said June, 'she said she'll contact you and she will. If you keep in touch with me, I'll get you back together. I can set it up.'

Ed grabbed her by the shoulders. 'You're a liar,' he screamed. 'She's gone for good, hasn't she? We were in love, for God's sake; we were made for each other. She was my world.'

'Ed, you're hurting me! You were her world too.'

'Then why?' he cried. 'I can't live without her.'

'Ed, let go of me,' said June. He let her go and she rubbed her shoulders, feeling that she'd have bruises tomorrow. 'Come on Ed, sit down. She'll be back. We're on the road together a lot; as soon as I see her, I'll let you know, just leave me a phone number.'

'Well, you'd better,' said Ed, calming down a little. 'Wherever she is, I'll find her. I don't care how long it takes. Have you got her agent's number?'

'He won't help unless she asks him to. Phone numbers are confidential and it's no good trying to find her in the phone book. You won't find anyone under the name of Gypsy.'

'Well, you must have it,' said Ed.

'I haven't,' lied June, 'or a surname, but she will contact me. I know it.'

Ed had his head in his hands. 'What am I going to do?' he asked.

June racked her brains. 'Let's discuss this over coffee.'

Ed stood up and took a swing at her. June ducked and he fell, landing with his arm doubled under him. As he got to his feet she could see blood seeping through the sleeve. He got to his feet and swore loudly. June faced him this time. She was angry and curious about that arm. 'Is that the way you treat women?' demanded June. 'Your arm's bleeding. Show me. Cathy's arm is in a bad state too.'

'She fell on some glass,' said Ed, 'and I got cut when I helped her up.' His anger had been replaced by guilt.

'Show me. What did you do to her?' She walked over to him. 'And what is that around your neck?' she added. Closer inspection revealed a small phial on a chain. June stared in horror. 'What's in that?' she gasped. 'It looks like blood.'

'Mind your own business,' said Ed.

'Ed, whose blood is that?' said June, though she thought she already knew.

'Okay,' said Ed, 'it's Cathy's.'

June was feeling faint and sat down. 'Show me your arm,' she said forcefully. Sheepishly, Ed unbuttoned the sleeve on his shirt and she saw the same bandage that she'd seen on Cathy. 'Fell on glass, did she?' said June incredulously, unwrapping the bandage. She looked at the laceration and felt the nausea rise in her throat. 'Matching pair,' she said. 'Glass? No way. Someone did this to you both. No prizes for guessing who. You stupid bastard; what have you done to my friend?'

Ed groaned and threw himself face down on the bed crying, 'I can't move on. I want her.'

'"I want, I want." Is that all you can say?' screamed June. 'God knows what Seth has unleashed on you.'

June was crying now. She had encouraged Cathy to go with Ed, but she never realised that he had developed this fixation, this obsession. She should have seen it coming. He had always been spoilt, and used women, and now that he'd finally met the woman of his dreams, he was determined to own her like a possession.

'My poor Cathy,' cried June, over and over again.

Ed sat up and angrily rounded on June. 'What about me?'

'What about you? She loved you, she trusted you, and you allowed that twisted bastard to perform some sort of ritual on her. Did you enjoy it, Ed? Cathy must have been out of it. She would never have let you do this to her if she was conscious. She told me before that she was scared of the occult. So you got off on it, did you?'

He shuddered at the thought of the ceremony the night before. 'It was horrible,' he said. 'I kept telling Seth to stop but he said it was too late and it could be dangerous to stop. So I had to go through with it. He said he'd given her to me and that not even death could separate us. He said that if she left me she'd always come back, so I suppose that's something.'

'Ed,' screamed June, 'don't you realise what you've done. There are no positive sides to this. I just hope that your cousin is full of shit and that he's making all this up just to boost his ego and to be revered by all his followers. I suppose they were all there too? As for you, well, what can I say? How on earth did he get involved anyway?'

'He married us,' said Ed.

'Was Cathy happy with that?' asked June. 'Or was she drugged for that too?'

'She was very happy,' said Ed, 'she told me she loved me, that she was leaving her family for me, and we had a great night.

She was with my nieces a lot of the time playing 'Simon says', and dancing with them. They love her to bits. Seth did the wedding ceremony for us and I just got talking about things. I said that I was so in love with her, and that the thought of her leaving terrified me. He said that he could fix a lifetime union, so I went for it.'

'So the fact that she'd told you she was leaving her family wasn't enough for you?' asked June, sarcastically. 'You had to drug her and let Seth cut her and do whatever else suited him. You see, even the position of that cut intrigues me. You must have been facing her when it was done. Enough said?'

Ed hung his head in shame. 'Yes, I shouldn't have done it.'

'Too right,' said June. 'She went home because her daughter needed her. Any mother would have done the same.'

'But I need her.'

'Ed, this isn't about what you want or need. She'll come back; even that poisoned cousin of yours said that and obviously you believe him. She really loves you, Ed, and there'll never be anyone else for her. Tony may live with her but their marriage was dead in the water long ago. I wish he was dead, he's top of my hit list.'

'Mine too,' said Ed. 'June, what am I going to do?'

'Work, you are going to throw yourself into work. That is the answer to most things and then when she does come back you'll be much stronger and you can pick up where you left off. She really loves you, and if you're meant to be together you will be, no matter how long it takes.'

Ed got to his feet. 'I can't move on,' he said. 'I need her.'

'You can,' said June, taking him in her arms. 'You got on before you met her and the graveyard's full of people that we can't live without. Now, let's get that coffee.' She kissed him on the forehead and added, 'if you must have a phial of her blood around your neck, then for God's sake get one that's not glass. Get a silver one or something, because it's going to raise a few eyebrows, and if you fall onto it you'll end up cutting yourself again, this time without Seth's help.'

Ed followed her downstairs and they went through to the kitchen. He stared around him. How many times had he stood in this kitchen with Cathy making coffee, laughing together, sharing a kiss, and making plans? It now felt cold and unfriendly; the atmosphere was different. They took their coffee out to the bar and sipped it, watching the decorators laying dustsheets down. Ed gazed across the dance floor and, in his mind's eye, could see the gypsy girl spin, dance, clap, and laugh. The tears started to flow again. He turned to June, and she read his thoughts.

'She used to devour that dance floor, didn't she?' she said. 'Used up every inch of space. She loved to dance, and loved Sandy, and then you came along and eclipsed everything. You made her truly happy.'

Ed searched in his pocket for a tissue and, finding none, wiped his eyes on his sleeve. 'I'll see her dance again,' he said. 'We will find her; we're meant to be together. I'll bombard her agent with calls. Give me his number, June. I'll search the entire country for her; she's mine and I have to find her.'

'I'll see her soon on the road; you'll be back together sooner than you think.' She wished she believed herself. She drained her coffee, scribbled down Cathy's agent's number on a beer mat, and was relieved when Ed said he had to leave. She was going home soon, and for the first time in her life she was happy about it. She gave Ed a hug and watched him drive away. 'Thank God,' she thought, and went back upstairs to resume packing.

Ed drove away; he felt freezing cold and his arm throbbed. He switched on his radio and tried to sing along with it. Out loud, he said, 'you won't escape me, Cathy; Seth gave you to me, you're mine. If I have to kill for you, I will; you're mine, all mine.' Dylan's voice filled the car so he changed stations. 'And you can shut up too,' he said. 'You can't have her either.' His obsession was growing worse. 'Bristol, here I come,' he said, and the tears flowed once more.

Chapter Six

5th August 1970

The Shelltones were shell-shocked. They were working in Norwich and had been kicking a football around in a park. They were in high spirits. Mick and the band manager, Doug, had gone to organise an important photo shoot for their new album. On returning to their digs they spotted a police car outside their front gate. They were sweating buckets as there was a stash of dope in the house, plus Romany had had sex with two underage girls the night before. They got out of the car and approached the police car. A very red-faced policeman stared up at them and asked if he could have a few words as he had some bad news. They agreed as there was a small crowd beginning to build up.

Once inside the house, the policeman introduced himself as PC Miller, and settled himself in a red leather armchair. Romany offered him some tea but the officer declined. He was used to being the one to bring bad news to people, maybe because he'd been in the force as long as he could remember. No one else wanted the job. He looked around the room at the anxious faces. He never found this easy as he suffered with high blood pressure, and even with medication it got no better. He was a tall man with a strong Norfolk accent, brown hair with a receding hair line, brown eyes, and several chins, but he never smiled. He pursed his thin lips and said, 'I'm sorry to bring you such dreadful news and there's no easy way to say this. There's been a car crash and two of your friends have been involved. Your manager is dead and Mick is on life support.'

The band members were ashen-faced; they just couldn't take it in. Death just didn't figure in their lives; they were invincible. Romany fell to the floor in shock, partly because he'd had a massive row with Mick that morning when he'd told him he wished he was dead, and now the poor devil was fighting for his life. Plus the fact that he appeared to have got away with those two underage girls.

'God,' he said, 'the only reason that he's not here was because we had a falling out and he decided to go with Doug, just to give us space.' He got to his feet and for once he was lost for words.

'I'll leave you with the phone number for the hospital,' said PC Miller, and dragged himself to his feet. He was badly out of condition due to his 'couch potato' nature and being overweight, and he knew his days in the police force were numbered. The band thanked him, and phoned the hospital as soon as he left. A phone call later, Romany faced the band. 'No singer, no manager. What's gonna happen to us?' he wondered aloud.

Gerry scratched his head. 'Well, I think we'd better go and see Mick,' he said. 'Doug may have been our manager but he's dead, and Mick isn't. Obviously tonight's concert is cancelled, and probably the rest of the tour, unless we can find a new manager and singer. Then again if we find neither, we'll have to disband.'

'I'll phone Doug's office,' said Romany, 'maybe they don't know yet.'

'Well, if they don't know by now, they will soon,' said Gerry. 'When we don't turn up tonight, they'll know, and anyway, Doug's cousin works for the same agency, so he'll have been notified by now.'

'Greasy Victor Lee,' said Romany. 'Money mad he is; he'll be in touch.'

'Come on guys, let's go and see Mick,' said Gerry, reaching for his coat. Secretly he would be happy if they disbanded; he was sick of touring, but he was a good keyboard player and at twenty-six felt he still had a good career in front of him. Touring did his marriage no good at all; the rules were no wives or girlfriends on tour and his marriage was suffering badly. Many times the thought of returning to his old job as a motor mechanic crossed his mind. He was a good looking man who had his fair share of groupie attention but he never got involved with them; he loved his wife Lisa and she was the only woman he wanted. Diminutive, but with a body like a Greek god, he was the best looking member of the group. Blonde, green eyed, a perfect nose, and full lips with a devilish smile; he was a groupie's dream, but none got close except for autographs.

Hours later, after visiting Mick, who was completely out of it on a life support machine, they'd returned home. Once more there was a car stationed outside their house. Romany held his breath; maybe he hadn't got away with it? Maybe this was an irate parent? His question was answered when the occupant got out of the car and followed them into the house.

They needed no introduction; it was the infamous Victor Lee. He was a fat, sweaty man who said, 'sorry to hear about your loss. As you know, Doug was my cousin. Apparently he died instantly, but Mick wasn't so lucky.' His beady eyes scrutinized the band through his horn-rimmed glasses, visualising pound signs. He'd always wanted to get his hands on this lot, and now it seemed as if it was about to come true. He grinned at them; he always grinned even when he was stressed. Romany viewed him as a fat, short, broad-shouldered, balding twat. Closer inspection didn't improve the image, and he stank of moth balls. His hair was thinning badly, he had dirty fingernails and he was very down at heel. He looked nothing like a manager at all, but as Romany knew, appearances could be deceptive. 'Well,' said Vic, 'can any of you sing?'

'Back up,' they said in unison.

'I can sing,' said Romany. 'I do some vocals, but not enough to hold a complete set.'

'Right,' said Vic, 'obviously the tour has to be cancelled. I would like to take over where Doug left off. Do any of you know of anyone good enough to step into Mick's shoes who also knows you and is familiar with your material?'

Romany grinned. 'I know just the man; he's playing at Caister-on-Sea tonight.'

'Right,' said Vic, 'let's go.'

The drive down to Caister wasn't a long one but it felt like it to Romany. Vic never stopped talking about his plans for the band and how he was going to glam them up and make them even bigger.

He asked about Ed, and Romany told him that he'd known him for most of his life and that he was with one of the support bands on their 1968 tour. He carefully omitted to tell him that since the tour Ed had become irrational, depressed, violent, and suicidal, having actually attempted to take his own life a year before. He thought that if anyone was going to divulge this information, it would have to be Ed himself. Arriving at Caister, it was a relief for Romany to get out of the car and away from Vic's disgusting stench.

At the clubhouse, Romany indicated the stage. 'There's your man,' he said.

'Okay,' said Vic, 'but I'll form my own opinions and give my diagnosis at the end of the gig. Now let's get some liquid refreshment.'

Ed stood on the stage, singing his heart out with Billy. Paddy, his drummer, beat out the tempo disinterestedly. Vic was impressed with Ed who sang well, had stage presence, looked good, and flirted with the audience. It was obvious that the girls adored him. At the end of the show, Vic approached the stage, and Romany conveyed the news. Ed was horrified; Mick was his friend and he asked which hospital he was in. Vic thrust a card into his hand. 'I need a replacement, and fast, so if you're interested, come and see me in the morning. I'm staying with the boys in Norwich for the next couple of days so you won't have far to come. Where are you staying?'

'In Bacton, in my brother's caravan,' said Ed.

'Oh well, not a huge distance away then. Romany's told me about you and how you supported them in '68, so you must know their songs inside out. Sleep on it, but I would like you to join the band.' With that he was gone, followed by Romany who was not looking forward to the drive back, and the odours that went with it.

Twenty-four hours later, Ed sat with Vic in the boys' living room. They'd gone back to the hospital again to see their friend and also to give Ed and Vic some privacy. Ed was doubled up in pain. His insides were killing him and Vic gave his diagnosis, 'probably a touch of irritable bowel syndrome,' he said. 'I get it a lot, bloody nuisance.'

'Well,' said Ed, 'if this is a touch, I'd hate to get the full blown version.'

Vic frowned. 'Have you thought about fronting the band?' he asked, not at all interested in Ed's pains.

Ed stared at Vic intently, 'I appreciate your offer, but what about my band? Can you find them work too?'

'No, they're losers. I only want you.'

'But I can't just leave them like that. I've got a contract to fulfil until October when the season ends, and they'll need a new vocalist.'

'I can get them a new vocalist,' said Vic. 'I'll get one today; he can rehearse with your band and when we all leave for London in a couple of days they'll be up and running. As for your contract, I can get you out of that, no problem. I can make the band bigger; I've spoken to Romany about glamming it up and changing direction. It's just about the right time to change; glam rock is going to be huge. I can get you fame, fortune, and as many lovely chicks as you can handle.'

'I dunno,' said Ed, 'I just want to make a bit of money; just enough to survive and settle down like my brother.'

'No problem, my boy,' said Vic, 'you'll find a special lady when the time is right.'

Ed doubled over as the pain was getting stronger. 'I did,' he said, 'but she left me, and there's not a day goes by when I don't think about her; she was the love of my life, still is. I can't get her out of my head. If someone could grant me a wish it would be to be with her, money or no money.' He tapped his forehead, 'she's still in there.'

'Early days,' said Vic, 'you'll get over it.'

'No I won't. It was two years ago and it feels like yesterday. She's married to a right bastard but she won't leave because of her daughter.'

Vic was getting frustrated. 'There'll be others and you'll have the world at your feet.'

Ed clutched his stomach. 'Fame means nothing. I need her.'

Vic's frustration was getting worse. 'Well, when you get famous, she'll probably come looking for you.'

'She's not materialistic,' replied Ed. He wished these pains would leave him. He looked at Vic; so pompous, so fat, and so smelly. If this is what money did to people, they could keep it. Vic lit up a cigarette and offered one to him. He could see the tears in his eyes but he wasn't sure if it was the stomach pain, or the pain that he was feeling over this girl. He guessed that it was the latter as physical pain was spasmodic, whereas emotional pain sometimes never left.

He needed to get this idiot under contract and guessed that there was probably only one way. He walked through to the kitchen, opened the fridge, and removed two lagers.

Returning to the front room, he handed one to Ed saying, 'if I can find this girl, do we have a deal?'

'You'll never find her,' replied Ed. 'I've been searching since she left. Her agent won't help and neither will her friend but I will find her one day, I have to. I can't sleep, and when I finally do, all I dream about is her.'

Vic pursed his lips and sighed; he needed Ed's signature so he had to convince him that he would find her. 'Okay Ed, I've more contacts than you, I'll find her. Have you got a photo?' he asked.

'Yep,' replied Ed, taking a photo from his wallet, 'I've got loads.'

Vic took the photo from Ed and whistled. 'Pretty girl,' he said, staring at a girl adorned with bangles, beads, flowers, a white dress and a veil. She was holding a bouquet of flowers and had a white shawl draped around her shoulders. 'Looks like she just got married,' said Vic.

'It was a hippy wedding,' replied Ed. 'She's mine and when I catch up with that husband of hers, I'm gonna kill him.' He snatched the photo back, adding, 'and when I find her, she'll never leave me again.'

'Of course,' said Vic, thinking that although this was an unhealthy obsession, he wanted Ed to front the band so he would agree to anything. 'Name?' he asked.

'Cathy, but she dances under the name of "Gypsy", and I don't have a phone number or surname.'

Vic furrowed his brow. 'Agent?' he pressed.

'Noddy Todd; lives at the Elephant and Castle, but he won't help, I've tried.'

'He owes me a few favours; he'll cave in, and what about this friend?'

'June Maclaine; she's a cabaret singer.'

'I know her; I'll pay her a visit. I have her phone number and she's done a few gigs for me. She'll be the key to your gypsy; women always exchange phone numbers.'

'She told me that she didn't have it,' Ed said dejectedly.

'Then she's lying; I'll get it.'

'I wish I had your faith.'

'I've got a few things on her that she won't want made public.'

'I thought she was my friend,' Ed said, shaking his head.

'Women... who needs them?' joked Vic.

'I need Cathy; I can't function without her.'

'I will deliver her to you gift-wrapped.'

'I love her so much.'

Vic lit a second cigarette and offered another one to Ed who declined. He puffed himself up saying, 'Ed, my boy, it's your job to become famous, and mine to supply you with whatever you want, and if it is this Gypsy, then that's what you'll get. Now come on, let's ditch these losers and make money. I promise I'll find your dream girl for you. I've only got to make a few phone calls and you'll get her in no time. Sign on the dotted line, ditch the losers, and then when your friend Romany returns you can give him the good news.'

As an afterthought, he added, 'Ed, can you give me one of those photos? It would help to see who we're looking for.' Secretly, however, he was thinking he'd like this girl's photo by the side of his bed. She looked like a horny bitch to him, and it would be nice to pleasure himself over this on cold nights. He would look for her, but first he wanted Ed to gel with the band as soon as possible so they could resume touring and cut an album. Then he would pressurise June Maclaine and Noddy Todd for information.

Ed nodded. 'Okay, I'll get you a photo, but not this one. It travels with me everywhere.'

'Great,' said Vic, 'now let's discuss your schedule.'

Ed stared straight ahead. 'Cathy's my soul mate,' he sighed.

Vic was getting impatient now; he wanted to discuss work and ways of making himself richer. 'I'll find her; I'll start looking tomorrow.' He'd say anything by this point to push Ed into the band.

Cathy was doing a bit of pushing herself. It was a hot August day and she was delivering a healthy baby boy. When her pain had subsided, miraculously Ed's stopped too at the same time. After the baby's birth, Cathy delivered her contraceptive coil.

Outside the delivery room, Tony was fuming. He did not want another child. His wife had been dancing but had had to stop four months ago, and who knew how long it would be before she was able to work again? The nurse called him in to the delivery room. 'You have a strong baby boy,' she said in a thick Irish accent.

Tony forced a smile. 'Great,' he said. He looked at Cathy who was tired but radiant. He kissed her on the forehead. 'Well done,' he said, as if she'd run a race.

Cathy smiled down at the baby she cradled in her arms. 'He's beautiful,' she said. 'I'd like to call him Steven.'

'Whatever,' said Tony who was bored already. 'When do you think you'll be able to get back to work?'

Cathy continued to gaze at her baby. 'Don't know,' she said, 'why don't you get a job until I can resume working.'

Tony recoiled in horror, 'because you make more money than I could, and it's a shame to waste your talent.'

'Well,' said Cathy, 'you'll have to sign on for a while then and we'll get a family allowance as this little one is our second child.'

'Yes, but when will you go back to work?'

'Not for at least nine months,' said Cathy. That thought at least had pleased her; more time with Sandy and her new baby.

Tony snapped angrily. 'What happened? You had the contraceptive coil?'

'Don't know,' said Cathy, 'it must have moved or something.'

'Well,' said Tony, glowering at her, 'you'll have to go back on the pill.'

'How about you get done?' suggested Cathy. 'Then we won't have to worry about it any more.'

'I can't believe you just said that. Are you trying to make me less of a man?'

Cathy giggled, finding his last remark very funny but ignored him anyway. She was happy even though the pregnancy had been unplanned. 'Tony, I'm tired. Maybe you should go home to Sandy.' Tony agreed and left.

After he'd gone, Cathy asked for the telephone, and a nurse wheeled it over. She rang June who was in pieces. 'I feel so helpless,' she cried. 'I want to be at Mick's bedside but I can't; it's too difficult. I'm calling the hospital everyday but I can't get to see him. I've got no work in Norwich, but loads in the north, some even in Scotland. Still I suppose it's good news for Ed; he's stepped into Mick's shoes now. That ghastly Victor Lee is going to manage the band. I spoke to Ed yesterday. He still asks about you, still wants you back. The only reason he joined the band was to get Vic Lee onside in helping to look for you. He's still besotted; he says he will find you.'

Cathy laughed, 'Vic Lee looking for me? Ed will be famous soon, and he'll forget me.'

'I wouldn't bet on it,' said June, 'it would take one phone call from you to make his life complete. He even attempted suicide last year, and says he can't exist without you.'

'Ed is used to getting his own way. I still love him, June, and I think about him everyday but if I go, Tony will take Sandy away from me. I can't leave, and now I've got my new baby that's the end of that. Anyway you said he attempted suicide. He probably got help before things got really bad or he wouldn't still be here. It's just another "I want" example, and this time "I want" didn't get. It had to happen. Give my love to Mick when you see him. I know you'll invent some imaginary gig in Norwich just to be with him.'

June laughed. 'You know me too well.'

'And you know me too well. Ed's better off without me, especially now that I've got Steven.'

'He'd take you no matter what the situation was,' said June. 'His obsession gets stronger by the day. He even keeps your photo in his wallet after two years. Tells everyone it's his wife.'

Cathy sighed. 'Well it was a lovely wedding. Simple but perfect.' Her mind recalled the scene and she added, 'Ed, Rusty, and Fawn did it as a surprise. You should have seen Amber and

Amethyst in their pretty pink dresses. They even sat up for most of the night making my veil. It was something that I'll never forget, unlike the following events.'

June went ice cold. How much had her friend remembered? Cathy continued, 'the man that married us was called Seth and we went back to his cottage for a nightcap. I had a couple of drinks of some strange tasting beverage; I guess it was herbal, and I remember getting sleepy and Ed cuddling me. Then I didn't remember any more until we were back at the club, but I keep getting flashbacks. It's silly really, but how rude of me to fall asleep like that; I really owe Seth an apology.'

June felt angry. Cathy was blaming herself when all the time both Seth and Ed had abused her. 'Well, Ed said you were stoned and drunk. How's your arm? I remember last time I saw you, you were still having problems.'

'Plays up now and again,' said Cathy. 'Really throbs at times; it was a nasty gash. Well, you saw it. The doctor even accused me of self-harming. Must have been a nasty piece of glass to do that to me. It healed, but like I say it can throb from time to time.'

June switched her thoughts to Mick. 'Mick's on life support, so unless he's improved overnight I guess he won't know that I'm there at all. I don't even know if they'll let me see him but I'm going to say that I'm family and hope they let me in. I'm leaving for Norwich after I've worked Newcastle. I've got a few spare days then but I won't tell the old man that.'

'Well, give my love to him, and wish him well.'

'Okay,' said June, 'but I'd rather you rang Ed. He really does love you.'

'No,' said Cathy, firmly. 'I love him but he's obsessed with someone he met two years ago, and obsession is not an attractive feature. Maybe some day our paths will cross, but by then I feel as though he'll be with someone else.'

'Cathy, you're so stubborn,' cried June. 'You were made for each other. Wake up!'

'I made my decision,' said Cathy, glancing over at her baby boy who was stirring. 'I'll be back on the circuit soon if Tony gets his own way.'

'Okay, I concede defeat, but keep in touch and congrats on your baby. I'll be sending something in the post. Bye.'

'Will do,' said Cathy, 'bye, June.'

Nine months later, Ed was beset with terrible sickness again. The doctor scanned him for a stomach ulcer, gallstones, bowel problems, liver problems, and just about every digestive symptom possible. He vomited profusely. It was always worse first thing in the mornings, and Romany joked that he'd been got at. 'You're pregnant,' he chortled, but Ed didn't find this funny at all.

He'd gelled with the band, and was making more money than he ever thought possible; he was Vic's golden boy, sometimes making the rest of the band take a back seat. This caused a little discontent with the rest of the band members, except with Romany. Now, however, he was getting all this stomach trouble which made life difficult, but by evening it eased again, making gigs possible. Each morning, the feeling would return with a vengeance once more.

At the same time, Cathy was pregnant again. Tony went crazy; just when he thought things were going to get better and she was about to return to work, this happened. He surveyed his wife who literally had her head over the toilet bowl most of the day until evenings. 'How did this happen?' he shouted, 'you're on the bloody pill.' Cathy couldn't come up with an answer. The only thing that she thought was possible was that previously she'd had such a bad attack of gastroenteritis that she'd had to be admitted to hospital for forty-eight hours. Nothing could be kept down in her stomach and obviously the pill would have been rejected too. When she voiced this to Tony, he exploded. 'Well, you'll have to have an abortion,' he yelled.

'Never, we'll manage. Maybe you should have put something on the end of it, Tony.' Tony let forth with a series of expletives and went out slamming the door, furious that now they had another nine months before the baby put in an appearance, and then probably another nine months before Cathy went back to work. He prayed every night that she'd miscarry.

Ed now had everything apart from his health. He had expensive cars, a mansion, and a steady flow of girlfriends. Then Vic found Faye and introduced her to Ed. She soon became a permanent fixture in Ed's life. She was the trophy girlfriend; beautiful, a body to die for, gorgeous features, long, ash blonde hair and something that only one other woman he'd been with had, her virginity. Ed installed her in his mansion immediately, and Vic sighed with relief, thinking the Gypsy saga was all over. Faye delighted Ed; he taught her how to pleasure him in every possible way. He didn't love her with the passion that he loved Cathy, but as he said to Vic, 'she'll do until you find Cathy.' Vic was dumbfounded. He thought that Faye was the answer to the problem, and was stunned at Ed's remarks.

'What is it with this girl. Has she got a gold-lined cunt?'

Ed just smiled and put his hand to his heart. 'She's in there. Don't worry Vic, I'll look after Faye and she'll have a good life for now; you worry too much.' He did give Faye everything, and in return she gave him her virginity.

To start with things were great; he was a gentle, considerate lover, but later, to her dismay, his sexual demands got greater. She was having to do things that she didn't like and, if Ed went out with Romany, she knew that he was gone for the night and that there were other women involved. To top that, no matter what time he got in she was subjected to a marathon sex session after being rudely awoken. They split up several times but always got back together again, driven by Ed's desire to have someone waiting at home for him and Faye's love of luxurious living. She didn't like the touring either. The rules were the same; no wives or girlfriends, so she either had to go as Ed's secretary and PR lady, or stay at home while he toured, getting up to God knows what. Her life wasn't as perfect as she thought it would be, but she realised that if she wanted to remain in this life of luxury, she'd have to put up with it.

On the day that baby Michael was born, Ed was beset with agonizing pains again, which once more disappeared as soon as the child put in an appearance. After that, his health returned. In mid-November, 1972, Cathy approached her agent, and sat in his office leafing through the different contracts. Noddy was enthusing over a dance contest in which the participants had to be able to do just about every kind of dance possible. He said that this was for her as she could do just about any style of dance and the prize money was good, with many opportunities for the winner.

Cathy agreed to do the competition as Noddy was always right. She valued any advice that he gave her. It was going to be hard going but she brushed up on her dancing at every level and every style. They'd called it a go-go competition, though it was anything but. True, they had to do one go-go dance in every stage of the competition, but the hidden agenda was the international styles. She moved in with Noddy some of the time as Tony was now spending more and more of his time at his mother's. His excuse was that it gave Cathy more time to practise, but she guessed the truth was that there must be a woman involved somewhere, so she concentrated on the competition. She sailed through the regional heats and then found herself in the final twelve.

Chapter Seven

Vic was frustrated. It was December, 1972, and still he had had no luck with this girl. He badly wanted to find her, and not just for Ed. He needed to know what all the fuss was about; she was just a woman after all. He masturbated regularly while focussing on that photo, but Ed was driving him nuts. Still the obsession went on, despite him having everything. Noddy Todd refused to help and wouldn't accept bribes. June stood her ground even when he threatened to expose her affair with Mick to her husband.

'Prove it,' she said, and laughed in his face. He'd spent a fortune over the last two years trying to find her. He'd had leads but they'd all been dead ends, and Ed was pressuring him the whole time. Ed knew nothing about her absence from the scene owing to two pregnancies.

Vic got out of bed and went downstairs just as the morning's post ended up on the mat. He bent down, picked the mail up and immediately wished he hadn't. His head was spinning; he'd had a skinful last night with his photographer friend Al. He walked into the kitchen and threw the letters on the table. After making himself a black coffee, he sat down and opened his mail. Bills, bills, more bills, and some bloody letter from Ted Taylor asking him to judge a dance competition on his show. He also wanted Ed to sing at the final. 'Bloody queen,' he muttered. In the envelope were some photos of a few entrants. Vic scanned through them absentmindedly, but one in particular intrigued him. He studied it thoroughly and compared it to his photo. The girl looked slightly older but he felt excitement growing in his stomach. This had to be his elusive Gypsy. He turned the photo over and read the details on the back. It read; 'Cathy Peterson aka Gypsy, speciality dancer'. That clinched it. There was even a phone number. Vic gave out a whoop of delight. 'Gotcha, Eddie baby, I am going to deliver.' He felt really horny now and returned to bed with his photos. He was going to have an orgy with these girls – a one-handed one.

A little later, he had an idea and rang Al who was in the midst of a pornographic shoot. He was an accomplished photographer but specialised in porn as he found that that was where most of the money was. He told his actors and actresses to take five and answered the telephone. Vic's voice boomed down the line. 'Al, I want a favour. I need you to charm a very special lady.'

Al liked the sound of that, thinking that this was another star in the making. He could always do with more actresses. 'Who is she?' he asked, wiping his forehead on a tissue; it had been a really steamy session.

'I need you to charm this lady into coming to my house tomorrow for a photo session, only I won't be in the room. I'll be looking at her through the mirror and she mustn't see me.'

'What is this, an off the wrist job for you?'

'No,' replied Vic, 'this is for Ed.'

'Pimping now, are we?'

'Don't ask so many questions, you'll be well paid. I want her here tomorrow; I've got her phone number. You've got to convince her that she needs a portfolio, and that she's been specially selected for a free photo shoot. I don't want her getting suspicious so put on your best telephone voice and manner and get her to me tomorrow.'

'Do you want film in the camera? Is she interested in porn?'

'Of course I want film in the camera, and no she's not into porn. Just do it, these photos are for Ed.'

Al was disappointed. 'What sort of photos?'

'Don't ask so many questions; you want to know the ins and outs of a duck's arse. Get round here when you've finished whatever you're doing and you can call from here so I can make sure you don't make any cock-ups.'

'Chance would be a fine thing. Okay, see you later.'

A couple of hours later, Al arrived at Vic's house. Vic plied him with drink and then handed over the phone number. 'Charm,' he said.

Al dialled the number and got a very disgruntled Tony. 'Hi,' said Al, 'I'm the photographer for the dance competition and we need Cathy for a photo shoot at the studio. If you can give me your address I'll get her picked up tomorrow morning.'

'Why can't you do it here?' asked Tony.

'Because it needs to be done in a studio with all the correct setting and lighting.'

'How much is she getting paid for this?'

Al reached for a pad and scribbled how much and waved it under Vic's nose. Vic mouthed £100 and Al repeated it to Tony. 'Okay,' said Tony, 'I'll get her.' He was glad he'd called in as he'd been staying at his mother's for the last few days. He'd come to get some cash from Cathy as he'd run out of money. This sounded interesting. It looked like his wife was about to get some more money just for posing for a few photos. It was the main prize that he had his eye on though, thinking that if only Cathy could win the whole thing, they'd be in clover. Well, he would anyway. Cathy would be too busy working to spend anything on herself. Seconds later, Cathy came to the phone.

'Hallo, can I help you?'

'No, doll, I can help you, you've just won a photo shoot for free. I'm the official photographer for the dance competition. You need a portfolio, and I've got you down for tomorrow. I can get you picked up at 10 o'clock if that's convenient, and we'll pay you £100 for your time.'

'Goodness, that's a lot of money. If they pay every girl that, it'll cost a fortune.' Al was lost for words, so Vic snatched the notepad and scribbled that they were choosing girls at random.

'Well,' said Al, 'they've selected three girls and you're one of them. You're being paid because we don't know how long you'll be at the studio.'

'Oh well, I suppose that's different. I guess I've struck lucky.'

'You sure have,' said Al. 'I've been looking at your photo. Would you be interested in doing films? You're very photogenic.'

Vic slapped him around the head and snatched the phone. 'Hallo,' he said, 'photographers should stick to taking photos. I'm the PR man.' Al grabbed the notebook and scribbled, 'that's right, PR stands for prick' and held it under Vic's nose.

'Oh,' said Cathy, 'I'm a bit confused by all this.'

Vic was going all hot and cold. It was her voice; she sounded so young. 'I noticed that you have three children, or so it says on your application.'

'That's right; does that make a difference?'

'No dear, it's just that you sounded so young.' He was getting agitated now. 'I'm pleased to say that you have been selected for a free portfolio, and we're fascinated by your stage name. Do you have a gypsy costume? It would be a good publicity angle with a nice little twist to it.'

'Yes, but won't you want go-go costumes too.'

'Of course, bring whatever you think will be appropriate but don't forget the gypsy outfit.' He couldn't believe that he was speaking to the love of Ed's life.

'Okay, what is your name?'

Vic was lost for words now and Al was laughing at him getting more and more flustered. He stared at the calendar in front of him and encircled in red biro was, 'phone Frank'. 'Mr Franks,' he blustered. 'I suppose you've loads of work at the moment.'

'No,' said Cathy. 'I've not worked for ages; I had two children in quick succession.'

Vic now understood why he hadn't been able to find her. She hadn't been on the bloody circuit at all. 'Oh well, I suppose they keep you busy.'

'Yes, but I'm ready to return now and my agent thinks this could open a few doors for me.'

'That's for sure,' said Vic, thinking: once Ed opens those doors, you're cornered. 'Well dear, I'll send someone round for you at ten tomorrow and I'm sure that we'll get some beautiful photos. Now what is your address?'

'Okay,' replied Cathy, 'will you be there?'

'No, not in the flesh, but in spirit.' He was smiling to himself, thinking: my spirit will be behind the two-way mirror.

'Oh, shame,' said Cathy, and she proceeded to read out her address, adding, 'well thank you for ringing, Mr Franks, I'll be ready for ten.' As an afterthought, she said, 'maybe I'll see you at the show, I'd love to meet you.'

Vic was at a loss for words. He'd forgotten he was Mr Franks. 'That's lovely, dear, I'm sure we will.' He replaced the receiver. 'Who's Mr Franks?' he asked Al.

'You are; you told her that was your name.'

'Of course,' said Vic, 'I was only joking.' He glared at Al. 'You were bloody useless, I said charm, not funny farm.'

'Well, you couldn't remember you were Mr Franks,' retorted Al.

'Who?' said a very confused Vic.

'Forget it, her photos will look great. I'm gonna ask her about making films again. Perhaps she'll do a bit tomorrow.'

Vic went blood-red. 'I told you, she's for Ed. The only thing she's doing tomorrow is a perfect set of photos, and I want them to be tastefully done. You can film her, but only dancing. I think Ed would like to see her moving.'

'Yes, but I could get some tasteful porn shots,' said Al, 'Ed might like them too.'

Vic opened another bottle of whiskey and poured two glasses; he was getting angry. He looked at Al who had brought a projector with him, and his latest porn film. Al was a dead ringer for Stan Laurel, even down to his mannerisms. 'Get that film started, I'm getting frustrated. As for Gypsy, no porn; don't even discuss it with her, treat her with respect if you know what that is.' Al scratched his head making his hair stand on end; he looked even more like Stan Laurel. He voiced his observations to Al who retorted that if Vic put on a black wig and wore a bowler hat, he would be a dead ringer for Oliver Hardy.

'We could do a porn movie together,' said Al, accepting the whiskey offered to him.

'Shut up and get that movie started.' Al grunted but obeyed; he'd got nothing better to do.

Suddenly the phone rang; it was Ed. 'Where have you been?' he shouted, 'This bloody album is a mess. It's a right shambles. I hate it.'

'Patience,' said Vic, 'everything will work out all right.'

'Well, I wouldn't buy this album if you paid me. I'm trying to write, and getting nowhere. I'm thinking about quitting the band.'

'You are not. I've got a new lead on your Gypsy and unless you knuckle down and get this album out, I won't bother to follow it up. You could be reunited in a couple of months; this is the first concrete lead I've had, and if you choose to blow it that's up to you. So if you want to leave, then do it; I've heard that Mick's on the mend. He might not be able to tour but he hasn't lost his voice and I'm sure he'd love to return; he's a great writer too. The fans would love to have him back. He's the main draw, always was, and he conducted himself properly too. He'd been with the band since its beginning and people still mention his name. You have yet to prove yourself even though you've struck lucky. The band carry you, it's not the other way around. You're just the vocalist and not a very good one lately either.'

Ed was about to voice his feelings in no uncertain terms when he remembered what Vic had said earlier. 'What concrete evidence? You've done this before and got false leads.'

'This time I have an address and photographs. You aren't getting either unless you get this album up and running for me, and you'd better get up close and personal with Kim Carter if you want your girl back.'

'Why?'

'Don't ask so many questions. I'll see you at the studio tomorrow afternoon, and then you can come over to my place twenty-four hours later and see the evidence for yourself. When I get to the studio tomorrow, I want to see a vast improvement. Try writing a love song for your girl and then you can sing it to her when you're reunited.'

'You're sure that it's her?' asked Ed, feeling the excitement starting to build up in his stomach.

'Let's put it this way: when I see a photo of a girl, and on the reverse it states: "Cathy Peterson aka Gypsy", then I think it's pretty solid evidence. That's where you and Kim come in. Kim's a judge on the panel of a dance contest, and your girl has managed to get herself into the final twelve which will be televised in two weeks' time. The final twelve will be eliminated until there is a winner. Oh and by the way, I'm another judge, and as for the other two, they owe me big time.

'They want you to sing on the final show too, so if we can get Gypsy into the final she'll be forced into your company anyway. The final is important, so get working on Kim pronto. Get her to the final, Ed; it doesn't matter if she loses then because we can get a hotel and meal included in the consolation prize and then it'll be your job to console her. We'll discuss it tomorrow; now go and charm Kim. I'm entertaining at the minute so piss off, you're cramping my style.'

Ed said contritely, 'Okay, give me Kim's number.'

Vic grinned and looked over at Al. Entertaining, he thought; here he was with this grinning idiot setting up the projector, and he had another idiot on the phone who would do anything to get this girl back. He found Kim's number, gave it to Ed, and then replaced the receiver. Al was on the floor with a lot of unwound film. 'What happened to the movie?' he asked.

Al rewound the film, oblivious to Vic's question.

'Who's coming round?' he asked, getting more and more agitated with the film that was winding itself around him like a serpent.

'No one, what the hell have you done with that reel of film?'

'Dunno, but don't panic, things will be fine.'

Another thirty minutes passed, and finally, another bottle of whiskey later, they sat down to watch the film. 'We're pissed,' said Vic, 'and it's all your fault. I'm going to have a massive hangover tomorrow and you'll probably have camera shake.'

'Not me,' said Al, and promptly passed out on the sofa.

'Lightweight,' muttered Vic, and settled down to watch his film.

The following day, Cathy was transported to Vic's house. She was greeted by Al. 'This your house?' she asked.

Al nodded, 'just bought it. Now follow me upstairs and I'll show you where we're going to do the photo shoot.'

Cathy followed him up to the bedroom that adjoined Vic's. Al had put a backcloth across a couple of the walls and in the corner was a small screen, behind which she could change. What she didn't know was that the mirror behind the screen was two-way. Vic had a perfect view of her as she disrobed. Behind the mirror, Vic gloated; he had Ed's pride and joy in his house and could view her in several stages of undress. Her photo hadn't done her justice; she posed as asked, unaware that she was being watched. In Vic's eyes, she was beautiful and sensual, but with this little girl-lost look. Al did his job efficiently despite a banger of a headache. He got the shots he wanted, and also footage of her dancing. He wanted to ask her about making movies but knew that Vic wouldn't pay him if he did, so he refrained.

That afternoon, having sent Al to take Cathy home with the agreed payment, Vic went to the recording studio. The session was going badly and even he had to agree that it wasn't good. Ed was flagging, and Vic called him to one side. His vocalist looked all washed up. 'I've been on the phone to Mick,' said Ed, 'and he says he'll give me a few of his songs to mull over. He was always better than me. I'm tired and I feel old, my eyes are stinging and I know the band is pissed off with me. Mick was spontaneous, and writing was second nature to him.' He rubbed his eyes as Vic handed him an envelope.

'If you want inspiration, look no further. This was sent to me a few days ago.' Ed opened the envelope with shaking hands and withdrew the photo.

'Where is she?' he gasped. His eyes had lit up; all tiredness gone. 'I was beginning to think she was dead.' He threw his arms around Vic knocking the breath out of him. 'When can I see her?'

Vic pushed him away. 'I told you, in about two months if you can persuade Kim to get her to the final. Get to work on her; she's madly in love with you and she'll be putty in your hands.'

Ed nodded vigorously. 'Anything you say Vic. Isn't she beautiful? I love her so much.'

'Yes, yes, now let's get this album off the ground, and let's make Kim happy.'

Ed grinned. 'I'll take her out tonight.'

Vic was amazed at the miraculous change in Ed. 'Come over to my house tomorrow night. I'll have more photos by then and some footage of her dancing.'

'Great, and I feel a song coming on, must go.' With that he hurried back to the band, laughing. 'Come on guys, let's get this show on the road.'

Vic was relieved, and decided that if this was what Ed needed then he was going to get it. He decided to call the other judges, and a short while later was a very happy man; he certainly had something over both of them. They couldn't disobey his instructions. He chuckled to himself. If the stupid pillocks got themselves into such dangerous situations while in his company, then that was their fault.

That night Ed did indeed charm Kim with all sorts of promises, none of which he intended keeping. It was as Vic had said; the girl was in love with him and after dinner at the Dorchester he took her to his bed and made her dreams come true. It hadn't been too bad. He'd had to listen to her spouting undying love and, wonder of wonders, she was also a virgin, like Faye. He couldn't believe his luck.

Twenty-four hours later he made his way over to Vic's house. Al was still there after setting up the projector and handing over the photos that he'd taken. He was swiftly dismissed though when Ed arrived, as Vic needed to speak to him privately. Vic had also had a row with Al that evening as he was still smarting from when he told Cathy that the house was his.

'The cheek of it!' he said. 'You couldn't afford anything like this; you are such a bloody fool. And there was no need to photograph her sprawled across the bed with the gypsy blouse off her shoulders; you could almost see her tits. The skirt was around her thighs as well; you just couldn't resist it, could you? You're a pervert.'

'Perfect photos,' retorted Al, 'and anyway, you're the pervert. When she was behind the screen, you must have been getting off just watching. I bet you were giving yourself one off the wrist.'

'I was not, I was watching to make sure the shots you were doing were good enough,' Vic retorted angrily.

'Then you should have put the screen on the opposite wall.' snapped Al. 'You were having your own private peep show.'

Vic drew himself up to his full height, which wasn't much. He'd been caught out. 'Well that shot on the bed leaves very little to the imagination, and you were straddling her to get it. Ed's not stupid you know, and at one moment during that shot I thought you were going to have sex with her.'

'I wish! She'd be perfect in one of my movies.'

'You're a bloody fool. You drank all my whiskey the other night, and tried to get some lewd photos out of that poor girl.' He placed his hands on his hips. 'I've got a good mind not to pay you.'

'Then I'm taking the footage and photos back,' said Al.

Vic thought Al looked even more like Stan Laurel than the man himself. He took his wallet from his pocket, and Al gloated as he counted out the money. He was more than happy with it and settled down on the sofa just as Ed knocked on the door. 'Right,' said Vic, 'now you can clear off.'

Al got to his feet, dejected. He'd wanted to see Ed's reaction to his handiwork, but, remembering Vic's words about the near porn photo, he decided it was probably a good idea to leave. 'Okay, I'll pick up the projector tomorrow.'

Vic let Al out and greeted Ed warmly. 'Come in, I'm sure you'll like what I've got in store for you.'

Ed seated himself in front of the screen, his excitement getting to bursting point. Vic poured out a couple of brandies; he scrutinized the bottle which was three quarters full. He was out of whiskey because of the idiot that had just left, and by the end of the night would probably be out of brandy too. He offered the drink to Ed and got out his cigarettes. 'How's the album going?' he asked, looking over at Ed who was gazing at the empty screen.

'Great, and Kim's great too. Come on Vic, I've waited long enough.' He drained his brandy in three gulps. Vic could see it was only a matter of time before the vodka would put in an appearance. He thrust the photos at Ed who enthused over them.

'Oh, she's so beautiful, so precious. Did Al take these?' Vic nodded and lit up a cigarette, watching Ed's reaction. He looked so happy. He studied the photo on the bed and whistled. 'That is hot; she looks so sensual. The look says it all; the way her lips are parted, the look in her eyes. She looks ready for me. Hold on though, how did he get that shot? How did he get her to get that expression? He must have been astride her. I don't like that; I don't want anyone else seeing her like that, and I hate the thought of that muppet getting so close. I'll have to have words with him.'

Vic frowned and started up the projector. Cathy's image leapt onto the screen, and Ed was transfixed, 'all mine,' he repeated over and over again. There was his very own angel in front of him. It was more than he could stand and he burst into a flood of tears.

Vic got to his feet and went over to him. 'Not long now and you'll be together again.'

Cathy was dancing and smiling at him, and he longed to touch her and feel that warmth again. He always felt cold nowadays, could never get warm, never felt well, but the emotion that he was feeling now was of a love that ate him alive.

The film ended abruptly with a close-up of Cathy smiling into the camera. 'Where was she?' he asked. 'Why could we never find her?'

Vic crossed to the bar and poured more brandy. 'Well, I don't know where she was to begin with, but since I've been searching, she hasn't been on the circuit; she's knocked out two more sprogs. She's been at home for a long time, not working at all. That's why I drew blanks.'

'Ouch,' said Ed. 'Tony's been busy. Still they're married, even though he's got a string of girlfriends. She can't say no, can she? I mean, I wouldn't let her say no to me. She tried before and I wasn't having any of it. She's mine, and if I wanted sex I expected it. Faye tries it on too but it doesn't wash with me. So, I've got a ready-made family, have I, Vic?'

'But Ed, what if she doesn't want to come back?'

Ed laughed. 'She's got no choice. She belongs to me, and once I get her back in bed, she'll remember it too.'

Vic was uneasy; it sounded like an obsession again. It was as if he wanted to possess her and take away any freedom of thought at all that she might have. That Ed thought he could just take the children away from their father was crazy, it was insane. He continued, 'when I get her back, she won't have to work any more, I'll make her and the kids happy.'

Vic changed the subject. 'The key word is surprise. She has to know nothing until you meet up, and then you'll have to act as if you've never met, or she'll be disqualified. The judges are fixed, they know that she has to reach the final, and you can throw in a hotel and a meal whether she wins or loses. Then it's down to you.'

Ed was remembering their first encounter, and relayed it to Vic. Halfway through, Vic fell asleep and fell off the sofa. He hit the floor with a thud, but Ed didn't seem to notice as he was so absorbed in his reverie. 'I have never had a feeling like it. It was weird; like sexual but also warm, secure and happy.'

Vic started and got to his feet having spilt his drink. That was sacrilege, and the bottle was nearly empty. 'Do you like vodka?' he asked. 'That bastard Al drank all my whiskey the other night.'

'Vodka's fine. The electricity between us was amazing, like a fusion, it was fantastic.'

'Lucky you, I've never felt like that.'

Ed sighed and added, 'she was going to leave Tony for me and then she just left me.' He felt June could have helped him, but he guessed that she was just being loyal to her friend.

'Do you want anything in the vodka?' called Vic. He'd have to go shopping tomorrow; that bloody Al had drunk all the whiskey, Ed had finished the brandy, and now the vodka was going to be hammered.

'Orange.'

Vic pretended that he'd heard all the conversation, not wanting to own up to having fallen asleep. It annoyed him though that Ed had not noticed him fall off the sofa. Could have been dead for all the notice he took of me, he thought. Handing the glass to Ed, he said, 'some lady, but you can have anyone you want. I mean, look at Faye, she's so gorgeous.'

'I know, but Cathy and I have a chemistry that's very different. She's adventurous and she keeps pace with me; anything goes.

She's always raring to go. Now Faye can't keep up and that makes me angry. Turns me into a right bastard at times. Anyway, in my eyes, Cathy's my wife and always will be. June said she left because her daughter had had an accident but I don't know if that was the truth.' What really worried him was that maybe she'd recalled the events with Seth because that might be enough to keep her running for the rest of her life.

'June's at Bognor Regis tomorrow night.'

'Really? I owe her a visit. I've known her for years. I was rotten to her when I realised that Cathy had left without me. Where is she Vic?'

'Butlins. Saturday night cabaret.'

'Good, I'll pay her a visit.'

Vic grinned. 'You can bring her back here. She won't want to travel back at that time of night. She lives up North, doesn't she?'

'Thanks Vic.' A plan was hatching in Ed's brain already. Vic was elated; the two-way mirror would be in use once more. Great stuff.

The first that June knew was when Ed jumped out at her from behind her dressing room door. She screamed, then after she'd composed herself and realised who it was, cried, 'Ed, how nice! What brings you this way?'

Ed seized her to him. 'I came to see you, of course. Vic said you were here.'

'I'm honoured. Shall we have a drink?'

'Better than that, babe, we're going for a meal and then back to Vic's for a nightcap.'

June laughed and began to change into her jeans and t-shirt. 'Still taking over,' she muttered.

'That's right, babe, it's the only way to be.'

After a meal that blew them both out, they headed for Vic's home. 'Nice house,' said June, 'shame about the owner. I won't stay long. I've got a long journey home.'

Ed walked over to Vic's bar and poured two drinks. Handing June a glass of brandy, he settled down beside her on the sofa. 'The night is young, babe, and you can stay. Vic won't mind.' Vic certainly wouldn't mind. He'd heard them come in and was waiting upstairs behind his two-way mirror, excitedly. Ed placed his arm around June's shoulders. 'Come on, babe, loosen up. You haven't changed since I first met you; you're just as beautiful.' He swallowed hard; he was lying to her.

Time hadn't been kind to her but she still had that sparkle. He was going to seduce her anyway. He knew what was in store for him as they'd been bedfellows for years. He wanted information no matter how he got it, and June was fun as a sexual partner. A few more brandies and they were very merry and giggly. June gazed into his eyes, and wondered how many more chances she would get like this? Ed now fronted the band, and here he was trying to get her into bed; why fight it? Ed could see that she was weakening, and plied her with more drink. A little later they ascended the stairs. 'Come on June, come through the gates of Eden and I'll take you to paradise.'

'Another pun on a Dylan song,' laughed June as she followed him into the bedroom. Vic was elated. He was wide awake behind his mirror and lapping up the performance. Ed kept his word; he did indeed take June to paradise several times, and the following day she awoke in his arms. That had been some night. She arose, showered, and when she came back into the bedroom, Ed was awake. He was a bit muddled. Why was he with June? Why was he in Vic's spare room? And then it all came flooding back. 'I've got to go,' said June, 'but I've got to ask you something.'

'Fire away,' yawned Ed.

'I noticed at the restaurant last night when you paid the bill that you still carry Cathy's photo in your wallet. Why? It's been four years.'

'She's my wife. She'll come back one day, and I still love her.' June perched herself on the edge of the bed.

'You've never given up, have you?'

'No, I know she had to go back for her daughter but I don't know why she never came back. She loved me, I know she did.'

June sighed. 'Okay, I swore I'd never tell you but unless I do, you'll never move on. Tony got wind of you. He rang a couple of times and was told that she was setting up home with you. So he told Cathy that Sandy had had an accident to get her home. She had never had an accident at all and he threatened Cathy that if she left he'd take Sandy away from her whilst she was touring. She also felt that if she left with Sandy, she'd slow your career down. She's got two more kids now, much to Tony's annoyance.'

'But he got her pregnant.'

'Yes but she was on the coil when she got pregnant with her boy, Steven, so he was unexpected. Then nine months later she got a severe bout of gastroenteritis and was in hospital on a drip so the pill failed too. Tony told her to get an abortion but she wouldn't.'

'He wanted her to kill her own baby?'

June nodded. 'So now she's got Michael too. Your name came up just after Steven was born and she says she still loves you and thinks that maybe one day your paths will cross, but she feels that you'll be with someone else by then.'

Ed was elated, but one question remained. 'She said that, but tell me June; what are the children's birthdates?'

'Steven's is 6th August, 1970, and Michael's 9th February, 1972,' she replied.

Ed laughed. 'Well the fact that she still loves me is very uplifting, but the dates coincide with something to do with my health which has been a mystery until now. 6th August 1970 was the day that I signed with Vic, and I was crippled with dreadful stomach pains that left me as quickly as they came. On 9th February this year, I was admitted to hospital for scans for gallstones, appendicitis, stomach ulcers, and God knows what else. Prior to that I'd been sick every day for about nine months.'

June laughed. 'So you suffered both pregnancies too. Cathy was very sick for the entire nine months. Just remember Ed, this conversation never happened, right?'

'Of course, thanks for telling me; that's cleared up an awful lot. I can cope now. I thought she didn't love me any more.'

'She thinks about you every day, but I must go.'

'Give us a cuddle,' said Ed, opening his arms to her. 'You've made me feel so much better, and last night was great. We must do it again sometime. Tell you what, give me thirty minutes and I'll run you to the station, but first cuddle.' So they cuddled, then Ed showered and dropped June off at the railway station.

On his return home, Ed was greeted by Faye. She realised that his absence all night was due to a woman, so thought there'd be no action, but to her dismay he had breakfast and then took her upstairs for a marathon sex session. Exhausted, she fell asleep, and through a haze heard him go downstairs, let himself out and drive off. She fell asleep once more and dreamed of her beauty queen days.

Ed drove over to Romany's house. He was well pleased with himself. June had volunteered the information with no pressure at all. He now understood the mystery. Women were a pushover, he thought, except the one he was still focused on, but she'd return. He couldn't lose. 'Cathy, babe,' he said out loud, 'you're coming home. There's nowhere to run to now.'

Cathy had never done so many styles of dance. The competition was advertised as a go-go contest though it was anything but, as many contestants discovered. They did have to do one go-go dance set, but the hidden agenda was different international styles of dance.

Cathy had to literally pull out everything that she knew. Among the dances were Spanish, hula-hula, Greek, belly dance, Irish, modern, jazz, classical, Indian, and just about any other style possible. The hard part about this was that when you attended auditions you were not told beforehand what you would be performing. Despite this, Cathy sailed through the regional heats, and Noddy Todd put her through her paces daily. Tony spent a lot of his time at his mother's so that she could, 'practise night and day without interruption'. Sadly, she agreed, and her heart sank when he added, 'just think, Cathy, the prize money is massive and with your talent, you can't lose.' Money was his God, but she threw herself into the contest and quite often slept at Noddy's flat in the Elephant and Castle. She went home now and again, as did Tony, and occasionally they met up but it was only on rare occasions. By the time Noddy had finished with her, every style was polished and he swelled with pride at her performances.

'Most dancers have strengths and weaknesses, but every style that you've done is now perfect,' he said. Cathy, however, didn't share his enthusiasm and was amazed to find herself in the final twelve. From then on it was televised every Saturday night on the Ted Taylor show, and for the first time the dancers were in front of a panel, whose main job was to weed out the weakest dancers and elevate the best. She was stunned to find herself in the final several weeks later. 'How did I do this?' she asked Noddy, 'I'm the oldest girl in the contest.'

'Because you're the best dancer and because we've worked non-stop.'

Over a coffee, they discussed the two speciality numbers that Cathy would do. This time, as it was the final, they were allowed to choose their own dances. 'I think we'll do flamenco and belly dance. I doubt the other girls will go down that route,' reasoned Noddy. 'The flamenco is full of passion and you've got this dance off to a fine art. Even if they do belly dance, it won't be as good as yours; you had the best teacher in the world. Nayana is fifty years old and still the finest in the land.'

Cathy smiled. 'I owe it all to you.'

'No, love, you're the best. Apart from Nayana, that is.'

Cathy asked pensively, 'what about the other two in the final?

They're both young, and Jasmine Summers is red hot and only nineteen.'

'But she doesn't have your experience.'

Cathy frowned. 'And Amber Chapman is very athletic and only seventeen.'

'Yes, and very raw around the edges. You see, these girls are very good but they don't have your finesse or charisma. You can win this. You've worked from morning till night and you deserve to win.'

'Thanks Noddy, now let's get some more work done.'

'Spoken like a true professional,' said Noddy, and together they resumed the routines.

Vic Lee was truly happy. He'd sat on the panel of judges for weeks eyeing the girls as they went through their routines. The judges had put Cathy through to the final and now it was up to her. She had to do this all by herself, although Kim had made her mind up that Cathy would get her vote as she got closer to Ed each time she did well. She believed that it was only a matter of time before he ditched Faye. She was so besotted, and Ed was very convincing.

Vic sat at home on his sofa. This contest had cost him a fortune in booze. Ed repeatedly brought Kim over to his house and they both liked a drink. He'd be glad when it was all over. His thoughts returned to the final that night. It was called the Gold and Silver show, and nobody knew why except Vic and Ted Taylor. Ted was going weak at the presence of Sammy Silver on his show. He was openly gay and had been frothing at the mouth when he knew that the number one teen idol was going to award the prize to the runner-up in third position. Ted wasn't interested in Ed Gold. He knew that he chased anything in a skirt, so he was a no-go area, but Sammy, well he'd like to find out if he was AC/DC. Vic's only concern was the photo shoot with Ed. The finalists had to have their photos taken with him before the show for publicity, and he hoped that Cathy wouldn't run, although he doubted she would. She was a professional after all. She'd probably accept it as part of the competition and act as if they'd never met. Vic had drummed it into Ed constantly, saying, 'remember you've never met; make one false move and you'll lose her and she'll be disqualified. You won't have to wait much longer.' Ed had agreed, he'd had to wait for years so a few more hours wouldn't make much difference. The clock was ticking and he was getting very excited. He'd taken care of Kim with endless promises, but that would finish tonight.

Later that night, Ed, Vic, and a photographer waited in another studio for the photo shoot. Amber was the first one in and she draped herself all over Ed, much to the photographer's delight. She was a pretty little Welsh girl with a childlike expression. She had long red hair and a beautiful smile. She was wearing a can-can dancer's outfit which suited her petite frame perfectly. She giggled as she placed her foot athletically on Ed's shoulder. The photographer got some great shots, as she loved the camera and the camera loved her.

Jasmine was next and strode in as Amber left the room. She was unfazed by Ed and posed as if she'd rather be somewhere else, but nevertheless the photographer got some good shots. She was a very fiery character with short, afro, black hair. She was black, slim, tall, and wiry, with a broad grin when she did smile, which wasn't often. Her brown eyes glittered at Ed as she posed in her short, American outfit. She also carried a baton and her knee high boots were silver. She never once spoke, and flounced out of the room, slamming the door as she left. Vic now held his breath, praying that Ed would not fall apart. Any second now, he and Cathy would set eyes on each other.

The door opened and in stepped Cathy, followed by Noddy. She was clad in her blue flamenco dress with fringes. Ed was sitting with his back to her staring in the mirror. She froze. None of the other girls had mentioned him, but then, Jasmine had almost knocked her over as she flounced out. She turned to Noddy, terrified that her past had caught up with her. Noddy whispered in her ear, 'come on, be a pro, he can't acknowledge you or you'll be disqualified.'

Ed turned around and, leaning back in his chair, surveyed her. Vic needed him to give an Oscar-winning performance and make this appear like a first encounter. Ed's mouth had gone dry. His heart was racing; there was the object of his desire. He wanted to take her in his arms, to love her and at the same time slap her for putting him through this torture. Vic watched both of them. The electricity between them was amazing. He could sense it even though he was on the other side of the room. Cathy wanted to throw herself into his arms, cry, beg his forgiveness, and run all at the same time. There was a deathly silence, and then Ed got to his feet and crossed the floor. He extended his hand and took hers in his. Cathy was shaking as he shook her hand and then kissed her fingertips. 'Hola senorita, comestas?' he said.

Cathy stuttered, 'Muy bien.'

'Mucho gusto, encantada.' Vic was frustrated that he'd never learnt Spanish. The photographer yawned as he was getting bored. Noddy wasn't happy either. Cathy was bearing up but he'd noticed that when Ed took her hand, it had been as if she'd received an electric shock. Vic noted her jump too; the girl looked petrified. Ed broke the silence saying, 'beautiful costume.'

'Thank you, cost a fortune but I've had it a long time. You get what you pay for.'

Noddy sighed with relief. Ed had diffused the situation by drawing her attention to her dress. The photographer wandered over and positioned the couple to face each other. 'Put your arm around her waist, Ed. Now Gypsy, strike a Spanish pose.'

Cathy extended one leg and raised her arms above her head. Ed laughed. 'I get all the best jobs!' The arm around Cathy's waist was bothering her; it was releasing pretty strong feelings. She prayed that this would soon be over. The photographer repositioned them again. Noddy wandered over to Vic as Cathy was being moved closer to Ed, the photographer telling her to look into his eyes and smile. She complied, finding this very hard, as the last thing that she wanted to do was to make close eye contact. Ed wasn't finding it very easy either. She was so close he could have kissed her.

'What a couple of pros,' muttered Noddy.

'Yes,' said Vic, 'they look good together.'

'One final shot,' said the photographer. 'Gypsy, stand in front of Ed with your hands on your hips. Now Ed, thread your arms through hers and hold her around the waist. That's lovely. Gypsy lean back onto him a bit.'

Vic was gobsmacked; he could see that Cathy was uneasy and guessed why. Ed's face was a picture of bliss.

Noddy chuckled. 'He's enjoying it.' Vic agreed and wished that the couple were in his house with him stationed behind his mirror. After tonight he was going to invite them both over, get them both pissed, and then upstairs. After settling them into the room adjoining his, he could sit back and enjoy the view. Cathy was uncomfortable; she could feel Ed growing against her.

Noddy turned to Vic. 'Are you going to say anything to anyone?'

'Course not. Ed didn't know she was in this contest, and she's got this far by her own merit anyway. Ed's not even a judge,' replied Vic.

'No,' said Noddy, 'but you are and you're not telling me that you didn't know who she was. You plagued me for years trying to bribe and threaten me for information.'

'Well, I shan't say anything, and neither will Ed. He wouldn't want her to lose and, looking at the other two, I think she'll win.'

'Hold it,' shouted the photographer, 'great, that's it.'

The couple separated and Ed remarked, 'maybe we should do that again, it might not come out.' The photographer agreed; you could never be too careful, and he placed the couple back into position again. Ed grinned and whispered into Cathy's ear, 'you're much more fun than the other girls.' She giggled as he'd blown into her ear and it tickled.

Finally the photographer was satisfied, and Ed almost was. Cathy moved away fast. She did not need stains on her dress and she knew it was a close call. 'There'll be one final shot after the winner's been announced,' said the photographer. 'Good luck, Gypsy.'

'Thank you,' replied Cathy. 'Come on, Noddy, you need to brief me again on the middle section. I'm still uncertain of the turns. I think I'm spinning too fast or too slow, but it's not right.'

'Always the perfectionist,' laughed Noddy, 'go on ahead; I'll be with you in a minute.'

'Okay, thank you, Ed, thank you, Mr Lee.' Then she left; spinning and playing the castanets as she went. They could still hear her as she progressed down the corridor.

'Adios Senorita,' shouted Ed and laughed.

Noddy shook Ed's hand. 'Thanks, see you later.'

They could still hear Cathy shouting: 'Oh damn, I've done it again. That's wrong. Noddy, Noddy!'

'Okay, I'm coming,' shouted Noddy and made a swift exit.

Vic frowned and uttered, 'and you nearly were, I hope it doesn't show up in the photo.'

'Yes, that was close.' Then he sat back at the dressing table and gazed into the mirror, murmuring, 'senorita gitana, te quiero, contigo siempre.'

'Will you speak English?' blustered Vic.

'Not long now. Have you booked the restaurant and the hotel?'

Vic nodded. 'She looked like a nice armful.'

'She is, and in a few hours' time, that's where she'll be.'

Vic strode to the door. 'Got to go and see that queen, Ted Taylor; rumour has it that Sammy Silver's making a guest appearance tonight. Still, you've got top billing so who cares.'

Ed groaned; he hated Sammy. However, the best part of the night was still to come and he was certainly going to enjoy that.

The show began and Ted Taylor took centre stage. He was a top television star but most people he worked with couldn't stand him. It wasn't just that he was gay; it was his whole manner. He had tantrums frequently, changed his sexual partners like other people changed their underwear and, despite being in his sixties, dressed like a teenager. He preyed on young boys. If they were over nineteen, they were too old; he liked them about seventeen. His grey hair was dyed jet black, his eyes were hooded owing to age, his nose was perfect due to plastic surgery, and his facelift done ten years previously was beginning to sag a bit. His lips were thin and he had a very shifty look about him. He was a very tall, thin man and wore mainly striped suits that made him look even thinner. He addressed the audience. 'Welcome to my show! Tonight the show is themed; it's our gold and silver night. There'll be one girl walking away with our gold prize, and one with silver. The theme also has a twist to it, but you'll find out about that later.' His mind shifted to Sammy Silver again, and his fantasy knocked in once more. 'The auditions were extensive. Thousands of dancers entered this competition, and many fell by the wayside. Tonight you will see three of the finest dancers in the country. A charming Welsh girl, a red hot raver, and a stay-at-home mum. So let's get this party started.'

The audience applauded as Ted continued, 'let's hear it for the judges who have had the most difficult job tonight – choosing the finalists. First, Victor Lee, impresario supreme, the main man for all the top acts in show biz including the Shelltones.' Vic walked out onto the stage and bowed to wild applause before taking his position on the panel. 'Second, the up and coming singing star, Kim Carter. Kim swept onto the stage and gave a cheesy smile. She was a very pretty girl who strongly resembled Diana Ross, apart from her nose which she was considering going under the knife for. She waved to the audience, curtseyed, and then walked daintily to her seat alongside Vic. 'Next we have Gerry Hunter, international choreographer, who has been involved with all the best musicals at home and abroad. Gerry strutted out onto the stage and did a few dance steps. Ted attempted to copy his steps and almost fell over.

Gerry laughed and said, 'who do you think you are, Bruce Forsythe?' He patted Ted on the back and took his seat. 'Finally,' muttered Ted, 'Nat Stevens, columnist, actor, writer, and ex-dancer international.'

Nat walked out onto the stage, pausing as he reached Ted and saying, 'great footwork, man, if we're not careful you'll be taking over from Rudolph Nureyev.' The audience laughed and Nat took his seat.

Ted waited for the applause to die down and then announced, 'bring on the girls. First up, a young lady from Wales who gets herself into some incredible positions. Let's hear it for Amber Chapman! Her theme is 'France', take it away Amber.'

Amber emerged in her can-can outfit, splaying her legs in all directions and squealing with delight as she danced. She finished her routine with the splits, done to perfection. The audience went wild; here was a star in the making.

Next up was Jasmine, and her theme was 'America'. She did a faultless modern jazz performance, ending up with the star spangled banner, and marching in time with the music.

'Great twist,' said Noddy, who had followed Cathy up to prepare for her performance. Jasmine was now twirling a baton as a girl behind her held aloft the American flag. She also ended in the splits, still twirling the baton. Cathy was uneasy. She didn't regard Amber as a threat, but Jasmine was another matter. The audience roared its approval as she finished her dance.

Finally, it was Cathy's turn and she stepped out to total silence. Behind her was sitting a flamenco guitarist whom she had worked with since deciding to make the flamenco one of her dances for the final. Cathy began to dance, slowly at first and then gradually building in tempo. In her mind's eye she could see her teacher, Madame Elsa, who trained her in the sixties. She could hear her shouting, 'Head up, Catalina, be proud, haughty, be poised, listen to the music, swish your skirts. And one and two, head up, turn now spin, faster.'

The audience faded and Cathy slipped into her own little private world, one where she could disappear into the dance completely. It was something she'd done as a child. She'd lose herself in the dance and become invisible. She got faster and faster, her feet beating out the rhythm. Sweat was pouring from her brow. Offstage, Jasmine remarked to Amber, 'Fuck, she's good.' They both knew that after the go-go section, one of them would be eliminated; so Cathy's performance was very unsettling. She was now concluding her routine, her feet getting faster by the second, coupled by spins and the sound of the castanets. The guitarist was also going full throttle. He was very old but a maestro in his discipline. His expertise outweighed his wrinkles. Cathy finished with a flourish, ending in a kneeling position with her arms above her head. There was a deathly silence and then the audience went crazy, giving her a standing ovation, and cries of, 'bravo!' Cathy got to her feet and extended her hand to the guitarist who stood up and bowed. She ran off to Noddy. 'Was it okay?' she cried, throwing herself into his arms.

'Fantastic,' he replied.

Vic was sweating buckets. The dance was too much for him, and the judges had given her a standing ovation too. 'I've never seen anything like it,' he said.

'I have,' said Kim. 'I was in Spain five months ago and she's as good as the Spanish girls. Maybe even better.' She was pleased now that she'd put Cathy through because, in her eyes, she was a winner. Vic was also pleased as Gerry and Nat enthused over the Flamenco number.

'Way out in front,' said Gerry.

'Brilliant,' agreed Nat.

Ted Taylor took centre stage again. 'While the girls are changing for their go-go set, we have the first of our guests. It's our silver special, all the way from America. You can start screaming now girls; it's Sammy Silver.' The girls in the audience cheered and screamed as Sammy strutted out on stage. He flashed a dazzling smile.

'Hi everyone,' he shouted. Ted gave him a hug. He wanted to do much more but knew that he had a show to do and would get a knock back anyway. He'd fancied this guy for ages. Sammy was a picture with black glossy hair, a perfect shaped nose, voluptuous lips, tall, slim, and wearing a jumpsuit encrusted with jewels. Best of all he was only sixteen years old. Ted released his hold on Sammy and asked what he thought of the girls.

'Amazing, they're all great.'

Backstage, Amber was all starry eyed. 'Oh, I love him.'

Jasmine flashed a pitying smile. 'He's too cheesy.' But Amber wasn't listening; she was enraptured watching Sammy on the monitor. Jasmine had fixed her gaze on the make-up girl, now that she did fancy. The girl was curvy, had long chestnut hair, huge boobs, a tiny waist, and broad hips. She had a wide mouth, snub nose, and dark brown eyes. Her outfit suited her – it was bright red, fitted – and she'd complemented the ensemble with a pair of red wedge shoes. Jasmine was going to make a move whatever the result tonight.

Sammy was now going into his latest single, *Schoolgirl Crush*, and Amber was in seventh heaven.

In another room, Ed cringed; how he detested Sammy. Fortunately the song was soon over and the girls were ready to perform again. Amber took to the stage, shaking every inch of her body. She wore a green sequinned leotard topped by a short layered matching skirt. She combined her routine with acrobatic moves, and her green knee high boots sparkled with just about every conceivable jewel. She was well received by the audience.

Next came Jasmine; she was all fire and passion. Her costume was composed of a sparkly leotard with red and gold tassels and embroidered black boots.

Finally Cathy took the stage in her navy bikini, covered with white fringes. Her white boots had fringes too. She threw herself into her routine with abandon and constantly smiled at everyone, her hair streaming out behind as she moved. She shook and shimmied, throwing in a few high kicks as well and ended her routine in the splits.

The girls now huddled together awaiting the result. One of them was about to leave. Ted called Sammy back onstage and then collected the envelope from the judges. Handing it to Sammy he said, 'can you give me the name of the girl who is leaving us?'

Sammy opened the envelope and sighed, 'sadly it's Amber Chapman. Come on out, darlin'.' Amber walked out on stage to tumultuous applause, and Ted seized the girl in a bear hug.

'What a wonderful contestant,' he said. 'Sammy, would you like to tell the young lady what she's got in store for her?' Sammy stepped forward and, placing his arm around Amber's shoulders, said, 'a holiday in the Canaries, a year's free dance lessons, my new album and, guess what?'

Amber was nearly fainting with happiness, 'what?' she asked breathlessly.

'Amber, where are you going after the show?'

'Back to Wales,' said Amber.

'Wrong, I'm taking you out for a meal, just the two of us. Then we're going to a club, and after that we have booked you into the Savoy hotel tonight. Then in the morning you can go back to Wales.'

Amber was delighted and threw her arms around Sammy. The audience cheered and whistled as the photographer took photos. 'What do you say to that?' asked Sammy.

Amber beamed, 'Well I won really, didn't I? I got the best prize.' She smiled at Sammy and hand in hand they left the stage.

'Let's hear it for Sammy Silver and Amber Chapman!' boomed Ted, before attempting to do a bit of stand up and sing (or murder) a Frank Sinatra song.

In the dressing room, Jasmine and Cathy were changing into their final costumes. Jasmine was dressed as a Brazilian Carnival dancer and she looked magnificent. Cathy remembered a photo that her mother had given her of a lady called Carmen Miranda wearing a similar costume. Cathy donned her belly dancer outfit and put on a sand dancer's costume over the top.

In Ed's room, he gazed at the monitor. 'Not much longer,' he said to himself. He wanted to go out and wish Cathy luck but knew he couldn't. She must be going through emotional trauma now, but he still couldn't acknowledge her. He intended to keep the pretence up over dinner too, and mention Faye a few times to throw her off the scent so that she would accept the hotel. He intended to chat her up as well, though just to see her response. He guessed that Noddy was giving her all the reassurance she needed at this moment. Jasmine was professional and flashy, but Cathy danced with her heart and soul. Control, that's what he had to have if things were going to go his way. Vic was right, surprise was the answer.

Jasmine went on to deafening applause. She didn't put a foot wrong until the end when she attempted to put in an extra spin that made her lose her balance and fall. Trying to get up, she caught her shoe in the hem of her dress and went down again. She recovered quickly but her confidence had suffered and the performance became lacklustre.

She finished to loud applause, and she hoped that Cathy would screw up too. As she went on the audience were uncertain of what was going to happen next as she was clad in the garb of a sand dancer. She did a little sand dancing and then stripped out of it, revealing her belly dance costume underneath. Removing a veil from the waist band she began to swirl it around expertly, and then discarded it. Vic's eyes were out on stalks; it was his birthday soon and this was the cabaret he wanted. Cathy now speeded up the rotation of her hips and moved her belly muscles up and down and side to side. She slowed down and sank to the floor into a backbend. Then lying on her back she began to ripple her stomach muscles again. Vic's jaw dropped, so much so that Kim asked him if he was catching flies. Back on her feet again, Cathy began to clap her hands and the audience joined in as she began to play the finger cymbals, speeding up the whole routine. As she finished, the audience were on their feet again clapping wildly. Her heart was racing and she threw herself at Noddy, sobbing. She just didn't know if it had been good enough. Ed passed by and said nothing. Ted Taylor was once more centre stage and cracking more corny jokes.

Vic was still catching flies, and in the end Kim nudged him and said, 'Vic, we've got to reach our decision soon.' Vic came down to earth and began conferring with his fellow judges.

After more corny jokes and an attempt at a Dean Martin song this time, Ted addressed the audience. 'And now, you lucky people, here's our gold section of the show. He turns the girls' legs to jelly when he sings, they faint when he smiles, everyone wants him to read them a bed time story, they hunger for his touch. He's the fantasy of every red-blooded female, the dream of schoolgirls, or at least that's what he told me; it's the one and only, Ed Gold.'

Ed strode out onto the stage, full of confidence, to cheers and screams. 'You weren't supposed to say that last bit,' he joked. Two chairs were brought on stage. Ed had forgotten that he had to be interviewed by Ted. The two men sat down and Ted began.

'Ed, how's it going? How's the new album? I'm curious about the new single. It's an old Dylan number, I believe.'

'My life couldn't be better, and the album's great; it'll be out in the shops next Monday. My entire life has been steeped in Dylan,' replied Ed.

Ted scrutinized him while he talked; he didn't like him. He'd met him six weeks previously, and the feeling was mutual. Ed didn't like gays, particularly ones that preyed on young men. He smiled at Ted as he was probed more about the new single. 'This song has a special connection for me,' said Ed. 'The band weren't keen at first, I think they thought I'd be sitting on a stool with an acoustic guitar and no backing which didn't please them.'

Ted sniggered, 'but that's what Dylan did, wasn't it.'

Ed leaned back in his seat. 'Obviously you're ignorant of Dylan's work. To begin with he did do that, but in 1966, he did a tour with an electric set for half of the show. A lot of his staunch followers didn't like it and booed him. They'd loved the first half of the show because it was acoustic, but as soon as he came on stage with the electric set, some of the fans heckled, booed, and gave him the slow hand clap. In the end, Dylan told them not to clap too loud and the rest of the fans cheered. Just before he did the song, *Like a Rolling Stone*, someone shouted "Judas!" and Bob replied, "I don't believe you, you're a liar". Then one of the band, or someone just offstage shouted, "Play fucking loud", and they did. That shut the others up. So you see young man, you don't know your Dylan and at your age you really should. Or perhaps you are a Sinatra fan, 'cos you murdered one of his songs tonight. Anyway to get back to where I started; when I explained to the band that we were doing the electric version they were quite happy with it. In fact, Romany even plays the mouthorgan on it.'

At the mention of Romany's name, there was more screaming from the audience. Ted was angered by some of Ed's comments and centred his conversation around Romany. 'Romany, the superstud,' he said laughing, as if he'd made a huge joke.

Ed shrugged. 'I've known Romany all my life, or the best part of it, and jokes like that about his sexual prowess annoy me. He's a brilliant guitarist and, yes, he likes the ladies. I guess he's watching this right now at home with a bottle in his hand and a girl either side of him, you know, just like your boys' nights in.'

Ted was seething with rage, but flashed a theatrical smile at the audience. 'Well Ed, will you treat us to a taste of your new single?'

'Sing? I thought I was just here to present the prize to the winning dancer. I thought Sammy was the singer tonight. Now, there's a nice young man, a very nice man, just up your street,' laughed Ed. Vic was cringing; sometimes Ed was a bit too honest. Ed stared at Ted. 'Well, I haven't rehearsed, but seeing as we're such old friends, I'll sing for you.'

The two men got to their feet, shook hands, and Ted gave Ed a hug, muttering, 'I'll fix you, you bastard.'

Ed laughed again and smiled at the audience. 'Isn't Ted a wonderful guy? It's an honour to sing on this show and to such a lovely audience too.' He gave Ted another hug and whispered in his ear: 'Just try it, you bloody old faggot.' Ted patted Ed on the back and headed for the judges. Ed took centre stage and picked up the microphone. 'This is from our new album. It's called, *I Don't Believe You, She Acts Like We Never Have Met*, and if you can get your tongue around that you can do anything. My tongue is very well trained and I can get it around anything and everything.'

Vic choked; he'd just taken a swig of water and spilled it everywhere as he coughed. Kim slapped him on the back and, Ted, horrified by Ed on stage, tripped over a cable and fell face down. Several people rushed to help him up and sat him on a vacant chair. 'I'll speak to you later,' he mouthed at Vic. Ed was finding this very funny and performed with gusto. He'd been joking about not rehearsing but he'd been at it all day. The song sent shivers down Cathy's spine; it was the very first song that he'd ever sung to her when she'd requested Dylan at the pub.

Once the song was over, Ted asked the judges if they'd made their decision, and Vic handed over the envelope. Cathy and Jasmine were called back on stage. They returned and stood hand in hand awaiting the verdict. Ed sidled over to Noddy, hoping that Cathy had won.

In a caravan in Norfolk, Rusty, Fawn, and the girls were glued to the television.

In Essex, Tony, his mother, and the children watched intently. Sandy was dancing with glee, 'Mummy's won,' she cried.

'Not yet,' said Tony, stubbing out a cigarette.

Sandy said indignantly, 'but she was the best.' Tony was getting excited; five thousand pounds was a lot of money and he had a feeling that Ed Gold was the guy who had tried to spirit Cathy away four years ago. He would have to keep his eye on that one just in case. Ed was welcome to her body but he wasn't having her taken away from him; he needed her here.

Ted opened the envelope, 'And the winner is…' There was a deathly silence as Ted deliberately kept the audience in suspense. Ted grinned, 'the winner is Gypsy!' Cathy stared around her, not seeing anyone. Did she hear right? Her mouth was dry and she felt dizzy. Had she really done it? A look across to the wings told her that she had. Noddy was jumping up and down with joy. Her tears began to flow. Ted Taylor had his arm around her shoulders. Jasmine had stormed off stage, and no one could get her to come back. Ted diffused the situation by saying, 'We'll get her back when she feels a bit better. It's hard to get this far and then lose.'

In Essex, Sandy was screaming with delight. 'Mummy's won!' she screeched, dancing around the large oak table. She would be the envy of all her school friends on Monday.

'Mummy's won!' echoed Steven, and joined Sandy dancing around the table.

Michael stared at the television. 'Mama!' he cried, staring up at his father who had him perched on his knee. Tony was happy; he'd sleep well tonight, and tomorrow evening he'd go home.

He was sick of his mother. Nag, nag, nag. 'Get a job, be a man, your father worked until the day he died.' Emily Peterson was a large woman approaching sixty seven with a wide smile, grey hair, and violet eyes. She was still very clued up, and annoyed with her son and his lifestyle. She liked Cathy and knew that she wanted to be a stay-at-home mum but she also knew that Tony would never change. She sighed and returned to the television.

In Norfolk, Fawn cracked open a bottle of bubbly. They were all over the moon with Cathy's win. Amber turned to her mother. 'Will Angel come back to Eden now?' she asked. 'I would love to see her. Maybe she could bring Sandy with her. I don't like Faye; she's stuck up. Maybe Eden could bring her to see us now that he's met her again.'

'Don't be silly,' said Amethyst, 'Eden's engaged to Faye.'

'But he's married to Angel, we were her bridesmaids.'

'Girls,' said Fawn, 'they'll be together one day. I know it. The cards never lie. Let's tell the others, and we'll have a little party.'

Amber was still glued to the television set. There was a close-up of Cathy. Amber let out a delighted shriek. 'Mummy, Angel's wearing our pendants.'

'That's lovely, dear.'

'She said she'd never forget us, and she hasn't.'

She was one happy little girl, and now felt sure that Cathy would visit. She skipped over to her mother and went to tell Sky and her current boyfriend her good news.

Back at the studio, Cathy was surrounded by people: the judges, Amber, Sammy Silver and photographers. The photographer that had taken the photos previously wanted an interview for the newspapers. Cathy agreed and promised that she would as soon as she'd changed. He was a handsome young man but Cathy hadn't really noticed him when she'd been posing with Ed, as she'd been too busy getting the shoot over and leaving the room. Ted called Ed back to present the cheque. They posed for more photos and then Ed kissed her on the cheek and handed the cheque to her. Cathy gazed at it. Five thousand pounds; she'd never held so much money in her hand. It still hadn't really sunk in. She stared into the wings and spotted her mentor. 'Noddy,' she cried. Noddy hesitated, so Cathy ran off and dragged him centre stage.

'And who are you?' asked Ted.

'My name is Bob Todd, better known as Noddy because I fall asleep all the time. Won't do it tonight though. I'm so proud.'

He looked at Cathy saying, 'I've had the pleasure of managing this lady since 1966. She was a classical dancer at the time with a bit of tap and modern, and she came to me wanting to learn. I sent her to all the best teachers and, one week after meeting her, she was working for me. She worked herself into the ground, but look at her now. I can give her any international style of dance and she'll make it perfect.'

The tears were forming in his eyes. 'Can't say any more, I'm filling up.' he pulled a hanky from his pocket and dabbed his eyes before giving Cathy a hug. Jasmine grudgingly came back and received her prize of two thousand pounds and various prizes of lessons, dancewear, a holiday, and other gratis items. She posed with Cathy and Sammy Silver, and was actually smiling. She'd pulled the make-up girl so she was very happy about that.

It wasn't long before the circus was over and Cathy faced the photographer in the dressing room with Noddy looking on. 'I'm Barry,' said the photographer. 'This interview is for the press.' Cathy stared at this handsome young man. He certainly had the looks, and Cathy thought he would have done better as an actor or model even. He had wavy red hair and a pale complexion which suited him and blended with his hair. When the light hit him, his hair revealed gold streaks. Cathy felt compelled to ask the shade, it was so attractive. Barry laughed, 'I'm always asked that, actually it's strawberry blonde. It's a lot darker now because it's winter but in summer it's a lot lighter. Hey I'm supposed to be asking you all the questions.' He laughed, his green eyes sparkling, and Cathy was beginning to sit up and notice this Adonis. His jaw line was firm, he had high cheek bones and his nose was small but perfect. Added to that he'd removed his jacket which revealed a firm, lithe body as his shirt was very tight fitting.

He smiled; all the girls admired his good looks. He was well aware of it and so was Ted who'd got him the job for his own reasons. Barry fired questions at the girl which she was quite happy to reply to; it meant she could keep her eyes on him. She couldn't believe herself. She was getting turned on by a stranger who sat just a few feet away. How on earth didn't she notice him? He'd been positioning her and Ed. She sighed and knew the answer; when Ed was in the room everyone else faded. She still felt the same. That electricity was still there, and by the feeling she'd sensed when she was leaning back against him, she guessed that she still turned him on if nothing else.

The interview over, Cathy prepared to leave with Noddy when Vic put in an appearance. 'Come on, babe. The Rolls is waiting,' he said.

Cathy looked at him in disbelief. 'Rolls?'

'Yep, you won the gold prize, didn't you? Ed and I are taking you and Noddy for a meal at a top restaurant. You're famous, babe, and you'd better get used to it.'

Cathy picked up her suitcase and stared at Noddy. 'I'm up for it,' he said. 'You've won it, so enjoy it.'

Cathy smiled; she'd do anything for Noddy. They left the studio and headed for the Rolls Royce. The chauffeur opened the door and Cathy got in the back with Noddy and Ed who was already inside. Ed congratulated her and then ignored her for the rest of the journey, speaking across her to Noddy. Cathy relaxed; maybe he had forgotten her after all this time. That made her happy; scenes she did not need, and anyway he was engaged to a beautiful girl. Cathy had seen her photo in the newspapers.

They drove to a very impressive eating house, and Ed ordered plenty of everything plus the best champagne. It wasn't long before Noddy lived up to his name and, after being blown out by a huge meal, fell asleep and started to snore. Ed turned to Cathy. 'Let's have a dance before I leave,' he said. Cathy didn't want to but didn't like to refuse as Vic had repeatedly played footsie under the table, and once or twice had placed his hand on her knee. The presence of the hand once more decided it for her and she got to her feet. They walked to the dance floor and Ed pulled her in closely. She pulled back slightly but he pulled her even closer.

'For such a good dancer, you're very tense at the moment,' he murmured, nuzzling into her neck. The reason was obvious; he was rock hard.

Cathy was lost for words, but managed to stammer, 'I'm not used to dancing with superstars.'

Ed laughed and his hands started to wander. 'Maybe we should alter that; I'm going to have a problem sitting down. How about we get ourselves a piece of action later?'

'I'm a married lady,' replied Cathy.

'They're the best; anyway, I didn't see any husband with you tonight,' he murmured, nuzzling into her neck again. He was enjoying this. She didn't know if he remembered her or not.

'He's busy, and you can forget any kind of action, when I leave here I shall be going home to him,' retorted Cathy.

'So what's wrong with me?' said Ed. He was blowing in her ear now, thoroughly enjoying himself.

'Why didn't you ask one of the other girls who were single?'

'Because I like blondes and, as I said, the married girls are best. I know a married lady who's great in the sack, her name's June.'

'Bully for you. I hate to dent your superstar ego, but I'm quite happy with my husband, thank you.' His last remark had hurt though. June constantly told her to return to Ed, and she appeared to be sleeping with him. Ed felt her stiffen; he knew that his remark had hurt her.

She glanced over at Noddy who was snoring so loudly that she could hear him from where she was. 'I think I should get him home.'

'Lives up to his name every time,' he said. 'So you don't want me or the hotel?'

'What hotel? No one mentioned a hotel to me.'

Ed's hands continued to wander. 'All part and parcel of the competition. If you don't believe me, ask Vic.'

Noddy awoke with a start and apologised profusely for falling asleep. He was surprised that Cathy had declined the offer but he told her to take it. 'You don't want to go home to an empty house, do you? I can't go as my son is visiting me tomorrow and it's very late now, but you should go, Cathy.'

Ed was delighted. Now he knew that she had an empty house, that made things even better. 'Empty houses are cold places. The hotel's luxurious and you've got the room until midday tomorrow. You could even put me up for the night. I'd spoil you.' Cathy blushed, and Ed laughed. 'I'm only joking, Faye will kill me if I stay out again tonight.' He kissed Cathy on the cheek. 'Take the hotel, babe, you've won it, or take me and put me out of my misery.'

Vic laughed. 'Come on Ed, Faye's waiting. I'll order you a minicab, Cathy; they'll drop you at the hotel and take Noddy home. Have you got everything?'

'Yes, my suitcase is in the cloakroom. Thanks for everything, Mr Lee, and you Ed.' Ed turned around, winked, and left with Vic.

Once she arrived at the hotel, Cathy gave the cab driver Noddy's address; she thought she should as he'd nodded off again. She asked the driver how much she owed him but he waved his hand and said Vic had paid for it.

A porter emerged from the hotel in uniform; he was about twenty with a very cheerful face and dark brown hair. As soon as she entered the hotel, the staff began applauding. They all knew who she was from her appearance on the television, plus a phone call from Vic describing her and telling them to send her up to Mr Gold's suite.

After checking in, she followed the porter to the lift. When they reached the room and the porter had let her in, she thought that she'd died and gone to heaven. She'd never seen such grandeur. 'This all for me?' she asked.

'Sure lady, you're the golden girl for tonight,' he said and winked. He held his hand out for a tip and, after receiving it, walked away grinning. He was in on the whole thing too.

Chapter Eight

Cathy closed the door and wandered further into the room. The whole thing was out of this world. Flowers seemed to be everywhere. It was unbelievable, and it was a complete suite. 'Beautiful,' she breathed out loud. Walking through to the bedroom, she gazed around her, and placed her suitcase on the floor. By the side of the bed were two glasses, and on a small table in the corner of the room there was champagne on ice. The burgundy drapes were sumptuous and her feet sank into the red carpet. She progressed to the en suite. The taps were gold and the large shower cubicle looked inviting. Walking back into the bedroom, she began to unpack her case.

She didn't hear the door open; she was too engrossed unpacking. Those costumes needed to go on hangers before they got too creased. She hung them up and was undecided between watching television, or showering, or soaking in the large bath. She decided on a shower. She had the room until midday, so there was plenty of time to enjoy the rest of the suite tomorrow. Closing the wardrobe doors, she turned to see Ed framed in the doorway.

'Hallo Gypsy,' he said. 'Long time, no see.'

Cathy was furious. 'You bastard, so you did recognise me. What a shabby trick.'

'Like the one you played on me years ago. You ripped the heart out of my body. Come on, honey, I'll forgive you, if you'll forgive me.'

He opened his arms to her. Cathy remained rooted to the spot as he advanced toward her. 'We're okay now, we're together again, and everything will be fine.' He took her in his arms.

'We're not together, you lunatic,' she cried.

'Yes we are, you're mine, you always were,' and his mouth came down on hers. Cathy was struggling, trying to force him off, and as Ed released her she caught him a stinging slap around the face. Alarmed, Ed jumped back. 'Christ, this is where I came in when we first met.' He tried again, 'Come on Cathy, don't fight it.'

He embraced her again; both kisses had inflamed him. What was wrong with her. She was struggling harder now. 'Calm down,' he shouted. Releasing her, he was rewarded with another slap.

Suddenly everything fell into place. 'I see,' Cathy said. 'This is your suite, and it never was included as a prize.'

'Well I had to get you here somehow, and you believed it.'

Cathy now felt like a prize idiot. Ed had retreated into the adjoining room to give her time to cool down. 'So you've had a laugh at my expense, now let me go,' cried Cathy.

'Never, I've got you back and I want you to stay.'

'Okay, so you wanted to screw the winner, let's get it over and done with, and then I can go, yes?'

'Stop making it sound so cold-blooded,' said Ed, coming back into the room. 'That's not the way I planned it and you know it. Anyway I'm pleased that you won tonight, you were the best.'

'Thanks, was that fixed too?'

'You know it wasn't, you won that fair and square. For God's sake, if you want to hate me so much, don't knock yourself. You won because you were the most talented. Now come and have a drink with me, at least.'

'I don't want a drink with you, I don't want this suite and I don't want anything to do with you. I'm leaving,' yelled Cathy.

Ed had had enough. He stormed over to her and, shocked, she backed away, ending up sprawled across the bed. He pinned her down. 'You're not leaving me again,' he cried. Cathy was now scared as he kissed her again.

There was no point in fighting, as ever he was stronger and bent on getting his own way. She lay still; her head was spinning, the kiss was getting to her as he still had the same control over her. 'That's better,' he soothed, 'I'm not going to force you because I wouldn't get any pleasure from it. Also I know I don't need to and you know it too.' He got off the bed and walked over to the table where the champagne was. He threw his wallet across the bed. 'Take that,' he said angrily.

'I don't want your money,' sobbed Cathy.

'Look inside,' shouted Ed. Cathy obeyed. She was too scared not to. She removed a rather dog-eared photo. 'Recognise her?' snapped Ed. 'Her name's Angel, my niece took the photo amongst many others. She keeps asking me if Sandy's better yet and when am I taking you to see her. She'll be glued to the television tonight willing you to win. Rusty and Fawn will be celebrating because you've won. They still love you, Angel. I still love you. I've carried this photo with me since you left, and I've always told people that you're my wife. That's true, isn't it? Or have you forgotten our hippy wedding ceremony?'

Tears were streaming down Cathy's face as she cried. 'How could I? But I had to go back. Tony said that Sandy had had an accident.'

Ed punched the table and glared at the sobbing figure on the bed. 'But the accident didn't last all this time, did it? And I've been told that it was just a ruse to get you back. When you realised that you'd been duped, you could have come back to me. I'd have sorted the bastard out, but no, you stay with that waste of space and have two more kids. You see Cathy, I've been doing my homework and don't say that you couldn't have found me. You only had to call June.' He walked over to her and picked up the two glasses by the bed. 'Do you know how hard it was for me tonight, having to keep my hands off you. I was going crazy.'

Cathy's bottom lip was trembling. 'It was just as bad for me; I was shocked when I first saw you. I wanted to run.'

'Yes, you're good at running out on me, but tonight's different. It's gonna be a long one so you might just as well join me in a drink.' He reached out his hand; she took it and they moved over to the table. Ed uncorked the bottle and poured out two glasses of bubbly. 'Right, now when are you gonna see sense?' he asked, handing her a glass. 'I've made it now, I've plenty of money, and you've just won five thousand pounds, plus contracts and mega prizes. We're set up.' They raised their glasses. 'To us,' said Ed.

Cathy was dumbfounded, 'There is no us. I've got three kids now, and you've got a beautiful fiancée; I've seen her in the papers.'

'I don't mind a ready-made family, and Faye's only attraction was that she was a virgin and beautiful.'

'I see, so you could teach her to pleasure you as you wanted?'

Ed shrugged. 'Is that so bad? She doesn't mind taking my money and living in my mansion. She does okay.' He put his glass down and stroked her face with his fingertips. 'Nobody does it better than you, Angel.'

'But it's such a mess, and Tony won't let me go. He threatened to take Sandy from me in 1968, and now I've got my two boys.'

'So, if you didn't have the kids, would you still be with him?'

'You know the answer to that. I'd never been unfaithful until I met you. You made me happy and I've never been unfaithful since.'

Ed laughed. 'Well at least that's bolstered my ego. Oh, and I didn't just carry the photo with me, I kept this too.' From his pocket he produced a box. Cathy was aghast as he opened it and removed the ring that he'd bought her while they were in Wales. He took her hand and placed the ring on her finger. 'I got it for you, so it's yours. I always knew the day would come when I'd put it back where it belongs. It was just a case of playing the waiting game.'

Cathy suddenly saw the funny side of it and giggled. 'So now you've got two women with rings on their fingers.'

'Yep, but I'll despatch the other one if you like. I'm not letting you get away again.' He cupped his hand under her chin, making her look at him. 'What we had was special, Cathy, and that's why you are scared, not because you want to run, but because you know that we were made for each other, and you know that you wouldn't take much persuading to restart where we left off.'

Cathy sighed. He'd found her and she was cornered. She tried to avert her eyes but he wasn't having it. 'Look at me, Cathy. Don't look away; look at me.' She knew that she was lost as he added, 'I still want you, girl, nothing's changed except now I want you even more.'

Cathy could feel her willpower beginning to leave her. 'No,' she cried. She picked up her glass and drained it. 'I'm tired, and it's been a long day. I need a shower.'

She got to her feet, and Ed took her in his arms. 'Okay, darling,' he said. Cathy leant up against him. All the old feelings were surfacing, the warmth, the feeling of security and lust. His lips came down on hers and she was lost.

She pulled away. 'Shower,' she said. 'I'm falling asleep.' Ed let her go and she headed for the en suite. Minutes later, he followed her in and got under the shower with her.

'Remember the waterfall, baby?' he murmured. Cathy nodded; she'd never forget that. She was suddenly wide awake as he started to caress her before sliding down to his knees and opening her up with his tongue. Her orgasm was almost instantaneous. It had been so long. She was in the throes of ecstasy and passion with Ed, blotting out everything apart from this beautiful sensation. She was falling, slipping, as her legs were giving way. Ed lowered her to the floor as she relaxed and then clung to him with the water still cascading over them both. He stood up and turned the water off, helping Cathy to her feet. He held her for a moment and then, taking a bath towel off the heated rail, dried himself and threw a towel to her. As she emerged from the cubicle, he picked her up and carried her to the bed. Laying her down gently, he whispered, 'I love you so much, Angel. I've been in agony since you left. I can't function properly without you; it's been a nightmare.'

He kissed her all over, taking his time, he wasn't going to hurry. He'd waited this long so a little longer wasn't going to make any difference. He marvelled at this lady, the one that he'd hungered for for so long. By now Cathy was stroking him back, her body moving slowly. She pulled his head down and kissed him. Her life was a complete disaster zone, and this was only for one night, wasn't it? After Ed had spent the night with her, he'd go back to his fiancée. He was only reliving their time together in 1968, but she found it odd that he'd spent so much time looking for her, keeping her photo and ring. She was feeling so good that she dismissed all of these thoughts and gave herself up to the moment. She felt him enter her slowly, and surrendered.

Afterwards, they lay side by side in silence, neither one of them believing what had happened. Ed broke the silence by asking her if she wanted another drink. She nodded. He poured the champagne and asked how she was feeling as he handed her the glass. 'Fantastic,' she replied as he got back in the bed.

Ed said exasperatedly. 'Then why deny yourself all this pleasure? Is it this good with Tony?'

'No, Tony has many girlfriends and he remembers that I'm his wife now and again, but he doesn't have your expertise.'

'Silly girl,' said Ed, stroking her hair. 'You'd be much happier with me; I'd give you the world.'

Cathy sipped her champagne slowly; it was hitting her. 'Let's forget Tony and enjoy tonight.'

'Okay, I'll ring room service later and get some more drink sent up and maybe something to eat.'

'I couldn't eat anything. That meal we had earlier has blown me out.'

Ed chuckled. 'Better work it off then,' he said, taking the glass from her hand and rolling her over, 'and I won't be as quick this time. I just couldn't hold back. I was like a schoolboy, really excited.'

Cathy giggled. 'So we're married, are we?'

'Yep, a hippy wedding is as legal as a church one. Seth married us and he used to be a preacher.'

'Some marriage. I'm committing bigamy and you're cheating on your fiancée.'

'Well, that's the way it is. I always did like to be different. Let's consummate our reunion.' Cathy smiled up at him, there was no way she was about to disagree. She held him to her as he took her again. For the rest of the night, they laughed, drank more champagne, reminisced, and made love over and over again. Cathy felt like they'd never been apart, and Ed felt whole again. He realised that the cold feeling had left him. She couldn't leave him again. This was it; the lost years were bearable. He could write more songs, he could climb a mountain, he could do anything.

'I love you, Angel,' he said, tears filling his eyes.

Cathy had her eyes closed and felt the tears running down onto her face. 'I love you too,' she said, and held him to her like a mother would hold a child needing reassurance. 'Everything will be fine now. We'll work something out.' Then she fell into a contented slumber.

The following morning she awoke to the sound of the shower running. Minutes later, Ed emerged from the en suite clad in a fluffy white bathrobe. 'I've ordered breakfast,' he said, 'should be here very soon.' Cathy got out of bed, gave Ed a kiss and then headed for the shower herself. She put on the shower hat and slowly came too as the water revived her. She heard the knock on the door and towelled herself dry, dressing in another white bathrobe. When she walked into the bedroom, Ed was seated at the table with a banquet set in front of him.

Cathy seated herself. 'This is some breakfast, the crème de la crème. I've never seen a breakfast like it!' There was orange juice, yoghurt, coffee, tea, and a plate of two fried eggs, three rashers of bacon, mushrooms, tomatoes, baked beans, three sausages, and something else that she didn't recognise. Ed said they were hash browns. Cathy stared at this mountain of food on her plate and wondered how she was going to get through it.

As if reading her thoughts, Ed said, 'just eat what you can. I didn't want you going hungry.' She picked up her knife and fork and began to eat. Ed poured the orange juice. 'You've got the room until noon,' he said. 'Enjoy it, anything you want, just ring for room service. I've got to do an interview for a girls' magazine. You'll be doing the same thing yourself soon, after last night you'll find that everyone wants you.'

Cathy picked up a slice of toast and spread some butter on it. 'Really, they'll want me?'

'Course. If you ring Noddy, he'll have tons of work waiting for you. You're the best thing since sliced bread at the minute, and it'll be like that for the next year. After that, it's up to you.'

'What a stupid title that contest had,' said Cathy. 'Go International, Go. Most of the girls thought it was a go-go contest until we got the entry forms, and then we found that it was really a dance contest of international styles. It made it easier for me but a lot of really good dancers just couldn't make the criteria. Noddy worked me into the ground; I didn't even have time to celebrate Michael's first birthday. I feel really bad about that, but then I suppose he didn't know that it was his birthday, and so if he has a belated one it won't make that much difference. And it was worth it, although I never thought I'd win.'

'I did, you were by far the best. Did you see that idiot Ted Taylor stack it?'

'I did,' replied Cathy. 'You really upset him; he was quite shocked by your reference to your tongue and your remarks about his boys' nights in.'

'Well it's true, and when he started going on about Romany, that finished it. I've no problems; it's Vic that'll have to take all the flack. Anyway, you've no problem with my tongue, have you?'

'Definitely not, but I thought your reference to Sammy Silver wasn't too kind.'

Ed was shovelling food into his mouth like there was no tomorrow. 'Well,' he said through mouthfuls. 'He's a dickhead, all bloody teeth and no talent; the all-American boy. God I hate him. And anyway, how did Ted take offence at my tongue comment? I could have been talking about foreign languages or my ability to talk non-stop. Bloody queen, I called him an old faggot too. He was the one that thought up the title of that dance contest, and his ignorance of Dylan was ridiculous.'

Cathy pushed her plate away. 'I can't eat any more. You've cleared your plate, where do you put it all? There's not an inch of fat on you.'

'An army marches on its stomach, and now that you're back I'm going to have to keep my strength up because I know you'll refuse to move in with me at present. So I've got to keep you and Faye happy. I guess it would look bad if you moved in at this stage, considering that Vic was on the panel and I was singing that night. But please don't keep me waiting too long, Cathy; I've waited an eternity for you.'

'You really are serious, aren't you? I thought you were just doing this for old time's sake. We can meet up whenever it's possible but I really find it hard to believe that you still want me to move in with you after all that's happened. What about Faye?'

'Just tell me when you're ready, and Faye goes the following day,' said Ed. 'We're soul mates, always have been. It's you I want.'

Cathy poured another glass of orange juice. 'Give me time to get my head around this.'

'As long as you don't run off again. Oh and I want you to work for me next month. I've got two gigs at Wembley and the second one coincides with Vic's birthday. He wants you for his cabaret, can't really refuse as he did find you in the end and he's spent a fortune in the process. It's being held at my house so you'll be able to see where you'll be living in the future.'

'That'll be nice, as long as that is what you want.'

'What I want is you, right now,' said Ed taking her hand and leading her to the bed. He pulled her on top of him. 'You go on top this time, I want to get a real good look at you.'

'Your obedient servant,' laughed Cathy and complied with his desire. They spent another two hours in bed, each one fuelled with the need to satisfy the other. It ended when there was an abrupt knock on the door. It was Victor. Cathy got under the bedclothes, pulling the duvet to her chin.

Vic marched in, and Ed dressed hurriedly. 'What is it with you?' he shouted. 'I told you to be ready. You've managed to upset Ted Taylor and Sammy Silver, and I've been waiting downstairs for thirty minutes. I don't know why I bother, the rest of the band is already at the office being interviewed and you're supposed to be there.'

'I was preoccupied,' said Ed. 'Cathy's going to do her act for you on your birthday. So that's one thing I've done for you. Be grateful.'

'I am, thank you, Cathy, but you should take these interviews more seriously, like the rest of the boys do.'

Ed laughed. 'They didn't have such a beautiful lady with them all night and, if they had, maybe they'd have been late too. Anyway I don't give a toss for Sammy or Ted. They're both wankers.'

'They are both highly respected individuals,' shouted Vic.

'Yep, Sammy by little girls, and Ted by gays. I caught Ted last night with the photographer, and what they were up to was hardly respectable, so if Ted is thinking of suing, tell him about that. I could make him front page news.' Cathy was taken aback; the photographer that she'd been drawn to was obviously gay.

Vic stormed out. He hated it when Ed spoke like that. 'Be

downstairs in five minutes,' was his parting shot.

Ed came over and sat on the bed. 'Got to go,' he said, giving Cathy a final kiss. 'Enjoy the rest of your stay here and I'll ring you later to fix up another meeting. Bye Angel, it's so good to have you back.' With that he was gone.

Cathy stretched out on the bed for a while, still not believing what had happened. Then she packed her costumes and other items into her case and ran a bath. She needed a long, hot soak to relax and to try to take this all in.

An hour later she checked out; she wanted to go. Home wasn't much but she preferred it to all of this luxury. She looked at the card that Ed had left by the bedside, but thought she wouldn't use it, she'd be too embarrassed. What if Faye answered the phone? No, she'd wait for him to call her, because at the back of her mind she still felt that it could have been a one-off. She doubted that it was though because he'd been very emotional, and you'd hardly try to find someone and then dump them after the reconciliation. Whatever the outcome, she was pleased to have seen him again after their last farewell. If he phoned, he phoned, and if he didn't then she'd have to deal with it like he had when she'd left him.

She smiled. No one could take away the fact that she'd won the contest, or the amazing night that she'd spent with her lover. Well, Tony had many, so she couldn't be blamed for having one, especially when they were as loving as Ed. Her thoughts turned to her children. They'd be coming home today and she had a birthday to plan for her youngest. She'd missed them so much. 'Lovely,' she said out loud as the mini cab arrived to take her to the railway station.

When she arrived home, she set to tidying the place up. She'd been home about two hours when her family arrived. Steven kept repeating, 'saw mummy on telly.' Cathy took Michael in her arms and gave him a kiss.

'Mummy's going to sort out a nice birthday party for you,' she said. The baby gurgled and snuggled into her shoulder.

Tony was adamant. 'Never mind parties, the kids all need new shoes.'

Sandy was bouncing around gleefully; she was going to be the centre of attention tomorrow at school. 'Was it nice at Nanny's?' asked Cathy.

'No,' replied Sandy. 'I missed school, and Nanny shouts a lot.'

'Oh Tony, why?' she cried.

'Couldn't wake up in time. Anyway I lost a lot of school days when I was young and it didn't do me any harm.'

Inwardly Cathy fumed. Sandy then fired a barrage of questions, mainly about Ed and Sammy Silver. She answered to the best of her ability, and her mind drifted back to the previous night. It seemed like a fantasy, but she was soon brought down to earth by Tony asking for money. Cathy felt the fantasy leave to be replaced by depression. She ignored him and began to answer another barrage of questions by her curious daughter.

Later that evening, Ed did phone her. 'Just called to say thank you for last night, and to tell you that I love you. I'm very tied up at this moment, but I said I'd call you and I have. I'll call you again tomorrow because I'd like to meet up later this week.'

'Great, I'll look forward to hearing from you.'

'Can't wait, but unfortunately I have to. Speak to you tomorrow, bye darling.'

'Bye Ed,' said Cathy, replacing the receiver. She was truly happy.

'Cathy!' shouted Tony, 'the baby's filled his nappy up.'

'Coming,' cried Cathy, and taking the baby from his father hurried upstairs.

The following day everything went wrong. Cathy awoke with a splitting headache and, while preparing breakfast, managed to let the milk boil over and burn the toast. She also managed to break two eggs, and after attempting to bring in the morning's milk delivery broke a bottle. Michael screamed repeatedly, and Tony seemed to be oblivious to it all, demanding breakfast in bed. Cathy yelled up the stairs that he could have it in bed if he wanted the contents of the saucepan poured over his head. There was no response and, after Sandy had eaten her breakfast, she left for school. Steven tugged at Cathy's skirt. 'Want toilet,' he moaned. Cathy turned her attention to him, and Michael began to scream even louder.

'What's the matter with that kid?' yelled Tony from the comfort of his bed.

'Come down and find out,' Cathy yelled back. There was a series of grunts and groans coming from Tony's direction, plus a loud burst of flatulence. He shuffled down the stairs, moaning once more about his breakfast. 'Cook it yourself,' snapped Cathy.

'You're my wife and you're supposed to cook for me.'

'You're my husband and you're supposed to go to work and keep me and the kids.' Angrily, Cathy went upstairs to tend to Steven and on her return found Tony sitting at the kitchen table eating burnt toast.

'Want some tea? There's plenty in the pot.'

'Save wasting it,' replied Cathy, seating herself at the table and wondering why he was so amiable again. She soon found out.

'I'm a bit short of cash,' said Tony. 'I'll pay you back.' Cathy gazed at him, wondering what on earth she'd ever seen in him. He was nearly fifty and had let himself go. He'd lost most of his hair, and what was left was almost grey. His florid complexion, large nose, and very thin lips left a lot to be desired, and yet he had more than his fair share of women. Obviously something drew females to him.

Tony stared back wondering why he didn't fancy his wife any more. She was very desirable but he had her and missed the thrill of the chase, finding her very boring but a little goldmine nevertheless. In a strange way he still loved Cathy, but preferred to pursue others, loving the chase and exciting surrenders. Already Cathy was reaching for her purse and offering a ten pound note. He pushed his luck asking for more and Cathy told him to get lost, which he promptly did.

Later she headed for the shops and the bank; she needed to get the cheque paid in and get some food. She had a twin buggy, and Steven soon fell asleep, but not for long as Michael whacked him a few times with his rattle.

She pushed the buggy into Mothercare and bought a few items for Michael; a teddy bear, a mirror which was deemed childproof and some clothing. Next stop was the bank. She handed the cheque across the counter and the girl paid it in. At the bakers she bought a small celebration cake with blue icing, and some fresh crusty rolls. Sainsbury's was her next stop for some much-needed groceries. Tony always waited until he'd run out of food before replacing it. Some birthday invitations and balloons later, she was able to return home. She met her next door neighbour as she opened her front door and they both went inside to discuss the local gossip and write out some birthday invitations.

Later that afternoon, Cathy put the children down for their regular nap and relaxed with a cheese roll and a cup of tea.

The phone rang about fifteen minutes later and it was Noddy. He was bubbling over with excitement about the work designated for Cathy. She hardly had a day free for the next month, and then there was a summer season looming, taking her from May to the end of October. 'You've got to go to Norfolk next week to meet the agent down there and fix up the venues for the season,' he said. 'It's only for one night but there's another agent in Suffolk who also wants you, so while you're down there you might just as well go and see him too. That way, you'll probably be able to work the two counties on your season, making it more than financially sound.'

'Great, I've never worked there before,' Cathy said, relishing the chance to go somewhere new.

'Stay for about a week. That'll give you plenty of room for manoeuvre, and as soon as you get some sort of deal struck, ring me and I'll negotiate the money.'

'Will do,' replied Cathy, and turned her thoughts to more important things like posting invitations for Michael's birthday party the following day.

After pushing the invites through letterboxes, she returned to the house and checked the boys. They were still sleeping, so she decided to join them. It didn't look like she'd be seeing much of them in the coming months. Michael stirred slightly in his cot and Steven still slumbered. Cuddling up to him in his single bed, she soon dozed too.

It was about five o clock when she awoke. Tony woke her up by slamming the door, which in turn woke the children. He was in a bad mood and had obviously had a bad day at the bookies, Cathy thought. She went downstairs with the children and started to prepare dinner. She wasn't working that night so there was no rush.

Ed rang about six wanting to arrange a meeting the following day, and was fascinated to hear about Norfolk. 'Think I'll join you,' he said. 'I've got about five days free next week. Where are you working tomorrow? Give me the address and I'll get you picked up.'

'The Acropolis, a Greek restaurant in Reading.'

'I know it. Romany celebrated his birthday there last week. Vic knows everyone there and he's got a thing going with one of the waitresses, so he'll be only too pleased to pick you up. What time are you going on?'

'Eleven, and then again at twelve thirty.'

'Good, too late for you to travel home on a train; it's not safe. Vic'll put us up. He's overjoyed that you're dancing at his party.'

'Talking of parties, I've got my son's to do tomorrow afternoon. I'm taking some photos on my Polaroid camera, so I'll bring the photos along.'

'That'll be great,' said Ed, and then went on to tell her how much he loved her and what he was going to do to her the following day. It was strictly X-rated and she found herself blushing on the end of the line. Twenty minutes later she replaced the receiver and relayed to Tony that she wouldn't be coming home the following night. Tony just shrugged; he was more interested in the money she was about to make.

He loved the idea of yet another summer season which left him free to do as he liked. 'Put the kettle on Cath,' he said contentedly.

One cup of tea later, Cathy settled down in front of the television and stayed there until the baby fell asleep. He'd had a bath earlier and it had made him very drowsy. She took him upstairs with Steven following behind and then decided on an early night herself. She called down to her husband but was answered by a grunt, and so headed for bed.

The next day, Sandy was up very early. She was blowing up balloons for the party. 'No wonder you went to bed before your brothers,' said Cathy. 'I was surprised, you've never gone to bed straight after dinner before.'

'I wanted to help before I went to school. I've already wrapped Mickey's present,' she told her mum proudly, and she held out a neatly wrapped parcel.

'Well done! What a clever girl you are. Let's have some breakfast. Your brothers are still asleep so we'll have some girly time.' The walked to the kitchen, and Sandy took her favourite cereal from the pantry and filled two dishes with it.

Pouring the milk over it, she said proudly, 'I've made you breakfast for a change.'

The day progressed in sheer chaos after Sandy left. Tony got up and decided to do a bit of balloon blowing himself, succeeding in bursting most of them. Steven managed to get the Weetabix from the pantry while Cathy was changing the baby and gleefully trod it into the carpet. He'd added some orange juice to it as well and left a trail of juice in the kitchen so that when Tony went into the kitchen to make coffee, he skidded on it and fell flat on his back. He yelled for Cathy who was still upstairs with the baby. The sight that met her eyes when she got downstairs was unbelievable.

The lounge carpet was a mess, there was juice all over the kitchen, and Tony was still on his back. He was shouting, 'Bloody kids!' repeatedly. Cathy suddenly saw the funny side of it and collapsed laughing. Steven added insult to injury by laughing and jumping all over his father. 'Get this bloody kid off me!' yelled Tony. Cathy lifted Steven off his father, shrieking with joy thinking that this was just a game. Tony got to his feet and then skidded, ending on his back again. By now both of the children were laughing, and Cathy was struggling to keep a straight face. She finally got Tony to his feet and began clearing up the mess. A little later he left for the betting shop, and Cathy began blowing up more balloons with Steven's help. He wasn't very successful but enjoyed it anyway.

At half past four, several toddlers and babies arrived with their mothers. Michael received many gifts of toys and clothes. All the children sang 'Happy Birthday', and Steven delightedly blew out the candles, as he said that his brother was too little to do it. Cathy had put on quite a spread, with jellies, iced biscuits, ham sandwiches, and a fruit flan. All of the children received a goody bag, and they all started to leave as Tony came home.

The neighbours liked Cathy but couldn't stand her work-shy, older husband. Everyone thanked her for the party, and finally the last child left about six. After bathing the children, Cathy put them to bed. She didn't know if they'd settle but now had to start getting herself ready for the evening's performance in Reading. When she was ready to leave, she kissed Sandy on the lips and cuddled her, telling her that she'd see her tomorrow evening as she was too far away to come home tonight and would be staying with a friend. Sandy nodded; she was used to her mother's absence so it was no big deal. She knew that her mum would always come back and merrily waved her off. A grunt was all she got from Tony; that's all it ever was, nowadays.

She went out, closing the garden gate behind her and walked to the bus stop. After boarding the bus, she sat down and gazed all around her. It seemed strange, all these people going to destinations that no one else knew about.

A short while later, she arrived at the main line station and boarded the train to Liverpool Street where she caught a connection to Reading. The cabaret went very well that evening, and she noticed Vic sitting at the bar when she'd finished her final spot. He followed her as she went to change and waited outside the door.

He was full of ideas, and when she re-emerged he told her that if she ever considered leaving her agent, he would be only too pleased to take her under his wing. She listened but didn't reply. As she left the room, she was about to see the manager about her money when Vic informed her that he already had it. 'Saves time,' he reassured her. 'And it's getting very late.'

As she got into Vic's car, Cathy put her foot on something. It was a used condom. 'Vic, I think someone's being doing naughties in your car.'

'What,' shouted Vic indignantly. He'd been putting Cathy's case in the boot, so he didn't see her get into the car. He got into the front and sat beside her. Previously he'd been enjoying sexual congress with his waitress friend and had forgotten about the condom. His 'friend' wasn't very pleased to know that she had to settle for just the car this time. She was used to coming back to his house, but tonight things were different. Vic had asked for a blowjob, but she'd refused so they'd had a quickie in the car. 'Disgusting,' said Vic. 'I do apologise. It's that bloody Al Simpkins. I let him borrow the car and look what he's done. Well, it's the last time I do him a favour.' He picked up the condom and threw it out of the car.

The drive back to Vic's house was a long one. Cathy dozed off intermittently and noticed that he placed his free hand on her thigh a couple of times, only to have it brushed off. When she arrived, she thought the place seemed very similar to the one she'd visited for her photo shoot. She voiced this to Vic, who said, 'the houses around here are very similar.' He let them both in and was greeted by Al.

'Oh Mr Simpkins, how nice,' said Cathy. 'Do you remember me? Are you a friend of Mr Lee? I thought you were Mr Franks' photographer.'

'Never mind that,' shouted Vic. 'You've left a used condom in the front of my car. Very embarrassing. I picked Cathy up and she put her foot on it. Where's Ed?'

'Upstairs taking a shower; and I haven't used your car.'

'Don't lie. What are you doing here anyway?'

Cathy was confused. Looking around her, she took a mental note of the place. She knew that this was indeed the same house that she'd visited. 'But Mr Simpkins,' said Cathy, 'I thought this was your house.'

'Another lie,' retorted Vic, 'all you do is lie.' He turned to Cathy. 'I put him up a short while ago and let him use the place for his photos, and he repays me by using my car and telling people that it's his house. Why are you here, Al?'

'I've got that new porn film you wanted,' said Al. 'Wish I hadn't bothered now; Ed's already thumped me.'

'Good, just what you needed. I told you about that photo and I did say he wouldn't be pleased.'

Cathy sat down on the sofa and wondered what was going to happen next. She didn't have to wait long. Ed appeared at the top of the stairs, rushed over to Cathy and grabbed her in a firm embrace. His hands were all over her. 'Like a bloody octopus,' said Al.

'Time you left,' said Vic, 'it's late.' He snatched the film from Al and shoved him towards the front door.

'But you said there'd be some action later,' Al whined. He and Vic both stopped in their tracks as there were moaning sounds coming from the sofa. They tiptoed over; Cathy was on her knees giving Ed a blowjob. Vic sank into his comfy red armchair while Al stood behind him mesmerized. Vic's jaw had dropped. Ed hadn't even said hallo to her yet and already they were engaged in oral sex.

As Cathy released her lover, Vic gasped, Al had an accident, and Ed lay back, totally satiated. Cathy got to her feet and straightened herself up, one breast hanging out of her top. She gazed at Vic in disbelief and, covering her breast with one hand, she shook Ed who was still lying with his eyes closed. He focused on the two spectators. 'Perverts!' he shouted. 'Is this how you both get off?'

Al had headed for the bar and poured himself a drink. Vic was still gazing at Cathy; there wasn't a sign of any sperm around her lips so she must have swallowed the lot. 'Would anyone like a drink?' was all he could say. Cathy was embarrassed and hid her face in the sofa.

Ed was incensed. 'Whiskey, and I told you, it's chemistry. It doesn't matter where or when but you two pervs shouldn't have been watching. You make me sick.' He would have felt sicker if he'd known about Vic's two-way mirror, but no one knew about that apart from Al and Vic himself. Ed took the whiskey handed to him by Vic, and said, 'Get that pathetic, Stan Laurel lookalike out of here before I clump him again. He's not only taken a near-porn shot of Cathy, but now he's witnessed her giving me a blow job. Bet he wished he'd got his camera with him.'

Al was about to admit to having one with him when Vic removed the glass from his hand and muttered, 'time to go.' Al was angry, but as Ed got to his feet he decided to make a swift exit. Vic let him out and then offered Cathy a drink. She accepted a rum and blackcurrant, and Vic said he was going to bed. A drink later, Cathy and Ed ascended the stairs, and Vic waited in anticipation. He wasn't disappointed. The couple made love all night long. They got into so many different positions, Vic thought that they entwined like a couple of snakes. Every move seemed choreographed, and just when it looked as if the session was about to end, Cathy simply blew Ed up to the point of desire once more. No wonder Ed didn't want to lose her. About half past five in the morning, the couple did sleep. Vic was shattered by this point. He'd seen Ed with various girls in this room but nothing like this. The girl certainly had talent, in more ways than one.

The following morning Cathy was awake early. She wanted to go home to her children. Ed stirred and took her straight away. Immediately afterwards, Cathy showered and made her way downstairs to make some coffee. She took a freshly made cup up to Ed, who guzzled it down and then reached for her again. Vic awoke and stared through his mirror. 'Not again,' he said out loud, and gazed at the couple so obviously absorbed in each other. When they'd finished, Vic took himself downstairs to sort some breakfast. Cathy and Ed came down about ten minutes later. They had some toast and then he drove her to the railway station before returning to an anxious Faye. He stayed out more and more these days and, although she didn't mind the lack of sex, she didn't like being on her own night after night. Ed reassured her that he'd fallen asleep at Vic's, and Vic backed him up.

Chapter Nine

Just over a week later, Cathy was on her way to Norfolk. She fell in love with the place straight away. The agent met her at Gunton Hall and was more than pleased with her performance. Ed turned up just before she went on. It was Friday night and Vic had told him that he'd switch some interviews in the following week so that Ed was free to spend five to six days there. Faye was told that he was visiting his brother, and as Ed knew that she wanted nothing to do with his family there was no protest. He'd given her plenty of money so she was happy.

Cathy thought that Gunton Hall was one of the most beautiful places she'd ever seen. Ed seemed to think that it used to be Lord Nelson's residence at one time and voiced this to Cathy. She replied that she didn't know but she would love to live in a place like this. 'You haven't seen my place yet,' said Ed, 'you could lose yourself in it.' They had a lovely meal of sole and jacket potato, with a side salad. Dessert was strawberry flan, one of Cathy's favourites. She was provided with accommodation for that night and the bed was one of the most comfortable that she'd ever slept in. She snuggled up to Ed after they'd made love and they fell asleep just like an old married couple.

They left Gunton Hall at twelve the following day and went sightseeing. Ed didn't seem bothered about looking for accommodation, which surprised Cathy, but she guessed that he had it all under control. Later that evening they drove into a place called Bacton which looked nice and quiet. They didn't need reporters getting involved. At the moment, Ed was hailed as a leading singer, and Cathy was in demand as a dancer. It was quite dark by now and she was surprised when he got out of the car and told her to wait where she was. He walked off, turned a corner and then returned about five minutes later. In his hand he had a black scarf. He bound Cathy's eyes with it saying, 'You've got to trust me, just walk.' He took her hand and she followed, as he guided her. Reaching their destination, he removed the blindfold and Cathy could not believe her eyes. Smiling at her were Rusty, Fawn, Amber, and Amethyst.

'Oh, how lovely. I've thought about you every day!' The family hugged her in turn, and Ed said to Amber, 'I told you I'd bring Cathy to see you, didn't I?'

Amber was delighted and remarked on the pendants that Cathy was wearing. 'They brought you luck with your dancing and now that you're back, Eden can send Faye away.' Cathy sighed; the child may have aged several years but her outlook on life was still very innocent. She held the little girl to her as she repeated excitedly, 'Angel's home.' Fawn beckoned Cathy inside the caravan. This was larger than the previous one and had three bedrooms and a small gas cooker. The lighting was gas too and the living area was much larger.

'Nice isn't it,' said Fawn, 'and we've struck really lucky this time. This is the land belonging to the lady next door in that bungalow. She's very kind to us and even lets us have use of her telephone in emergencies. The other caravan belongs to her but she lets Sky rent it. It's empty at the moment because Sky has gone to Ibiza. You two can have it for as long as you need. Of course if you want to bunk in with us you can but I know that Eden likes his privacy. You can still eat with us though and there's a nice little pub just down the road where we occasionally go to refresh ourselves.' She pointed to the television and added, 'see, all mod cons.'

Cathy was feeling very happy. She had thought that she'd be in some hotel most of the time avoiding photographers, as she felt that being caught on camera with Ed would lose her title of 'Miss Go International, Go'. What a mouthful! Ted Taylor must have been on something at the time when he dreamed that one up; probably the handsome young man that was taking the photos at the contest. Ed may not have been a judge but Vic certainly was. Fawn made some bacon sandwiches and they tucked in hungrily. Cathy could relax now as nobody would find them here; it was perfect.

The following morning, Cathy went with Rusty to the local school. The girls had attended it since they'd arrived in Norfolk. Fawn felt that education was paramount, even though Sky was a qualified teacher and could have taught them at home. Amber was so happy, and introduced Cathy to her friends. 'This is Angel, she's my sister.' The child still believed that everyone on the planet was her brother or sister. Cathy guessed this was because she had lived in a commune for so long. She waved the little girls off as they went into the school building, and returned with Rusty to the caravan. On the way back they stopped at the village shop and bought some provisions. Cathy was amazed at how helpful and friendly all the people were. In Essex, she'd encountered many a surly or downright rude shopkeeper, but she imagined that this was because here they were village people, whereas at home she lived in an impersonal town.

Arriving back at the caravan, she found Ed and Fawn deep in conversation. Fawn told Rusty about Cathy's forthcoming summer season. 'You can stay here,' said Rusty. 'I can ferry you back and forth to venues. We'll look after you and Ed can visit whenever.'

Fawn nodded. 'It would be nice for the girls too. We could take them to watch the shows sometimes.'

'Well, that would be lovely, but most of my work is quite a way further down the coast. I would pay Rusty to take me as I don't drive. I'd love that.'

'Just pay my petrol. I'd be more than happy to look after my brother's wife, and I think Eden would feel much better if he knew we were looking after you.'

Cathy sighed. They still regarded her as Ed's wife even though she was still married to Tony. 'The only thing is, I always bring Sandy away for a week when I do a season. So that would be another body for you to put up.'

'No problem,' Rusty assured her. 'We'd love to see her and so would the girls.' Cathy felt so happy that she thought she was going to cry. She was so looking forward to staying in Norfolk. Some scrambled eggs and toast later, they all set off for the beach. It was March, so they still needed fairly warm clothes but it was very pleasant.

Over the next few days, Cathy was amazed at the change in Ed. He was more relaxed, he didn't demand sex as much, and he just seemed content to be with her. They still made love every night, but then fell asleep in each others arms; none of these sexual marathons. They went to Corton to see the agent that also wanted her, and struck a happy contract.

She was to do Pakefield, Corton, Lowestoft, and Hopton for him. Then for the agent she'd met at Gunton Hall, she was also to do Great Yarmouth, Caister, Scratby, Hemsby, and several others. She left the agent Noddy's number and said goodbye. She wondered if she'd have to do a show for him before she left, but he informed her that he had no need to see her as he'd seen her on television.

Cathy was elated. She loved the area, she had Fawn and Rusty watching out for her, Ed to visit when possible, and best of all she could bring Sandy away to stay in a real hippy caravan. Better than that even, was the fact that Sandy would have two playmates while she was staying, which was nicer for her as she normally trailed around all the venues with her mother, even when she didn't want to. Now she had Fawn's two daughters to occupy her. They spent five days in all at Bacton and had a very carefree time. They visited village pubs, and frequently went to the beach which was just nearby to the caravan. They were sited on the cliff top and there was a metal ladder which made the beach accessible.

Cathy loved the caravan. It had cooking facilities, two bedrooms, one of which was made by pulling the bed out of the wall, and a small single room. It would be perfect for her and Sandy, the only thing that it lacked was a toilet, but there was an outside one nearby, and as Fawn and Rusty were only a few feet away, she would have anything extra that she needed.

Rusty had never seen his brother so happy. Obviously Cathy was responsible for most of it, but there was also something else. Many times he'd tried to get Ed to try his style of hippy living and he'd always sat on the fence over it. Looking at him in these last few days made him think that maybe Ed was now ready for it. He knew that, money aside, the life that Ed lived was an unhealthy one. Victor Lee was a nasty, perverted man, Romany was pure evil, fans were fickle, and as for his fiancée, well that was another story. Beautiful, manipulative, money mad, vain, and stuck up. She'd openly called Fawn frumpy, Rusty an ageing mess, and the girls dirty little gypsies. All of which was untrue. Fawn was only starting to spread around the middle and wore hippy style clothes. Rusty dressed to please himself and was spotlessly clean and, as for the girls, well, they wore school uniform weekdays, and at weekends wore the clothes they wanted, all of which were clean.

She'd said Sky was a tramp because she had a love child and made it obvious that Ed would never get a child with her as she didn't want her body ruined. Rusty felt sure that if Faye had met Ed in his hippy days, she wouldn't have given him a second look. He stared over at his brother who was enjoying the winter sun. He was stretched out on the grass on a tartan blanket with Cathy at his side. Now there was the ideal couple. He knew that Ed still had his tantrums but he seemed much calmer this time. Here was a match made in heaven. Fawn had read the cards and told him that Ed and Cathy were soul mates and that they'd always end up together. She intended doing a reading for Cathy when she returned to do her season in order to try and get more information. Rusty smiled; at least Ed was more relaxed away from the circus that he lived in.

On the final night, they all went to the nearby pub that Rusty frequented and had a meal. After returning home, Ed wanted a late night stroll and so, hand in hand, they walked along the deserted country lane.

Ed was dreaming, and Cathy, confused by his silence, enquired if anything was wrong. He didn't want to give her back to Tony; he wanted her to stay with him as he was unhappy without her. Cathy replied that she was unhappy without him too, but they still had to wait due to work commitments as well as the horrific mess that they were surrounded by. For once he agreed with her that to do things properly took time, and he guessed that if he was seeing her regularly each week then it was better than the years without her. 'Are you happy with me?' he asked, stopping and hugging her close. Cathy nodded. 'I'm prepared to wait,' he added. 'We've got Vic's place to meet at, but it's the end result that I'm thinking about, and this week has opened my eyes. I keep thinking about the open road and you and me and the kids. How about it?'

'I'd love it. Rusty and Fawn look well on it but until we've fulfilled our contracts I don't see that we can do it. You've got a tour soon, and Noddy's got so much work for me. I'm judging talent contests, doing commercials for shampoos, opening supermarkets and new dance studios, modelling sweaters, the summer season which you know about, and Noddy's even talking about a pantomime and ice show in the future. On top of that, when I go home I've got to go to Wakefield for a week, followed by Newcastle. Then it'll be London until I start the season.'

'I want out,' said Ed, 'but I guess you're right. I always want everything yesterday. I thought it would be great to take Mick's place but it's not, apart from the money. I was much happier when I first met you. I was enjoying the hippy lifestyle, and the only reason that I wanted to make it big was because I wanted to give you the best of everything, and that backfired.'

'Then we'll have to wait, and as soon as we can we'll do it. You could sing with Rusty, and I could probably be fitted in as a dancer sometimes. Maybe Fawn could teach me to read the cards.'

Ed held her at arms length and she could see the excitement in his eyes. 'You mean it, you really mean it?'

'Yes, I want to be with you. By the time we finish our contracts, the kids will be older. It'll take at least another couple of years. Noddy's got work for me right into the end of 1975 and I'm sure that there'll be more. If I can't get custody, I will still go with you. We can provide for the kids better than Tony, unless he gets a job which I'm sure he won't.'

Ed picked her up and swung her around. 'You have made me so happy. Do you know I suffered both of your pregnancies?'

Cathy furrowed her brow. 'How's that?'

'June gave me the dates; the first date was when I signed with Vic. I was in agony all afternoon and as for 19th February, I was admitted to hospital and they nearly operated on me. Plus I'd been sick for nine months. So I'll never forget their birthdates, will I?'

Cathy found it hilarious. 'God knows what will happen if we have one of our own.'

'Can't wait to find out; let's get started,' said Ed.

'Okay, race you back to the caravan!' She felt that at last they had a goal to go for. She hated the world that Ed existed in but if he gave it all up when the work was honoured, they could both opt out and live together in privacy with the children. No more Tony, no more Faye, they'd travel until they finally found where they wanted to live and then they would disappear into insignificance.

Back inside the pretty caravan with all Sky's eye-catching decorations, dream-catchers, wind-chimes, and cosy ambience, they had a drink and then prepared for bed. 'I'm tired,' yawned Cathy.

Ed silenced her with a kiss and then rolled her over onto her back. 'Sleep later, right now I want you.' Cathy struggled at first but it soon became half-hearted and she pulled him to her.

Ed laughed. 'See, you want me as much as I want you.' Cathy said nothing; she was unaware of anything except the pleasure that was engulfing her. Finally she reached orgasm and she felt her muscles contract as all the tension evaporated into a state of contentment. Immediately afterwards, Ed set to arousing her again. She pushed him away. 'What is it with you? You seem to have a permanent hard on.'

Ed chuckled. 'Only happens with you.'

'Liar, what about Faye and all those groupies? Oh, and June.'

Ed turned a deaf ear to her. He was determined to arouse her again and he did. She experienced orgasm after orgasm. A little later she lay back feeling completely drained, as once again he'd deliberately held back until she felt sore. It was then and only then that Ed released himself.

After a conversation about their future they both slept until about eight o'clock when they were woken by Amber knocking on the caravan door. Cathy got up and opened it, welcoming Amber and Amethyst with a tray of coffee and toast. They were excited about Cathy coming to stay with them for five months. 'We can go to Yarmouth,' said Amber, 'and we can go to the Pleasure Beach and go on all the rides.'

Amethyst was more interested in the shows. She liked Peters and Lee and knew that they were on the same circuit as Cathy. 'Will you let us come and see you dance?' she asked.

'Of course,' replied Cathy.

'And will you bring Sandy in the school holidays?' Amber enquired.

'Of course.' The girls were really pleased.

Amber flung her arms around Ed's neck. 'Thank you for bringing Angel back,' she cried.

Ed was still half asleep; he scratched his tousled head and sat up in the bed. 'That's okay, baby,' he said. 'You'll see more of her when she starts work down here.'

Amethyst checked her watch and took her sister's hand. 'Come on, Dad's waiting in the car, we mustn't be late for school.' They exchanged hugs and left the caravan while Ed and Cathy devoured the coffee and toast.

They left Norfolk about one o'clock and headed back to their homes. It was Wednesday and they made arrangements to meet up at the weekend, as Cathy would be up North for the following two weeks. Ed reminded her about Vic's birthday, which she'd completely forgotten about. She informed Noddy straight away to make sure she didn't have a booking that night and invited him along to the Wembley gig and party. Cathy had informed Vic that she wouldn't perform unless Noddy came too. Vic was happy to oblige, after all he was getting his own private show every time she stayed overnight with Ed. He encouraged Ed to get the girl to stay there more often. The couple were only too happy about it and Vic was elated. He gloated to Al about it but never invited him over on those nights. He said that Ed was still calling him a pervert and wanted to get his hands on him and Al decided not to push his luck.

Arriving home, Cathy was confronted by an angry Tony. 'The kids have driven me nuts.'

'I'll make a nice cup of tea,' she said, putting her suitcase on the hall floor.

'I should think so. I've been slaving away all week while you've been enjoying yourself.'

'Actually it was five days,' said Cathy, eyeing the pile of dirty cups and plates that decorated the draining board in the kitchen.

The nappy bucket was overflowing with dirty nappies, and the linen basket was full too. 'I can see that you've been busy. When was the last time you did any washing up, or dirty nappies, or washing? The floor's filthy too. Come to think of it, when's the last time you did anything?'

She switched the kettle on, and Tony mumbled that the kids had kept him busy and that was why things had piled up. 'Hey,' he said, 'I don't suppose you'd have a few quid spare, would you?'

'Going out, are we?' asked Cathy.

'Well I think I've earned it, and I've been in all the time that you've been away,' moaned Tony. Cathy reached for her purse and taking out a five pound note gave it to her husband.

'I'm having an early night.'

'You're a good girl, Cathy, a real hard worker. I'm lucky to have a wife like you,' simpered Tony.

Sure, thought Cathy, what you really mean is you're lucky that you married a fool. The kettle boiled and she made the tea as her stomach rumbled with hunger. When she opened the pantry door it came as no shock to find it empty. At the back of the shelf she found some fish paste and a packet of custard cream biscuits. In the bread bin was half a loaf which was starting to go stale. As that was all the edible food there, she had to eat it. Apart from that the only other thing was a packet of Farley's rusks and some Sugar Puffs. She looked for butter but there was none. Spreading the fish paste onto the dry bread she decided that it didn't look too appetising, but it was better than nothing.

'A few of the lads are holding a card school tonight,' Tony said, 'so if I win, would you like me to bring in some Chinese food?'

'Might be an idea,' replied Cathy, trying to force the sandwich down her throat. 'This paste is awful without butter. How long have you had it?'

'Can't remember, I hate shopping. That's women's work.' He kissed her cheek and then smiling said, 'thanks for the fiver. If I win I'll see you all right.' He walked to the hall and put on his coat. 'If I win and you're in bed when I get home, shall I wake you up?'

'Yes, I can't eat any more of this.' She put down the half-eaten sandwich and drank her tea. As Tony went out, Cathy decided to make a start on the nappies. 'What more could you want than a bucket of nappies?' she said out loud. Obviously the children were at Tony's mother's as they were nowhere in sight. Cathy sighed; an early night was definitely on the cards.

When Tony arrived home, Cathy was in bed, but the smell of the take-away drifted up the stairs and made her mouth water. 'I see you got lucky,' she said, watching Tony making his way to the kitchen as she came downstairs. He piled the food onto two plates.

He was glad to see that the mountain of dishes had gone, and the nappy bucket was empty. 'You should have left it all until tomorrow,' he said, indicating the empty sink.

'Then it would have been waiting for me tomorrow,' said Cathy, wearily. Tony gazed at his wife; she really was a delectable girl, and in that negligee she was a dish.

After their meal they went to bed, and Cathy lay back and waited. She was always waiting and not receiving, but tonight Tony did make love to her. She felt nothing and afterwards, when he turned his back to her, she wept silently. She moved her pillow slightly to get comfortable and a lipstick clattered to the floor. It wasn't hers and she wept until she slept. How had her life disintegrated into this mess and web of deceit?

Faye Beaumont awoke and felt the vacant pillow beside her. She sighed with relief knowing that once more she'd spent the night alone. She was happy; Ed was far too sex hungry for her liking. She loved him but couldn't keep up with his demands, so his absence pleased her. She turned over onto her back and gazed at her reflection in the mirrored ceiling. She pushed the satin sheet from herself and admired her body. It drove Ed crazy and she knew that it was her greatest asset. Sex she liked, but not as much as he did. He could never seem to get enough and he adored all night sessions. To cap it all, he wanted kids and she did not. Still, she had this lovely house and all the trappings that go with it, with just about everything money could buy. She knew that he wasn't faithful but had never caught him out. Ed was too clever for that. Groupies were a part of the pop scene but with a face and figure like hers, Ed would never stray long.

She heard a car pull up and wondered if he was back, but then she heard Romany's voice and realised that Ed must have phoned him and let him know that he was on his way home. She hated Romany but knew that he desired her and so got some sort of sick satisfaction out of flaunting herself in front of him. She got out of bed, showered and made her way to the stairs. She had dressed in a low-necked, clingy top and a black mini skirt, making herself up as if she was going out on the town. She went to greet Romany and stood framed in the doorway, posing as if she was having a photo shoot. 'He's not here,' she said. Romany had his back to her but at the sound of her voice turned around.

He drew his breath with admiration. 'I know, he rang me earlier and told me to come over and wait.'

'Really? He didn't ring me.'

'Probably didn't want to wake you; after all, you do spend most of your time in bed. I suppose you've only just got up.'

'Nothing else to do.'

'I could find you something to do.'

'Really,' replied Faye, seating herself on a nearby sofa. She bent seductively to pick up a magazine, giving Romany an eyeful of cleavage.

He knew what she was doing. 'Why do you play games?'

Faye gave him a wide-eyed, innocent look. 'Whatever do you mean?' she asked, sweetly.

'Flaunting yourself in front of me, just like a silly little girl. I pity Ed at times.'

'Ed and I have a very full sex life.'

'Sure, that's why he rang me and told me that he'd spent five days on the East coast.'

'He's been recording.'

'Then why wasn't the rest of the band there?'

'He was doing some solo recording.'

'Vic never knew about it.'

'Well, I believe him.'

'Look he's having fun, why don't you? I'd take care of you.' He leered and then joined Faye on the sofa. He slid his hands under her top saying, 'what a body you've got.'

'How dare you,' screamed Faye, pushing his hands away.

In anger, Romany pulled her to him. 'How dare I?' he said. 'That's a good one.' Faye shivered as he ran his hands over her body. 'It's what you want; you've dressed to get me going. You do it all the time, only this time I've had enough, this time you're getting what you asked for.' Faye was petrified, yet fascinated at the same time but she guessed that Romany was just trying to scare her.

So she decided to play along with him. 'Come on then, are you all talk or are you serious?' She got up and headed for the stairs with Romany in hot pursuit. He was confused. He wanted her like crazy but felt sick; this was Ed's house, Ed's girl, and he'd only meant to scare her to teach her a lesson. Faye led him to a guest room and sat on the bed smiling at him. He turned the key in the lock and sat down beside her. She was okay at first and allowed him to kiss her but when he tried to get her to open her legs she began to struggle.

If there was one thing that Romany hated it was being given the green light and then seeing it change to red. He increased his caressing and kissing and Faye began to sob. A car pulled up outside and he let her go. Faye straightened her clothing and slapped him around his face. The slap hurt and he jumped up quickly. 'And you call yourself his best friend,' she cried.

Romany fiddled with the key in the lock. 'What does that make you then,' he sneered. He swore as Faye left the room adding, 'little girls shouldn't play games they can't finish.' The couple hurried downstairs just as Ed entered the house. Faye flung her arms around his neck but Ed took one look at her and ordered her to change into something more fitting. He flopped down on the sofa and asked Romany if he'd like a drink. 'Can a duck swim?' he replied. Ed laughed and told him that he would have to get himself one as he was fagged out.

'Fagged or shagged?' laughed Romany, 'who was she?'

Ed chuckled. 'I've been working hard.'

'I should have gone with you. I've never seen you so relaxed and contented.'

Faye returned. 'Who's contented?' she asked.

'Well I'm not when I come home and find you dressed like that. Your tits were nearly hanging out of that thing.' Faye flushed scarlet, remarking that whenever she saw him photographed with girls, they usually had less on. Ed retorted that he wasn't engaged to them and he wasn't having every Tom, Dick, and Harry staring at her. 'I'm the only one allowed to see your body, so you just remember it,' he added.

'But there's only Romany and the staff here,' protested Faye.

'It doesn't matter; you're the lady of the house, so act like one.'

Faye was hurt, 'I do try,' she said sadly.

'Sure you do, but the staff has to view you with respect, and they can't if you float around half naked.'

'I wasn't; I had a top and skirt on.'

Ed ruffled her hair. 'Only just, anyway you look much nicer in jeans and a shirt, doesn't she, Romany?' Romany nodded, he thought the girl looked stunning in anything. Ed turned to Faye, 'Okay, how much have you spent while I've been away?' he asked.

Faye looked down. 'Three hundred pounds, roughly,' she said. She knew it was nearer six but wasn't going to own up to it.

'Three hundred quid,' cried Ed. 'I'm gone for five days and you go through three hundred quid! What did you buy?'

'A dress for Wembley, some shoes, perfume, a bracelet, and some lovely underwear.'

'Oh well, I'll see the underwear later and I suppose I can afford it,' he laughed. 'Oh, and while we're on the subject of Wembley, we're holding a party here straight after it.'

'Why?'

'Vic's birthday.'

'Thanks for telling me at this late date; I'd better inform the housekeeper. Faye left the room grumbling, and Romany poured out another drink for himself and Ed.

'Have the invitations been sent out?' he asked.

Ed ignored him. He was thinking about Cathy and his short break in Norfolk. He'd felt reborn, and the open road beckoned.

Romany repeated his question and waved his hand in front of Ed's face. Ed came back down to earth. 'Yeah, the usual bores have been invited, and Gypsy.'

'How is she?' asked Romany. 'Did you have a good time?'

'How did you know?' said Ed.

'I didn't, but I do now.'

'I haven't seen Cathy since the dance contest.'

Romany drained his glass and smirked.

Faye flounced into the room. 'I've given Mrs Shores the necessary instructions, but I felt a bit of a fool when I rang the caterers and they already knew about it.' She seated herself beside Ed and began to fondle him under his shirt. Romany stared in amazement; he would have had her upstairs by now but Ed seemed unfazed. Faye looked like a child. She was so fresh and lovely. She continued to fondle him until he took her hand and led her to the stairs.

'Cue to leave?' said Romany.

'Not if you don't mind waiting,' replied Ed. 'Help yourself to drinks.'

Upstairs, Faye allowed herself to be positioned this way and that, caressed by Ed who laboured over her body. The problem was simple; he brought her to orgasm too quickly. She enjoyed it, but then wanted to stop immediately which he never did. He'd hold back until she begged him to stop. Then and only then, he'd allow himself to come.

When this happened she felt so drained that she was unable to respond any more and then she'd be accused of being cold and selfish. Nowadays she faked orgasm regularly, hoping to get it over more quickly. She'd sigh and moan making him believe that he was ringing all these cries from her when all the time she was acting. She cast her mind back to Romany and wondered if they were more compatible. She doubted it, after all he was the great lover of the group and probably worse than Ed. How she wished that she could find a rich old man who wouldn't demand sex. Ed rolled off her and headed for the shower.

She wondered if there were girls who would like the treatment she'd just had. Her nightmare was not yet over as Ed started on her again after drying his hair. She pushed him away saying, 'no Ed, I don't want to.'

'Course you do, you don't fool me.'

Faye felt like she was going crazy. 'Please stop, I can't.' In desperation she tugged on his hair. 'Stop it!' she sobbed.

'Want to fight, do you?' yelled Ed. The girl struggled violently but to no avail. Ed seized a handful of her hair and jerked her head back.

'I can't,' screamed Faye.

'Don't you ever say, "can't", to me,' Ed snarled. 'I look after you real good and all you have to do is keep me happy. You love all this luxury around you, don't you? If you want to keep it, you'd better start being friendly. There are thousands of girls who would love to be in your place.'

'I love you, Ed,' sobbed Faye, 'but, really, I just can't keep up with you.'

Ed yanked her head back harder. 'Then you'd better learn, hadn't you? Well, you may have finished but I haven't.' He forced her to her knees. 'Kneel,' he commanded. This was what Faye hated most of all but she took him in her mouth, the tears still stinging her eyes. Fortunately it didn't take long and immediately after, she tore herself free and vomited in the toilet. Ed left the room, slamming the door as he went.

Downstairs, Romany had nodded off, so Ed increased the volume on the television and he awoke with a start. He stared around him in confusion and then, realising where he was, said, 'I wasn't asleep really, I was just resting with my eyes closed. Where's Faye?'

'I wore her out,' said Ed, with a wicked grin. He was angry; every time they had oral sex, Faye threw up.

'Same old you,' laughed Romany. 'You've netted yourself a stunner there. Faye's really something, isn't she?'

'Yeah,' replied Ed, getting more and more bored by the second. 'I'm the lucky one.' There was a silence and then he added, 'I didn't ask you to come over here to discuss women, I wanted to run through a few numbers.'

'You brought me here to work? Just as well I brought my guitar.'

'Yeah, but let's have a drink first.'

'Great idea, let's see off that bottle of whiskey.'

'Leave off, this week's cost me enough already, what with Faye's spending and Cathy's fee.'

'What a way to go, both of them together. You can't lose. It'll be a great party. You will whistle if you can't manage, won't you?'

'My dear Romany, Cathy and I are finished,' said Ed, pouring out two glasses of whiskey and offering one to his friend.

'Maybe I should take care of her at the party then,' joked Romany.

'Just try it and I'll slit your throat.'

Romany drank his whiskey in two gulps. 'You never were a good liar.'

'You bastard,' chuckled Ed. 'Now, how about a run through of our latest single.' Eden the 'happy hippy' had left, and Ed the controlling, chauvinistic superstar was back.

Upstairs, Faye wept, and later she heard the door slam and raised voices laughing hysterically. Ed and his best friend were gone for the night. She tiptoed downstairs and switched on the television. She watched every programme until daylight and then went back to bed.

Thursday and Friday flew by for Cathy. She had to open a supermarket, give a speech and dance at a women's guild before preparing for a gig at Southend-on-Sea. On the Friday she had to travel up to Whitby for two shows, so the travelling itself was exhausting, plus she had the return journey to contend with. She finally got to bed at about three thirty in the morning and was awoken Saturday morning by Steven who jumped all over her. As usual Tony moaned. She'd woken him up when she got back in the early hours of the morning and now Steven had woken him up. He was sick of his life. He deserved better, or so he thought. Cathy suggested that he found some work and then his troubles would be over. He replied with a tirade of abuse, so she got out of bed and took Steven with her.

Downstairs, Sandy was preparing for her ballet class, and a little later left with her friend who lived next door. The day sped by and soon Cathy was on her way to Ilford. She had a further show to do later at South Woodford, and Ed had instructed her to wait for Vic who would be picking her up.

Vic arrived at about one o'clock and hastily drove to his house with Cathy sitting in the back of the car this time. She said she would rather sit there as she was feeling a bit queasy and didn't want to throw up all over him, but the real reason was that she didn't like the way his hand frequently ended up on her knee. Vic wasn't bothered; he was going to get a free show later anyway.

Ed was already installed in Vic's house; he hadn't been home since Wednesday. He was intending to teach Faye a lesson.

Arriving at Vic's house, Cathy followed him inside. Ed was lying on the sofa and got to his feet as Cathy approached him. He grasped her in a bear hug and then presented her with a gift-wrapped box which Cathy unwrapped excitedly. Inside was a bottle of 'Joy' perfume. Cathy was in seventh heaven. She'd tried the testers in the shops but never thought that she'd actually ever be able to buy it; it was very expensive. She opened the bottle and applied some to her wrists, it was beautiful. She kissed Ed and thanked him; he was so generous to her. What she didn't know was that it was Ed's favourite, and that it was just another way of controlling what perfume she wore. He handed her another box and, on opening it, she beheld a diamond necklace. She nearly dropped it with shock. It must have cost a fortune. She was speechless as Ed placed it around her neck and fastened it. 'But I can't accept this,' she cried, 'it's far too good for me.'

'Nothing's too good for you. Now let's have a drink and we'll go to bed.' Vic was on his feet in an instant, making his way to the bar. He placed two glasses on the bar and asked, 'what's your poison, kids?'

'Brandy for both of us.'

'Can I have some lemonade in mine?' asked Cathy.

'Of course,' replied Vic, feeling his temperature rising. Already he was visualising the scene that he was going to witness. He poured the drinks, handed them to his guests, and then told them that he was off to bed.

He knew he wouldn't have to wait long as already Ed's hand was creeping up Cathy's thigh and she had that same expression that she had given in the photo. It wasn't long before he was stationed at his mirror watching the couple go through the same routine that he'd seen before. The only difference was that they kept it up all night this time, and Vic's eyes were smarting at trying to keep them open.

He didn't hear Cathy leave; he had fallen asleep after his exhausting all-night vigil. Ed returned later that day and woke him up when he came in. He'd just dropped Cathy at the railway station and was considering ringing Faye. He knew that he wouldn't be seeing Cathy for two weeks and he still needed female company but he lay down on the sofa and fell asleep.

Faye was distraught. It was Sunday morning and Ed still hadn't returned. It was bad enough that he'd been absent for five days the previous week, but now he'd been gone for another four. In desperation, she rang her mother who rushed around to her straight away. Mrs Sara Beaumont was a very well preserved woman, always smartly dressed and very youthful looking for her age. She'd been forty when she'd given birth to her daughter but they looked more like sisters, except for the fact that Sara wore too much make up.

She tried to console her unhappy daughter. 'Come on,' she soothed, 'last time I saw you, you were on top of the world. What is it this time?'

'I'm losing Ed,' Faye wailed.

'Hardly surprising; you spend his money like it's water. I told you last week that you'd overdone it and I bet you haven't owned up to half the things you bought. He's not a walking bank.'

'It's not that. I'm not sexy enough for him.'

Sara threw up her hands in horror. 'What sort of talk is that coming from you?'

'It's true,' cried Faye, becoming hysterical.

'Hush, dear,' whispered Sara, 'we don't want the hired help to hear you.' She surveyed her daughter. 'When did you last eat?'

'Two days ago, I think,' sniffled Faye. 'I can't remember.'

'Right, smarten yourself up; you're coming with me to a restaurant. You're far too pallid for my liking.'

'But Ed might ring,' wailed Faye.

'Then the wanderer will have to wait, won't he? If you think you're losing him then you'll have to fight back. You don't want to lose this beautiful house, do you?'

'No, but he will come back, I know he will. He was gone almost a week, and now he's gone off with Romany.'

'Then they're probably boozing,' said Sara, fiddling with her nail in a bored manner. Just then the phone rang, and Faye rushed to it. 'Oh no,' said Sara, 'I'll take it.' She lifted the receiver.

'Is it Ed?' squealed Faye. Her mother nodded.

'Hallo,' said Sara. 'No you can't speak to Faye, she's not very well, but don't concern yourself. I'm taking her out to get something to eat. She's worried about you, though I can't understand why. The way you treat her is disgusting.'

Faye snatched the receiver from her mother's hand. 'Ed, please come home, I'll do anything.' The line went dead and Sara shook her head sadly.

'You shouldn't have done that,' she said. 'If you had let me speak to him longer I could have helped, but now you've spoilt everything by crawling to him again.'

'But it's not his fault; it's just that the girls throw themselves at him because he's so good looking.'

'And he's rich,' snapped Sara. 'You're far too good for him. I did warn you, didn't I?'

'I think that sex is all he cares about, and I can't keep up with him,' cried Faye, cuddling up to her mother.

'To most men it is,' sighed Sara. 'You don't refuse do you?'

Faye shook her head. She could feel her stomach beginning to grumble, and listened as her mother went on, 'You must decide whether you want to stay here or come home to me; my door is always open.'

'I can't give up all of this,' Faye wailed in horror.

'Faye, is it Ed you want, or his money?' She wished her daughter would make up her mind, she was getting very hungry.

'I want both,' cried Faye like a spoilt child.

'Then as you've made your bed, you must lie in it. Now what

we'll do is go for a meal, and then we'll come back here and get you looking even more beautiful, so that when he walks in tonight he'll forget all his other distractions. You'll also be ready, willing and able. Now get ready,' she ordered, 'I'm very hungry.'

Faye dried her tears and ran upstairs; she was feeling hungry as well now. 'Won't be long,' she shouted down but her mother wasn't listening, she was too busy searching for her nail file.

When Ed returned that night, Faye greeted him in a low cut evening gown. He took one look at her and dragged her upstairs. Once inside the bedroom, he tore the dress from her. Faye winced. The dress had cost a fortune but she remembered what her mother had said and let herself be positioned this way and that. She felt sick, but sighed, moaned, heaved, and panted knowing that that was what he wanted to hear. She wanted to scream but acted as if she was caught up in some raging passion. In the end they both fell asleep exhausted, but in the morning he took her as soon as he awoke. Afterwards he smiled at her. 'That was better,' he said, 'just like it used to be.' A car pulled up outside. 'That's Romany and I've got rehearsal. Do you want to come?' Faye shook her head and closed her eyes again. Ed reached for his wallet and threw some money at her adding, 'get yourself some new clothes for Wembley and the party.'

Faye's inside felt red raw, but she smiled; that was just what she wanted to hear. She knew that Ed had various interviews to do this week and then he was off to Ireland for the following week. After that it would be Wembley, and the girl from the dance contest was being brought in for Vic's party. She'd watched the show from the start and felt that she'd known her all her life. It would be nice to have a female at the party to talk to. She'd wondered if Ed fancied her; it was just the way that he'd looked at her in the photo after the winner had been announced. It was as if he was proud of her. She dismissed the thought, rolled over and went back to sleep.

Chapter Ten

Cathy meanwhile was travelling up North. She was overjoyed when she found herself on the same bill as June, and they had a really girly week. They were on the same bill at Newcastle too, but sadly June met up with a young man from her past and spent much of her time with him. Cathy busied herself with work, buying presents for her children and having early nights. She spent a lot of time walking up and down Northumberland Street, gazing in all the shop windows.

Soon be home time, she thought, and Vic's party. She giggled, thinking about Vic and Al. She was now convinced that Vic was the elusive Mr Franks and that there had been no free photo shoot at all.

Still, what was done was done and nothing could change it. She'd gained the title through her own efforts and she had her hippy boyfriend back, even if it was part time. The feelings that she had towards Ed were strange. She loved him and she knew that he loved her. The sex was great; the intensity of it was sometimes too much to bear but they were very compatible and she could never get enough of him.

It was something else though; she felt that she had to be with him. It was like a bond that made both of them miserable when they were apart. Often the feeling was being ill, though not seriously, and even when they had been apart, she'd thought of him every single day. He'd just never gone away. It was very strange. She wasn't feeling too good now, and wondered if he felt the same. When she returned home she felt worse and hoped that she wouldn't show herself up at the party by giving a bad performance.

Meanwhile Ed had returned from Ireland and played his first concert at Wembley. He wasn't well; he'd felt lousy towards the end of the week whilst in the Emerald Isle. Vic wasn't sure that he should perform but found a drug dealer that helped out partially. The Wembley gig was a disaster. Ed forgot his words several times and gazed around him with a vacant expression. There was no sparkle at all. This gig would certainly go down as one of the worst that the band had played.

When he reached home afterwards, he just fell asleep on the settee. He didn't even have the energy to climb the stairs. However, the following day was a different story. He knew he'd given a bad performance and was on edge all day, making Faye's life a misery. He was insufferably moody, and she would be relieved when it was time to leave for the show. The final straw came when he decided he wanted her just as she was getting into the shower. She had already started running the water and objected fiercely.

Ed dragged her, soaking wet, onto the bedroom carpet and practically raped her. 'What is it with you, you animal?' she screamed.

She got to her feet, and Ed slapped her around the face, pushing her down for the second time. 'Don't you ever call me that again; you can be replaced any time.' Faye was crying and pleading to him, telling him that they'd be late. He answered by telling her that he was the star and the audience would have to wait. Faye fought as if her life depended on it.

'I've got to shower,' she screamed.

'Well, bloody shower then,' yelled Ed and backed the girl into the shower. 'No, no, no,' pleaded Faye, 'not again, please not again.' Ed pushed her under the shower and tried to take her standing up but had no success at all. He slapped her over and over again as she begged him to leave her alone.

Finally he left her under the shower crying and said callously, 'Okay then you frigid bitch, get ready. I don't want you looking a mess with your eyes all puffy. I've got a show to do.'

Faye showered and made herself presentable in the short time left. After being informed that the car was ready, the couple went downstairs. 'You look lovely, Miss,' said Mrs Shores, the housekeeper. 'Really lovely. Everything's under control with the caterers, and the band has just turned up. I think they play at the local Greek restaurant. I believe they're for the young lady that is going to dance here. She's very good I've been told. My husband is outside in the car and, like I said, everything's fine here. When you get back everything will be ready.'

Faye smiled, Ed scowled, and on the drive to Wembley they sat in silence. On their arrival, Faye retreated to a corner of the dressing room while Ed and Romany played cards.

When Cathy and Noddy arrived, Romany felt a draught on his back. 'Who opened that door? I'm cold.'

'Turn around,' laughed Ed.

'You must be joking. You only want me to turn around so that you can see my hand or pinch my cards while I'm not looking.' Cathy walked around in front of him and he dropped all his cards on the floor. 'Cathy! And to what do I owe this pleasure?'

'Well, I heard that you're the best in the country so I've come to listen.'

'True,' said Romany, and pulled her onto his knee. 'You always did have good taste, young lady, though you should have run off with me years ago. Then you could have heard me every day.'

Faye got to her feet. 'Hi Cathy, I'm Faye.'

'Clear off,' said Romany.

Faye sauntered over to Ed. 'I wish you'd have a word with him; he's got no idea how to behave when a lady's in the room.'

'Can't see one,' said Romany. 'Oh correction, I apologise, Cathy.'

Ed was uncomfortable. Romany was being his usual sarcastic self, and also he didn't like the sight of Cathy sitting on his knee. 'Let's run through our new number; we'll use the room next door.' Romany nodded and followed Ed out of the dressing room. Faye had retreated into the corner again while Cathy and Noddy tried to console her.

The press arrived shortly after and it was evident that Ed was in a bad mood. Cathy didn't realise that he was tanked up on drugs. She had seen tantrums in 1968 when he'd had to have his own way but nothing like this. He raged, he yelled, he was down right rude, and Faye took most of the brunt of it. She stood there meekly being verbally abused while Ed rained insult after insult on her. Cathy was relieved when the show began and heard a massive cheer as the band trouped out on stage. She could recall the days when the same sound had echoed through the auditoriums for the band when they a different lead vocalist.

The performance that followed left Cathy in no doubt of Ed's brilliance. He was terrific; he clowned with the audience and sang and danced to perfection. During one number, he sprawled across the keyboard and sang to Cathy and Faye. Noddy was sitting next to them and chuckled. 'First time a bloke's sung a love song to me.' The band excelled itself and gave two encores.

When they finally left the stage, the fans stormed it, so Ed and his entourage had to leave very quickly. He was soaked in sweat, and Vic wrapped a towel around him. Vic was unusually quiet; it was his birthday and he tried to forget it. He was well into his forties and wondered what tonight's party would be like.

Everyone drove off into the night. Faye had insisted that Cathy share their car, so Noddy sat in front with the chauffeur while Ed sandwiched himself in between the two girls. He liked this position; a woman either side of him. He felt quite capable of taking them both on, one after the other. It would be great, but better still, how about the two together? Noddy broke the silence, 'great show, Ed,' he said.

'Thanks,' replied Ed, 'it'll be a great party too.'

'Could you teach me how to belly dance, Cathy?' asked Faye.

'I'd be delighted to, if I can find time to fit it in.' She stretched her leg out, she was getting cramp.

'I suppose the contest has brought you plenty of work?'

Cathy nodded, 'yes, but my children keep me busy too.'

'I can't think how you manage,' said Faye, fiddling with an expensive looking ring. 'I don't ever want children. I don't want to put weight on and get stretch marks. I want to keep my figure, and I'm sure that childbirth is painful.' She flashed the ring right under Cathy's nose. 'Beautiful, isn't it?' she added. 'Cost a small fortune.'

'Very nice.'

Ed was still sitting in silence. He was still visualising the possibility of having the two girls at the same time. 'You will stay overnight, won't you Cathy? She must, mustn't she Ed?'

'Of course, darling,' said Ed; already a plan was hatching in his mind.

Arriving at Ed's mansion, Cathy noted that the house was ablaze with lights. She wondered how on earth the bills got paid, but then mused that with Ed's wealth, the problem was probably nothing. Faye was like a giggling schoolgirl getting out of the car. She took Cathy's hand, wanting to show her their beautiful home.

Inside, Cathy glanced around the master bedroom where everything seemed to be designer labelled. Faye said that her drapes were specially made in France and the bedspread was too. There was a full mirrored ceiling which Faye said she didn't like, but Cathy thought that secretly she did. With a body like that, you wouldn't mind gazing up at yourself. Faye began to witter on about her horses, dogs, homes abroad, and just about every possession that she had. Cathy just wasn't materialistic so the conversation left her cold.

Downstairs they were greeted by Romany who said, 'wow, let me escort you to the dining room.' Faye beamed thinking that he meant her and was hurt when he took Cathy's arm. As they walked away he called back, almost as an afterthought, 'Ed's looking for you, Faye.'

Faye flounced off; she wasn't used to being upstaged. Arriving in the spacious dining area, Cathy found herself seated by Mrs Beaumont who smiled and introduced herself. 'You're sitting next to Romany and opposite Mr Todd,' she said. She was feeling quite stressed tonight, and had already been upset by Ed's attitude to her.

'Great,' said Romany. Cathy looked around the table; she'd never seen so many famous faces. Every rock star seemed to have been invited. The room was heaving with select groupies, freaks, starlets, and musicians.

'Doesn't Faye look terrific?' said Cathy.

'Top show, of that I'm certain.'

'Why are you so nasty, and how would you know?'

'Just do,' replied Romany, sipping his red wine. 'They've got problems and, as there's no shortage of money, there's nothing else that it can be.'

'Well it doesn't have to be what your mind is conjuring up,' said Cathy.

Romany leered at her. 'He disappears for five days, comes home and disappears again like last week.' He rubbed his leg up against hers and added, 'don't pretend, you don't fool me.'

'Pretend what?' asked Noddy, who had just been seated.

'Nothing,' replied Cathy. 'Just Romany shooting his mouth off.'

Romany scowled. 'If I really shot my mouth off tonight, both you and Ed would be very uncomfortable.'

Ed toasted his manager and then, after dinner, entered another room where the DJ was setting up. It didn't take him long, and soon couples were on the floor dancing. 'Dance, Cathy?' asked Romany.

'Good idea,' she replied, and led Noddy out onto the floor. Romany was dumbfounded, but was soon approached by a tall, good looking redhead. 'Hi, I'm Barbie,' she said.

'Well Barbie, this is your lucky day,' replied Romany and swept the girl into his arms. About half an hour later, Ed came looking for Cathy to tell her it was time to get ready for her spot. He found her sitting in a corner with Noddy who was giving her last minute instructions.

'May I cut in?' he asked. 'It's nearly time for Cathy to get ready, but before that I'd like to give her a whirl around the floor.'

'Be my guest,' replied Noddy. 'I'll go and check out the Greek band.' Ed led Cathy to the dance floor. The Stones were on the turn table singing *Let's Spend the Night Together*.

'That's appropriate,' said Ed, and Cathy laughed, dancing to the music. Ed moved as he alone knew how to. When the record was over, she left the floor but was guided back by Ed 'You of all people should know that once of anything is not enough for me,' he said. The Troggs were on the turntable now singing *Love Is All Around*. 'Remember this?' asked Ed.

Cathy smiled, 'Yes, it was played at the Shelltones' last party night in 1968. I remember it well,' she said.

Ed held her very close. 'Oh babe, I'm nearly coming just holding you, I think we should slip off somewhere. The house is plenty big enough, or there's the garden.' He was nuzzling her neck now, and Faye looked on quite unconcerned.

'No, I've been paid to dance, and your fiancée is staring at us.'

'Let her, and anyone else, I don't care.'

'Well I do. I didn't come here to upset Faye, I came to work.'

'Okay, but don't lock your door tonight.'

The record over, Cathy made her way over to Faye. 'I've got to change,' she said, 'can you give me a hand? I have problems with zips and things.'

'Of course,' replied Faye, and together they went upstairs. She changed rapidly with Faye's help, who once more wittered on about her perfume, clothes, how much money Ed earned and what he was going to buy her. In short, when it was time to go downstairs, she was relieved as Faye's conversation had bored her. Having left Cathy upstairs, Faye went looking for Romany and found him at the bar. 'About the other day,' she purred.

'Forget it, I already have.'

'I wanted to apologise,' said Faye, leaning up against him.

'Don't bother, just remember not to play kid's games, I don't play with little girls.'

'Supposing the little girl grows up,' breathed Faye.

The Greek band struck up the music and Cathy glided onto the floor. Every male in the room was transfixed as she swayed to the music.

'All woman,' said Romany, 'oozing sex appeal from every pore; this act is strictly for the adults.'

Faye saw it too; she was even feeling aroused herself. She didn't feel Romany's arm snake around her waist and didn't hear him say, 'did you mean that about growing up?'

Cathy sank to her knees and began to gyrate as she lay on her back. Faye was now very aroused and wanted to screw badly. The crowd surged forward as Ed approached Cathy on the floor. Taking a ten pound note from his pocket he folded it and tucked it into the belt on her costume. He cleared a nearby table and lifted her up onto it. Then everyone wanted to be in on the act and Cathy had notes crammed into her belt and bra. Noddy made the whole audience roar with laughter when he demanded ten per cent.

Sara Beaumont looked for her daughter and was angry to see her with Romany. She needn't have worried though as Romany sauntered over to Cathy, lifted her down from the table and then began to imitate her movements. Noddy threw him a pair of finger cymbals. 'Try these on for size.'

'What am I supposed to do with these?' asked Romany.

Vic raised his glass, 'you don't want me to tell you, do you?'

Several people offered suggestions, all of which Romany declined to try.

Noddy took his shirt off. 'I'll show you how to dance,' he said. The whole episode ended with a pile up of bodies with the unfortunate Romany on the bottom.

Vic was delighted. 'Best cabaret I've seen for ages.'

Sara was horrified. 'How can you allow such goings on?' she chided Faye.

'I didn't know what was going to happen,' cried Faye, wishing that her irate mother would go home.

'Glad it did,' said Romany, en route for the bar. 'There was a bird that landed on me and she had enormous boobs.' Sara was furious. She hated these parties; you never knew what was going to happen. To her left she could see a couple openly taking coke. Faye ran upstairs to join Cathy who was still in the throes of changing. There was money everywhere; it lay partly on the bed and the rest on the floor. Cathy shook her costume and a few more notes landed on the floor.

Faye was like an excited little girl again. 'I loved your act,' she said, sitting on the bed. 'Do you want me to show you where you're sleeping now or shall we leave it till later?'

Cathy smiled and began to pick up the money, she felt very hot and sticky. 'You can leave it till later,' she said, 'but I would like to shower, it was hot out there and the pile up didn't help.'

'Great, shower's through there; Ed likes to shower as soon as he gets up in the morning so we had one put in here.' She indicated a room leading off the bedroom. 'See you later,' she added, 'you shouldn't be disturbed.' Then with a smile she was gone.

Downstairs, Ed was fuming. Faye's mother had had a right go at him. He was slightly stoned and had just taken a handful of something that he didn't recognise. Romany had told him it was good stuff so he'd taken it. Also, his manager had fallen into the swimming pool and had to be fished out because he couldn't swim, and to top it all he couldn't find Faye. He stormed upstairs in a furious temper. Still no sign, and in desperation he went into his bedroom and flopped down on his bed. He laid there for a few more seconds and then was aware of the shower running.

The dividing door was closed but he could definitely hear water. Getting to his feet he strode to the door and opened it yelling, 'Bitch, you must have heard me calling you,' but he stopped dead in his tracks when he viewed Cathy and not Faye behind the shower screen. His legs gave way and he sank to his knees crooning, 'Oh my angel, my very own angel.' He stepped into the shower; the water drenching him as it cascaded onto his clothing. Pressing his lips to Cathy's stomach he noted that her skin glistened, the water having given it a sheen. Ed traced a pattern on her skin with his tongue around her neck, breasts, stomach, hips, and pelvis before finally slipping his tongue inside her. He grasped her so hard that his fingernails dug into her flesh. She began to moan with pleasure and she begged him to take her as Ed tuned her up to a fine pitch. Cathy gave herself up to every sensation and was soon reaching out for her climax.

By now Ed was saturated and it suddenly hit him that he was fully clothed. With extreme difficulty he struggled with his zip; the satin suit was a tight one and his erection wasn't helping. The satin stuck to him like a second skin. Finally he was able to move the zip, but couldn't remove his trousers, so apart from getting his throbbing cock out he couldn't do much else. He guessed that he might need to be cut out of this outfit but realised that he'd reached the point of no return, so he lifted Cathy and straddled her around him. He was angry with himself for not removing his clothing earlier as the satin stuck to him like mad. He felt Cathy flinch as she wound herself around him and her legs felt the wet satin, it was so cold. Ed was relieved that he wasn't wearing underpants; the zip was bad enough but underpants would have been a catastrophe. Cathy was scared that someone would come in but clung to him as she rode along with the sensations. Ed felt as if his mind was about to blow and then suddenly he came with a terrific explosion. Seconds later Cathy pulled free and ran into the bedroom snatching a bath towel as she left the en suite.

Ed slumped to the floor under the shower; he was soaked to the skin but was quite content to let the water rain down on him. God he felt good. Cathy dried herself, dressed, and then went in search of Faye. Ed heard the door slam and smiled to himself; he felt out of this world.

Cathy was confused as there were so many doorways in the house. She had to find Faye as her hair was soaking wet and needed drying. This was some party; it was crazy and nothing seemed real to her.

Ed was obviously out of his head; someone had supplied him with drugs. His eyes looked strange and he was unsteady on his feet, not himself at all. She thought at one time that he was going to topple over in the shower.

Halfway down the stairs, Cathy ran into Sara Beaumont. 'Have you seen my daughter?' she asked, looking very flustered.

'No, I was looking for her myself.'

'Your hair is wet; don't say that you fell into the pool too.'

'No,' laughed Cathy. 'I've washed my hair and I don't know where Faye put my case.'

'Oh well, if that's your only problem I can help you. I have no idea where Faye is but I do know where she keeps her hairdryer.' They headed to the bedroom where Cathy had just fled from.

As they entered, Ed shouted above the noise of the shower, 'that you, babe? Come back for more, have you?'

Sara was very angry and began to rummage through the dressing table drawers.

'Depends on who you're calling to, you pig,' she replied.

Ed laughed out loud. 'Not you lady, I'm not that hard up.' He attempted to do his zip up and couldn't, so he did the button up and hoped that Sara wouldn't notice his gaping flies. He swayed all over the place. He hadn't a clue what Romany had given him but it certainly was good. He staggered to the adjoining door and stood framed in it. Sara noted everything, the wet suit and his condition, plus other extremities that she'd rather have missed.

'You really are disgusting, and you're partially exposed.'

'Thanks,' replied Ed, 'you're not so bad yourself.'

Sara looked from Cathy to her future son-in-law and felt sick. 'Do you usually take showers with your clothes on?'

'Depends on who's in here with me,' he replied.

Sara stood with her hands on her hips. 'Are you trying to tell me that Faye is in there with you?'

Ed swayed once more and nearly fell over. 'I haven't seen your lovely daughter since before the cabaret, and anyway, what are you doing in my room? Are you prying? I bet you're looking for some grass or coke.'

Sara glared at Ed who looked as if he would fall at any second. 'I'm looking for a hairdryer for Cathy; do you know where I can find one?'

'Yeah, your house. Why don't you go home and get it.'

'I suppose it's impossible to get anything out of you in your state,' sighed Sara. 'When you're not drugged up, you're incoherent, but like this you're no more than a zombie. Anyway my concern is to get Cathy's hair dry.'

Ed swayed even more, the room was spinning. 'Tell you what, I've got a better idea, she could come in the shower with me and get the rest of her wet.'

'You really are a disgusting animal, aren't you?' said Sara as she searched in the top of a nearby wardrobe. She found the elusive hair dryer and handed it to Cathy. She glared at Ed, who stared back at her with a silly grin on his face. 'For God's sake, dry yourself and put some other clothes on. You'll catch a cold, or worse still pneumonia.'

'Make a lot of people happy, including you,' replied Ed, swaying even more and crashing across the dressing table, scattering perfume, make-up and trinkets onto the floor. Disgusted, Sara tried to help him up but he swayed again and slumped onto the floor.

'Piss off,' he said, 'I want to talk to Cathy.'

Sara eyed Cathy with pity. 'I hope you know what you're doing, I'm going to find Faye. If this pig tries anything, knee him, that'll cool his ardour,' she said as she left the room. Ed was beginning to feel sick and dragged himself to the toilet. Once in there, he felt worse and vomited profusely, cuddling the toilet bowl. Cathy plugged the hairdryer into the wall socket and began to dry her hair. She felt no sympathy for Ed; she knew that no one twisted his arm to take drugs and that he did it because he wanted to. He struggled to his feet. He was feeling a bit better but still unsteady.

He flopped onto the bed. 'Silly old cow, she tells you to knee me and hasn't got the sense to realise that you were under the shower with me in the first place.'

'Not everyone's mind works the same way as yours,' said Cathy.

With her help, Ed got out of his wet clothes and dried his hair on a towel. He found another suit, and then crossed to Cathy who was brushing her hair. 'Cathy, babe, I feel terrific. Let's lock the door and make love for the rest of the night.'

'Don't be silly,' said Cathy, pushing him away as he started to nuzzle into her neck. 'We'd be missed, or at least you would.'

Ed tried again. 'Just once more,' he murmured, kissing her bare arm.

'No.'

'Why does everyone say no to me, especially my fiancée?'

'I've no desire to pry into your private life.'

Ed pushed her over onto her back and then lost his balance and fell to the floor. 'What have you taken?'

'Dunno, feels great though, come on down here.'

Cathy helped him up and back onto the bed. 'Where is Faye?' she asked, switching the hairdryer back on.

'Fuck Faye, cold bitch.'

'You're out of your head and you don't know what you're

saying. Now get that suit off of its hanger and onto your back,' sighed Cathy. The last thing she needed was Sara or Faye coming into the room and finding Ed starkers with her sitting on the bed drying her hair.

'I know everything that I'm saying, come to bed,' murmured Ed, kissing her neck.

'Vic will be wondering where you are; it's his birthday and you should put in an appearance for his sake.'

'Silly old bastard fell into my swimming pool.'

'Yes, but you are the host.'

'I don't want to go downstairs.'

'You owe it to Vic and the rest of your guests, now get that suit on.'

'On two conditions.'

Cathy put the hairdryer down after switching it off. 'With most people it would be one,' she said, picking up her hairbrush again.

'Yeah, but I'm greedy.'

'Tell me about it.'

'I'll go downstairs if you promise me that we'll get together later, and I'll make sure that no one finds out.'

Cathy put her hairbrush back into her bag. 'Okay, but you'd better make sure that nobody does find out.' She got to her feet adding, 'I'm going downstairs to find Faye, and I need to know where my case is and where I'm sleeping.'

'Darling, I said two conditions.'

Cathy turned back wondering what was next; he still hadn't got into his dry suit. 'So you did,' she said resignedly. 'Now will you get that bloody suit on.'

Ed staggered to the door and locked it, 'kneel,' he said. His mouth was dry as he waited for her to either refuse or comply with his wishes. Cathy's answer was a passionate kiss and then she slowly dropped to her knees.

'Is that all?' she said.

Ed looked down at the golden head and nodded. He felt her mouth make contact and sighed blissfully. 'Oh Cathy,' he murmured.

When she finally went downstairs, there was still no sign of Faye. She caught sight of Noddy telling a couple of young musicians the story of his life. Looking around the room she noticed that everyone seemed to be stoned or drunk. Many people were now openly snorting coke or smoking pot. Cathy felt like the odd one out. If you can't beat 'em, join 'em, she thought, taking a glass of champagne from a passing waiter. 'Can I have another one?' she asked.

'Lady, you can have the lot,' he replied, handing her the tray and staggering away, collapsing on a nearby sofa. She went over to Noddy with the tray deciding that she could endure the story of his life one more time.

Outside, Sara was still looking for her daughter, and by now she was very hot and bothered. Faye couldn't just disappear into thin air. She walked over to the parking area, delighted that every other car was a Rolls Royce, Bentley, Mercedes, or Lamborghini.

She detested Ed and his friends, but realised that Faye's liaison with him had raised her standard of living. Her daughter was so beautiful and so different from these party goers. Faye had class which was more than could be said for anyone else at this crazy gathering. She would never indulge in the perverted ways of the others, never degrade herself.

Suddenly she heard Faye's voice. 'Oh that's wonderful,' she gasped, 'do it again.'

Sara froze. She felt nauseous; the voice was coming from Romany's Mercedes. Why on earth had Ed brought Faye out here to have sex when the mansion had several comfortable bedrooms? And why in Romany's car? Had Ed completely flipped? He looked half-crazed when she'd seen him upstairs but the whole situation was ludicrous. It made it even more ridiculous to think that her daughter was playing along with it.

Disappointed with Faye's behaviour, Sara walked back into the house again. Noddy asked her if she'd like to dance but she declined his offer and looked around the room. She nearly fainted when she saw Ed and Cathy practically locked together on the dance floor. Her feeling of disgust turned to horror. If Cathy was dancing with Ed, then who was Faye out there with? She went outside again just in time to see Faye emerge from the car with Romany.

Numb with shock, she stepped back inside the house so they didn't see her. It couldn't be true; there had to be some mistake. She had to be seeing things. Seconds later, Romany walked past her and headed for the bar. A few minutes later, Faye arrived and received a slap from her mother around her face.

'You've shamed me,' cried Sara, 'you're no daughter of mine.'

'What do you mean?' retorted Faye, flushing crimson.

'You behaved like a little tramp, and with Ed's best friend too. Heaven help him from his worst.' She stormed out of the house with Faye in hot pursuit, pleading with her mother to stay and forgive her. From the bar, Romany gazed around the room. Faye had been one hell of a let down; he was anything but satisfied and tried to focus on something that might be more satisfying. His eye came to rest on the girl wrapped in Ed's embrace. He'd wanted to screw that one for a long time. He'd been thwarted years before and that was not going to happen tonight. Tonight he was going to have her; he didn't know how but it was going to happen. He drained his glass and felt in his pockets. He grinned. Cathy wasn't into drugs which meant that her body would react in a hell of a way.

He saw Sara return with Faye and point an accusing finger at Ed and Cathy, and knew that it was just a matter of time before they were split up. It wasn't long. He saw Cathy disentangle herself from Ed's grasp and Faye take her place. He watched as Cathy made her way into the garden, and then followed her at a distance. He stalked his quarry as she walked in the garden and sat down on a bench. Her head was ringing; it had been some night and she wondered what else was in store for her. She wasn't aware of Romany's presence until he sat down beside her and she caught a whiff of his aftershave. She recognised it as the same as Ed's.

'Great show,' said Romany.

'Thanks, I'm shattered and I've had too much to drink.' Romany's eyes glinted with lust. That made things easier for him. Alcohol didn't mix well with drugs, and what he had in his pocket would knock her for six. Cathy closed her eyes, she was so sleepy. He leaned over and kissed her neck. 'I told you before that we could make great music together. I can satisfy you better than Ed.'

'No,' cried Cathy, suddenly wide awake and aware of Romany's lewd intentions. 'I don't think so.'

'I do,' said Romany, nuzzling into her neck. Cathy attempted to rise but he pulled her back down again and made her face him. 'Don't fight it. I knew from the beginning that you and I had an understanding, and I can see by looking into your eyes that you've woken up to it too.' He forced his lips down on hers and shook with desire.

Cathy didn't know what had hit her. She broke free and ran back to the house. She was ashamed of herself. Romany stirred up feelings that she'd rather not own up to. Faye was inside arguing with her mother.

'I hate to cut in,' she said, 'but I have a raging headache. Can you show me to my room so that I can lie down for a while?'

'Of course,' replied Faye. 'Come with me.' Cathy followed Faye upstairs where she was shown her room. 'Your case is already in here; I should have brought you up earlier, sorry. This is a lovely room; it's got an en suite too if you need a shower.'

Cathy gazed around the room; it was very pink and girly. 'It's very nice,' she said, thinking about her drab bedroom at home.

'Thank you so much.' Faye walked over to the bed and pressed the switch on the bedside lamp. It flickered and then went out. 'Oh, the bulb's gone; I'll have to get you another one.'

'Don't worry, I'm better off in the dark at the minute; my head is throbbing.'

'You poor thing, I'll get you some painkillers, but I can't stay up here with you because mother's in such a state. I'll be back in a trice.' Faye left the room, and Cathy lay down and shut her eyes. She felt awful.

As Faye was on her way back with the pain killers, she ran into Romany. 'How's Cathy?' he asked. 'She said she wasn't feeling too good?'

At that moment, a terrific scream pierced the air. Sara Beaumont was in a full blown argument with Ed. 'I've never been so insulted,' she screeched. 'How dare you speak to me like that.'

Faye handed the pain killers and glass of water to a very happy Romany. 'It sounds like World War Three down there,' she said. 'Take these to Cathy, will you, Romany, and tell her that I'll fix the light bulb later.'

There was the sound of breaking glass, and a horrified Faye rushed downstairs. 'My pleasure,' Romany said to himself, smiling. This was brilliant and so simple. All he had to do was switch the pills. It was going to be a good night, and Faye would get the blame if Cathy reacted badly.

He tapped on the nearest door and heard Cathy's voice, 'Come in'. The room was in darkness so he switched the light on which was just behind the door.

'Special delivery from Faye,' he said. Cathy shielded her eyes from the light and accepted the pills and water from a grinning Romany, who was now perched on the edge of the bed. He'd switched the pills over prior to entering the room.

'Strange looking pain killers,' said Cathy.

Romany lit up a joint, 'well, little miss droopy drawers has to have the best. Ed's probably paid through the nose for them but they must be magical. You'll probably feel better in no time. I'm sorry about earlier; I was out of order but you can't blame me for trying. Drag on this; it'll help your pain too.' Cathy swallowed the pills and swigged the water down. She accepted the joint from Romany and took a drag from it. 'Faye's going to bring you up a light bulb later, but she's tied up at the minute; Ed and Sara are downstairs trading insults, and poor Faye's in the middle of it.'

'Nice girl,' said Cathy, handing the joint back. 'I think I'm going to have a shower and then try to sleep. You will switch the light off when you leave, won't you? It's killing my eyes.'

'Sure, babe, I've got a hot date waiting for me so I've got to go anyway, but hope you feel better soon.' He got up and left, switching the light off as he went. Cathy dragged herself from the bed and had a shower. It made her feel a little more refreshed and, after drying herself thoroughly, she went back to bed. She drifted into a near comatose state, but a while later was wide awake and rushing to the toilet. The contents of her stomach spewed up until there was nothing left and, feeling exhausted, she dragged herself back to bed, hoping sleep would come. It was impossible as she could still hear the music downstairs.

Everything was now muddled, and she kept seeing bright lights inside her head. Suddenly the music changed and she could hear Bob Dylan's voice floating up when the door opened. Cathy could only make out a figure as the light outside her door made the person a mere silhouette. She attempted to switch on the bedside light but couldn't, recalling that the bulb had blown. She closed her eyes again and felt as if she was dropping down into an abyss.

'Ed, is that you?' The only response she got was a series of whispered shushes. Cathy wondered if Faye was hovering nearby and so kept silent. The figure closed the door and locked it before approaching the bed. Cathy inhaled his aftershave as colours began flashing like a kaleidoscope, and then felt her neck being kissed. She shivered as her lover kissed her all over; she was floating and getting a delicious tingle. He progressed to her feet and began to suck each toe individually. This was a new thing but Cathy liked it, then she felt him get off the bed and kneel by the side of it; hooking her legs over his shoulders and giving her an exquisite helping of head. She was floating, lifting, feeling as if she was about to lift out of her earthly body. She was sobbing as she climaxed, never before had she reached such heights. Then she was being rolled over onto her belly and being given a massage. This was pure luxury; Ed was really going for it tonight. He then raised her to a kneeling position on all fours and took her doggy fashion. He felt enormous, and Cathy wondered if it was just the drugs that made him feel larger. She climaxed again, and then found herself being swivelled around until she was in a sixty-nine position. Her lover's head forced itself between her thighs and she took him in her mouth, wondering why she was nearly being choked.

He felt different as he stopped moving and pulled out of her mouth, rolling over onto his back and pulling her on top of him.

He bucked under her like a bronco and Cathy continued to ride him, as over and over again he took her over the edge of excitement and into ecstasy. He took her with fire and passion until her passion matched his own. Cathy's body was aching but she was unable to stop, it was like being on a roller coaster. He pulled out of her once more, giving her yet another helping of head. She didn't feel as if she could take another orgasm, but her partner wasn't giving up, and gradually her body accepted it. She tried to speak but words failed her as she received multiple orgasms. The colours in her head were now disintegrating into coloured shards. Was her lover never going to give up? She was feeling sore now, images were flashing across her vision. She tried to speak again but it all came out garbled as her lover now forced himself into her, gasping, 'I can really feel you pulling me now, come on, girl, come with me.'

Cathy was now getting a second wind, 'harder, harder!' she cried, clawing at his back. Ed's voice sounded three dimensional and quite unlike him at all. They were both caught up in a raging passion, and Cathy screamed 'more, more!' Another orgasm overtook her as he thrust away inside her. He was coming now, and Cathy was once more going with him. They reached a simultaneous orgasm together as he collapsed across her and lay still. They both said nothing until Cathy, who had just come back down to earth, said, 'I don't know what you were on but you were fantastic.' He didn't answer so Cathy held him to her. 'You were brilliant, you're the best, Ed.' The man in her arms began to laugh and kissed her full on her lips.

'I always was, and let's hope that this isn't an isolated incident. We created a symphony; I told you we could make great music together.' He got off the bed and walked over to the door. Switching on the light, he said, 'beautiful, baby, really beautiful. Boy, do you know how to suck a cock, and you move just like me too. Now that is what I call a union.'

He began to dress, and Cathy burst into tears. She was in shock, shamed, and feeling stupid. The worse thing was that, drugs or no drugs, she had enjoyed it and she'd betrayed Ed in the process.

'What happened to your hot date? I suppose you made that up,' she sobbed. Romany finished dressing and brushed himself down.

'No babe, that was you,' he laughed. He went back to her and kissed her cheek. 'Thanks, babe, best fuck I've had in ages. See you downstairs.' He left and blew her a kiss. Cathy rushed to the shower. She wanted to wash him off her. She showered, feeling very unsteady on her feet, and a short while later made her way back downstairs again. Everyone's voice seemed distorted.

'Good party,' said Noddy, creeping up behind her. On his arm he had a girl of no more than eighteen; he was having a ball. Cathy saw everything in sepia but, now and again, brilliant colours flashed across her vision. She couldn't believe what she'd done.

How could she be that stupid to let Romany fool her like that? There'd been no tenderness, no love, just pure dirty sex.

Something brushed past her legs, making her jump, and when she look looked down she saw a beautiful golden retriever looking up at her. She bent down and stroked it. It offered her its paw, and then another dog bounded over. Cathy made a fuss of both of them and then, noticing that the French doors were open, headed for the garden in an attempt to get some fresh air, trailed by the dogs. She felt a real mess and the fresh air gave little respite. The trees were moving now, and the water feature that was running clear water seemed to change into several luminous colours. She walked further into the garden and stopped by a pond of fabulous koi carp.

Faye passed by, walking past a small tent with a sign that read, 'Madame Karina'. Cathy sat on a bench beside the pond and, minutes later, Faye returned with Ed, who was protesting violently about having his fortune told. Angrily he walked towards the tent and went in. Faye approached Cathy, 'still not feeling right?'

Cathy put her head in her hands; Faye's voice seemed unusually loud as she was such a softly spoken individual. 'No,' she replied.

At that moment, Sara Beaumont came storming out of the house. 'Faye will you come back inside? People are leaving and as the hostess you should be here.' Faye got to her feet, groaning, telling Cathy that she'd catch up with her later.

Inside the tent, Ed surveyed the clairvoyant. She was a lady in her sixties with piercing blue eyes, a thin mouth, sallow skin, and a wiry frame; she was well known to most. 'Okay,' Ed grunted. 'I'll shut up and then you can tell me a few lies.'

Karina took a look at his palm. 'Great wealth,' she said.

Ed laughed. 'Everyone knows that.'

'You will marry and have a fine son and a daughter, but beware the dark man.'

'Sod the dark man.'

'The dark man desires everything that is yours; he brings misfortune of the blackest kind and you would do well to remove him from your circle.'

Ed was getting bored now. 'Sounds like a nasty chap.'

'Don't mock me, sir, you will achieve everything that your heart desires but misfortune will follow if the dark man remains.'

Ed sighed. 'This really is mumbo jumbo, isn't it?'

Karina's eyes blazed angrily. 'He will destroy you.'

Ed got to his feet. 'I know hundreds of dark men, and my fiancée will never give me children. You're talking in riddles.'

'You will have a fine son and daughter by someone else, and you will marry that person.'

Ed was ready to leave now. 'Look, I only did this to humour Faye. I read cards myself and so does my sister-in-law, and this has never been mentioned. If you're so good, tell me the name of my future wife.'

'Please sit down, and I'll consult the crystal ball.' She stared into the crystal and went deathly white. She looked up at Ed in horror. 'You are joined to her, I cannot continue.' Ed sat down and felt shock waves sweep over him. Karina was visibly shaking.

'Tell me,' yelled Ed, scared that this woman was no fake.

'I cannot, this is evil.'

Ed got to his feet and towered over the frightened woman. 'Tell me!' he screamed once more.

Karina took a deep breath. 'The goat, chanting, an orgy, the girl is lifeless and subject to many perverse practises. There is a knife, you are screaming for it all to stop, no I cannot carry on, this reading is over.' She slumped back in her chair, gazing up at Ed who still towered over her.

'Tell me my future wife's name, I didn't ask for the wittering of a crazy woman.'

Karina gave a deep sigh. 'She has three names. The one she was born with, one you gave her, and a stage name.' Ed sat back down again and waited as Karina said, after a lengthy pause. 'She was born Catherine, her stage name is Gypsy, and you gave her the name of Angel.'

Satisfied, Ed got to his feet again and threw fifty pounds at the clairvoyant before leaving. He was deflated; Karina had uncovered something which he'd hoped was dead and buried in 1968. He looked around the garden for Cathy. She'd been by the koi pond when he'd been en route to the clairvoyant, but she'd gone now. He could hear her laughing and hid behind the shed as she came into view. Cathy was running with the dogs, her headache had left her and she was experiencing the upper side of the drugs with a new found energy. She held her shoes in her hand as she ran barefoot in the grass. The laughter turned to a scream when Ed jumped out at her and seized her. Her heart was racing, for a moment she'd thought she was about to be murdered, what with so many strange people at the party. However, held in Ed's embrace she felt warm and safe.

They were interrupted by Romany coughing. 'Piss off, you inconsiderate bastard,' snapped Ed.

'Thanks, but I only came to warn you that Sara's heading this way,' replied Romany.

Suddenly Sara's voice pierced the air, but Ed paid no heed to it. He kissed Cathy with such passion that they both ended up on the grass. Sara came into view with Faye, 'Good heavens, have you two been fighting?' Sara spied Cathy and asked why she was also on the grass.

'Well actually, Cathy and I were having a bit of slap and tickle,' Romany lied. 'Until Ed fell over us, that is; clumsy sod.' He winked at Ed who could now breathe easily again. Faye was hurt, wondering why Romany would go with her and still feel the need to go after Cathy. She helped Ed up and, arm in arm, they strode back to the house. Cathy got to her feet and put her shoes back on. Sara stared from Romany to Cathy, and then turned on her heels and returned to the house, deciding to give her future son-in-law another ear bashing. Cathy headed in the same direction; she had no desire to be alone with Romany. Once inside the house, she went in search of Noddy. She looked everywhere but couldn't find him, so after about fifteen minutes of fruitless searching she gave up.

Suddenly, pandemonium broke out and everyone rushed to the swimming pool. Ed had been arguing with his mother-in-law-to-be and had tried to walk away from her but Sara, in her usual way, had refused to let him go and followed him to the pool area. The two dogs had rushed in, full of high spirits and knocked both Ed and Sara over. Ed had managed to save himself by grabbing a rail but Sara went flat on her back into the pool. Ed was in hysterics, 'I always knew those dogs would come in useful one day,' he laughed, almost in tears.

Faye screamed as her mother splashed out. 'You beast,' she screamed, pummelling her fists on Ed's chest. 'How could you do this to my mother?'

'I didn't touch her, the dogs did it; give 'em a bone each.'

Romany hurried in, followed by a crowd, and when he saw Sara in the pool, he leaned over, saying, 'why Sara, you're all wet.'

Sara reached over and grabbed his ankle, pulling him into the pool. 'I'll teach you,' she cried. Minutes later he heaved himself out, soaking wet.

'Old cow, my suit's ruined,' he snapped.

Faye openly began to laugh at him, but Romany removed the smile from her face by pushing her in too. 'Ed!' she screamed. Ed couldn't help; he was doubled up in laughter and then he jumped in himself. Cathy was dumbfounded as Sara's wig floated away. The dogs looked on barking and when their master called them they were only too glad to jump in for a swim. Ed noticed Sara's wig floating away from its anguished owner.

'Fetch,' he yelled, and the dogs obliged. Cathy had seen enough and returned to the lounge where she found Noddy in an armchair.

'I'm going to bed,' she said, 'I think the swimming pool incident is going to turn nasty.'

'Okay love,' he replied and dozed once more.

Once upstairs, Cathy fell into a deep sleep.

The next day, Cathy was very surprised to wake up in another room. This was a double bed and she'd fallen asleep in a single. She wondered if she was still dreaming as the room felt alien. She stared up at the ceiling and her reflection stared back at her. Wondering what was going on, she sat up, but was immediately pulled back down again. 'Morning babe,' yawned Ed.

'Where's Faye?'

'Gone home with mummy.'

'Why?'

'I upset her and her mother, she'll be back later.'

'When?'

'Dunno, tonight, tomorrow, next week, next month, who cares?'

'I do, she could walk in any second. How did I get here?'

'I waited until everyone had left and then carried you in here. God knows what you'd taken but you were right out of it.'

'I don't know. Faye went to get me some painkillers but it was Romany who actually put them into my hand. Faye had to go downstairs to separate you and Sara.'

'Faye could have got the pills mixed up, but then again Romany may have switched them. Either way the intention would have been to take the pain away. Neither one of them would harm you; I trust Romany with my life.' Recalling last night's events, Cathy realised just how evil Romany could be.

'Give me a cuddle,' said Ed, 'then I'll give you a massage.'

Soon enough the two became the two-headed monster once more as Ed gave Cathy his undivided attention. Fully satisfied, Ed headed for the shower and, once inside the en suite, he stepped back in amazement. 'Come here Cathy, look at the state of this,' he laughed. Cathy got out of bed and walked over to Ed. She gasped as she saw Romany sound asleep in the bath. Ed gave a wicked grin. 'Back to bed,' he ordered. Cathy dived back into bed and a few seconds later heard water running which was followed by a string of verbal abuse. Ed emerged from the en suite followed by a soaking wet Romany. He was very angry.

'Who told you that you could sleep in my bath?' laughed Ed.

'Came in here for my own safety, that old cow Beaumont was going to kill me; she came after me with a kitchen knife because of her wig, but it's okay, I told her that you'd buy her a new one.' He eyed the hump in the bed where Cathy had completely covered herself up and, as he left the room in a dry set of Ed's clothes, he said, 'I'm gonna fix a drink. Do you want one Cathy?' Cathy remained covered up but after he'd left the room, she surfaced.

Ed was convulsed with laughter. He'd forgotten Sara's wig and couldn't understand why Cathy didn't find it amusing.

She was concerned that Romany knew it was her in the bed. Staring at Ed who was now rolling around on the carpet with tears in his eyes, laughing hysterically, she said, 'is it that obvious?'

Ed laughed. 'Of course, even Vic helped. He drove Faye and her mother home.' Cathy gazed at Ed feeling very guilty and told him that she thought it was time she left. He sat on the bed and took her hand, kissing her fingertips. 'You've no reason to feel guilty, none of this was your doing and, secondly, I haven't paid you yet. Plus, before you leave, I intend to give you a conducted tour of my house and to delay you as long as possible.'

'My family will be getting worried.'

'All taken care of, Noddy agreed to ring Tony this morning and tell him that you wouldn't be home till later. And now that Romany's out of the bath, we can shower.' Cathy got out of bed, took his hand and he led her to the shower. As the water rained down upon them, she voiced her feelings that Faye seemed such a lovely person and she still felt guilty. 'She's twenty five with the maturity of a ten-year-old, and she's a spoilt brat. Only fine when she gets her own way, so forget her. I already have.' Cathy nodded and continued to soap herself. She needed to wash herself clean after the sex in the shower when Ed was stoned, the sex with Romany, and then the session that she'd had with Ed this morning. She felt like a walking sperm bank.

Downstairs, Noddy was tucking into eggs, bacon, sausages, and bread rolls. Romany sat in the corner of the room with a glass of vodka. 'Don't you do anything else?' asked Ed.

Romany muttered something under his breath and leered at Cathy. 'I hear you own horses, Ed,' remarked Noddy.

'Two. Dunno why I bother really, never seem to get the time. I might today though, if Cathy will join me.'

A young Irish girl of about seventeen entered the room and asked if Ed or Cathy wanted breakfast. 'Doubt it,' said Romany, 'they've already had their afters; still, I wouldn't mind having you for my breakfast.' The girl flushed crimson. She was a very pretty, slim blonde and had only been in service for three weeks.

'Leave her alone,' barked Ed. 'No wonder I have to keep hiring new staff with you around.' He turned to Cathy and asked her if she wanted anything. She replied that she would love scrambled egg on toast and a coffee, and Ed told the girl that he would have the same. The girl left and returned a short while later with their breakfast.

Noddy sat back and patted his stomach. 'Eat and grow fat,' he laughed. He was having a great time. Ed surveyed the contented old man.

'Tell you what, I'll get a horse saddled for you; that'll burn off some calories.'

Noddy pushed his plate away and glanced at his watch. 'Thanks Ed, but I'd probably fall off. Plus, time is marching on.'

'Okay, I'll get my chauffeur to drive you home in the Rolls.'

Noddy beamed. 'Can't wait to see everyone's faces when I arrive home in a Rolls Royce, thanks.'

'Any time,' said Ed, shaking his hand.

Romany was about to pour himself another drink when Ed removed the glass from his hand. 'You can go too.'

'Why?' retorted Romany, 'I've nothing to do at home.'

Ed helped him to his feet. 'See you later, pal.'

'Nice to know you're wanted,' Romany protested and left, reluctantly.

Ed's chauffeur was summoned, and soon Noddy was on board the white Rolls Royce. He beckoned Cathy over. 'Don't be a fool all of your life, love. You're right in there, if only you realised it.'

'Maybe one day,' Cathy sighed, not wanting to disclose the plans that she'd made with Ed at Bacton. Noddy kissed her as the chauffeur started up the car, and the old man waved as they drove away. Ed swept Cathy into his arms while Mrs Shores looked on disapprovingly. She clicked her tongue as Cathy passed her. Her mistress was away and she didn't like what was happening before her eyes. Ed was in his element; he'd dreamed of this day for ages.

'I've got a housekeeper, chauffeur, cook, gardener, two domestics, and you can move in as soon as you want.'

'It's a dream,' said Cathy, as Ed gave her a full tour of the mansion. 'Faye's very lucky.'

'Forget her for five minutes. Come on, we're going riding.'

They headed for the stables and saddled up the two horses. After a very enjoyable ride they made their way back to the house. 'I enjoyed that,' said Cathy. 'I haven't been on a horse for over three years.' Her face was flushed with happiness.

Ed looked longingly at her. He knew that there was little time together now and he'd have to let her go. 'Come on, upstairs, I guess you're getting bored with me now.'

Cathy was horrified. 'How can you say that? Don't spoil things.'

'Okay, let's pay you your money. Everyone loved your dancing, and Vic said it was the best present he'd ever had.'

Cathy followed him into his bedroom and when he locked the door from the inside she felt afraid. His countenance had changed and he seemed very morose. 'Why did you lock the door?'

'Keep the servants out,' he muttered, putting the key in his pocket. He crossed to the dressing table and took out an envelope. 'One hundred pounds,' he said, and handed it to her. Then he took her in his arms and cursed as the phone rang. They sat on the bed and Ed lifted the receiver, caressing Cathy's breast with his free hand. The voice on the other end of the line was distraught. 'Don't cry to me, lady, you were the one that walked out,' he snarled. Cathy pulled away but was hauled back sharply by an Ed that she didn't recognise. His face was convulsed with fury as he listened to the sobbing voice. 'What do you mean, you want to come back. I don't care if you never come back.'

Cathy felt a stab of pain inside her. There for the grace of God go I, she thought, and visibly flinched. She pulled away again and Ed slammed the receiver down. Cathy got to her feet. 'I'm leaving. Faye's coming home and I don't want to hurt her.'

She was scared and shrank back towards the door as Ed moved towards her with an evil expression. 'By that time, we'll be tucked up in bed together to greet her. She's been your understudy for years and you know it.'

Cathy swallowed hard. 'You can't do that, it's cruel.'

Ed advanced and pressed her against the door. 'This is your home and I'm not letting you leave, not ever, I can't. When Faye arrives, she'll make headlines of it; she loves publicity, and Tony won't want you back. I'll see to that.'

Cathy was filled with terror as he steered her back towards the bed. 'You don't know what you're saying,' she cried. 'What about the plans we made?' He threw her across the bed and tugged at her clothing.

'You belong to me,' he shouted, forcing her to a submissive position.

'You're hurting me!'

'Hurting you?' laughed Ed. 'What about you leaving me all those years ago? That was a hurt that I had to learn to live with.'

Cathy lay still. 'Okay, at this minute we'll play it your way, but if I lose my children over this, I'll never see you again. This behaviour is not binding me to you.' Ed tore at her underwear and she felt him enter her roughly. Cathy clenched her teeth and when he collapsed across her, pushed him away and headed for the bathroom. She felt sore, bruised, and dirty. After a good wash, she began to gather her things.

Ed was on the bed looking very guilty. 'I'm sorry, really sorry, but don't you realise that I need you with me all the time?' He stood up and put his arms around her. 'I love you so much. I'll make it up to you.'

Cathy gave him an icy stare and pushed him away. 'Love!' she cried. 'What the hell do you know about love? Years ago you did, but now all you know is lust. I'll tell you what love is, Mr Big Shot; love is innocence, the kind of innocence that I share with my kids who, incidentally, I've only seen for about twelve hours recently owing to two weeks up North and Vic's party. You even want to deny me that.'

'But Cathy, I'm sick when you're not with me.'

'Snap,' shouted Cathy, 'and I don't know why. I was ill part of last week, didn't feel one hundred per cent last night but I'd promised you that I'd attend Vic's party and I kept my word; shame you can't keep yours. I thought that we'd planned our future but I was wrong, you lied to me.'

'But Cathy, we belong together.'

'Really? At least you always run to form; every time we get together I'm trapped. You trapped me in a field in Wales because I had no idea where I was and had no way of getting back to the club, you trapped me after the dance contest in the hotel and you're doing it again now as you've locked me in. You manipulate people, Ed. The difference is that this time you're wrong about Tony. Whatever you told him wouldn't make any difference. He doesn't love me but he needs me to keep the money coming in, so this is one time that you've lost. You can't keep me here for ever, and I'll run as soon as I get the opportunity. Love, you know nothing of any more. As I said before, love is two little sticky hands grasping your own. A sweet smile as my proud daughter hands me something that she's spent all day making, or if Steven falls over and hurts himself he'll run to me as if I'm the only one that can make him better in the whole world. Michael needs me to comfort him, help him through life, trusts me and his father and loves us both because we are ourselves. That's love, Ed, and I thought that's what you and I had and were striving for in a couple of years.

'Obviously I was wrong. Love doesn't exist in your plastic world; it only has room for plastic people. You and Faye have a wonderful arrangement. You tell her that you love her and buy her just about everything that you can in exchange for her body. She trades in and bleeds as much as she can out of you. You must really love her if you want to move me in before she gets home; some homecoming! You don't understand love at all.'

She walked over to the window and gazed out across the spacious grounds. There was silence until Cathy heard sobbing coming from Ed's direction. She turned and saw him face down on the bed and crying his eyes out. It was unbelievable. Here was the idol of millions crying just because she'd given him a few home truths. She clenched her fists hard and closed her eyes, not knowing what to do. A few seconds later she discovered that her palms were wet. Investigation proved that she'd dug her nails into her flesh without realising it. Blood trickled from the wounds, and Cathy stood there helpless. It seemed that every time they got together, one of them upset the other.

She walked to the door, forgetting that Ed had locked it and, after trying the door, felt extremely dumb. As calmly as she could, she said, 'Ed, please unlock the door, I've got to go. I won't come back again, it's pointless. Every time we meet, one of us gets cut up. You can forget me; you've got Faye and if you're tired of her, there are dozens of others ready to fill her shoes.'

Cathy wasn't prepared for what happened next. Ed stopped crying and stared at her wild-eyed. 'No!' he cried, over and over again.

'Ed, I want to leave, give me the key please.'

Ed got to his feet and, with a half-crazed look, cried, 'you can't leave me. Name your price; you can have anything.'

Shaking, and with fear in a voice that threatened to let her down any minute, Cathy said 'Ed, the key please.'

Suddenly Ed threw himself at her, as if giving a rugby tackle, and knocked her against the door. 'Don't leave me, you can't, I won't let you.' He was grovelling at her feet. 'You're right about my plastic world; I lost the ability to love when you left. I punished every woman that I met because of you. I tried to trace you and failed, so I turned to booze and drugs to try to forget but I still couldn't. I still love you, Cathy, and nothing's going to change that. You've brought me back to life by coming back into my circle. I still want to marry you and I couldn't take it if you leave. I might as well be dead, I need you.'

Cathy stroked the top of his head, feeling only pity now. 'But we have to wait until we're free of contracts and other distractions, and my children need me more,' she said.

'But you can all come and live with me.'

'I know, but I've no intention of removing them from their father until we're out of this plastic, materialistic world of yours. I don't want their minds scrambled.'

Ed got to his feet, saying contritely, 'I keep forgetting you're so close. It must be great. I wouldn't know but I wish I did.' He kissed her on her cheek. 'This party wouldn't have been the same without you.' He spread his arms wide and crossed to the window. 'All this and it means nothing: the mansion, the life, the girls, Faye. Nothing. Cathy stared at the floor, listening to Ed who still rambled on about them both continuing to spend Saturday nights at Vic's, and Cathy's summer season, delighting in the fact that she would be staying with his brother so he could turn up at any time. He went on, promising her that there would be no more scenes like this one. 'I've never had to share a woman before, but in your case I guess I'll have to make an exception.' Cathy sighed with relief; it seemed as if their plans were back on again. Two years seemed a long time, but she guessed that Vic would let them meet up a little bit more if asked. She loved Ed, but they were caught up in a trap of their own making and would have to wait. Ed walked over to the bed and motioned Cathy over. She sat down beside him. He kissed her and the phone rang again. Ed picked up the receiver. Faye was sobbing again. He listened and said, 'we've been through all of this; if you come home, something else will go wrong, won't it?'

Cathy lay back; she had no desire to listen to his conversation and couldn't leave as the door was still locked. Sensing this, Ed leaned over and pressed a switch and a tape began to play. It was Dylan, and Cathy closed her eyes letting the music sweep over her. Ed tried to reason with Faye and focus on Cathy at the same time. A rush of desire hit him; he wanted this call over as soon as possible. 'So you want to come back?'

'I'll do anything if you let me come home,' replied Faye. Ed stared at Cathy, he wanted to come too, but in a different sense to the way that Faye meant.

'I think we should split,' Ed told her. There was more sobbing, and then Ed added, 'but maybe we could give it one last attempt.' Cathy's eyes snapped open and she nodded her approval. 'Okay.' He grinned at Cathy. He rested his hand upon her thigh and she smiled at him. Damn, he thought; he could refuse this golden-haired lady nothing. His hand travelled higher and he noted the flush appear on Cathy's face. He listened to Faye and the music. It had changed to Hendrix now, and Faye was muttering all kinds of endearments. He was muttering several back, but not to her. Cathy was moving now. The track was *Angel*, and Ed wanted to plunge into his sweet angel now, but still Faye poured her heart out to him.

'I love you,' she sighed. Ed beheld the glassy-eyed lady beside him.

'I love you, Angel,' he murmured. Cathy could feel herself approaching orgasm and pushed his hand away. Hendrix was singing about being taken over yonder and that's where Ed wanted to go.

He unzipped himself as Faye cried, 'I really miss you, and I'll be back tonight.'

'I'll send the car,' said Ed as he slid into Cathy's welcoming body.

'I really do want to come,' replied Faye.

'Yes darling, I know,' murmured Ed, replacing the receiver and moving with the body beneath him. 'So do I, and so does Cathy.' He shook and shuddered; this Angel was taking him over yonder.

Before Cathy left, she agreed to meet him on Saturday at Vic's. Shortly after, Ed played the tape again. He closed his eyes and began to get all kinds of visions. A white, floaty angel danced around him while he sang. A plan was hatching; one which he would voice to Vic and Noddy when the time was right. 'Cathy, babe, we are going on tour together 'cause if you don't go, then I won't either.' He knew that between Vic and Noddy, big things could happen. He recalled 1968 when she'd gone on stage to help him when he was being heckled. It worked then and it would work again. Forget *Green Tambourine*, he was now going to help her, and Angel would be big; he knew it. He'd cracked it; they would be in each other's company day and night. Laughing, he headed for the shower; the ice maiden would be home soon, so he had to get ready.

Chapter Eleven

May 1973

Vic wasn't happy; he'd known nothing of Cathy's summer season, and realised that the mirror would be inactive for five months. He'd got used to Ed and her performing for him most Saturday nights, and was well miffed. To make matters worse, Ed had told him that she was staying with his brother, so he would be visiting her down there when he wasn't working. He became very moody, and when Ed enquired about his bad temper he realised that he could hardly tell him. Still, he had this tour for the band to organise that kicked off in June. The rules still were in force; no wives or girlfriends which caused a few more domestic arguments.

Ed scanned the list of dates; Birmingham, Bristol, Brighton, Cambridge, Ipswich, Norwich, Nottingham, Cardiff, Oxford, Southend-on-Sea, and two final concerts in London. He hated touring, but as Cathy was going to be in Norfolk for quite a long time it pleased him to know that, although he wouldn't see her as much as he'd like to, Tony wouldn't be seeing her either. She had told him that she was taking Sandy to the caravan in August and he knew that the tour would be well and truly over by then. He looked forward to meeting the child as he hoped to be her stepfather in the future.

Vic had also annoyed the band by changing their name to the Z Tones instead of Shelltones, insisting that the name was far too 'sixties'. He was changing their image too; they were more and more glammed up. They were in glittery outfits and sequins like all the other bands out there. They drew the line at tights though. Vic wanted them all in tights, white shiny ones, but they agreed to do it on one condition, Vic had to wear them too. The idea was shelved very quickly and Vic decided to get them to wear extra make-up instead.

Cathy was a very happy lady; she loved Norfolk and was seriously considering moving up there when she'd finished the season. She was talked out of it by a fellow artiste who lived there, telling her that Caister-on-Sea may look lovely now, but that she should see it in the winter when it would be very cold and very quiet. The first week she spent at a guest house in Great Yarmouth as she needed to get her bearings and meet fellow artistes, managers, compères and other people connected with the entertainment scene. She loved Great Yarmouth; it was a lively place. The sand was beautiful to walk on, the shops were great, the market fantastic, and the people friendly. She was fascinated by the rock shop; you could see it being made there.

At the end of the first week she returned to Essex, laden with gifts for the children, and spent a very happy day with them. The following day she was on her way back to Yarmouth and was met by Rusty at the railway station. They headed for the Seashore Holiday Village where they had a bite to eat and then Cathy went through her routine.

She was surprised to find that Billy and Paddy comprised the backing band alongside a keyboard player called Danny and a vocalist called Paul. They greeted her warmly and were pleased to know that she was a regular act there once a week. Billy recalled the *Green Tambourine* incident, remarking that Cathy had been a life-saver that night. He was less happy with Ed though and voiced the strong opinions of the band.

'All those years helping him and taking him on when it wasn't even him we wanted. He pleaded with us to give him a chance, and then he just gets up and goes, leaving us to get on with it,' said Paddy. 'I don't want to see him again. I'm glad you left him; it really cut him up. He even tried to kill himself at one point. Shame he didn't succeed.'

Billy agreed and then congratulated Cathy on her performance in the dance contest. 'We knew you'd win, and we loved watching Ed pretending that he didn't know you. It was great.' Cathy made a mental note to keep Ed away from the Seashore.

Back at Bacton, Fawn had laid on quite the spread for everyone. After consuming it, plus a bottle of wine or two, Cathy made her way to Sky's caravan, promising the girls that she would go to school with them the following day. Fawn had cleaned the caravan and put fresh new sheets on Cathy's bed. She went to sleep inhaling the delicate scent of the washing powder.

Ed arrived for two consecutive weekends and then started his tour at the beginning of June. He managed to creep into the caravan when he was performing in Norwich and Ipswich. It was very late on both occasions but Cathy knew he was coming and had stayed up into the early hours. He made two further appearances when the band were at Cambridge and the final London gig, then, as the tour was over, stayed for a further week. He didn't attend many of Cathy's bookings, realising that if he got recognised it could cause hassle, so he stayed behind with Fawn and let Rusty continue to ferry her back and forth.

Whenever he arrived, he was very uptight and very aggressive with his love-making, but when he stayed for the whole week he reverted to Ed the happy hippy again, playing with his nieces and enjoying the local pub and days out. It was evident that the life as a superstar was no good at all, and the open road was his salvation. He worshiped Cathy with a love that was so intense even Rusty was astounded. They seemed even more in love than before. Rusty was happy, and he so wanted his brother to be happy too. He knew that Cathy was the answer.

The weeks turned into months, and Cathy felt as if she was on holiday every day. It was fantastic; she was gelling with Fawn and her family who showed her how to read the tarot cards. She also had Ed putting in unexpected appearances all the time.

Sandy arrived in August. Tony had wanted her to stay for a month instead of a week, and Cathy said that if Sandy wanted to stay for a month she could, but if she didn't then she would return home after a week. She said that she would call him at the end of the week to let him know what was happening, and then she left with a very excited little girl. To Sandy this was a great adventure. She made friends with Amber and Amethyst, and they played, danced, and painted the scenery on three little easels that belonged to Sky.

They also went to the pleasure beach in Great Yarmouth and went for a ride in a horse-drawn carriage. The adults stood to one side as the girls went on all the rides but found themselves being badgered into the Merry-Go-Round. Sandy whispered to Cathy as they spun on the carousel that she didn't ever want to go home. Rusty went onto the rifle range and won a teddy which he gave to Sandy. The girls eyed up the water chute, but as they'd just eaten candyfloss and beef burgers, Fawn decided that it was definitely off limits. There was no sign of Ed yet; he was giving Sandy time to settle in.

He did arrive midweek, after a fierce argument with Vic who wanted him to do a charity event. He replied that charity begins at home and that's where he was headed to see Cathy and his future step daughter. Vic was angry and said that he couldn't just make up his own rules, but he replied that he had for most of his life so he wasn't going to change now. Vic fumed but knew that it was pointless to argue. 'When will you be back?'

'Dunno, when do you want me?'

'Now! For the charity event.'

'Tough, you've got the phone number where you can contact me, now I'm off to meet Sandy. Bye Vic,' and with that he was gone. Vic swore out loud, Ed's constant bad behaviour unsettled the band. They were fed up with him disappearing just to suit himself. They wanted Mick back and hoped that he would recover fully soon.

Arriving at Bacton, Ed was greeted by his nieces who hugged him in excitement. They adored their uncle and fussed over him, kissing him as Sandy hung back. It was one thing to hear about Uncle Eden but quite another to see him in the flesh. Ed gazed at the child; she was a perfect miniature of her mother. So this was the child that Cathy had left him for; she was very blonde, very pretty with the same full bottom lip that her mother had. She was dainty, and turned to her mother, waiting for her to tell her what to do. Amber and Amethyst were clinging to Ed as Sandy took small steps towards him. She'd seen him on the television and the instinct was to hug him, but she wasn't sure if that was the right thing to do. After all, even though she was only eight, her friends had fantasised over him. Amber was now taking her hand and Ed bent down to bring himself to her level.

'Hallo Sandy, do I get a hug?' She nodded and suddenly threw herself at him, knocking him over. They both ended up on the grass with Sandy on top of him and everyone else in hysterics. Cathy hurried over and helped her daughter to her feet as Ed laughed. 'That's a fantastic greeting. I wish your mamma had done that when I first met her.'

Sandy giggled; she found the whole thing funny. 'Are you staying with us for a while?' asked Amber, 'Daddy told us that you would take us to the Pleasure beach and go on the rides with us.'

Fawn smiled. 'Actually it was my idea, and Rusty just went along with it.'

'As I always do,' said Rusty. 'Come on, let's eat.'

'I can probably stay for a while. Vic knows where I am and I gave him your neighbour's phone number, so if I'm needed urgently he can reach me,' Ed informed them.

'What about Faye?' asked Rusty. 'Won't she be worried?'

'No, she knows where I am and as you know, she's neither hippy nor caravan friendly.'

'She's a snob,' said Amber, 'she called us dirty gypsies.'

'Where will you sleep?' asked Sandy.

Everyone held their breath until Fawn said, 'with you and your mother.'

Sandy wandered over to Ed. 'You can have my bed and I can bunk in with Amber; her bed's bigger than mine. Then you'll have a bed to yourself, or you could share Mummy's bed if she doesn't mind.'

'Sandy,' cried Cathy, feeling very embarrassed.

'When Daddy's friends stay, they share his bed,' replied Sandy, 'and anyway I only slept in the other caravan because I didn't want you to be lonely. I want to sleep in Amber's room.'

'That's settled then,' said Rusty, 'to everyone's satisfaction, I should imagine.'

Ed grinned. This was going to be a good vacation and the child was something else.

It wasn't surprising that Sandy decided to stay for the month. She had everything she could possibly want; her mother, her new friends, the beach, and she was learning new skills every day.

A bond was also developing with Ed and she got upset when he had to return to London to work, but he always came back, usually with gifts for everyone. They got to see a few of Cathy's shows, and Amethyst got to see Peters and Lee, getting a signed photograph when at Pontins, and they saw several children's entertainers too. For Sandy, this was much better than sitting at home with the television on night and day. Her artwork was coming on in leaps and bounds and her paper flowers rivalled the girls. She'd learnt to embroider, make a corn dolly and even shown an interest in the tarot cards.

Ed had taken them all to the Pleasure beach but had dressed in some of Rusty's clothes, and wore a floppy hat. He didn't get recognised once, and was delighted. The rest of the entourage dressed as hippies and so they were ignored too. The public viewed them as villagers on a day outing, who dressed a bit odd.

A month later and Sandy had to return home because of school. She was heartbroken but was told that she could visit again during the next school holiday if Cathy wasn't working. Cathy knew she had a pantomime coming up but kept quiet as she could see her daughter was upset enough. On the train home, Sandy repeatedly looked at her photographs. She'd had several taken with Ed, a couple with Ed, her mother and herself, and many taken of the whole group. At least she had those to look at when she got home.

Cathy's summer season came to a close mid-October, and she found herself giving a tearful goodbye to her new family. She'd been so happy. Ed had consoled her, telling her that it would only be another eighteen months and then they could go back for good if she wanted. He knew Sandy would, given the choice. Cathy's reign as the winner of the dance contest would be over in March, so if they went public after that it wouldn't matter.

By 1975, Ed figured that Cathy would be divorced with custody of Sandy, and he would be out of the band. He wasn't going to say anything yet to Vic, in case he got angry and took Cathy's title away. He was still doing very well in commercials work, guest appearances, modelling, and other entertainments. He hated waiting though, and now just tolerated Faye but had to wait before he could give her the elbow. They were rowing constantly about his absences and sexual demands.

Cathy began the pantomime in late November. This was something new for her and it was completely different. It was a nice experience, especially the children's reaction to the show. The production was Aladdin, and she danced several times during the show. She tried to get Tony to bring the children to see her but he said it was too far away. Sandy was not really interested; she'd hoped to go to the caravan for Christmas, and Cathy's pantomime had got in the way. She cheered up a bit and began writing out Christmas cards when her mother told her that she would take her there at Easter when the weather would be nicer, and she would instruct Noddy to keep her work-free for two weeks.

Christmas was well on the way, and Ed knew that he would have to endure Christmas day at his future mother-in-laws. He'd decided that it was the better option, as he could make an excuse and leave if he got fed-up, not like the previous year when she had visited him and stayed all day and Boxing Day as well. That was not going to happen again.

He wanted to wake up with Cathy on Christmas day and spoke to Vic about it. Vic said to bring her to his place after she'd finished the show on Christmas Eve so that she could pick up her presents and, as there was no pantomime on Christmas day, she could stay over and be driven home the following day. That way she had Ed on Christmas Eve and her children the following day. Cathy was uncertain; she reminded Ed that she had to cook the dinner so couldn't afford to get back late.

'Neither can I,' said Ed, 'Faye's gonna wake up on her own and I've got to go to Sara Beaumont's house for Christmas dinner. We've both got to rush but it'll be worth it just to wake up beside you on Christmas day.' Cathy agreed; there was nothing better in her eyes, so she was happy with the situation.

Vic picked her up at the theatre on Christmas Eve, and together they headed for his house. He'd put up a huge Christmas tree, and Al Simpkins was trying to get the fairy lights to work. He was having no success and decided to leave when Ed put in an appearance. He'd told Faye that he was going out with the boys for a Christmas drink and might be out all night, insisting that he wouldn't drive home if he'd had too much to drink. She seemed satisfied. She was happy dreaming of her Christmas presents and a sex-free night. Ed had a huge sack with him, and Cathy guessed that it was full of gifts. 'That looks heavy.'

'Call me Santa Claus. This is for you and your family, and I've even splashed out on a bottle of brandy for your old man.'

Cathy was flabbergasted; he was buying for her family now. He seated himself on the sofa, and Cathy settled herself beside him. Vic had the coffee table loaded with nibbles and chocolates. He poured some drinks for his guests and then handed her a small wrapped box.

'Oh Vic,' cried Cathy, 'I haven't got you anything.'

Vic grinned; he'd get his present later behind his mirror. Cathy got to her feet and hugged him. His blood pressure soared. She was turning him on even though it was just a friendly hug.

Ed caught on though. 'Hey come back, you're making me jealous.' Cathy laughed and rejoined him on the sofa.

Several drinks later they were all merry and headed for bed, with Vic in his usual position. The couple sucked, licked, and entwined in their usual fashion, totally absorbed in each other. The clock struck midnight. 'Merry Christmas, Angel,' said Ed, 'I love you.'

'Merry Christmas, Ed, I love you too.'

'Merry Christmas,' muttered Vic to himself and gazed through the mirror, waiting for the couple to continue. He didn't have to wait long and was enthralled with the scene before him which continued until five thirty in the morning. Ed and Cathy slept for about two hours. They'd both got what they'd wanted, and they were able to wake up on Christmas morning, together and happy.

Ed made love to her even though she was half asleep, and then after a shower they went downstairs for breakfast. Breakfast over, Ed drove Cathy home and dropped her on the corner of her road. He'd wanted to take her to the front door but Cathy didn't want the neighbours to see, so they agreed to meet up again a week later at Vic's and, after a loving kiss, Ed drove off and she staggered around the corner with the huge sack.

Ed drove away feeling empty; he didn't want to leave her. Once a week wasn't enough, he wanted more. He was going to go flat hunting next week with Vic on the pretence of needing a residence in London for him and Faye. He'd tell Vic the truth once he'd found something and clinched a deal. Christmas had started beautifully but now he had to face Sara Beaumont and his lovely fiancée.

Cathy let herself in to her home and set to putting the chicken in the oven. Tony was stretched out in front of the television; his appearance gave the impression of someone who'd been up all night. Cathy guessed that he just hadn't bothered to get undressed before going to bed. He nodded to her and told her to put the kettle on. Sandy was upstairs listening to music and hurried downstairs when she heard her mother arrive. Tony eyed the huge sack in the hall. 'Suppose that's from lover boy,' he grunted.

'Does it matter?' replied Cathy.

Tony headed for the sack, grinning. 'No, if he's stupid enough to spend money on us, that's up to him. Saves me spending my money. Let's open the presents; there might be something in there worth flogging.'

'Where are the boys?' Cathy enquired.

'In bed. Hey, look at this, my name's on this one.' Cathy ascended the stairs. Michael was rattling the bars in his cot, and Steven still slumbered. She carried Michael downstairs and sat him in his high chair while she and a very excited Sandy took out all of the presents and stacked them under the tree. Tony had found not only a bottle of brandy, but a bottle of vodka too; he was well pleased.

'You know, you should hang on to this Ed bloke; he seems very generous. Stick with him and bleed the bastard dry.' Sandy was buzzing around like a mother hen. She wanted to help with the dinner so Cathy found the potato peeler and handed it to the little girl. Sandy happily started peeling potatoes and singing to herself. About midday the phone rang. It was Amber who wished Cathy a Merry Christmas and then asked to speak to Sandy. Sandy rushed to the phone and chattered away happily, making plans for Easter. Cathy went upstairs and ran the bath. She'd changed Michael earlier but he smelt as if he needed a bath.

Steven by now was up and jumping all over his father shouting 'Merry Christmas!' at the top of his voice.

'Bloody kids,' shouted Tony. 'Get him off me.'

'Can't. Michael needs a bath.'

At three o'clock, the family sat around the table to eat their Christmas dinner.

In Surrey, Ed was doing the same, accompanied by all of Faye's relatives. Sara Beaumont had put on a magnificent spread, but it meant nothing to Ed who wished he was in Essex sitting with Cathy and the kids. He hadn't met the other two yet but he was working on it. Once he had the flat, things would start moving. Faye was offering Ed a cracker, and he pulled it with her, getting the lion's share.

'You won,' laughed Faye.

'I always do,' replied Ed, making Faye uneasy.

After finishing their dinner back in Essex, everyone opened their presents. Tony had already got his, but he was looking at everyone else's in case he could sell it. Sandy opened hers; she had new clothes, records, books, and many other small items. When she opened the presents from Ed she was thrilled. He'd got her an easel, canvases and oil paints, plus water colours and many different brushes. In another parcel was a watch which she put straight onto her wrist. However, it was the final box that really delighted her; a gold charm bracelet with about four charms on it. Tony eyed this with great interest. 'That's real gold,' he said examining the hallmark. 'That'll be worth a few bob.'

'I love it,' cried Sandy. 'It's the best present I've ever had, and I can paint again.' She was a very happy little girl. Ed had bought Michael a huge teddy bear; it was bigger than him and his eyes opened wide as he laughed hugging it. Steven had a train set; he could spend many hours annoying his father with that, and he also had a children's game.

'Puts my gifts in the shade,' said Cathy.

'Yeah well, that's what moneyed people do,' replied Tony. 'They try to buy people's company. Never worked with me though. Tell you what; let's open that hamper that was in the sack.'

'Did you like my presents?' asked Sandy, still gazing at her bracelet.

'They were lovely,' replied Cathy. Tony said nothing; he'd eaten the box of chocolates from Sandy that morning in front of the television. He had his eye on Cathy's too but she read his mind and removed them from sight. She opened her presents from Ed as Sandy looked on in anticipation. One box was huge, and on opening it she discovered a white, fake fur coat.

'Try it on,' cried Sandy. Cathy put the coat on and posed for her daughter.

'Is it real?' asked Tony.

'No, thank God. I hate real fur; butchering animals for glamour is disgusting. This is lovely though.'

'Probably fake because he's too tight to buy the real thing,' said Tony. Cathy ignored him and opened another parcel; it was another bottle of 'Joy' perfume, so obviously Ed was a fan of it. Her third parcel was a Cartier watch. Cathy reeled in shock. She'd seen this watch in a shop when she'd had a rare trip out with Ed, and told him that it was beautiful, but she hadn't expected it to end up on her wrist.

'Tight?' she said, waving the watch under Tony's nose.

Tony was gobsmacked. 'Well, aren't you and Sandy the golden girls? I know where to come if I'm a bit short.' Cathy smiled and thought of the gifts she'd bought Ed. Aftershave and a Dylan box set; there was no comparison, but at least it was the aftershave that he used, and he had dropped a few hints about the Dylan records. Cathy had bought Tony a sweater and a couple of shirts which he'd unwrapped, and they lay on the floor.

'Didn't feel well enough to get out or I'd have bought you

something,' he said. Cathy was unfazed; he never remembered her birthday so how was he going to buy her a Christmas present?

Ed was pleased when Christmas Day was over. Sara kept asking if they'd fixed a wedding date yet, and Ed avoided the question. All of Faye's relatives kept asking too, so in the end Ed invented a headache and was back home by seven thirty. Faye said that he had insulted her mother by leaving so early, and Ed replied that he couldn't care less. 'I was ill,' he said. 'You could have stayed. I would have picked you up in the morning.'

'But we could have stayed overnight.'

'You could. I wouldn't stay with those toffee-nosed prats. No wonder I felt ill. I'm a working class boy. I might have to rub shoulders with them, but I hate the bastards. I would have had more fun at Vic's.' He pictured Vic and Al sitting and watching porn films and pulling crackers or maybe fixing fairy lights.

Faye kissed him. 'I loved my presents, darling, thank you,' she murmured.

'Cost me enough. I'm still feeling lousy though so how about you try and make me feel better?'

'Shall we have an early night?'

Ed stared at the beautiful girl before him. 'No,' he said. 'Kneel. If I feel a bit better later, I might go out. Faye knelt before him, tears filling her eyes; it was no use protesting. If she wanted to hang onto him, she had to obey.

The pantomime finally drew to a close and Cathy found herself back on the cabaret circuit in London. She still saw Vic and Ed once a week but the situation was going to change. Vic had found a place in Chelsea for Ed, and things moved very fast. Ed furnished it to his specification, and then, after everything was sorted, he told Vic to pick Cathy up at the nightclub and bring her over to the apartment in Chelsea. 'I'll meet you there,' he said.

Vic was beginning to smell a rat. Why did Cathy have to see it? He thought it was for Ed and Faye. The reality was frightening;

no more mirror. Still, he thought, if he were wrong, things would still be great. Maybe Ed only wanted female advice on the place before Faye saw it.

Cathy was amazed when she was told of her destination, but followed Vic inside the building. Ed was already there. She wandered around the hall. The carpet was plush and peach coloured; there were two bedrooms, one with an en suite. The kitchen was beautifully fitted; the units were pine, and the bathroom had a pink bath suite and shower unit. From the terrace there was a brilliant view across London. 'What do you think?' asked Ed.

'Very nice, but shouldn't Faye be here to see what she thinks?'

'Wouldn't be a surprise then, would it?' replied Ed. 'Do you think she'll like it?'

Cathy smiled, 'well I would, it's even fully furnished. It's absolutely beautiful. I couldn't afford anything like it; it's straight out of a magazine.' Vic swallowed hard. He now knew that his worst fears were about to be realised. He looked over and Ed and forced a smile. Cathy saw his expression. 'What's making you so happy?'

Vic laughed, feeling sick inside. 'Tell her,' he said, staring at his rather smug superstar. Ed put his arm around Cathy's waist.

'Well, it's like this, I got it for us.'

Cathy was in shock. 'For me? For us?'

'Yep, now let's christen the bed.' He picked her up and carried her through to the bedroom. 'Thanks Vic,' he shouted back, 'we'll still see you Saturdays, if that's okay?'

Vic grinned, that had been a close call. He picked up his car keys. 'Anytime,' he replied. He got no answer. He could see into the bedroom from where he was standing and noted the couple already entwined. Silently he let himself out.

Side by side a little later, they stared at each other. This time they'd reached even greater heights. 'So when did you organize this?' asked Cathy, propping herself up on one elbow.

'Couple of weeks ago, I think,' replied Ed. 'Vic's Mr Fixit.'

'Certainly looks out for you. I love this place.'

Ed kissed her gently. 'Can you stay tonight?'

'Should be okay; the kids will be in bed by now. I don't usually get home until about three o clock in the morning anyway. I'll ring home.' One phone call later, a very happy Cathy smiled at an even happier Ed. 'He's happy,' laughed Cathy. 'He was sozzled and I heard a female voice in the background so he's not alone.'

Ed rolled Cathy onto her back. 'Our first night in the flat together,' he said. 'I love you so much.'

'I love you too,' replied Cathy, and gave herself up to him.

The following morning, Cathy awoke in her strange surroundings. Getting up, she made her way to the kitchen where Ed was making breakfast. He ordered her back to bed, and minutes later appeared with a tray of two cooked breakfasts. Handing the tray to Cathy, he got back into bed and they both tucked in.

'You're spoiling me,' said Cathy.

'A husband has to look after his wife.'

'Maybe someone should tell that to Tony.'

'Maybe someone should kill him,' snapped Ed. He'd seriously considered doing it, but said nothing. After breakfast they made love again, and then a little later he drove Cathy to the railway station where she boarded her train.

As Ed drove away, he smiled to himself. Now that he had the flat, he could see Cathy more often; it was more convenient. He knew that Tony wouldn't object; he didn't care where she was as long as she was bringing the money in. Faye would be happy to cut down on her sexual duties, so everyone was happy. He had every man's dream. His soul mate in his flat, and his model fiancée in his house.

Tomorrow, Cathy would be getting a new wardrobe. He wanted her to be dressed in clothes that he'd chosen for her, and if that was what he wanted, that's what he'd get. By going back to her family through the day, Cathy would think that she was in control, but the need to make her dependent on him grew stronger by the day. Most women came and went, but he'd always thought of Cathy as his very own possession. To his mind, Seth had cemented this by the ritual. He'd told him that she was all his, and Ed regarded her as such. She belonged to him and always would. He adored her. One day they'd be together properly to raise a family. It was a beautiful dream that he would never give up on.

When he arrived home, he found Faye in the garden with the gardener. She was discussing a new rose garden, and he listened to suggestions and agreed with everything. He gave Faye a hug, 'I'm going to bed, I'm really tired.' Faye waited for him to lead her upstairs and was surprised when he went up on his own.

'Ed, do you want me to come up?'

'No, babe,' he replied. 'Go shopping and treat yourself, charge it to me.'

Faye smiled; that was just what she had wanted to hear.

When Cathy arrived home, Sandy had already left for school. Tony was moaning about everything and gave her the third degree. She explained that a friend had offered to put her up for the night to save her travelling home in the morning. The station was packed with seedy characters and lately she didn't feel safe. Tony agreed; he felt that she'd be better off staying too and told her to do it all week. A new neighbour had just moved in across the road, and Tony had his tongue hanging out.

'Great idea,' he said, 'you'll still see the kids through the day and be safe at night. Have you got any spare cash? I fancy some red hot favourites today. If I win, I'll get us something nice for dinner.'

Cathy fumbled in her purse and handed him five pounds. 'Could you make it ten?' he asked. Cathy gave him another five pounds, and he pecked her on her cheek. 'You're a good girl, Cathy; you stay as many nights as you want. You work hard and we don't want to add the extra strain of travelling to it.' Then he put on his coat and left.

Michael was crying upstairs, 'I'm coming Mickey,' called Cathy.

March came and Cathy's reign was over. She was interviewed on Ted Taylor's show to tell everyone about her fruitful year. She answered to the best of her ability, collected her payment, and made her way to Chelsea to get prepared for her evening show. She arrived back at the apartment about one o'clock and, seeing Ed asleep on the sofa, unpacked her costume and headed for the shower. When she came out, Ed was awake and poured her a drink which she accepted gratefully. When they'd finished the bottle they cuddled up on the sofa.

'Just like an old married couple,' said Ed. He was so content; just like he had been in 1968. Cathy felt even closer to him now. She closed her eyes and slept in his arms.

They both awoke a short time later. The television was still on and they continued to watch it for a while before heading to bed, where they made love for the remainder of the night.

Easter arrived, and Cathy and Sandy travelled back to Bacton. Sky still hadn't returned from Ibiza, so Cathy had the caravan to herself as Sandy still wanted to sleep with Amber. Ed arrived at the weekend and stayed for a week. Sandy absolutely adored him and painted him a picture. 'This is me, you, and Mummy,' she said, proudly. Ed scrutinized the painting and smiled at her.

'I think that's the best painting I've ever owned,' he said, giving her a hug. They spent an idyllic week with the whole family and once more lived as happy hippies.

A month later, Ed informed Vic that he was leaving. Vic was seething. He'd raised Ed to stardom and now, years later, he wanted out to become a hippy and travel the open road. 'Come round on Saturday and we'll discuss it,' he said. If Ed thought he was walking away that easily, he was mistaken, and on the following Saturday Vic faced the loved up couple at his house. He was going to ply them with drink and some very large joints of wacky baccy. Putting his feet up and reclining in his comfy chair, he addressed Ed who was indulging heavily in the brandy and dope offered by Vic.

'I want out. I'll honour anything that can't be changed, but that's it.'

Vic puffed on a cigar and studied the list of dates in his hand. 'You can be out of everything by January 1976.'

Ed shook his head. 'I want out before that.'

Vic sat up and handed the list to Ed. 'See for yourself, I can't make these dates go away. I need you, and so does the band; you owe it to them. Your dream may be appealing now, but if you opt out you'll be soon forgotten. Look at Mick; no one knows who he is any more.'

Ed read the list. 'Is there no way out of this?'

Vic pulled a face. 'Well, if you were a member of the band and not a lead vocalist, it would be easy, but the public want you and you'd be letting down the band badly. You've got a new album to do, a European tour, a tour of Great Britain, several television shows, a couple of charity events, and then there's the American tour next August, plus another Irish one, and the Isle of Wight.' Vic smiled. He could see that Ed was getting groggy; his speech was becoming slurred too.

'I want out, you lousy bastard.'

Vic got another round of drinks and sat down again. 'Look at Cathy; she's delectable. Don't you want the best for her?' Ed got to his feet, staggered, and fell back onto the sofa.

'The best thing for her would be to get out of this bloody business completely,' he slurred.

Cathy giggled. This joint sure was making her feel strange. Ed downed the brandy and gazed across at Cathy who was beginning to slump slightly across him.

'You look lovely, babe, really lovely,' he said, leaning over her and then crashing over onto the carpet and knocking her drink from her hand.

Vic was incensed, not only was the alcohol pure brandy but he'd slipped some pills into it too and now the contents were all over his new beige carpet. Ed was lying there with a smug look on his face. Vic's face had gone blood red. He hauled Ed to his feet, but he promptly slumped onto Cathy. 'I think you two should go to bed.'

Cathy didn't answer; she was out for the count. Ed wasn't happy at all. 'Look at the state of her; what the fuck have you been giving us and why is my glass empty?'

'Your glass is empty because you drank everything, which is more than can be said for Cathy's; you knocked her glass out of her hand and the contents of that is now all over my new carpet.'

'It's only a carpet. Listen, I don't want to go to America.'

'Tough, you're going. I'll cancel what I can.'

'Okay, but Cathy comes too as part of the band.'

'Have you completely lost the plot?'

'No, I can sing and she can dance alongside me in a couple of numbers. If you're uncertain, try it out at one of the charity gigs.'

'We'll discuss this tomorrow when you're sober.'

'Okay, but that's the deal, and if it works, I might be persuaded to stay a bit longer or until you've got a new vocalist.'

'What about her?'

'She'll do as I say, she always does. Now, how about some black coffee?'

'Coming up,' replied Vic striding towards the kitchen. He grinned. When January 1976 arrived, the date for Ed's 'get out of jail free', he'd find a way to stall him and make him stay. Ed's idea might be a good one though. America loved specialities and if it worked he'd have both of them under his wing. He'd love Cathy under him in any way. He could hear her throwing up; that was good. She'd wake up and once more the mirror would be useful. Fuck the carpet, he could buy another one. He made the coffee and took it through to his guests. 'Feeling better?' he asked a very red-faced Cathy.

She nodded and indicated the fruit bowl she was holding. 'I'm sorry Vic, but there was nothing else handy.' Vic felt a bit queasy looking at the bowl full of vomit.

He took it from her, forcing a smile. 'Get yourself to bed; Ed can't drive in his condition.'

'I'll clean it out for you,' said Cathy, getting to her feet.

Vic shook his head. 'I'll deal with it, just get yourself to bed. He was visualising his favourite couple entertaining him and, once in the kitchen, tipped the bowl's contents into the waste disposal. He'd never liked this fruit bowl, a fan of Ed's had given it to him. It was a gaudy mish-mash of colours and it clashed with just about everything else in his home. He rinsed it and was about to throw it out when he had an idea. Al had a birthday coming up soon, and that would save him buying a present for him. Al quite liked the thing actually. Yes, that was it, he would give it a good clean and then offer it to Al Simpkins as an early present tomorrow.

Cathy was already halfway up the stairs with Ed in hot pursuit, even though he was walking like a drunk. Upstairs, Cathy had partially recovered and was giving Ed her full attention. He was just lying back and enjoying it. The drugs were really kicking in now, and he was on cloud nine; just when he thought sex couldn't get better, Cathy always surprised him and took him to another level of ecstasy.

Next door, Vic was eyeing the performance enviously; he'd love to be in Ed's position. America was food for thought; it was a different ball game. Ed would have to keep Faye happy so maybe Cathy might be at a loose end now and again. If he could introduce her to the wonderful world of drug heaven, she might be grateful to Uncle Vic and spread her legs for him now and again. Yes, it was a very good idea and Ed couldn't keep an eye on her twenty-four seven. Ed was getting very vocal now, and

Vic was getting excited. One minute, Cathy had been throwing up, and the next, eating his superstar alive. 'Lucky bastard,' muttered Vic, and took himself in hand.

The following morning, Cathy headed home. It was Sunday, and the only full day that she got with her children now, owing to work. She left in a mini cab, as Vic said he needed to speak to Ed before he went home to Faye. The two men faced each other across the kitchen table, drinking endless cups of coffee. 'Right,' said Vic, 'now tell me what this vision of yours contains.'

'Well, did you ever see Elvis in *Roustabout*?'

'Of course I did, but what's that got to do with the tour?'

'Presley did a number in it called *Little Egypt*, about a dancer.'

Vic sighed. 'Go on.'

'I can do that and she can dance, but it's the other number that freaks me out, it will be a biggy.'

'Go on.'

'*Angel* by Hendrix. A floaty, white angel, a classical ballet piece with me singing, her dancing, and the band singing the chorus while I dance with her.'

'I thought you didn't want to wear tights.'

'I don't, you're not getting the full picture.'

'Thank God for that, you really have lost the plot.'

'It'll be great; all we need is a choreographer.'

'All you need is a brain transplant.'

Ed continued to witter on and Vic listened. By the time he left, Vic had food for thought and he rang Noddy to arrange a lunch at which they could discuss Ed's new idea.

After lunch was over, the two managers went their separate ways, with Vic deciding to include Cathy in the charity gig.

In September, Tony drew Cathy's attention to the holiday that she'd won in the dance contest. 'You have to fly before the 31st of December,' he said, a plan hatching in his mind.

'Well I can't go, why don't you go with your mother?' replied Cathy. 'I'll write a letter telling the travel firm that I can't go and they'll transfer the holiday to you.'

Tony was jubilant, and after Cathy wrote a letter, took off for the travel agents. On his return, he said that he'd booked for mid-December, as he thought that his mother would like Christmas in the Canaries. 'Great,' said Cathy, 'it'll be nice having the kids to myself for a whole fortnight.' Cathy doubted that Tony was taking his mother; it was probably a new girlfriend, but she felt that it was better that the tickets were used rather than being thrown away. That night she informed Ed of Tony's holiday.

'Great. I now need to book a holiday for Faye and her mother on the same dates.'

'Faye won't go without you.'

'She will when I tell her that I'm inviting Rusty and his brood over for Christmas. You won't see her back for dust.' He was right and, faced with the prospect of Ed's hippy family for yuletide, Faye accepted Ed's offer to a four star hotel in Tenerife with her mother.

Autumn passed, and winter reared its head. It wasn't long before Tony left for his holiday, and Cathy was picked up by Vic. Michael slept for most of the journey, and Steven for part of it. Sandy never stopped chattering, and by the time they'd arrived at Ed's mansion, Vic had a splitting headache. Rusty and co. had already arrived, and greeted Cathy and her children warmly. In the corner sat a couple with two children. Cathy didn't know them but Fawn made the introductions.

'This is Barry and Rosaleen,' she said, 'and the kids are Garry and Susie. We've known Rosaleen for years, even before our hippy days.' Cathy extended her hand to Barry and kissed Rosaleen on her cheek. The children scampered off with Amber and Amethyst. Michael awoke from his slumber and gazed around the vast room. He began to cry, and Fawn took him from Cathy. The child immediately stopped crying and began to play with the shell necklace around her neck. Steven had his eye on the grand piano and whispered to his mother that he would like to play it. Ed suddenly swept into the room and took Cathy in his arms. Steven took the opportunity to let go of his mother's hand and head for the piano. He clambered up onto the piano stool and began to finger the keys.

Out of the corner of her eye, Cathy spotted him. 'No Steven, you mustn't.' Ed laughed and went over to the child. He sat down beside him on the stool and played a little whilst Steven joined in with a few notes of his own. After a little while he tired of this and ran back to his mother.

'How would you like to play the guitar?' Ed asked him.

'Yeah,' replied the child, 'like T-Rex.'

'If you like, but not until after dinner. Now where are all the kids, there's a massive Christmas tree in the lounge, and my housekeeper and her husband need some extra hands to decorate it.' As if in answer, the children all came rushing into the room. Amber threw herself at Ed along with Amethyst and Sandy.

'He has this effect on women,' laughed Rusty. 'Come on kids, the tree needs decorating.' Everyone headed for the lounge and Ed slipped his arm around Cathy's waist.

'This is going to be the best Christmas ever, baby. This house will come alive with the kids' laughter. A house needs kids at Christmas, that's what it's all about and I'm one big kid anyway, but I'll be getting my present later.'

Cathy surveyed the scene in front of her; brightly coloured baubles, tinsel, fairy lights, miniature crackers, a Christmas fairy, foil covered chocolate Santas, and other trimmings were being added to the huge pine Christmas tree. Michael toddled around laughing and clapping his hands, while his brother wrapped tinsel around the tree. Sandy smiled at her mother and Ed, looking truly happy.

Ed was right, it was a wonderful Christmas but it passed too quickly and soon it was time to return to reality. Cathy had been able to honour all of her bookings as Fawn and Rosaleen looked after the children for her. Cathy liked Rosaleen; she was warm and funny, but Barry was a bit of a misery. He was tall and dark, a bit like Romany, but plumper. Rosaleen was a mirror image of Cathy, and she wondered where she figured in Ed's life but never asked. His past was his concern.

On Christmas day, Vic had dressed up as Santa Claus and handed out gifts. Ed had been his usual generous self, and Cathy found herself the recipient of gold, perfume, and many expensive clothes and gifts. Sandy had a gold locket, Michael a rocking horse, and Steven a small pedal car. Ed spent hours playing with the children. He gave both of the boys piggy backs and read them bedtime stories, and he let Sandy ride one of the horses while he led it around the field. Ed noted Steven's interest in pop music; he was only four years old but knew all of the current hits and doted on T-Rex. During their stay, Ed had shown him some basics on his acoustic guitar and he learnt very quickly. 'Star in the making,' said Ed, handing Steven a signed and framed photo of Marc Bolan.

There was one question that had bothered Cathy since her return to Norfolk; there was no sign of Summer, and when she'd asked about her, everyone clammed up. She wondered if maybe she'd gone to Ibiza too but expected her to be present at this family gathering.

She voiced her feelings to Ed who replied that the beautiful, young girl was dead. Cathy was horrified. 'How awful. She was such a healthy, beautiful girl. What happened?'

'Heart attack in 1969. She was laughing one minute and dropped dead the next. I think my family is cursed. My father and mother died the following year in a car crash, which wiped me out. I was still trying to get over you, and then Summer died, followed by Mum and Dad a bit later. Sky's living with Fawn and Rusty now; she's Rusty's love child. She was born just before he met Fawn. Sky's mother wanted her baby but not Rusty. He was devastated as he loved Sky's mother, but then he met Fawn and the rest is history.'

'So Sky is Amber and Amethyst's half sister?'

'That's right. She looks after Blue now as well as her other kids. Nobody sees her that much owing to her love of Ibiza. In fact, I haven't seen her since I brought Faye down to meet my family.

'Sky was friendly to Faye, but Faye was nasty to her. She called her a tramp because some of her kids were born out of wedlock, and Sky was too polite to retaliate. Faye added that she would never have any screaming brats of her own; that would ruin her figure. I wonder what she'd have thought if she'd seen this lot running around her house.'

'Probably would have had a fit,' laughed Cathy. 'But I am sorry about Summer. I can't believe it's New Year's Eve already; I'll be going back home soon.'

'That's right, forget the past, let's party and celebrate. I've had a great Christmas with you and the kids. I love them, and I worship you with my heart and soul. Next year will be hard but Vic has managed to cancel a few dates and says I can leave in January 1976, so we'll just have to ride it out. Then you can get your divorce and make my dreams come true.'

Ruby the housemaid bustled into the room. 'Dinner will be served in about thirty minutes.'

Ed took Cathy's hand. 'Let's go up and get changed darling. We've got time for a quick cuddle too.'

'Your obedient servant, sir,' said Cathy, and hand in hand they ascended the stairs.

After a magnificent dinner, everyone went into the huge lounge where a DJ had set up. Rosaleen had put Michael to bed for Cathy, and sat in a corner beside her miserable husband. 'Come on Rosie,' cried Ed, 'come and dance.'

Rosaleen sat still; it seemed as if her husband controlled her. In the end, Ed dragged her to her feet and got her dancing. She became a changed person once she was dancing with Ed, and she moved with him perfectly. After three dances, she returned to her husband who was glowering at Ed. 'Lovely mover,' said Cathy, 'you move well together.'

Ed shrugged his shoulders and took her into his arms. 'Not as well as you and I together. I love you.'

Cathy looked over at Rosaleen; she looked so sad it reminded her of her own relationship with Tony. At ten o'clock, all the children were put to bed. They were all going home tomorrow, and so needed their sleep. Everyone raised their glasses as midnight arrived, and wished each other a happy New Year. The dancing continued, and Ed said, 'Happy New Year everyone, my new year starts now.' Then he picked Cathy up and carried her upstairs. As he did so, Cathy glanced over her shoulder and swore that she could see tears trickling from Rosaleen's eyes.

The following morning was hectic. The kids were playing up, and several times Cathy was in tears. She didn't want to go home but knew it was inevitable. Sandy was inconsolable; she'd had a wonderful time and adored Ed. He picked her up saying, 'don't cry baby, you know I love you and we'll all be together soon but now you must go home to your father and friends.'

Rusty and his family had already left, and Rosaleen and her husband were loading up their car. Her children hovered nearby. She approached Cathy and hugged her. 'You will look after him, won't you? That Faye's such a bitch.'

'Of course,' Cathy reassured her. 'You look after yourself, maybe we can meet up in the future.' They were interrupted by Barry shouting at his wife to get a move on. Rosaleen let go of Cathy and walked away meekly, getting into the car with her children and then driving away. 'What a shame,' said Cathy.

'She made her choice,' snapped Ed. Cathy kept silent; she didn't want to follow up this conversation. Vic arrived, and Sandy and Steven loaded their presents into his car.

The housekeeper approached Cathy with Ruby, who held three

wrapped parcels. She handed them to Cathy. 'These are for the children,' she said. 'We've all loved having them here; this house needs children.'

Ada Shores agreed. 'Yes,' she said, 'it was lovely to hear children's laughter, it reminded me so much of the days when my children were young; it was a real family gathering.' Cathy thought it was a lovely gesture and said so, hugging both of the women before they retired to the kitchen.

Ed held Cathy in his arms. 'And now for the hard bit. I don't want to let you go but I know I have to. There's still the flat. Will you be back there tomorrow night? I'm going to miss the kids too; they've really opened my eyes to what's important in life.'

Cathy could feel tears welling up in her eyes. 'Wild horses won't stop me. I'll see you tomorrow, and I've had a lovely time, thank you.'

Ed stroked her hair. 'The pleasure was all mine, honey.' They clung together and, after one last kiss, Cathy picked up Michael who was sound asleep on the sofa and headed for Vic's car. Ed went back inside the house; he couldn't watch her drive away. He stared around the house; it seemed so cold now. Faye would be home soon. He caught sight of Ruby and instructed her to change the sheets in his room so that Faye could have fresh bed linen.

Ruby winked at him. 'Yes sir.'

In February, Noddy broke the news about America to Cathy. He'd told her before that she was going to Devon for a summer circuit, but as *Angel* needed to be tackled, and the tour kicked off in August, rehearsals needed to start. Over lunch he told her the truth. Cathy was stunned. 'I'm not good enough for America,' she said.

'Just continue with your daily classical ballet class and you'll be fine, you're a pro. You're dancing with Ed in this ballet number.'

'Ed? I didn't know he was a dancer.'

'He isn't, but you're dancing as he's singing, and he's doing a few minor holds as he supports you.' Cathy's head spun; if he was supporting her she had to hope that he wasn't out of his head at the time. This could become a real *faux pas* instead of a *pas de deux*.

The band were unhappy; they didn't want a new addition, but Cathy was in a daze. Nothing made sense any more as she worked through a routine with a choreographer. As they went on rehearsing, Ed soon realised that the performance was beginning to resemble something rather lovely.

In June, Cathy was confronted one morning by a tall, willowy blonde. At first she thought the girl was selling something, but then she introduced herself. 'I am Ingrid Larsen and I have come to au pair for you,' she said. 'I have the excellent, how you say, references. I am nineteen years of age.' She swept past a very confused Cathy as if she owned the place.

'Who sent you?' asked Cathy.

'Victor Lee,' replied the girl. 'May I see the children, please? I am a qualified nanny as well.'

'Of course,' replied Cathy, wondering why she hadn't been consulted about this. Ingrid was thrusting her references at Cathy who took them and read them; they were indeed excellent.

'Which way kitchen? I will make you a cup of tea. You sit down, from now on I work for you and Mr Lee pays.'

Even more dazed, Cathy sat down. 'First on the right.' Michael began to cry and Cathy got to her feet.

'I will see to him, you come first, baby second. I will bring him downstairs,' said Ingrid. She gave Cathy a hot cup of tea and then went upstairs.

Unfortunately, she went into the wrong room and Tony let forth with a tirade of abuse. 'Cathy,' he yelled, 'I was just getting up and this blonde bird walked in. Who is she?' Cathy chuckled, but laughed even more when he came downstairs in his y-fronts which were on back to front. She was amazed at the speed with which this girl had entered her life and taken over. It was nice to be waited on, but secretly she wasn't sure if this was what she really wanted. The prospect of going to America was mind-blowing, especially as part of Ed's entourage, but the whole thing scared her.

All she wanted was to be a wife and mother, yet that was denied her. Tony had met her when she was eighteen, swept her off her feet, knocked her up, and then done the decent thing and married her. As soon as Sandy was born, she'd had to resume work, as Tony gave up his job and encouraged her to pursue her career once more. He blamed her for getting pregnant, and said that although he could have done a lot worse, he didn't love her and never had.

'You were young and very desirable,' he had told her, 'and I didn't want any child of mine being born illegitimately; that's the reason I married you. But love? Forget it, it only exists in fairy tales, so does fidelity so don't expect that either. You'll have a lot of fun; sex is rampant in show business. I won't stop you having fun, but just remember that we are married, and don't ever consider divorce because if you do, I'll make sure you lose custody of our child and any others that you might conceive.'

Cathy had remembered that speech as if it were yesterday; it was the day that her bubble had burst. Was she never going to get her cottage in the country, her cosy little home with roses around the door? Tony had shattered her vision completely and, shortly after Sandy's birth, she was back at work while her husband played mother. Contrary to what Tony had said, she'd never played around until that fateful gig in Wales.

Her mind switched to Ed; she was crazy about him but scared to admit it to herself. At times she thought he might tire of her and that made her feel sick. She liked Faye, and yet here she was deceiving her. It made her feel guilty, but Ed drew her to him so strongly and their time together was out of this world. She was brought back to reality by Ingrid returning with Michael in her arms. The child gave a toothy grin and seemed quite unfazed by Ingrid.

Tony went back upstairs moaning, and was met by Steven, who took one look at his father and pulled his y-fronts down around his ankles. 'Bloody kids,' shouted Tony. 'Go and see your mother.'

Ingrid frowned. 'It is difficult to know who is the child,' she said, smiling at Steven who was now downstairs.

'Daddy's pants are back to front,' he said, and then he gave an infectious laugh that caused the two women to chuckle.

'I shall cook you lunch,' said Ingrid. 'You don't need do any more cooking. I am, how you say, honoured to work for you. You work very hard; you will be a star. I have never worked for a star, but now I do. I am very lucky and I will be a good cooker and very good scrubber and look after the children. My English is not good but I will learn.'

'I'm no star,' said Cathy. Ingrid headed for the kitchen and then looked in the fridge.

'But you will be, I know it, and now I will fix lunch.' Cathy smiled, she liked this girl.

Later, she rang Ed. 'I can't make it tonight; I've got to settle the au pair in.'

'Okay, but I'm gonna miss you.'

'You'll survive.'

'Suppose I'll have to, still I'm glad that she turned up. She was the best we could get. I couldn't have just anyone looking after my little angel.'

'So my daughter is my rival.'

'Well, she was a lot more responsive than you on our first meeting, wasn't she?'

'Lucky man; Faye, me, and Sandy.'

'Fuck Faye.'

'You'll have to in America; she'll be in your bed, not me.'

'Don't remind me, but I'll work something out, you'll see.'

'I love you, Ed.'

'Love you too, baby, I'm getting a hard on just talking to you.'

'Lucky Faye.'

'No chance, see you tomorrow. I'll save it and ravish you until you beg me to stop.'

'Sounds good to me. See you tomorrow, bye Ed.'

'Bye, Angel.' Ed replaced the receiver, his dream was coming true. The American tour loomed; then there were a couple of short British ones, Cathy's divorce, and the open road. 'I am one lucky guy,' he said, pouring himself a brandy and relaxing in front of the television.

Vic soon had everything under control. Passports, press coverage, new stage outfits for the band, two beautiful new costumes for Cathy, plus a mountain of ballet shoes. Romany was amused; the rest of the band confused, and Cathy's feelings were mixed. Noddy was getting excited.

'It's your big chance, and you may never get another one like this. I know I certainly won't.' Vic pressured Cathy as only he knew how, and he was helped by Faye who really did want Cathy to go.

Ingrid had settled in well, and the children loved her, so did Tony. Sandy had told all of her friends that her mother was the best dancer in the world, and that she was going to tour in America with the Z Tones. As Cathy packed her case she began to wonder where this was all going to lead. If she'd had the answer, she would have unpacked.

Faye had checked her wardrobe over and over again. She'd gone on her usual spending spree and bought a lot of things that she would never wear. A close friend had discovered the identity of the Chelsea flat occupants, and informed Faye. She had smiled, 'that's nice for them both.'

'Aren't you bothered?' her friend had replied.

'Course not, I live in Ed's house and he'll tire of her, given time, so now can you leave? I've got a lot to do.' With friends like that who needed enemies thought Faye. Her friend left dejected.

It was the evening before the tour, and Ed suggested an early night. 'America tomorrow,' he said, and went upstairs.

Faye followed him. She was feeling quite excited; he hadn't touched her in two weeks. 'I'm coming,' she said, knowing that very soon she would be.

Chapter Twelve

Ed drove to the airport in the Rolls with Faye. He was bored with yet another tour. Still, at least he had Cathy on board with this one. He looked over at Faye; so beautiful, so immaculate, and so cold. His mind flashed back to their previous night's love making; it had been a total disaster. It was ridiculous; all the groupies and starlets creamed themselves just getting a glimpse of him, and here he was engaged to an ex-beauty queen with a million hang-ups. The press waited on the tarmac with Vic, and Ed's bodyguard Karl. The plane was loaded with just about everything that Vic had ordered. As Ed got out of the Rolls, the press moved in. Faye clung to his arm and posed, picture-box fashion. Vic checked his watch. 'Come on Ed, we've got to go.'

Cathy was nervous and snuggled up to Noddy as the plane took off. 'Don't worry,' he said, 'everything will be fine.'

'Wish I had your faith.'

About halfway into the journey, Faye fell asleep. Ed looked behind him and noted that Noddy had done the same. Vic watched as Ed got to his feet and approached Cathy. He knew what was going to happen. Ed headed for the toilet, and a few seconds later Cathy got up and followed him. Vic saw the toilet door open, and Cathy follow Ed inside. He got to his feet and stood outside the toilet, wishing that he could see what was going on inside there. He knew more or less, by the sounds that were coming through the door, but just wished that he had x-ray vision. When the occupants emerged, Vic stepped away from the door. Cathy looked flushed and happy, and Ed very smug with a glazed expression in his eyes.

'Pervert,' he snapped at Vic. Vic tried to excuse himself by saying that he was *on guard*. Ed surveyed the bulge in Vic's trousers, muttering that it was more like *on hard*. He pushed past his manager and rejoined Faye who was still sound asleep. Cathy went back to her seat and picked up a magazine, glancing over at Noddy who was snoring his head off.

In New York, there were enormous crowds, and Cathy was petrified. The band was whisked away and then Cathy and Noddy followed on in a waiting car. On reaching the hotel, Cathy went straight to bed and slept fully clothed. Ed's first night show was a sell out. Cathy shook as she was helped into her angel costume by Faye; she was unable to do anything up as her fingers refused to move. Faye even had to help her with her make-up.

'You're a bag of nerves,' she said, 'don't worry.' Cathy struggled to tie up the ribbons on her pink satin ballet shoes. Never had she been so scared. About five minutes later she managed it after a lot of fumbling. There was a knock on the door and Ed entered with the press and assorted hangers-on. 'Well,' said Faye, 'how does she look?'

'Beautiful,' replied Ed, and wolf whistled.

'Real cute,' said a photographer. 'Baby, you are the cutest thing I've ever seen.'

'Hey young lady, could you pose with Ed for me? It'll be front page news tomorrow.' Cathy felt numb as she was positioned alongside Ed.

Ed was feeling jittery; he knew he'd need something before the night was out. The phone rang and Vic picked up the receiver; the caller immediately hung up. 'Fuck it,' said Vic, 'haven't I got enough problems without cranks?' He ushered the press from the room and stared at Ed who was already soaked in a nervous sweat. 'Okay Ed?'

'Yeah, but I need something.'

'I'll get it,' replied Vic, knowing exactly what his superstar was asking for. He felt sure that the tour would be a success, but the ballet bothered him. Cathy was doing all the dancing, but in the chorus the band was taking over and Ed was involving himself in the dance. Vic was scared that the couple might get tangled up in cables. He wished now that he hadn't let Ed get his own way with this one, but then realised that if it was a success it would be great publicity. It had to be a first; a rock star and a ballet dancer on stage together, with the rock star actually participating. His head began to ache as he left the dressing room with Ed and headed for the stage.

The band had already gone into their first number. Vic had decided that it was a good idea for them to do a couple of numbers without Ed. It gave Gerry a chance to sing, and Romany a chance to show off his brilliance as a lead guitarist. Both the numbers were given a terrific reception, after which Romany announced: 'Here he is, here's Eddie.'

The audience screamed, and Vic slapped Ed on the back. 'Go out and knock 'em dead.'

Ed strode out and the audience went wild. Off stage, Cathy waited with Faye and, turning to her, Faye said, 'There's something I've been wanting to ask you.'

Cathy was staring straight ahead of her, trembling with stage fright. 'What's that?' she asked.

'Have you and Ed ever been lovers?' she asked casually, as if she was asking the time. Cathy was shocked and about to deny it when Faye giggled. 'It's okay, I don't mind, really I don't. I'm glad that you're here. Ed's far too oversexed for me; if you only knew the agonies that I go through just to keep him happy.'

'But Faye,' Cathy faltered, 'how can you…?'

'I'd rather it was you,' replied Faye. 'He's too much for me.'

At that moment, Noddy and Vic came over. 'Ready, Cathy?'

Cathy nodded. Romany stepped up to the microphone and

announced: 'Now for something completely different.' He then struck the opening chords to *Angel*, and Cathy was bathed in the spotlight. Ed began to sing and Cathy travelled en pointe towards him. He knelt down as she came up beside him and, holding his shoulder, she balanced in a perfect arabesque with her cheek resting against his. The audience were silent as the ballet continued. Out front, Al Simpkins was happy with the shots he was getting; they were marvellous. Young girls were weeping, and screaming at the top of their lungs.

Vic was sweating. 'So far, so good,' he said to Noddy. As the final chorus arrived, he held his breath and closed his eyes. Cathy turned a double pirouette, and Ed caught her just right. Vic opened one eye and wondered if things were all right. The look on Faye's face told him that it was. Poised on one leg, Cathy faced the audience until Ed, standing behind her, brought her arms from above her head down in front of her. He then leaned back so that Cathy, still en pointe, leaned against him, and cheek to cheek he swayed her to and fro. The audience now had linked arms and were swaying to the music.

'One more time,' called Romany, and this time the audience sang the chorus alone. Slowly, Ed and Cathy sank to the ground, facing each other with arms outstretched, finishing with Cathy's head on Ed's shoulder while he held her to him in an embrace. There was a deathly silence, and then the crowd went wild. There were cheers, whistles, screams, cries of more, and girls fainting. Al fired away with his camera as Ed raised Cathy to her feet, kissed her hand and addressed the crowd saying, 'she'll be back later.' Cathy rushed off and straight into Faye's arms.

'Beautiful,' she gushed. Ed shot a sidelong glance over to the wings and smiled. He was glad that the girls were getting on; it made life a lot easier for him. Cathy was on Vic's payroll so she couldn't just walk away when she felt like it. This carousel turned because Vic made it turn, and no one would wriggle out of a contract of his.

The support band was a trio; the so-called Cupid Stunts, which caused great mirth. Several girls out front tried to get on stage, but Ed's entourage prevented it. Romany laughed; he'd seen this before, first with Mick and now Ed. A young girl at the front was getting crushed and was pulled out of the crowd and taken to safety.

Ed gazed down at the crowd. Some of the kids were real jailbait but he wouldn't need them this time; he had two ladies to keep him happy. No problems with underage kids, and no nasty rashes either. This was going to be some tour.

Back in the dressing room, Faye helped Cathy into her *Little Egypt* costume. She stood back and looked at Cathy. 'Looks great, I'll just brush your hair. Oh, and I'm sorry if I shocked you before but I meant every word of it. There's a party tonight at the hotel, and one at Romany's brother's place tomorrow night. He lives just a few blocks from here, and tomorrow I'm hoping to be able to disappear during the course of the party. So feel free, you'll be doing me a favour.'

Cathy was stunned and listened as she continued. 'Look out for the little people of Shangri-La; you're very tense and they'll soon find you. They sense it, and believe me they will make a beeline for you. If you want it, they've got the key to making you feel great. They'll tell you that you're entitled to it and I'd hate to see you caught up in that scene. I do care for you, I look on you as a close friend and you'll find that the first time you snort cocaine you won't really feel any difference after the trip has passed. It can take a long time before you cross the line, and by then your mind won't know the difference between fantasy and reality. Then your brain won't be able to function properly and you'll be addicted. After several suicide attempts you'll want out, and get it with pills or a gun shot in the head.'

Cathy shuddered. 'I don't intend to start.'

Faye sat down. 'I know you don't, but you're in America now, not the UK. You'll find rolled up joints beside plates at some dinner parties, and if all else fails they can always put it in your drink. Stick with me; I don't indulge apart from mild stuff.'

There was a tap on the door and Vic entered, his gaze lingering on Cathy. He kissed her on her lips, and Cathy noted that he reeked of whisky. 'Darling, you were sensational. Now we mustn't keep Ed waiting, must we? There's one more number and then you're on again.'

Cathy took his extended hand, and as a parting shot, Faye said, 'watch him Cathy; he's the most evil thing on two legs.'

Vic blew her a kiss and then leered at her. 'What's the matter, Faye, Ed too tired to fuck last night?' Faye said nothing and followed Cathy and Vic from the room. He crossed to a roadie, whispered something and then turned back to Faye and grinned. The roadie disappeared and then returned about five minutes later with a large black man who looked as if he was in his thirties.

Faye was obviously distressed as she implored Vic to send him away. He ignored her and stared at Ed, who was obviously in need of a boost.

'What is it Faye?' asked Cathy.

Faye uttered, 'Shangri-La,' she sobbed.

On stage, Ed felt as if his body was about to collapse, his mouth was dry, his knees were giving way his head hurt and he had a sour taste in his mouth. There was a ringing noise in his ears and he felt that one minute he was growing taller and the next shrinking. He didn't know how he was going to carry on and glanced over at the wings to see Cathy. Somehow he had to get through *Little Egypt*, and then he saw Chico who had supplied him many times. He was saved, and heard Romany announce, 'it's *Little Egypt*.' Ed thought that Romany's voice sounded a million miles away.

As Cathy made her entrance, Vic hissed, 'bring him off with you and tell Romany to fill in with some lead.' Cathy nodded and moved over to Romany giving him Vic's instructions. The sight of the man with the briefcase had unsettled her as much as Faye, and the sight of Ed didn't help either. Ed wondered if the microphone had packed up, he was singing but he couldn't hear himself. All he could see was colours, lots of them, and the reflections of the mirrored sequins on Cathy's costume. As soon as the number was over, Cathy led Ed off stage where he promptly collapsed. Vic and the black man got him to his feet and helped him to the dressing room. Faye would not be consoled, and she followed with Cathy to Ed's room. Karl, his bodyguard, stood outside.

Chico stared into Ed's pupils and said to Vic, 'He's okay, just needs a drop of magic, that's all.' Faye wept even more when Chico took a length of rubber and wound it around Ed's arm, just above his elbow.

'You're a murderer, Vic,' she cried.

'Shut your mouth,' he snapped, and watched as the hypodermic needle came into view. 'He's got to have this.'

'Ed, don't let him do this, listen to me,' cried Faye. Ed was beyond listening to anyone; he couldn't hear a thing and didn't feel the needle enter his arm. He gazed into space seeing nothing. Minutes later, he came out of his dream-like state and looked around at all the anxious faces.

'What the hell's the matter with you all? You should be happy; we're doing a great show.' He felt terrific and looked it too. 'Pay him, Vic, this stuff's great.'

Drying her eyes, Faye demanded, 'can't you see what this is doing to you?'

Ed laughed, 'don't be such a stick in the mud, Faye,' and taking her arm, he led her out of the room and towards the stage. 'Come on, I've got a show to finish.'

Chico's eyes came to rest on Cathy. 'What about you, doll? I'm sure Uncle Vic would love to treat you too.'

'No thanks,' replied Cathy.

'Okay, but I'll be at the party later so just whistle if you change your mind; you look as if you need relaxing. Cathy walked over to Noddy and hugged him.

'Good job I've got you,' she said, feeling safe in his arms. The change that had come over Ed was electric. He was building fans up and exciting them, singing with everything he could transmit to them. He reeled off one song after another and had to give two encores.

Once the show was over, he was very distant and was whisked to a waiting car with Vic and Karl. Faye, Cathy, and Noddy followed on just after and found the hotel lobby full of reporters and hangers-on. A tall, thin man with red hair stepped out in front of them. He wore a tweed suit, brown leather shoes, a cream shirt, and a stetson, with horn rimmed glasses that completed the picture. He gazed at Cathy with adoration and fell to his knees. 'My name is Kenny Carson… I saw the show… you were great,' he gushed. 'I've got a cosy little pad just three blocks away and I'd love it if you would honour me with your presence tonight.'

He took her hand and kissed it as Cathy stammered, 'I've got to go,' and withdrew her hand. She was horrified. She'd only done one show and she was already being hit on.

'I'll wait for you,' said a very lovesick Kenny. Cathy turned away and went upstairs with Faye.

'What a creep,' giggled Faye. 'You'd better get used to this because you'll have many men interested in you now. The girls fantasise over Ed, so the guys will do the same with you.' They entered the large hotel room that had been designated for Ed and Faye, and surveyed Ed, who was basking in the limelight surrounded by many photographers, groupies, and several people who appeared to be attached to the papers. He held his arms open to the two women and kissed them both.

'Hallo, my angels,' he exclaimed. 'This tour is going to be great, really great.'

Flash bulbs popped, and Faye winked at Cathy. 'Sure is,' she said.

The following night was Rick's party night, and anyone who was not connected to the band was not invited, although Rick had invited several starlets, hookers, and groupies, plus some very pretty boys. Rick was nothing like Romany, apart from his build. He wore his black hair very long and dressed like a hippy. He loved blue movies, much to Al's delight, who already felt at home. Vic was pounced on by two redheads who were hoping to get closer to Ed.

The trio disappeared into another room; how Vic loved New York. Rick was bisexual. He wasn't bothered if his partner was male or female; he'd just spot someone and pounce. He flung his arms around his brother and greeted Ed and Faye warmly. Then turning to Cathy, asked, 'how do you like New York?'

Cathy gazed at Rick and smiled, feeling quite out of place. 'Hardly had a chance to see it yet,' she replied. She followed the others and found herself in a huge room, the kind you see in celebrity magazines. There was obviously no shortage of money here, no expense had been spared with the furnishings and decor. Doors led to a terrace which gave beautiful views of the city. Rick offered champagne all round and then escorted Cathy to a scarlet sofa. Cathy was getting nervous. Rick scared her, but she managed to murmur, 'You have a beautiful place,' and then took a sip of champagne.

Rick liked what he saw; Romany had already informed him of the girl's potential in bed. 'Thank you,' he replied. 'You have the most beautiful eyes I have ever seen.' He slid his arm along the back of the sofa adding, 'you have the most kissable mouth that I have ever encountered, and I would love to drown in your hair. Here or the bedroom, darling? Your choice.' Cathy felt right out of her depth until Faye beckoned her over. She got to her feet, relieved to be out of Rick's clutches. He disappeared and returned a few moments later with a tray loaded with more champagne and caviar.

As Faye had said, they were rolling up joints en masse. Romany lit one up. 'How about some Dylan?' he asked 'Cathy loves him.' Ed shifted uncomfortably in his seat and groaned as

Rick said, 'I know him well, maybe Cathy would like an introduction? I could fix it.'

'No way,' snapped Ed. 'We've got a tour to do.' Cathy dipped a small cracker into her caviar and smiled as Rick placed the *Blonde on Blonde* album on the turntable and Dylan's voice filled the room. Vic emerged from the bedroom with the two redheads in tow; he'd had a great time. Al was still in the bedroom; he was really snap-happy tonight and he'd got some great shots of many bodies in the act of love. The best thing of all though was that he'd got some great shots of Vic and the two redheads, and Vic didn't even know as he'd been too engrossed in the girls. These photos would be going into Al's private collection, and what made things better was that he knew both girls were hookers and had been well paid by Rick. Vic was in the dark about this though and that's the way things would stay.

Faye spotted Gerry the keyboard player and he looked pissed off. He was missing his wife and had voiced his feelings. Faye sympathised with him and decided that once the night began to swing, she'd stick by his side. He could be her knight in shining armour if anyone got too close to her, and she desperately needed to get Ed and Cathy together so that she'd be free of any sexual activities. Romany was dancing around naked, and Rick had disappeared into another room where an orgy was in progress. Drugs and drink were abundant and making themselves felt amongst many.

Cathy felt very odd and sick. She had once more had her drink spiked and was losing all sense of reality. 'Watch this space,' said Vic to Al. 'I hope you've got plenty of film in your camera, this is going to be better than any of your blue films. Ed's nearly out of it and Cathy seems close.'

Cathy was now like a zombie; she had no idea where she was, kept seeing bright lights and wanted to laugh out loud, doing so several times. Faye moved over to her and hugged her, and for a second Vic thought that he was going to get some girl-on-girl action. The two girls were kissing and groping each other. Faye took Cathy's hand, helped her to her feet and seated her beside Ed who had his eyes closed. Another joint appeared and Cathy took it in a trance. She looked up at the donor; it was Rick who had just returned from his orgy whilst Romany had wandered in to his bedroom and taken over. Faye was smiling and stroking Cathy's left breast which was now exposed. Cathy was beginning to feel numb.

Ed awoke and stared to his right, watching Faye caressing Cathy's breast. He was uncertain if he was going to get a threesome, but he doubted it. Vic wandered over, 'Ed, Cathy looks tired,' he said. 'Why don't we help her into one of the bedrooms so she can sleep; we don't want her falling over on stage, do we?' Al was getting excited; he was finally going to see the girl in action. Rick looked on with interest; he had some amyl nitrate in his pocket. Ed touched Cathy and she flinched as if she'd burned herself. Faye got up and left the room in search of Gerry as Dylan's voice echoed in Cathy's ears and she thought that she could actually see him.

Vic was speaking to her but it was garbled. The sight of Al made her laugh; he looked even more like Stan Laurel. Ed leaned over and kissed her, everything was in slow motion and the kiss seemed to last forever. She felt fantastic as she staggered to her feet and lolled against Vic, before being steered with a very groggy Ed into another bedroom. The lights hurt her eyes and it seemed as if the ceiling was caving in. When she lay down she felt as if she was on a moving carousel. Strong arms encircled her, then she was being rolled over on her stomach and someone was unzipping her dress and undoing her bra. She was rolled back over again as a hand slid over her thighs and her panties were removed. It seemed as if her lover had acquired an extra pair of hands. It was Ed's lips upon hers and his arms around her, but someone's head was between her legs, sucking and probing at her. The whole thing was too much. She gasped as Ed entered her, he felt huge. She achieved one orgasm after another as Ed took her again and again.

Al filmed away, and by his side Vic was once more taking himself in hand. Romany staggered into the room, climbed onto the bed and crashed straight away, oblivious to the action beside him. Ed sent Cathy into a frenzy, making her twist and writhe. Al was beginning to get cramp as he'd been filming for ages, while Vic was slumped dazed in the corner, and Rick was hovering around the couple on the bed. He approached the bed whispering, 'I've just the thing for you, young lady, as he saw the contorted look on her face. Cathy was reaching orgasm yet again. Ed was still rock hard and she felt as if her mind was about to blow. She pulled him closer, clawing at his back as Rick snapped a capsule under her nose. The orgasm was slow and seemed never ending, and then she lapsed into nothing.

Vic eyed the couple. He had footage of them; they weren't going anywhere, and Ed would be on his payroll forever now. He wouldn't want footage like that shown to the public, and neither would Cathy. 'Great show, kids,' he said as they both slumbered.

'Do you think he'll remember?' asked Al anxiously.

Vic laughed. 'Considering what they've been given tonight, I'll be very surprised if either of them ever opens their eyes again. Come on, let's find Faye; it's safe for her to come to bed now.' He pulled the covers over the lovers and left the room with a bleary eyed Al.

When Cathy awoke the following morning, Rick was lying next to her propped up on one elbow and gazing at her. Everyone appeared to be in a heap on the bed, and although it was huge, Cathy knew it was far too crowded. Ed lay the other side of her and Faye was spread-eagled across him while Romany was hanging halfway off the bed. Cathy shut her eyes; she couldn't recall a thing about the previous night. She pulled the covers up higher and tried to go back to sleep. Rick snuggled under with her. 'You're some girl,' he said, his hands parting her thighs. Cathy pushed his hands away and drifted back to sleep once more, but Rick was persistent and Cathy awoke with him astride her. She tried to push him off but to no avail. Faye decided that she was feeling some strange vibrations so she thought that she was dreaming. However, the vibrations were getting stronger and more realistic as the bed began to move. Opening one eye she saw Rick astride Cathy. The girls made eye contact and Faye could see that Cathy was frozen with fear. It was over quickly and when Rick rolled off the terrified girl, he accidently knocked Romany onto the floor. Romany swore loudly as he hit the floor.

'Why didn't you wake me?' he yelled at his brother. 'We've got an interview this morning.' He stared over at Ed. 'Someone wake him up; get your arse in gear, Faye.' Karl, Ed's bodyguard, was waiting for them in the kitchen. He'd had a pretty good night with the females that Rick had invited but he'd not indulged in any drugs; his job was to protect Ed so he had to stay alert. Ed suddenly awoke and stared around him. The sight of Cathy one side of him, and Faye on the other, made him wonder if he'd had a threesome after all; he couldn't remember a thing.

Vic was running around like a mother hen. Cathy was up and dressed as quickly as she could, then she hurried downstairs with the others, deciding that she'd have a long soak in the bath when she returned to the hotel. Faye had to glam herself so they'd just have to wait. She washed and began to apply her make-up, but didn't hear the door open behind her or hear it lock, and the first inkling she had that she was not alone was when an arm snaked around her waist. She was held in a firm embrace. 'Open your legs,' grunted Romany, hiking her dress up around her hips.

'Leave off!' Faye cried, trying to pull her dress down again. Using brute force, Romany took her standing up after he'd literally torn her lace panties from her. Downstairs, the occupants of the car were hooting loudly.

From the window, Rick saw Vic leave the car and move toward the front door. 'Romany, come on, Vic's coming,' said Rick.

Romany increased his hold on Faye. 'Jeez,' he murmured, 'so am I.' Afterwards, Romany tore himself away and Faye gazed into the mirror sobbing and wondering where it had all gone wrong. She'd met Ed in 1971, and he'd told her that he loved her, got engaged to her, moved her into his home and given her everything. Then he'd changed, taking more drugs and becoming sexually insatiable. She felt so unhappy as she put on her damaged panties and tried to repair her make-up.

Vic was now at Rick's door. He stuck his head in. 'Come on, we're waiting,' he bawled. Faye picked up her bag, still sobbing, and left as fast as she could.

Back at the hotel, Cathy did indeed soak in the bath, and she was beginning to feel half human when there was a knock on the door. 'Just a minute,' she called getting out of the bath and wrapping the beige fluffy dressing gown around her. She opened the door to find a very dishevelled Faye. 'What's wrong?' cried Cathy, as Faye threw herself into Cathy's arms.

'I'm so unhappy,' she sobbed. 'It's Ed, he's changed so much. He's so heavily into drugs now and he's always wanting sex. It's as if he likes humiliating me, and Romany won't leave me alone. If I threaten him and say I'll tell Ed he just grins and says he wouldn't believe me. He's right, Ed can see no wrong in him; he's his best friend and seems more important than me.' Cathy seated the shaking girl on her bed, knowing that Faye was right; Ed would always believe his best friend above anyone else. Faye broke down. 'Vic Lee's circus is evil,' she sobbed. 'I saw what happened to you with Rick this morning and I know that you didn't encourage him.' Cathy shuddered at the thought of it. 'Look,' cried Faye, pulling her dress up. 'This underwear cost a fortune and now it's ruined.' Cathy was shocked at what she saw.

'Ed did this?' she asked in disbelief.

'No,' replied Faye. 'When you all went downstairs, Romany came into the bathroom and grabbed me from behind and this is the result.'

Inwardly, Cathy fumed. 'Animal.'

'What made it worse was that Rick was outside the door and he didn't help me.'

Cathy put her arm around Faye's shoulders. 'Try and put it behind you. Why are we letting them get to us? Let's get painted up and hit the shops. Don't forget I've not been to New York before; you can introduce me to the best places. We can get you some new underwear, in fact I might even get some myself, and then we'll have lunch and enjoy ourselves with no men around.'

Faye smiled and dabbed her eyes. 'Thanks,' she said, giving Cathy a hug.

'What for?'

'Listening to me.'

'Any time. Come on, get your face on.'

'Okay,' laughed Faye. 'I'm going to spend, spend, spend, and I'm going to pay for anything that you want. Wait till Ed gets the bill. Still after last night I think we need to treat ourselves.'

Cathy was feeling better already.

Vic's circus continued to concerts far and wide. In Philadelphia the band received rave reviews. Cathy got used to seeing herself in the papers, and was now doing interviews. At first it seemed strange but soon it became a way of life. She didn't kid herself though. Here she was getting the star treatment because of Ed's show, but in England she was just another speciality dancer. As the tour continued, she avoided as many parties as possible. The ones that she couldn't wriggle out of she'd attend and then disappear as soon as possible complaining of a headache or something similar.

On stage she worked with Ed, off stage she avoided him as much as she could. New York had unsettled her. If drugs and sex were part of Ed's life, they weren't hers. She needed sex like any other woman, but group sex? Definitely not. As for getting into the drug scene, there was no way.

In Miami, Vic pursued her. 'Honey, how would you like to record?'

Cathy laughed. 'With my voice?'

'Can't be that bad, and by the time we put on double tracking, back up vocals, and special effects, you'll sound great.'

'No thanks,' replied Cathy, 'I'm not interested. I just want to get back to England once this tour's over, then Ed can complete his commitments to you and we can start a new life together.' She was lying in the sun, attempting to get a tan. Nearby, Noddy looked his usual self, a typical advert for a first-time Englishman abroad. He had his socks on, trousers rolled up, no shirt, and a handkerchief knotted around his head.

Vic viewed him with disgust and wondered why Cathy didn't get rid of him. He crouched down beside her. 'Honey, don't you realise what I'm offering you?' he said. 'Fame, fortune, a long list of young studs. Tell you what. We'll get you to a clinic so you can lose some weight. We'll turn your hair silvery-blonde and get you a whole new wardrobe. Ed won't mind paying, how does that sound?'

'Awful,' replied Cathy. 'Go away Vic, you're standing in my sun.' Nearby on a sun lounger, Noddy began to snore as Cathy lapped up the sunshine. The place was full of chinless wonders and has-beens, but the weather outweighed the vile, ageing Casanovas and misfits.

Ed was a happy man; Cathy and Faye had bonded and were having quite a girly time. At night he partied with Faye, came home with Faye, went to bed with Faye, but during the night he crept out and joined his beloved downstairs spending the rest of the night with her. Faye was happy too, it certainly helped her having Cathy on board. The lack of sexual activity was great and Cathy was just like a big sister.

In Chicago, the band played a blinding concert. Ed was on top form and the audience loved the new addition to the band. Cathy was sought after, especially by a certain Sammy Silver. He bombarded her with flowers, gifts, and phone calls but Vic wasn't happy and began to intercept Sammy's calls. As for the flowers, he took the gift card out and told Cathy that they were from him in appreciation for her hard work. Cathy was unaware that Sammy had had a fixation for her since the Ted Taylor show, and delighted in Vic's generosity.

In Memphis, however, things turned nasty. Some guy managed to get up onto the stage during *Angel*. One minute Cathy was in Ed's arms, and the next she was being wrenched away by a stranger. There was confusion everywhere, and Ed hit the man with his microphone stand. Security removed the dazed man and he had to be carted off to the nearest hospital. After the show, Ed rounded on Vic. 'Where the fuck was security? Or Karl for that matter? That could have been nasty.'

'It was nasty. You could get done for assault.'

'Fuck you,' Ed retorted. 'That guy could have had a gun, knife, or anything, and what kind of tour is this anyway. We always start in Ottawa, and yet this time we started in New York and we're travelling like a crazy spaghetti junction, the tour's all over the place.'

Vic felt as if he was about to have a nervous breakdown as Ed left the room kicking over a table and causing the vase on it to hit the floor. 'That doesn't help,' snapped Vic.

'Neither does security!' yelled Ed, slamming the door. Vic was worried; Ed's consumption of drugs was increasing daily. He needed drugs to help him sleep, drugs to wake him up, drugs to calm him down, drugs to get him high, and more drugs to get a good show out of him. The only thing that he didn't need drugs for was sex. Apart from that, Ed wanted to do more Dylan material and perform alone on acoustic guitar. Vic wasn't having it as lately Ed had had problems remembering the words to regular songs, so there was no way that new material was going to be added. Half of the time he couldn't even recall what he'd done the previous day.

Vic gave a deep sigh and wondered when Mick would make a full recovery.

Houston was a smash, but in Nashville, Ed's possessive streak reared its head. Hank Benson was in town and Cathy had worked with him for many years in the past. Noddy encouraged him to hang around as it was he who had got Hank his first big break. Ed seethed as Hank gushed all over Cathy and showered her with gifts and flowers. A very angry Ed questioned his beloved about her history with this singing cowboy but got little feedback. 'What is he to you? What are you trying to do to me?' he cried as they lay in bed after making love.

'A friend,' sighed Cathy. 'Just a friend.' Ed got out of bed and paced the floor, erotic images floated before his eyes. 'Ed come back to bed, it's you I love, I don't need this!' she cried.

Ed continued to pace, and punched the wall. 'If he touches you, I'll kill him,' he yelled. Cathy got out of bed and surveyed her lover who was now seated on the edge of the bed with his head in his hands sobbing. There was only one way to calm him, so, sinking to her knees she took his member in her mouth and felt him begin to relax. His hand stroked the back of her head.

'I love you so much,' he murmured. 'I get jealous because I can't stand the thought of you with anyone else.' Cathy said nothing, how could she? Her mouth was full and, shortly after, Ed apologised. They went back to bed. Cathy had got rid of his tension and fears and together they slept.

The following day, however, Ed's fears had returned. When he was on stage with Cathy, he saw Hank in the wings armed with a massive bouquet of flowers. It was obvious who they were for and as Cathy wiggled past Ed in her *Little Egypt* costume, he grabbed her wrist hard. He was going to show the cowboy who Cathy belonged to. Cathy attempted to break free but Ed swung the girl round to face him and brought her to her knees. Alarmed, Vic yelled, 'let her go,' as Faye gasped. She'd seen this side of Ed many times but she had no idea of what

Cathy had done wrong. Tears were forming in Cathy's eyes as Ed increased his grip. He continued to sing holding the scared girl in a submissive position at his feet.

Noddy elbowed Vic. 'He's lost it,' he said. 'Do something or we're on the next flight home. She's not here to be abused by some moronic junkie.'

Faye was trying to get Ed's attention. 'Let her go!' she screamed. Hank held his breath; he didn't understand why Ed was doing this.

'I said, do something,' snapped a very irate Noddy, 'or I will.' Blood was now trickling from Cathy's wrist, but Vic didn't know what to do. 'Did you hear me? Do something,' repeated Noddy. 'It's obvious that he's lost the plot with his consumption of drugs.' Blood was now running down Cathy's arm but still Ed held her in the same position.

Vic shouted over to a very confused Romany, 'stop him!'

Romany trudged over to Ed and mouthed 'She's bleeding.' A very startled Ed finally released Cathy. He hadn't meant to hurt her, just show her who was boss. Cathy got to her feet and continued to dance despite the blood which was now very visible. As soon as the number was over she rushed off stage and threw herself into Noddy's arms.

'What's he on?' snapped Noddy. Vic turned to Faye, trying to shift the blame and asked her the same question. 'I don't know,' she cried, 'you supply him.' Then she fled in tears. Cathy's wrist had now stopped bleeding as it was just a surface gash and looked worse than it was. Ed was now halfway through Free's *All right Now* and, noting Vic's anxiety, just grinned and carried on singing.

When the show was over, Ed asked Vic where Cathy was.

'Gone to Hank's party,' replied Vic, puffing on a cigar. 'What happened earlier? You scared her.'

Ed towelled his hair and stared at his inquisitive manager. 'Mind your own business,' he replied. 'I need some stuff, let's party.' They left the concert hall, followed by a moody Karl who was fed up with Ed. He'd minded a few in his time but this one was a real idiot.

At the party, an elderly man attempted to make a move on Faye and guided her away into a corner. Ed was furious as the old man was filling her head with nonsense, telling her that she'd be an overnight sensation in the movies. Ed moved in. 'Yeah, overnight star and nothing in the morning,' he snapped. 'Come on, Faye, I want to dance.' He saw Cathy go upstairs, and saw Hank follow about three minutes later. The knife within began to twist. Faye was gorgeous but the girl that he wanted was upstairs.

Cathy was in the powder room doing her make-up when Hank surprised her. 'You can't improve on perfection,' he said. 'You look the same as you did ten years ago.' Hank embraced her, running his hands through her hair. 'My wife lives in England now,' he added.

Cathy stiffened as he began to run his hands up and down her body. She removed his hands. 'Look,' she said, 'I'm flattered but…'

Hank pulled her in close. 'You're driving me wild, stay the night. I'm very discreet,' he murmured. 'No one will know. Come with me, you know you want to.' He took her hand and led her into his bedroom. She pulled back but he smiled and seated her on his bed. 'Now my darling, I've got everything here that you could possibly want: coke, amphetamine, grass, booze, and an experience in the art of love that you'll never forget.' Cathy groaned. How many times had she heard the last bit? She'd stopped counting. He flicked a switch and immediately two figures appeared on the video screen. They were locked together in a naked, passionate embrace.

'Switch it off!' cried Cathy.

'Okay,' replied Hank, 'I will if it disturbs you.' He crossed to the dressing table and took out a small oblong maroon box. 'How's your wrist now?' he queried.

'Okay,' replied Cathy, 'but I don't know why he did it.'

'I do,' said Hank. 'He wants you as much as I do, as if you didn't know.' Cathy said nothing as she took the box from Hank. She opened it and gazed at a gold bracelet; it was beautiful but she didn't think she could accept it. She felt sure that this was a gift and that it came with a price; a price that she wasn't prepared to pay. Hank kissed her again and she resisted, so he held her to him. 'Okay Cathy, I'm a patient man, I won't rush you but just let me hold you for a moment.'

Cathy relaxed as he held her. How good it felt. Ed meant everything to her; if he'd cut her wrist off she'd still have loved him, but Hank's embrace was very pleasant. She pulled away, 'I'm going downstairs.'

'Okay,' replied Hank, 'but keep the bracelet and if you change your mind about staying…'

'I won't,' she said and went downstairs.

The minute she arrived downstairs she was pounced on by a scruffy middle-aged man. 'I've been looking for you,' he said.

'Really?' asked Cathy. 'Have we met before then?'

'In dreams, babe,' replied the man, steering her into the corner. 'I've got the key to heaven.' Cathy eyed the man suspiciously. From his pocket he produced a cellophane packet with white powder in it. 'Take it,' he said, 'it's on me this time.'

'No thanks, I don't need it.'

'Hey, babe, you don't understand, don't knock it if you haven't tried it,' the scruffy man insisted.

'No thanks.'

'There's nothing to it; you'll feel terrific, girlie, really great. Isn't that how you want to feel? Everyone else does.'

'I said no and I meant no,' said Cathy firmly, turning away.

The man took her arm. 'But babe, you're entitled to a little fun, you need to relax.' He pointed over to Vic who was conversing with Ed. 'Look at old Vic,' he continued. 'Rich, fat, and making a load of dough out of you, Ed, and the boys. After he's taken his cut out, you get the left-overs. Come on honey, wise up.'

Cathy laughed. 'That's my agent over there,' she said, pointing to where Noddy sat with Faye.

The man threw back his head and laughed. 'That creep?' he said. 'By the look of him I'd better get over there fast and see if he wants a trip to Shangri-La.' He ambled over to Noddy but was waylaid en route by Romany. Sammy Silver chose that moment to arrive and he apologised to everyone for his lateness.

'Probably couldn't tell the time on his Mickey Mouse watch. Who invited that moron?' asked Ed. On Sammy's arm was an ageing movie star of about forty-five. She'd squeezed her size sixteen body into a size twelve dress and there were rolls of fat everywhere. She wore a low-necked gown and her breasts were spilling out of the bodice. The skirt was split to the thigh revealing masses of cellulite, plus the fact that she wasn't wearing any briefs under it.

'Get a load of that,' laughed Ed as Hank greeted Sammy Silver warmly.

'What's bugging you?' asked Vic, drinking a glass of champagne.

'Nothing,' replied Ed. 'Except I wish that cowboy would drop down dead.'

'What the fuck's he done to you?' asked Vic, worried by Ed's outburst.

'He's moving in on my lady.

'On Faye? I'll sort him out, don't worry.'

Ed scowled. 'Don't act ignorant. It's not Faye.'

'Oh,' said Vic, 'so that's what it was all about on stage earlier. Now keep away from Cathy, you scared her before.'

'Vic, I don't know what you're talking about,' replied Ed. The truth was that he didn't as he'd been on a cocktail of drugs tonight and only just about knew his own name. Somewhere in the recesses of his mind he knew that Hank was enamoured with Cathy, but other than that everything was blank, so he hadn't a clue what Vic was going on about. He left Vic, uttering 'get stuffed', and wandered over to Sammy. 'Come and have a drink, kiddo,' he slurred, 'I'll introduce you to my fiancée; she's a fan of yours.'

'Great,' replied Sammy. 'I've been trying to catch your show but without any success.'

'See Vic about tickets,' Ed replied.

'Great show tonight,' said Hank, coming up behind him. 'Can I get you anything Ed?'

Ed shot him a look of pure hatred and nodded. Taking him by the arm he growled, 'yeah cowboy, keep away from Cathy.'

Hank frowned, replying, 'I think I'll mingle,' as he brushed Ed's hand away. Faye got to her feet as Sammy approached her.

Vic was perplexed. Hadn't Ed remembered about the incident on stage? Romany was at his side. 'Have you got anything, Vic?' he asked.

'There's a dealer here, but the last lot of stuff I had from him was rubbish,' Vic replied.

Romany laughed. 'Guess what, Sammy's date is in the next room offering head to any one who wants it.'

'Really?' inquired Vic. 'I might get a helping myself later. I'll see what I can do. Ed desperately needs something.'

Ed did need something; his mind was a total blank. He was sitting on a leopard skin covered couch and staring over at Cathy who was surrounded by a group of young men. He ached to go over to her, but Vic had told him to stay away as he'd scared her. What the hell was that all about? His problem was that he didn't know what to say because he really had no idea what he'd done. Sammy was asking him if he could dance with Faye. 'Go ahead,' he replied. His mind was racing; he had to be somewhere but didn't know where. Did he have a show to do? Had he already done it? Who had he got to see? It was no good asking Vic as he'd already told him to stay away from Cathy, so he must have done something. He watched as Cathy left the group of men and went upstairs. Minutes later he followed her up.

It was while she was in the powder room that Cathy

discovered her necklace missing. Hearing footsteps outside the door made her think that Hank had come upstairs as they continued into the bedroom. Cathy walked to the bedroom and tapped on the door. 'Hank, I'm leaving now but I've lost my necklace. It's a pendant; if you find it, can you give it to Ed or Faye?' There was silence, and Cathy pushed the door open. 'Hank?' she called again.

A voice whispered, 'come here.' Cathy was puzzled and walked inside the room. Suddenly an arm enclosed her from behind gasping, 'I need you.' She tried to scream but her voice failed her. She was panic stricken as Ed slammed the door shut with his foot, and her heart beat wildly. He pressed up against her. Shivers were racking her body and then Ed turned her to face him. Cathy was terrified. He'd cut her wrist, and now what was next? Ed's eyes bored into her and she realised that his mental state was unhinged; if she fought back she was destroying his fantasy, whatever it was.

The vomit was rising in her throat as he led her to the bed and pushed her onto it. She was weeping and felt sure that he was going to kill her; any false move could cost her her life. Instinctively she held him to her in a reassuring embrace and comforted him as if he were a baby. 'I love you,' he whispered, kissing her. Cathy stared up at him. His eyes were glazed and he was obviously sicker than she'd first thought. 'Come on,' he slurred, 'let's get that dress off you.'

'I can't,' cried Cathy, 'you're holding me down.' Ed relaxed his hold slightly to allow her to remove her dress. She wriggled out of it slowly praying that someone would come in, but Ed got impatient and tore it from her body. She was wearing nothing under it as it was clingy and made underwear impossible. This excited him even more and he was now struggling with his trousers. 'Ed I'm tired,' Cathy insisted, 'please, let's go home.'

Ed stared at her with a crazed expression on his face. 'Okay,' he relented, 'we'll wait.' He got to his feet and helped Cathy up.

He stared at her for a minute and then held her close. Cathy sighed with relief, but not for long though. As she attempted to put on her clothing he suddenly slapped her around her face hard. She cried out and he struck her again. 'Bitch!' he shouted. 'Fucking bitch, you whore!' Once more he struck her, this time sending her backwards across the bed. Cathy was terrified as he towered above her. He'd never struck her before. What was happening to him? She attempted to rise but he pushed her back down again. Cathy was frozen with fear and as she watched him remove his trousers; it was as if she was paralyzed. He screamed all kinds of obscenities at her and then humiliated her by raping her. She was sobbing as she was violated. He was hurting her and she felt as if there was worse to come. The look on his face was one of crazed anger and hate, and Cathy wondered if he was going to kill her. She pictured her three children with their innocent little faces; how she wanted to go home.

Suddenly Ed's countenance changed. He stood up and dressed, staring at a motionless Cathy. She was too scared to move, and then he smiled at her, saying, 'Come on, baby, let's go home. Rusty, Fawn, and the girls will be waiting.' Downstairs, Vic had noted the couple's absence and began to worry. The worry became shock as Ed and Cathy came downstairs. Cathy's dress was torn, she appeared frightened, and her mascara had run into rivulets down her cheeks. Ed had a silly, happy expression on his face and approached Vic. 'We're leaving,' he slurred. 'We have to get back to the caravan.'

Vic went blood red in the face and swore, 'Fucking arsehole!' he bellowed 'I told you to stay away from her.'

'Why?' replied Ed. 'We just got married, isn't she beautiful?' Vic surveyed Cathy. She looked as if she'd been raped, probably had, but then Ed's moods were unpredictable. He summoned Karl and ordered him to take the couple back to the hotel. Cathy shook her head, but Vic pretended he hadn't seen it and bundled her into the limo outside alongside Ed. Karl felt sorry for her, but orders were orders. Mr Lee would put things right in the morning by sending the girl flowers, several gifts, and buying her a new dress, but he'd probably supply Ed with more drugs too, spoiling the whole thing, and he felt sure that there was no way that Cathy would get an apology.

Vic watched them drive away and then went back inside the house. He informed Faye that Ed had left with Cathy. She replied that she would stay on a bit longer as she was enjoying herself. 'Stupid cunt,' muttered Vic, and went in search of Sammy's date; he could do with a blow job.

Back at the hotel, Cathy went straight to bed, still weeping as Ed followed her into her room. Karl stood in the doorway asking if he was finished for the night. 'Yes,' muttered Ed, 'piss off.'

Concerned, Karl asked Cathy if she needed anything and if she was okay, and when she replied, 'I think I'm all right,' he hesitated in the doorway.

'I'll be right outside, if you need me,' he reassured her, 'goodnight.' He closed the door quietly and stationed himself outside the door on a chair. He'd sleep there for the rest of the night, and if he heard the girl crying or screaming or in any kind of distress, he would go in and teach that motherfucker a lesson. He may be paid to help Ed out when situations got nasty but this was one time when Cathy appeared to be the one that needed protection, and if she did need it, he would see that she got it. One thing was sure, he would never work for Ed again; the guy was a drug addict and totally out of control.

In bed, Cathy lay on her side, terrified, wondering what Ed would do next. He was on the edge of insanity and dangerous, she felt him snuggle up to her, murmuring, 'I love you, baby', and then he was silent. Still weeping, Cathy fell into a deep slumber.

The following morning, Cathy awoke with a start as the events of the previous night came flooding back to her. Outside her room, Vic was stunned when he saw Karl stationed by the door. 'Why are you here?' he asked, 'you should be in bed, I'll need you to be alert later today.'

'I'll leave when you check to see if they're both all right,' replied Karl. 'Ed was out of it last night and Cathy was very distressed.'

Vic went blood red. 'Thank you, you're a real pro. Now get some shuteye, you're back on duty at two thirty this afternoon.' He tapped on the door, needing to know if Cathy was still alive, or Ed for that matter. He'd certainly spouted some rubbish last night, something about marriage and caravans. If they were both dead he was doing a runner right now and blaming the whole thing on Al Simpkins. 'Cathy,' he called, 'You've both got a photo session this afternoon.'

It was Ed's voice that responded in less than dulcet tones. 'Please leave me alone Vic, I've got a banger, piss off.'

'Charming,' said Vic, pushing the door open and entering. 'Good day, Cathy. Are you all bright-eyed and bushy-tailed?' He turned back to Karl and gave him the thumbs up, but the bodyguard wanted to see for himself so poked his head around the door. Seeing Cathy sitting up in bed glowering at Vic made him laugh so he wandered off to his room. 'Don't stay in bed too long, I want these photos to be perfect. Oh and Faye's gone out,' said Vic, opening the drapes and letting the sun stream in. Ed let out a scream, his eyes were killing him, his head felt fit to burst and he had an evil taste in his mouth. He picked up one of his shoes and aimed it at Vic. Fortunately for Vic it missed, but unfortunately it smashed a vase of flowers, spilling water and rose petals everywhere. The vase lay in half.

'Fuck you, and fuck Faye!' screamed Ed. 'Now fuck off.' Vic bid a hasty retreat, fuming at the fact that now he would have to pay for a vase and damage to the carpet. He now wished that both of his acts had died, and he could have made a 'Romeo and Juliet' type headline for the press.

His thoughts were interrupted by Sammy Silver approaching.

'Hi Vic,' he said brightly, revealing perfect white teeth as he smiled. 'Cathy doesn't return my calls, acknowledge my gifts or flowers, and she even ignored me at the party last night. I thought I'd come and see her to find out what I've done wrong. I only wanted a date, nothing more.'

Vic was horrified, and he could feel his blood pressure soaring. 'Bad time,' he said. 'She came back from the party feeling ill and I don't want her disturbed, she has a show to do tonight. I'll tell you what, we'll be in Los Angeles very soon and we won't be so busy then. I'll speak to her later and make sure that you get your date when we arrive there but at the moment her personal life is dreadful, she's got a lot on her mind. That's probably why she didn't speak to you last night, she probably didn't see you.'

Sammy was dejected, but smiled, 'Okay Vic, I'll leave it to you.' Then he walked sadly away.

Chapter Thirteen

As the show wound itself across the states, everyone was tired and getting bored, but as they approached Los Angeles they perked up. Romany knew he would be seeing Rick again, Noddy had always wanted to take one of his acts there, and Ed knew that it was only a matter of time before Faye disappeared to stay with her friends. As the plane landed, the police had to hold back the surging crowds. Ed appeared on the steps with Faye who posed in her usual fashion. Cameras flashed as one fan gushed to her friend, 'doesn't Ed look great, and isn't Faye gorgeous?' Her friend nodded, wishing she had a gun so she could shoot Faye down in cold blood.

Cathy gazed around her as the band was whisked away with Karl. 'This is the biggest turn-out yet,' she said to Noddy excitedly.

He grinned. 'California, here I come!' Cathy took to Los Angeles, and soon found herself rubbing shoulders with many celebrities. The weather was fantastic too, and everyone seemed so friendly.

Vic paid her a visit. 'Enjoying yourself?' he asked.

'I love the place,' replied a beaming Cathy.

'This is my domain, anything you want, just whistle,' said Vic. 'Oh and Sammy Silver requests your presence one night. I think he wants to show you the sights and take you to the best restaurant.' He gave her arm an affectionate squeeze and Cathy giggled, finding the very suggestion of a date with Sammy funny.

'I don't think so,' she laughed.

'Well then, dear, let me know if you change your mind, and don't you forget what I said about me making you into a star.'

'I won't forget, Vic, and tell Sammy that I'm too busy.'

'Okay babe, get some rest. Tomorrow's concert is sold out,' said Vic as he turned to leave.

Cathy watched Vic walk away, and yawned. She decided to take his advice; there was another party to attend tonight and he had told her that this one was compulsory. At least she could get a few hours' sleep. She walked over to her luxurious bed and lay down, wondering why Tony never replied to her letters or phone calls. It upset her but she guessed that Tony was playing his usual mind games. Closing her eyes, she soon lapsed into a dream where she was back home playing with her children.

The party that evening was a very grand affair. Rick was there and made a beeline for Cathy. 'Remember me?' he asked.

'You're Romany's brother,' replied Cathy.

'That was some scene in New York, wasn't it? I'm holding a party tomorrow night, and you're invited.' He moved to kiss her on the cheek but Cathy pulled away.

Romany wandered over and leered at Cathy, undressing her with his eyes. 'Brother dear, what are you doing to our Cathy?' he asked.

'Inviting her to my party. With Ed of course,' Rick replied.

'Of course, must have Superprick,' sneered Romany.

Cathy was in awe of the house; it belonged to a record producer and was on the beach. Suddenly Ed appeared at Cathy's side. 'Fancy a walk on the beach?' he asked, 'Faye wants to mingle.' Cathy nodded and they wandered out onto the beach, kicked their shoes off, and strolled along hand in hand as if they didn't have a care in the world. They walked to the water's edge and sat down on the sand recalling the sixties, Dylan, their hippy wedding, Cathy's children, the memorable Christmas that they had spent together in Ed's mansion, and thoughts of the future. Ed said he could either keep her in luxury or they could resume their dream of the open road. 'We'll do whatever you want,' said Ed. 'I'm your slave.'

Not the other night, thought Cathy to herself. He'd terrified her, slapped her and taken her by force. His brain was scrambled that night and it was obvious that he could recall none of it or he would have apologised by now. Cathy turned the conversation back to the open road and a little later they returned to the house.

Ed sought out Faye. 'I'm leaving,' he said. 'Tomorrow night's show is sold out and I'm tired.'

'But I'm having so much fun,' replied Faye. 'Cathy can look after you.' Her circle of friends stared in disbelief as Ed and Cathy left, and Faye giggled, flirted, and danced. Nearby, Rick overheard the conversation and decided that he'd look after Faye himself.

The concert the following night was one of the best the band had done. By now, Cathy was getting her own following but tried to stay out of the spotlight as much as possible. She didn't want to attend Rick's party, and told Vic that she didn't feel well, but Vic was adamant. 'Faye fucked off to Sacramento earlier,' he snapped, 'and Ed wants you with him. Don't argue, you're going. If you feel that ill I'll get you something.' Cathy sighed. There was no point in protesting but she was feeling so homesick and wanted this tour over as soon as possible. She didn't like the lifestyle and ached to cuddle her children.

Rick's party was about the freakiest thing that Cathy had attended. There were porn stars, gays, transvestites, starlets, movie moguls, record producers, closet queens, psychics, ageing movie and rock stars, and many other freaks. The women were scantily clad, the dress code being optional, and as for the men, some of them were half undressed already. One ageing actress lay on a couch with her dress hiked up around her thighs, revealing the fact that she hadn't bothered to put underwear on, and propositioned every male that passed. Cathy looked away and sat beside Ed, listening to him giving an interview. She feared both Rick and Romany, so had been drinking only orange juice, wanting to stay sober and ready to leave early.

The wine flowed freely and the drugs were in abundance as usual. She turned to her left and saw an old man of about eighty masturbating and staring at her. Vic was flustered as he'd just chatted up a lovely young blonde and disappeared into a bedroom with her, but closer examination made him squirm because although the lady was willing, *she* was a *he*. He sat down beside Cathy for a while and made polite conversation before heading for the back room where he knew there was an orgy in progress. As he left Cathy's side, Romany appeared with a couple of drinks for her and Ed. The reporter had had enough and headed for the bar as Romany sat down alongside Ed. He handed Cathy her orange juice and she eyed it suspiciously, wondering if it was doctored.

Romany noted this. 'Pure orange juice,' he lied, handing Ed a brandy. 'Tell you what though, I've got some top grade stuff here. Rick's just got it.' Cathy grimaced. She hated the drug scene and wanted to go back to the hotel but Ed wanted to try the stuff, and indulged. 'Sure you don't want any?' asked Romany. 'It'll make you feel great, Cathy; it's out of this world.' Cathy shook her head, not realising that her drink was indeed fixed by a very devious Rick. Romany got up and wandered off as Ed and Cathy watched the antics of some of the party goers. In a corner, a group of people were trying to build a human pyramid but didn't get very far.

One young girl paced the room looking down her trousers. 'I can't find them!' she wailed. 'They've gone.' Cathy was beginning to feel tired, and Ed's speech was becoming slurred so she knew that she wasn't going to get her early night now unless she could ring for a cab or find Karl. Trying to get to her feet she fell onto the floor and gazed up at Ed who now was slumped across the sofa, staring up at the ceiling. Rick was close at hand and helped Cathy back onto her feet and onto the sofa alongside the now glassy-eyed Ed. Her eyes were stinging so she closed them as another glass of orange juice was being thrust into her hand. Cathy opened her eyes once more, and Rick stared into her pupils as a watchful Romany eyed Ed. To Cathy, it was as if she was viewing the room, and everyone in it, through a giant kaleidoscope. Her mouth was dry and she gulped the orange juice down. The next thing she saw was Rick and Romany helping Ed to his feet; he stared ahead of him, oblivious of anything or anyone around him. Once more Cathy attempted to rise but fell back onto the sofa, and watched as Ed was helped from the room. He staggered, supported by the two brothers and called Cathy's name.

'It's okay Ed, we'll come back for Cathy,' Rick reassured him, 'but first, we need to get you to bed and then you can snuggle up together.' Cathy closed her eyes once more; she was drifting in and out of consciousness. She didn't know how long she'd been in this state but was awoken by Rick gently shaking her. 'We've put Ed to bed, honey, and we're going to take you to join him. Do you need me to carry you?' Cathy shook her head, wondering why Rick's face looked three dimensional. She got to her feet and began to walk with Rick's help, but then hit the floor once more. He scooped her up into his arms and headed towards the bedroom, or so Cathy thought. She was quite surprised when, on reaching the room, there was no sign of Ed. Rick laid her on the bed and began to undress her, but Cathy stopped him, maintaining that she could do it herself and inquiring as to where Ed was. Rick didn't answer.

'Just go to sleep,' he said soothingly.

She closed her eyes and heard the door open. Thinking that it was Ed she asked, 'where have you been? I've been worried.' There was no answer, and Cathy felt the bed move as a body sat on it. She felt a kiss on her cheek and opened her eyes to see, not

Ed but Romany. This was her worst nightmare and she felt her own adrenalin begin to kick in.

'Come to Daddy!' cried Romany. 'We're going to have our own private party, all three of us. My brother and I like to party hard, very hard.' The tiredness was beginning to lift, and Cathy shook with fear as she begged, pleaded, and protested when Rick came towards her. He pulled her to him and stripped her with Romany's help. She struggled, petrified at the thought of the ordeal before her. She pushed Rick away but as she did so, Romany was upon her, and as she repelled Romany, Rick was back.

Rick glowered at Romany; he was getting angry. 'She must have the staying power of a horse,' he snapped. 'I'm not raping her; there's no fun in that.' Cathy managed to break free of Romany and got off the bed, but unfortunately as soon as she got into a standing position, her legs gave way and the room spun once more. Romany picked her up and laid her on the bed again. Cathy's conscious state was in doubt and she closed her eyes.

A slap around her face brought her round again and she sat up, staring at the two brothers who both leered at her. 'Let's party!' bellowed Rick. 'The room's locked and soundproofed so you ain't going nowhere. I've got some coke here, that'll loosen you up and put you on top of the world.'

'No drugs,' cried Cathy. 'Take me to Ed, please.'

Rick laughed. 'You're loaded already. We've been supplying you and Ed all night. He's had enough to kill two men, so maybe tonight will be the last show that brings the curtain down for good.' He found the coke and brought it to the bedside. 'Snort it,' he ordered, 'or I'll fill your fucking veins with heroin.' Cathy obeyed. She was too scared to do anything else and it wasn't long before her groggy state began to leave her, replaced by a feeling of wellbeing and elation. She could feel her heart speed up and began to sense her body beginning to perspire. Rick gazed into her eyes and noted the dilation of her pupils.

'She's almost ready,' he said to Romany. Cathy lay inert as

Rick began to kiss her all over, finally sliding down and forcing his head between her legs. Lust was now taking over as Rick slipped his tongue inside her, and Romany sucked on her nipples. Very soon, Rick mounted her and Romany forced his engorged penis into her mouth.

'Ed's little angel, if he could only see her now,' he laughed. Rick was riding her as if his life depended on it.

'Call my name, cry, scream, I don't care which but I want to hear you call my name,' he yelled. 'Come on.' Unable to stop herself, Cathy arched towards him as her orgasm loomed, and seconds later she did indeed cry out to him, much to his satisfaction. A happy, satisfied Rick rolled off her and let Romany take his place. Cathy gazed up at Romany and saw the glint in his eyes. As soon as he entered her she climaxed.

'Good girl,' sneered Romany. 'Let's go.' He stared at the girl beneath him, she was moving in time with him urging him on and driving him wild, he wished that he could put this to music; last time had been great, this time was better. Cathy was thrashing around in wild abandon, caught up in a raging passion. Romany increased his efforts and stared down at his partner. Her expression was wild, her body sweet and red hot, she was coming over and over again; her energy was amazing. 'Come to Daddy!' cried Romany. 'One more time, just for Daddy, you want to, don't you?'

Cathy writhed beneath him, much to his satisfaction. She was coming again, and he could feel it. She clawed at his back crying, 'More, Romany, more.' The sensations that she was experiencing were out of this world and she dug her fingernails into his back, to the point where blood began to seep from the abrasions as she held Romany in a vice-like grip. Together they reached a simultaneous orgasm and then Romany moved off and was replaced by his brother.

For the next two hours, the fornication carried on. They'd gone through just about every sexual deviation possible, except one, and that was one that Rick was saving until the end. To introduce it earlier could have stopped play as he wasn't sure how Cathy would react. He nodded at his brother and Romany lay on his back and pulled Cathy astride him. To begin with everything was fine until Rick went behind her and then pushed her forward onto Romany. The next thing Cathy felt was unbearable pain, and she screamed out loud as the two men took her at the same time. Throughout her ordeal she cried, screamed, and begged them to stop but to no avail as they increased their efforts. Repeatedly she cried out to Ed, but in another room he still slumbered. Fully satisfied, Rick pulled away from Cathy and she collapsed across Romany who promptly pulled out of her and forced her head into his groin.

'Come on, baby, I'm fit to burst,' he groaned. 'Suck me.' Cathy's tears fell onto him which quite excited him. This was great; she was completely humiliated and the tears added to his pleasure.

He finally did burst, and the exhausted Cathy gave a sigh of relief. She pulled her clothes back on and took the drink that Rick offered her. Eyeing it suspiciously, she asked if there was anything in it.

'Pure orange juice,' replied Rick, 'don't need drugs now, you're going to bed.' He'd completely lost interest in Cathy now and wanted her out of his bedroom, but he was pleased that he'd saved the best till last and joked, 'you lost your virginity to me tonight, pretty lady. Take her back to Ed, Romany.'

Romany did as he was bade, and joked to Cathy. 'Let's hope that Ed doesn't wake up; you know how virile he is. You have my sympathy.' Cathy didn't answer; she was in too much pain. Back in bed with Ed, she snuggled up to him and, exhausted, slept.

The following morning she could recall nothing of the night before and wondered where she was. Ed stirred and rolled over with his eyes still closed. Cathy felt as if she'd been in a fight and attempted to sit up. Her insides were killing her and she slid down under the sheets again. Half asleep, Ed was already reaching out for her so she slid under the bedclothes and took him in her mouth; intercourse was out of the question. She teased him with her tongue and neither of them heard Rick enter the room with coffee. He heard Ed groan as Cathy took him deeper into her mouth. It didn't take long to release him and soon Cathy surfaced from under the bedclothes.

Rick cleared his throat, 'Coffee,' he said, placing two mugs of steaming hot coffee on the bedside table.

'I feel as if I've been in a fight,' said Cathy inquisitively. 'Did someone attack me, or did I fall over and hurt myself? I can't remember a thing. I remember arriving here and listening to Ed's interviews but after that everything's a blank.'

Ed scratched his head and stared at Cathy, 'I don't even remember getting here, it's crazy.' He got out of bed and headed for the en suite.

Rick seated himself on the edge of the bed and gazed into Cathy's eyes. 'The reason that you don't recall anything is because you both indulged very heavily last night,' he informed her. 'Sometimes drugs cause memory loss.'

Suddenly the door opened and Vic Lee stormed in looking shattered and very disgruntled. 'Move it Ed!' he yelled. 'You've got an interview later.' Ed emerged from the en suite, muttering about injustice.

'The only injustice is that I discovered you,' cried Vic.

'You look healthy and extremely wealthy on it.'

Vic punched the wall, 'I dragged you up from nothing to what you are today. If I hadn't found you, you'd still be nothing. I've given you a lifetime's devotion.'

'All of five years,' Ed quipped.

'It feels like a lifetime. Sometimes I've had to go down on my knees to procure contracts for you... and then there's Cathy. You tell everyone that there's nothing going on, and then send Faye to Sacramento and display Cathy on your arm. I cover up for you and then you fuck up. Don't you realise that every time you're photographed with her in Faye's absence, you are sending out very strong signals to the press, giving her husband grounds for adultery if he wants a divorce.'

'Don't know, don't care. Cathy wants a divorce anyway,' replied Ed.

'Not like this,' cried Vic. 'She has to be squeaky clean to get the court on her side and get custody of her kids.'

Cathy burst into a flood of tears. 'I've written home since I came to America,' she sobbed. 'Tony's not answering the phone or made any form of contact. I think my family's forgotten me.'

'Rubbish,' replied Vic, placing his arm around Cathy's naked shoulders. 'They must be very proud of you. I'll ring later; Tony won't ignore me. I'll fix it for you.' Cathy dried her eyes; if anyone could fix things, it was Vic. Vic turned to Ed. 'Come on,' he bawled, 'it's show time.' Rick left the room and went in search of his brother. He wanted everyone out including him.

After Los Angeles came Las Vegas. It left Cathy cold; the tall showgirls made her feel inferior, as did the dancers and the cocktail waitresses. Vegas was in the middle of nowhere, and Cathy couldn't wait to get out of it. It was a city but not the kind that Cathy wanted to see again, and she was getting more and more homesick by the second. A letter for her arrived the following day, and Noddy stuffed it into his pocket. He would give it to Cathy later in case the contents might unsettle her, as he knew just how unpredictable Tony was. He stretched out in his hotel room feeling tired, he always felt tired these days. Closing his eyes, he dozed off.

That night, Cathy limbered up backstage as Ed, surrounded by beautiful women, basked in the limelight. In a corner, Romany sat with a showgirl either side of him as he strummed his guitar. The rest of the band attempted to crack jokes, but they were starting to resent Cathy as every time they opened a newspaper

Ed was in it with her. The impression given was that they were back-up musicians to a double act. When Mick had been with them they were a unit, and even Romany was taking a back seat lately. They sighed as they saw Ed leave the room. They knew where he was headed and it wasn't for a rehearsal, although God knows he needed it.

Last night's show had been a near disaster. Ed kept forgetting his words, and clowning around made himself look a right idiot. He went into the wrong key in *Suspicious Minds*, and fell over during *Angel*, making Cathy put her foot down sharply as he wasn't there to catch her as she turned a double pirouette. The real faux pas of the night was when Ed forgot all of the words to *Little Egypt* and mumbled something incoherent. Fortunately Romany had saved the day by taking on the lead vocal. He wasn't a good singer, but without him the show would have been a complete fiasco. Ed was booed several times that night but didn't seem to notice.

Ed tapped on Cathy's door. 'Hi,' he said as he entered, 'I need to run through *Angel*, I've been told that I ballsed it up last night.'

'I'll second that,' snapped Noddy

'No one noticed,' replied Ed, indignantly.

'Well I did, as did the rest of the band. Anyway, I'll leave you to rehearse but make sure that it is a run through of *Angel* and not a run through of Cathy. She's a professional and gives one hundred per cent of herself to the audience; you appear to be giving one hundred per cent to the drug dealers. Vic's even disgusted with you, and wants Mick back; he never let the band down. Anyway you rehearse, that is if you can control that animal lust of yours. Where's Vic anyway?'

Ed looked shamefaced and stared at the floor. 'In my dressing room,' he mumbled.

'Yours, I thought it was the band's?' He went out slamming the door. Karl was stationed outside. 'Why are you here?' asked Noddy.

'Orders,' replied Karl. Noddy grunted and walked away.

A short while later, an angry Vic Lee headed for Cathy's room. His anger knew no bounds when he saw Karl stationed outside the door and, on entering the room, saw Ed servicing Cathy up against the wall. 'Some fucking 'Angel',' he snapped. 'Supposing I'd had the press with me?'

Ed ignored him and carried on until he'd reached his goal. Then he kissed Cathy, did his zip up and rounded on Vic. 'Don't you ever knock?' he said angrily.

'What is it with you two?' Vic exploded. 'It's bloody obscene.'

'Hold your horses,' said Ed defensively. 'Cathy, come here. Let's show our good friend, Vic, what we were doing earlier, apart from what he saw.' Cathy obliged, turned a perfect double pirouette and Ed caught her. 'See,' said Ed, 'It's not all sex.'

'Maybe not,' replied Vic, looking miserable, 'but the band isn't happy; you're not a unit any more.'

Ed stared at his manager and grinned. 'Okay,' said Ed, 'I'll go and see them right now, calm down.' He left the room, and Vic was gobsmacked.

'Never known him that helpful,' he said, stunned.

That night, Ed was a sensation; he put his all into the show. Romany and he were as one, and the band were infected with the feeling and played their hearts out. Things changed, however, about halfway through the concert. Ed started to feel ill. He didn't convey this to his audience but had a venomous taste in his mouth, colours flashed in front of his eyes, and his ears were ringing. Romany appeared to have three heads, Vic had shrunk, Noddy didn't have a head at all, and he felt certain that the band were about to attack him. His teeth ached and he was getting smaller, plus something inside his stomach had burst and he wanted to spew up. His legs were giving way and he wondered if he was actually singing. His mouth was moving so he guessed that he was, but his body was red hot and it felt as if a terrific flush had come over it. He saw Cathy in the wings waiting to go on, and tears began to run down his cheeks. He wanted to go to bed, to sleep; how he longed for sleep. His chest felt tight and his heart beat wildly; he was scared. The song over, the crowd went wild and then he heard Romany announce *Little Egypt*, and Cathy appeared on stage. The rate at which his heart was beating made him think that it was about to explode into a thousand pieces. He was terrified as he could feel the life draining away from him. He needed a fix, and fast, but a smile from Cathy gave him a new surge of energy and he continued to sing.

After the song was over, and Cathy had left the stage, he spotted Hank talking to the lead singer of the Cupid Stunts. The bloody cowboy was back and he was too ill to be able to do anything about it. The colours were brighter now; they burned his eyes and the taste in his mouth had got worse. He soldiered on and, as the show finished a little later, he left the stage without a goodnight to the crowd. There would be no encore tonight. As he left he felt as if he was on a skating rink. Vic's voice boomed in his ears, 'good show tonight,' then his face became a blur as Ed's legs gave way and he fell into Karl's arms.

After *Little Egypt*, Noddy followed Cathy to her dressing room and handed her the letter. She flopped down onto a chair and opened it. After reading the contents, she gave a broken cry and went deathly white. 'Tony wants a separation; he's citing Ed as breaking up his marriage and saying I'm a bad mother. In fact, he's saying that I'm unfit and unbalanced. I mean, I want a divorce but not like this, I can't defend myself while I'm over here. He's added that, although Sandy wants to live with me, he intends to take all of my children away from me. He wants me to remove myself and all of my belongings when I return to the UK.'

'We'll fight it when we get back home,' said Noddy, sympathetically. 'Probably by then he'll be sick of whoever he's with and want you back. I can't get you out of this contract, Vic won't let you go, but I'll have a word with him. Ed will get the best lawyers; you won't lose the kids.'

'Come on baby, let's hit the nearest roulette table,' said Hank, breezing into the room as if he'd never been away.

Noddy shook his head. 'Bad news from England.'

'Well, crying in America won't help the situation in England,' replied Hank. 'You'd be better off going out rather than sitting here beating yourself up. Come on, I'll help if I can, let's all three of us go out.' He squeezed Cathy's hand, adding, 'We don't have to stay there too long.' Cathy reached for the tissue box and dried her eyes. She agreed, she had nothing to lose, having already lost what mattered, and her heart and soul were broken. She'd have a word with Vic later, he was Mr Fixit.

Later at the tables, she rolled the dice for Hank and they hit a winning streak. 'I knew you'd bring me luck!' he cried. They moved to the roulette wheel and their luck continued to hold. Cathy fell asleep on the drive back to the hotel so Hank didn't disturb her, he just dropped Noddy off and drove Cathy over to his place, leaving Noddy with his address and phone number in case of emergency. Arriving at his place, he woke Cathy and helped her out of his car.

'I should be at the hotel,' she said sleepily. 'Ed will be worried.' Hank stroked her hair saying that he would take her home after a night cap. She began to cry and relayed the contents of her letter.

'I'll help you, honey,' said Hank. 'Even if it means coming to England myself.' He held her to him and kissed her eyelids. 'I can't wait any longer,' he added.

Cathy was still weeping; tears ran down her face in rivulets. 'Take me home,' she sobbed. 'Ed will be getting worried.' It was obvious that Hank hadn't brought her here just for a night cap, he could have woken her up when they'd arrived at the hotel. She was worried. She liked Hank but didn't want to sleep with him; the only man that she wanted was back at the hotel. She declined his offer of alcohol, so Hank made her a coffee. 'I really need to go,' she said, drinking the cup of black coffee.

'Baby, you don't, he doesn't own you,' Hank told her.

'But I love him.'

'And I love you, always have done, and I'm prepared to help you.' Cathy swallowed hard as Hank began to caress her.

'No I really don't want to,' she implored.

'I do,' replied Hank. 'Come on, and then I'll take you home.' Cathy sighed, she wanted to get back to Ed. Maybe this would be over quickly. Hank was a lot older than her, like Tony, and with him it was always over very fast. She smiled and let him carry her to his bedroom. Once inside she lay there immobile as he began to release the tension in her. 'Just like a little Venus,' muttered Hank, undressing her. Cathy let him take her and then he fell asleep, so she dressed and rang the hotel, asking for Vic Lee.

Meanwhile, a doctor had been summoned for Ed. 'Complete rest,' he ordered.

'Impossible,' replied Vic, breaking out in a nervous sweat. The tour was starting to bug him, as was the doctor. 'Dope him, do something. We've got a huge charity event in forty-eight hours and then we fly back to Los Angeles again for more gigs, we haven't completed our tour yet. He can rest when we get back to England.'

'I can't work miracles,' replied the doctor. 'He's been thoroughly abused by drugs, probably self-inflicted but he's surrounded by too many people who encourage him to continue destroying himself. The only answer is rest and away from this circus.'

Vic wrung his hands. 'He's okay.'

'People usually are until they're found dead; cancel the rest of the tour.'

Suddenly Ed stirred. 'I'll kill him.'

'Kill who?' asked Romany, who sat by the bed. Ed felt the vacant spot beside him and began to call for Cathy.

'She's downstairs, she's asleep.' Ed gazed around him; Romany, Vic, Karl, and a guy that he didn't recognise were gathered around the bed. He didn't recall the trip back to the hotel; all he remembered was falling into Karl's arms.

'Get Cathy,' demanded Ed. The concert came back to him slowly. 'Get her, damn you.' Nobody moved. 'You can't, can you? She's with that fucking cowboy. I'll kill him, I'll kill her, I'll kill the whole bloody lot of you. I saw that cowboy, he was in the wings talking to Ken, the lead singer of the 'Stupid Cunts', while I was on stage. I saw him'.

The doctor raised his eyebrows at the band's name. 'Cupid Stunts,' said Vic. He watched as the doctor prepared the syringe.

'Now, our good friend here is going to give you one hell of a fix; you'll feel really good and then I'll go downstairs and get Cathy,' said Romany. 'Good eh?' Ed nodded as the doctor approached his patient and Romany swallowed hard, hoping that the tranquilliser would work fast. The drug was administered and Ed slowly closed his eyes.

'Always could rely on you, Romany. Get Cathy for me,' he said. He lay still and Vic offered up a silent prayer; now he had to find the girl. His prayers were answered once more when he received a phone call and found Cathy on the other end of the line. She explained what had happened and gave Vic the address and phone number just in case he got lost. Vic drove off at top speed and found her waiting on the doorstep outside.

'Ed's like a raving lunatic,' he said as Cathy got into his car.

'What happened?' asked Cathy as Vic took off at a breakneck speed.

'Never mind that. Where the fuck were you?'

'At the casino.'

'Who with?'

'Noddy and Hank.'

'So Ed was right.'

Cathy burst into tears and revealed the contents of her letter. His free hand rested on her thigh. 'I'll fix it for you,' he said. 'I can turn Tony around for a price, I'll have him eating out of my hand, and when you start divorce proceedings he won't know what's hit him. Then you and Ed can live happily ever after, know what I mean, baby?' Cathy was about to remove his hand when he repeated, 'you do understand what I want, don't you?' and his hand travelled higher, groping her. Cathy felt sick, but nodded. Vic reached the hotel in record time and got Cathy into bed with Ed just as fast. Cathy snuggled up to him and, closing her eyes, began to slumber.

The couple slept for over twenty-four hours. Vic looked in a couple of times and decided not to intervene. He wasn't cancelling any gigs, and thought that if Ed rested it would put him back on top. As the day of the rehearsal for the charity concert arrived, he tapped on the door and entered. He felt that Ed had rested enough and the show must go on. Sure enough, Ed was on top but not in the way that Vic wanted. He closed the door silently and wandered off to get the rest of the band.

'Where's Ed?' asked Gerry. 'We can't go without him.'

'Resting,' replied Vic.

Romany ran his fingers through his hair, making it stand up on end. 'Resting? Come off it Vic, after all that sleep, he'll be getting his rocks off.'

Gerry stubbed out his cigarette. 'I'm sick of all of this,' he snapped. 'I came here to work as a band not as an appendage to a double act. Not only that, we can't bring our wives here, but Ed dangles Faye on his arm as his private secretary which is the greatest farce of all time, and screws Cathy at every opportunity. It's bloody unfair.'

Vic stamped his foot angrily. 'Wives are not allowed on this tour, but Ed's not married. Faye is his secretary, and Cathy's his dancer.'

'So?' replied Gerry, heading for the elevator. 'That's rubbish, he's still screwing 'em both. As he reached the elevator door, he turned back and faced Vic. 'Of course, that's it, we're not a band any more. Ed's the superstar; we're nothing.' The other members followed him to the elevator.

'Lads…' protested Vic.

'Go fuck yourself, Vic,' snapped Gerry. 'You might enjoy it.' Vic said nothing and decided to get Ed and Cathy moving.

Arriving at the venue, Vic studied the running order. It was full of stars, and Ed was closing the first half of the show. To Vic's dismay, he saw that Hank was opening the second half. He hadn't even known that Hank was on the bill, and noted that Sammy Silver was booked too. At that minute he wished that he was a car salesman, or factory worker, or sales assistant, or cloakroom attendant, or anything other than Ed's manager.

The band was furious when they saw the songs that they were performing. Gerry swore out loud. 'I knew it, four numbers and she's in two of them. What's next Vic? A performing seal? What happened to the band?'

Vic's mouth formed a tight line, and he was about to reply when Hank breezed in. Cathy was limbering up and knew nothing until her eyes were covered up and a small box thrust into her hands. Vic shot to Ed's side but he wasn't quick enough to restrain him. Furiously, Ed swung Hank around by his shoulder bringing them face to face. 'I warned you!' he screamed.

Noddy intervened quickly. 'Don't be a fool, Ed,' he yelled, restraining him.

'Leave me alone!' shouted Ed. 'I'm gonna kill him.'

'Calm down, buddy, I don't want to hurt you,' replied Hank, calmly.

The whole episode ended as Sammy Silver made an entrance dressed in purple velvet. Ed's fury evaporated and he burst into laughter. Sammy looked ridiculous; purple was not his colour and as for his silver high-heeled boots, they were so high that he was in danger of falling off them. Ed greeted him with enthusiasm. 'Sammy, baby,' he laughed. 'You look great, real swell.' He was obviously taking the piss, and everyone saw it except for Sammy.

'Had my teeth capped too,' boasted Sammy.

'Great,' replied Ed, 'you'll really dazzle us now.'

Gerry nudged Romany. 'It's a real circus now, maybe we should try jumping through hoops?'

The rehearsal began and Hank was up first. He began to sing and Ed winced. 'I hate cowboy songs,' he said.

Noddy grunted. 'He's got to where he is by hard work; he deserves his success. He used to be a lorry driver.' He nudged Vic, 'very good friend of Dean Martin.'

'I'd like an introduction,' replied Vic. Hank finished his western number and began to sing a country song.

'Bloody hell,' yawned Ed, 'I'm bored stiff, he's doing country songs now.'

'So?'

'Trucking, country music, and Deano,' sneered Ed.

'Well,' chipped in Romany, 'we know the way you prefer it.'

Ed was interested. 'Really?'

Romany leered, 'well if he likes trucking, country music, and Deano, your interest is fucking, cunt, and vino.' He laughed at his own joke, and Ed went into hysterics. He started to fondle Cathy who had just joined him.

'Stop it,' hissed Cathy. 'People are watching.'

'People?' cried Ed, 'you mean that bloody cowboy, don't you? You're mine.'

Hank left the stage having finished his songs and approached the couple. 'You don't have to simulate sex to impress me Ed, Cathy's a lady and she deserves to be treated like one, not made to look like a cheap whore which is what you appear to be doing. She's also got a mind of her own so all of your threats won't make any difference.' He kissed Cathy. 'See you later, honey.'

'Over my dead body,' snapped Ed.

'Maybe.'

'Maybe it'll be yours, it could be arranged.'

'So arrange it, bye.'

'Come on Ed,' fussed Vic, 'for god's sake.'

The rehearsal went well and, later on, back at the hotel, Faye put in an unexpected appearance. Cathy made an excuse to leave, saying they must have lots to talk about. Ed turned to Faye and looked her up and down. 'What brought you back? Run out of money, did you? I didn't expect to see you again until we hit LA.'

'I missed you,' replied Faye.

Ed held her at arms' length; she looked good. 'I missed you too,' he lied, running his hands over her body. Inwardly, Faye cried because in truth she had run out of money and the charity thing was a huge occasion. She liked being photographed with Ed at this sort of event. Whilst in Sacramento, she'd had a great time with an ageing millionaire. He'd asked nothing of her and gave her everything she could possibly want. He even wanted her to marry him and promised to write to her when she returned to England. In her eyes she'd found Mr Perfect. Ed guided her to the bed and she felt him start to undress her, so she spread her legs and let him take her. What a bore this was, but if she wanted more money, then this was the price she had to pay.

Meanwhile, downstairs, Cathy opened the box that Hank had given her. Inside was a ring with a note attached to it that read, 'I love you'.

Noddy whistled. 'It's a beauty.' Cathy put it on her finger. 'Got two of them after you now, lucky you. How about some shuteye? Big event tonight.' Cathy nodded. She was petrified at the thought of it, and it was some event. She decided to go to bed and drifted into a dream in which her life was perfect and not the usual muddle she was becoming accustomed to.

The show that night was a very big concern. Film stars mingled with rock stars, managers, starlets, and film producers. Vic was pleased; this was one time when he was proud to be Ed's manager. Before the show there was a bomb scare which turned out to be a hoax. Backstage in the dressing room reserved for Vic's entourage, tension ran high. Faye was out front, seated with Ed's publicity man. Vic and Noddy stayed backstage to take charge of any problems that might arise. Ed was nervous; he paced the stage several times and didn't even see Hank arrive. Marcia Malone, the film star, tapped Ed on the shoulder. 'Nerves?' she asked.

Ed turned to face the sex goddess of the movies. 'A bit,' he replied.

'You'll be great.'

'Sure,' said Ed, wishing that he believed it. Normally he would have tried to chat her up but he really didn't feel well at all. He guessed that he needed a fix and decided to find Romany; he could always rely on him. He walked back to the dressing room and was totally unprepared for the sight that met his eyes. Cathy had her back to him and was held firmly by Hank. Suddenly something inside him snapped. He wrenched Cathy out of Hank's arms. 'You whore,' he screamed. Cathy fell, and Noddy helped her to her feet as Ed threw himself at Hank.

'Cool it,' shouted Hank, holding him off. Vic restrained a furious Ed who shouted all kinds of obscenities at Hank. 'I was wishing her luck, that's all.'

'Come on Ed, we've got a show to do,' Romany reminded him, 'Do you think I'd stand around and let anything happen?' Ed shook his head.

'Shake on it,' said Vic.

'Never,' said Ed, furiously.

'Do I go or stay, Cathy?' asked Hank.

'Go and get ready,' replied Cathy. 'I'm fine.'

'You're never to see him again!' yelled Ed, crossing over to Cathy and pulling her around to face him. Cathy pulled away and presented her back to him.

'Leave me alone, Ed,' she said softly.

Noddy took Ed to one side. 'Ed, she's stressed, just like you. She's upset.'

'She's upset?' yelled Ed. 'What about me?'

'Because of you, you arrogant bastard, she has big problems in England and she could lose everything that she loves.'

'Good, I hope she does. I'm glad. Maybe now she'll realise where her place is.'

'Where's that? With you so that you can behave like a spoilt child every time she looks sideways at someone?'

Faye entered the room and ducked as Ed threw a bottle at the door as he shouted, 'clear off and mix with the beautiful people.' Faye retreated faster than she'd entered, and Ed turned back to Cathy. 'I'll kill anyone that lays a finger on her,' he shouted, 'including that make believe Gene Autrey.'

Vic seized Ed by the shoulders and shook him. 'Stop it,' he ordered, but Ed was having none of it and knocked Vic to the ground, causing him to sprawl onto his fat belly on the floor. Ed grasped Cathy's hand, and then noticed the ring on her finger.

'I'll kill him,' he screeched.

Noddy laughed mockingly and marched over. 'How long have you fancied suicide? Hank could break you with one hand.'

Vic staggered to his feet as Ed's voice reached a crescendo, 'Break me!' he screamed. 'No one can break me, just let anyone try, I'll take you all on.' He tore at Cathy's dress, revealing one of her breasts. 'She belongs to me,' he yelled triumphantly.

Cathy slapped him around the face, 'I've had it with you,' she cried, pulling away from an enraged Ed.

'Then my angel, you've had it with everyone,' he screamed, dragging her back to face him. Placing his hands around her throat he began to squeeze. Cathy began to splutter, and Karl stepped in. Ed was hauled from Cathy and then he slumped on the floor, sobs racking his body. 'Get out, all of you except her,' he cried. Vic knew better than to argue, they had a show to do and he ushered everyone else out. Noddy was reluctant to leave, but Cathy assured him that she was okay so he followed the others outside. Cathy did a quick repair job on her costume and approached the snivelling wreck on the floor. Ed shifted to a kneeling position and took her hand. 'Cathy,' he begged, 'don't leave me, I'm sorry about the trouble in England, I'll get Vic to sort it out, I'll even phone myself if you like but don't leave me.' He got to his feet and took her in his arms. 'You're mine, Seth gave you to me. I can't live without you. If I thought that you loved someone else I'd kill both of us. When we're together, I'm complete, you're my other half. Say you love me or I'm nothing.'

Cathy shuddered inside. 'Seth married us, that's all,' she whispered.

'No, he bonded us in a special ceremony, you are mine.'

'Ed, you're scaring me.'

'You know I love you, there is no one else, never will be. Come on we've got a show to do.' She pulled away from him and left the room. Everyone was clustered outside the dressing room door.

'You okay?' asked Vic.

Cathy closed the door. 'Fine, but you've got a very sick man in there, he needs treatment.' Vic grunted and entered the dressing room with his entourage as Cathy walked away.

Cathy found Hank waiting in the wings watching America's newest comedian on stage. 'You okay?' he asked, concerned.

'Ed's very sick; I think it's the drugs that everyone's giving him. He's raving on about some ritual that we both did. I don't recall it at all.' The comedian left the stage and was followed by an all-black, girl group. Noddy was watching nearby and didn't like them so wandered off.

'I see Faye's back, that's good news for us,' said Hank. Neither of them heard Ed approach as Hank kissed her on the back of her neck. 'Can you get away tonight? The other night was beautiful, you were wonderful.'

'No,' replied Cathy, 'it shouldn't have happened and it won't again.'

'But honey, I'll need you around when I ring England,' murmured Hank.

'No, Vic will fix it, but thanks anyway.' As she pulled away, Ed felt as if he'd been kicked in the stomach. How he hurt inside.

Something had happened and now the cowboy had to go; he'd just sealed his fate. He smiled as a plan entered his head. Hank was going to open the second part of the show and would need his microphone set up. He knew that Hank refused to use any other mic but his own, and as he used no backing there would be no one else on stage. He also insisted on setting it up himself as he didn't trust anyone else to do it. How many times had Vic yelled at Ed to check his equipment? Sudden death, he called it. Ed never bothered, he had other people to do it but in Hank's case, well that was just perfect. He moved closer to the couple and kissed Cathy on her cheek.

'Noddy's looking for you; maybe he has news from England.' Turning to Hank, Ed extended his hand. 'Sorry about earlier,' he said. 'I was way out of line. According to the doctor I'm suffering from exhaustion, and things get a bit distorted at times. I've known Cathy for years and I was afraid that you might try to take advantage of her, seeing that she's very low over this problem in England. I don't want her hurt.'

Hank grasped Ed's hand firmly in his own. 'Let's shake on it and get a drink. I know what it's like to have exhaustion; it's no joke.'

'Great,' replied Ed. 'I'd love a drink.'

They walked away from the wings and nearly collided with Vic and the rest of the band. Vic stared open-mouthed at Ed and Hank with their arms around each other. 'Now what's happening?' he asked.

'Going to get a drink,' replied Ed. 'Won't be long.'

Vic was worried. Ed was a lot sicker than he had first thought. His temperament was worrying, and his mood swings were impossible to deal with. Then he spotted Noddy and Cathy and remembered that he had to ring England. He'd tried earlier with no success, but at least he'd got through to Ingrid and left a message telling Tony to be by the phone at ten as he needed to speak to him. Vic was intending to get the result that he wanted because he felt that if he helped Cathy, she might be grateful and give him a bit of the treatment that Ed got.

Romany brought him back to earth. 'I don't believe it, one minute he wants to kill the guy and now they're the best of friends.'

'That's showbiz,' laughed Vic, uneasily.

Ed and the band played a good set that night, and Cathy danced like a dream. After two curtain calls, Ed left the stage and, turning to Hank said, 'thought I saw Dean Martin out there.'

'Really?' said Vic. 'I'd love to meet him.'

'Very good friend of mine,' interjected Hank. 'I'd introduce you to him now but I have to set up my mic and check it.'

'Very sensible, I'm always on at Ed about that.'

'Yep, just like a worn out record,' joked Ed.

'Never mind,' said Vic ruefully. 'Maybe I'll meet him some other time.'

'Chances are he's backstage now, or at the bar,' said Hank.

Ed took his chance. 'Tell you what, I'll do it for you. I'd like to make up for my stupid, thick head earlier.' Hank stared at Vic who really did want to meet Dean, but wasn't sure if Ed's suggestion was a good one.

'That would be great,' Hank said, finally. 'Come on, Vic.'

Vic hesitated but knew that Ed knew his job, and he did seem okay again. The matter was clinched when Ed offered to pay for drinks as Vic really fancied a whiskey. Nearby, Al was taking photos but put his camera down when Ed offered him a free drink too. He ambled after Vic, wondering why Ed was so friendly all of a sudden. Who cared? He was getting a drink from someone who hated him. Ed waited until the stage was clear and the curtain down, then he set to work. '"Friends, pals",' he muttered. 'No way, buddy.'

The intermission nearly over, Cathy stood in the wings with Hank's arm around her waist. Ed looked over with building excitement engulfing him. Noddy and Vic stood nearby. 'Hank,' called Noddy, 'have you checked your mic?'

Hank smiled. 'All taken care of,' he replied. The curtains opened and Hank strode onto the stage to deafening applause.

Ed sidled over to Cathy. From behind he placed his arms around her waist and pulled her back onto him. 'Love you, baby,' he whispered. Sammy Silver was sulking. He'd wanted to open the second half of the show, not follow Hank. Cathy turned to speak to Ed when it happened. There was a sudden flash as Hank touched the microphone, and in an instant he was thrown backwards to the floor. He was writhing in agony.

'No!' screamed Cathy, having to be held firmly by Ed to prevent her rushing to Hank's aid.

'Oh my God,' gasped Vic, staring at Ed who was unmoved by it all. Noddy buried his head in his hands and, nearby, Sammy wet himself. The purple suit would never be the same again and now he was pleased that he hadn't opened the second half.

Ed was silent. He held a tear-stained Cathy to him. He stroked her hair and muttered under his breath, 'Mine.' Cathy gazed from Ed to Vic, to Noddy, to Sammy who had just been sick in the wings, and then all the faces merged and everything swam before her eyes.

Back at the hotel, she was sedated and slept. Every time she awoke, she cried, and Noddy attempted to soothe her. He was beginning to think that the tour was a bad move. What with Ed's jealousy, the problems in England, and now Hank's death, life had become unbearable to Cathy. She didn't remember getting on the plane and flying back to Los Angeles as she was so heavily sedated, she didn't even know her own name. Vic had some good news though, and told Cathy that she would be getting a phone call. Upon hearing this she was pleased for a minute, but quickly lapsed back into a state of melancholy. She'd been like that since Hank's death.

At the hotel she answered the phone and heard her husband's voice. 'How are you?' he asked.

'I wish I'd never come here,' replied Cathy. 'I wish I were dead.'

'Sorry about Hank,' said Tony sympathetically. 'I always liked him.' There was a long silence and then he said, 'I'm sorry my letter distressed you, it's just that I've been a bit silly since you've been gone.'

'Silly? How do you mean silly?'

'Silly, silly. I'll explain when you come home.'

'Home? I thought you wanted a divorce and wanted me out of the house and that you were going to take me to court claiming that I was an unfit mother.'

There was another silence and then Tony added, 'I was uptight when I wrote that letter. When you get back we'll try and work something out.' Cathy felt new life begin to surge into her as Tony added. 'I'm going now; I'll see you when you get back.' Then the line went dead.

Cathy sighed and Noddy looked up. 'Okay?' he enquired.

Cathy nodded. Noddy sat down beside her and gave her a hug. 'You know that Ed has a violent temper,' he said. 'But I'm convinced that it's because he's terrified of losing you, he panics when you're not around. There's nothing that he wouldn't do for you but he's so insecure…'

'And sick,' interrupted Cathy.

Later, at a chat show for television, Cathy was made up by the make-up assistant. The girl, a tall gangly blonde, couldn't believe her eyes. Cathy looked so ill, it took ages to get the girl to look healthy. Ed looked even worse, in fact the only one who looked well was Victor. The girl was quite pleased that she'd never entered show business if this was what it did to you. Sammy Silver on the other hand looked a picture of health but then she expected that it was his youth that gave that effect. The band got a quick make-up job although they weren't even being interviewed; they were there simply there to play *Angel* for Ed and Cathy. There was an aura of discontent about them. Vic could feel it and chatted to Sammy's manager. In the background, Faye hovered, getting in everyone's way. Repeatedly, she was told to move as she wasn't wanted on camera. Dejectedly, she sat in the corner out of focus and fiddled with her nails.

Nelson Remo hosted the show and began with Sammy. He got all the answers that he wanted plus a song, and then he turned to Ed. He asked if Ed had ever considered living in America permanently. Ed replied that lately he'd given it a lot of thought and was looking for a home at the minute. Everyone in Ed's entourage was surprised, as he'd never mentioned it before. Later he was asked about *Angel* and if he thought that Hendrix would approve of this version. 'Dunno,' said Ed, 'I don't converse with the dead but I would think that he would. I love the song; it's beautiful, and classical ballet is one of the highest forms of art, isn't it?'

'You use Cathy in *Little Egypt* too, don't you? Why?'

'Seemed like a good idea at the time,' replied Ed. The interview continued as Cathy was asked for her opinion on Hendrix, Elvis, Dylan, and others. When asked for her all-time favourites, she surprised everyone by naming Steve Marriot as the best in the universe, Dylan her hero, and that she had a soft spot for a guy called David Essex. She also added that when Rod Stewart had recorded *Angel*, she'd gone out and bought it as it was such a lovely version. Ed was miffed. She'd never mentioned Essex before, and as for saying that Rod's version was lovely when she should have praised his, made him really upset. He left the studio in a huff, with Faye on his arm.

As Cathy left, she was waylaid by Sammy Silver. 'I've been trying to get your attention for ages,' he said. 'Could I take you out for a bite to eat later tonight? I hope you liked my gifts and flowers. I've been calling almost every day but never been able to get through.'

Cathy was about to refuse when Vic put in an appearance. 'Rick's hosting another party tonight.'

'Can't go,' replied Cathy. 'I've just accepted a date with Sammy.'

'Oh, never mind, there'll be other parties. What shall I tell Ed?'

Cathy shrugged her shoulders and then laughed at the annoyed Vic. 'Tell him whatever you want,' she replied, 'I'm sick of parties, especially the kind that Rick hosts. There's no show tonight so I'm not needed, in fact I think that Ed's sulking over my comments about *Angel* so I guess it'll take him a while to forgive me.' She turned to Sammy. She needed to know more about these gifts that he'd sent her as she had known nothing about it. After making arrangements with Sammy, she left the studio with Vic and went back to the hotel for a nap.

Later that night, Sammy picked Cathy up and she was feeling quite carefree. It flattered her that Sammy desired her company, and he remarked on her bracelet and evening dress. 'They make you look a million dollars, and I see that you're wearing the necklace too, I'm so glad that you liked them.' Cathy was shocked and unhappy about this revelation. Vic had told her that the gifts had come from fans and the flowers from him. She realised that Vic was even more of a slime ball than she'd originally thought he was. She sighed but was determined to enjoy her night out.

After a beautiful meal at which Sammy toasted her success in America, they left and drove along a coastal road to a disco. All eyes were on her as she danced with Sammy. She could feel his young body pressed up against hers and she began to feel quite light-headed. Later, in the back of his limousine, they talked about many subjects and they appeared to like the same things despite the age gap. Sammy was the perfect gentleman and, after taking her back to the hotel, kissed her on her cheek and said he'd ring her the following afternoon. Cathy felt much better. The night out had lifted some of her home sickness and depression. Once inside her room she took her pills and then got into bed, falling asleep almost immediately.

The following morning she was awoken by an argument. Ed's room was immediately above hers and she could hear Faye crying and Ed shouting at her. Getting out of bed, Cathy wandered over to her window just in time to see Faye get into a yellow cab and drive away. Minutes later, Vic arrived. He tapped on her door and entered. 'Hi honey, Ed wants to look at some property and he wants you with him,' he said, eyeing Cathy's naked body.

Cathy rubbed her eyes, yawned, and pulled her dressing gown on. 'Oh, is he speaking to me now? Has he got over his sulking? If he needs to view property, he needs to view it with Faye.'

'Faye doesn't make the bells ring for him like you do,' Vic replied.

'When can I go home? You said I only had a few more bookings to do and then the band would continue the rest of the tour without me.'

'Patience, darling, there are many loose ends to tie up. You've got three days of interviews and photo shoots plus a television special to do, and then there are extra bookings that have just been added. I need you for all of that.'

'Bastard,' spat Cathy, 'you told me that I was almost finished.'

'Work is work. I never turn anything down that is good for work. Not only that, Ed is worrying me; he's sick, and to remove you could make him worse and that is a risk that I refuse to take. You might now have to complete the entire tour.'

Cathy put on her dressing gown and reached for her pills. 'How much longer do I have to take this junk? I'm sick of it,' she asked.

'Until the doctor says you can stop. I'll get you a glass of water and, besides, you owe me.' He leered at her and headed for the en suite, laughing. Minutes later he returned with a glass of water and handed it to her. She put the pills into her mouth and swallowed them, washing them down with the water. Vic leaned over and kissed her on her lips. 'Besides, my darling, I helped you out and I would like a bit of gratitude. From the moment you appeared in that dance contest I've lusted after you; surely you won't spoil my fantasy?' He fondled her left breast and opened up her dressing gown, gazing on her nudity once more. 'You and

I will get a nice little scene going in the future but until then you will do exactly as I say. I smoothed over troubled waters for you and got you and Tony talking once more but remember that I'm quite capable of making huge waves too, and that could be bad news for you. You do understand me, don't you darling?'

Trying to change the subject, Cathy said, 'I don't want these pills any more.'

Vic took her head in his hands. 'I said, you do understand me, don't you darling?'

'Yes, you bastard, I do.'

'There's a good girl, now get dressed and you can go house hunting with Ed.'

Cathy wanted to scream, it seemed so unfair, and tears of sheer frustration filled her eyes. 'I hate men!' she cried.

Vic laughed, 'Not what Ed says, or Romany, or Rick.'

'If Ed talks behind my back, he's no gentleman. Romany never was one, and as for Rick, he climbed onto me while I was asleep in New York,' said Cathy, beginning to dress.

'What about Rick's pad when we hit Los Angeles for the first time? You remember Rick's party, don't you?'

Bewildered, Cathy sat on the bed. 'I remember arriving at the party and Ed giving interviews, but after that I don't recall much at all apart from waking up beside Ed the following morning. What has any of this got to do with Rick or Romany?'

'You had a ménage-a-trois.'

'Impossible, I'd remember. The only thing that puzzled me was that when I woke up I felt as if I'd been in a fight. I know that Ed can be violent occasionally when he makes love but I've never felt in that much pain before.'

'They both had you together, darling. Rick had been drugging you and Ed all night; Ed collapsed and was completely out of it. They took him to bed and then returned for you. Instead of taking you to Ed, they took you to Rick's room. Rick says that you put up quite a struggle; you snorted coke that night too.'

'Then why don't you tell Ed? He'd sort them out.'

'He'd kill them both but I imagine Romany would heap the blame on you so it's hardly worth it. Plus I need Romany for the tour. I can't risk it.'

'But why don't I remember it?'

'Drugs, darling, and anyway Rick says you were a willing partner once you'd snorted the coke. Apparently, you were insatiable.'

Cathy sobbed her heart out as Vic left the room. He was back five minutes later with Ed in tow . Ed looked pale and drugged as usual, but Vic was determined to keep him upright while work poured in. Now fully dressed, Cathy left the hotel with the two men, wondering why her memory was giving up on her. Downstairs, Karl opened the car door for them. He was feeling very sorry for himself as he hadn't had enough sleep, but Cathy looked as if she'd been crying and Ed looked completely dazed. He stumbled into the side of the car and the door slammed, almost jamming his hand in it. He steadied Ed, and once more opened the door, and this time Ed managed to get into the car without falling while Cathy followed him inside. 'Enjoy yourselves,' cried Vic. 'Have fun.' He handed over some keys and gave Karl directions to the properties that Ed was viewing.

Ed was pleased he had Cathy to himself again; they'd hardly spoken since Hank's death and he knew that it had hit Cathy hard but he felt that his actions were justified. He'd purposely picked a fight with Faye to get rid of her, and it had been music to his ears when he'd heard the door slam and she'd left. He began to fondle Cathy, and at first she objected, but soon responded to his touch. Whatever he did, she loved him with all of her heart.

Both of the mansions were huge and spectacular. The couple wandered from room to room, enthusing over the possibilities of the places. Ed couldn't choose. 'Which one?' he asked.

'Ask Faye, it's nothing to do with me,' replied Cathy.

'Don't act dumb, it's got everything to do with you. I'm buying a home out here for you and me. We can have a great life.'

'My home is England.'

'Stay with me and I'll lay the world at your feet.'

'What happened to the open road?'

'I'll get you the best lawyers; you will get custody of the kids and then we'll be together forever.' Ed took Cathy into his arms but Cathy tore herself free.

'I don't want to live here!' she cried.

'And I don't want you in Tony's bed, or Faye in mine; you're the only person that's keeping me going.'

'Really? So you can rape me, cut my wrist onstage, rip my costume, be jealous of Hank, and degrade me in front of everyone? And what is this about a ritual with Seth, I don't recall it?'

Ed was horrified. 'Rape you? I would never rape you, when?'

'Hank's party, ask Vic.'

'I don't recall this; it must be the drugs. I could never harm you.'

'At one stage, just before you raped me, I thought you were going to kill me. I was so frightened.' Tears were stinging her eyes.

Ed held her to him. 'My baby, my poor baby, but you are mine, and nobody will take you away from me. There's nothing that I wouldn't do for you, I'd kill for you. God help me, I have killed for you.' Cathy recoiled in horror. What did he mean? He'd killed for her? 'And I'd kill again for you if I had to.'

Cathy trembled, her legs felt as if they were about to give way. 'You don't know what you're saying, you're sick.'

Ed shook her and held her at arms' length as he gazed at her with the same glazed expression that she'd seen just before he'd raped her. 'I know exactly what I'm saying, I killed for you. There was no fault on Hank's mic that night. I set it up for him, I killed him and I'm glad. Damn you, Cathy, I'll never be able to let you go now. We're both caught in a trap.' Cathy pulled away from him. She wanted to scream, hit him, run, or anything but stay in his company. Ed pulled her back to face him, and once more she wondered in terror if he was about to kill her too.

Hoping that her voice wouldn't betray her, Cathy mumbled, 'I can't take this in, let's go back to the hotel. I need to lie down and I think you're the best person to soothe me.' Ed's expression changed from desperation to happiness and, in no time at all, Karl had whisked them both back to the hotel where Ed reverted to the happy loving individual that Cathy knew so well.

After making love, she fell asleep and was awoken some time later by Ed yelling into the bedside phone. 'Fuck off, you wanker.'

She sat up as Ed replaced the receiver. 'Who was that?' she asked.

'Sammy Silver wanting to take you out,' he grunted.

Cathy was hurt. 'You could have asked me if I wanted to go.'

'Why, do you want him dead too?'

'You wouldn't.'

'Keep away from that little runt unless you want him dead too.' Ed kissed her forehead, adding, 'I told you that you're mine.' His eyes were wild and staring, and the next moment glazed. Then his eyelids began to droop and he fell into a deep sleep.

Cathy waited for a while and then got up and went looking for Noddy. He'd know what to do, he always did. As she left the room, her head was crammed with a million thoughts. Did Vic know? Did Faye, or had Ed only confessed to her? Her lover was a murderer, or was it the drugs talking? Did he really kill for her? Reaching Noddy's door, she tapped on it and entered. Noddy listened in disbelief. 'It must be the drugs making him say that.'

Cathy fiddled with her hair and told him, 'Sammy rang a short while ago, and Ed told me that he'd kill him if I went anywhere near him. I'm scared for him now.'

'I'll speak to Vic tomorrow,' Noddy said, giving her a hug.

The following day, Cathy got a visit from Vic. He could see how stressed she was and put his arms around her as she sobbed and told him she wanted to go home. 'Ed couldn't kill anyone,' said Vic, 'he's very tired and needs a holiday. We can be out of here in a couple of weeks, and you look tired too.'

'I am; I just want to go home.'

Vic stroked her hair. 'Don't worry, honey, everything's okay.'

'I love Ed, but he scares me now.'

Secretly, Vic was concerned. He knew that it was Ed who had set up Hank's mic that night, so he had certainly had the opportunity to tamper with it. He also recalled that Ed had made threats to the victim and shown no remorse at his death. The best course of action was to get out of America as soon as possible, but there was still more money to be made before they flew home. He knew that Sammy was interested in Cathy but decided that the risk to him was minor. 'Dry your eyes, Cathy, the show must go on,' he said. He was getting bored now and left her, still sobbing, on the bed.

The concert that night was sold out. Vic was enraged as Ed carried out his threat and did an acoustic Dylan number. The band had trouped off stage and left Ed centre stage, sitting on a stool, with a mouth organ, acoustic guitar and microphone. Ed addressed the audience. 'Who loves the great Bob Dylan?' he asked. The crowd roared its approval. 'I love him too, and I hope that this song meets with your approval. I haven't sung this song for many years and I'm going to dedicate it to a very good friend of mine. I've been treating her badly recently so this is an apology to her, and also to show you all that I can sing without backing. I can never match the great Mr Dylan but I'll do my best. So here goes; this one's for you, baby, I'm sorry.'

Vic's blood pressure was going through the roof, and the band was pissed off. Cathy was elated. 'He can do this Vic,' she whispered, 'you'll see, he'll be great.'

'I suppose you put him up to this,' snarled Vic.

'She knew nothing about it,' retorted Noddy, 'but she's right, he never was cut out to front a band, he's a first class solo artist.'

The audience was silent as Ed began to sing and play his guitar. Faye shrieked, 'He needs the band, how could you let him do this?' She wandered over to Vic and kicked him in the shins, causing him to let out a yell and collapse onto Al Simpkins who had just emerged from the dressing room. Ed was midway through *It's All Over Now, Baby Blue*. He kept looking over at Cathy who was waiting in the wings in her angel costume. Ed's heart and soul were being projected into the song and, just for a moment, Cathy was transported back to Wales with her hippy lover. The spell was broken as the song ended and then there was a brief silence before the crowd were on their feet, cheering for more. Cathy wept tears of joy; this was the guy she loved, the guy that sang with every fibre of his body.

As the band regrouped onstage and began their latest single, Cathy turned to Vic and mouthed, 'told you so.'

Chapter Fourteen

The following week, Sammy Silver hosted a party. Ed wanted both Faye and Cathy on his arm, but in fact neither girl wanted to go. Faye because she wanted to go to a different party where her best friend lived, and Cathy because she was concerned for Sammy's safety. The girls eventually gave in and, as usual, Ed got his way. Sammy greeted the trio warmly, but Ed ignored him, recalling the phone call in which Sammy had requested a date with Cathy. It had unsettled him and he intended to watch Sammy's every move. 'A girl on each arm,' laughed Sammy, 'lucky guy.'

'Yep, and I'm keeping 'em both close, so don't get any ideas.' Sammy was hurt and confused as he didn't know what he'd done wrong. He liked Cathy and had enjoyed their date so much that he was hoping for another one. He'd had a soft spot for her since the dance contest, and had bought a couple of photos of her that night from Al Simpkins. Ed's attitude puzzled him as he knew that he was engaged to Faye.

He waited until Ed's attention was taken with a music promoter and headed for Cathy who was at the bar. She was pleased to chat with him, and when he offered to show her his house and grounds she was happy to accompany him.

It was about half an hour later that Ed noticed Cathy's absence. Sammy was missing too, and Ed felt the knife within him start to twist. He continued his conversation with the promoter, not really getting the drift of anything that was being spoken about.

Erotic pictures flashed before his eyes and he felt sick. Suddenly the missing couple came into his vision and he noted that they were both laughing. Ed got to his feet. 'Cathy, we're leaving,' he snapped, and taking her hand hauled her outside towards his car where Karl was in the driving seat reading a book. Disgruntled, Faye followed with no idea what had got into Ed; he was in a real lather. Vic was fuming; he had a new producer waiting to see Ed and now this had happened. Making excuses to everyone, none of which made any sense, he left.

Noddy chose to remain. He'd seen the way that Ed had behaved towards Sammy, and he was staying just in case Ed returned. Meanwhile, Sammy was very miffed as he was being prevented from having Cathy in his company.

A press man hovered nearby and began to ask questions about his music, fans, and touring dates. He also asked if Sammy had a special lady in his life. Angered by Ed's behaviour, Sammy said yes, there was, but she'd just left. She was part of Ed Gold's entourage but they were keeping things quiet for now. They'd had a few dates and he thought he was in love with the lady. 'We'll go public when Ed's tour finishes,' he said, 'but for now it's a secret.' He knew that this would be front page tomorrow, and wanted Ed to see it.

'Got any photos?' asked the reporter.

'Yep,' replied Sammy. 'I'll get you some if you're not in a hurry.'

'Got all the time in the world, Sammy,' said a very happy reporter. He'd already got some photos of the couple when they'd been out on their date, but had shelved them as he thought it had been a one-off meeting. He was always taking shots of Sammy with ageing starlets and Barbie-type, young girls, but this revelation was very interesting. He'd visit the girl tomorrow and get her side of the story. Meanwhile the photos that he had in his possession would do very nicely, plus anything else that Sammy owned. He'd got a scoop here. The teeny bop idol actually saying that he was in love. 'I love showbiz,' he said out loud as he watched Sammy ascend the stairs.

Back at the hotel, Cathy went straight to bed. Ed ignored her and dragged Faye upstairs. In bed, he attempted to make love to her and, after many futile attempts, he pushed her head down into his groin. Fifteen minutes later and he still couldn't come, so he shoved Faye away exclaiming, 'cold bitch.' Making his way down to Cathy's room, he still fumed. Faye had to go, that was for sure. Cathy lay in bed sobbing. She didn't understand anything any more. All she wanted was to go home, and she cringed with fear as she saw her door open. She knew who her visitor was; Ed had a spare key. He'd demanded one and got it. Cathy had no privacy any more. She shook as he disrobed and got into bed with her. Kissing her, he could feel that her cheeks were wet. He began to soothe her, and minutes later they were making love. Afterwards, Cathy closed her eyes, praying that sleep would come, and luckily it did. Unfortunately, so did the morning papers.

The following morning, Ed was in a strange mood and it was obvious something was bothering him. Cathy turned over and went back to sleep, but not for long, as a short while later she was awoken by Faye screaming and Ed shouting. Faye sounded terrified so Cathy felt that she had to go to her aid. She dressed as fast as she could and hurried upstairs. She pushed open the door and beheld Faye, cringing in the corner of the room, with Ed towering over her. 'Fucking whore,' yelled Ed. 'Are you fucking Silver too? Because that whore downstairs is. No wonder you don't want me, you'd both rather suck that wanker's cock. I'm just the prat who keeps you in luxury; all you do is take the piss out of me.'

'I left with you last night,' cried Faye.

'Sure, but what about all the other times that you've stayed behind? How many others have you fucked?'

'I've just been giving you more time with Cathy.'

'Cathy, Cathy, another whore, yes I want more time with Cathy but not so as you can fuck half of America.' She looked on in horror as Ed dragged the sobbing Faye to her feet and repeatedly slapped her around her face. She had to find Vic, and fast. She backed out of the room and rushed downstairs where she found Vic having a heated argument with Al over the contents of the newspapers.

'You idiot!' he yelled. 'If Ed sees this, you'll be flying home in a coffin.' He stormed off and collided with a very scared Cathy.

'Vic, help, Ed's lost the plot and he's beating up Faye,' she cried.

'That's nothing compared to what he'll do to Al Simpkins. I won't intervene; it's just a domestic problem,' replied Vic.

'If you don't, she'll be beaten to a pulp.'

'You're such a drama queen, Cathy, she'll be fine. Now how about you and I get cosy while Ed's busying himself with Faye.' Angrily, Cathy scurried back upstairs, if Vic wasn't going to do anything, she would. Entering Ed's room, she surveyed a terrified Faye who was cowering in the corner of the room.

Cathy stormed across the room. 'Leave her alone,' she ordered Ed who towered over a sobbing, puffy-faced Faye. 'She's done nothing.'

Ed rounded on her now. 'How do you know? Have you been having some girlie fun? Can I watch? I could do with a laugh; better still how about a threesome? Does Silver get in between you when you're pleasuring each other?'

'Ed, what's wrong with you? Faye loves you; she wouldn't cheat.'

'So she loves me, and you don't?'

'You're twisting my words. I never said that.'

Faye got to her feet and rushed over to Cathy, sobbing her heart out and clinging to her. Cathy edged towards the door as Ed screamed out every obscenity possible and advanced towards the two women with a crazed expression. Managing to get the door open, Cathy pushed Faye through it and faced a furious Ed. 'Get Karl,' she cried, as Faye ran off.

'Yeah, run little girl, you've never been any good,' yelled Ed. It was then that Cathy noticed the knife in his hand and froze; she desperately hoped that help would come soon.

Downstairs, Faye crashed on Vic's door screaming, 'Vic, Ed's got a knife.' Vic opened his door and surveyed the wreck before him. She was a total mess; hair all over the place, swollen eyes, and her very puffy face was streaked with running mascara. Obviously Ed had seen the morning papers, and someone's head would roll, probably Al's. He wanted to turn his back on the whole episode, and then recalled that he needed both Ed and Cathy for a concert that very night, so sent Faye off to find Karl and made his way upstairs.

In Ed's room, things were heating up as he threw Cathy to the ground before dragging her up again by her hair. 'Better than me, is he? You two-timing bitch. What is it that he does for you that you love so much? How much better than me, is he?'

He slapped her around her face and then threw her across the bed. 'I don't know what you're talking about. I love you.' cried Cathy.

'Really? Well I recall a certain phone call that I took where he'd asked to take you out. And why did you both disappear last night when I was talking to that promoter? I can't remember what the deal was or what his name was; I was too absorbed wondering where you'd gone.'

'Sammy was showing me around his house.'

'You were gone for ages.'

'We weren't.'

'You were; what did he do to you?'

'Nothing.' Terrified, Cathy watched Ed pace the floor and then suddenly he threw himself across her, wielding the knife.

He ran the blade of the knife across her throat. 'Feel good, honey, does it? I used to know a guy who specialised in snuff movies; he said that when the blade of the knife goes in, the look on the face of the victim is priceless. After all the build up and fear, the thing is actually happening; they are going to die and nobody can stop it. What a feeling, babe. Tell you what, stick the knife in me, and then I'll do it to you. That way, as we both fade we'll see that look. What a way to go.'

'If you've got the guts to kill me, why not get on with it? Why prolong it?' sobbed Cathy.

Ed gazed at her and then began to laugh. Removing the knife from her throat, he said, 'kill you, I was only joking. If I killed you, I'd have to kill myself, but you need to be taught a lesson and so does someone else who shall remain nameless.' His anger seemed to have evaporated as he kissed her on her cheek. 'Let's have a drink of the most beautiful nectar you've ever tasted. I'll bring it over to the bed; you just relax.'

Cathy was uneasy but lay still as he left her side. She believed any false move could push him over the edge again, and she watched as he walked away and returned, minutes later, with a bottle of opened red wine and two glasses. Placing them on the bedside table, he lay down beside her and began to kiss her, this time on her lips. Then he straddled her.

'Close your eyes, honey, and I'll transport you back to our wedding day.' Cathy obeyed; it would be foolhardy to do anything else. 'Now, keep your eyes closed until I tell you to open them,' murmured Ed.

Cathy lay in silence, she could feel his weight on top of her but he'd gone quiet. Suddenly she felt him grasp her wrist and felt a very sharp pain in the palm of her hand. Her hand and wrist were wet and, opening her eyes, she saw Ed who was still straddled across her, with the palm of his hand covered in blood. He forced their palms together, mixing their blood which was now running down their arms and into a glass that Ed had positioned to catch it. The blade of the knife was also covered in their blood. Cathy stared at Ed and then fainted.

Vic had stood outside Ed's door for a while wondering what to do. There was no noise coming from the room, and he was about to go downstairs when Faye appeared. 'Have you been into the room?' she asked.

'No, you stupid bint, it's quiet. I told you it was nothing,' replied Vic. Faye was angry. She hadn't been able to find Karl and the silence scared her. Cathy had pushed her to safety and she had to find out if she was okay. She pushed open the door and screamed at the sight before her. Ed was straddling the unconscious Cathy and, hearing Faye scream, turned his head and smiled. 'Hi baby,' he cooed. 'Cathy and I are having so much fun.'

Hearing Faye's distress, Vic rushed into the room and gasped at the bloodstained occupants and bed. 'What have you done?' he yelled at a very bemused Ed.

'Chill out, Vic, Cathy's so relaxed that she's fallen asleep,' replied Ed. Vic stared in horror as the mingled blood trickled into the glass. He walked to the en suite and opened the medicine cabinet; he needed bandages and possibly a trip to the hospital so that Cathy could have stitches in her hand. Faye was throwing up in the toilet; the only one unaffected was Ed, who still grasped Cathy's hand, seemingly transfixed by the flow of blood.

Vic approached the bed with a bandage. 'Let go of her hand, I've got to stem the bleeding.'

'No,' retorted Ed. 'I haven't got enough yet.'

'Enough what?'

'Blood.'

'You really are nuts, aren't you? Now let go of her hand.'

'No, you don't know how this works.'

'I don't want to; let go of her hand.' Vic insisted. There was a knock on the door and Romany entered. He was shocked at the scene before him. Faye staggered out of the en suite covered in puke, Cathy was out for the count, and Ed appeared to have embarked on a blood letting ceremony.

Cathy opened her eyes, stared up at Ed, and then saw the blood. She began to struggle, 'Get off me, you lunatic!' she cried.

'Just a few more minutes, babe,' said Ed, and, noting that the flow of blood was ebbing, began to suck on the wound. Cathy yelped; every suck was agonizing but Ed ignored her and continued to draw as much blood as possible from the wound. Romany was in shock; this was just like something out of a small-budget, horror movie.

Vic attempted to pull Ed away from Cathy but lost his footing and ended up flat on his back. 'Where the fuck is Karl?' he yelled. 'What the fuck am I paying him for?'

'Couldn't find him,' replied Faye, crossing to the side of the bed with a glass of water for Cathy in her hand.

Romany was rooted to the spot and watched as Faye attempted to get Cathy to drink some water before remembering why he'd come upstairs. 'There's a reporter downstairs who wants to interview Cathy,' he informed the group. 'Come on Ed, let her have her fifteen minutes of fame.'

Ed stopped sucking Cathy's hand and gazed up at his friend. Romany thought that Ed looked like Dracula, his face was covered in blood. He climbed off the terrified girl and placed the glass containing the intermingled blood by the side of the bed. 'Better clean up then, but first let's have a drink.' Cathy closed her eyes; this had to be a nightmare. Vic wound the bandage around Cathy's hand and secured it, telling Romany to go downstairs to the reporter and inform him that Cathy was asleep but would be available in an hour. He felt that the wound definitely needed stitches but as the bleeding had abated, he decided that the interview was more important. He went to the en suite to wash his hands and as he ran the taps he heard Cathy spluttering. He rushed back into the room and saw Ed trying to force the girl to drink the blood in the glass. It was dribbling down her face.

'No!' she cried in between splutters.

Vic had had enough. 'Are you trying to choke her now? Have you completely lost the plot, or is this a new crazy phase that you're embarking on?' he bellowed.

Faye had stripped out of her dress and was about to shower

when she heard Ed give out a screech. As she turned back and went back into the room, Ed began to laugh like a maniac and raised the glass. 'Cheers,' he shouted. 'Cathy, you are such a lightweight.' He put the glass to his lips and drained the lot in one go. 'Nectar,' he repeated over and over again. This time it was Faye who fainted as Vic held a sobbing, frightened Cathy to him.

An hour later, everyone was cleaned up and Cathy faced the press. Ed had insisted on accompanying her as he wanted to get to the core of this statement from Sammy about him and Cathy. Also, he told Vic he wanted to be present in case Cathy got out of her depth, so that he would be there for support if she needed it. Cathy seemed to be the only one who hadn't seen the morning paper, and she was stunned to see the headlines.

'I'm in love says Sammy,
Cathy has captivated my heart.'

The reporter had dug out the photos that he'd taken on the couple's night out. Cathy stared at them; there were shots of them at the plush restaurant, some of them dancing at the disco and at the very top of the page the risqué photo that Al had taken for the dance contest. Cathy laughed, 'It was just a night out. Romany's brother was hosting a party and I was going to have an early night, but Sammy turned up and asked me out. Vic okayed it and I had quite a pleasant evening with Sammy away from the party scene. He's a nice guy but much too young for me, and anyway I have a husband in the UK so I have no interest in any kind of relationship with Mr Silver. He appears to have read too much into our night out. This is just silly gossip, and as for the photo of me on the bed, that was taken years ago when I entered a dance contest.'

Ed was simmering inside. Vic had okayed the date, and Al had obviously given Sammy the old photo, so why were they ganging up on him. There were a few questions that needed answering. He believed Cathy was innocent now but it appeared that Sammy viewed her as someone that he had wanted to get involved with. Reporters made fires, that was true, but they needed sparks to ignite it.

Cathy was getting rather flustered, as it was now being suggested that she'd used Sammy to further her career. 'That shot on the bed is hot,' said the reporter. 'You'll get offers of screen tests now.'

'But I'm not interested in screen tests, I'm touring with the Z Tones, and when the tour is over I shall return to my husband and children in England.' She was upset now; all she'd done was to go out for a meal and she'd been punished by Ed, and now hailed as manipulative by giving Sammy false hopes of a relationship.

Ed stepped in. 'This interview is over; Cathy's upset. I'm a good friend of her husband, and you could say that I look out for her. If Vic thought that the date was okay, it was. As for the photos at the disco, so what? If I take a woman to a disco, I dance with her; it would be insulting not to. Sammy's a good friend of mine and a perfect gent too. The photo on the bed was taken a few years ago, it's not recent. I guess Sammy probably got one on the night of the show. He was a guest that night as well as me. You can take it from me there is no Cathy and Sammy, unless it exists in his imagination. Maybe he's obsessed with her or has some kind of odd fantasy, and if that's the case, it would probably be a good idea for him to stay away from her. I won't have this lady's honour defiled while I draw breath.'

The reporter viewed Cathy's bandaged hand. 'Accident?' he enquired.

'Yes,' replied Ed. 'She was trying to open a bottle and the glass neck snapped into her hand. Typical America.' He put his arm around Cathy's shoulders. 'Any more questions, ask me. Oh, and we would like an apology for this tacky story. Goodbye.' Taking Cathy's hand in his, he led her from the room.

Later that day, the whole entourage sunbathed around the pool, taking in the glorious sunshine. 'This is the life,' Ed sighed, basking in the rays. He was buoyant, but angry inside. He'd defended Cathy, but that phone call that Sammy had made unsettled him. Sammy had wanted a second date, so it was obvious that his interest in Cathy was not platonic. This matter needed addressing, and if nobody was going to act then he would have to. He turned his mind to the concert that night and decided to take both girls out to a top restaurant. He liked that kind of publicity and knew that he would be sure to get it. 'Good performance, good restaurant, good club, good publicity, good sex, and then goodnight Mr Silver,' he thought to himself. Sammy had overstepped the mark and he had to pay for it.

Noddy rang Cathy just before she'd left for the show. 'I'm staying on a little longer. Sammy's an idiot, he gave that story to the press to upset Ed and I should imagine that he's succeeded. After what you told me about Hank, I need to be here to witness anything if it happens. Ed's unhinged and I think capable of anything. Is everything okay your end?'

'Fine,' Cathy lied, 'you stay.' When she replaced the receiver, she wished that she believed herself, and longed for the day when she could return to her family. She sighed and prepared herself for the evening's show, plus the frivolities that were sure to follow.

The trio got back to the hotel about two o'clock in the morning and Faye went straight to bed. Ed followed Cathy to her room and was full of apologies for his behaviour that day, trying to justify his actions. Cathy wasn't listening; she was sick of his behaviour. A sex marathon later, she fell asleep in the arms of the guy that professed to love her. She was awoken later by the phone and groped for the receiver. Finding it, she lifted the receiver and sleepily mumbled, 'hallo?'

On the other end of the line was a very anguished Noddy, 'Cathy, is Ed with you?'

'Yes,' replied Cathy, not even bothering to look as her eyelids began to droop. 'Is that all?'

'Are you sure he's there?' asked Noddy.

Cathy reached out her arm and felt the pillow beside her. Her heart jolted, the pillow was vacant. She was panic stricken. 'What's happened?' she cried.

There was silence and then Noddy replied, 'someone's just tried to top Sammy. I didn't intend to fall asleep but I did and when I awoke everyone had gone. I suppose Sammy didn't want to wake me and had gone to bed. I noticed that the French doors were open and when I attempted to switch on the lights nothing happened. Then I heard a scream from upstairs and decided to investigate. As I went upstairs, I heard a pistol shot and then someone charged out of a bedroom and knocked me down the stairs. I banged my head and the intruder shot past me and ran out into the grounds. I called out to Sammy and at first there was no answer. My heart was full of dread, and then Sammy called out that he was okay. The noise awoke the staff, and between us we managed to get the lights back on. We searched the grounds but found nobody.'

Cathy shook with fear; surely Ed hadn't done this awful thing? 'Is Sammy wounded?' she asked.

'No, but he has a few minor lacerations where the knife caught him, and his throat has scratches on it; so it has to be someone with fairly long nails.'

'Knife?' cried Cathy. 'You said pistol shot?'

'Sammy sleeps with a gun under his pillow for his protection. He doesn't want the police involved, which makes me think that he knows who his evil assailant is. The important question is: where is Ed?'

'Asleep,' she lied.

'Wake him; I want to hear his voice.'

'I can't, you know how drugged up and sick he is.'

'True, but I'm not so senile that I get that close to someone and am unable to recognise them. I know who it was, and so does Sammy. If he really is there, put him on the line.'

Cathy began to sob, and Noddy added, 'don't lie to me; you're now shielding a murderer. He's killed once and just attempted a second. Don't you realise that Tony will be next, and how safe are the kids?'

'He wouldn't.'

'Silly girl, he wants you all to himself, no one can come near you. I'll speak to Vic tomorrow. We need to go home.' The receiver went down and Cathy reached for her pills; she really needed them now. She doubled the dose but sleep refused to come.

Time passed. Cathy didn't know if it was an hour or two, when the key turned in the lock. Her pills were knocking in now, and all she wanted to do was sleep. She heard Ed go into the en suite and guessed that he was cleaning himself up, if Noddy was correct. When Ed got into bed, Cathy feigned sleep, but it was to no avail. Ed made love to her expertly, and before long she responded. Ed blotted out everything else, locked in the embrace. Cathy uttered, 'I love you, God help me, I'm going to hell.'

Ed offered up a silent prayer before gasping, 'mine'. While he breathed life, no one was going to touch her.

Cathy awoke the following morning to the sound of knocking on her door. She glanced over to where Ed had been, and noticed that once more he'd gone. There was a note on the bedside table that read, 'I have to do an interview with the band, I didn't want to wake you, see you later, I love you.' The knocking got louder, and Cathy got out of bed, donned her robe and opened the door to a very flustered Vic.

'You're going home early,' he said. 'I'll take care of everything but you've got two more concerts first and a television show. On your final concert, you will come off after *Little Egypt*, change, and a car will be waiting to take you to the airport with Noddy.'

Cathy threw her arms around Vic's neck. 'Oh thank you, I'm so happy!' she cried.

Vic hugged her. She was a lovely armful. 'Don't thank me, honey, that's Noddy's price for his silence. If I had my way, you and Ed would never separate; he needs you. Why don't you join me for lunch, I could do with some female company.'

Cathy nodded, for the first time in ages she actually had something to look forward to. 'See you downstairs,' she said, breaking free of Vic's grubby little arms. His hands had begun to wander, and she knew at some stage she'd have to bed him but she was determined to delay it as long as possible.

As the television special loomed, Cathy was counting the days to returning home. She couldn't cope with Ed's mood swings any more. Hank's death, Sammy's near one, the rape, humiliation, degradation, and the fact that he'd cut her had convinced her that his drug taking was too much for her to handle. Until he sorted this out, he was not father material. She had to protect her children at all costs.

The television special was a huge success, as was the concert the following day. Ed spent nearly all his time in her company, with Faye taking a back seat. She wasn't bothered. Since she'd seen Ed drinking Cathy's blood, she'd avoided him as much as possible. The day of the final concert arrived. Cathy had had a reasonably early night and awoke feeling refreshed. Ed was still asleep and she cuddled into him. She wondered what would happen if Ed found out about her escape plans; that was a scary thought. Ed stirred and began to make love to her even though he was half asleep.

Vic tapped on the door. 'Ed, are you up yet?' he called.

'Yep, but not in the way you mean.'

'Be serious, I thought that you two might like a guided tour of Hollywood. I've cancelled everything today, so that you can spend the whole day together. The weather's glorious, the birds are singing, and Uncle Vic has a very heavy wallet filled with cash to spend on you both. My treat, nothing's too good for you two, and we'll be back in time for tonight's concert.'

There was a silence, and then Ed answered, 'hold on Vic, be with you in a minute.' Vic waited a short while and then heard Cathy cry out in her usual way. Minutes later Ed came to the door clad in a dressing gown looking very happy. 'Great idea, who's taking us?'

'Me of course, and Karl in case someone tries to get too close for comfort.'

'What about her?' said Ed, pointing his finger skyward.

Vic laughed. 'She's doing an article for a magazine on what it's like to be your fiancée; they picked her up hours ago.'

Ed smiled. 'Good.'

The day in Hollywood was a good one, Vic pointed out all the film stars' houses and film studios, the couple listened but neither of them took much in, they only had eyes for each other. Vic treated them to a slap up meal; he thought it was the least he could do. He took many photos of them and marvelled at their love. He felt quite choked and emotional; he'd spent all that time finding Cathy, making Ed complete again, and now he was about to snatch her away from him once more. He took Ed to one side. 'You really love her, don't you?' he said, sadly.

'Yeah,' said Ed, 'I love her more than anything, and I'm not going to lose her again; without her, I'm nothing.'

Vic took the point; if only, he thought. He knew that in Cathy's company, Ed needed neither drugs nor drink, she was all he needed. He swallowed hard. The decision to remove her was Noddy's, but for everyone's safety she had to go. Ed's obsession was dangerous. 'Come on kids,' he said, 'let's have fun.'

Much later, Cathy lay in Ed's arms sobbing as if her heart would break. They'd just made love, and Ed mistook her tears for tears of happiness. These days he found it hard to tell the difference between anguish and joy; his mind continued to break down and fail him. The drugs kept him going, plus Cathy's love, but he knew that he wasn't well. As time wore on he was getting more and more possessive about the girl. Rather than let anyone take her away, he'd kill her himself if he had to. He vowed to tell Faye that it was all over tonight, and that she could have property, anything, just as long as he could have Cathy. As soon as Cathy's divorce was sorted, they'd live in his house, or maybe abroad, and if she objected, then she'd have to learn that her place was by his side.

Cathy had stopped crying now and clung to Ed as if her life depended on it. She didn't want to go. She loved Ed more than life itself but he was sick; his mind was deranged. He should be getting help now, but Vic was intent on making as much money as possible out of him. The holiday would be pushed further and further away until Ed broke down completely. 'Come on, kids,' called Vic from the other side of the door. 'Time to get ready; it's party time'.

Ed sighed and rolled Cathy over again. 'Just this one last time,' he said. If only he'd realised the significance of his remark, heads would have rolled.

At the venue, Cathy dressed in her *Angel* costume. Noddy had stayed behind at the hotel to pack everything. Before Vic left the hotel, he had told Noddy that he'd pulled *Little Egypt*, as the flight had been brought forward and Cathy needed to be on it. 'I don't want any tearful goodbyes; I want everything to move as fast as possible. I don't want her to have time to reconsider.' Noddy was in agreement, and said he'd call Vic as soon as he got back to England.

Backstage, Cathy's stomach was churning, she felt terrible and her heart was heavy as she made her entrance. During the ballet, her legs were heavy and she had difficulty in dancing at all. She floated one minute and was earth bound the next. When she sank to the ground with Ed at the end of the number, she rested her head on his shoulder as normal and then looked up at him. Their lips met in a passionate embrace in front of the huge audience. Cathy gasped, 'I love you, I always will.' Ed returned the fervour of her kiss, feeling unsettled.

He wondered what had possessed her to do it. He was glad that she had but couldn't understand why. The applause was deafening, and Vic signalled to Romany to begin the next number. Cathy was jolted back to reality and left the stage in a hurry. Stunned, Ed began to sing. It was as if she was saying goodbye. He dismissed the thought; no one walked out on Victor Lee.

In the dressing room, Cathy met Noddy. 'You're early,' she said. 'Come to watch my final number in America?'

'You're not doing it,' replied Noddy, wishing the ground would swallow him up. 'The flight is earlier than we thought. Change, and leave your costume on the hanger. Vic will bring it when he returns to England. Trembling, Cathy obeyed. She had hoped to see Ed one last time and now that was being denied her. The face that she loved would only gaze at her from newspapers, and the warmth of his body would become just a memory.

She hung up her costume and turned to Noddy. 'It's funny, I feel as if I've done this before,' Her mind flashed back to 1968 when she'd clung to Ed saying practically the same thing that she'd just uttered on stage. She'd left then and only met up again in 1973. It was 1975 now, and once more she was leaving.

Vic appeared and kissed her on her cheek. 'Sorry to see you go, honey, but it is for the best.'

Tearfully, Cathy replied, 'break it as gently as you can, won't you, and let me know how he takes it. I'm truly worried. I don't want to go but I'm scared.'

'Sure honey, I'll keep in touch. He'll be fine; when he realises what he's done to you and others he'll be running to your front door begging forgiveness. He just needs a vacation.'

As Cathy left, she added, 'thanks for everything.'

'My pleasure, honey, bye.'

Cathy walked out into the night air with Noddy and got into

the waiting car, which immediately left for the airport. Once on board, Cathy sobbed into Noddy's shoulder. The stewardess asked if there was anything that she could do, and Noddy replied that Cathy was sad because she was leaving America. Cathy forced a half smile and agreed. She attempted to read a magazine, but it wasn't long before the print became a blur and finally she fell asleep.

Back at the concert, Romany was surprised when Vic shouted, 'no *Little Egypt* tonight.' The band continued as normal; they didn't understand it but were past caring.

Ed kept looking into the wings and, hearing Romany go into their final number, realised that something was wrong. There was no sign of Cathy and he was panic stricken. Was she ill? With the show now over, he made for Cathy's dressing room. It was empty apart from her *Angel* dress. He turned to Vic. 'Cathy sick?'

Vic ignored him. 'Come on, we've got another party to go to.'

Cathy was still nowhere to be seen. 'Cathy gone on ahead?' asked Ed.

Vic ignored his question. 'I want to get out fast. There's a huge crowd outside; now hurry.' Confused, Ed obeyed, and back at the hotel made straight for Cathy's room. 'Leave it,' said Vic, 'she's not there. Go upstairs. Faye might be with her.'

Upstairs, Faye awaited Ed's arrival; she was immaculately dressed as usual. 'Seen Cathy?' asked Ed.

'No,' replied Faye. 'Maybe she's gone on to the party.'

Ed was uneasy but thought that Faye was probably right. He left with Faye on his arm and, once there, tried to enjoy himself. It was hopeless, however, as there was still no sign of Cathy or Noddy. He excused himself and went back to his hotel. He began to look for her, thinking that maybe she'd come back and was waiting for him. Switching on the light he called her name. There was no reply. Dejectedly he sat on his bed, racking his brains for an answer. Nothing tied up. They'd had a wonderful day, and the way that she'd clung to him on stage had made him feel like a king. Suddenly, something caught his eye; it was white and hung on the clothes rail next to his lame suit. Vic must have put it there by mistake.

Getting to his feet, he decided to take it downstairs. The *Angel* costume was a beautiful garment and he could still smell the scent of Cathy's body on it. He went downstairs and entered Cathy's room. Feeling around in her wardrobe, he found plenty of empty hangers. Something was wrong, every hanger was empty; there were none of her clothes in there at all. In a choked voice, he cried, 'Cathy, where are you?' He felt as if someone had just cut him to ribbons. 'No,' he sobbed, 'she wouldn't, she couldn't.'

The truth had now struck home. His darling was gone and the kiss on stage was a farewell one. His head spun and he raced upstairs still clutching Cathy's costume. Once inside his room, he flung himself down on his bed and sobbed his heart out. Then, in a blind fury he tore the curtains from the windows and smashed everything in sight. He turned around and saw Karl and Vic framed in the doorway. Vic tried to calm him but to no avail. 'Why Vic, why? You knew, didn't you, you bastard? Why didn't you try to stop her?'

Angrily, he threw a bottle at a mirror, shattering it. Karl held Ed in a vice-like grip as Vic replied, 'yes I knew about it, she was running away from you. She was scared for herself, scared for her friends, and any male acquaintance; she was even scared for her husband and kids.' Ed stopped struggling, unable to take the last remark. 'Oh God!' he cried. 'Did she really think that I would harm the kids?'

'Yes, she was terrified of you, that's why I let her go. Plus the fact that her departure was the price of Noddy's silence over your attack on Silver, we know you did it, Ed. I arranged it; it was me that got things moving, Ed, not her. She didn't want to go, but at least she knew that it would stop you being locked up. We both know that you would have killed Silver if he hadn't had that pistol under his pillow.'

'You,' cried Ed, 'I'll kill you!'

'Sure, you're pathetic, rather than lose her, you'll kill every person that she dares to smile at.' He picked up the telephone. 'Get me a doctor, fast,' he ordered. 'Mr Gold is sick.'

With a fit of superhuman strength, Ed broke free from Karl's grasp and smashed another bottle. Holding the jagged end he advanced on Vic. 'Get me on a plane to England!'

Romany, Rick, and Faye chose that moment to arrive, and the sight before them was not a pretty one. Karl was attempting to pull Ed away from Vic. One false move and all Vic's problems would be over. The jagged edge of glass was a hair's breadth away from Vic's throat. Romany strode over to Ed. 'Come on pal, give it to me. I don't know what's bothering you but I'll sort it. Now give the bottle to me.' He hoped that Ed wouldn't turn the force of his wrath upon him, but knew that if he didn't intervene, Vic was as good as dead.

'Where's Cathy?' asked Rick, knowing that if anyone could talk Ed out of this it was her.

'Good question,' Ed cried. 'This bastard put her on a plane to the UK. He's sent her away from me.' Romany flinched. No wonder Ed was angry and, in this state of mind, he was liable to kill anyone. Karl, despite his strength, was having difficulty holding him until Ed's eyes glazed over and he sank to the ground clutching Cathy's dress to him. He released his hold on the bottle, and Romany grabbed it, placing it on one of the few remaining tables that Ed hadn't smashed.

When the doctor arrived, they couldn't prise the dress from him. They put him to bed, and the doctor examined him. 'I don't know what's been keeping him going, but whatever it is, it's not done any good. You people lay your hands on good and bad drugs, don't you? As long as this man stands up, you can pump any old rubbish into him. I advise hospital, but I can't enforce it.'

Vic swallowed hard. 'No hospital, he needs rest, that's all.'

The doctor administered the sedative, and sighed, 'hospital.'

'No,' asserted Vic.

Romany leaned over Ed who still clutched Cathy's dress to him, murmuring, 'Cathy I love you, come back.' He stared up at Romany, not really seeing him or anyone else for that matter. All he could see was him and Cathy, and as he felt the needle enter his arm a tear trickled from his eye. He wondered what they were putting into him this time; he felt like a walking pin cushion these days. He fingered the white dress. 'My angel,' he repeated over and over again. Gradually the drug took effect and he closed his eyes, still clutching the dress.

Romany broke down. 'You bastard, Vic. They told you in Vegas that he should rest but you wouldn't allow it. If he can stand tomorrow, you'll get a show out of him. Well Mr Big, if you want a show, you get another lead guitarist because I'm not working again until he's fit, if the poor devil ever is.'

Oblivious to everything, Ed slept, and Vic said nothing. What could he say? He was surveying the wreckage and wondering how much this was going to cost.

Chapter Fifteen

Back in England, Cathy let herself into her house. She knew immediately what Tony meant by being silly. Ingrid, in a flood of tears, told her that she was going to have Tony's baby. Cathy, calm at first, erupted at her husband who attempted to kiss her on her cheek as if he'd done nothing wrong. Ingrid left the room as Cathy rounded on her husband. 'You can't run from this one,' she scolded. 'I'll move out and support my children, but not Ingrid's. You'll have to get a job.'

'Let the state take care of her, and we'll stay together,' said Tony. 'I didn't even fancy her really; she was just here.'

'No,' asserted Cathy. 'I've had enough of being used. Whether you stay with Ingrid or not, I'm leaving. The kids never see me because I'm always touring. You've made your bed, so now you must lie in it. If I stay, I'll still be keeping you. No, Tony, enough is enough.'

'But we could stay together for the kids.'

'No, your duty is to Ingrid now.'

'I read the papers; you were a smash.'

'No, it was Ed the fans paid to see.'

'So why are you home, and he's still out there?'

'I got homesick, and Vic only needed the band. I want a divorce, Tony. We're never together, and like I said, Ingrid needs you. We'll have to let the courts decide about custody, but if I lose, I want access, regular access. I can't live this life any longer.'

'So you're going to desert us and go and live with Ed?'

'No I'm not; he's engaged to a lovely girl. I'm going to live on my own for a while. I was thinking of us trying again, but not now. Ingrid's your priority.'

'I'll send her away.'

'No, she deserves better than that, she's carrying your child.'

'What about the kids?'

'Okay, I'll stay for a month until we get some kind of structure, and I'll sleep in the boys' room. Ingrid needn't move out of your bed.'

'But Cathy…'

'No "but Cathy", I'm tired and going to bed.'

'But I'm your husband.'

'You should have thought of that before making Ingrid pregnant.' With that, Cathy turned on her heel and went upstairs. Suddenly she felt a lot stronger.

Back in America, Ed awoke from his sedated state and stared around him. For a second he wondered where he was and why he was feeling groggy. Beside him, Faye slumbered peacefully. Beautiful, but cold, he thought, not like Cathy. She was beautiful and red hot. He decided to get up and creep downstairs into his beloved's arms. He felt a delicious tingle come over him, and then he recalled that she wasn't there. He was scared. Where was she by now? Would he ever see her again? He needed her so badly. Anger mounted in him as he thought of Vic.

He wanted to kill him and anyone else who dared to come between them. Then suddenly he felt lost. Maybe she didn't want him any more? He couldn't take that. Then it struck him; instead of killing everyone else, why not kill himself? If his love was in vain, then there was no point existing. Seth had said that they were joined beyond death, so if that were the case then he could come looking for her and literally spirit her away. This was so much simpler; he wandered over to the en suite and found his pills. After washing them down with a glass of water, he went back to bed. The bottle had been half full so he guessed that he'd taken enough to remove him from the earthly plain. A friend had told him once that if you took too many, the body would react and throw the pills back up again. That would be no good, he wanted to die; to go to sleep and die. As he got back into bed, Faye stirred and then turned over onto her side. Ed looked at the lovely girl, and now felt bad about the way he had treated her in the past. He reached out to her and she awoke with a start. 'Ed!' she cried. 'Are you okay?'

'I'm fine, baby. I'm feeling friendly, are you?' Faye was lost. She wanted to go to sleep but felt obliged to placate him as she knew that Cathy's exit had hit him hard. She turned to him and they kissed. Ed's head was reeling. He felt strange, the pills were starting to work. He was pleased and then it struck him. He loved sex, so what better way to die? He could die in the embrace of this beautiful girl; that was wonderful. He began to caress Faye slowly and gently, taking his time. Faye was baffled; where was the lusty passion? This wasn't the Ed that she knew, something was wrong. Ed raised himself above her and slid into her body. He was moving very slowly, and then his speech was becoming garbled. His mind was elsewhere.

'My beautiful baby, my wonderful gypsy, dance for me gypsy, I can't live without you, I love you.' Faye was indignant. She didn't mind comforting him, but this was too much. Suddenly he slumped across her, he seemed heavier than usual. She pulled away from him and wriggled out from underneath his body. He appeared to have gone to sleep, and Faye wanted to wash him off her.

She got up and headed for the en suite, knowing that a shower was just what she needed. Crossing to the medicine cabinet, she opened it and looked inside for her favourite shower gel. It was then she noticed the empty bottle that had contained Ed's sleeping pills. She'd knocked the bottle over earlier and knew that it had been half full. Rushing back to the bed, she attempted to wake Ed. She shook him, slapped him, and screamed at him. He half-opened his eyes. 'Whasssamatter, baby?' he slurred, 'I feel great.'

Horrified, Faye threw on her robe and rushed downstairs to Vic's room. She pummelled on his door with her fists. 'Vic!' she cried, 'I think Ed's overdosed.'

Vic rushed to his phone. 'Get me an ambulance fast,' he yelled. 'Ed Gold's suite.'

The press on both sides of the Atlantic screamed: 'Ed Gold overdose mystery.'

Vic rang Cathy. 'The press are exaggerating,' he said. 'Ed had been drinking and took one pill too many. We'll meet up when I get back to England. Ed's writing to you. He's sorry for what he's done and can't wait to see you again.' The receiver was replaced, and an uneasy Cathy sobbed. She didn't believe Vic at all.

The following day brought another shock. Calling in at Noddy's office, she found his daughter behind the desk. 'Dad died this morning,' she said tearfully, 'It was a heart attack.' Cathy's world had now disintegrated. Noddy had been her friend, advisor, and a brilliant manager. Now he was gone.

Sadly, she left the office and, later in the day, received another call from Vic. 'I guess I'm your manager now. I'm flying back to the UK on Friday; we can have lunch and discuss your future. Sorry about Noddy, a colleague told me the news.'

'How's Ed?'

'Tell you Friday, dear; be at my office at twelve thirty.'

Cathy felt numb. She guessed that Vic would now want payment in kind. Her heart was heavy as she knew that her time of avoiding Vic's advances had run out.

Friday arrived, and so did Cathy. She was punctual, and over lunch enquired after Ed's condition. Vic replied that he was on vacation in Rio de Janeiro. He patted Cathy's knee under the table. 'Let's talk work,' he said, leaning across the table and eyeing her lustily. 'I've got you a good venue in London, and a recording contract is in the works. You'll never look back now that I'm in control.'

'I've seen a solicitor. I'm divorcing Tony but it's going to cost a fortune.'

'But of course, I'll help you. Ed will be pleased that things are moving; he loves you. He nearly killed me when he found out that you'd gone. Came at me with a broken bottle and held it to my throat. Then later took an overdose.'

'You said he was on vacation? You love making people squirm. What is the real truth?'

'He's having psychiatric treatment in LA, but he'll be well soon.'

The waiter brought their meals to the table, and Vic cut into his steak. The blood oozed out, and Cathy wondered how much more he was intending to squeeze out of her or Ed if she signed up with him. They continued their meal in silence and, after Vic had paid the bill, he amazed Cathy by getting to his feet, grinning and saying, 'thanks for your company, Cathy, now I have a lot of work to do so I'll have to leave you. Oh, and I haven't forgotten our little agreement, honey, bye. Get yourself a mini cab and charge it to me.'

The following day, Cathy took Sandy shopping and on her return was surprised to see a Rolls parked outside her house. Sandy was happy, thinking that maybe Ed had returned from America and had come to see her. However, they were confronted by Vic and Tony. In the kitchen, Ingrid was up to her elbows in soap suds, and Vic was making himself at home, with Michael perched on his knee. Ingrid dried her hands and began to make coffee.

'It's your lucky day, Cathy,' said Tony. He was in his usual attire; shirt unbuttoned, sleeves rolled up with old trousers on and a fag in his mouth. He rambled on, 'Vic's got work in London, followed by a road show and a recording contract.'

'Bully for Vic, but I'm not interested.'

Michael was tugging on a gold medallion which Vic wore around his neck. He seemed intent on strangling him with it. Cathy lifted the child from Vic's lap. 'He's okay,' said Vic. 'Tell you what, son, would you like a ride in my car?' Michael beamed and nodded enthusiastically.

'And my bruvver, and Sandy,' said the very happy child.

'Okay,' said Vic, 'but I need to speak to Mummy first. Ingrid, could you occupy the children, please?' Ingrid took the children through to the kitchen.

'I'm not interested,' repeated Cathy, drinking her coffee.

'You can't retire,' said Tony, indignantly.

Vic fixed her with a steely gaze. 'Five months in London, dancing by night, studying with a good vocal coach by day, and then the road show. By then Ed should be well enough to tour again and we'll build on that. You can repeat *Angel* and *Little Egypt*, and then you can start to duet with Ed on a few simple numbers. As you get vocally stronger, you can work with the Z Tones, and solo with a ready-made band; then lo and behold, you'll be a superstar.'

'And all of that without being heard singing. You don't even know if I can.'

Vic laughed. 'In this business, who cares? It's not what you do, it's who you know, and you've got a head start as you've actually got talent.'

'Take it, Cathy. I'm sure if you don't like it, Vic will let you out of the contract,' said Tony, lighting another cigarette.

'Sure,' said Vic. Secretly, however, he thought, no way. He put down his coffee and got to his feet. 'Kids,' he shouted, 'Uncle Vic's ready.' He extended his hand to Tony. 'Nice to have met you, Tony. I hope it won't be the last time. We must all get together soon and discuss the American tour. Boy, there's some tales I could tell, eh Cathy?' Cathy nodded, knowing that the wrong information fed to Tony could jeopardise her divorce.

She followed the children out to the car and got in with her excited family. They went for a spin, and when Vic dropped them back at the front door he turned to the unhappy girl. 'See you in my office tomorrow, Cathy. Don't let me down and I won't let you down, understand sweetie? See you at midday.' She agreed, and dejectedly went back into the house, followed by her happy brood.

The following day, Cathy met Vic and signed the contract he'd prepared. Through his intercom, Vic told his secretary that he was not to be disturbed at any cost, and then turned to the shaking girl. 'Okay baby, you're under contract to me. You will sail through your divorce, and we're both gonna get rich. Now how about a bit of gratitude?' He leered at her, adding, 'let's see what drove Ed out of his mind.' Cathy was revolted as Vic removed his clothes and his fat body came into view, but she closed her eyes throughout the whole episode, keeping a mental note of three small innocent faces. They were worth any sacrifice.

Afterwards, a well satiated Vic rose from his casting couch. He dressed and crossed to his desk, searching in the drawers for the London venue. He thrust the paperwork into her hand. 'You start tomorrow,' he told her. 'No need to audition; my word is law in this place.' He kissed her on her cheek, saying, 'I'm gonna have a lot of fun making you into a superstar, much more fun than I had with Ed. We'll have a great time.'

Cathy donned her clothes. 'What does it matter what I think? Obviously you own a percentage of me.' She left his office feeling completely numb. The sex hadn't been too bad, but as she passed a record shop she saw a record sleeve in the window of 'Ed and the Z Tones'. Ed's face smiled at her and she hurried past the shop, her heart heavy. Suddenly it began to rain, the rain drops mingling with her tears. 'Even heaven's crying now,' she said out loud. 'From now on it's hell all the way. Thank God for my three little angels.'

In his office, Vic gloated. He now had Cathy under him, and he needn't stay in England any longer. He'd already booked a flight to LA. He needed to check on Ed and, until he was better, get the record company to re-release some of his records. Now he was going to launch Cathy. He'd have fun with her; she'd do anything to keep those children. He could play with her and, in time, get her back with Ed. That would be some force. He'd get rich and work both of them into the ground. He rubbed his hands together, placed his feet on his desk, lit a cigar, and sat back, relaxed. It was a shame about Noddy, but the old boy's death had helped him. 'Ed, Cathy, me, and money,' he sighed contentedly and closed his eyes.

Time passed, and Ed was making a very slow recovery. He never felt well, was always cold, and at times his mind failed him. He'd spent six weeks in a hospital for the insane, been moved to another hospital to recuperate for another six weeks, and was then sent by Vic to the Seychelles for a vacation. Faye was still with him, but she was also dallying with her rich, old sugar daddy. Ed of course knew nothing of this.

Cathy was by now making a lot of money, and Vic had introduced her to Kevin, a singer ten years her junior. The first time they'd met was at Vic's abode. He introduced him as, 'a young buck with a brilliant voice,' but said that he had no idea what to do with him as he didn't want to go solo, and didn't want to front a band either. 'Romeo, meet Juliet,' continued Vic. 'You'll be perfect together.' Kevin dropped onto one knee and kissed Cathy's hand. Cathy was unsettled. This guy was the image of Ed when he was younger, and even his actions were similar. Cathy felt that maybe Vic had groomed him and told him of Ed's mannerisms. 'You're both on the same roadshow,' Vic informed her, 'so you'll have plenty of time to polish your act between working. Now, what I want is Nancy Sinatra and Lee Hazelwood, Johnny Cash and June Carter, Ike and Tina Turner, plus Cathy to dance in a couple of numbers. Get my drift?' The couple nodded, but weren't sure if it would work.

It did, however, and soon they had an act that was almost ready. Kevin adored Cathy. Here he was with Ed Gold's lady, and he was besotted. Cathy liked him; he was funny and so like Ed that she had to remind herself that he was ten years her junior, but he made her feel so young.

Her divorce was coming along nicely, and then it happened. Sandy got knocked down by a car and was killed instantly. Cathy was inconsolable. She moved in with Vic and whilst there slashed her wrists. Vic got her to hospital in time, and when Ed received the news he did the same thing and once more found himself back in a mental hospital. He didn't help himself when asked why he'd done it. He explained that this was a sign that he had to take his own life because his future step-daughter had been taken, and he needed to die like Cathy, so that they'd become a family forever. The doctor shook his head, especially when he went on about being bonded for life and death with the child's mother.

Cathy lost custody of her remaining two children. The court said she was an unfit mother by her actions, and she was granted access but only with supervision. Ingrid had had her baby and was now pregnant again. Tony shocked everyone by getting a job and holding it down. Cathy threw herself into her work, and Vic regularly threw himself on Cathy. She was now taking drugs; they helped for her sex sessions with Vic. She'd get spaced out and become a very athletic lover. Vic was delighted and made sure that she had a regular supply.

In the following weeks, Vic worked Cathy and Kevin at an alarming pace. They slept very little and hardly rested at all. Cathy didn't need to diet any more; she hardly had time to eat.

Six weeks later, Ed returned to England, seemingly recovered. He'd stopped taking drugs by now and was drinking less. Slowly, Vic eased him back into work and promptly sent Cathy and Kevin abroad. Time and time again Ed tried to contact Cathy but was thwarted by Vic every time. Faye had left him, and really dented his ego by marrying a guy old enough to be her grandfather. Vic threw many girls in Ed's direction but he ignored them all, saying yesterday was gone and the only girl he wanted was Cathy. He was thirty-one now and if the fortune teller was right about Cathy giving him a son, then he believed they'd better get it on soon.

In France, Cathy had trouble with her leg; it hurt like crazy. The doctor ordered immediate rest, and confiscated her birth control pills. Vic allowed her to give the dancing a rest, but was determined that she would still sing. She sang with her leg strapped up, and with the help of pain killers. Cathy was very worried about ceasing her birth control. 'Now what do I do?' she asked Vic. 'Abstain or get pregnant?'

'Depends, honey, on who you're screwing. I don't know what time you send Kevin home.'

'Considering that you're the only one, you amaze me,' retorted Cathy.

'I didn't know that,' laughed Vic. 'Baby, you haven't got a problem. I've been sterile all my life. I can't get you pregnant, but if you fool around it might happen.' He raised her to her feet from the sofa where she'd been resting her leg. 'You, my dear, are a very lusty girl. I've never encountered anyone with a sex drive like yours, apart from Ed and Romany. You and Ed are made for each other. Oh and by the way, he's back in England and asking to see you. I'll have to go and check on him, but meanwhile Kevin'll keep you company. Just be careful though, he looks a lot like Ed when he was your young lover, doesn't he? I'll be back in about forty-eight hours.'

The next step, when Vic returned, was the recording studio. Cathy was amazed how Vic made wheels turn, but once they were back in England, the record had a very slow start. However, Vic sent so many people out to buy the disc that suddenly it was in the charts. He also gave Kevin and Cathy masses of publicity, and mentioned that Ed Gold was so impressed with the duo that he was writing a song especially for them.

Stunned, Ed phoned Vic. 'What the fuck is this all about? I knew nothing about it,' he raved.

Impatiently, Vic muttered, 'do you want her back or not?'

'Course I do.'

'Well, get off that lazy backside of yours and start writing. It may start off as a duet for Cathy and Kevin, but it'll end up as a permanent double act for you and Cathy.'

'You're using Kevin as a pawn?'

'Why, have you suddenly got a conscience?'

'He seems like a nice guy.'

'He is, that's why he's easy to manipulate.'

'Is he Cathy's lover?'

'No. Now get writing, I'm sending the press round later, so make sure that you come up with all the right answers. Oh, and do you know *River Deep* by Ike and Tina?'

'Course I do'

'Right, well polish it up'

'Why?'

Vic was fuming. Why did people ask so many questions? Ed should know that this was in his own interest. 'Just do it,' and with that Vic slammed down the receiver.

Within the next fortnight, Cathy and Kevin's single had shot up the charts. Vic's efforts had borne fruit, and 'Top of the Pops' had worked wonders. Now was the time, thought Vic, to let Ed and Cathy catch an occasional glimpse of each other. He wanted Ed to salivate a little. Z Tones were number one, and Cathy and Kevin number two.

Before the show started, Ed was briefed. 'Give her a friendly kiss and nothing more,' Vic told him. 'Then we're all going out for a meal to discuss a certain concert to end all concerts that I intend fixing. Be polite to Kevin. He's a nice guy, a bit like you when you were younger. In fact, he looks like he could be your younger brother. Cathy's been to hell and back since you last saw her as well, so don't blow it.'

Ed reluctantly agreed; playing the gentleman was not his scene. He was even more annoyed when he realised that Vic had set him up with a dinner date. The girl gushed all over him. 'Ooh, Eddie baby, you're the greatest,' she cooed, all bleached blonde hair and big boobs. 'Why did you pick me?'

'I didn't,' replied Ed curtly. 'We got you from some bloody escort agency. Deflated, but not completely rebuffed, the girl clung to his arm as Ed fixed her with an icy smile. 'Top of the Pops' began, and Kevin and Cathy went through *Ladybird*. It was a catchy number, and Cathy swung along nicely to the melody with Kevin complementing her well. Ed ached to touch Cathy. In his eyes, she was everything, but he controlled himself.

When Ed took to the floor with the band, Cathy couldn't watch and walked away. Vic dabbed her eyes. 'Chin up, honey, what would Noddy have said? Be a pro.'

Cathy forced a smile. 'I know, but I'm so scared.'

'No need to be. You won't be alone, apart from the dance floor later.'

Later at dinner, Cathy found it hard to force any food down her throat. She nudged Vic. 'Got anything?' she whispered.

Vic ignored her request and turned to Ed. 'How's the new song coming on?'

'Nearly finished.' Ed knocked back a glass of Blue Nun in one gulp. He gazed at Cathy who was clearly distressed, and reached across the table taking her hand. He kissed her fingertips. 'It's lovely to see you again,' he said. Cathy withdrew her hand, feeling that same sensation like an electric shock.

The starlet was wriggling in her seat., 'Oooh, Eddie babe, let's dance,' she trilled in her little girl voice.

'Later,' replied Ed. 'I've got business to discuss, right Vic?' Vic nodded, and began to outline the plan for the event that he was going to promote. Ed said it sounded pretty normal really.

'There will be guest appearances too, and your set will have a fantastic finale, Ed.'

'Well, now that we know what it's all about, I'd like to dance,' said Ed. The starlet wriggled around in anticipation, and was disappointed when Ed reached across the table once more and took Cathy's hand in his own. They made their way to the dance floor, and Kevin decided to take the starlet for a whirl. Vic looked on happily as his favourite couple clung together. Cathy felt as if she was being engulfed with red hot flames, and as for Ed, she could definitely feel him growing against her. Vic smiled, he saw that Ed was getting extremely horny, and the enraptured look on Cathy's face said it all. This was great. Ed was getting Cathy aroused, and yet it was he who would get the full strength of Cathy's lust tonight.

Later that night, Vic got the full force of her passion. He plied her with drugs galore and plenty of booze, then he just lay back and enjoyed himself. She was writhing around, and her eyes were wild and staring. 'Wanna fuck, baby?' he asked, as he entered her heaving body. 'Come on, baby, fuck, come on, fuck,' he said.

Earlier that day he'd purchased some cream that was guaranteed to make him last. He hoped it would, as he knew that it would be only a matter of time before Ed spirited her away. He wanted to get right inside her head and didn't think it would be hard as she was heavily drugged. They tossed around on his water bed and rolled right off of it, still joined together with the girl in a torrent of passion. The cream was working as he thrust at her again and again.

She was screaming like a banshee as he pulled out of her, opened a bottle of champagne and sprayed it all over her. She moaned as if in pain as the drink hit her body. 'My star,' groaned Vic as he knelt down and began to lick the liquid from her. Her eyes were glazed as he released her with his tongue then he tried her in every conceivable position with no protest at all.

When daybreak finally crept into the room, Vic had had three orgasms, and Cathy countless. He rolled over on to his back, more than satiated, but already she was giving him another helping of head. He closed his eyes. You are too much, honey; you and Ed belong with each other.'

Cathy stopped and sat bolt upright. 'Ed, Ed?' The name registered but her head was fuzzy and nothing made sense. Vic's eyes snapped open and he stared at the confused girl. He really had got her right out of her head, she didn't even know who Ed was. He reached over to the cassette player beside the bed and switched it on. Ed's voice burst forth singing one of his sexiest songs. Cathy lay down again and closed her eyes as Vic began to caress her body with his fingertips. Cathy sighed as he progressed; she had opened her eyes but appeared to see nothing.

He spoke to her but there was no response as the tape was getting to her. She still stared blankly ahead as he raised himself above her. He felt as if this was going to be like the fourth of July, and he wasn't wrong. Cathy began to sob as he took her and, at the height of her passion, she cried out, 'oh Ed, I love you so much.' Vic smiled. Any other man would have been very insulted, but he was elated. He knew how much Ed loved Cathy, and now he knew that she felt the same way. After all the heartache, she was ready to reunite with Ed once more.

As Cathy relaxed, she fell asleep, and Vic pulled the covers over them both. He switched the cassette off. 'Success,' he murmured. 'Ed gets Cathy and, between the two of them, I make big bucks.'

If Vic's problem was excessive sex that night, Ed's was the reverse. He'd taken the starlet back to his house, but Cathy had really got him going. He was still being patient with her, but since seeing her in this latest encounter, he was going crazy. He'd led the girl to his bedroom and she'd remarked on the blow-up photograph of Cathy above his bed; the very same photo that he'd chided Al for. Al had got it blown up after dodging Ed's fury in LA, and given it to him as a peace offering, saying that the newspaper item had nothing to do with him. He told Ed that the teeny bop idol had bought the photo off him at the night of the dance contest, which enraged him even more. They had settled their differences since as Ed realised that Cathy had been the victim of a publicity stunt just for Sammy's ego. Mr Silver sure had some apologising to do.

'She's beautiful,' remarked the starlet, who said her name was Susie May. 'Won't she mind me being here?'

'Shut up and fuck,' snapped Ed.

The girl removed her clothes and embraced him. 'Be gentle,' she whispered in his ear, 'it's my first time.'

'Not my problem. I don't know how much Vic paid for you but you'd better be worth it. Now, no talking, just fuck.'

A tear trickled from Susie. 'Everyone says I look like Marilyn Monroe.'

'You don't. Now, just fuck, you're starting to bore me.'

'But everyone says you're a great lover.'

'I am. Now are we fucking or shall I send you away and get Vic's money back?' The girl stationed herself on Ed's huge bed and spread her legs. Ed forced her head down but he was so huge that she thought she was going to choke. 'Do it, or out,' ordered Ed. The girl complied, but fifteen minutes later Ed still couldn't come.

'It's all lies,' cried Susie. 'You, a Superstud? Never in a million years.' Furiously, Ed rolled her onto her back and forced himself into her. Susie was delighted; at last he'd made contact with her. She'd have liked some foreplay but at least she was getting some form of love. Ed held the girl to him whilst focusing on the blow up photo above his bed. How he wanted Cathy, how he needed her. His stomach was knotting up and he felt the first stirrings of desire. He ignored the girl beneath him and fantasised about the photo.

Susie was crying. This really was her first time and Ed was hurting her. 'Stop, please,' she gasped, 'you're hurting me.'

Ed ignored her cries, he just didn't care. He pounded away at her for a good ten minutes and held her in a vice like grip. His heart beat wildly. 'Oh honey, oh my angel,' he gasped, his orgasm not far away. The girl was in agony but the words that he uttered made it all worthwhile. He must really care, it was wonderful. She wept tears of joy as Ed continued. 'I need you, you're wonderful, my very own angel, I love you.' The girl was thrilled, but in seconds he'd shattered her dream as he cried out, 'oh Cathy, I love you!' Susie felt as if he'd slapped her. She broke down in tears. How could he take her nubile body while thinking of another woman? He still held her in a vice like grip until he finally rolled off her.

He suddenly noticed that she was crying. 'What's the matter?' he asked impatiently. 'You got what you wanted, didn't you?' Susie was broken-hearted, but a thoroughly bored Ed shouted, 'shut up and get out, I'm tired.' Susie dressed and left, still crying, feeling thoroughly humiliated.

The following morning, Ed sent two huge bouquets to Cathy, and an invite for dinner. She accepted, much to Vic's annoyance. 'Okay go, but ring when you're ready to leave and I'll pick you up. Ed's off drugs and you are poised to be something big with Kevin, I don't want things going pear-shaped because of any kind of emotional trauma.' Cathy agreed and, later that evening, was greeted by Ed at a plush restaurant, where he'd booked a table far away from prying eyes.

The conversation was strained. They both still loved each other but weren't sure of each other's feelings. After deserting Ed in America when he was sick, Cathy wasn't sure if Ed still wanted her, apart from as a friend, but Ed was scared of making a move too soon. Now that he was drug free, apart from an occasional joint, he saw a much clearer picture and was very ashamed at the way he'd treated her. He kissed her hand. 'Vic's building you up just like he did me. Watch him.'

Cathy smiled; she knew exactly what he meant. Vic was using her in every possible way. She'd wanted to move out months ago, and was ready to resume living back in the Chelsea flat until Vic informed her that he'd let it out to Kevin. She was seriously considering asking Kevin if she could share the flat with him; after all the flat did belong to her and Ed. She was caught between the devil and the deep blue sea, as she was now aware that Kevin was infatuated with her. Her life was beginning to get entangled with men again.

Ed was her knight in shining armour, but had he changed? If she fell for his charms again, would he use her? Was this new gentleman Ed just an act? He might just want to humiliate her by hooking her on the end of his line and then cast her away. She couldn't risk it.

Throughout dinner, Ed was very talkative. 'So why are you living with Vic?'

'Nowhere else to go.'

'What about our flat?'

'Vic's rented it to Kevin.'

'He's rented out our flat? Crafty bastard, he could have asked me first. He's a total bastard. Has he come on to you?'

'No,' lied Cathy.

'He'd better not either if he knows what's good for him,' said Ed angrily. 'I can't believe he's charging Kevin rent and I'm not getting any of it. Suppose that was his way of keeping you with him. God knows he's got no friends. Well apart from the fair weather ones and Al Simpkins.'

'Don't mention that name to me,' snorted Cathy.

'If you're talking about America, he was innocent. It was all Mr Silver's fault; he wanted publicity and also wanted to hurt me because I'd been nasty to him so he invented the whole thing for his own ego.'

'So how did he get that old photo?'

'He bought it on the night of the dance contest. He fancied

you even then and you really helped him with his fantasy the night you went out with him.'

'But nothing happened and it was never going to.'

'No, but in his eyes it was, that's why he rang the following day. He was expecting the works.'

'He wouldn't have got it.'

'Yeah, but at that time my head was fucked up and he was a lot younger than me. I was feeling insecure and I thought I was going to lose you.'

'But I loved you too much to cheat on you.'

'Past tense, Cathy; does that mean you don't any more?'

'Of course not, it's just that, since I left you, there's been so much shit. I got my divorce, but I lost my kids so I fell apart, and before that Sandy died and my whole world collapsed.'

'Well, I would like to say I was there for you but I was in and out of mental institutions since you left. I did write to you almost every week. I had the mail sent to Vic as I didn't know where you were living, and knew that he would pass them on.'

'I haven't had any letters.'

'Then the bastard kept them. I cut my wrists when I heard about Sandy, and ended up back in another funny farm.'

Cathy was shocked. 'Oh Ed, I knew nothing about that. Did Vic know?'

'Yep, he was the one that certified me as loony and got me put away again.'

Cathy sighed. 'I cut my wrists too. That's why I lost my two other kids; they said I was an unfit mother.'

'So we've both been through the mill, and the only one still benefitting is Vic. Get away from him, Cathy, he's evil. I know that first hand.'

'Kevin and I are under contract with him.'

'Kevin, yes. Another interesting individual.'

'Don't you like him?'

'Actually I do, he reminds me of myself when I was his age.

I remember what I was like at his age, and I've noticed the way he looks at you.'

'Don't be silly.'

'I'm not, that guy's in love with you. Devotion pours out of his eyes and, given the opportunity, he'd marry you tomorrow.'

Cathy laughed. 'You're being silly,' she said. 'Besides, I'm still in love with you.'

'And I still want to marry you, baby. I'll never stop asking you.'

'But I was responsible for your breakdown, it was my fault.'

'No it was mine, honey. I drove you away but I've grown up a bit now.'

'But Ed... Vic's got me hooked on drugs… I want to marry you but…

'Okay, I can wait, I don't want anyone else. Come to me when you're ready, but don't stay too long with Vic or you'll end up just like I was. Now, finish your meal and we'll go dancing.'

'Plenty of dancing tomorrow. Vic told me that he wants us both to run through *Angel* and *Little Egypt*.

'Some manager, I still get told nothing. Oh well, that's cool, now let's party, at least that's one way of getting my arms around you even if I can't do anything else.'

'Okay,' said Cathy excitedly, 'I'm ready.'

'You always were,' laughed Ed.

The following day, Vic watched as Ed and Cathy went through the two routines. He was pleased with what he saw. It was mid-October and the gig to end all gigs was scheduled for Christmas Eve, with the after party to be held at Ed's house. He could see that Ed and Cathy were getting closer, but wasn't too upset; Cathy was just another woman to him. He loved having sex with her, but he liked making money out of her more. He'd just clinched a deal with a promoter for Kevin and Cathy in the Canary Islands. They were to work for six weeks between Tenerife and Gran

Canaria. The Z Tones were going to embark on another UK tour; Vic had only just informed both of his acts that morning.

The band protested. 'It would have been nice to have been informed earlier,' said Gerry indignantly. 'I was going on a family holiday in two weeks.'

'You'll have to postpone it then,' sneered Vic. 'While you're with me, you jump when I say so.'

Cathy and Kevin were surprised too; they'd thought they were going to the West Country. Vic certainly moved in mysterious ways. He'd designed it so that both parties would be back in time for his famous gig, and decided to book a holiday for himself. It was just what he needed; a couple of weeks in Mexico would be ideal. Cathy and Kevin were leaving in a couple of days, but the band weren't going for another fortnight. Yes, a holiday was definitely on the cards.

Cathy and Kevin returned in December, but Ed and the band were still on the road. The day of Vic's gig arrived and Cathy spent a lazy day around the house, not realising that this day was about to turn her life around. At two-thirty, Vic excused himself and went out. Cathy took her chance. She wanted to find those letters that Ed had written. So far she hadn't had a chance as Vic never went out unless she was with him; he liked having her on his arm.

She ascended the stairs and began to look around Vic's bedroom. She finally found a large envelope about fifteen minutes later with her name on it, plus Vic's address. It was in with a pile of her contracts. Opening the envelope she was amazed to see about fifty or so letters written by Ed. Some were short and to the point, one of them consisted of only a few words, it read, 'Cathy, this is not the end, just the beginning.' The date on it was shortly after she'd left America.

Several letters were muddled, owing to his state of mind, and many of them so loving that they made her cry. How could she have ever doubted him? He truly loved her. There was even one that he'd written just after Sandy's death where he stated that there was no purpose in living now, and that he was going to join Sandy and come back for her so that they could be a real family.

She put the envelope back in the drawer with all the contracts and decided to call Ed and tell him that she loved him, and that she now wanted to spend the rest of her life with him. She dialled his number, excitement building in her stomach, and was told by his housekeeper that he was out and meeting Mr Lee. Cathy replaced the receiver and decided to take a nap.

Vic woke her about two hours later, armed with a bottle of champagne and a huge bouquet of roses, 'for my star,' he said, uncorking the champagne which gave out a mini explosion. He poured two glasses of the bubbly mixture and raised his glass. 'Cheers, are you nervous?' Cathy nodded and accepted her glass of champagne. She gazed around the room. Vic was the only person she knew who had a well-stocked cocktail cabinet in his bedroom. Vic seated himself beside her on the bed and placed his hand on her knee. 'You'll be great,' he reassured her.

Cathy sighed; the fact that he'd kept her letters had really upset her. She knew that he was expecting sex as he hadn't touched her since her return from the Canaries, and it was obvious, by the way he was looking at her now, what he wanted. She'd decided that today would be the last time she would have sex with him.

When he got her out of her head it wasn't too bad because she'd be too stoned to know who he was; most of the time she was too far gone to even know who she was. The problem was that at the moment she was stone cold sober and knew everything, so the prospect of sex with Vic was very nauseating.

Tonight she was going to leave and, if Ed didn't want her, then she was going to flat share with Kevin. It was her flat so she had everything in her favour, but she'd have to lay down a few ground rules before she moved in. Kevin would have to know that there was no future for them romantically. Vic's hand moved higher and he began to grope.

'Ready at any time, aren't you?' he said, inserting his finger into her dampness. He leaned over and unbuttoned her blouse. 'I won't disappoint you,' he added, taking her breast in his mouth. Her body was responding and she began to emit little cries as her body gave up its precious fluid. The phone began to ring and Vic picked it up angrily.

'Is that all!' he cried. 'She'll find out later tonight.'

'What about Kevin?' came the reply on the other end of the phone.

'Fuck Kevin, and fuck you, Ed, I'll speak to you later.'

Vic slammed the phone down and returned to Cathy. 'Come on, star, let's have some of that star quality.'

Cathy sighed as Vic undressed and spread himself on the bed. This is most definitely the last time, Mr Forty-Per-Cent, she thought, and attended to the heaving blob before her. He didn't take too long and, immediately afterwards, Cathy headed for the shower. She could hear the cleaner singing to herself and cleaning Vic's spare room.

After showering, Cathy went looking for her hair dryer. It wasn't in its usual place, so she called down to Vic who was on the phone but he didn't seem to hear her. She decided to search for it herself. She finally found it in a wardrobe on the opposite wall and plugged it in. As she was drying her hair she stared into the huge mirror by the wardrobe and sat in Vic's easy chair. Usually she sat at the dressing table on the opposite wall which was her side of the bed, but she thought that Vic wouldn't mind her sitting in his chair, so she sat back, holding the dryer in her hand. It was a huge mirror, but then, Vic was a huge man. She leaned forward and gazed right into it. She could hear the cleaner next door, and then it struck her, not only could she hear her, she could see her too. This was no ordinary mirror; it was two-way. Cathy's heart sank; the spare room was the one that she'd slept in with Ed when they'd stayed. No wonder Vic wanted them to stay; he'd been watching them every time they'd made love.

It also meant that when she'd done the photo shoot years ago, he would have seen her disrobing if he'd been in his room at the time, which she felt sure he was. She vowed never to return here, and wondered how many guests had fallen foul of the mirror. She dried her hair and then, finding Ed's letters again, stuffed them into her case with her costumes. 'Fuck you, Vic,' she said out loud, 'I'm out of here.' After the show she would be gone.

At the theatre, nerves overtook her. Vic had given her a joint before leaving which helped slightly, but she was still jumpy. She smoked one cigarette after another, and the arrival of Romany didn't help. He seized her in a bear hug. 'Hi babe, you look good enough to eat. Actually I think I might take a bite later if Ed doesn't beat me to it.'

Cathy disentangled herself from him. 'You haven't met Kevin, have you?' indicating the young man who was tuning his guitar in between lovesick glances at Cathy.

'Seen him on stage. Hi Kevin, I guess you and me have got something in common.'

'Really?'

'Yeah, well we're both guitarists supreme, and our Cathy loves a guitarist, don't you darling? Tell you what, if you need loosening up just whistle and I'll be there. Well I guess I'd better find Ed. He plays the guitar sometimes and he gets some great sounds out of our Cathy.' Kevin said nothing, but he adored Cathy and hated to hear her spoken about like that.

'Creep,' muttered Cathy, and she began to fix Kevin's bow tie. Vic appeared and handed Kevin the running order. 'What happened to *River Deep*, Vic?' asked Kevin.

'Running time,' replied Vic, staring at the floor.

Romany smirked at the puzzled couple. He knew all about the missing song, and was about to add some smart remark when Ed arrived. He was accompanied by a man who was snowed under by flowers and champagne. Ed kissed Cathy on her cheek. 'To my angel, the next superstar in Vic Lee's stable.' He shook Kevin's hand and stared at the young man who resembled him so much when he was younger. 'Good luck Kevin, you're tipped for stardom too, I hear.'

'Thanks Ed,' stammered Kevin, completely overawed.

The Hotheads were on stage tuning up. 'I've heard these before,' said Romany, 'they're awful. What happened to all these top names you were on about, Vic?'

'Other commitments,' replied Vic.

'A likely story,' snorted Ed. 'Nobody else wants to work for you except us, and even we don't really.'

Vic ignored Ed and puffed on a cigar. 'May I remind you that you lot sounded like these boys before I groomed you.'

'No way,' said Gerry. 'We were stars before you came along. Doug did all the spade work, and Mick was the greatest. Let's face it, Vic, we've been around since 1965.'

'The Stones were around before that and they're still rocking brilliantly,' Vic reminded them.

The Hotheads were now onstage and went into their first number. 'What a din,' scowled Romany. 'I'm going for a drink.'

Ed flinched. 'They should be called the Tone Deaf Fatheads.' Suddenly there was silence. 'Someone's pulled the plug out.'

'Thank God,' said Gerry, relieved.

The curtain came down and the band stormed off. Vic was sweating buckets, but soon the problem was sorted out and the band resumed playing. Once they had finished their set, Sammy Silver put in an appearance. 'Who the fuck invited him,' snarled Ed.

'I did,' said Vic, defensively.

'Somebody shoot him,' joked Ed, raising his eyes to heaven, 'give me a gun.'

'Yes,' chuckled Cathy, 'and I'll fire it for you.' Ed laughed, at least Cathy was joking about the American episode now.

Sammy's stage act still wowed the young girls; they loved

him. As soon as he left the stage, Kevin and Cathy prepared to go on. They got a huge cheer when they appeared and went straight into *Ladybird* followed by *Jambalaya*. Cathy then delivered Dolly Parton's *Down from Dover* with so much pathos that several girls in the audience started crying, before Kevin picked up the beat with *Memphis* followed by *Johnny B Goode*. The audience were rocking along and Romany whispered, 'I had no idea they were that good.'

The song over, Kevin announced: 'Now we would like to do a number written especially for us by our very good friend, Ed Gold. It's a great song, and Cathy and I will try to do it justice. It's called *Just Good Friends*.'

The song was very catchy and the audience sang along with it. It received a great ovation, and Cathy followed up with *Sugartown*, encouraging the audience to join in vocally. *Jackson* was next, and then Kevin swung into a sixties medley, including *Green Tambourine*.

'Takes me back,' said Ed, reminiscing. 'Those were the days.' Cathy had now removed her skirt and, clothed in the garb of a go-go dancer was freaking out.

'Jeez,' said Romany, 'crafty old Vic.'

Moments later, Kevin and Cathy finished to wild applause. Vic took them back to the dressing room. 'My children, beautiful, wonderful!' he cried.

Romany grunted. 'What about us?'

'Dunno,' replied Ed. 'Don't care either. Anyway I've got to get some photos done with Cathy for the *Angel* sequence.' He felt guilty about *River Deep*. He knew that Kevin had worked really hard with Cathy on it, and Vic was repaying him by taking the song away from him. It was underhand, but then, everything Vic did was underhand.

In the dressing room, Cathy changed rapidly. 'Damn, I have a ladder in my tights. Kevin could you get me the spare pair in my case, and my ballet shoes. Kevin did so and then watched the transformation as his singing partner became the beautiful angel. He wanted to blurt out his feelings now, but held back, wondering if the time was right. 'How do I look?' asked Cathy, doing a twirl.

'Beautiful,' replied Kevin and, trembling, advanced on her. At that moment the door opened and in came Vic, Ed, and the photographer. Kevin backed into the corner.

Vic embraced her. 'Just like a princess,' he murmured. 'Now listen, you two. I want the same performance that you gave in LA on your final show.'

Ed grinned. 'You sure about that?' he asked, remembering the fervent embrace at the end of the number.

'I just said so,' replied Vic. 'Is there something wrong with your ears?'

He'd completely lost his memory of the kiss. 'Okay Vic, I'll give it everything.' The photos were taken and Ed prepared himself to go on stage.

A handful of celebrities were out front, and many rock stars were in the audience. Romany laughed. 'Vic, these guys should be on stage, not just observing.' Vic went blood red and made his way back to Cathy. Sammy hovered nearby, and Ed felt his stomach turn; this kid made him feel sick. All these rhinestone suits, capped teeth, and his immaculate grooming, made him feel old, and so did Kevin. In fact, recently, everyone did. He followed the band on stage after their equipment was set up. These roadies sure worked hard. Ed had had his microphone checked twice tonight just in case Sammy tried to get his own back.

The band took their positions and the curtain went up. Tonight they all seemed infected with a sense of fun. *Angel* went down a storm; the British public hadn't seen it before and, as Ed and Cathy sank to the ground and embraced, the audience went wild. Cathy felt as if she'd touched a bare wire, and Ed was extremely overheated. Once his lips were on his lady, he wouldn't let go of her, and the kiss seemed to last forever. Vic fumed; the two performers were still locked together urged on by the crowd. In the end, Vic signalled to Romany who crossed to the couple on the floor and tapped his friend on the shoulder, indicating the very happy audience and the very angry Vic. Ed reluctantly released his angel, helped Cathy to her feet and, turning to the audience, shouted, 'I needed that.' The crowd cheered, and Cathy made her way to the dressing room.

Kevin had watched everything from the wings, and now wondered if it was worth telling Cathy how he felt about her, as the kiss on stage said a lot about where her heart was. He followed her to the dressing room and helped her to prepare for *Little Egypt*. As her body came into view he felt as if he wouldn't be able to restrain his feelings for her any longer. He helped her to do up the jewelled bra and longed to run his hands over her body, but managed to keep his emotions in check. Cathy turned around and placed her arms around his neck. 'You were great, Kevin,' she said. 'I couldn't have managed any of this without you, really I couldn't.'

With his arms around her, he said in a shaky voice that threatened to give up any time now, 'it was you who was great. You could sing with anyone.'

Cathy kissed him in a sisterly fashion. 'Come on, I'll be on again soon.' They left the dressing room and Kevin sighed, he'd had his chance and blown it.

Little Egypt was a roaring success. Cathy dragged Vic onstage halfway through the number and dressed him up as a sand dancer. Romany filled in with some extra lead, and the band produced Tommy Cooper hats. Ed, not wanting to be left out, joined Vic in sand dancing and then took him in his arms and waltzed around the stage with him. After being called back for several bows, Cathy ran back to the dressing room and flopped down in a chair giggling. 'I enjoyed that,' she gushed to Kevin. 'I guess I can get changed now that I'm finished.'

'Oh no you can't,' said Vic, rushing into the room and peeling off the sand dancer outfit. 'Change into this.' He produced a beautiful jewelled dress which matched Ed's costume that he was wearing on stage.

'That's not mine,' responded Cathy, 'unless it's an early gift from Ed, seeing as it's Christmas day tomorrow. Can't I try it on later?'

'No,' snapped Vic, 'get it on as quickly as possible and come with me, and put these on too.' He threw a pair of high-heeled, jewelled, ankle strap shoes at her.

'But why?'

'Don't argue, just do as I say.'

Puzzled, Cathy obeyed, watched by an equally puzzled Kevin. Cathy was distressed, something was wrong, something was going on that she knew nothing about and she didn't like it. Vic practically dragged her back to the wings. Ed was delivering his latest single and stared over at Cathy standing with Kevin and Vic. Finishing the number, he addressed the audience. 'This next song is our final one tonight, take it away Romany.' Then he began *Sweet Little Rock 'N' Roller*. Cathy relaxed, maybe all she had to was take a curtain call or something, but it seemed a bit silly to dress up like this purely for a curtain call. The band ended their set to overwhelming applause; there had to be an encore.

As the band took to the stage again, Ed took Cathy's hand and hauled her onstage before she could object. She was terrified, wondering what was happening. Ed kissed her on the cheek. 'That's for luck, now sing.' Cathy was panic stricken, wondering what she had to sing, and then heard the intro to *River Deep*. Now she understood; she was victim to another of Vic's tricks. She began to sing with Ed, and the nerves soon left her as they both belted the song out. As a couple they matched perfectly, the costumes, the voices, everything. Vic was overjoyed, the press had a field day, and in the wings, Kevin sobbed quietly to himself.

The following party was a very noisy one. Cathy apologised profusely to Kevin, denying any knowledge of the finale to the concert. 'It's okay,' mumbled Kevin, 'it doesn't matter; I could never have done it as well as Ed.' Cathy felt terrible. No matter what Kevin said, she could see that he was hurt. Romany made things worse by congratulating them both on their performance, adding, 'shame you weren't in the finale, Kevin.'

Kevin ignored him and led Cathy to the dance floor. She was shaking with rage at Romany's last remarks, knowing that the aim was to hurt Kevin. 'Calm down,' soothed Kevin, 'he's just stupid, now get in close to me and we'll upset him a bit.' Cathy snuggled up close, and Romany stormed off in a huff. 'See?' chuckled Kevin. 'We've bruised his ego; for some reason he seems to think that he's got some sort of monopoly on you when Ed's not around.'

Reaching the door, Romany looked back just in time to see Cathy kiss Kevin on the lips. He made his way back to the couple and tapped Cathy on her shoulder. 'Dance?'

'No thanks,' replied Cathy, 'I've got a partner.'

Kevin released her. 'Go on, let's see if his dancing matches his mouth.'

Cathy dropped Romany a mock curtsey. 'Okay.'

Romany pulled her to him closely. 'You bitch, you loved that, didn't you? You like making me suffer, don't you? You got me all horny on stage, but I still want to take you somewhere and remind you what a good fuck is like.'

Cathy shot him a wide-eyed, innocent look. 'I don't know what you're talking about; I'm at a party with Kevin, that's all.'

'And what sort of setup is that?' grunted Romany, pulling her even closer.

'Perfectly platonic, as Ed's song goes, *Just Good Friends*.'

They danced together twice, with Romany trying to steer her in the direction of the garden and Cathy steering him back to the dance floor again. 'Let's fuck,' said Romany.

'No way,' replied Cathy. 'I'm going to find Kevin.' With that she wrenched herself from his grasp.

'Looking for someone?' asked Gerry as she passed him.

Cathy nodded, 'Kevin,' she replied. 'I can't find him.'

'Went that-a-way,' directed Gerry, pointing to the garden. Cathy hurried outside, looking over her shoulder just in case Romany was behind her. However, Romany had found his way through the dancers and, with his usual cunning, had managed to take a short cut and lay in wait for her in the garden. She saw him at the last minute and turned back to run but he was faster and dragged her into the darkness.

'Let me go!' she cried.

'Don't scream,' ordered Romany, pushing her over onto the grass. He kissed her hard, 'lousy, rotten bitch,' he growled, reaching under her dress. Summoning all of her strength, Cathy brought her knee up hard. It made contact and Romany let her go and rolled around in agony on the grass. Getting to her feet, Cathy brushed herself down and ran back to the house colliding with Vic and Ed. Faces became blurred, and then she slumped to the floor. Ed picked her up and carried her upstairs

'Mine I think,' he said to Vic who shrugged and headed for the bar.

When Cathy regained consciousness, she was lying on Ed's bed with him beside her. She turned her head into the pillow and began to sob. 'My life is such a mess. Vic's turning me into something that I don't want to be. I'm so unhappy. I'm useless. I was a bad wife and mother. America scared me, you scared me, and now I've lost everything. I thought I had nothing to lose by letting Vic advance my career, but I hate it and him. I found all of your letters; he'd hidden them so I put them in my case and I'm not going back with him tonight. Can I stay in one of your rooms? Any one will do.'

Ed stroked her hair and turned her to face him. 'Baby, you've been through more than most people go through in a lifetime, and I'm sorry to say that I put you through some of it, but you see I couldn't bear the thought of anyone else touching you or getting close to you. I'm sorry, I really am, but I guess I'll never change.

I suppose that's why Faye took off. You see, I can't change my feelings for you. I've loved you since the first time I saw you and that won't go away. We're bonded for life, so you can't escape me. I'll follow you to the end of the earth if I have to and I'll always find you. Of course you can stay here, but not just in any room, you can stay in this one with me and when you're ready you can move in permanently. There's no Tony, no Faye, we can do anything now. There's no one to stop us, not even old Vic. Isn't that wonderful?'

He kissed her gently at first and then began to caress her, but Cathy pulled away. 'Let's go downstairs, it's Christmas Eve and there's a party going on.'

'And it looks like it could be a good one. Come on, let's mingle.' He took her hand and raised her from the bed. 'Whatever happens, I'll always love you.'

It was then that Cathy noticed the huge photo on the wall. 'How long have you had that?'

'Since I returned to England,' replied Ed. 'Al Simpkins did it for me, nice eh?'

'Clever old Al,' replied Cathy, and they left hand in hand and went downstairs.

Downstairs, Vic was drunk and tottered around the dance floor before collapsing on a buxom blonde. He had to be helped onto a nearby settee where he slept soundly. Kevin gazed at Cathy. He had the feeling that she was about to be taken away from him at any second. He spotted Sammy Silver who looked a bit lost and walked over to him.

Meanwhile, Ed and Cathy clung together in one smoochy dance after another. Ed was now edging her closer and closer to the stairs. He eyed the clock on the wall. It was eleven fifty-five. He waited until midnight and then shouted, 'Merry Christmas everyone!' and as the poppers and streamers went off, he carried Cathy upstairs to his bedroom.

Once inside the room, he laid the unresisting girl on his bed and began to kiss her very slowly. 'My angel,' he said, tears filling his eyes. Cathy kissed him back. What was the point in denying each other? He'd put her through agonies in America and, without realising it, she'd put him through just as much. They belonged together, they'd always belonged together. Every kiss, every embrace was a testimony of love. His tears fell upon her face. He was still crying. So many tears had been shed, so much heartache had been endured. Wasn't it time for a little happiness? She wanted to be loved and to be able to love him back. She wanted… she wanted to… she wasn't even sure now what she wanted as Ed began to undress her. Her body trembled, it was so beautiful, and she felt like she was floating on a cloud as his hands slid over her body. 'All mine,' he murmured, 'all mine.'

Cathy gasped, feeling her body beginning to tense up. 'Yes darling, all yours, forever and ever.' Within seconds she passed over the threshold in sheer ecstasy.

Minutes later, she groaned, 'I forgot,' as Ed rolled off her.

'Forgot what?' asked Ed, puzzled.

'The doctors took away my birth control; I should have taken precautions.'

Ed's eyes were sparkling as he felt a fresh course of desire burning through his body. 'That's wonderful, darling, I'll have to make an honest woman of you.'

'Do you still want to marry me after all the pain I've put you through?' cried Cathy.

'Of course, I love you and I can't wait for the next set of labour pains.'

Cathy giggled and, as Ed took her again, experienced a strange and beautiful sensation, and knew that at that moment of sheer heaven, she'd conceived his child. 'I love you, Ed,' she sighed.

'Love you too, baby,' he replied, then they snuggled up together and drifted off to sleep.

Downstairs, the party was breaking up. A dejected Kevin made small talk with Sammy Silver, who by now was as sloshed as

Vic. Romany passed by. 'Shouldn't wait for Cathy, she's with Ed. I reckon the party's over in their eyes. I've got a couple of cuties waiting for me. Want a lift?'

'No thanks,' replied Kevin, 'I'll stay.'

'Please yourself, the party's over, people,' said Romany, and left, whistling.

Vic sat up and flopped back down again. 'Where is everyone?' Kevin was appalled, thinking that people in Vic's position should never allow themselves to get into this state. Vic tried to focus, and through a haze saw Kevin. Drunk or not, he was feeling horny. 'Where's Cathy?'

'With Ed,' replied Kevin, the words choking him.

'Shit,' snapped Vic. Catching sight of a waitress, he decided to try his luck and offer her a lift. The girl accepted, thinking that it would save her the cost of a mini cab, plus the fact that Vic looked too drunk to try anything. On the drive home, however, he passed out, receiving nothing, not even the girl's phone number.

Kevin, Sammy, and his chauffeur left together, Kevin wishing that this day had never come. It might be the season of goodwill but he felt anything but merry. He noticed all the houses lit up with fairy lights and Christmas trees, and stared at a few late night revellers from the limousine. He wished that he'd told Cathy of his feelings but knew that it was too late now.

His dream state was cruelly brought to a halt by Sammy spewing up everywhere; the stench was horrific. 'Merry Christmas, Sammy, and a happy New Year,' he muttered, opening the window. There was no answer. Sammy flopped back into his seat and fell asleep, covered in puke.

Ed made headlines in the press. He'd informed every newspaper about his forthcoming marriage. He wanted as many people as possible to attend, but because of the work commitments of several guests, most of which were entertainers, the wedding had to be put back until May. Cathy would have been happy with simple plans, but Ed insisted on a fairytale wedding. By now, Cathy was pregnant, with an anxious Ed watching her every move in case she overdid things.

Cathy had been on cloud nine since moving in with Ed. On Christmas day, she awoke to find herself in Ed's arms and embarking on a totally new life. She had to pinch herself so many times as she wandered around the palatial mansion and huge grounds. She couldn't believe that it was all true, and her cup of happiness overflowed.

They saw the New Year in together alone. Ed didn't want anyone else around. He was now with the love of his life, and she was all he needed.

Shortly after, Vic got the couple to record *River Deep* which was a smash hit. Kevin had been launched on a solo career, and Ed had now got him on a tenancy agreement, stopping Vic from receiving any money. He also told Vic to put the place on the market, and made Kevin understand that as soon as he found a buyer he would personally re-house him. Cathy had become pregnant almost immediately after moving in, so Ed told Vic that as soon as she started to show, she was to be eased out of any work at all. In fact, after thinking about it in more depth, he decided that apart from recording, all other work was to stop pronto.

'Why?' yelled an infuriated Vic. 'I've made her part of your band now. When she had her other kids she was working up to five months, she told me.'

'But this is my kid,' retorted Ed, 'and I want to look after her.' Vic swore. Cathy was coming to be a nuisance. He'd be pleased when she had the kid because he intended to get her back into harness immediately.

The wedding was going to cost a small fortune, and the amount they were spending on the reception was going through the roof. Ed was useless with money; he was spending a fortune on his lady. Vic could think of much better things to do with it. Wedding invitations were sent out, and Cathy insisted on the same format as she had with her hippy wedding. Ed was happy to oblige, but added Romany as best man, reminding Cathy that Rusty had played two roles in 1968. An invite was sent to Tony and Ingrid, as Cathy wanted her sons there. They accepted, Ingrid happily, and Tony wanting to see where his ex-wife was living to see if there was anything in it for him.

Meanwhile, in Wales, someone was reading the newspapers with building excitement. 'Megan!' shouted Seth. 'Megan, who was scrubbing the floor in the kitchen, pushed her hair from her eyes. She was shattered. All she did was clean up after Seth and fetch and carry for him. She was scared of him these days; he seemed to have completely lost the plot. She'd lost count of the times that she'd run away, but Seth always found her and punished her, beating her soundly. She thought that maybe one day he'd kill her, so had decided to stay and be a live coward rather than a dead hero.

'Megan, come here, you worthless piece of shit, come here at once.' Seth's voice was getting louder and angrier by the second. Megan got to her feet and wandered into the sitting room where Seth was lounging in an easy chair with his feet up. He threw the daily paper at her. 'Dig out your best dress; that arsehole of a cousin is getting wed. I'm gonna deliver him the best wedding gift ever, and it's gonna cost him. We are about to come into some money.'

Megan was confused, 'but we don't have an invite, do we?'

'Don't need one, I gave him everything he wanted and now it's pay back time. He'd want me there, probably thinks that I moved on like Rusty.' Megan shuddered, knowing that something bad was afoot.

Chapter Sixteen

May arrived, and Cathy got her fairytale wedding. She was five months gone and showing, but her designer dress disguised her bump well. Fawn and her daughters were dressed in pastel pink, and Amber and Amethyst turned the heads of the younger males in the party. Rusty was happy. At last his brother was tying the knot with the girl of his dreams. He hoped that Ed would be as happy as himself and Fawn. While her beauty was fading, he still loved her more than life itself. Amber was gazing at Cathy's bouquet and expensive wedding dress.

'Do you remember our flowers?' she asked a nervous Cathy.

'Of course, and your bridesmaids' dresses. You were pretty little girls then, but now you're lovely. You and your sister will break many hearts.'

Amber smiled; she was just starting to take an interest in boys. Rusty strolled over. 'So, pretty lady, I'm giving you away for the second time, but this time with a love child in your belly.' His attention was suddenly taken by two people he had not expected to see. Seth and Megan stood apart from everyone else, and Rusty wasn't happy, but assumed that Ed must have sent out invites to all of his family, unfortunately. He gritted his teeth. Seth was always bad news, and hated his brother, so why was he here? It didn't make any sense.

Still, it was Ed's wedding and it was obvious that he'd given Seth the news, perhaps in an attempt to build bridges. Ed must have sent him an invite so he decided to concentrate on giving Cathy away. He helped Cathy into the horse-drawn carriage and got in beside her. Fawn and her children followed in the limousine behind.

The wedding over. Ed stood outside to be photographed with his new wife and family, and then they headed back to his house. No expense had been spared, and Vic was tearing his hair out. It was a banquet fit for a king and queen, and the band that Ed had booked were headliners. 'Gary Turner and the Dazzlers' were hot property and mega-expensive.

There was a star cabaret too with June Maclaine, Hal Perkins, Ross Dozier, Kim Carter, a dance troupe called The Sparklers, and two surprise guests, none other than Kevin, and Mick, the original Shelltones front man. The latter two were giving their services free as a wedding gift.

Steven and Michael hugged their mother warmly. They were overawed by all of the splendour, and asked their mother if they could live with her. Tony was not amused, saying that money meant nothing. Ingrid, however, was enamoured with everything and decided that it might be a good idea to let the boys spend more time with their mother.

'Why should they be denied all of this when their mother would love to see more of them? It was also about time that Cathy was allowed access without supervision.' She approached Cathy and suggested it. She was delighted, and wandered over to Tony with Ed on her arm. Ed extended his hand which Tony accepted after being nudged in the ribs by Ingrid.

Tony said he would think about it. 'You stole my wife,' he said, and fixed Ed with an accusing look.

Ed laughed. 'You divorced your wife when you got Ingrid pregnant and wanted to marry her. You got married a while ago and, as you can see, we've only just tied the knot.'

Tony gazed at the floor, cursing the fact that he'd ever had anything to do with Ingrid. He was sick of work, but Ingrid was determined to keep him employed. The boys clung to their father.

'Please, Dad,' appealed Steven, 'we could come here weekends if Ed lets us.' He was now seven and was taking an interest in the guitar. 'Ed could help me with my playing.' Michael, now a lively five-year-old, charged into the garden with Ingrid in hot pursuit. How glad she was that her other children were with Tony's mother. You had to have eyes in the back of your head to deal with Michael.

The cabaret commenced, and everyone turned their attention to the stage. It was June who noticed Seth lurking in a corner, stuffing his face from a plate piled high with food. Megan sat beside him, wishing that she was anywhere but where she was. June was surprised. She didn't expect to see someone who she thought Ed would rather forget. She went in search of Ed, and was just in time to see him get up onto the dais and dedicate a song to his wife. He smiled at his guests.

'When I first met my wife, she was a big fan of the Small Faces. She was out for the night celebrating our good friend's birthday. Mr Hal Perkins, who tonight has had us in stitches, and our lovely songbird, June Maclaine, were also with her that night in '68. The two of them demanded 'Small Faces' songs, so my brother Rusty and I did our best to comply. And that night I fell in love. I've loved that lady ever since. Work commitments and other distractions have kept us apart over the years, but now my dream has come true and we'll be together forever. I kind of realise that I'll never be able to deliver this song as well as Steve Marriot, but I'm giving it my best shot. This one's for you, Cathy, and thank you for everything.'

He began to sing *Afterglow of your Love* and Cathy felt as if her heart would burst with happiness.

'He's making me feel sick,' snapped Tony, opening a bag and stuffing as much food as he could get into it.

Ingrid looked on horrified. 'I think it is very romantic, which you are not. No wonder she left you to be with him. For God's sake stop filling that plastic bag with food.' Tony scowled. There were one or two other things in the bag too, like a couple of porcelain figurines and a pair of candlesticks which looked as if they could be real silver. Maybe the boys could come and stay after all, and he could grab a few other items when he picked them up. Al Simpkins looked on in amazement, but was too drunk to intervene.

Later that evening, June drew Ed's attention to Seth. Ed had no idea he was there, and moved across to his cousin who was still in the same spot that he'd been in all evening. Seth got to his feet. 'Eden,' he cried, throwing his arms around Ed. 'Lovely wedding, wouldn't have missed it for the world.'

Ed disengaged himself from Seth's bear hug, wondering what his cousin wanted. 'I didn't invite you.'

Seth shrugged his shoulders. 'Oversight, I guess. Is there somewhere we could go and speak in private?'

Ed glanced across the room. Cathy was surrounded by a group people, and he wasn't sure if he wanted Cathy to sit in on his conversation anyway. 'Okay,' he said, 'follow me.' He walked to the drawing room and seated himself on the cherry-red chesterfield.

Seth paced the floor after sending Megan away. 'Great set-up you've got here, cousin.'

'I like it,' replied Ed.

'Maybe you should think about sharing a bit of your wealth with the rest of your family.'

'Spit it out, Seth. I guess you want a loan?'

'No cousin, I want a gift. I gave you the gift that you wanted, and I think that you should find some way of repaying me.'

'How much is this gift?'

'Twenty grand. I've made your dreams come true, haven't I?'

'You can whistle for it.'

'Don't be too hasty. Your beautiful wife still knows nothing, does she? Because that's the way I fixed it, but I could always refresh her memory. You see, cousin, the night that I bonded you, one of my followers was filming you. You wanted it filmed, remember? It's great viewing. I can see the headlines now: "Rock star marries girl of his dreams". Then another headline: "Look what Ed did in '68 after hippy wedding". Great publicity, cousin. What do you think Cathy would make of that? I don't think she'd like it, and I also think that it could push her over the edge, and she might lose that spawn of the devil in her belly.'

Ed got to his feet and swung out at Seth, who laughed. 'I want twenty grand and you get the film. Great wedding gift, eh?'

'A gift? How do I know that you're not full of shit? Maybe you've no powers at all? Maybe we're not bonded at all? You could just be a charlatan.'

'When I gave her to you, you gave yourself to me. Just for example, I can tell you everything that you've done since the last time that you left me.'

'Prove it.'

'Okay, she left you and you got back together at a dance contest.'

'Anyone could know that. The show got publicity; it was in every newspaper.'

Seth continued. 'You managed to get her over to America with you. You killed a man even though the papers said it was an accident. I saw you tinker with that microphone. You nearly killed another man, and that wasn't in the papers, and, oh my, what a mess you made of cutting your beloved's hand. You should have been a butcher. Is that enough for you, cousin?'

'Shut up.'

'And then your beloved left you again and lost her daughter. She attempted suicide, so did you. I told you, cousin, you are bonded, even with illness and even down to labour pains, remember them?'

'I could get the police.'

'And I could show the press the film. There is a copy, Ed. There's more than one. Twenty grand says that you will get the film I have, and the copy. I gave you everything; even in death you won't be parted. Isn't love grand? Now you write me out a cheque for twenty grand, or get me the cash, in fact I'd prefer cash, that way I haven't got to hang around waiting for the cheque to clear before you could put a stop on it. Yes, cash.'

'Do you think I carry that sort of money?'

'No cousin, that's why you're going to put me up until you get it, and if you can't get it tomorrow you can put me up every day until you do.'

Ed was lost for words. He called Vic in who was next door. He was inebriated as per normal. At the news, his jaw dropped. 'Twenty grand?' he spluttered. 'What for?'

'My cousin is down on his luck and his girlfriend is pregnant. They're getting kicked out of their house and have seen a small cottage they would like to buy. He was a great help to me when I had nothing, and I've never repaid him,' lied Ed.

'I could raise it tomorrow,' Vic told him, 'but why not just write out a cheque now?'

'The owner of the house wants payment in cash,' Seth answered, 'and there are others interested in it. I'd hate to lose it; Megan's set her heart on the cottage and as she's in the same state as Cathy, preparing to give birth. It would be nice to be settled sooner rather than later.'

'Okay,' said Vic. 'Ed's in a generous mood today. I'll get onto it first thing tomorrow.'

He left the room and went in search of Al Simpkins. Many glossy magazines had outbid each other to get an exclusive on this wedding, but he still preferred Al's photos, and believed that his shots would be just as good as the chosen publication.

Ed eyed Seth, suspiciously. 'I want you out as soon as you have the money, and I don't want to ever see you again.'

Seth was jubilant. 'The feeling's mutual. I'll see you in the morning. Great wedding, cousin... so glad you invited me.' He walked from the drawing room. 'Don't forget we're sleeping here tonight, will you?' Ed grunted and went in search of Cathy and his family.

The reception went on until the early hours of the morning. Cathy was glowing, she felt so good. Tony had said he would think about giving her more access to her sons, Ed had given her the perfect day, and she felt so warm in Rusty and Fawn's company again. She snuggled up to her new husband at the end of the day, thoroughly content. Life was good; it had never been so good.

After getting his money, Seth left with Megan in tow. He'd handed over the two reels of film to Ed who promptly took them to his library room and watched both of them just to make sure they were indeed the films of the ritual. 'We'll both sit here until I'm satisfied that this is the real thing, and then you'll get your money.' Seth was unfazed and settled himself into the nearest armchair. These were the kind of movies he loved.

Ed watched the films. He was feeling very nauseous, and couldn't believe that he'd actually partaken in this awful scene. He had pushed it to the back of his mind, but now Seth had resurrected it and he felt dreadful. After viewing both films, Ed rang Vic, and about thirty minutes later he arrived with the money in a large brown box. There were twenty piles of notes, each pile containing a thousand pounds. Seth was suspicious and counted each and every note. Satisfied, he slapped Ed on the back. 'Thanks buddy, I hope you and Cathy have a long and prosperous life. Where is she?'

'Resting,' replied Ed, 'and I don't want her bothered. June's with her, I think.'

'Oh, June Maclaine. Oh well, I suppose you've got to keep ex-lovers close just in case.' He laughed and headed for the door. As Seth left the house with Megan trailing along behind, he turned to Ed. 'Enjoy your marriage while you can, because given time you will screw the whole thing up. You will fuck up big time. Bye.'

Ed closed the front door and went back to the library. 'What the fuck's this really about?' asked Vic suspiciously.

'It's called blackmail,' replied Ed. 'He filmed me years ago with Cathy, and I've had to pay him to stop him taking the films to the press.'

'Why the fuck didn't you say, we could have topped the bastard. Don't you realise blackmailers never stop?'

'Well, I've got the evidence now,' replied Ed, 'and a copy.'

Vic was exasperated. 'There could be other copies,' he exploded.

Ed shrugged. 'Well, we'll cross that bridge when we get to it.' He was feeling very stupid, and Vic was probably right, but now he wanted to get upstairs to Cathy. She and their unborn child were the only important people in his life, and they were off on honeymoon at the end of the week.

Cathy went into labour in September. Ed was away at the time, but realised as soon as the pains hit him that their child was on the way. He drove at breakneck speed to the hospital even though he was in agony. He arrived just as she was giving birth, and the nurse allowed him to cut the cord of the afterbirth. The baby, a boy, weighed in at nine pounds.

Ed gazed at the baby that lay unwashed in his mother's arms. 'I love you,' he said, kissing a very tired Cathy. 'You have just made my world complete.'

'I read in the press that this was your best tour yet.'

Ed nodded. 'Yeah, it's been one hell of a tour, but the press still try to put me down. Well, the ones that I refuse interviews, so they lie and photograph me with stupid starlets and invent crazy stories. It's like a bad dream sometimes. I don't want any of these girls; you're all I want.' He added the last sentence as he was feeling rather guilty. His eye had started to rove again, and he had taken an occasional girl to his bed, but he wouldn't let Cathy know that.

Cathy sighed, 'Some of the girls that I see in the papers are irresistible.'

Sister Forbes came into the room and took the baby from Cathy's arms. 'I need to get this young man cleaned up. Oh, they've still not taken the afterbirth away.'

Ed stared at the afterbirth and asked her if he could take it home. Sister Forbes agreed, although she thought it was a strange request. Ed replied that he was fascinated by it and would keep it overnight and then dispose of it himself. Sister Forbes took the baby to be bathed and thought that these rock stars had some very strange ideas.

Reaching home, Ed went straight into the kitchen carrying the afterbirth. He sampled a small piece, then ate some more. He smoked a few joints and then headed for bed; the rest of the tour could wait. He rang Vic. 'Cathy's had a nine pound baby boy and I think I'm going down with something; my throat's red raw,' he lied. 'I need a few days off.'

Vic was angry, but knew there was no use in arguing. If Ed really had got a bad throat, he didn't want him damaging his vocal cords. 'Okay, Ed,' he said. 'Congratulations on your son; hope Cathy's well. I'll send something to the hospital. Ring me when your throat eases up.'

'Will do,' said Ed, and poured himself a brandy.

The following day he headed for the hospital, delighting in his son. He watched as Cathy fed him, fascinated by the milk dripping from her breast. In the later months of her pregnancy, he'd often got a mouthful himself and envied his son for the amount that he was getting. He couldn't believe what he'd done the night before; he'd eaten the afterbirth raw. In fact, it wasn't until he was chewing it that he realised what he was doing.

'What shall we name him?' he asked a radiant Cathy.

'After you, of course,' replied Cathy. 'Then I'll have two fabulous men with the same name.'

Ed laughed. 'He can be Edward, but never Eden, I hate that name. I'm taking you both home today. I've taken on a new nanny so we can still tour and have time to ourselves.'

Cathy smiled, but inside felt sad. She had all but forgotten the open road.

Throughout 1977, Ed was the model family man. He took his wife and son everywhere with him. He watched Cathy feed him and worried every time the child cried. He told everyone that every time his son smiled, he was smiling at him, even though everyone else knew it was wind. He changed nappies and was quite happy to be photographed doing so. He doted on his wife and son, swamping Cathy with expensive gifts. They travelled far and wide to exotic holiday locations, and he refused to tour without her.

He also bought a pony for his son and a huge tortoise, big enough for the child to ride on. When they'd spent their honeymoon in the Seychelles, a paradise destination chosen by Ed, they'd seen these massive reptiles and Ed decided to buy one on his return to the UK. He'd wanted an Aldabran tortoise, but after speaking to a reptile expert decided to buy an African Sulcata. It was also a giant but was easier to keep. It was three feet in length and slept in a stable with heating all year round as it didn't hibernate like Mediterranean species.

Unfortunately, Ed was beginning to have the odd indiscretion. He still adored his wife, but sometimes the eye candy was just too much to resist, and he felt that as long as Cathy didn't find out, it was okay.

Chapter Seventeen

By February 1978, he was back on drugs and becoming extremely anxious. At first Cathy didn't notice, but gradually she noticed the change and began to discover packets of white powder all over the house. He was staying out later and later, and sometimes didn't come home at all. Her heart sank. Was her dream over already? Every time he stayed out, he was always laden with gifts for her, but she recognised the pattern. He'd done this with Faye.

Kevin was a regular visitor; he used to come to the house every Friday with the rent money. Cathy always used to explain that Ed was recording. That was the excuse that Vic gave, and she had to admit there was a new album in the works. She recalled that when she'd recorded her album with Kevin, sometimes they'd sleep in the studio, simply too tired to go home. She kept a brave face while Kevin was around, but one day when he arrived she was very distraught. She cried on his shoulder and poured her heart out to him. Kevin tried to soothe her, saying that Ed worked very hard, and that if Vic said he was recording then he must be. Cathy shook her head sadly. 'What about all these girls he's always photographed with? It can't be publicity every time, can it?'

'Course it can.'

'I don't believe it.'

'Cathy, he worships you.'

'When he remembers who I am and where he lives.'

Kevin thought Cathy was probably right, but didn't want to distress her further. He tugged on her hair playfully. 'Tell you what, we'll phone Vic, find out where he is, and pay him a surprise visit. Can I use your phone?'

Cathy nodded. Ed had been missing for four days now. Kevin lifted the receiver and dialled. He listened and then replaced the receiver seconds later. 'It went to answer phone.'

'I've got the address of the recording studio. It's the one that I was in last month. We won't ring; we'll just turn up.' Cathy was uncertain, but taking her in his arms, Kevin said, 'you smarten yourself up and we'll drive to the studio. If Ed's too busy, you and I will have a night on the town.'

Cathy smiled. 'Okay, I could do with a break. Ed never takes me out any more.' She went upstairs, and about thirty minutes later emerged from her bedroom looking stunning.

Kevin stared at her open mouthed. 'You look amazing. I shall be proud to have you on my arm tonight.'

Cathy giggled. It seemed like ages since she'd received a compliment. True, when Ed was at home he'd make love to her and make her feel special, but then she knew that Faye had received exactly the same treatment. Their marathon sex sessions didn't necessarily mean that he was being faithful as he had such a high sex drive. 'You don't look so bad yourself,' teased Cathy.

'I make the effort when I'm in your company,' replied Kevin. She looked so lovely that he couldn't resist the urge to pull her into his arms and kiss her passionately. He held her tightly; his whole body aflame. He wanted to tell her how much he loved her but knew that it was pointless, and felt her begin to struggle. He released her and she was breathless.

'Hey!' she exclaimed. 'Slow down, I'm a married lady.' Kevin apologised and said it wouldn't happen again.

Cathy repaired her make-up and brushed her hair. 'Let's go.'

Arriving at the studio, Kevin told Cathy to wait in the car. 'Shan't be long. I'll tell him that you're worried and send him out.' Cathy switched on the radio, and Brian Ferry's voice burst forth. As his voice faded, Fleetwood Mac followed with *Dreams*. Cathy sang along with it. She loved the band and was always singing their songs. Vic had remarked that she sounded a lot like Stevie Nicks and wanted to get her to do a couple of their songs on stage. However, Ed said that he didn't want her on stage or recording, he wanted her at home out of the public eye.

Inside the building, Kevin found Vic on the phone. 'Where's Ed?' he asked. Vic pointed to another door and Kevin opened it. Romany and Ed were together, but not recording. Romany lay on a rather battered blue settee; he was naked, and stretched out beside him was a young girl smothering him with kisses. Kneeling by his side was another girl who had her mouth full. Kevin couldn't see very well as the room was dimly lit, but he could make out the shape of a mattress on the floor. There seemed to be several bodies on it. A female voice pierced the air. 'Come on Ed, let's fuck,' she moaned.

A voice that Kevin recognised, as Ed grunted throatily, 'okay, I guess you've earned it.'

Kevin knelt down beside the mattress after picking his way through bodies and discarded clothing. Anxiously he said, 'c'mon Ed, let's split right now. Cathy's in the car outside.'

Ed laughed out loud and flicked a switch. Immediately disco-type lights began to flash. 'Who are you kidding, Kevin?' he said as a blonde straddled him. He lay on his back, quite content to let the girl do all the work.

The disco-lights illuminated the room as they flickered on and off, and Kevin could see that not only did Ed have a girl on top of him, he also had a girl either side of him too.

The girl nearest to Kevin turned to him. 'Don't I know you?'

'I doubt it,' replied Kevin. 'I'm fussy who I screw.'

Ed was trying to concentrate. It wasn't easy as he'd been drinking and it was taking its toll on him. 'Oh Eddie, you're too much,' cried the girl astride him.

Kevin shook Ed by the shoulder. 'For Christ's sake, come on. Cathy really is outside; do you want her to walk in on this?'

Ed stared at Kevin disbelievingly, before the girl astride him reached her climax and collapsed across him. He pushed her away and pulled the girl to his left onto him. 'Don't try that line with me,' he mumbled, 'it doesn't amuse me in the slightest. Now piss off and stay away. We don't want you here; I'm having fun.'

'Yeah,' shouted Romany, from the corner. 'Kevin's always sniffing around Cathy. Watch him or he'll tell her. When he's around her, he behaves as if she's a bitch on heat.'

Kevin got to his feet and faced Romany. 'Don't stir it. She's outside and I don't want her barging in on this little lot.'

Ed was now very angry; the last bit of Romany's shot at Kevin had got to him. 'You stay away from my wife. If you lay one finger on her, I'll kill you. She belongs to me.'

Kevin stood his ground and surveyed the scene around him, feeling disgusted at these sick individuals. 'As a matter of fact, Ed, I'm taking her out tonight as you don't seem to have the time to give her the attention she deserves. She's worried about your absence; she thinks that you're recording. She loves you so much that she'll believe anything you or Vic tells her. We stopped off here because she hoped that you might have finished recording for the day and that you might take her out socially, but if you're not available, I'll take her.' A naked girl threw her arms around Kevin's neck, and he pushed her away as he continued. 'Cathy's a woman, Ed, and an attractive one at that.'

'Don't you think I know that?' snapped Ed. 'That's why I'm warning you to keep away from her. Touch her and you're dead.'

Romany rose from the settee and began to dress as the two girls that had been with him piled onto the mattress with Ed. 'Shall I fix him, Ed?' he said menacingly.

'No,' replied Ed, 'but check outside just in case the bastard's telling the truth.'

Romany zipped up his jeans and buckled his belt as Vic entered the room. 'Going so soon, Romany? Quite unlike you. Hey Kevin, have you got a preference? Come for a piece of action? We've got blondes, brunettes, or redheads; a good selection today. I hand picked them myself.' He placed his arm around Kevin's shoulders and Kevin brushed it off. He could feel nausea rising in his throat as Romany opened the door, went through it and closed it behind him. Vic began to strip off, and Kevin made a final plea to Ed, but it was useless. All he received was a two finger signal.

There was a commotion outside the door, and Romany shouted, 'No, you can't go in there!' There were sounds of a scuffle, and Ed, thinking it was more girls, shouted, 'let 'em in, the more the merrier.' He sighed; at last he could feel himself starting to come.

Suddenly, Romany let out a yelp. 'You bitch!' Alarmed, Kevin stared at the door, wishing that there was something he could do to ease the situation. The girl astride Ed was in the throes of orgasm when the door opened and the light was switched on. Kevin wasn't fast enough, and Cathy stood framed in the doorway. She gave a broken cry as her eyes met those of her husband's, and Ed felt as if something inside him had died as he held her gaze and she stared him out.

Then it was total mayhem. Ed flung the girl from him and made a desperate attempt to cover himself up. Romany staggered into the room with an agonised look on his face, clutching himself between his legs. Vic turned the air blue, and the girls began searching for their clothes.

Cathy was sobbing as if her heart would break and, flinging her arms around Kevin's neck, cried, 'take me home, take me anywhere but get me out of here.' Kevin glared at Ed who looked back very shamefaced. 'Cathy, it meant nothing, believe me, please believe me.'

Kevin ushered Cathy to the door. 'Shut up, Ed,' he yelled. 'You've done enough harm already.' Once outside and in the car, Cathy dried her eyes and repaired her make-up, informing Kevin that she needed that night out even more now.

Kevin drove her to her favourite club and, once inside, she saw a face from the past. 'Look Kevin, there's a blast from the past. See that guy in the grey suit and black hair who's waving at us? What memories that brings back, visions of Wales and flower power.' Kevin recalled the guy from Cathy's wedding who immediately took Cathy in his arms and kissed her.

The press were out in force that night; rumour had it that a certain David Essex was going to be attending the club, but as he hadn't shown yet they felt that Cathy was a suitable target for their attention as she was without her husband and in the company of two young men. This was a snip for the press; the guy in the suit was all over her, and her former singing partner gazed at her with true love pouring out of his eyes. A few questions were asked and it became apparent that the guy in the suit was none other than the original member and lead vocalist with the Shelltones in the sixties. Throughout the rest of the night, Cathy danced with both men, much to the delight of the press, and she consumed champagne as if it were water.

At about five in the morning, Kevin drove her home. She asked him in for coffee, and they discussed the events of the night. 'The photographer got some great shots,' laughed Kevin. 'Ed'll come running home when he sees the morning papers.'

Cathy kicked her shoes off and yawned. 'I've had far too much to drink,' she groaned. 'I'm quite tipsy.' She closed her eyes for a second and Kevin leaned over and kissed her eyelids. She opened her eyes and gazed into his. Kevin's heart beat wildly. He longed to hold her, kiss her, take her, and above all love her. He kissed her gently and she did not object, but when he kissed her again he noticed tears began to trickle from her eyes.

'Come on, darling, it's all right,' soothed Kevin. She lay passive, and then he felt her arms creep around his neck. He wondered if it was the drink or Ed's infidelity, but he didn't really care, he had her in his arms at last and that's exactly what he wanted. He was about to voice his feelings for her when the phone rang. He sat up wanting to kill whoever was on the end of the line as Cathy stretched out her hand and reached for the receiver. She listened for a minute and then said, 'oh, it's you Ed.' She glanced at her watch. 'Just gone to bed, have you? Whose bed is it this time?'

Kevin sighed and buttoned up his jacket. Ed sounded very concerned. 'I rang earlier and you weren't home, I was worried.'

Cathy giggled. 'You must be to ring at this time, unless you've just satisfied about six different girls and can't sleep. I mean, what's better than ringing your wife up after you've actually remembered you have one?' She lit a cigarette and inhaled deeply.

'Cathy, I'm sorry, I'd like to come home.'

'Come home? Have you left me then? I thought that you were in the studio recording.'

The line went silent for a moment, and Cathy thought he'd hung up and was about to replace the receiver when Ed replied, 'I was recording... I could never leave you... You're the only one I've ever wanted.'

'Really? Then who were those five girls? What recording was it? A blue movie with you and Romany taking starring roles, not forgetting dear old Vic in a supporting role? I think you should all get an Oscar for it, preferably over your skulls.'

'I've said I'm sorry. I want to come home,' replied Ed meekly.

'So why ask me? It's your house, you own everything in it. You've even paid for everything I've got on my back. If anyone should leave, it should be me. Then you can move in as many girls as you like.'

Ed gave a strangled cry. 'Don't leave me, Cathy. I'll do anything you say but don't leave me.'

Cathy yawned. 'I'm going to bed now. I can't tell you what to do. It's your house, not mine.'

'Give me another chance. I promise that it'll never happen again; I love you.'

Cathy yawned again. 'I can't keep my eyes open, goodnight, Ed.' She replaced the receiver and staggered across to Kevin.

'You're leaving? I've got plenty of spare bedrooms.' Kevin was tempted, but ignored her and helped her upstairs. Her head was reeling by the time they got to the top of the stairs, so Kevin carried her the rest of the way. As he laid her on her bed, she spread her arms wide. 'Hey Kevin, I'm on a merry-go-round, it's fun,' she mumbled.

Seconds later she was asleep, and Kevin pulled the covers over her. 'Sleep, my darling,' he said, kissing her on her cheek. He went downstairs and let himself out of the house quietly.

The following morning's papers left Ed with a very sour taste in his mouth. Cathy was front page with Kevin and Mick. The second paper offered a shot of her kissing Mick with a caption that read: 'Cathy on the town with heart throb Mick and toy boy Kevin. Where's Ed?'

The third paper really got to Ed; it showed Kevin and Cathy sitting together in a secluded area of the club with glasses in their hands full of champagne. It appeared as if they were toasting someone, and this time there was a story which read:

'Last night, Cathy Gold had a choice of two young companions. One, the original member of the Shelltones who has fully recovered from his dreadful accident in 1970. The other, Kevin Howard, Cathy's vocal partner when they made up the popular double act, Platinum. Cathy appeared to be having a wonderful night out; she kept Mick on his feet most of the night on the dance floor. The couple seemed to delight in each other's company. Nice to see Mick standing up again. Kevin on the other hand stepped in when Mick stopped dancing, and left much later with Cathy on his arm. Asked where Ed was, his wife replied, 'I don't know, he hasn't been home for nearly five days. Recording I'm told, but he hasn't rung me since the last time I saw him so I haven't a clue, and as you can see I'm not short of male company, so why should I care?'

There was also full length photo of Cathy and Mick smooching, and it was noticeable that Mick really was standing up. Ed threw the newspapers down in a fury and swore profusely, waking Romany. 'What the fuck is she trying to do?' Ed bellowed. 'And what's this about Mick being young; he's older than me. He's standing up all right, you can see it. Bastard. I'll fucking put him back into his wheelchair again when I see him. As for Kevin, I might terminate his tenancy after last night. How would you like to be fucking and have that prat crouched down beside you?'

'As long as he didn't fuck Cathy, what does it matter?' replied Romany, half opening his eyes. He felt terrible. The phone rang and Romany answered it, still half asleep. He flinched as Vic yelled into the receiver, and handed the phone to Ed. 'For you, it's the boss and he's not happy.'

Ed snatched the phone out of Romany's hand. He listened for a while and then uttered, 'well how the hell was I to know how things would turn out. Cathy's completely out of character.'

'Some bloody superstar. You're pathetic. You can't even handle your own wife. I suppose I'll have to go over and smooth things over as usual?' screamed Vic.

'No need, I've sent flowers to her.'

'And that cures everything, does it?' snorted Vic. 'Don't you realise that you paid her the greatest insult ever? Sometimes I wonder if you have any intelligence at all.'

Ed felt lost. He was sick with fear that he might have lost his wife. 'I rang several times last night and early this morning.'

'Really, what did she say?'

'She said that she was going to bed.'

'Hmmm, the point is who with?'

'What do you mean?' Ed was petrified now.

Vic laughed. 'She's got a lot to offer, and Kevin's head over heels in love with her. I don't know about Mick but they looked quite cosy together.'

Ed swallowed hard; he remembered the time when Mick had suggested swapping around. 'It's all lies, and Kevin's no more than a good friend.'

'You think so? You're half-blind, you fool. In fact, I think, given the chance, Romany would give her a bang if he thought he'd get away with it.' Vic omitted the fact that he'd sampled the delights of her body before Ed had married her.

Ed shot a sidelong glance at his friend who had now gone back to sleep. 'I'll drive straight over.'

'No you won't. I'll do it and I promise you that Cathy will be back with you by tonight.'

'We've got a gig tonight.'

'I know, and your lovely wife will be in attendance with Mick and Kevin.'

'She might not want to attend.'

'Trust me. I'll ring June Maclaine too. That'll keep Mick busy. Leave everything to me, I'll ring you later.'

Ed put the phone down and shook Romany. 'Got any coke?'

Romany grunted and said sleepily, 'might be some over there behind the clock. There's definitely some in the bookcase.'

Ed began to search. 'Thanks, pal,' he said, once he had found some, but there was no answer, his friend had gone back to sleep.

By the time Vic arrived at the Gold residence, Cathy was in the grounds romping around with Ed junior and her two dogs. Nearby, the nanny sat knitting as usual. Cathy didn't hear Vic approach; her hair streamed out behind her and her laughter was piercing the air. She was dressed casually in blue jeans and a blue checked shirt, and Vic couldn't believe how young she looked. He lit up a cigar and the dogs bounded up to him, smothering his clothes with dog hairs. Cathy, now aware of Vic's presence, scolded the dogs and they ran off. Vic brushed his clothes down. 'This is a new suit.'

'Oh,' said Cathy cheerily, 'it wasn't your suit I was worried about. I'm fussy what my dogs touch; I don't want them catching any nasty diseases.' She giggled. 'Oh I forgot, they're not my dogs, are they? They're Ed's; they belong to him just like everything else here.' She handed her son over to the nanny, asking her to make some coffee and bring it through to the lounge. The nanny, a Scottish lady in her forties, nodded and took the little boy inside the house with her.

Cathy took Vic's arm. 'My, my, my, quite the blue movie star aren't you, Vic? I didn't realise how talented you were.'

'You're not funny.'

'I know, but I just wanted to let you know that I don't blame Ed entirely. You see I caught a glimpse of you in the room yesterday, and you were half-naked. Then there was Romany, who must have been more than a spectator.'

'Ed's very hurt; the morning papers have upset him.' He reached for an ashtray and flicked cigar ash into it.

'Really? Can't have him upset, can we? I mustn't be upset when I walk into a full-scale orgy, but when he reads a load of mumbo-jumbo, he has to be sheltered.'

'Was it mumbo-jumbo? You weren't short of male attention last night.'

'I had a great time.'

'Did you sleep alone?'

Cathy wrinkled her brow. 'Depends on what you mean. Do you mean, "did I sleep alone?", or "did I fuck first and then sleep alone?", or "did I go to bed, fuck, and then send the guy home?" Then again, maybe what you meant was "did I take the guy to bed, fuck, then sleep with the guy and send him home this morning?". Say what you mean, Vic.'

She gazed at Vic provocatively, sending his blood pressure soaring. 'Don't, you know what that does to me.' Cathy began to unbutton her shirt. 'I said don't, this situation is bad enough without you giving me the come on.'

Cathy kicked her shoes off and swung her legs up onto the settee, leaning forward so that Vic got an eyeful of cleavage. 'Don't worry Vic; there's no way I'd have sex with you after what I saw yesterday. You've probably got the groupie clap. Come to think of it, so must Ed. Make sure he sees a doctor, will you?'

Vic spluttered on his cigar; he hadn't thought of that. That was all he needed to make this a real faux pas. Ruby brought in the coffee and asked if she should pour it. Cathy shook her head and she left the room. There was a silence before Vic stammered, 'the question is, are you going to take him back?'

Cathy spread her arms wide, finding the question hilarious. 'Ed asked me that. The only reason I'm here is because I'm his wife and it seems as if he's tired of me, so if anyone should go, it should be me. If he wants his freedom…' she said and began to sing the first verse of *Dreams*.

Vic was impressed. 'I wish you'd record that; you sound so much like Stevie Nicks. Look, it was just a silly lapse; he didn't even know that the girls were going to turn up. He'd been in the recording studio for four nights, and I thought he needed some recreation.'

'So you put temptation in his way? I know what happens; you and Romany egg him on. I can hear it now: "Come on Ed, have fun, Cathy won't find out, you're a star, you chicken or something. Let's snort coke, let's go out on the town, look at those birds. Just have a dance with that redhead, she fancies you, you've got time for a quick fuck, we'll invent an alibi for you". So you see the poor devil doesn't want to be labelled chicken, he wants to be the same as his friends, so he snorts coke, adds a few girls to his list of conquests, parties with you, hopes that I won't find out, and you continue to manipulate him to suit your own needs. Those girls were only there for Ed. You didn't think they wanted you, did you? Ed has always been the main attraction.'

Vic said nothing. What could he say? Cathy knew everything. The phone rang and she answered the caller. Minutes later she put the phone down and, then, turning to Vic said, 'out of this mess comes something special.'

Vic drank his coffee and put the cup down. 'You're talking in riddles, but I want you at Ed's gig tonight.'

'Does Ed want me there? Or is this Vic's marriage guidance?'

Vic stood up. 'Course he wants you there; he's unhappy and he needs you.'

'I wish I could believe you. He destroyed me yesterday, but the phone call clinched it. Can you keep a secret?'

'Are you coming to Ed's gig?'

'Only if you can keep a secret…' replied Cathy, her eyes sparkling as Ruby entered the room.

'More flowers have arrived,' she said.

Cathy clapped her hands together and giggled like a schoolgirl. In her arms, Ruby had a huge bouquet that held just about every possible bloom available for the season. Vic looked on in amusement as Cathy took the flowers from her housemaid and smelled them. 'Beautiful fragrance. Ed must be worried; these flowers must be costing him a small fortune,' she laughed. 'Flowers have been arriving since I got up.'

Ruby looked on, sniffing the beautiful blooms, her face a picture. 'I love flowers. The house looks like a florists.'

'Then they're yours,' said Cathy. 'A gift from me.'

'But…' protested Ruby.

'No "buts",' ordered Cathy. 'Take them and go.' Ruby was overcome with emotion and gave Cathy a dozen 'thank yous' before she left the room. Cathy smiled as the door closed, then bobbed a mock curtsey to Vic before spinning around on her toes like a ballet dancer, laughing deliriously. 'Oh Vic,' she cried, 'if he broke every bone in my body, I'd still love him.'

'God forbid. I want you back at work soon; have I got plans for you.'

Cathy's mood changed, and she stared at Vic. 'Sure you do, Vic, even when people don't want plans made for them; you're a great organiser.' She extended both hands to him and he took them in his own. 'I can't stay angry with him for too long, my feelings are just confused at the minute so maybe I shouldn't go tonight. If I do, I'll fall into his arms, and what I saw yesterday really hurt.' Vic gazed into her eyes; he was feeling aroused.

'He really loves you, and he is sorry, Cathy,' he repeated. 'Now shall we go upstairs?'

'I beg your pardon!' snapped Cathy, her eyes flashing wildly.

Vic laughed. 'Not for that, to find out what you're going to wear tonight. But if you like, I'll give you as much head as you want; that way I can't infect you if I am indeed infected.'

Together they went upstairs and rummaged through her wardrobe. Whatever she suggested, Vic disagreed. Bored, she lay down on the bed and let him sort it out. Finally he found what he wanted. A maxi dress, halter neck plain and simple, and best of all pure white. 'This one,' he said, holding up the dress.

'Okay,' agreed Cathy, 'anything you say.'

'Virginal white, just perfect.'

Cathy closed her eyes. 'I suppose Ed will be dressed in scarlet then if we're hinting at morals. Even so I should think that white was pushing it a bit in my case, wouldn't you say?'

Vic put the dress back into the wardrobe and crossed to the bed. Slowly he ran his hand under her shirt and murmured, 'I don't think so, Cathy. If you lock the door and get out of your clothes, I'll pleasure you, but then I know you won't let me.'

Cathy sat up. 'Why? Ed's been playing around. Why is it wrong for me? I've got needs too.'

'It wouldn't be, Cathy, would it? And I'll prove it.' He began to fiddle with the button on her jeans. 'Come on; let's see how far we get, shall we?'

'Don't,' cried Cathy, as Vic attempted to undo her zip.

'Why? Because you know just how much you want to screw? Or is it because you remember what good times we had together before you married Ed?'

'Don't,' replied Cathy, swallowing hard.

Vic slid the zip down, adding, 'Maybe there's another reason; why don't you admit it?'

'Admit what?' replied Cathy, her mouth feeling dry. Vic tried to slip his hand inside her jeans and she slapped his wrist.

Vic got up and grinned smugly. 'Admit that Ed is the only one you will allow to touch you.'

'I wasn't short of male company last night.'

'No, but you left the club with Kevin, and I know Mick stayed on much longer.'

'What about Kevin?' persisted Cathy, zipping up her jeans.

Vic walked to the door. 'Kevin respects you too much to take advantage of you. No you haven't been unfaithful to Ed since the day you got wed.'

Cathy got to her feet and followed Vic downstairs. 'Is it that obvious?'

'To me, yes. To others, including Ed, no.' As they walked through the hall and towards the front door, Vic took Cathy's arm. 'Now listen to me, tonight you turn up halfway through Ed's gig, not at the beginning. Dress as I told you to. We don't want him thinking that you're too keen. Kevin will be your escort, and Mick will be there too. After the gig we're having a get together at my place and, during the course of the night, you will mingle. When you dance, you divide yourself between Mick and Kevin. Oh, and Sammy Silver will be in attendance too, so give him a smooch as well.'

'But I hate Sammy after America.'

'Put your feelings on hold. The sight of you with these guys will bring Ed to heel and, before the night's over, he'll be on his knees begging your forgiveness.' Cathy was just about to open the front door when Vic remembered the phone call. 'Hey babe, what about your secret?'

Cathy glowed with pride. 'I'm pregnant,' she said.

Vic seized the girl in his arms and swung her around. 'That's terrific, babe.'

Cathy wriggled free. 'Hey, steady, or it'll never get born.'

Vic kissed her hand and smiled at the radiant girl. 'I guess you'll want to be the first one to tell him, so your secret's safe with me, you gorgeous creature.'

Cathy pecked him on the cheek, feeling as if things were now going to work. 'See you later.'

Vic left the house, and Kevin drove up just as he was about to drive off. He glowered at Vic as he got out of the car and found his route to the front door blocked. 'Get out of the way, Vic.'

'Fine way for an artiste to greet his manager,' said Vic, raising his eyebrows.

'After what I saw yesterday, I feel ashamed to have any contact with you.'

Vic looked away and coughed. 'I was on my way to see you.'

'Saved you a visit then; now get out of my way.'

Vic grabbed Kevin's arm. 'What is the purpose of your visit?'

'Could ask you the same thing.'

'Sure you could, but my visit is to ensure that Cathy is reunited with her husband tonight. I imagine yours is more personal.'

'Mind your own business.'

'Okay, you nobody, but I'm warning you to lay off Cathy.'

'Why? You don't care about her, and neither does Ed. Yes, I'm a nobody, and I'm glad because if being a somebody means you're stoned half of the time so your brain can't function, and you have to screw around to prove that you're a somebody, then you can stuff it. I enjoy my work, and when I'm onstage I have to do everything you say, but offstage, I don't. Now let go of my arm, Vic, before I make you.'

Vic released Kevin's arm and eyed a package in Kevin's car. 'That for Cathy?'

'No, it's for Eddie; it's a present from me.' He walked to his car and produced not only the package, but a huge bouquet too.

Vic laughed. 'Shouldn't bother, the house is starting to look like a florist's dream. I suppose if you can get around the child, you might get round the mother. I should give up though, you can't win. There's only one man for Cathy, so lay off.'

'I can't. I've loved her since the moment we first met.'

'Then you have my sympathy, because if Ed finds out he'll kill you, and if Cathy finds out, she'll reject you. Still if you like being rejected and risking your head being split open, go ahead. Now I've given Cathy instructions about tonight so make sure you get to the gig halfway through.' Undeterred, Kevin rang the door bell as Vic drove away.

Later that night, Vic was having a near heart attack. A big time Hollywood starlet was in England, and on Romany's arm, whilst making it very obvious that Ed was her target and hovering around him. Vic took Romany to one side. 'What the fuck are you doing?' he yelled. 'I want Ed reunited with Cathy tonight.'

'What the hell for? She's a drag; we had a great time yesterday before she turned up.'

'Fuck yesterday; keep your whore to yourself tonight. I've gone to a lot of trouble to set things up and, anyway, if she's such a drag, why did you and that scummy brother of yours bother with her in America? You said she was a great lay.'

'Yeah, but I can't lay her now, can I? She's married to Ed and she cramps his style badly.'

'Do as I say Romany, keep that whore under control. If things fail because of you, I might find that my memory gets a jolt about a couple of incidents in the States, and Ed might just rearrange your features.'

'What do you mean?' asked Romany, stubbing out a cigarette.

Vic picked up a beer can and tugged on the ring pull. 'If things go wrong, I will tell Ed about you and Cathy, and I don't think he'll be very pleased. In fact, you might end up stiff, and we're not talking about the trouser department. He wants a reunion, and if it doesn't happen he'll need someone to vent his anger on.'

'He can have anyone he wants,' sneered Romany.

Vic took a swig from the can. 'Sure he can, but he wants his wife. Maybe you don't know Ed as well as you think you do. With Cathy he's possessive, over-possessive. He's quite capable of killing for her. Don't you remember Hank?'

Romany went deathly white and plucked at his guitar. 'Accident,' he mumbled.

'Was it? Now be a good boy and keep that tart under control, will you?' He took another swig of beer, and noted that for the first time ever he'd managed to instil fear into the man that Cathy had named 'the devil's own'. 'Disobey me and I'll make sure he hears of your liaison with Cathy, and if he doesn't mess up your face, I will.'

Romany was lost for words and licked his lips nervously. 'Okay, I'll see to it,' he said, and wandered over to Ed and Karen.

When Cathy arrived on Kevin's arm, she was dressed exactly as Vic had told her. She wore the white dress, and had also put a flower in her hair which cascaded down her back in a mass of curls. Kevin had complemented her by wearing a white suit. They made a charming couple, except that Cathy was on edge and Kevin was far from happy. He'd pleaded with Cathy not to attend, knowing that the very moment she set eyes on Ed she'd be lost in the magic that he weaved. Kevin didn't want them reconciled, he wanted Cathy to notice him and forget Ed altogether.

Cathy stared around her. There was the usual assortment of roadies, and the hard-faced groupies seemed to be out in force. She caught sight of Karen Keen, the movie star, who had eyes for nobody but Ed. Cathy nudged Kevin. 'Maybe that's Ed's bed mate for the night.'

Kevin looked over, wishing it were true, but said reassuringly, 'darling, when he claps eyes on you there will be no competition.' Cathy wasn't so sure. Karen was a real star, and the groupies looked pretty good too. It appeared to be a contest for the girl who could show more cleavage or thigh or, as in the case of Karen, both.

On stage, Ed was a knockout. He was dressed in electric blue satin which clung to him like a second skin. Karen was getting excited, and so was Vic. He looked up from her plunging neckline and, catching sight of Cathy, felt that it might be a good idea to remove Karen from the scene for a while. 'Really fancy him, don't you?' he said.

'And how, honey,' she replied.

Vic planted a kiss on her bare shoulder. 'Just how badly do you want to bed him?'

'I'll do anything,' Karen replied, her breasts heaving.

Craftily, Vic worked out a plan. One where he would gain everything and her nothing. 'I'll see what I can do; let's go somewhere quiet where we can talk.' Karen nodded. She didn't like Vic much but she understood what he meant and, if that was the price to be paid, then she would pay it. Like a small dog, she followed Vic to a nearby room. Once inside, Vic's mood changed as he leered and unzipped his fly. She looked at him, her eyes filled with dismay.

'Right, you cunt, if you want to bed my superstar, you kneel for me.' Karen knelt reluctantly, taking him into her mouth. Vic was happy, he couldn't lose. These women were all stupid and he could make them do anything. Like zombies they obeyed, all for the promise of a fuck with Ed. He smiled. 'Suck, honey, and just think of the night of love you'll get with Ed.'

On stage, Ed looked toward the wings many times, hoping to see Cathy but seeing only groupies. Halfway through *Ruby Tuesday*, however, he saw her. She outshone everyone, dressed all in white. Her hair had a wild, tangled look to it, making her look even more sensual than usual. The white flower in her hair reminded him of '68 and a waterfall, and he could almost feel the water on his body now. He sidled over to Romany, asking him to fill in with extra lead, then he rushed off stage and practically threw himself at his wife. He dropped to one knee, kissed her hand and gazed up at her.

'I love you,' he said, and Cathy felt her stomach begin to churn. She knew that she was lost and drowning in his eyes.

Kevin was in agony. He'd lost again, Cathy was clearly enraptured. How different from the day before which had been one of sheer agony. Ed had won again and always would. How he wished Ed would drop down dead.

He slipped away unnoticed and went into the dressing room. Sitting down, he gazed at his reflection in the mirror. He sighed. What else could he offer Cathy besides undying love and his youth? Ed was rich, owned a palatial mansion, fathered a child with her, and professed to love her. She appeared to love her husband with her whole being, and was completely blind to the agonies that he was going through. It seemed as if his love for her was in vain, and he wondered, if Ed was dead, maybe she would notice him and maybe they could resume their double act as the always popular Platinum?

He stayed in front of the mirror for a while and then, bored with his own reflection, wandered back to the wings. Ed was onstage now and Cathy stood alone. Kevin tiptoed up behind her and planted a kiss on the back of her neck. 'Okay?' he asked, enfolding her in his arms from behind.

'Isn't he the greatest?' she sighed, not bothering to turn around.

Kevin stared at Ed, who was delighting his audience. 'Yes, he's the best. There's not another singer to touch him.'

'Kevin, would you like me to share a secret with you?'

'A secret, of course I would.'

Cathy turned to face him smiling. 'Ed doesn't know yet, but I'm pregnant again.'

Kevin went icy cold. If there had been a glimmer of hope before, there was certainly none now. Hiding his feelings, he mumbled, 'I'm very happy for you,' and embraced her. Cathy opened her mouth to say something, when her attention was drawn back to the stage. Ed was dedicating his next song to the most wonderful lady in his life.

Karen, who'd just returned with Vic said, 'I think he means me.'

'Stupid cunt,' muttered Vic.

'What's that, honey?'

'I said there's a good crowd up front,' he lied.

'Yeah, I think he's fallen in love with me.'

Vic was silent and heard Ed begin *Help Me Make It Through The Night*. He wandered over to Cathy several times during the song, blowing kisses. Karen was confused. 'I wonder why he keeps going over to that side?' she said. 'Maybe I've got a rival.'

Vic shuffled from one foot to the other. 'Maybe.'

Ed was putting his all into the song, and every other song that followed. Meanwhile, Karen had worked her away across to the other side of the stage and gazed at Cathy. 'You a celebrity, honey?' she asked.

Cathy shook her head. 'Not me.'

'No,' said Kevin, kissing her on the cheek. 'She's just a happy wife and mother.'

Meanwhile, Sammy Silver appeared and joined Ed onstage as the audience went wild. They loved him; he was still the idol of millions even though he was outgrowing his teeny bop looks. He sang a couple of old Everly brothers songs to a delighted audience, and a very angry Ed. He still hated Sammy and wished he'd done the job properly in America. They did all the theatrics of a great friendship, but away from the mic Ed hugged him and whispered, 'I hate your guts, and so does my wife. Keep away from her or I might take it upon myself to pay you another visit. We both know what we're talking about, don't we?' Sammy nodded and quickly left the stage.

'Great!' exclaimed Vic. 'What a great performance. You wowed 'em, Sammy. I'm having a get together after the show; you can stay if you wish.'

Sammy made his way to the dressing room, passing Cathy on the way. 'Hi beautiful,' he said.

'Don't speak to me,' retorted Cathy. She suddenly felt someone grasp her around her waist, and hands were placed over her eyes.

'Guess who?' said a female voice that Cathy recognised.

'June!' she cried. The hands were removed and Cathy turned

to face both June and Mick. She threw her arms around them both as Karen looked on with interest. The groupies were also hovering around, wondering who Mick was. He was dressed like a pop star but they dismissed him as not important enough; they were all far too young to remember him. Ed was a non-starter because Cathy was there, but Sammy; well that was a different case. He was now the prime target. They giggled at Karen. Was she really that stupid that she didn't know who Cathy was? Whatever the situation, she was making herself out to be a prize idiot. One or two cast their eyes over Kevin, but didn't follow it up. He never seemed to have a girlfriend, and several groupies thought that he was possibly gay.

Karen had also eyed Kevin up, but thought he was with Cathy so concentrated on the main person that she was going to try and captivate. She never read newspapers, so had no idea that Cathy was Ed's wife. The only time she bothered to buy one was if she was on the front page, so she was very disillusioned when Ed charged off the stage running towards her. He was soaked in sweat and she spread her arms wide, smiling her best smile ever. Any second he'd be in her arms; she'd already seen the love light in his eyes. Her heart beat wildly and she waited. She could smell his aftershave as he drew level with her, and then she closed her eyes and grasped… nothing. She opened her eyes and looked behind her. Cathy and Ed were locked in a passionate embrace.

'Hey!' she cried, but no one was listening. Mick and June stared at her as if she was out of her head. Ed meanwhile had steered Cathy into the dressing room. 'Hey!' cried Karen again, 'what is this?' Everyone ignored her, and she walked over to Kevin. 'I'm going in there,' she said.

Kevin grasped her arm. 'Better not,' he said, 'they're probably occupied.'

'You crazy?' screeched Karen. 'Do you usually let your wife screw other men?'

Kevin shrugged his shoulders. 'No,' he replied.

'Well do something then. I had to suck Vic's cock to get to Ed tonight.'

Kevin laughed. 'Bet he enjoyed it.'

Karen was even more exasperated when she saw Romany arrive, and he was also barred from entering the room. 'Cathy and Ed in there?' he asked, and Vic nodded. 'Shit, I guess I'll have to wait until they've finished.'

Annoyed, Karen tore herself free of Kevin and headed for the door. 'I sucked Vic's fat cock,' she yelled at the top of her voice. 'He said I could sleep with Ed if I did it.' Romany went into hysterics at this, and Vic went blood red. The groupies giggled amongst themselves, and June and Mick stifled their laughter as best they could. Crossing to Romany, Karen slapped him hard around the face. After checking to see if his teeth were intact, Romany returned the favour.

'I've never been so humiliated in my life,' cried Karen.

'First time for everything, babe,' laughed Kevin.

Karen rounded on him. 'As for you, you should be ashamed of yourself.'

Sammy ambled over. 'Can't think why?' he said, disengaging himself from two blonde groupies.

'He let his wife go in there with Ed,' cried Karen.

Romany doubled up in another fit of hysterics. 'His wife?' he chortled. 'When did you get married, Kevin?'

Vic was losing patience. 'Look, you stupid cunt, if you have to make a scene, go somewhere else and do it.' The roadies nearby were having a field day; this was some conversation.

Karen, renewing her attempts to get past Vic's bulk, yelled, 'She's not taking him away from me!' Her efforts were futile, however, and she began to cry. 'Whose wife is she then?' she sobbed.

Vic rubbed his hands together feeling the palms reach their usual clammy state. He was in such a nervous state that his shirt and underpants were sticking to him. He felt embarrassed. It was one thing Karen stating what had happened but to scream it at the top of her voice was quite another.

Romany ambled over. 'Come with me, lady fair,' he said. Karen answered with another slap to his face. After checking his teeth for a second time, Romany snarled, 'you're anybody's. If you're waiting for Ed, you've got a long wait. He won't want you; he's got a real woman in there with him, not a painted doll. You look like a walking Aunt Sally; your make-up's awful, you look like an ad for a wig commercial, your boobs look like a silicone job, and your arse has got a touch of the droops. Even your false eyelashes look like a couple of spiders that escaped from the zoo. You're cheap, lady, even down to that wig, really cheap.'

'It's my own hair,' screeched Karen. She threw herself at Vic and clung to him. 'Why?' she cried. 'Why?'

Vic was feeling even worse now; Karen was gazing up at him with a look that he'd only seen once before. He'd been a kid then and his spaniel puppy had chewed up all his Air Fix kits that he'd spent hours making. He'd beaten the puppy soundly and it had given him this same injured look that Karen was giving him.

The bystanders were in their element now. The groupies gathered around Romany who by now was enraged. Karen continued to cling to Vic, and he started wish he was a car salesman, or a milkman, or a coalman, or even a dustman. At the moment, even being a loo attendant seemed preferable to his job. The height of his embarrassment came when Karen turned to face Romany again. One eyelash hung precariously, and the other had attached itself to Vic's shirt.

He flicked the eyelash onto the floor in disgust and said to Romany, 'take her somewhere quiet and reveal Cathy's identity so she can have a good scream.'

Reluctantly, Karen allowed herself to be led away. She knew that her face was a mess and wanted to tidy herself up for when Ed did emerge from the room. She still believed that once he saw her, he'd forget Cathy, whoever she was. It wasn't long before a scream pierced the air, and a little later Romany returned alone. Vic smiled. 'Crisis over.'

Inside the dressing room, Ed was elated; he hadn't realised it would be this easy. Cathy had other ideas, however, and was going to make this anything but easy. She'd responded to all of his kisses and caresses passionately, but had decided that sex was out of the question. The groupie clap she did not need, and she also had to consider the health of her unborn baby. 'I can never forget that look you gave me yesterday. I didn't mean to hurt you; you're my world, you know that,' he whispered.

Cathy listened but her mind was on other things. 'Go down on me,' she ordered.

Ed obeyed, if that was what she wanted then that was what she'd get. He had an awful lot of making up to do. 'It's the drugs, I can't help it,' he murmured. He slid down her body and knelt at her feet.

'I know, I know.' She gasped as Ed's hands slid over her thighs and removed her panties; then she began to moan as his tongue found its mark. She reached orgasm very quickly, and Ed shifted his head once he felt her relax. Cathy shifted him back. 'Again,' she gasped, breathing heavily.

Puzzled, Ed complied. He needed to take her badly, and he found this strange, usually she couldn't wait to have him inside her. The blue satin trousers were tight enough normally, but at the moment they were fit to burst. She climaxed again and Ed got to his feet. 'I need you,' he said, fiddling with the zip on his tight trousers. He was astonished when she pulled away and stepped back into her panties. 'What are you doing?' he cried, 'I haven't even started yet. Stop playing games.'

Cathy smoothed her dress down. 'I'm finished; see you at the party.'

Ed was fuming and grabbed her arm. 'I want to fuck, and after what I've just done to you I think I've earned it.'

Cathy pulled away and met his gaze. 'Well, my darling

husband, if you want to fuck, I suggest you see a doctor first. Besides, I would have thought the action you had yesterday was enough to keep you going for ages; any more and it would have dropped off.'

'You know I always use protection, and you're my wife, you seem to forget that.'

'Strange that you forgot you had a wife yesterday.'

'It's the drugs.'

'Really? Then maybe I'll try some and then when you find me with five men I can use the same excuse.'

'What's got into you?'

'It's more a case of what is not going into me until you've seen a doctor. Well, I'm off to the party now, see you later, bye.'

She emerged from the room looking radiant and, slotting her arm through Kevin's, said, 'shall we go?'

Kevin was delighted; he'd hung around in the hope that he might see her, but never expected this. Vic was astonished; he guessed that Cathy was up to something but hoped it wouldn't make Ed too jealous. He needed both Ed and Kevin for his forthcoming European tour, and if Ed decided to dismember Kevin he'd be one act short, or maybe two. He decided to have a long chat later with Mick and to bring Cathy back onboard for a while. He could sense a migraine coming on. Most people had already left for his party and the only person remaining apart from himself and Ed was a very tear-stained Karen. His migraine was making itself felt now, and he shook his head at the girl. 'Go home, honey, everyone's gone.'

Karen was about to take his advice when the dressing room door opened and Ed emerged, his eyes blazing. Vic noted the bulge in his trousers and watched helplessly as Ed took one look at Karen and yanked her inside the room. Once inside he took her in his arms roughly. 'I knew it was me you wanted,' cooed Karen.

Ed grunted. 'You look like a dog so I'm going to treat you like one. Get across that table right now.'

'But aren't we going somewhere more comfortable?'

'Shut up, bitch, I don't want to look at you. Turn round and get across that table.'

Cathy had only driven a little way when she decided that she wanted to go back. Just when Kevin thought that things were going his way, he was being slapped down again. Arriving back at the venue, she noted Vic going into the gents. As she approached the dressing room, she could hear noises.

Inside, Karen was beginning to wish that she'd gone home. She'd been forced across the table and had both her dress and underwear ripped. Ed had just forced into her with no consideration for her feelings at all. She felt degraded as he called for Cathy over and over again.

Cathy froze in her tracks hearing, 'oh baby, I need you, oh Cathy.' She turned to Kevin and then marched into the ladies, emerging with a bucket of water.

Kevin was horrified. 'You can't!'

'Just watch me; he's made a fool of me for the last time.' Cathy replied. She marched to the dressing room and opened the door as quietly as possible. The sight that met her eyes was exactly what she expected. Karen saw her first and squealed.

Ed noticed nothing until he felt the contents of the bucket drench him. 'I could see that you both needed cooling down, so I thought I'd help you out,' said Cathy. Then she turned on her heel and stormed out.

Vic rushed out of the gents with his trousers at half mast. Hearing the noise of Karen squealing, he rushed to the dressing room. He turned the air blue as he collided with Cathy. 'I thought... you'd... left,' he stammered, attempting to cover his lower half.

'I did,' replied Cathy, 'but I forgot something.'

Vic heaved his trousers up and yanked on the zip but it refused to budge. One extra hard heave and it moved in a way that it shouldn't. Vic let out an anguished shriek, followed by a few swear words. 'Forgot what?'

'Nothing much, just my husband.'

Vic's blood pressure was going over the top. He was going to have a stroke any minute; he knew it. Any second now and his suffering would be over. He would be confined to a wheelchair, or better still dead. His head reeled as Cathy said, 'there's a dog and a bitch on heat in there. My mother used to say that the best way to separate them was to throw a bucket of water over them, so I did just that. Anyway, I'm going again. Oh, and I hope that that zip hasn't done you any harm because that bitch in there looks as if she could handle another dog. Blue movie queen of the future there; get in quick.' She laughed and left once more. Vic opened the dressing room door and nearly collapsed when he saw the drenched occupants. Distraught, he offered up a prayer for deliverance.

At the party, Cathy was very much the centre of attention. Al Simpkins hovered nearby as he'd been left in charge of greeting the guests until Vic turned up, and already he was drunk. Mick repeatedly left June's side to dance with Cathy, but June was unfazed and mingled. Mick was overheated. 'Shame Ed beat me to you,' he said. 'How about we split for a while? I'll have you twitching around in no time.'

'I love Ed,' replied Cathy, wondering if she did any more.

'A slice from a cut loaf is never missed.'

'June would never forgive you.'

'June would never find out.' His hands were straying all over her.

Cathy gazed at him. He drew her too much as she'd fancied him before she'd ever met him. He was the main draw of the Shelltones in the sixties. She levered herself from his grasp. 'I'd like a drink.'

One drink later and Mick had her back on the dance floor, just as Ed made his entrance with Vic. He scowled when he saw Cathy in Mick's arms. Vic could sense trouble. 'Cool it. You're hardly in a position to chastise her, are you?'

Ed shot Mick a killing look and seated himself in an armchair. He did not like the way Mick was holding his wife, and noted the way that his hands strayed. He was about to cut in when Kevin beat him to it. Mick wandered over. 'Hey Ed, what's up?' he said, attempting to shake Ed's hand.

Ed pulled his hand away. 'It's more a case of what was nearly up,' he snapped. 'Keep away from my wife.'

Vic intervened. He could sense trouble ahead. 'Boys, let's have a drink, we're all pals together,' he said, but Ed wasn't listening. He approached the dancing couple and pushed Kevin over.

Kevin got up, brushed himself down and walked away. He wasn't going to get involved in any punch-ups. Ed held his wife to him so closely that she could hardly breathe, 'Vic says that you've got something important to tell me.'

'Really?' said Cathy. 'I see you've changed; get wet did you?'

'Don't play games with me, I don't like it.'

'I didn't like what I saw earlier; that's two days on the trot that I've caught you out.'

'It wasn't my fault this time, it was yours. You got me going and then walked out. What was I supposed to do?'

'You could have given yourself one off the wrist.'

'I don't trust Kevin or Mick.'

'Don't be stupid, Ed. I don't fool around.'

Kevin was looking on and wasn't surprised when Ed began to kiss Cathy passionately and run his hands over her body. He knew that it was for his benefit, and a little later Ed approached him. 'Keep away from her,' he shouted. 'That's a warning, and if you don't listen I'll do more than warn you.'

Vic staggered across the floor towards them, sloshed. 'Great party,' he said. 'Cathy told you yet?'

'No,' replied Ed. 'Do you know what the mystery is?'

Vic nodded. 'My lips are sealed. How are you two boys getting on? It won't be long before the tour starts. You'll get on like a house on fire.'

'Yeah,' replied Ed. 'Put Kevin in the house and I'll set light to it and pour paraffin on.'

Vic collected his thoughts. The prospect of being a loo cleaner became more appealing every day. He handed Ed a small package, and Kevin guessed it was drugs of some kind because as soon as Ed had the package in his hand he was doing a disappearing act.

Kevin followed him. 'Wise up, Ed, isn't it that that's doing the damage?'

'I need it,' retorted Ed, making for the stairs.

Kevin restrained him. 'Don't destroy yourself. If you could kick it, you and Cathy could make a new start.'

'Fuck off, Kevin, we don't need to start again. There is no split and no separation. Our marriage is great, never been better, and if I want to get high I don't need your permission. I love Cathy and she loves me. You may have brought her here tonight but she'll leave on my arm and sleep in my bed. Now piss off and leave us alone.' He barged up the stairs and left Kevin at the bottom.

As the night wore on, Ed kept his wife at his side but he indulged heavily in drink and drugs. As the party drew to its end he was slumped on a sofa, stoned. Cathy was upset; she'd wanted them to leave together. 'What do I do?' she asked Romany.

'Leave him here and come upstairs with me,' he replied.

'Never give up, do you?' said Kevin.

'Maybe I don't have to try,' said Romany, leering at Cathy.

Vic yawned. 'He'd better spend the night here,' he said. 'We can't move him. You go home and I'll bring him home when he's slept it all off.' Sadly, Cathy agreed. She'd wanted him with her so that she could tell him about the baby, and tell him that was the only reason that she'd refused him sex. The prospect of a new baby might give him the strength to kick the drugs again.

'You will explain that I didn't want to leave him here, won't you, Vic?' she said. 'And tell him that I want him to come home as soon as possible.'

'Will do, babe. Now go home and make yourself beautiful for him; you look very tired. Shuteye is what you need, and then you can give him your news. That'll really put a spring in his step.'

'And if Vic's asleep, I'll tell him. I'm gonna curl up in that armchair over there,' said Romany. Reluctantly, Cathy left with Kevin.

Arriving home, Cathy invited him in for coffee, but she stressed that it wouldn't be a good idea for him to stay over, as Ed could come out of his stupor earlier than expected and get annoyed with him. Kevin announced that he was shattered and didn't feel safe enough to drive to Chelsea. After a disagreement, and a promise that he would stay out of sight, Cathy showed him to one of the guest rooms.

He tried to sleep but couldn't, so he got up and dressed, wondering if Cathy could do with a coffee or drink. He tapped on her door and could hear a Dylan cassette playing softly. Cathy declined his offer and said that the only thing she needed was sleep. Tentatively, he pushed her door open and beheld her sitting in front of her dressing table brushing her hair. The moonlight streamed through the windows, bathing her in its beam of light. She was dressed in a frothy pink negligee, making her look very feminine. She'd brushed all the curls out of her hair and it streamed in its usual wild, abandoned way down her back. She got to her feet as Kevin entered, and the moonlight made the negligee transparent. Kevin gulped; she was so near, yet so far. A blonde Venus with a husband who didn't seem to care about her. 'I couldn't sleep,' said Kevin.

Cathy appeared to be in some sort of dream-like state as she crossed to the window and gazed out. 'Bob Dylan,' sighed Cathy. 'He's been my idol for years.'

Kevin followed her to the window and stood behind her. She rested her head on his shoulder and leaned back against him. He relaxed, feeling the warmth of her body against him. His hands were actually on bare flesh as the negligee gaped slightly at the front. As she'd leaned back, his hands had managed to get beneath the material. It wasn't intentional, it had just happened that way. He was shaking as his hands slid upwards and encountered the swell of her breasts. Cathy didn't appear to mind. She just stayed in the same position with her head still on his shoulder. Kevin wanted to cry with joy; this was the moment he'd dreamed about actually happening. 'Cathy…' he whispered.

She didn't appear to hear him and, keeping one hand on her breast, Kevin slid his other hand downward. His pulse was racing and then Cathy spoke, 'don't, please don't. I can't betray Ed, I love him, and it's too much drink that's making you behave this way. It's not me that you want; I'm many years older than you and I know that if we continue we'll both be sorry in the morning.'

She pushed his hands away and turned to face him. Kevin gazed into her eyes. 'It's not the drink,' he said.

'Hush, don't let's mention it again. Furthermore, I think that your idea of a coffee is a good one. I could murder one at the moment.'

Deflated, Kevin let her go. She settled herself back at the dressing table again and resumed brushing her hair. 'Cathy, I… I…'

'Hush, coffee.' Kevin forced a smile and left the room to make the drinks.

When he returned, Cathy was laying on the bed with a very pained expression haunting her features. Kevin saw it at once. He set the coffee down by the side of the bed and was at her side immediately. 'What is it?' he asked, noticing that her eyes were full of tears.

'My baby,' she cried. 'I think I'm losing my baby.'

'Do you want a doctor?' asked Kevin, taking her hand in his.

Cathy winced, clutching her stomach. 'Probably nothing,' she muttered.

'It won't take a moment to phone the doctor.'

'No, the pain's subsiding. Can you hand me my coffee?' Kevin handed the beverage over and Cathy sipped it. 'Thanks Kevin, you're a true friend, the best ever.' She drank her coffee and then headed to the en suite, returning a few seconds later with a glass of water and a couple of pills. 'I think I need help tonight,' she said, 'especially as I've just drunk that coffee.'

Kevin drained his coffee and eyed the pills. 'What are they?' he asked.

'Valium,' replied Cathy, swallowing the pills and washing them down with the water. 'I'm going to bed now, I really think that you should go because if Ed returns before you've left, the sight of your car will be enough to freak him out.'

'Okay,' replied Kevin. 'I'll take these cups downstairs to the kitchen; try to sleep.' He left the room as Cathy murmured a slurred goodnight, and went downstairs. He put the cups into the dishwasher and was about to leave when he had second thoughts. Cathy had said that the servants were away that night, so what if she miscarried and needed help? There was no one there to help her, and Ed might not come back until much later. He couldn't leave her on her own. He'd check on her in the morning and then if she was fine he'd leave, hopefully before Ed arrived. He wandered back upstairs and pushed Cathy's door open. She was in a deep sleep. He lay on top of the covers and snuggled up to her. He wasn't going to sleep, just watch over her.

Ed awoke about seven o'clock in the morning. He stared about him and saw Romany slumped in an armchair. He got to his feet and elbowed him. 'Cathy, where is she?' he asked.

'Dunno,' replied Romany, his eyes heavy with sleep. 'Gone home, I think.'

Ed was feeling terrible; he had no memory of the previous night's party at all. He nudged Romany again. 'Where's Mick?'

Romany opened his eyes again; he felt as if someone was putting red hot needles into them. 'Dunno, what is this, twenty questions?'

Ed was getting more anxious by the second; his mouth was dry. 'I need a drink,' he said.

'Well, get a drink then, but for Christ's sake leave me alone. If you want more answers, ask Vic.'

'Where is Vic?'

'It is twenty fucking questions. Look, I'll play later but now I'm too bloody tired. Vic's in bed where we should all be.'

Ed mounted the stairs and went in search of Vic. He opened Vic's bedroom door, switched on the light, and shook him. Vic let out a yell; he thought he was about to be murdered in his own bed. 'Where's Mick, Kevin, and Cathy?' asked Ed.

After the initial shock had worn off, Vic awoke and stared at Ed towering over him. 'How the fuck do I know?' he said. 'Piss off, Ed.'

Ed parked himself on the edge of the bed. 'I want answers. Where's my wife?'

Vic rubbed his eyes; he had been having a lovely dream. He was an old-aged pensioner sitting in a rocking chair in front of an open fire. His wife, a buxom blonde of about twenty-five, waited on him hand and foot, and nearby in a cage a canary sang its heart out, while on the hearthrug a black cat was curled up asleep. He wanted to get back into that dream and away from Ed.

Ed, however, was not going until he got answers. 'Sammy,' he said, 'where's that prick, Sammy?'

'Next door, why? Do you fancy him all of a sudden?'

'Talk sense.' He shook Vic once again.

Vic stared over at his alarm clock, bleary-eyed. 'I can't talk sense at this time of day.'

'Well try. Where's Mick?'

'Went home with June just before you crashed.'

'Where's Kevin; where is the bastard?'

'Gone home. Can I go back to sleep now?'

'Where's Cathy?'

Vic closed his eyes and once more began to dream. It wasn't

for long though as Ed began to pace the floor and once more crossed to the bed and shook Vic. 'Did she leave alone?'

'Who?'

'Cathy!' screeched Ed.

Vic attempted to sit up. He half made it and then banged his head on the headboard. 'Please go away,' he pleaded.

'Answer me then, did she leave alone?' Vic racked his brains. He knew that he was supposed to tell Ed something but couldn't recall what it was. Cathy had mentioned something, but what was it? 'Vic, did she leave alone or with Kevin?'

'Yes'

'What? Alone or with Kevin?'

'Kevin drove her home.'

The noise had awoken Sammy next door. 'Everything okay?' he asked. Ed felt sick. He couldn't think of anything worse than hearing that voice first thing in the morning. Actually he could, the thought of seeing that face first thing in the morning. Sammy banged on the wall. 'You okay, Vic?' he called.

'Fuck off, you retard,' yelled Ed. He was about to throw something at the wall when he realised to his horror that not only could he hear Sammy but he could see him as well. He could actually see Sammy through the mirror. He picked up the alarm clock and aimed it at Vic's head. 'Fucking pervert,' he yelled. 'No wonder you wanted me, Cathy, Kim, and June to sleep here. You've been eyeballing me for years. You and Simpkins must have had a great time. I don't care too much about the other two, but you've been perving over my wife, you slimy bastard. You're dead.'

Fortunately for Vic, the clock missed its mark but he ducked under the covers as Ed stormed out of the room.

Sammy was on the landing. 'You okay? I could hear you shouting. Is Vic okay? Can I do anything?'

Ed stared at him, and then hit him in the mouth. 'Yes, drop dead,' he said and ran downstairs.

Sammy put his hands to his face; he was covered in blood. 'Vic,' he shouted. 'Vic, Ed's lost it.'

Vic wasn't listening, he was under the covers and was going to stay there for a while. Downstairs, Romany opened one eye. He'd heard the commotion but had decided to stay downstairs and let everyone get on with it. 'Did you get your answers?' he asked Ed.

'Yeah, I'm gonna kill the bastard.'

'Who?' asked Romany, reaching for his cigarettes.

'Kevin. I'm not having him fooling with my wife. It's a good job I can trust her.'

'I never liked him, sly little bastard. He's very young; wonder if he's any good in the sack? Suppose he might just boost Cathy's ego. You haven't exactly been the squeaky clean husband lately.'

'Don't rub it in.'

'Let's have a drink.' Romany flicked cigarette ash into his shoe which lay nearby and, finding a half full bottle of whiskey by the side of Al Simpkins who was asleep on the floor, poured a glass for him and Ed. 'Bottoms up,' he said, 'as long as it's not Cathy's.'

Ed was fuming inwardly. He knew he shouldn't have indulged so heavily last night, but that was nothing compared to Vic's mirror and the sight of that grinning idiot, Silver. 'Cathy wouldn't cheat on me,' said Ed, swigging the whiskey down.

'They looked brilliant on stage though. Kevin looks like your younger brother. I guess he must remind her of you when you were younger, and you have had a few problems lately. I suppose nobody could blame him for trying,' smirked Romany.

Ed got to his feet, crossed to the fireplace and removed a statuette from the mantelpiece. Romany was alarmed, wondering if Ed intended hitting him with it. 'What are you doing?' he cried, cringing away.

'I'm gonna kill Kevin,' yelled Ed, hurling the statuette through Vic's colour television. The glass shattered and Romany backed off, knowing that he'd said a little too much this time. Upstairs, Vic heard the crash and got out of bed, thinking that he'd been burgled. In a daze, he struggled into his trousers, lost his balance, and stubbed his toe on the castor of the divan base. His big toe and the one next to it had separated, and Vic hopped around on one leg holding his injured foot. The air turned blue as his trousers fell around his ankles, and he tripped and fell with a terrific crash on the floor, cursing the entertainment scene and everyone in it.

Romany didn't know which way to turn. Ed had just ruined Vic's television, and now there was this crash upstairs which sounded as if it needed some kind of investigation. 'Ed, cool it, everything's fine,' he said. He'd dropped his cigarette end on the floor in shock and noted that it had burnt a hole in Vic's carpet. It was brought to his attention when he put his foot on it and burnt his sole. Ed refused to listen and charged out of Vic's house as if the devil were after him. On his way out, he managed to break a vase and an ornament of a German Shepherd dog that Vic cherished, before he roared off in his car.

Vic stumbled downstairs, and when he saw the television he nearly had a seizure. One look at Romany's face told him all he needed to know. 'What did you say?' he bellowed.

'Never mind that, we'd better follow him. He says that he's going to kill Kevin.'

'Well don't just stand there gaping, Romany, let's go. I need both Ed and Kevin for Europe.'

Ed drove like a lunatic on his way home, nearly crashing three times. His heart was full of hatred for Kevin, and the sight of his car parked outside didn't help. He let himself in with his heart thumping. He was terrified at the thought of the sight that might meet his eyes but clung to the belief that Cathy would never cheat on him. Romany had fired the seed of doubt into him though and now he was ready for anything.

Silently, he climbed the stairs and made for his bedroom. Opening the door he looked in. Cathy lay on the bed with a contented smile on her lips. Ed sat down on the bed and gazed at his wife wondering how on earth he could have doubted her fidelity. He was about to undress and get into bed with her when she opened her eyes. 'I'm sleepy, I took two Valium. You looked bad last night. Are you better now?'

'Better for seeing you,' replied Ed. 'What was it that you wanted to tell me?'

Cathy attempted to open her eyes, but was far too tired to do so. 'Baby,' she murmured. 'We're going to have another baby,' and then she drifted back into a deep sleep again.

Ed's heart was full of joy. Now he knew why she hadn't wanted sex with him the previous day. How he loved her. He was never going to cheat again, ever. However, his blood soon turned to ice when he entered the en suite and found Kevin hiding in the shower cubicle. Kevin had intended leaving much earlier but had fallen asleep beside Cathy and not awoken until he heard Ed outside the bedroom door. There was nowhere to hide. He'd hoped that Ed might go straight to bed or maybe back downstairs, giving him the opportunity to slip away but his luck was out. Ed headed for the en suite and could see Kevin's outline crouched on the floor of the cubicle. There was no escape. All of Ed's hatred surfaced. He hit Kevin on the chin, knocking him down and followed up with a series of blows to his head.

'It's not what you think,' cried Kevin, trying to defend himself. But he didn't stand a chance. Ed was much too fast and powerful for him. They fought on the floor, rolling over and smashing several items. Kevin was fighting for his life. 'Ask Cathy, she'll tell you,' he pleaded.

'Don't need too, she's drugged up. Was that your plan? To wait until she was out of it and then take her? There are many bathrooms in this house, why did you feel the need to use this one, huh? Why, you crafty bastard? I warned you and you wouldn't listen.' He hit Kevin again and again. 'You slept with her, didn't you? You waited until she was out of it, and then you took her and you were just about to slink away unnoticed. You might look like a man but you fight like a girl. Kevin struck his head on the corner of the shower cubicle and went limp. Thinking that he'd knocked him out, Ed headed for Cathy but Kevin was faking and, yanking on Ed's ankle, felled him.

'Bastard,' swore Ed, 'I'll fix you.' He got up, dragged Kevin to his feet and then hit him so hard that the force of the blow knocked him backwards and into the bath where he struck his head on one of the taps. Kevin put his hand to his head, felt the blood begin to trickle down the side of his face, then he lapsed into temporary unconsciousness.

Ed strode out of the bathroom and back into the bedroom where Cathy slept. She was in a very deep sleep, oblivious to what was going on, and the first thing she knew of any of the disturbance was when she felt hands upon her caressing her body. She thought she was dreaming, a dream in which Ed was making love to her. The only thing was the dream was becoming rather realistic. Her body was responding far too well for a dream. Her eyes snapped open. 'Oh God, no!' she cried.

Ed was above her and in desperation she tried to push him away, but he slapped her around the face and snarled, 'if you think that you can fool around with someone else and then deny me, you're mistaken.'

'No!' screamed Cathy, 'think of the baby.'

'Whose baby? Yours and Kevin's?' sneered Ed.

'No,' cried Cathy, 'he never touched me.'

Cathy's screams brought Kevin round, and he heaved himself out of the bath and fell to the floor. He dragged himself from the bathroom to the bed on his stomach. He tried to stand but couldn't so he continued to crawl. 'Leave her alone,' he cried with all the strength that he could muster before keeling over onto his back. Ed threw the covers off himself and Cathy, forcing Kevin to watch their reflections in the mirrored ceiling. Kevin was in agony. He could see Cathy's body reflected in its nudity. He watched as Ed tore into his wife, and he wept. The woman he adored was being violated by her own husband.

'Watch, lover-boy,' commanded Ed. 'At the moment she hates me, but that won't last. She's mine, do you hear me, mine.'

Cathy continued to struggle and scream, and then got her first look at Kevin on the floor. His face was puffy and very swollen. 'Oh my God, what have you done to him?'

'I haven't finished with him yet,' replied Ed, breathing heavily. 'I'm gonna finish him off when I've finished with you.'

'Run, Kevin, run,' screamed Cathy. But Kevin couldn't run, he couldn't even stand. He was seeing stars, and felt himself blacking out again. Darkness was enveloping him as Cathy reached out her hand for the telephone. She grasped the receiver but Ed knocked it from her hand. The phone clattered to the floor and she knew that her screams would be futile. Her housekeeper was visiting her children with her husband and wouldn't be back until later that day, Ruby the housemaid slept like a log, and as for the rest of the staff, they lived out. There was just her, Ed, and Kevin. She thought she heard a car pull up outside and prayed that she had.

As Ed continued to ravish her, Kevin awoke from the darkness and dragged himself on his stomach towards the door. Cathy saw this and hoped that he would make it before Ed had finished with her. She held Ed to her urging him on knowing that this was the one thing that would make him hold back and give Kevin more time. 'That's better, baby,' murmured Ed, 'it's just you and me and that's the way it's always going to be. I can really feel you moving now, give yourself to me, baby. That's it, that's beautiful. You're beautiful.'

Now that Vic and Romany had reached Ed's house, they stood staring at each other. 'Now what do we do? Ring the door bell?' blustered Vic. 'He's hardly likely to open the door, is he?'

'I've got a key,' said Romany.

'Why didn't you say so, you idiot?'

'Sssh,' said Romany, 'we don't want him to hear us.'

Vic was shaking. He'd noticed both Ed's and Kevin's cars outside and wondered if he was about to walk in on a blood bath. Once inside, Romany went upstairs while Vic remained downstairs, worried by the silence. Then a scream pierced the air. 'Don't touch him, he's innocent.'

Vic rushed up the stairs, passing Romany as if he was in a life or death race. As he drew level with Ed's bedroom, Kevin crawled through the doorway covered in blood. Horrified, Vic helped him to his feet and supported him. Romany went into the room and beheld Cathy, clad only in a negligee, wrestling with Ed. 'You're not going to harm him,' cried Cathy.

Ed backhanded her down to the floor. 'I'm gonna kill the bastard,' he yelled and, catching sight of Romany, added, 'get out of my house, this is a private conversation.' He strode over to the en suite. 'I'm gonna carve him up, and Cathy's gonna watch me do it.' He opened the bathroom cabinet and extracted a cut throat razor. Cathy was on her feet in an instant. Her reflex was fast; she slammed the dividing door on him and locked it. In a rage, Ed battered on the locked door. 'Let me out,' he bellowed. 'I'm gonna kill him.'

Cathy turned to Romany. 'Get Kevin out of here.' Open-mouthed, he obeyed, hurrying from the room and helping Vic to get Kevin downstairs.

Minutes later, Ed broke the door down and emerged with the razor in his hand. Cathy stood on the landing and faced him as he screamed, 'let me at him.'

She barred his way. 'You'll have to go through me first.'

'Get out of my way,' screeched Ed, brandishing the razor, but Cathy stood her ground. She still felt woozy but wasn't going to allow her husband to carve up an innocent man. They began to struggle as Vic laid Kevin on a sofa and dialled for an ambulance.

Romany started back upstairs. 'Calm down, Ed, nothing happened. Let me have the razor.'

'If you come any closer, I'll let you have it right across your throat,' yelled Ed.

Vic was rubbing his hands together. 'Ed, we've got to get Kevin to hospital,' he pleaded.

'Pointless, he'll need an undertaker by the time I've finished with him. Get off me, Cathy.' She was pulling his hair, doing just about everything she could to prevent him reaching Kevin.

'Ed, I'll call the police.' Vic's voice was shaking.

'Shut up, pervert. You've been spying on me for months through that poxy mirror of yours; maybe I'll fix you too. I bet all that time Cathy lived at your place you were perving at her through it.'

Vic was shaking in his boots now. If Ed really knew what he'd done with Cathy, he'd definitely be on his hit list. Romany was scared too. If this is what his friend did to people that he'd thought might be messing with his wife, what would he do to people who actually had? Cathy was still struggling with Ed, and her hands had been cut as she'd tried to take the razor from him. She was losing the fight and, in sheer desperation, brought her knee up into his groin. Ed shrieked and lost his grip on her, causing her to lose her balance and hurtle from top to bottom of the stairs, coming to rest with a sickening thud. 'No!' screamed Ed. 'No!'

She seemed to fall in slow motion; he saw every move on her face. She lay still and, sick with fear, Vic leaned over her. 'Oh my God, Ed, what have you done?' he whispered. He was too scared to move Cathy, remembering her pregnancy.

Ed stood at the top of the stairs, speechless. He dropped the razor and rushed down to his wife's side. He pushed Vic out of the way and knelt beside her. 'Cathy, for God's sake, speak to me,' he wailed.

A long, drawn out sigh escaped Cathy's lips, followed by a moan. 'My baby,' she murmured. 'You've killed our baby.' Then she lapsed into unconsciousness.

'Cathy,' screamed Ed, but there was no response. He felt for a pulse, a heartbeat, anything, but in his disturbed state found nothing. His gaze fell upon Kevin. His face was very swollen; in fact one of his eyes appeared to have closed up completely.

Seth's words echoed in Ed's ears, 'you will fuck up big time.' There was no sign of life from Cathy, and Ed threw himself across her prostrate body. There was no point in living now. He'd killed her and their unborn baby. Getting to his feet, he went back upstairs.

Romany and Vic didn't see him go; they were too engrossed in helping Kevin and Cathy. As Ed ascended the stairs, he thought he could hear Sandy calling him; yes he could hear her and now he could see her. He entered his bedroom and headed for the en suite. The dividing door hung at an angle. 'I'm coming, honey,' he said. 'I'm here, Sandy.'

When the ambulance arrived, Cathy was taken out on a stretcher alongside Kevin. It was then that Romany noticed Ed's absence. 'Where's Ed?' he asked Vic. 'He'll have to go with Cathy.'

Vic sneered. 'Probably upstairs feeling sorry for himself. I'll go and get him; tell the ambulance driver to wait.' He went upstairs, his feet dragging every step of the way. He noted the blood stains on the landing carpet where Kevin had crawled along it. There was no sign of Ed, but Vic noticed that there was blood on the dividing door leading to the en suite. Even in a crisis like this, Ed was liable to be in the bath relaxing.

'Come on, arsehole,' he yelled as he walked through the doorway, 'your wife needs you.' Then he gasped at the sight before him. Ed was kneeling by the side of the bath with the upper part of his body draped in it, and blood everywhere. The cut throat razor lay on the floor. 'Not again,' cried Vic. He spewed all over the carpet and then rushed out onto the landing. 'Romany,' he shrieked, 'get those guys up here pronto and tell them to make room for one more.'

He couldn't believe it, three of his headliners practically wiped out, and all of them looked as if they'd been involved in a massacre.

Chapter Eighteen

Vic wanted Ed sectioned. 'He's mega loony now,' he said. 'How many times can I cover up for him? I'm exhausted. He might kill you next time. You can't give him any more chances.'

'And of course, you are completely blameless in all of this,' Cathy responded sarcastically. 'You don't procure women for him, like the time at the recording studio, do you? That was the trigger, Vic, I caught him out and it had a knock on effect. He believed that as he'd cheated, I would do the same, especially after the Karen incident. You told me to dance with Mick and Kevin at your party to make him jealous and bring him to heel, and after you'd plied him with drink and drugs he became immobile. So the fact that I left with Kevin drove him crazy and it pushed him over the edge. You turned up with Romany which makes me think that he probably wound him up. You're as guilty as sin, both of you.'

Vic put his arm around Cathy's shoulders, trying to look concerned. 'You have to section him. Kevin could front the band, and you could do a few numbers too, just to keep your hand in.'

Cathy removed his arm from around her. 'I'm going to visit him this afternoon,' she said. 'Do you want to come?'

Vic lit up a cigar and shook his head, saying that he was too busy and had to leave. He got to his feet and immediately fell over the giant tortoise which had come in through the French doors and tripped him up. Eddie ran in, followed by his nanny. He was nearly two now and Cathy was determined to have Ed home by his birthday.

Vic got up and the giant reptile lumbered towards him, settling itself across Vic's feet and resting its weight upon him. 'Get him off me, I can't move. He's a ton weight.'

Cathy was in stitches. 'He likes you. Come here, Wacky.' She took an apple from the fruit bowl and held it out to the tortoise, who promptly moved away from Vic and took it in his mouth. Vic made his escape. Cathy scooped Eddie up into her arms. 'Let's go and see the fish, Eddie,' she said. It was a lovely August day and she walked towards the koi pond with the nanny. Wacky brought up the rear; he lumbered behind hoping for another apple.

That afternoon Cathy made her way to the hospital which was set in the centre of some woodland. Squirrels were everywhere and the scene was picturesque, but once inside the building, reality kicked in. There were several secure doors to go through, and Cathy was led to Ed's room by his doctor. He was sedated, but very pleased to see his wife and held out his arms to her, embracing her warmly.

'I thought I'd lost you... I killed our baby... I hate myself,' he sobbed. The doctor smiled at his patient. He felt that Ed was still suicidal and needed a lot of specialist treatment as the drugs had taken their toll badly. He looked at Ed's medical notes and then decided to leave the couple alone for a while saying that he'd be back in about thirty minutes.

Cathy put some fruit that she'd bought in a farm shop into a bowl which stood on top of Ed's bedside cabinet. 'You'll be home soon,' said Cathy. 'It's almost Eddie's birthday.'

Ed was relieved. He wasn't sure if she'd want him back. He took her hand. 'I'm so sorry, baby. I don't suppose I'll ever be able to make it up to you but I'd like to try.'

Cathy gazed into Ed's eyes. 'Vic's bought Kevin off, but what worries me is who's next on your list. You even killed our baby by your actions.'

'Maybe Vic himself. Did you know about that mirror?'

'Found out about it on the day I moved in with you. I was disgusted, but that's all in the past now. When you're better he wants you to do another tour with me on board again.'

'Great idea, maybe we could record more together.'

'Any particular ideas?'

'Well, *Je T'aime* would be a good one; come to bed and I'll borrow a tape recorder.'

They were interrupted by a young, black nurse who had come in to administer Ed's medication. 'He's a model patient,' she said.

'I'm a model husband too; ask my wife,' said Ed.

Cathy said nothing and a little later the doctor returned. The questions fired at Ed were answered to the doctor's satisfaction, until he was asked why he had tried to take his life.

'I had to, my wife fell down the stairs and I thought she was dead. I couldn't find any signs of life so I had to die, and Sandy was calling to me.'

'Sandy?'

'Yes, Cathy's daughter, she died in a hit and run accident. If Cathy dies then so do I, and vice-versa.'

'But it doesn't work like that, Ed.'

'Yes it does, Cathy and I are bonded.'

'Bonded?'

'Yes, we went through a ritual with my cousin in 1968. We're bonded through life and death, and Sandy's our daughter so when we both die, we'll be a proper family again.'

The doctor shook his head sadly and glanced at Cathy. 'Can you confirm this?'

Cathy was shaken by Ed's words. She recalled nothing of this but he was so focused on the event that it was hard to dismiss it. She addressed the doctor: 'I wish I could, but I have to say that I'm starting to believe it. Ed is not insane; he's driven by some sort of force. In 1968, it was all free love and drugs, so maybe something could have happened if I was stoned at the time.'

She looked over at Ed, feeling only pity. What had happened to that strong, loveable person she knew? He was being used by everyone and becoming like a mechanical doll. The doctor checked his notes. 'There's something wrong with his blood too,' he said. 'I've never seen anything like it before. We should run more tests so I'd like to keep him here for another month.'

Cathy shook her head. 'And I would like to take him home, so a month is out of the question. Whatever it is that's driving him will not be cured in here. We'll visit his brother in Norfolk; the sea air and relaxed way of living will do him much more good.'

'But Mr Lee feels that he is a danger to himself and others; he needs a lot of medication.'

'Mr Lee is not related. I am his wife and next of kin, and I want him to be discharged. I realise that this cannot be done immediately, but I will be back in forty-eight hours and I want him ready to leave with me.'

'But he's very sick.'

'I know, and I will nurse him.'

Grudgingly, the doctor agreed and left the room. 'After all I've done, you're the only one who fights my corner,' Ed cried.

Cathy sat on the bed and hugged him tightly. She kissed him gently. 'It's called love, Ed,' she replied. 'Besides, who's going to fight my corner if you're not around? I need looking after too.' They lay side by side on the bed until Ed drifted off to sleep, then she rang home and waited for her chauffeur outside.

When Vic heard the news, he was furious, but Cathy was adamant, and forty-eight hours later left the hospital with Ed and his medication. He fell asleep on Cathy during the drive home. His words on the ritual were disturbing, but she pushed them to the back of her mind. She had Ed back and that was all that counted.

Nearing home, Ed awoke and sat up. 'If you hadn't stepped in, Vic would have left me in there and thrown away the key.'

'Forget him,' said Cathy. 'No doubt he'll rear his ugly head again when he thinks that you're well enough to work.'

Ed laughed. 'Guess so, I can't wait to get home, see Eddie, then take you upstairs for the longest cuddle you've ever had.'

Cathy smiled. 'Sounds good to me, and next week we're going to visit Rusty. The girls haven't met Eddie yet, have they? They'll love him; he could even spend his birthday there.'

Ed loved the idea. 'I love you, Mrs Gold, I really do.'

The following week they left for Norfolk. Eddie was in tears as he wanted to take his tortoise with him and would not be consoled. Finally he fell asleep and didn't open his eyes again until they reached Bacton. They spent three weeks in the caravan and, on his return to Surrey, Ed again voiced his feelings on the open road. Cathy said she'd never given up on the idea but felt that Vic would be a hard nut to crack. They'd had a great time in Bacton. The sea air had done Ed and Cathy the world of good, and the pressure of touring and recording seemed a distant memory.

Cathy wasn't wrong. When Vic found out that once more the pair was making a bid for freedom, he exploded. 'I made both of you,' he yelled. 'You were both nothing until I moulded you. You fucked up in America and gave me a monster problem with the promoters over there. I built Cathy up with Kevin, and you've ruined any chance of him playing with you again. You smashed out a couple of Silver's teeth and I'm picking up the tab for that too as he was going to expose you to the press. Kevin's cost me a small fortune for his silence. Mick thinks that you're loony, as I do, and God knows what you'll do next. You're a liability; look at the cover-ups I had to do in the States. Well now it's pay back time. I want an album from you as soon as possible, the European tour to be honoured, an English tour, four days in France, and then as far as I'm concerned you can both fuck off into oblivion.'

Cathy smiled calmly. 'Am I included on these gigs?'

'Too right you are. I want you to pay me back too for grooming you for stardom, and I want you at Ed's side just in case he goes loony again.' Cathy laughed, but Vic looked very stressed.

Ed had been silent throughout the conversation. 'Can I have that in writing?' he laughed.

The tortoise put in an appearance again and, as Vic stood up, it rammed his ankles, causing him to sprawl face down on the carpet. 'Fucking thing,' he yelled, as the reptile attempted to walk over him. 'Why can't you get a cat like everyone else?' Ed and Cathy were in hysterics as Vic staggered to his feet. 'I'll see you later,' he grunted and stormed out.

It wasn't long before the album was cut and the European tour commenced. This time Cathy wasn't dancing, she was just singing alongside Ed doing several Fleetwood Mac numbers, *River Deep* and many others. Returning home, Cathy found herself pregnant, but two months later lost the baby. After a blood test, the hospital diagnosed Cathy as also having a strange mutation in her blood. She ignored requests for tests, and later in the year began the English tour. Once more she became pregnant, and Ed was delighted; he and Cathy were almost at the end of their contract. They avoided parties and kept themselves to themselves, and were very happy when the final night arrived in London. That morning, Ed took Cathy shopping and bought her a fabulous cocktail dress which flared under the bust and gradually got fuller and fuller until there were yards of chiffon at the ankles. 'It's beautiful,' exclaimed Cathy, 'but I won't be able to wear it after I've had the baby.'

'Who cares, and what's money? Anyway you might need it in the future.' He winked at the salesgirl. 'That dress was designed with you in mind.'

As they left the store, Ed decided that Cathy needed new shoes, an evening bag, gloves, and new perfume. 'But I don't need them,' cried Cathy.

Ed wasn't listening. 'After the show, we'll go to a brand new restaurant that I discovered the other night. They've got a belly dancer there, should bring back a few old memories.'

'You're spoiling me.'

'And why not? If I get pleasure from giving, why can't you accept without protesting?'

'I'm sorry,' said Cathy, and got into the Rolls while the chauffeur held the door open for her.

Later at Wembley, Ed collected some fan mail, opened a couple, and then left the rest on the table. Vic breezed into the room. 'Great party tonight.'

'Not going,' replied Ed. 'I'm taking Cathy out.'

'You've got to go; you're the main attraction.'

'I want a quiet evening with my wife.'

'But you've got an interview to do.'

'No, you're not fucking up my plans.'

'But you have to go.'

'I'm not interested in your interview, and if you give me any more shit, I'll leave and you won't have a show.'

The situation was made worse by a photographer entering the room accompanied by two beautiful, young blonde girls. Cathy had left the room minutes earlier to get some drinks and was horrified on her return to find the two girls undressing a protesting Ed. One of the girls was on her knees unzipping his trousers and, for a minute, Cathy thought she'd walked in on another orgy.

She placed the tray down on a table, being careful not to spill the drinks, grabbed the girl by her hair, and propelled her across the room. The angry girl protested that she was trying to help Ed into his Lurex suit, to which Cathy responded sarcastically, 'and you have to kneel down to do it?'

The ruffled girl got to her feet, and Cathy thought she was going to retaliate. Noticing Cathy's condition, she didn't, but still fawned over Ed who yelled at Vic, 'get 'em out.'

Vic ushered the girls out. They were furious. It had been Vic who had set up the photo session. One of the girls shouted, 'freaks, rejects, sixties has-beens, boring old men.'

'Silly cows,' grunted Romany, combing his hair.

'Those "silly cows" are your public,' said Vic, scathingly.

'Fuck off, Vic,' snapped Ed, donning his Lurex ensemble.

Cathy collapsed into a chair; this pregnancy was tiring her. Earlier in her pregnancy she'd received bad news. She had cancer of her uterus, and the doctor had wanted a termination carried out. He was unable to treat the cancer because of the baby and felt that if she continued the pregnancy, she was putting her own life in danger. He wanted Ed to step in, but Cathy said that he was not to be told and that the treatment could begin once the baby was born. 'My husband has been under a lot of strain lately and he's set his heart on this baby. If you remove my womb, there will be no more children and it's alien to me to abort a human life.'

Her doctor was not happy. 'What about the risk to your life?'

'The baby's life is more important to me,' replied Cathy, placing her hands on her stomach.

The doctor realised that Cathy was determined, and offered her an alternative. 'We can perform a caesarean when you are seven months gone. Most babies can survive with care at that stage, and we'll remove your uterus and baby at the same time. Meanwhile we'll monitor the cancer and, if it puts on a spurt, you may wish to reconsider your decision.'

Cathy was scared but she was determined that the baby would not be aborted. She shook her head as the doctor added, 'it's your body, but I want you to know that we're here for you just in case you later want to reconsider your decision.'

Cathy told the consultant, 'I won't, but I will agree to your second version. I'm strong and I'm already three months gone. I feel fine and it's only another four months. I don't think it'll grow that fast. Could it harm the baby?'

'No, you're the one at risk.'

Cathy shook the doctor's hand. 'That's okay then.'

Ed brought her back to earth from her recollection, saying, 'come on baby, time to go.' She smiled, and they headed for the stage.

As the curtain went up there was a huge cheer. They opened with *The Chain* by Fleetwood Mac, followed by *Dreams*, and then Cathy left the stage and sat on a chair, thoughtfully provided by a roadie. She was able to rest for twenty minutes, and reflected on her desire to keep the cancer a secret from Ed. And she wondered why he was so secretive about the safe in the library. It seemed as if there was a sinister secret being hidden there.

She was six months gone now and would be glad when the surgery was carried out. According to the doctor, the baby was fine and the operation date had been set. Ed would be told that the baby was stressed so that there would be no questions asked. Vic nudged her. 'Come on, honey,' he said.

Cathy got to her feet; her back hurt, her ankles were swollen, and she was so looking forward to a quiet night with her husband instead of the usual final night razzamatazz. She smiled and strode out on stage to the opening bars of *River Deep, Mountain High*.

The performance was hot; they both put their heart and soul into it. Vic had talked Ed into attending the party for the interview, and he had relented on the understanding that he left as soon as it was over. Vic grunted, and said that if that was the best on offer then he would have to accept it.

He was unsettled though; Ed and Cathy were great on stage together and he hated the idea of them leaving his stable. He wished that Cathy had left Ed in the mental hospital. He could have put her with anyone and she'd still sound good. Right now she was rivalling Ed with her voice.

He sat close as the interview was conducted, chipping in now and again. Ed wanted this over as soon as possible and ignored all of the booze and drugs that were on offer. The usual questions were asked, and then the reporter addressed Cathy. He spoke of their son, and then asked how much contact Cathy had with her other two sons. She replied that she saw them every other weekend at her home. 'They adore their step-brother, and Michael loves riding the pony. As for Steven, Ed is teaching him to play the guitar. We've taken them to Disneyland and many other places so I think everyone is happy on that note.'

'But you've travelled extensively with Ed on tours. Rumour has it that you knew him from the sixties and that you've been conducting an affair ever since.'

'Rumour is wrong,' said Cathy.

'Interview over,' said Ed. 'We're leaving.'

'Didn't you have another child, Cathy?' the interviewer felt as if he'd touched a nerve.

Cathy flinched, thinking how dare he speak of my deceased daughter.

The photographer was hovering nearby and noticed Ed getting rather twitchy. 'My wife's past has nothing to do with our gig tonight,' he said. 'Goodbye.'

He helped Cathy to her feet, and they walked towards the door with the reporter and photographer in hot pursuit. 'But shouldn't the other kids live with you? Ed's loaded, and how did your daughter die?' Cathy was really getting stressed now. The reporter stood in front of Cathy blocking her path. 'Can't you give me an answer?' he said.

'Move or you'll get your answer,' snapped Ed.

The reporter moved and then restrained Cathy by grabbing her arm. 'Get off my wife,' warned Ed.

Feeling the tension in the air, the photographer moved closer. Seconds later, he got his front page photo. Ed hit the reporter on the jaw in a fury, which knocked him over and broke his glasses, leaving him dazed. Romany laughed. 'That livened things up.'

After an enjoyable cabaret and first class meal, Cathy and Ed drove home and peeked in at the nursery. Cathy smiled when she saw her son asleep; he'd kicked his covers off so she tucked him in. He looked so peaceful, angelic, and secure that her thoughts went back to her other sons. Tears filled her eyes as she thought about them and the reporter's comments. 'Hey honey, you mustn't distress yourself. What is it?'

'Nothing,' lied Cathy. 'I'm fine.'

Ed turned her to face him. 'Don't worry, this really is the end. When we get back from France, we'll be free.' They left the nursery, and after a nightcap went to bed. Ed reached for Cathy. 'How's junior?' he asked.

'Kicks a lot,' she replied, kissing Ed's cheek.

'Hey, what kind of a kiss is that for a wife to give her husband? Perhaps I should go back to the party if that's the best you can do.' Cathy raised her hand to slap him, but he caught her wrists and kissed her passionately. She responded immediately, kissing him fervently and causing Ed to shake with desire. His hands slid over her breasts and she moaned with pleasure as he kissed her all over. Every sensation possible built up inside her, and her breathing speeded up as his tongue found her. She was already climaxing as Ed entered her, and she convulsed as he penetrated deep inside her. She felt him growing before bursting inside her, and she passed over the threshold, feeling as if she were dying. She almost lifted out of herself when Ed launched himself for the final time. She arched towards him and then sank with him.

'I love you,' he said, stroking her hair. Cathy snuggled up to him; she had a peculiar feeling in her belly. It unnerved her but she put it down to the after-effects of passion. Instead, she praised him for their gig and told him how proud she was of him.

France was just two weeks away. Vic had said they could leave as soon as they'd finished there, but Cathy wasn't going to hold her breath. So far there had been no mention of a replacement for Ed as lead vocalist, and Cathy felt certain that Vic would do his best to find them more work. Nobody seemed to know that they were using their get-out-of-jail-free card, not even Romany had been told. She wasn't feeling well and wished that the operation date could be brought forward, but she knew that France had to be honoured and so busied herself around the house and played with her son.

As France drew closer, Cathy felt worse. She was so exhausted that she wondered if she'd be able to work on stage at all, but somehow managing to find some hidden reserves of energy. What she couldn't understand was that the act of sex actually soothed her; it was the one thing that she felt might cause her some problems, but it had quite the reverse effect. In her husband's embrace, she felt better; pain-free and reborn. If she'd known the precise details of Seth's ritual, she would have understood.

Ed, however, knew exactly how it worked; they had to be together. One could not exist without the other and, joined together in the act of love, they were one. This was the complete bond, apart they became ill, couldn't function properly, and each one felt the other's physical pain. Consequently the sex act progressed as usual, much to Ed's delight. Cathy was becoming much bigger but as she was still just as enthusiastic about it, he continued to make love to her as much as she wanted.

The day before travelling to France, Ed drove over to Vic's to make sure that these were indeed to be their final performances. Cathy was packing, helped by her housekeeper. Mrs Shores gave a concerned look. 'You look very pale. Are you feeling all right?'

Cathy gave a wan smile. 'I'm very tired and there are only a few months to go now. I'm six and a half months gone, and I think they may be inducing the baby in a couple of weeks as I'm not carrying it very well.'

'Too much work,' said Mrs Shores. 'You need a good rest, not another tour.'

She went to the kitchen, and returned with a cup of coffee for Cathy. On her return, however, she found her doubled up on the floor moaning in pain. She was clutching at her stomach. 'It can't be,' she cried. 'It's much too late for a miscarriage. God it hurts.'

Mrs Shores helped her onto the bed. 'Shall I get an ambulance?'

Cathy shook her head; she was deathly white. 'No, I'm fine,' she insisted, but let out an agonizing scream. 'I think I'm in labour,

I've never had pains this bad. I think you should call an ambulance after all. I feel so weak.'

The housekeeper called her husband, who took one look at Cathy and realised that there was no time to wait for an ambulance, so he decided to take Cathy to hospital himself. They managed to get Cathy downstairs. She was screaming with pain and, once inside the Rolls, darkness enfolded her.

Ed had just reached Vic's house when he was beset by agonising pains. 'Got to go,' he said, realising immediately what this meant. 'Cathy's in trouble.'

Vic was amazed. 'I'll come with you,' he said, hoping that this was a false alarm as he wanted Ed and Cathy for France.

Ed was driving like a maniac, and Vic expected to crash at any minute. 'Slow down!' he yelled, 'or you'll kill both of us.'

Arriving at the hospital, Ed raced up and down corridors, scattering anyone that got in his way, leaving Vic to follow at a more leisurely pace. After discovering his wife's whereabouts, Ed rushed to her room. A doctor barred his way as he tried to enter. 'I'm Ed Gold, and I demand to know what is happening. Get out of my way,' he yelled.

The doctor eyed him with suspicion. 'I don't care if you're God,' he said in a thick Australian accent. 'I'm Doctor Hogan and I've got a very sick patient in there who needs immediate surgery; every second counts. Lunatics who scream their heads off don't help either.'

The door opened and a tall, sandy-haired man emerged. 'Which one of you is Ed Gold? I need a signature.'

Vic was astonished. Which one? Wasn't it obvious? Had they no idea who Ed was? 'He is,' he said, indicating Ed.

'How is she?' Ed asked, in a panic stricken voice.

'Critical,' replied Doctor Hogan, casually. He'd taken an instant dislike to Ed. In his eyes he stood for just about everything that he hated: tight trousers, coloured streaks in his hair, and even a touch of make-up. Was this a rock idol? Was it? He worked long hours himself as a dedicated doctor and as far as he was concerned, Cathy need not ever have been in this situation.

A young nurse was pushing a form into Ed's hand. 'Sign here.'

Ed stared at the doctor still stationed outside Cathy's room. 'Can I see her?' he asked.

Dr Hogan nodded and moved away from the door. Cathy lay motionless; she was so pale. Her eyes flicked open. 'Ed, I'm sorry,' she said softly.

Ed could feel a lump in his throat. 'You've nothing to be sorry about,' he said, taking her hand in his. 'I love you, and everything will be fine as soon as they've delivered our baby.'

Doctor Hogan cleared his throat. 'We have to give her a hysterectomy, her cancer has moved on faster than we thought.'

Ed could feel his legs giving way. He grabbed the doctor. 'What cancer? Why hasn't this been dealt with earlier?'

Vic restrained him and guided him to a nearby chair. 'I'm sorry,' he said, addressing the doctor. 'He knew nothing, no one did.'

The pre-med was kicking in now and Cathy was drifting into a contented slumber. The pain had been taken care of by drugs, and all she wanted to do now was sleep. The young nurse was doing last minute adjustments to the drip attached to Cathy's arm.

Ed was distraught, 'She will be okay… once the baby is delivered… I mean… won't she?' he stuttered. 'Why didn't she let you operate earlier?'

Doctor Hogan opened the door and Cathy was wheeled through it. 'In answer to your first question, I don't know. There are some things that money can't buy, and one of them is life. In answer to the second, she wouldn't let us abort the baby because she knew how much you wanted it. Once we remove her uterus, there'll be no more children and Cathy knew that. Her last miscarriage destroyed her. She felt that she'd let you down and was determined to give this baby the chance of life.'

Sobbing, Ed got to his feet and walked alongside his wife who by now was unaware of anyone. 'Can I go with her?' he asked.

'As far as the operating theatre and no further,' replied the doctor. 'I apologise for being a bit off-hand, but this should never have happened. However, you'll be pleased to know that your finances have made it possible to get the best possible surgeon. He's the top man in cases like this; if anyone can fix her up, he can.'

Ed shook his hand and then made a very unusual request. 'I want the placenta.'

The doctor shrugged his shoulders. 'If you're sure that's what you want then you can have it, but I would have thought that at this moment in time you'd rather have a coffee.'

'Coffee would be fine,' said Vic.

Doctor Hogan turned on his heel. 'Okay, I'll get the nurse to get some coffee and pass on your request to the surgeon. Never tried it myself but I gather it's full of nutrients.' He laughed at his own joke and left.

'Prick,' said Ed as a nurse ushered him and Vic to a vacant room. Ed got to his knees and started praying between sobs. Vic was praying too, but only that Ed would get to his feet; he looked a sight. He was grovelling to God.

'Get up,' he said. 'It's a bit late in the day for praying with your track record.'

Ed was becoming hysterical. 'You can't take her, I'm nothing without her. Please listen to me, if you're really up there.'

Vic's patience was exhausted. 'Get up, you're pathetic,' he growled. 'You're trying to barter with someone who has the power to take her away from you, who you can't beat up or murder. There's always someone bigger, you stupid bastard.'

Ed got to his feet and rounded on Vic, screaming a tirade of abuse at him. Vic's answer was to slap Ed hard around his face, the force of which knocked Ed to the floor. 'Pull yourself together; supposing the press show up? I can hear someone coming. Come on, be strong for Cathy.'

Ed got to his feet just as the nurse arrived with the coffee. He stared out of the window. 'She will live, won't she, Vic?'

'Of course, you just prayed, didn't you? Who is going to refuse the great Ed Gold anything?'

Ed sighed. He knew that Vic was trying to cheer him up, but somehow it wasn't working.

Later, Sir Guy Hartley came to see Ed. He shook Ed's hand. 'You have a daughter. The operation was a success and I think we've got all the cancer. I removed her ovaries and fallopian tubes too just to be on the safe side. Her uterus was in a bad way, but she's strong and she'll make a complete recovery given time. She's sleeping now but if you want to look in on her, that's okay.'

'I'd like that,' said Ed, and together they headed for Cathy's room. Vic went looking for the phone; he had cancellations to make now. Cathy was clearly unfit to go to France, and he could see that Ed wasn't going anywhere without her. For a second, he wished that Cathy had succumbed to the anaesthetic and died.

Inside Cathy's room, a young nurse was at the side of her bed. She left the room to let Ed have a little privacy with his wife. Cathy looked like a dead person; Ed hardly recognised her. Tubes and drip feeds were many, and she lay motionless. He kissed her and felt an overwhelming force of love envelope him.

'We've got a daughter,' he whispered. 'I wanted to be the first one to tell you even though I know you can't hear me. I love you so much and I'm now feeling the same as my brother. My family is all that matters. I've been selfish and vain and materialistic, but that's all over now. We can do anything you want, anything. You come first, the children second, and I'm a poor third. Please get better, Cathy, then we can concentrate on raising our kids. I thought Amara would be a nice name for our little girl if that's okay with you. It means 'love', and this little girl was made with so much love, wasn't she?'

He left the room as the nurse came in and resumed her position. 'I'll be back tomorrow morning,' he said to the nurse. 'I'm going to see my daughter now, and then go home to see my son.'

The nurse checked all the drip feeds and monitors, then nodded. 'Get some rest. I'll look after her.' He headed for the nursery and saw his daughter for the first time. She lay very still in an incubator; a miniature Cathy.

Vic stared at the baby. 'Daddy's girl.'

Ed wiped a tear from his eye. 'Cathy was prepared to forfeit her life to give me this beautiful little girl. I think I've finally grown up. All I want now is to get my wife and this little miracle home and live like a normal family.'

Vic listened, but inside felt that this was a five minute wonder. Ed collected the afterbirth and together they left the hospital.

Arriving home, Ed poured himself a whiskey and ate some of the placenta with relish. He actually loved it; he had started to get a real fetish for raw meat lately. Ruby the maid was horrified one day to see him tucking into raw chicken livers. She reported it to the housekeeper who told her to keep her nose out.

For the next forty-eight hours, Ed kept a constant vigil at Cathy's side. At times she appeared to be drifting away as if she was going into a coma. She didn't seem to recognise him which added to his concerns. When he had voiced his fears, he was told that it was still early days.

As the week drew on, Ed decided that he could make her respond using music. 'Get me all of the Small Faces tracks,' he ordered Vic. 'And as much Fleetwood Mac and Bob Dylan as you can, as well as some of our stuff.'

Vic was really pissed now. 'Anything else?' he said, thinking that if he kept Ed sweet, he might just change his mind about leaving.

'Yep, an art sketch pad and other drawing materials.'

'Why? Is she going to sketch in her sleep?'

'No, I'm going to sketch some pictures that might jog her memory when she does wake up. I'll do anything. She opens her eyes but doesn't seem to see or recognise me.' Vic grunted and left the room. That evening he returned with everything Ed had asked for.

Meanwhile in Wales, a happy Seth gloated. Cathy wasn't responding because Seth was holding her in a trance. He'd let her go when he was ready, but he loved the idea of Ed suffering.

Ed tried everything he knew. She was awake but not seeing. His efforts were rewarded, however, one afternoon when he'd gone to get himself a drink. As he returned to her room he could hear Stevie Nicks singing *Dreams*, but it sounded different. He could hear another voice. He pushed the door open and beheld his wife sitting up in bed singing along to the music, and in her hands she had the sketches that Ed had done. 'These are really good,' she said. How long have I been here? How's our baby?'

Ed was overjoyed; his darling was back with him. After three long weeks, the suffering was over. He put his drink down and took her in his arms. 'Oh Cathy, I thought I'd lost you,' he cried. 'Our little girl is beautiful. I'll get them to bring her to you.'

Cathy remained in hospital for another forty-eight hours, and Ed stayed by her side until she was discharged. However, the baby was to stay in hospital for a further week. To the couple, it seemed like the longest week of their lives, but the day finally arrived when they could take their precious bundle home.

The following year passed quickly. Ed and Cathy still did the odd gig for Vic, and recorded, but drew the line at touring. He still hadn't found a replacement for Ed; no one he'd seen had that special quality that he wanted. Mick wasn't really interested, and was quite happy working with a new band that he'd formed. Vic was watching them with interest. He also tried Kevin but he declined the offer as well.

Ed had never been happier. He really had grown up at last, and now shunned the social scene completely. Little Amara really was Daddy's girl and he thought the world of her, spoiling her rotten as he did the others. They went everywhere together, helped by the fact that Tony was much more flexible now. He could see the benefits of letting the children visit more often. It was 1981, and Steven, now eleven, was becoming a very good guitarist. He knew that the entertainment scene always needed good guitarists, and that with Ed's help he could certainly go places. Michael on the other hand was mad on photography, and Ed always saw that he got the latest and most expensive equipment.

Cathy and Ed were devoted to each other. They were now preparing to live their dream, sell up, and finally take to the road. The idea was to join Rusty and his family to start with, and at a later date move off when the time was right. Ed had picked out some state-of-the-art caravans, but Cathy still dreamed of a horse-drawn Romany caravan. It was only a dream though, and she realised that while the children were young they would have different needs. They finally picked out the ideal mobile home and prepared to make their dream a reality. Ed sorted out final gigs and recording deals with Vic, and Kevin agreed to front the band for a six month trial.

Vic was happy. He felt that Kevin could be the next 'best act of all time'. He was young and flexible; in fact he was Vic's perfect front man. However, Romany wasn't happy. He didn't like Kevin, but the rest of the band gelled with him. He was informed that if he didn't like it he could leave, but that he should seriously think it over as he wasn't getting any younger. Grudgingly, Romany agreed to stay.

All went well until December. Cathy caught a cold which turned to flu, and she was ill for about two weeks while steadily getting worse. In the end, she couldn't breathe properly and had to be taken to hospital where she was diagnosed with pneumonia. Ed was distraught. Here they were, about to fulfil their dreams in a few months' time, and once more they were thwarted.

In the end he left the children in the care of their nanny, and once more kept a constant vigil at his wife's side. He returned home at night, and on occasions Vic or Romany stopped by to keep him company. They tried to cheer him up but all he wanted was Cathy. He felt the need to return home every evening as he didn't want the children to suffer. It was bad enough Cathy being absent, so to remove himself entirely from them would be too much. He was always there to say goodnight and read them a bedtime story which Eddie loved, while Amara just listened, being too young to understand much.

Eventually, Cathy seemed to be on the mend but the consultant said her heart had been under a great deal of stress and that he wanted to run a few tests before he discharged her. 'You can pick her up late afternoon tomorrow,' he said.

Ed agreed, and after a long conversation with Cathy about future plans, he left the hospital much later than usual. He'd have to read two bedtime stories tomorrow.

Arriving home, Ed let himself in. His housekeeper was still up, waiting on news of Cathy. 'She's doing well and coming home tomorrow after more tests,' Ed informed her. 'I see that Romany's here; I'd recognise that Merc anywhere. Is he alone?'

'No,' replied Ada, 'he has two young ladies with him upstairs. He said that you'd told him it was all right. We didn't approve, but couldn't really argue as we're only staff.'

'I'm off to bed,' said Ed. 'He can let himself out. Goodnight.'

'Goodnight, sir. She watched him climb the stairs and decided to go to bed herself. Ed went to the nursery and lay down on the spare bed. He fell asleep, but was soon awoken by a real racket.

Romany was shouting at a sobbing girl that she was a stupid bitch and that he didn't play kids' games. Another girl complained that she wanted to see Ed. Turning on his side, Ed began to doze and heard Romany go downstairs, followed by his playmates. There was silence, and then more shouting and sobbing. Romany's voice boomed out. 'Go home if you don't want to play.'

'I can't,' cried a female voice. 'I've no money.'

'Hard luck then. You'll have to wait until I've finished with your mate,' shouted Romany. 'Come on, babe, let's have fun. I'm the best stud around.'

Ed rose from the bed. Romany was very loud tonight and keeping him from sleeping. He was going to break this little party up as he didn't want his children to be woken. Enough was enough. He wanted Romany out of his home so he could get some sleep. He was still fully clothed and went downstairs to the kitchen. He opened the fridge, and poured some orange juice. After drinking it, he walked towards the lounge.

'When do we meet Ed?' asked one of the girls.

'What do you want him for?' said Romany. He crossed to the bar and poured himself a whiskey.

'Don't we get a drink?' asked a girl.

Ed stood outside the door; from where he was standing he could see Romany's dates. One had bleached blonde hair that resembled candy floss, and the other was a very attractive brunette. Ed was about to enter the room, but stopped when Romany started boasting about his conquests.

'The trouble is that you young girls don't know what it's all about. Ed's not that great. I've had all of his birds and they've all loved it.' Ed froze in his tracks, wondering why his so-called friend was telling these lies. 'I fucked that stuck up model girlfriend of his several times. She didn't know what had hit her. Ed's always had the best women, the lead singer always does.'

Ed was stunned. He couldn't understand why Romany was talking this way, and wondered if it was the booze talking. Romany laughed. 'Faye was a beautiful girl but as cold as ice, hadn't got a fucking clue. I think my brother Rick might have had a hand in that sweetie jar too. Every bird that Ed's had has had their eyes opened once I've been with them.'

Ed was angry; he was slagging off his sexual prowess. How dare he, and what did he mean, every bird? He couldn't include Cathy; Romany had always known that Cathy was off limits. The girls wanted to leave and had asked to use the phone to call a mini cab as it was Ed they'd wanted to see. 'I suppose Ed might be at the hospital,' said the brunette. 'The papers said Cathy had got pneumonia. I hope she gets better soon. She seems so nice; Ed must really love her.'

Romany ignored the request for the phone and slumped into an armchair. 'He does love her,' he said. 'The beautiful Cathy. I first set eyes on her in 1968, fancied her like crazy, but she only had eyes for Ed. I tried hard but she wouldn't respond to me. I was gutted; thought this one had all the allure of a real horny bitch.'

They listened as Romany continued. 'I almost gave up, and then in 1973 my dream came true. Cathy wasn't into drugs so when I gave her some pills for a headache she went under pretty quickly, in fact, so much so that she thought I was Ed. After the most mind-blowing sex, she burst into tears when I switched on the light and revealed my true identity. I told her that she was the best fuck I'd had in ages and she was horrified; you should have seen her face. I thought it was hilarious, the fact that the silly cow was crying her eyes out when she'd just experienced multiple orgasms and been tearing at my back, screaming for more.'

'We don't believe you,' said the girls in unison. 'Can we use the phone for a cab, or are you taking us home?'

'No way,' replied Romany. 'You were both bloody useless. The phone's in the hall.'

Ed slipped out of the front door, shutting it quietly behind him. He wanted to pulverise Romany, but needed the girls out first. Seconds later, he came back in again and slammed the door as though he had just arrived. He walked into the lounge. The two girls looked bored out of their skulls, but brightened when they saw him, saying that they'd been fans for years.

'Well that's nice,' Ed said, 'but it's very late and I'm bringing my wife home in the morning. I must get some sleep. We'll have to do this another time when Cathy's here.'

'We need a cab,' said Beryl, the blonde girl.

'Isn't Romany going to take you home then?' he asked. The girls shook their heads. 'Oh of course he's not, he never does. He screws what he can, and then leaves them to their own devices. He's a user; still, looking at him I don't think he'd be safe behind the wheel. Tell you what, I'll ring for a cab for you.'

Romany was uneasy. Ed had never spoken about him like that before. He wondered if Ed had been there the whole time. He hoped not, as he'd been pretty graphic about Cathy. Ed left the room and called for a cab, then returned with some autographed photographs. The girls were over the moon with them, and very soon their cab arrived. Ed kissed them both goodbye, and then returned to his friend in the lounge. Closing the door, he walked to the bar and poured himself a whiskey. He eyed his friend, feeling only hatred. 'Let's talk,' he said, pacing the floor.

Romany grinned. 'Okay pal, fire away.'

Ed sank the whiskey in two gulps and poured himself another. He continued to pace, making Romany very uneasy. 'Romany, my good friend, we've been best mates most of our life, right?'

Romany was now getting very anxious. Ed was looking at him in quite a menacing way. 'Right, close mates, and we've always shared everything,' he replied.

'So have you ever been jealous of me? My brother and his wife always thought you were.'

'No, I never needed to be jealous; we've always been honest with each other.'

'Are you sure?'

'Best mates don't get jealous.'

'What about women?'

'I've had my share, and most of yours when you've passed them on.'

'But what about the ones I haven't passed on?'

'You're talking in riddles.'

'Am I? Are you sure? I mean, haven't you sometimes wished that you could have a bite when I wasn't looking?'

'Well, Faye was a turn on but she was with you, so although it was very tempting I couldn't betray you.'

'Really? Because I was here earlier and had to go out to the car as I'd left my jacket in there, and I could have sworn I heard you say that you'd fucked her several times.'

'I said that to impress the chicks. I wanted some action, that's all. How's Cathy? Great that she's coming home tomorrow.'

'Did you know that I once killed a man for wanting her? That was Hank's big mistake. I always said that I'd kill anyone who tried to touch her, so I snuffed his life out. I attempted to do the same to Silver, and as for poor Kevin, well he was innocent and look what I did to him. So what do you think I'd do to someone who actually had taken advantage of her?'

'It was a joke, Ed.'

'Disrespecting my wife is a joke? Drugging her is a joke? And fucking her while she's so out of it that she thinks you're me is an even bigger joke? Can you remember what Kevin's face looked like? You were there at the time, weren't you?'

'Hank was electrocuted. Sammy fancied her, and so does Kevin.'

'I fixed Hank's mic. I would have cut Silver up if he hadn't had a pistol under his pillow, and I was wrong about Kevin. He stayed because he thought that Cathy might miscarry.'

'You've only got his word for that.'

'I've got Cathy's too. Now get up.' Romany got to his feet and Ed struck him on his jaw, knocking him back down again.

'Get up,' screeched Ed. Romany staggered to his feet.

'It didn't happen,' he cried.

'Liar!' screamed Ed. 'Tell the truth.' He hit Romany over and over again until his face was a bloody mess. He slumped to the floor, terrified, as Ed yanked him to his feet and hit him yet again. This time he crashed through a display cabinet, smashing several items and causing glass to fall everywhere. Ed yanked him to his feet and hit him so hard that he half somersaulted over the sofa. He was flat on the floor as Ed rained blow after blow on him.

'No more,' screamed Romany. The noise awoke the staff, and they rushed into the room as Romany once more staggered to his feet. 'Ed, no more,' he pleaded.

But Ed wasn't listening. 'So Cathy screams for more, does she? Well, you're going to scream until you're dead.'

The staff looked on, not knowing what to do. They didn't know whether to call the police, or let Ed continue to batter the man that everyone hated. Ed's chauffeur tried to get in between them and caught an unlucky blow as Romany tried to defend himself. Ada screamed as her husband fell and hit his head. His wife bent over him and looked up at Ed. 'Leave him, Mr Gold. He's not worth it, he never was,' she sobbed. Ed's concern was now for his chauffeur, and the fight went out of him. He sat down deflated as Romany ran, or rather staggered out of the room.

After checking that his chauffeur was all right, Ed wandered out into the garden; he needed fresh air badly. About ten minutes later, Romany followed him, having cleaned his face up as best he could. 'Ed, I'm sorry, I'd had too much to drink. I didn't know what I was saying.'

He extended his hand but Ed turned away. 'Get out,' he cried. 'I quit everything, and you can tell Vic why.'

Romany tried once more to reconcile, attempting to put his arm around Ed's shoulders but he was shoved away and knocked to the ground. He got to his feet. 'But Ed, nothing happened.'

'Romany, leave now while you're in one piece or I won't be responsible for my actions. You took the only thing in life that was precious to me, and if I ever see you again, I'll kill you. Cathy is my everything; you didn't need to do what you did. I guess my brother was right about you. He said if I had something, you had to take it away because you were jealous of me. Tell me, did you fuck Jenny and Rosaleen too?'

Romany could feel blood running down his cheek again. 'No,' he replied, 'or Faye or Cathy; it was just talk.'

'Really, well Faye and Cathy were both scared of you, and I used to think that they were overreacting but I know different now. Get out. I don't ever want to see you again.'

Once more, Romany extended his hand but Ed turned his back and walked towards the house. He went white with anger and swung Ed around. 'Okay,' he said. 'Just for the record it did happen. I wasn't interested in Jenny or Rosaleen, but the other two I was. I had your wife twice and if I'd had my way it would have been more. Remember Vic's birthday in 1973? Yes, I had Faye that night and several times after and, as for Cathy, I got her so out of her head that she really thought that I was you. She was great, and the only reason she cried was that she felt guilty when she realised her mistake. But you see Ed, it gets better. In Los Angeles, my brother and I both had her. The funniest thing was that we fed you a drug cocktail, and you were so doped up that you didn't even notice. She protested but we told her that if she wouldn't play we'd tell you she was the one who had initiated it, so she was scared shitless and heavily drugged. We even made her snort coke that night. God, how that woman can suck a cock; it's out of this world. She had multiple orgasms that night until Rick decided to spice things up a bit.'

Ed stared at Romany, trying to believe that he was lying. 'What did you do to her, you evil, twisted bastard?'

Romany burst into laughter. 'What do you think?'

'Tell me, you fucking sicko,' cried Ed.

Romany couldn't stand up for laughing. 'Well, you see, I pulled Cathy on top of me and as you know Rick is bi-sexual, so he decided to treat her as if she were a guy. She was screaming, telling Rick to stop. She said that he was hurting her and in the end she was pleading and begging, tears were streaming down her cheeks. He really gave it to her Ed; she hated it and was screaming for you to come and help her, but as usual you were out of it. Rick kept going and so did I, she was a great sandwich. We let her go in the end when we'd had our fun; she was in such a state of shock when Rick pulled out. She was in a lot of pain too, but I still made her give me head, even though she was crying. In fact it was quite nice feeling her sucking and her tears trickling onto me at the same time. Rick thought it was hilarious; he's a bit of a sadist and told her that he'd taken her virginity. Funny, eh? So you see Ed, we had our fun and you were none the wiser.'

'For the last time, get out or you're dead!' screamed Ed.

Romany turned on his heel and left. Stunned and speechless, Ed returned to the house. He poured himself a stiff drink. He certainly needed one. Ada was on her hands and knees with a dustpan and brush attempting to clear up the broken glass around and inside the display cabinet.

He swigged his whiskey down and then returned to the nursery. Amara awoke and started to cry. Ed picked her up and held her to him. 'Daddy's here, and Mummy's coming home tomorrow.' He soothed her and soon she drifted off to sleep and he put her back to bed. He gazed at his child. Cathy had risked her own life to give him this little girl. How he loved her. Whatever Romany had done, changed nothing. If the twisted guitarist had thought that by revealing her secret, it might tear them apart, he was wrong. Cathy was the victim. She had cried out for him to come to her aid and he hadn't heard her. He'd let her down, but then he had never believed that Romany could be so evil.

His head was aching and his eyes stinging, he was past being ready to sleep and all he could picture was Cathy screaming for help as she was being abused. He decided to go back downstairs and make some black coffee. Ada was still clearing up in the lounge when the phone rang. Ed answered it, and moments later replaced the receiver, ashen faced. Ada got to her feet, asking if he needed anything, but Ed shook his head. 'Cathy's had a relapse and she's asking for me. I have to go.'

Ada put her hand to her mouth, shocked. 'Shall I wake my husband; he can drive you.'

Ed shook his head. 'Let him sleep,' He picked up his car keys and went out. Getting into his sports car, he roared off at top speed. He was scared, tears were streaming down his cheeks. He felt confused and his mind switched to the very first encounter with his beloved. The smiling gypsy girl who had delighted at his rendering of all of her favourite songs, the field where they'd first made love to *Itchycoo Park*, their hippy wedding, the encounter with Seth, the pain when he'd found out that she'd left him, the joy on reconciliation. He remembered his first encounter with Sandy when she'd knocked him flat at Bacton, the happy days spent at the caravan, their delight in finding the Chelsea flat, and the sadness of his descent into insanity and controlling jealousy. He was starting to get chest pains that he'd never had before. He recalled America, Hank, Sammy, drugs, and paranoia.

The chest pains were getting worse so he tried to ignore them as his mind reverted to Sandy's death and his attempted suicide. Kevin and Cathy as Platinum, his joy in his dream wedding to Cathy, Eddie's birth, his stupidity in playing around, the haunted look as Cathy discovered him mid-orgy. He'd never forget the agonized look on her face, and his attempt to end Kevin's life because he thought he was having an affair with his wife. After struggling with him, she'd fallen down the stairs and lost their baby. He had killed that baby; what a sicko he was.

She'd lost yet another baby only months later, and throughout all of his outrageous behaviour, she'd stood by him. All he'd given her was stress and, even when she had cancer, she'd put the life of her unborn baby before her own because she knew how much he'd wanted one. She was an angel.

The chest pains were getting unbearable. He accelerated; he had to reach the hospital. He wished now that he'd let his chauffeur drive him. The pain stabbed at him again. What had the clairvoyant said about a dark man destroying him? Romany was dark. He'd been nursing a viper to his bosom for years.

There was that pain again. He was soaked in sweat, and felt as if someone was building a brick wall upon his chest. He had to make it to the hospital. 'Please God, help me,' he cried. Everything was spinning around him now and he realised what was happening to him. It was his heart. 'No!' he screamed. 'No!'

Through his fading vision he could see the gypsy girl laughing and spinning. 'I love you, Cathy,' he cried before slumping across the wheel as the car spun out of control and crashed.

Chapter Nineteen

Cathy had been sedated, and appeared to have gone to sleep as the nurse at her bedside watched her carefully. Suddenly her heart stopped; the alarm sounded and the doctor was there like greased lightning. As he worked on her, Ed died by the roadside.

A passer-by found the crashed sports car on the country road. It was too late to do anything. The driver was beyond helping. Cathy gazed at the ceiling; her husband seemed to be drifting above her holding his arms wide open. She wanted to get to him and felt herself begin to lift upwards. She stretched out her arms to him and, for a second, they were almost touching before she was being dragged backwards and downwards. The doctor sighed with relief; she was back with them again. 'Nearly lost her,' he said. I think we can breathe easy now, but keep an eye on her.' The nurse nodded and she resumed her place at the bedside.

Vic Lee surveyed the newspaper and handed it to a shame-faced Romany. 'Been in a brawl, have you?' he said. 'It's about time someone slugged you, the way you behave. You should grow up.'

Romany said nothing and looked away, then after a pause he said, 'I don't believe he's dead, Vic.'

Vic leafed through a book of phone numbers. 'Well he is. Ed was far too irresponsible. He was only in his thirties; the papers say it was a heart attack. Do you think Cathy might come back now and front the band with Kevin?'

'Ed is barely cold and you're talking about Cathy getting back into the fold? Don't you care at all?'

Vic leaned back into his chair and lit a cigar. 'Business is business. Of course I'll attend the funeral out of respect, but I shan't be visiting Cathy unless she does decide to front the band. Maybe you could mention it to her when you visit her. I think I'll ring Kevin; he may be able to persuade her. We have to look to the future. Life doesn't stop because Ed dies.'

Romany twiddled his fingers. 'It may have stopped for Cathy. She loved him.'

'What do you know of love?'

'Not much, but I do know they were both very much in love.'

'Oh well, she'll recover. Kevin can help her. I'll get him to pay her a visit in hospital. Both of her parents are dead so she'll need someone there. I doubt that she even knows yet.'

Romany left. He couldn't believe his conversation with Vic. The guy was just callous; he had no feelings at all. He knew that Kevin would rush to Cathy's side as soon as he heard the news of Ed's death so decided to go home and nurse his wounds.

Cathy was propped up in bed when Kevin arrived. She looked very tired, but was pleased to see him. 'Kevin,' she cried, 'what brings you here?'

Kevin kissed her forehead and seated himself beside her bed. 'Came to see how you were.'

'I've got to stay in for a bit longer, for more tests. I was going home today but apparently I had a heart attack last night. Can you bring the children in to see me? Ed can't.'

'Why did you say that?' asked Kevin, alarm bells going off in his head.

In a choked voice, Cathy said, 'because he's dead. I know it.'

'Who told you this?'

'The children are all I've got now,' she sobbed. 'Hold me, just for a minute.'

Kevin held the sobbing girl to him and he could feel his own cheeks getting wet. 'Last night they thought I would die, and right now I wish I had. I must have died for a short while because I remember seeing the doctor working on me and I was floating. Everything was blurred one minute and crystal clear the next. Ed was above me and I floated up towards him, we almost touched and then I was being pulled away with such a force that I had to leave him. Then he faded away and I looked up at this doctor who was smiling at me.'

Alarmed, Kevin got to his feet, and Cathy panicked. 'Don't go. He is dead, isn't he?' she cried.

Kevin nodded and Cathy stretched out her hand to him. 'Please stay. I need your strength.'

Kevin sat down; what else could he do. 'I'll stay overnight if you like, or as long as you want.' He was as good as his word, and remained overnight in a room next to Cathy's. At about twelve o'clock, he was awoken by something tapping on the window. He opened it and, seeing nothing, closed it again.

He looked in on Cathy and saw her sleeping soundly. Then, all of a sudden he was freezing cold, lost his balance, and fell. 'I need sleep,' he said to himself, 'but I could have sworn that someone pushed me.'

He then returned to his own room and went back to bed. Suddenly he heard Cathy sighing, and she began to giggle. Kevin thought she was probably dreaming and went back to investigate. He sat on the bed but hit the floor again, feeling as if he'd been pushed as an icy blast hit him. He was wide awake now and saw that Cathy was still giggling and that her window was opening itself. As he got to his feet another freezing blast of cold air hit him and he fell, hitting his head on a bedside cabinet. Cathy rose from her bed and walked towards the window as if in a trance. She stopped in front of the open window and raised her arms as if embracing someone. She then appeared to be lifted up onto the window sill; she certainly didn't climb. Kevin approached her quickly and dragged her from the window, he knew that it was dangerous to wake someone up if they were sleepwalking but he also knew that they were three floors up and that she was as good as dead if he didn't intervene. She awoke in sheer terror, but Kevin held her close. 'You had a bad dream,' he whispered. After settling her back into bed, Kevin closed the window and heard laughter. Sick with fear, he went back to bed.

The following morning, Fawn and Rusty arrived. Rusty to make funeral arrangements, and Fawn to be Cathy's constant companion until she was well enough to go home. Kevin mentioned the previous night's happenings to Fawn, but as a clairvoyant, she felt that it was only natural for Ed to visit Cathy. 'Don't worry,' she said, 'I'll take care of her and I'll converse with Eden too.'

Kevin left feeling very uneasy. A few days later, Cathy was home and very happy to be in her own surroundings. Rusty had arranged everything, and decided that instead of hymns they would have songs. He and Cathy got their heads together on this, and it was arranged that Fawn and her daughters would perform *It's All Over, Baby Blue*, and that a tape would be played of *Afterglow of Your Love*, by the Small Faces. The minister was quite happy with that, and Rusty agreed to make a short speech about his brother's life and what he meant to him. Cathy insisted on having the coffin at home with the lid off. It was put into the library so that any of Ed's fans could pay their respects. They had to install a couple of burly gentlemen to keep guard in shifts, but although many people found this all rather macabre, it was what she wanted, so everyone agreed.

Cathy spent a lot of time in the library. She would have slept there if she could, but realised that she had a duty to her children too, so divided her time between them and her beloved husband. Many times she gazed at him, not believing that he was really dead. Here was the man who had pursued her everywhere, loved her, abused her, given her two beautiful children, and made love to her passionately. Now he was gone and she didn't know why or how. It was a mystery. It seemed impossible that a heart attack was the only cause. Many times she kissed him on his lips, wondering if he would wake up like the fairytale of Sleeping Beauty. He was stone cold, but she felt sure that if they were truly bonded as Ed had insisted, he would wake up for her.

She traced the contours of his face. 'You are so handsome,' she said. 'I don't know how I'll manage without you. I'll always love you, and there'll never be anyone else.' Her heart felt as if it'd been ripped out of her body, but she had to keep going for the children's sake.

There was a huge turnout at the funeral, and security was out in full force. The floral tributes were magnificent, and several rock stars put in an appearance. As the congregation entered the chapel they were greeted by a rendition of *It's All Over, Baby Blue* by Fawn and her daughters, with Rusty on acoustic guitar. Cathy heard and saw nothing, however, her eyes were fixed on the coffin. Rusty gave a beautiful speech, saying that his loveable rogue of a brother had finally found happiness as a family man, and he brought tears to several people's eyes when he recalled their childhood and escapades. He moved on to their hippy days and admitted that Eden was a ladies' man and had broken many hearts, but from the moment he'd set eyes on Cathy, he became besotted.

'He told me on stage the first time they met, "I want her", and guess what? In the end, he got her. My sister-in-law is one of the kindest, most beautiful people that I have had the privilege to meet, and her children, Edward and Amara, were the most wonderful gift to my brother. He lives on through them.' His voice was quivering as he continued his speech, and he broke down in tears as he left the rostrum. As he passed Cathy, he took her hand and kissed it. 'Thank you for everything you did for him.'

Cathy barely heard him; her attention focused only on the coffin. Suddenly, she could see Ed standing behind it. Her eyes opened wide. He wasn't dead, he was right there in front of her.

As *Afterglow* was played, he moved across to the minister, and Cathy felt as if he was joining in the song. Then the curtains closed around the coffin and it began its journey into the furnace. Cathy's eyes were fixed on the spectre, but then it was gone too and she heard a voice in her ear say, 'I love you.' She began to sob and had to be supported by Rusty as she left the chapel. Her heart was breaking, but she had confirmation that he was still with her.

Outside the chapel, she thanked everyone for coming and then headed home to find that Mrs Shores had prepared some 'refreshments', as she called them. Cathy thought it looked more like a banquet, and wasn't surprised to see her ex-husband, Tony, there as he loved free lunches. Steven and Michael ran to their mother and hugged her. They had bonded with Ed and were feeling a sense of loss too. 'Didn't bring them to the funeral,' said Tony. 'Didn't think it was a good idea.'

Cathy agreed, telling Tony that funerals were no place for children. 'Where's Ingrid?' she asked.

Tony was stuffing his face with sandwiches. 'At home,' he managed to say. 'Worse thing I ever did, getting involved with her.' Cathy walked away; she really didn't want to listen to his moans.

Eddie was with Kevin. He'd known him since birth and they had bonded a long time ago. Cathy thought that the striking resemblance of Kevin to Eddie's father helped. Even her other two children had asked if Kevin was Ed's younger brother. Cathy was in a trance. Wherever she looked she saw Ed. Fawn noted this. 'Yes, it's him; he'll never be far away. I'm so glad that you can see. True love never ends at the grave.'

Cathy took Fawn's hand and gave a wan smile. 'I thought I was going mad,' she said, and excused herself. 'Must go and see Eddie, he's such a little terror, but so loveable. I caught him the other day trying to put a saddle on his giant tortoise Wacky. The tortoise wasn't very impressed but I guess that while he's having fun he's not depressed. God knows what it must be doing to him inside; he loved his father so much. Amara worries me though; she won't eat and cries for her father constantly. She really was Daddy's girl and, although she's very young, she knows that he's gone. Sometimes she gazes into space and lifts her arms up, but when I try to pick her up she screams and points to something behind me.'

Fawn put her arms around Cathy and gave her a hug. 'Give her time.'

However, time wasn't on Amara's side, and forty-eight hours later, her nanny found her, stone cold, in her little bed. Cathy broke down. 'Why?' she cried, over and over again. The coroner's verdict was a sudden heart attack. 'There was nothing wrong with her heart,' sobbed Cathy. 'The only thing wrong with her heart was that it was broken.'

Everyone told her that sometimes this happens to a normal, healthy individual, whether child or adult. Fawn had remained with Cathy after Ed's funeral and now, once more, found herself comforting her sister-in-law. She'd had a premonition that this would happen, but couldn't tell Cathy as she was still reeling from the shock of losing Ed. She'd spent a lot of time in the nursery, and noted that Amara would scream non-stop and then suddenly stop, give a toothy grin, and settle. Fawn was aware that the child only stopped when she saw Ed's presence in the room. She felt quite sure that the only time the child would be out of her misery would be when she was reunited with her father. She often heard Ed singing to his daughter, and on one occasion had walked into the nursery to see Amara sitting up in bed clapping her hands and laughing. 'Daddy,' she cried to Fawn. 'Daddy.'

Out loud, Fawn had said, 'please don't take her, Eden,' but all she got was a blast of cold air and a chuckle which she recognised. Then the singing continued and Amara lapsed into a contented sleep.

A week later and Cathy found herself at another funeral. Fawn did her best but couldn't console her. The doctor gave her tranquillisers and other medication, but nothing worked. Many times, Kevin would be speaking to her and she'd go into a trance like state. He rang Vic and voiced his fears, at which Vic laughed loudly. 'She's gone loony just like Ed. If I were you I'd stay well clear.' Kevin slammed the phone down. Somehow he thought that would be Vic's response.

Cathy's recovery was a slow one, and Kevin moved in with her. He noted her response to her son; loving and clinging to him one minute, and losing interest the next. Vic began to visit and started pressuring her to return to work. She listened but declined to have anything to do with the entertainment scene.

One evening, Cathy spotted a light coming from the swimming pool area. She decided to investigate and heard someone call her name, but the pool was empty, or so it seemed. Switching the light off, she noticed a luminous glow coming from the pool itself. Kneeling down, she stared into the water and heard her name being called once more. It was getting louder and was coming from the pool and yet no one was there. As the voice grew louder, her ears began to hurt. Suddenly the outer door blew open and she was caught up in a gale force wind. Terrified, Cathy clung to the rail and attempted to stand up but found herself losing her balance as the voice thundered in her ears. The luminous glow was taking shape, a face stared back at her and she screamed as Ed rose from the water. Cathy tried to get to her feet once more but could feel herself being pushed from behind. She screamed as she hit the water and struggled as she was dragged under. 'No, Ed,' she cried, 'no.'

Kevin was getting concerned. Cathy had been missing for a while, and he decided to look for her. Just as he was getting up, Ruby the housemaid rushed into the room. 'Come quick,' she cried. 'Mrs Gold is drowning and I can't swim. I'm scared. She's screaming at somebody.'

Kevin ran to the pool and dived in fully clothed. Vic followed at a distance and found himself flat on his back as a strong gust of wind took his legs. Getting to his feet he watched as Kevin surfaced with Cathy. His jaw dropped when he saw that Kevin appeared to be wrestling with something he couldn't see. Ruby was terrified. 'He's come back,' she cried. 'I hear him every night, and Mrs Shores says it's just my imagination.'

Vic rubbed his hands together as if he were trying to wear them out or at least rub holes in his palms. With Ruby's help, he hauled Cathy out of the pool. Just as the wind had risen, it dropped, and Kevin swam over and got out of the water dripping wet. Vic went cold as laughter echoed around them, and he knew exactly whose voice it was. Terrified, Ruby fled, screaming at the top of her voice.

Vic rarely visited after that, and Kevin never let Cathy out of his sight. She was sedated most of the time but insisted that she spoke to Ed. She spent most of her time pacing up and down the marble hallway, around the garden and back to her bedroom.

She appeared to have retreated into her own little world, and Eddie hardly saw her now as Cathy never bothered with him at all any more. The bond between the child and Kevin grew stronger every day.

Cathy's mood swings were getting impossible. One minute she would enthuse over something, and the next deny any knowledge of it. Her condition deteriorated rapidly and the doctor said she was suffering from manic depression. His theory was born out a week later when she tried to slash her wrists, but Kevin managed to stop her just in time and ended up with a nasty gash himself. Fortunately, Romany was there at the time and managed to disarm her. 'Cathy, you're not well,' he said. 'Ed's not here; it's your imagination working overtime.'

Cathy lashed out at him. 'Get away from me,' she screeched. 'You're the cause of everything. You told him, didn't you? You killed him, you're evil, and you've destroyed Ed and me.' She stared at Romany, her eyes blazing with fury. 'Ed told me,' she cried.

Romany shuddered, and for a second thought he could see Ed standing by the door. He pulled Cathy to him. 'Ed's dead,' he snapped, over and over again. He shook her, but Cathy kicked him in the shins and broke free, then she ran into the garden, collapsing on the grass crying. 'Ed, help me.' The doctor was quickly summoned and he administered yet another sedative.

Kevin was miserable; his life had become meaningless. He loved Cathy, but she didn't return his love. However, he was not about to give up on her, and the next day talked her into going to London with Eddie. They had an enjoyable day, and for the first time in ages, Cathy did things spontaneously. He also persuaded her to go out with him the following night for a slap up meal. Vic by now had talked Cathy into singing again. He told her that it was good therapy, plus he knew it would swell his bank balance.

Meanwhile, Cathy wanted to know what was in the library safe. Ed had refused to give her the combination and Cathy felt that, as he was dead, she had a right to see what was inside. She rang Vic and asked him to send someone round who could get the safe open. She was curious, and Vic thought that there might be a fortune stashed away in it.

The very next day, the locksmith arrived to attend to the safe. Mick arrived at the same time, and Cathy threw her arms around him. Nearby, Kevin scowled. Cathy had never hidden her feelings for Mick. She adored him but showed Kevin no affection at all, other than the sisterly kind. Once the safe was open, Cathy looked inside and was confused by its contents. 'What is it?' she asked Kevin. 'Why would Ed keep all of this? I thought it was Seth that kept this sort of thing?'

'I don't know,' replied Kevin, 'but it needs an expert to divine it. Don't touch any of it. Ring Fawn; she'll know what it is.'

Cathy was scared and confused, and wondered if Ed was

into the occult. He'd never spoken of it, so she rang Fawn and then went into the garden, seating herself by the koi pond. Mick followed her out and found her gazing at the colourful fish. She smiled at him and pointed at them. 'That's a sanke and that's a kohaku. That one over there is a showa and the very large one is my favourite; it's a goromo. He's beautiful; they call it a goromo because it's a pattern that resembles a shroud. I guess the word is Japanese for shroud and that one is…'

Mick placed his arm around her shoulders. 'Forget the fish; I'm taking you out to dinner tonight. I've a hunch that Vic might be able to throw some light on that safe. He's a slimy bastard, and Ed probably confided in him so I'm going to ring him.'

They could see Wacky the tortoise approaching slowly from the nearby stable block. 'Okay,' said Cathy, 'but let's go back inside. If Wacky gets into the house we'll never get him out again. The gardener has to use a sack barrow to move him and, as Eddie encourages him to come in, the tortoise knows no different.'

Mick laughed. 'He's speeding up,' he said, as the huge reptile almost broke into a trot. Once inside, Kevin gave Cathy a hug. He felt she needed it as the contents of the safe were enough to upset anyone, especially Cathy who'd been denied the combination by her husband.

Mick rang Vic who agreed to meet the couple for dinner. Kevin once more felt left out as Cathy didn't invite him along. He saw the signs and felt cold inside. 'I'll wait up for you,' he said. 'Eddie will keep me busy.'

'No, don't bother,' replied Cathy. 'We might go onto a club later so I don't know what time I'll be home. You and I can go out tomorrow.' Kevin sighed. It was obvious why Cathy didn't want him to wait up for her as she still had this thing with Mick, and he guessed that tonight they wanted him out of the way for a reason.

That night over dinner, Vic asked about the safe. He said that he knew about the two reels of film but nothing else. Mick recalled

1968 and told them that Ed had been obsessed with Cathy, but that he wasn't aware of anything relating to the occult. 'He had a crazy cousin,' he said. 'I thought that he was the one who dabbled in that sort of thing. Ed's only concern was that he'd lose you, Cathy, and he wouldn't let anyone near her. He even accused me of trying it on with you, even though I never sampled the delights of your body, plus I was with June most of the time.' The waiter brought their starter which looked, and tasted, delicious.

'Ed spoke of a bonding ceremony,' said Cathy, dipping her spoon into the starter. 'He said that Seth did it. I remember visiting the cottage and toasting our marriage but the rest is blank. Ed said I fell over and cut my arm, and that he was also bleeding when he helped me up. Must have been a big piece of glass to have given me a scar this size, and Ed's scar was even bigger.'

'I think you were cut,' said Vic. 'Remember that Sammy Silver fiasco? Ed cut you then, and he seemed to remember more than you do, plus the fact that he appeared to know how to do it. I think you must have been drugged. Did you drink anything?'

'Yes, some strange concoction. It was rather nice. I had two glasses of it and then I remember nothing until I awoke outside the cabaret club. I did notice after we had the toast that Ed and Seth just sipped their drinks, and the last thing I remember was noticing that their glasses were practically full. Maybe you're right, Vic.'

'I think this Seth bloke is a charlatan. He made Ed part with twenty thousand pounds on your wedding day for two reels of film, and Ed didn't flinch.'

Mick pushed his plate away. 'Obviously something on them that he didn't want anyone to see.'

Cathy's mind was racing; she couldn't make sense of this. The films were both in the safe, so why hadn't Ed destroyed them? Something wasn't right.

'Cathy, you know that Ed was loony,' Vic said, sitting back so the waiter could remove their empty plates.

'Well, maybe Fawn can shed light on it, as well the other items in the safe. He wasn't loony, Vic, just disturbed,' insisted Cathy.

'Well, he had a fetish for afterbirths. He told me he'd taken Eddie's home and was going to eat it. I was even there in person when he was given Amara's. If that's not loony, I don't know what is,' said Vic.

The waiter brought the main course and refilled their glasses with champagne as Cathy and Mick stared at each other in amazement. 'Why?' cried Cathy.

'Because he was a complete lunatic,' said Vic, cutting into his steak. 'He said they were nutritious.'

'But I had cancer when I carried Amara. Let's change the subject; let's talk about work,' said Cathy, suddenly feeling rather sick as she watched Vic stuff a huge lump of steak into his mouth. Work was his favourite subject after all.

After swallowing the steak he said that he was going to stage a concert in Ed's memory, which delighted Cathy. 'You'll take part, won't you, Mick?' said Cathy.

'Of course,' he replied, 'how about you me and June getting a set together as a trio?'

Cathy nodded vigorously; she loved the idea. Vic scoffed his meal down and took Cathy's hand across the table. 'You will work with Z Tones doing some Fleetwood Mac numbers, and I want you to reform Platinum with Kevin. Oh, and I want you to do another ballet, this time with Romany. *Albatross* springs to mind.'

'Lovely number,' said Mick. 'We used to do it years ago; it's one of Fleetwood Mac's finest.'

Vic still held Cathy's hand and smiled at her. 'I want your son too,' he said. 'I know he's young, but Ed taught him how to play the guitar and I know Kevin still helps him. Just one simple number; it'll boost his confidence no end.'

He let go of her hand as the waiter appeared once more and cleared their plates from the table.

'I'll speak to Tony about it,' replied Cathy excitedly. 'What a tribute.'

'Now, what about Kevin? He might not want to do it after that mad attack Ed unleashed on him,' asked Mick.

'Don't worry, Kevin will do anything for Cathy,' laughed Vic. 'Don't you feel anything for him, Cathy? The poor sod's head-over-heels in love with you.'

'I do,' replied Cathy. 'He's brilliant with Eddie and my other kids, but I can't take things further because he'd want commitment, marriage, and fidelity. I went through all of that with Ed and I don't want it again, so I can't take him to bed for straight, uncomplicated sex as I'd end up hurting him. Of course I'm tempted, he is so like Ed when he was younger but I don't want to hurt him.' Mick took Cathy's hand under the table. Uncomplicated sex he could supply, and he hoped that finally he might have her. As they left the restaurant, Mick suggested going onto a club. Vic declined so, hand-in-hand with Mick, Cathy left and got into his Volvo.

After several dances and another bottle of champagne, the couple left the club in the early hours of the morning. Cathy had almost been swooning in Mick's arms during the slow numbers, and she was on fire when Mick whispered, 'is this finally going to happen, Cathy?' She sighed and nodded seductively. Time was standing still. Cathy had desired Mick since The Shelltones days, and now her idol of the sixties was taking her home for what looked like a very promising night of passion. 'I guess it's back to my place,' said Mick. 'You won't want anyone in your bed unless it's Ed, so I think that we'd both feel better at my humble abode.' Cathy nodded and hoped he didn't live too far out as she was so excited; how she needed sex. She felt guilty but, she told herself, she was a widow so she wasn't committing adultery. She still loved Ed, but knew that if he were in her situation he wouldn't have thought twice about satisfying his lust.

As Mick sped off into the night, Cathy closed her eyes and

was suddenly aware of Mick's hand on her knee. She opened her eyes and gazed at him, seeing desire in his. His hand moved higher, making her squirm, and they were both relieved when Mick pulled up outside a block of flats. After locking his car, Mick took Cathy's hand and led her inside the dingy building, where, once inside the lift, they were all over each other before the lift doors had even closed. Their lips were locked in a passionate embrace, and they were half undressed by the time they reached the third floor.

Mick's hands were shaking as he tried to get his key in the lock of his front door. He felt like a teenager again. Once the door was open, they tumbled into Mick's bedroom as they both shook with a raging passion. Cathy lay across the bed and felt him begin to kiss her all over. In Wales, he'd turned her legs to jelly and now she actually had him. Cathy was aware that this night was built entirely on lust, but it was just what she needed. They were both hot for each other and very compatible sexually. Mick couldn't recall the last time that he'd had a sex marathon, but kept pace with his lust crazed partner; she was insatiable.

The couple finally dozed off at about six o'clock in the morning and awoke about two hours later. After coffee and toast, Mick drove Cathy home before speeding off. He needed some sleep.

At home, Cathy opened her mail and was greeted by Kevin. 'Like some coffee?' he asked. She nodded, and Kevin noticed how happy and glowing she seemed. He headed for the kitchen and wondered if she would ever see him as more than a good friend.

Fawn arrived late afternoon and wasn't happy with the contents of the safe. 'This is the work of someone who hasn't a clue what he's doing,' she sighed. 'People shouldn't dabble.' Cathy surveyed the contents. There were various tarot cards, a beautiful gold locket which held two locks of hair entwined in it, a small box with a pile of what looked like finger nail clippings, two photos in gilt frames of the hippy wedding, and two wooden dolls with chains around their necks. In another box were two reels of film, and Cathy guessed that this was what Ed had paid for to silence Seth. Fawn explained that one of the tarot cards, the one of the devil, was not always a bad card.

'It can signify bondage, but it can mean self-bondage, and if you look closely at it you can see that the chains around the necks of the two people are loose so they can be removed at any time. As that card is right behind the dolls, I can only think that Eden read something else into it. Maybe he thought that it bound you two together or that he could make spells. He's giving me the impression that he was trying to manifest something, but I don't really know what. He was always interested in the occult, and Seth encouraged him. They practised lots of things which Rusty and I disapproved of. He read books on voodoo and sat with Seth many times with an ouija board. We tried to help him but you know what he was like, once he got the bit between his teeth there was no controlling him.'

'Seth's always been trouble,' said Rusty. 'He believes he's some kind of god. Megan used to say that on Sundays he would erect a cross, get his helpers to put him on it and leave him there for hours. He's crazy but clever. He brainwashes people into believing he has some sort of power. In actual fact he has none apart from a very uncanny vision that can project worldwide. If he gets inside your mind he has radar vision and will find you wherever you are. When he was about ten years old, he fell and knocked himself out and when he woke up he started to see all kinds of visions and predict happenings. I suppose some might say that he's some sort of seer, but not clairvoyant in the normal sense. He once held Eli in a trance for six weeks, and only let him go when he got bored, but he said he was teaching him a lesson. He certainly has control over people, and unfortunately Eden was gullible, so Seth was able to contact him just as if he was using the telephone.'

Fawn picked up the wooden dolls. 'Do you want me to dispose of these, Cathy? Tell you what, take what you want and I'll get rid of the rest.'

Cathy picked up the golden locket and put it on. 'I'll keep this,' she said, 'and I'll leave the two locks of hair inside. I find it quite moving that Ed had this. If I wear it, I'll still have a part of him, won't I? It may be only a lock of his hair but it's his and, as he'd entwined it with one of mine, we're still together. Oh, and I'll keep the wedding photos too. I suppose we'd better burn those two reels of film.'

Rusty was intrigued, and asked if they were blue movies, but Cathy's reply shocked him. 'Ed paid Seth twenty thousand pounds for those films,' she said.

Rusty was incensed. He'd wondered why Seth was at the wedding. That must have been his reason for showing up. 'Did this happen when you got married?' he asked, angrily.

Cathy nodded, saying that Seth hadn't been invited but turned up and demanded the money. She added that she'd been denied the combination to the safe, and Ed's secretive behaviour had concerned her. 'Ed said that the contents were private, and I thought it was probably porn, but last night over dinner Vic told me that he had paid twenty thousand pounds for two films, and that Seth was the beneficiary.'

'We need to view it,' said Rusty. 'There could be incriminating evidence on that film, and if Seth involved my brother in something demonic, I need to know. I'll use his bonding knife on him if that's the case.' Cathy was uncertain about the film's contents, but curiosity got the better of her and she felt that if she watched it, she could put the whole bonding thing behind her. It was either on the film, or it wasn't. She located the projector and settled down with Kevin on the cherry red chesterfield. Rusty set up the projector and film, and seated himself in the nearest armchair.

As the film unfolded, Cathy couldn't believe her eyes. The whole thing was nauseating, and she watched as Ed carried her into the room, completely naked and unconscious. Figures danced to tinny music, and as it slowed down they threw off their clothes and began to fornicate. A hooded figure dressed in long robes moved around the group carrying something in his hands.

'There's your cameraman,' said Kevin. 'This whole thing is fake; rituals are secretive. You don't film them; it wouldn't be allowed. I know very little about the occult, but I had a friend who did. He said that nobody even speaks about rituals, so a genuine member of any sect certainly wouldn't film it. Though why Ed would expose you to this I don't know.' Cathy didn't know either. She didn't understand this spectacle at all.

In the film, three females had now stripped Ed, after he'd laid Cathy down on a bed. Three males approached her and then there was a lot of swirling coloured fog making it impossible to see anything. Ed was panicking. He couldn't see anything either, and was worried about what might be going on around Cathy. He began to struggle with the three girls who were all over him.

'Seth!' he screamed, 'don't let them touch her.'

Seth had been standing behind Cathy throughout the whole episode, and he was now gloating, knowing that Ed was in distress. When the fog cleared, Seth's head appeared to have changed to that of a goat's. Its red slanting eyes glowed like the embers in a fire. He approached her, and the three men surrounding her moved away, joining the girls in an orgy. The whole thing got out of hand as Seth got onto the bed and mounted her, lifting his robes and giving the appearance of sexual congress.

Ed was like a raving lunatic, screaming, cursing, and sobbing while he was restrained by several girls who licked and stroked him. He nearly broke free at one point but others joined in restraining him, forcing him to watch Seth.

Rusty swore out loud seeing his brother's distress, and Cathy was upset. 'Tell me this is fake,' she cried. 'It can't be happening.'

Seth appeared to be having an orgasm as the cameraman filmed away. There was yet another swirl of fog and when it had cleared, he was standing behind Cathy once more. He pointed a bony finger at Ed, saying, 'Eden, take her, she is waiting, she needs you.'

Ed fell to his knees as his restrainers released him. 'I can't,' he cried, 'she looks dead. I want this stopped.'

Seth was joined by another figure, a female who had one breast exposed. She was very slim and wore long golden robes that trailed the floor. She had the head of a cat, and in her hand she carried a knife. Seth was cackling away and beckoned to Ed, who was still in a kneeling position, his body wracked with sobs. 'Eden,' snapped Seth, 'she's not dead, but she's as good as dead if you don't take her.'

'I can't.'

'She'll die if you don't; take her. I command you.'

With tears streaming from his eyes, Ed approached the bed and climbed onto it. He embraced Cathy's inert body. 'I'm so sorry,' he sobbed, and slid into her.

Seth was cackling and dancing. He was very excited. 'Raise your head when you are approaching fulfilment,' he cried, taking the knife from the cat lady.

The cameraman moved closer, taking in every expression on Ed's face. All eyes were upon him as he moved in and out of Cathy's lifeless body. Seth fixed his cousin with his one eye, and as Ed raised his head, he raised Cathy's arm. Cat Lady knelt down beside her with a small jug in her hand. As Ed made eye contact with Seth, the blade of the knife flashed and blood trickled down Cathy's arm and into the jug. Seconds later the process was repeated with Ed and the blood was mixed.

'Ed did this to me in America,' cried Cathy. 'How could he?'

Kevin cuddled her to him. He was disgusted with Ed. The music, dancing and orgy continued and some of the mixed blood was poured into a goblet and forced between Cathy's lips as Cat Woman sat her upright. It trickled over her lips so her mouth was forced open and the blood was poured down her throat. She began to choke and just for a minute, opened her eyes wide, staring at Ed who was still straddled across her. Then her eyes closed and she was laid down again. Ed drank the blood with relish as Seth informed him that he was now conjoined for life with the woman he loved. More coloured fog descended as Ed carried his beloved from the room, followed closely by the camera man.

Cathy arose from the sofa in a daze as the film ended, and Rusty put the second film onto the projector to check it was the same. 'Grand illusion,' said Rusty angrily. 'If my brother was in front of me now I'd give him the hiding of his life.'

'Illusion?' shouted Cathy. 'They both raped me.'

'Seth faked it. I bet he still had his pants on under that robe. He just did it to freak Eden out. He succeeded though; Ed was too scared not to obey him. I mean, he thought that you were going to die. Do you think that he wanted to have sex with you in that situation? No man would.'

'But Seth appeared to become a goat; the eyes were slanting and glowing like hot coals.'

'It's a mask; he would have put it on when the fog filled the room. That film has been spliced to add more special effects. He didn't need to drug you or put on a show. He's bonded several hippies, and the usual procedure is a cut on the hand, a prayer, and a toast. He's an illusionist and a sicko.'

'And Ed's as bad,' said Kevin. 'Rape is bad enough, but to drug the victim first so that she submits to it is worse.'

Rusty stroked his beard, deep in thought. 'I need to confront Seth with this. Could you drive us there, Kevin? If you can do that, I'll drive back. I know Seth is still at the same address because Megan keeps in touch with Fawn, so I know where he'll be.'

'My pleasure,' replied Kevin. 'This needs addressing.'

Cathy said very little. She was feeling guilty about her indiscretion with Mick, and she wondered if Ed would punish her somehow. He didn't, but that night Mick was involved in an accident and his car was written off.

The following morning, the trio left for Wales, and Fawn stayed behind to supervise Eddie. Driving through the beautiful countryside, they passed the cabaret club and stopped off to have lunch and to refuel the car. Cathy was feeling quite nostalgic.

After lunch, they headed for Seth's cottage and had to pass the farm where Rusty had lived for several years. He pointed to the empty field. 'Cathy had her hippy wedding there; it was a beautiful ceremony.'

Cathy then went into detail about it, making Kevin feel sick inside. It was as if Ed had never died. Rusty interrupted his train of thought. 'The cottage is just around the corner,' he said as they headed for a sharp bend in the road. Seconds later, the cottage came into view and Kevin pulled up. It was in a bad state. The porch looked as if it was about to fall down, paint was peeling everywhere, and tiles were missing from the roof. There were also several boarded up windows. 'Obviously the landlord doesn't visit that often,' remarked Rusty, getting out of the car.

Kevin got out and held the door open for Cathy, who looked around her. Rusty knocked on the door, and a very tired Megan answered it. 'He's indisposed,' she said, when he asked to see Seth, eyeing her visitors with suspicion.

Cathy felt sympathy for Megan; she wasn't very old but had the appearance of a fifty-year-old woman. Her clothes were drab, she had a pot belly, greasy, straggly dark hair, and her complexion was sallow. Rusty pushed past her. 'We'll wait,' he said. 'We've driven here from Surrey, and Cathy needs a few questions answered.'

Megan shrugged her shoulders. 'He's out there,' she said, pointing to the garden.

Rusty crossed to the window and began to laugh. He beckoned his companions over. 'Look, he must think he's Jesus Christ.'

Cathy followed his gaze and saw Seth bound to a huge cross. 'Look at him,' said Megan. 'I'm sick of this; it takes us ages to get him up onto that cross, and even longer to get him down. One day I'll leave him up there; he's bloody crazy. Tomorrow he's doing a kids' party with magic and balloons. Today he's the Messiah, and tomorrow he'll be the God of Hellfire!'

Cathy's memory was now beginning to kick in. She recalled the sofa with the goatskin across the back of it, and then she noticed the goat's head on the wall. Rusty removed it from the wall and put it on. He pressed a switch and immediately the eyes glowed. 'You shouldn't touch that,' snapped Megan.

'Just putting Cathy's mind to rest,' he replied, handing Megan the mask and opening the back door. Marching to the cross he shouted, 'get down, you son of a bitch.'

Seth was startled, but quickly recovered his composure and grinned. 'Cousin Rusty,' he cried, 'sorry to hear about Eden. Tell Megan to get my friends out here and get me down. I don't get visitors that often.'

Rusty marched back to the house, wishing he had an axe to chop the cross down so he could leave Seth flat on his face; he was disgusted with his crazy cousin. Megan met him at the back door. 'Suppose he wants to come down now; sometimes he stays up there all night.' Rusty nodded and Megan shouted up the stairs to Seth's friends.

Forty minutes later, Seth appeared, followed by his friends. 'Cathy,' he cried, 'what a wonderful surprise.' He sat down beside her and hugged her. Cathy recoiled, thinking that he could do with a good bath. Seth wound a tendril of her hair around his finger. 'You look so lovely,' he said, in barely more than a whisper. 'Sorry to hear about Eden; we all loved him.'

Rusty glowered at Seth. He wanted to knock him senseless, but needed answers first. Seth adjusted his eye patch and stroked Cathy's face. Kevin hated this man. 'Get off her,' he cried.

'Touchy, aren't we? Do you have designs on my cousin's widow? Because if you do, Ed will never allow it. I must say, Rusty, you're looking angry. I would have thought that finding a younger half-brother would have delighted you? Your daddy must have been busy; this guy is the spitting image of Eden.'

Rusty dragged Seth to his feet. He was fuming at Seth's last remark. 'Listen, you fake, don't insult my dead father. What did you do to Eden and Cathy in 1968?'

Seth pushed Rusty away, laughing, and spread his arms. 'Eden, take her, she's waiting, take her, or she'll die. The bastard obeyed me. I cut Cathy and then slashed him. I gave her to him. He's the demon, not me. I don't think he was too happy when the guys starting stroking his lady though, and when I slipped into her he went crazy. He begged me to stop. I wonder if Miriam cried out the same thing to him? I thought my performance was great, and Eden should have got an Oscar.'

'You sick bastard. You put him through hell that day and you simulated sex with Cathy which was killing him.'

'Simulated? Why do you say that?'

'You kept your robes on. If you'd had sex you would have been naked so everyone could see.'

'Clever, aren't you? I did as my cousin asked. He wanted it filmed; it wasn't my idea. He'll be back for her, you know.'

'I think you're sick and don't have any real power,' said Cathy, stung by Seth's parody of the ritual.

'Really? Then why did you always feel each other's pain? Feel the need to reunite every time you split up? Were ill whenever you were apart?' replied Seth, fixing his one good eye on her. 'You are a fool. He visits you often, and he'll come back for you and take you just like he took your baby girl.'

Cathy began to sob, and Kevin held her to him as Rusty grabbed Seth's arm. 'We could go to the police; blackmail is a serious offence. You conned Eden out of his money, not to mention the rape which is also a serious offence.'

Seth removed his arm from Rusty's grasp. 'But you said I didn't rape her. I'm a magician, a clairvoyant, a preacher, and a hypnotist, and I do bond people. In this case, things were different and Eden wanted spectacle so I gave it to him. The film looked pretty good. It was spliced to add special effects, and most people would have been taken in by it. Eden even left here with a phial of blood around his neck. He may have been upset earlier but he was over the moon when he left. He had the girl of his dreams and knew that she was powerless to escape him.'

'Mumbo jumbo,' muttered Rusty.

Cathy was shell-shocked and turned to Kevin. 'Maybe Ed did dabble,' she said. 'I don't know what to believe any more.'

'Believe what you like. You can dismiss it as Rusty does, or you can believe that none of this was illusion and that I slipped into that beautiful wet body of yours while an entity took possession of mine,' cackled Seth, smugly.

Rusty balled his hands into fists as Cathy stood up and faced him. 'Did you fuck me?' she cried.

Seth fixed the girl with an evil stare. 'Look into my eyes.'

A very pent up Cathy stared into his one eye before slapping him hard across the face. Seth reeled from the blow as Cathy struck him a second time.

'The first one's from me, the second one's from Ed,' she cried.

Seth was now howling like an injured animal. 'Ed? Ed? What about justice for Miriam?'

This was the second time Cathy had heard that name and it unsettled her. Rusty was fuming. 'Shut the fuck up Seth, or I'll shut you up,' he bellowed.

Cathy was shaking. Obviously there was a skeleton in the cupboard that he wanted hidden. Seth grabbed her by her shoulders. 'You want the truth? Well I'll give it to you. Eden wanted to ensure that he had you in life and in death. I did everything that he asked me to. I pulled out all the stops, including the film, but he never returned for it owing to the fact that you'd left him and he was all over the place. I saw him kill Hank and attack Mr Silver. As for your companion here, he would have been dead if you hadn't put a stop to it. He raped you, cut you, you lost your daughter in a road accident, and do you recall how you never responded after having your baby girl? You couldn't because I held you in a trance, I wanted Eden to suffer and he did. The money was nothing compared with what I did for him. Miriam was my twin sister, and Eden murdered her.'

He let go of her and she began to wail as Rusty ordered Kevin to take her back to the car. She was hysterical. 'If he's fake, how does he know all of these things?' she cried.

'It's all over now, Cathy,' whispered Kevin, reassuringly. 'Everything's going to be okay.'

Rusty emerged from the cottage, followed by a very distraught Seth who was staggering, his face covered in blood. He tapped on the car window and Kevin opened it a crack. 'The film was tampered with, but Eden was the evil one. Ask Jenny or Rosaleen; they'll tell you. He killed my sister; I saw him do it. He will return for you, and you will have to go to him and…' Seth's voice tailed off as Rusty started the car and left him standing in the middle of the road, waving his arms about.

Back at home, Cathy went straight to bed without saying a word. The following morning she was up early and glowing, enthusing about Vic's gig. 'Ed's life is to be played out,' she said, 'and as you're family I would like it if I had you on board. I want everyone that he was associated with in his career to perform.'

They were seated around the table eating breakfast. Eddie had already left for school. Fawn finished her toast and asked if she could use the phone. As she left the room, Cathy turned to Rusty. 'We need to talk; tell me about Miriam.'

Kevin got to his feet. He had no desire to listen to anything concerning Ed. Excusing himself, he left the room and Rusty faced her. He sighed and grudgingly began.

'It was 1951, and Seth and Miriam were celebrating their birthday. Their home was in Norfolk at the top of a cliff, and over the years the sea had reclaimed much of their back garden. Anyway, my parents took us to see them for their birthday party. The twins had been given many presents, and I think we gave Miriam a doll, and Seth a train set. Someone had bought Miriam a kaleidoscope, and she let Eden look through it. He loved it and didn't want to give it back, so he went into a strop, screaming how much he wanted it. We'd had a great time until then, party food, games, birthday cake and all that, but Eden wouldn't shut up. Mother tried to placate him, saying that she'd buy him a kaleidoscope the following day, but he just got worse. He pulled Miriam's hair, kicked her, yelled, and threw jelly everywhere until she handed it over, just to keep him quiet. We carried on playing musical chairs, you know, the usual stuff, and it was a good party. Seth's parents had booked a magician, but he arrived late and we got tired, so we stayed overnight instead of driving home.

'The following day, everyone slept in apart from Miriam. She was always up early and liked to stroll along the cliffs before breakfast. She was a sensible girl, so her parents knew that she wouldn't come to any harm. The adults decided on a picnic on the beach, and mother decided to stay on for a bit longer. My aunt was packing the picnic hamper when she realised that Miriam was still out and Eden had gone missing. Mother was terrified; she hadn't seen Eden disappear and was scared that he might fall over the cliffs. She rushed out of the house and went to search for him. About ten minutes later, she returned with Eden, screaming that Miriam had had an accident and we were to call an ambulance. Everyone was panicking, apart from Eden, who just sat on the floor with the kaleidoscope. I went with my aunt and we looked over the cliffs and saw Miriam lying motionless below on a small beach. It was a huge drop; no one could have survived a fall like that. My aunt and uncle were in shock. They couldn't understand how it could have happened. Miriam took this walk every day. How could she fall? It was unthinkable. Seth had come looking for his sister before her accident, and he must have witnessed something as they found him lying unconscious on the cliff top. He didn't speak a word for six weeks, and began to suffer memory loss. The picnic was forgotten, and Eden and I left with our parents to go home.

'Later that night, I heard my mother go into Eden's room. She was cuddling him, crying, "oh my God, Eden, what have you done? Poor Miriam". That's the story, Cathy. The jury's still out on that one, but I don't think Eden was responsible; he was only six years old.'

Tears were streaming down Cathy's face; she felt that Ed was capable of just about anything. 'Seth mentioned Jenny. I've already met Rosaleen, haven't I, at the mansion when we all spent Christmas together?'

Rusty sat back in his chair. 'Jenny was your predecessor. Eden met her when she was sixteen and they hung out together for years. She was a dancer and a folk singer. Eden treated her badly but she loved him so she allowed herself to be used. When he wanted a shoulder to cry on, he always went looking for Jenny. She was at the commune the night you married my brother. It must have hurt her as she always thought they'd end up together.'

'Then if she can sing, we need her at the concert. She'll be well paid.'

'She might not want to meet you, and she lives in Scotland now.'

'Well, she can deal with Vic then, but if she wants to meet me, she can stay here for a few days.'

Rusty gave a very deep sigh. Cathy was like his brother. When she set her mind to something, she saw it through to the end. 'Okay,' he said. 'I'll get Fawn to ring her.'

Fawn came bustling into the room. 'The girls think it's wonderful,' she said.

Cathy got to her feet. 'Lots of preparation to be done. I need to get started and make some phone calls.'

Rusty glanced at his watch. 'Time to hit the road, Mamma, thanks for your company, Cathy, and for coming with me to Wales. I've sorted out that evil cousin of mine, and I feel so much better.'

Cathy felt sad as the couple left. The house was far too big for her, and now it felt cold and empty. With Eddie at school, Kevin was her only companion, and he was driving her crazy with his gestures of love, such as the candlelit dinners, the flowers, and the surprise gifts.

Three days later, Cathy received a letter from Megan. Sitting down in her favourite armchair, Cathy opened the letter and started to read.

> *Dear Cathy,*
> *Seth keeps me in the background so I was unable to voice my opinions on your conversation. However, I was in the next room and heard every word. Seth is not into anything demonic, he suffers from paranoia and is unhinged, but it was your husband that was into the occult. They became blood brothers when they were in their teens, cutting their wrists and mixing their blood. In 1968, Seth intended to bond you just as he had others but Eden wanted a spectacle, something he could watch on film in private. He did kill Miriam, Seth witnessed the whole thing and it was covered up by Eden's mother. After that day he was mute for six weeks and he has never truly recovered from his twin's death. I know you think that he had sex with you but it never happened, the whole thing was simulated. Even the guys that were clustered around you were actors enjoying a free orgy with the girls. You were never in any danger but Seth had convinced Eden that you were. You were bonded, that part is true and it made Seth's day when he was able to convince Eden that you'd die if he didn't take you.*
>
> *Seth is clever and possesses a strange gift that enables him to get inside people's heads. He'd*

managed to do that to his cousin years ago and at times could control his every move. If you don't believe me about the true occultist, I suggest that you contact Jenny or Rosaleen as they spent many years with your husband and could tell you a lot. Seth should never have extorted money from Eden but many others would have done the same thing if they'd had the film in their possession. We make a humble living from our road show dealing in magic, illusion, spectacle and kids' balloon parties.

Remember it was your husband that wanted you unconscious and filmed, not Seth. Eden was the one that violated you while you were asleep. The rest of us were just putting on a show for him, most of them out-of-work actors and actresses. Please don't write back to me as Seth will open the letter and I will be punished.

Yours sincerely,
Megan

Kevin came into the room and she handed him the letter. After he had finished reading, she asked him what his opinions were. He kissed her on the forehead. 'You've got closure. Ed made you the victim in this film so obviously he wasn't the great guy you thought he was.'

He instantly regretted saying this as Cathy snatched the letter from him and screamed. 'How dare you talk about my husband like that. I loved him and he loved me.' She stormed off upstairs, leaving a very crestfallen Kevin in the lounge. She was angry, but he was right, she had been made a victim in Ed's twisted film. Saying that he wanted to watch it in private made Cathy feel sick, and she wondered if, on the nights he'd been working late and not come straight to bed, he might have been in the library watching it. It didn't make sense that he hadn't destroyed it, anyone else would have done. Ed was a control freak, an occultist and a sicko, but for all that she still loved him.

That afternoon, Kevin drove Cathy to the hospital, as a few weeks previously she'd been doubled up in pain and had had some tests done. Her doctor believed the pain to be caused by gall stones but wanted to run a series of tests to be sure, particularly as she hadn't been attending check-ups for the cancer that she'd had years earlier. She walked into the room with a smile on her face believing that her gall bladder was the culprit, and knowing that a simple operation would cure the problem. She left the room with the surgeon's words echoing in her ears, 'inoperable, six months, maybe nine with chemotherapy.'

Walking outside, she found Kevin sitting in the car. He looked concerned, but Cathy was not going to reveal the truth to him, knowing that he would be devastated by the news. Instead she got into the car smiling. 'Gall stones,' she told him. 'I've told the doctor I'll have the surgery after the memorial concert.'

'Is that wise?'

'Yes, I just need to change my diet and I'll be fine until the operation, and he's given me some pain killers. I'm in no danger, Kevin. You worry too much.' Cathy's mind was racing. She was going to die and she was never going to see her children grow up. There were so many things she wanted to do and experience, and just as she was beginning to recover from her husband's death, her life was about to be snuffed out. She sat in silence on the drive home alongside a miserable Kevin, who thought that she was ignoring him because of the way he criticised Ed that morning. Back home, a very scared Cathy went straight to bed and sobbed her heart out.

A month later, Cathy got a call from Jenny who said she would love to come and visit and that she would be honoured to take part in the concert. A week later she was on Cathy's doorstep with her face wreathed in smiles. She was attractive, with red, full lips, brown eyes, a small nose, and long blonde hair which was streaked with grey. Her appearance was that of someone who was caught in a time warp; her gypsy clothes reflected the sixties' hippy days but they really suited her and were colourful. Cathy bonded with her straight away and they discussed the set that she was going to do. They decided eventually that she would do a Joni Mitchell set, with Paddy and Billy backing her.

A car drew up outside, and Eddie entered with the chauffeur. He walked to the kitchen and returned with a pack of spring greens and an apple. 'Feeding time at the zoo,' said Cathy. 'Come and meet Patch and Wacky.' Eddie opened the French doors and skipped out into the garden, with Cathy and Jenny laughing and following close behind. Jenny was amazed at the size of the tortoise; he was huge and she watched as Eddie hand fed him. 'This is Daddy's friend, Jenny,' said Cathy.

Eddie smiled and looked up. 'Hallo, Jenny,' he said as he continued to feed his pet. Moving away from his tortoise, Eddie took Jenny to see his pony and said that she could ride him if she wanted to. Jenny declined, saying that she would be too heavy for the poor thing. 'Okay,' said Eddie, 'but we can go for a swim.' He ran back to the house, and shortly after returned with Kevin.

'Kevin, this is Daddy's friend, Jenny. Let's swim.' Cathy agreed that it would be a very good idea indeed, and very soon the quartet were splashing around happily in the pool. Jenny was struck with Kevin's resemblance to Ed; it was as if she was experiencing déja vu. She saw the way he stared at Cathy with love shining from his eyes, and felt sorry for him. She knew what it felt like to love someone and not have those feelings reciprocated.

After a swim, the foursome prepared for dinner, and then seated themselves at the dining table. Jenny felt out of place. The furniture was state-of-the-art; on one wall there were beautiful murals and on another expensive framed photos. Antique lamps adorned polished side tables, and on top of a mahogany bookcase was a large portrait of Ed and Cathy. The huge fireplace had an easy chair either side of it, and above it was a large family portrait. The easy chairs looked antique too; Ed certainly had provided his wife with a beautiful home.

Jenny wasn't used to all this finery and prayed that she wouldn't spill any wine on the highly polished dining table. The glass in her hand sparkled and looked rather expensive, her dinner plate was Wedgewood, and her knife and fork were real silver.

After dinner, Cathy opened another bottle of wine and beckoned her to the fireside. Cathy poured her a glass of wine. 'Let's have a girly chat. What was Ed like at sixteen?'

Jenny took a deep breath. 'Impetuous, had to have his own way, sprung things on you, loving one minute, unfaithful the next, and took off when it suited him. He decided to tour the Med and never told me or Rosaleen about it. When he came back, Rosaleen was married and he was extremely angry, so as usual he used my shoulder to cry on.'

'He didn't change much. He pursued me from the minute I met him. We hung out together for a week and, knowing his reputation as a bad boy, I thought we were just having a fling, but suddenly I had a ring on my finger and found myself getting married in a hippy ceremony. After that I was drugged and went through a bonding ceremony which I've only just found out about.'

'Nasty. Did Seth do it? He was always weird, but he doesn't usually drug people to bond them. He was a bit of a dabbler, but then Ed was right into that sort of thing. He played ouija boards, bought voodoo dolls, chanted, read the tarot and books. Sometimes he really scared me, the whole thing was creepy. I didn't like it at all.'

Cathy sighed; it appeared that Seth was right. She listened as Jenny continued, 'I saw your wedding. Ed looked very happy. I always dreamed of marrying him, but then I was a fool.'

'I knew nothing about you.'

'Well you wouldn't. He always gave girls the impression that he was unattached, but then I was just the shoulder to cry on, wasn't I?'

'He should have told me about you.'

'How could he? He'd fallen in love and wanted you. He changed that night; he came home early with Rusty and was very quiet. I was surprised; normally he'd be out late bedding some girl who wanted an intro to Romany.'

'Risky, you could have caught all sorts.'

'I never worried; he always used protection.'

'June said that, but he always went bareback with me.'

'Because you were the chosen one. The night he met you I thought he'd come back to be with me, but he went straight to Rusty's van to read his nieces a bedtime story. He came to me later and we cuddled up, but then he turned his back on me. Later, when he woke up, we did make love but he was very distant and for the rest of the night he was tossing and turning in bed muttering in his sleep: "Come to me, gypsy girl, I want you so much, I'd die for you, I'm so in love with you". Well I knew it wasn't me he was dreaming of, and the rest is history.'

'I left the day after our wedding due to problems at home.'

'I know, and when he returned from Bristol he called me and used my shoulder once more. He made it clear he was going to get you back, and then a few years later, Mick had his accident and he got lucky. Then he met Faye, and once more I was out in the cold, apart from the occasions when they split up. As soon as they reunited though, I was forgotten again.

'When I saw you in that dance competition, I knew he'd get you back because he'd never given up on you. When you won that night, and he was on the same bill, I knew you were cornered and that he'd get his own way. He used to say that you were soul mates and destined to be together, so of course when you went to America with him as his dancer, I knew it was a cover-up and that you were lovers again. I was surprised when he returned without you though. I guessed something was wrong, and he was still with Faye. Later that night he rang and then turned up on my doorstep, pouring his heart out and, of course, I gave him a bed for the night with me in it. What a fool I was.

'A few weeks later, I saw that Vic had a new act called Platinum and that you were one half of the duo. I realised that Vic was working you on the same bill as Ed quite a lot and I could see what was going to happen, so I decided that my shoulder had had enough, especially when you later got married and had a baby. I'd hoped to have an invite to the wedding, but I guess Ed didn't think enough of me to send me one.

'I moved to Scotland, but you had a bit of a bust up. I guess someone gave him my number because he used me like an agony aunt. He told me that you'd caught him out and he didn't know what to do. I replied that he needed to grow up, sort it out, and apologise, even to crawl and beg if he had to. I told him I had a new boyfriend and wanted to sort my own life out. He didn't like that though, and gave me a tirade of verbal abuse, said he wished he'd never met me, and slammed the phone down. That was the last time I heard from him.

'I'm happy now. I'm married; we don't have any kids but I have a son, Dylan, who was born when I was in the commune. He's fifteen now.'

'Oh, is he…? Maybe I shouldn't ask.'

Jenny laughed. 'He's not Ed's, Cathy, and I told you, he always used protection, even with me. I think in your case he was trying to get you pregnant so that you would never leave him. He truly loved you.'

Cathy felt very sad for Jenny and, after showing her where she would sleep for the night, decided they both needed a night out. She found Kevin settling in front of the television. 'Think you can handle two hot ladies?' We fancy going clubbing.'

'Anything for you, fair lady,' he replied, and went upstairs to get ready.

Later that night, while having a slow dance with Kevin, Jenny asked him how he felt about Cathy. 'I love her with all of my heart,' he said, 'but she doesn't see it, and I can't tell her because she's still grieving for Ed. She loved him more than life itself.'

'Give it time,' replied Jenny. 'I wish I were ten years younger.' Kevin laughed, but his heart was crying out to Cathy.

Jenny left three days later, and promised to return a week before the concert so that she could rehearse with Billy and Paddy. Kevin and Cathy now began to put in more and more rehearsal time; they were the two artists doing more than anyone else. Kevin had to spread himself between two acts. He had a whole set to do as Platinum, and also two sets fronting the Z Tones. As for Cathy, she had to perform with Billy and Paddy, dance to *Green Tambourine*, join Mick and June in a sixties medley, perform some Fleetwood Mac songs with Z Tones, and the ballet with Romany, a whole set with Kevin as Platinum, more songs with Z Tones in their second set, and finish with the Fleetwood Mac song *Gypsy*. Vic said it had to be the encore at the finish.

'When you met Ed you were dressed as a gypsy. You entered the dance contest under that name, and you always wanted to travel and lead a nomadic life so the whole thing's perfect.' Cathy agreed for once. Vic had finally come up with an idea she liked.

In total, Vic had fifteen acts plus guest artists. It should be a success, he thought, and after that he wanted to get Cathy back fronting the band with Kevin.

Kevin, meanwhile, was worried that Cathy was doing too much, but she assured him she was fine. She surprised him one day when she asked him to run her to the solicitors, but he didn't like to question her about it. When she came out she was beaming. 'That's done,' she said. 'I can rest easy now.'

'Good,' said Kevin. 'If you're happy, I'm happy.'

Cathy gave him a hug. 'You're great, Kevin. Now let's get home and rehearse.'

Everything went well until the week prior to the concert. Mick turned up to rehearse with Cathy, but Kevin was very suspicious as June hadn't arrived, and he was informed that she would not be showing up until the following day. Kevin wasn't very happy, and guessed that Mick had known about this all the time and was just trying to get Cathy alone before she arrived. He looked on as they performed *Everlasting Love*, an old sixties favourite, and *Bend Me, Shape Me*, finishing with *Love Is All Around.* Kevin thought the performance was good and that, as soon as June's voice was added, it would sound even better.

Mick joked, 'with those two standing next to me, love will be all around me.' Kevin forced a smile but he felt uncomfortable when Mick asked Cathy out to dinner and didn't include him as he knew what was going to happen. He was proved right when Cathy stayed returned the following morning looking very happy.

June turned up later that day, and Kevin relaxed. The four of them went out that night, and he noted that upon their return, Cathy was in a pensive mood. She was on edge and asked him to bring a drink up to her so he went downstairs to get one. His heart jolted when he reached the bedroom door and saw Cathy at the window, it was wide open and she was crying. She said to someone he couldn't see, 'how much longer? Don't torment me.'

Kevin crossed to the window and looked across the grounds. He could make out a figure under the tree and turned to Cathy who didn't appear to see him. 'Cathy,' he said, gently, 'Cathy.'

He guided her away from the window and sat her down on the bed; she appeared to be in a trance. He kissed her on the lips, and suddenly the window slammed shut. Cathy snapped out of her trancelike state and rushed to the window. 'No,' she screamed. 'Don't go, please don't go, I've waited for you for so long.'

Kevin made his way over to the window; he'd waited too long himself but for something entirely different. He pushed Cathy away from the window and opened it to get a better look. He caught his breath and felt his heart miss a beat. There was no mistake. He'd seen Ed cremated nearly a year ago, but there he was, under the tree looking up. In desperation, he shouted, 'go away, leave her alone. Would you deprive your son of his mother?'

As if in answer, the apparition faded away and Cathy slapped Kevin's face.

'You lousy, rotten bastard,' she screamed. 'Do you know how many nights and days I've waited for him. He's come for me.'

'Well, he's not having you,' said Kevin, pushing her back onto the bed and covering her with kisses as all of his pent up emotion exploded. He caressed her and murmured. 'He's gone, Cathy. You've got to live. I love you.'

Cathy lay back, her golden hair spilling onto the pillow like a mane, and Kevin thought he'd never seen her so beautiful. Her eyes were yielding as she said, 'we need to discuss this.' She sat up and reached for the drink that Kevin had brought for her. 'I'm very flattered that you want me; you're very young and handsome but I can't give myself to you. I love Ed and I know he still wants me; he was my husband and still is.'

Kevin took the glass from her. 'So you had a great marriage and you have wonderful memories, but you've got to go on living.'

Cathy picked up a cigarette and lit it. 'Great memories and bad vibes,' she said. 'Did you know that Romany and I were lovers? If you can even call it that?'

Kevin shook his head, deeply concerned. 'No, I knew there was something but I didn't realise it was that.' He felt bitterly unhappy now; he'd thought Romany was just bluffing.

Cathy inhaled. 'Well you wouldn't, I wasn't married to Ed at the time. Romany got me out of my head, using drugs at Vic's party in 1973. I was in bed as I had a fearsome headache and he told me that he'd go and find Ed for me. He came back a bit later and pretended to be Ed, but I was so high that I didn't know the difference until after when he switched the light on and laughed at me. Vic says we had a swinging time in America, but I really don't remember it. Apparently there was an occasion where I had a rather raunchy threesome with Romany and his brother, but I was high again and I don't remember anything about it. So you see Kevin, I'm not quite the lovely, untainted lady that you thought I was. The first time was a bad mistake, but I must confess the guy is everything he makes himself out to be, and more.'

Kevin averted his eyes. 'What about Mick?'

Cathy felt a flush coming to her cheeks. 'Before I met him, I had a huge crush on him, and when we did meet eventually, Ed had already claimed me. It didn't stop me fancying him though, and he asked me to join him on his tour. I didn't, but by then I'd gone back home and to be quite honest had forgotten him. It was only when we went out to that club the night after we discovered Ed in mid-orgy that I realised my feelings for him were still there. We've had a great couple of nights since, but it's just sex, that's all.'

'Would you do it again?'

'Yes, of course I would. Your problem is that you can't tell the difference between love and sex. You want the whole package, and something like that only happens once in a lifetime. It happened with me and Ed, and even though at times he acted badly towards me, I always forgave him. That's the real deal, Kevin. He used to say that we were one person, and now I'm starting to believe it.'

'I love you, Cathy.'

'No you don't, it's just an infatuation.'

Kevin grasped her to him. 'I said I love you, and I really do.'

'Then promise me something if you really do love me.'

'Anything, I promise.' Desire was washing over him. He cupped her breasts and Cathy felt a sudden thrill run through her. 'Raise Eddie as your own if anything happens to me.'

'Nothing's going to happen to you; we can raise him together. I'll take care of you from now on.'

'You've got to promise, really promise.'

'Okay. Oh Cathy, you're so beautiful.'

'I'm not. You've taken over as front man now, and Vic will introduce you to all the top people. Girls are already falling over themselves to get to you.'

'He can keep all the top people. I only want you.' He continued to caress her, adding, 'I've always loved you, right from the start but you never noticed.'

Suddenly the wind rose again as it had before, and Ed could be heard, plaintively calling Cathy's name. She pushed Kevin away and half rose, but he pushed her down and crossed to the window. Closing it, he came back to the bed where Cathy lay terrified. 'Don't touch me,' she cried, 'something bad will happen to you.'

Kevin held her down with the weight of his body and wrapped his arms around her tightly as the voice increased in volume. He held her, stroking her hair and telling her over and over again that he loved her. 'He'll harm you,' cried Cathy. 'Mick's had his car written off, and he and June were in a near-miss accident yesterday. It's like he always said, no one else will touch me. I'm not mad, I see him. He visits me at night and we talk. I can hear him now.'

'You're as sane as me, and I've seen him too. He was there in the swimming pool that night you nearly drowned. I've seen him several times, and at the moment he's trying to deafen me.'

Cathy wept tears of sorrow. She tried in vain to fight off Kevin, but this time he was determined that Ed was not going to win, whatever the outcome. The voice outside was deafening, and the window shook visibly. 'I'll marry you; I want you,' he gasped. He slid his hands down her body and could feel her weakening.

Cathy gazed at the window. Her dead husband stared back at her, begging her not to give in. Ed's voice was ringing in her ears, and she felt that any second now the window would shatter and her ear drums with it. Kevin could see how terrified Cathy was. He couldn't remove the face from the window, but he could do something about the noise. He switched on the stereo which drowned out Ed's voice and the rattling window. Cathy pushed him away and once more made her way to the window. Her eyes met Ed's and she cried out to him, 'help me!'

Seconds later, Kevin had her back on the bed, flat on her back, and he began to run his hands over her thighs. All willpower gone, Cathy pulled him to her. She marvelled at the youthful body before her. He was so like Ed when they'd first met. She gave a last look at the window, and attempted to rise, but Kevin pushed her down again and averted her eyes by kissing her passionately.

'I'll be gentle,' he murmured as he travelled down her body with his tongue. She was moaning and shivering now as he went down on her. After he felt her orgasm, he took her. She was his at last. With a deep sense of guilt, Cathy surrendered, and then she felt it, the rush of shamed pleasure that lifted her to alarming heights of ecstasy until she sank with her lover. The window ceased rattling, and Kevin held her close telling her that he loved her, after which he fell asleep almost immediately.

Cathy got up and crossed to the window. She could see Ed under the tree, holding out his arms to her, and then suddenly he was gone.

She went back to bed and snuggled up to Kevin. Half awake, he kissed her but quickly went back to sleep. Cathy began to drift off to sleep until suddenly she felt hands around her throat. She was choking to death and felt her life draining away. As she tried to move the unseen hands from her throat, she awoke Kevin with her struggles. 'What is it?' he cried.

The pressure eased from Cathy's throat and she sat up, wondering if it had been a nightmare. Kevin switched on the light, and Cathy got out of bed and rushed to the mirror in the en suite. Her reflection told her everything; she could see the finger marks on her neck. She trembled as she realised that this was no nightmare. At last she knew her destiny; Ed wanted her to die. There was no more confusion. She went back to bed, 'I'm cold, Kevin. I had a nightmare and I'm scared.'

Kevin stared at the open window, wondering how it could have opened itself. He got out of bed and, after closing it, snuggled up to Cathy. They finally slept, but not before they heard that familiar laugh again.

The following morning, Cathy awoke to the sound of Romany's car. She shook Kevin who immediately rolled her over and made love to her. A disgruntled Romany grew impatient and stomped up the stairs. He tapped on Kevin's door and, after getting no answer, opened the door and went in. He swore out loud when he found the room empty, and barged into Cathy's room.

'Hi babe,' he said, fixing her with a lecherous grin. 'Thought I'd give you an early morning call and put a smile on your face, if you'll let me. Let's fuck.' At that moment, Kevin surfaced from under the bed clothes, making his jaw drop. 'Ah, well, Kevin, I guess it's about time,' he laughed and left the room whistling.

Kevin had forgotten that they were supposed to be rehearsing. He washed, dressed, and hurried downstairs. Cathy lay in bed for a further ten minutes and then got up and showered. She noted the bruising on her neck and applied a concealer. She felt ill. Nowadays, she always felt ill and she imagined that the cancer was now really taking hold.

She'd refused the offer of chemotherapy; it would only have extended her life for a few months. So far she'd held up, but she felt exhausted most of the time and had only told Fawn about her condition. She donned a long black skirt and a red polo neck top with long sleeves, and then went downstairs and into the garden. She walked to the large oak tree where she'd seen Ed the night before and, placing her arms around its trunk, she cuddled it as if it were a lover. She could feel Ed's aura around her, so she sat beneath the tree, hoping to get a glimpse of him.

She sat there for about thirty minutes before spotting Romany walking in her direction. As usual he had a drink in his hand, and she felt his eyes boring into her. 'You look great,' he said. 'So, is he better than me, Cathy?'

He felt confident, knowing that, sexually at least; he was hard to beat. 'He's younger than you,' replied Cathy.

'Tell you what; you could spend the night at my place after the concert. I'm the best and you know it, so if you're sexually active again we could have a great little scene.'

'What makes you feel so confident?'

'Well, I recall a certain party thrown for Vic in which I had you screaming for more during a fantastic threesome in the states.'

'I don't remember; I was out of it.'

'Yeah, but you loved it while it was happening. It's making me feel horny just thinking about it. Feel this.'

Romany guided Cathy's hand to his groin and she snatched her hand away in disgust. 'You're nauseating.'

'Yeah babe, that's why you're drawn to me. I'm singing *Lay Lady, Lay* at the concert. I'll sing it especially for you and then lay you at my place later.'

'Okay.' Why not? She was going to die anyway, she thought.

'What?'

'I think my memory is returning; you were fantastic.' Getting to her feet, Cathy laughed. 'Come on, rehearsal time.'

They headed back to the house and there was no sign of Kevin. Romany took his chance and kissed her passionately. He was very surprised when she kissed him back. He slid his hand under her skirt, groping her. 'We could slip away during the intermission and screw in your car. That would be exciting. We could even get caught,' she said.

'Bit risky.'

'Where's your spirit of adventure, Romany, or are you getting too old for that sort of thing?'

'I'll never grow old. Okay, if that's what you want, I'll deliver.'

He released her just in time as Kevin came downstairs. Cathy kissed him and said that she had a headache and was going to lie down. After she'd left the room, Romany turned to him, asking what the set-up was with Cathy. Kevin replied that he wanted to marry her. 'You're a headliner now; you can have anyone you want. Why spoil it for yourself?' said Romany.

Kevin ignored him and continued to rehearse. 'You're not going to spoil this for me,' he said defiantly. 'I only want Cathy; you can keep your groupies.' Romany smiled to himself, remembering what Cathy had said, and resumed rehearsing.

Chapter Twenty

The day of the concert dawned and everyone was feeling very jittery. Mick and June were arguing; Jenny kept bursting into tears; Sky had a sore throat, and Amber and Amethyst had fallen out. It was left to Fawn to sort her family out as Rusty had decided to take Eddie for a walk. Upstairs, Cathy and Kevin were resting; they knew they had a gruelling schedule. Kevin bubbled over with plans for their future, but Cathy felt ill and knew her future was to be short-lived. Still she listened as he rambled on. She didn't want to live without Ed. He was right, they were one person and the future without him was bleak. She hoped that tonight he would spirit her away. The pains were really bad now and she was on very strong painkillers.

'Cathy.' Kevin broke her reverie. 'Will you marry me?'

Before she could say anything, the window shattered, splintering glass everywhere. Kevin suffered several abrasions and the sound of laughter echoed around the room once more. Mr Shores was summoned, and he boarded up the window muttering, 'the work of the devil.'

Arriving at the theatre, Kevin was mobbed as he got out of the car. Cathy went inside the building and sought out an empty room. 'It's just for a while,' she said. 'I want to relive some old memories.' Kevin agreed, and joined the rest of the band in the main dressing room. Cathy gazed into the mirror and spoke softly, 'I know you're there, Ed; it was your arm around me in the car;

your arms that pushed me to safety when Kevin was mobbed; and your hands around my throat, trying to drain the life from me.'

She felt an arm around her shoulders but looked up at nothing. She felt a kiss on her cheek, heard a whispered, 'I love you' that made her shiver. Just for a second, she saw him, but he quickly faded, making her weep.

Minutes later she dried her eyes and headed for her dressing room that she was to share with Kevin. Vic crept up behind her. 'Congratulations!' he said. 'Kevin's just told me you're getting married.'

Cathy jerked away violently. 'Don't you touch me,' she snapped. 'I don't want you anywhere near me; I'm doing this show in remembrance of Ed, not for you. I still hold you partly responsible for his death. It was you that made him spiral into a life of drugs, and everything else that stands for decadence. He couldn't cope, and you didn't just demand a percentage of his money, you demanded his blood and his soul, just as you intend to do with Kevin.'

Vic drew in his breath; he wasn't used to being spoken to like that. 'What happened to you?' he said, stepping back in amazement.

'Good question, Vic. Exactly what did happen to me? I don't even know myself lately. Who am I? Oh I remember, just someone for you to manipulate. I suppose now Kevin's your greatest find, hmm? I seem to recall how you made him stay up all night learning *River Deep*, only to snatch it away from him and give it to Ed. And now all of a sudden you're going to make him the biggest thing since Elvis.'

Vic recoiled in horror, then pulled her to him roughly. 'I want you,' he grunted, 'just this one last time. Come to my office tomorrow and I'll give you the best contract you've ever seen. Then Kevin can have you until he tires of you. Shouldn't be long, given the age gap.'

'Great morale-booster, aren't you?' snapped Cathy. 'I love Ed, so I can't marry Kevin anyway.'

Vic was shaking; he hadn't felt this horny for ages. 'You have to move on Cathy. Ed's dead, and Kevin's in love with you. You could both front the band; just think how great it would be? I can see it now, Platinum KC. It'd be great.'

'Oh, the band's going to change its name again? They hated it when you changed the name from Shell to Z Tones. At least you kept the tones in then, but now you want to remove it? I'm sure they'll be delighted. Gerry always said that Z sounded like Ed and that you were making him the headliner, forcing the rest of the band to take a back seat. Let's face it, Vic, they can't keep going much longer. There are new and upcoming bands emerging everyday.'

'The Stones are still rolling.'

'But they're unique, they'll always be around. Most sixties bands are now working in holiday camps, and that's what'll happen here given time.'

'Not with you and Kevin fronting them. We'll build the band around you.'

'But that's what I said; the band will be taking a back seat again.'

'I don't agree.'

'The band has been around since 1965. It's now January, 1983, and their time is running out. Anyway, as I said, I'm not marrying Kevin because I still love Ed. Do you know that he would have been thirty-eight tomorrow if he was alive?'

Vic released her and she wandered over to the mirror to brush her hair. 'Ed's dead, honey,' said Vic. 'Are you that much out of your head that you believe he's still here?'

'Ask Kevin, he's seen him. He calls to me, wants me to go to him. He's lonely. I'm not mad, Vic.'

'It must be the stress catching up with you, but if Ed really is watching he'd want you to marry Kevin. If you stay at home and opt out of show business you'll be unhappy. I'll prepare a dream contract for you, and I'll tear it up if you don't like it. My office tomorrow, the contract will be waiting and so will I.'

Vic leaned over her and cupped her breasts in his hands. Cathy got to her feet, removing his hands as she did so. 'Got to go now,' she said. 'The kids need to briefed on their performance. They should be here by now. Fawn's bringing Eddie too. He's looking forward to playing his wash board in the kiddy skiffle group; it should be a riot.'

She left the room leaving Vic rubbing his hands together in his usual way. From his pocket he produced his speech and read it to his own reflection in the mirror.

Backstage nerves were kicking in with just about everyone, and Jenny was bursting into tears at the slightest remark; it was all too much for her. Cathy introduced herself to the forties-style girl band, The Sweethearts, and although she didn't really want to talk, she was polite.

The show began at four o'clock, and Vic stepped out in front of the curtain to cheers from the audience. He told them that he was going to take them on a journey through Ed's life from cradle to grave. 'We begin in the forties,' he said, introducing The Sweethearts. They were well known on the cabaret circuit as the best forties-style trio around. They did a twenty-minute spot before the curtain came down. An easel had been set up with a board which read 1945, and when the curtain went up again, Sky was seated in a small nursing chair. She began to sing, her body padded out to appear pregnant. Behind her stood Rusty, who was supposed to be his own father.

After one song, Sky left the stage, but soon returned, this time minus padding. Her youngest child accompanied her, supposedly Rusty as a child, and she had with her a doll wrapped in a blanket that was supposed to be the newly born Ed. Her child knelt down by her feet and, once again seated in the nursing chair, Sky sang a lullaby to her newly born baby. Rusty was bored. He was not happy with what he was doing, but was getting paid for it, so he played and harmonised with Sky, feeling very relieved when it was all over.

Michael was in control of the blackboard, and erased 1945, replacing it with 1950. When the curtain went up again the Kiddytones were on stage. Eddie made his own special entrance with his mother on Vic's instructions. Kiddytones consisted of drums, rattles, whistles, saucepans, and Eddie's wash board. He was in his element, and the audience had cheered when he'd made his entrance with his mother; they loved the little chap. When the music began, it was quite a din.

'Punk Skiffle,' Vic called it. Eddie played his wash board with enthusiasm, as did the other children with their instruments. They delighted in the music they were making, especially the boy on drums. The girl with the whistle blew it repeatedly while her companion banged a couple of saucepans together, and Sky's younger children shook their rattles with relish. Behind them, Rusty attempted to pick out a melody.

After the din had abated, Rusty stepped up to the microphone. 'That was supposed to be, *Does Your Chewing Gum Lose Its Flavour on the Bed Post Overnight*. It'll probably be number one next week.'

The kids took a bow, and then Amber, Amethyst, and Blue came onstage and put them through their paces playing 'Simon Says'. Afterwards, they all went back behind the curtain, except Eddie, who was having a ball up there. He bowed over and over again to loud cheers until his mother came onstage for him and scooped him up. 'Just like his father,' she said, and carried the happy child off as he waved to the crowd. The easel now read 1955, and a rock and roll band took to the stage. They were well received and had to do an encore.

Steven was next up, and was shaking with nerves in the wings. Cathy hugged him and told him that he'd be okay, and that Ed would be proud of him. 'Do this for Ed,' she said, 'he'll be watching over you.' He took a deep breath and stepped out onto the stage. Sitting in the front row was Tony who was glowing with pride. 'That's my son,' he told anyone who would listen to him.

Steven began to play *Greensleeves*, and there was a hush in the theatre; you could have heard a pin drop. Cathy was very tearful, knowing that she would never see her son become an adult and realise his ambition to be a lead guitarist. She wiped away a tear and thought of Eddie. He'd already lost his father, and soon he'd be an orphan. Michael stood by her side with his camera; he wanted to get as many photos of his brother as possible. As Steven finished his number, there was a brief moment of silence before the audience leapt to its feet as one, cheering and clapping. Vic walked back onstage. 'What's your name, young man?' he asked.

'Steven,' he replied, still quaking with nerves and excitement from the audience's reaction.

'And who is your mother?'

'Cathy Gold.'

'Proving that talent runs in the family. Tell me Steven, who taught you to play?'

'I taught myself until my mother married Ed, then he helped me improve, and now Kevin teaches me.'

'Well, you've had the best teachers possible then. How about that ladies and gentlemen? Here's a star of the future. I give you Steven.'

The audience cheered and hollered as Steven bowed and left the stage. Cathy was extremely proud and hugged her son tightly. 'You were brilliant,' she gushed. Michael scurried past; he had to change the date on the blackboard again. It now read 'the Swinging Sixties'.

Rusty and his family took the stage with a selection of Dylan, Joan Baez, and many other sixties numbers. They were to close the first section of the show, and Jenny, still shaking with nerves, was to open the second section.

Kevin was enthusing over Steven's playing. 'He's great,' he said to Cathy, who held her son to her, knowing that she'd probably never see him again.

'I am so proud of you,' she cried, 'so very proud.' Steven freed himself from his mother's embrace. Now that his nerves were gone, he was feeling great and decided to go out front and join his father so that he could watch the rest of the show.

After the intermission, Jenny took her place on stage and the curtains opened. Billy and Paddy were backing her and she tried hard to smile, especially after Vic's build up. His introduction had made her feel worse; Vic had stated that she was an international singing star who had played Las Vegas and become a sensation. Jenny felt sick. She'd never even been abroad, but she went through her Joni Mitchell repertoire without incident and finished to rapturous applause.

As she left the stage, Billy and Paddy began their own set and had the audience singing along with them on several numbers. Just before their final number, Billy addressed the audience. 'In 1968 we had the pleasure of supporting the Shelltones as back-up. They were the hottest band around and sometimes audiences get a bit miffed listening to support bands. They get impatient, waiting for the headliners to come on. Ed was our lead singer in those days, and one night the audience were so pissed off they started throwing things at us. It wasn't very pleasant, but then this vision of loveliness appeared on stage and saved the day. From that moment, the crowd were on our side. Tonight we're going to re-create the same scene, but don't throw anything, we've been there before.' He struck up the opening bars to *Green Tambourine*, and Cathy went onstage to a huge cheer. The number went down a storm and, as the curtain came down, Mick began to set up his band behind it.

Vic went back on again and bored everyone with his jokes before building Mick up as the original lead singer of the Shelltones. He stated that if Mick hadn't had his accident, Ed would never become the front man for the band. He went into detail about his fame, and soon the audience were yawning, as was Mick. He was set up already and waiting for the curtain to go up. Finally,

Vic left the stage and Mick began his set, which was probably the best one of the night. He had such a terrific personality and was so adventurous with the music, but he pulled it off.

When he introduced June and Cathy halfway through his set, he said that they were his two favourite women. 'If I were shipwrecked on a desert island, these are the two people that I would love to be with.'

The trio reeled off the three numbers, and Kevin thoroughly enjoyed it until Mick kissed both women on the lips before mopping his brow. 'Love really was all around me then, and what a love. I'll tell you what guys, these two would kill you.'

The audience took it as intended, but Kevin stormed off to the dressing room, and by the time Cathy had joined him he had whipped himself up into a frenzy. 'Why did he say that?' he yelled at her.

'Who?' she replied, quite taken aback.

'Mick. He made it obvious that you were an item.'

'Don't be silly.'

'I'm not, he more or less said that you and June were rampant.'

'He was joking, June's been his off and on girlfriend for years, and you know about me. The audience took it as a joke, why can't you?'

'Because you're with me now, and I don't like it.'

'You're starting to sound like Ed. This concert is in his honour, and I'm not having it spoilt by someone who is obviously so insecure. I don't need it, Kevin.'

'Well, maybe now I know how Ed felt.'

At this, Cathy struck him a stinging blow to his face. 'You have no idea how Ed used to feel, how dare you. I tried to put you off, but you just kept coming. I knew that it was a mistake to sleep with you; you're paranoid. I'd be better off with Mick, or Romany for that matter, at least they know what they want, and so do I. I'll tell you what I don't need. I don't need a possessive boyfriend, and most definitely not another possessive husband.'

Kevin was shocked. He still had his hand to his face where Cathy had struck him. 'I'm sorry,' he cried.

Cathy was fuming, 'Sorry? Do you know how many times I've heard that? Sorry doesn't put things right. Ed thought it did, but I don't buy it any more.'

Kevin was sobbing as Cathy began to change. She was upset. How could such a stupid remark cause all of this? She faced Kevin clad only in a silk pink wrap. 'You've got a show to do,' she said. 'You've taken his place in the band, and you are behaving just like him. I want you to perform for him and you're in no state to do it. Ed had many strops, and I dealt with each one the same way. Sit down over there.' She indicated a nearby chair and Kevin wondered what was coming next, but he was pleasantly surprised when she knelt down and unzipped his trousers. She removed his manhood from his pants and began to suck on it as Kevin closed his eyes and gave himself up to her, realising that this was just another reason that Ed had wanted to keep her with him. He'd have to choose his words a little more carefully in future, but this lady was amazing. After releasing him, Cathy got to her feet. 'Now get out there, you've got a show to do,' she said.

Kevin zipped himself up and left the room. 'Kevin,' Cathy shouted to the retreating figure, 'welcome to the world of rock and roll; you've just been initiated.' He smiled; he'd never had a blow job like that before. He joined the other members of Z Tones and waited to go on stage.

Cathy changed into her negligee for *Albatross* and, putting her robe on top of it, headed for the wings. As she approached, she could feel somebody with her but couldn't see them. Vic sidled over. 'The boys are playing a blinder,' he said. She could feel arms around her waist and glanced sideways at Vic. He had his hands in his pockets, and no one else was around. She realised that Ed was back.

Kevin left the stage as Romany took over. 'This next song is dedicated to a truly beautiful lady who is not too far away from me,' he said, gazing over at Cathy. Kevin shot him a killing look as he began to play *Lay Lady, Lay*. Romany grinned, he could see that he was winding him up, and he made it worse as he kept looking over at her. Sometimes he would wander over and direct the song only to her. The lusty look in his eyes said it all and Kevin could see it clearly.

Anger boiled up inside of him, but he kept calm, remembering the row that he had had with Cathy earlier. As the song ended, Kevin went back out and took centre stage. He was determined not to cause waves, and continued the set.

Cathy was riveted to the spot. She could see Ed behind Kevin. This was crazy; couldn't anyone else see him? She grabbed Vic's arm. 'He's on stage.'

'Who, babe?' replied Vic distractedly. 'Kevin? Yes, he's great tonight, isn't he?'

'No, Ed' cried Cathy. 'Do something.'

The roadies nearby couldn't suppress their laughter; everyone knew that Ed's widow was crazy. Vic, however, was concerned. Cathy was definitely losing it; Ed was dead. The only time that he'd had his doubts was that night at the swimming pool, and he'd put that down to too much alcohol. He thought he'd better humour her. 'Probably helping Kevin get through the next number. Ed was the only one who could deliver that song. He wrote it for you, and it was his very own creation. I can't even think why Kevin's doing it.'

Kevin began to sing *My Secret Gypsy Lover* and delivered it in Ed's voice. Vic was struck dumb, and so was the audience; it was as if Ed was back. If Kevin was adored now, he was about to be hero worshipped. Romany was uneasy; he knew that Kevin couldn't sing that well and the voice was unmistakeable. A sidelong glance at Cathy, however, who had just removed her robe made him feel that he wanted some action now, and he forgot all about Kevin and Ed, hoping that this set would be over soon.

Cathy waited in the wings, clad in her white, frothy negligee and waited for Romany to seat himself on the stool for *Albatross*. Just as she was about to go on, Kevin came off and was immediately all over Cathy with a passion that left nothing to the imagination. Vic was fuming and tore the couple apart. 'Stop it,' he yelled at Kevin. 'She's got to go on.'

Kevin had grabbed Cathy again, and he separated them once more. 'What's come over you?' Kevin reached out again but Vic brushed him aside. Romany had a very good view of what was going on and could not believe his eyes. Cathy smoothed her negligee down and made her entrance.

Kevin was in shock. He didn't understand himself either. He recalled starting the last number but couldn't remember singing it, and as for his passionate embrace with Cathy, he was shocked at himself. He usually liked to keep those sorts of things private; it was as if he'd been fired up with an uncontrollable lust. The roadies were having a field day, first there was crazy Cathy, and now lusty Kevin. They were laughing and smirking until one of them fell flat on his back. 'Hey, who pushed me?' said the victim, looking round and seeing nothing.

'Dunno,' said his friend. 'I thought you just fell over.'

The ballet finished and Cathy went back to the dressing room to change. Kevin's embrace hadn't surprised her at all; she knew it wasn't from him any more than the voice on stage was. Ed was here once more.

Rosaleen was seated in the audience. She was going to sing in the Platinum set, but Vic knew nothing about it. She was doing two numbers, *Ruby Tuesday* and *Brand New Key*, both by Melanie. Kevin and Cathy had visited her the previous day, and had both of the songs off perfectly.

Once dressed, Cathy made her way outside; she needed some air. Tears were filling her eyes and she was scared. Everyone thought she was crazy, and she was beginning to think that maybe they were right. Pulling her coat around her tightly she headed for the parking area at the back of the theatre. She sat on a bench and could hear Z Tones winding up their first set. Suddenly, she realised that she wasn't alone any more, and she spoke to the invisible form. 'It was always you, Ed. There never was anyone else for me; you were the only one who held my heart. You could have snapped me in half like a twig if it pleased you, the one who could crush me with a single word, and the only one who taught me how to give and receive love. We're twin souls, and I know that the only way for either of us to find peace is for me to join you. No one can live or die without their soul.'

She could hear someone approaching. It was Vic, accompanied by Romany. She hadn't even realised that Z Tones had finished. Romany strode over and grabbed her to him. She was alarmed; she'd completely forgotten about their tryst. Vic swore. He had to go and keep Kevin occupied.

In the dressing room, a stunned Kevin was surrounded by reporters and photographers. He answered a barrage of questions, and Vic opened a bottle of champagne. 'Incredible, Kevin,' he said. 'It was as if… well, Ed couldn't have sung it better. Have I got plans for you?' He remembered that he hadn't brought the photos that he'd gone to his car for. The sight of Romany and Cathy together had made him forget. 'Back in a trice,' he said. 'I've got some great new shots in the car.'

He was freezing cold once he was outside in the parking area, and he heard Cathy giggling nearby. It was alarming how her moods changed so quickly. Vic felt icy cold. True, it was January, but it was more than a normal chill, it was uncanny and it was making the hairs on the back of his neck stand up. In fact, he also felt as if he were being watched. He noted the couple still locked in an embrace. He crossed to his car and started rummaging around, finding the photos on the back seat. As he looked up, he focused on Romany and Cathy, and to his alarm saw a third figure. He prayed that it wasn't Kevin, as Romany led her to his car which was unfortunately parked right next to his own. As the third figure came into view, he was struck dumb. He dropped all the photos onto the floor as the couple stopped just outside his car. They didn't appear to see him, so he crouched down into the foot-well out of sight.

Vic was mesmerised by this shadowy third figure which was approaching the couple. Romany had his back turned so didn't see it but he felt sure that Cathy had. Horrified, he realised that, not only was she seeing it, she was communicating with it. Romany was crazed with lust, but Cathy stared straight ahead. 'Come to me now,' she said lustily, and the figure drew closer. Vic felt sure that his guitarist was as good as dead as the figure drew closer. He opened his mouth to shout but words failed him; he couldn't move either. His body was like a lump of lead and he felt near to collapse as the figure appeared to go straight into Romany and remain there. Romany slumped onto Cathy, and the change that came over her was so fast that if Vic had blinked he would have missed it. 'I've missed you,' cried Cathy.

Romany lifted his head and stared straight at Vic. He spoke, but the voice that came out was not his own, in fact Vic recognised it immediately. 'I'm lonely, babe,' said Ed's voice.

Vic's nervous system went wild. 'Oh my God,' he cried.

He waited for the couple to get into the car, gathered up the photos, got out of his car and rushed into the theatre as fast as his little, fat legs could carry him. Back in the band's dressing room, he poured himself a large rum and coke. The reporter eyed him with interest. 'You look as if you've seen a ghost,' he said, eyeing Vic's shaking hands and shocked expression.

Gulping down his drink, Vic muttered, 'I think I just did.'

Even more interested, the reporter moved closer. 'Could you repeat that?'

Feeling a fool, Vic replied. 'When Kevin sang tonight, it was as if Ed was singing for him.'

Kevin was still in the dressing room, but he was worried and constantly looking around him. 'Where's Cathy, Vic?' he asked. 'She went missing before I'd finished the set.'

Vic was lost for words, and he rubbed his sweaty hands together. 'Don't know,' he replied shakily, 'but don't worry about her, you and I have a lot to discuss.'

What he'd experienced in the parking area defied explanation. Either he was going crazy, or Cathy wasn't crazy at all. How the hell did Ed take over Romany's body? It's not possible. Maybe he'd had too much to drink, or not enough. Kevin voiced his fears again. 'She could be anywhere; you know how her mind is at this minute. I need to run through a few songs in the Platinum set too.'

Vic agreed, saying that he'd go and look for her, but as he left the room Gerry informed them that Romany was missing too. Kevin's stomach knotted up as the first pangs of suspicion hit him; how it hurt to love somebody. Now he definitely knew how Ed had felt. Suspicion was a nasty thing, and he was beginning to feel as his predecessor had, that Cathy was his personal possession.

Vic went outside into the cold night air and stared at Romany's car. It was visibly moving and he could hear Cathy sighing and crying in a way he recognised all too well. Her voice reached a crescendo, and was followed by silence. Minutes later the couple emerged from the car and embraced. Once more he saw this figure as it emerged from Romany and retreated into the shadows. He shouted, 'come on you two, everyone's looking for you.'

Romany appeared dazed and sauntered over to him. Cathy appeared to be in a trance and didn't seem to know where she was. Vic was concerned. 'You okay?' he asked. She nodded. 'Are you sure? What happened?'

'Don't you know, Vic? I thought it was obvious?'

'Nothing's obvious any more; your state of mind is bugging me.'

'Can't think why. You never worried before. Guess who I was in the car with? The sex really blew my mind; I haven't come down to earth yet.'

'I thought you were with Romany, but just for a second I thought... no, it's too silly to mention.'

Cathy threw back her head and laughed. 'You thought I was with Ed, didn't you, Vic? And I thought I was the crazy one. Actually I was, but don't tell anyone or they'll think you're mad too.'

Vic shook her, and her hair fell over her eyes in a tangled mess. 'Talk sense,' snapped Vic.

Cathy straightened herself up. 'You thought I was with Ed? Don't be silly, Vic, Ed's dead; everyone knows that.'

Vic turned to Romany who looked completely out of it. 'Tidy up, you've both got a show to do.'

'Yes sir, anything you say, sir,' laughed Cathy, and she gave him a mock salute. Vic swore. He didn't want to upset her too much, but a few more remarks like that and he'd give her a slap. He controlled himself. He wanted her under his new contract and then, in his ultimate wisdom, would bleed her dry alongside Kevin. He walked back inside the theatre with Romany close behind.

Kevin was still concerned as he took Cathy in his arms. She was back, but where had she been? The final section had just begun with Dirty Dave and the Razors opening it. It had taken a lot of wrangling to get this world famous group, but Dave himself had met Ed in the mid-seventies and agreed to perform for the right salary. Vic wanted all kinds of music covered as it was a cradle to grave tribute, even though Ed had never performed punk. Kevin eyed Romany and gave him a killing look, but he just grinned, even when Kevin mouthed a visible 'bastard' at him. He wasn't bothered. He'd done this once before and, if doing it to his best friend hadn't pricked his conscience, he certainly wasn't concerned about Kevin's feelings. He was unfazed, and he had a very nice rendezvous to keep with Cathy later.

Rosaleen tapped on the door and Cathy greeted her warmly. Vic still knew nothing about her being included in the Platinum set and wouldn't realise until the girl was on stage. Kevin and the girls left for an empty room to run through a few numbers, and Vic walked to the wings to watch Dave. After Rosaleen had had a final run through of her songs, she headed back to her seat in the audience. Kevin was going to call her up when the time was right so that Vic didn't notice anything was amiss. He turned Cathy to face him as they began to change into their costumes. 'Will you marry me?' he asked again.

'No,' replied Cathy.

'Why not? Aren't I as good in the bedroom as Ed or Mick or Romany, or any of your previous lovers?'

'Kevin, what is wrong with you? Why are you so insecure?'

'Why won't you marry me?'

'Because I still love Ed. What we had was magic. Our love affair conquered everything. It's chemistry; everything just fell into place. It was the real deal and worth fighting for. No matter how long we were apart we always got back together again. On drugs, Ed was a nightmare, off drugs he was the kindest, most loving, and most beautiful person that you could wish to meet. I still love him and always will. There's no future for us, Kevin. Why can't you understand that?'

'Because I don't want to. I could make you happy. I'm sorry about earlier. I don't know what came over me; I just couldn't resist. I must have ruined your costume and make-up.'

'Well, the roadies certainly got an eyeful, and Vic nearly had a heart attack, but that's show biz and Ed's done much worse in the past.'

She smiled and gazed at her young lover. He really loved her, but inside she was crying and dying. The pains had been really bad today, and she'd upped the dose on her painkillers once more. There was no future with Kevin or anyone, and she longed to lie down and rest, but as Noddy would have said, 'the show must go on.' This show was all about her beloved husband.

She changed into her costume, and then walked towards the wings with Kevin for their set. Vic was happy; he loved these two together and believed that if Ed hadn't married Cathy, this act would have eclipsed every act that he had. He still could see them in Las Vegas. They would have been great, and maybe Cathy would have still been under him in more ways than one.

The curtain came down and Dave got a standing ovation. Cathy and Kevin took their places on stage, and Vic built them up with a magnificent introduction. They're style was middle of the road, so there was something for everyone. They did Cash/Carter, Nancy Sinatra and Lee Hazelwood, Ike and Tina Turner, plus sixties and seventies material. Kevin was adored, and Cathy kept the guys happy with her skimpy outfits for her dance numbers. Vocally they merged beautifully, and Vic was as proud as a peacock until Kevin introduced Rosaleen, saying that she'd sung with Ed in the early sixties. The shy girl left the audience and walked up the steps onto the stage. Vic was fuming until he heard her sing, and then he smiled as his rage quickly subsided, thinking that maybe this was another easy target he could manipulate. She was good, very good in fact. The crowd clapped along to *Brand New Key* and when Rosaleen delivered *Ruby Tuesday*, Vic was gob smacked. He'd have to have words with this girl before someone else snapped her up.

As Rosaleen left the stage, Kevin and Cathy continued with their set. Cathy was feeling very tired now and her pains were returning sharply; they stabbed at her like knives, and the pain was radiating from her abdomen right through to her back. Somehow she stayed upright, and the pain eased a little, but she knew it was only a matter of time before she would be admitted to hospital for much stronger painkillers. She gave a sigh of relief when Kevin struck up the opening bars of *River Deep, Mountain High*, the last song in the set. The couple had the audience on its feet, cheering when it concluded. Vic was delighted and jumped up and down, hugging his act as they came off stage. Cathy pulled free from Vic's suffocating embrace. She was sweating buckets, partly from exhaustion and partly from pain. She hurried to the dressing room to freshen up, followed by Kevin, and about fifteen minutes later, the couple headed back towards the stage.

In front of the curtain, Rusty and his family performed a medley of Ed's favourite songs, and behind it the roadies checked everything was in order in preparation for Z Tone's final set of the night. Soon the curtain went up to a massive cheer from the crowd. This was the one they had all been waiting for; several big names would be joining the band, as it was the final act of the night, making this set even more interesting. The band began with the Fleetwood Mac section, and *The Chain* was first up followed by *Dreams*. Cathy sang this number plaintively after telling the audience she used to sing it to Ed every time he got bored and believed the grass to be greener on the other side of the fence. 'It did work sometimes,' she laughed.

Yesterday's Gone was next, and then she and Kevin gave a beautiful rendition of *Landslide* which was sung without any backing apart from Kevin on acoustic guitar. It was a very touchy feely version which was charming, and the crowd loved it. Kevin kissed her hand as she left the stage. 'Great, great, great,' enthused Vic, 'there's so much charisma between you two.'

Cathy smiled, telling him it was just theatrics and affection. The band rocked on and she made her way to the dressing room. Fawn was gathering a few things together and noted her pallor. 'Pain bad?' she asked, as Cathy flopped into an armchair.

Cathy nodded. 'If he comes for me tonight, I will go with him. The pains are getting unbearable. I don't want to go to hospital for any chemotherapy; I know it can only prolong my life for about another three months, and I'm taking the pain killers like sweets so I just don't see the point. You understand, don't you? Because everyone else believes I've got gall stones and that my gall bladder is to be removed to make me well again. You're the only person I've told. I feel bad about leaving Eddie and my other two boys, but I've only got a short time left, so the end is inevitable anyway.'

Fawn put her arms around Cathy. 'Of course I do. Is there anything that I can do?'

'Organise my funeral; you did a wonderful job at Ed's funeral, and I want the same but I want you to sing *Woodstock* for me, and I want *Autumn Stone* played just before my coffin heads for the furnace. Tell Kevin to learn *Autumn Stone*. If he listens to the words, he'll know how I felt about him. We have a copy of the song at home. Ed and I adored the Small Faces so you'll be able to play the record at my funeral.' She glanced at her watch, groaning. 'Five more minutes and I'm on again; I hope Ed appreciates this concert. Where's Eddie?'

'With Sky and the other children. Don't worry, Cathy. I'll take care of everything.'

'Could you travel home with me and Eddie tonight? I need a friend to leave with.'

'Of course I will; Rusty and Sky can take care of the kids.'

Cathy winced as another pang of pain shot through her. This was unbearable, and Fawn felt helpless. Cathy looked so tired and ill.

Cathy got to her feet and took her gypsy dress from its hanger. 'I wore this in 1968 and it still fits,' she said 'Vic wanted me to get a new one but I wouldn't. I wanted the original outfit that I wore when I met Ed. This is one argument that I actually won.'

She began to change, aided by Fawn, and made her way back to the stage where Vic was waiting in the wings. She sat on a stool beside him, awaiting her cue. On stage, Kevin was unhappy as he saw Romany blow Cathy a kiss. He sidled over to him. 'If you mess with Cathy, I'll kill you,' he warned.

Romany looked up and grinned; he wasn't bothered. A pain struck Cathy, and immediately Vic was on his feet, shaking as she doubled up in agony. 'The sooner your gall bladder's out, the better,' he said. 'You should have had it done a few months ago.'

Cathy felt sick and prayed that the pains would leave her so she could finish this concert. She got to her feet, feeling her strength draining from her. Vic supported her and held her to him, stroking her hair. 'You'll be fine, baby,' he said. 'Come on, Kevin's waiting.'

Cathy summoned up all her strength and walked out onto the stage. She sang a couple of Dolly Parton numbers, *Down from Dover* and *Gypsy, Joe and Me*, then her role was over until the finale. Turning to Vic, she announced that she was going to put her feet up, and asked him to come and find her once the band were on their last song. He agreed and she settled herself down in a comfy armchair in the dressing room.

She dozed off, and a short while later was awoken by Vic shaking her. Dazed, she walked to the mirror and fixed her make-up. Following Vic, she heard Kevin announce that this would be the final song of the night. He thanked everyone for coming, and then began *Rock 'n' Roll Raver*. It was a real hit and had the crowd on their feet dancing. Cathy laughed. She could see Tony, and he was actually dancing with Al Simpkins as Steven made his way backstage.

The band wound up the song and, as they left the stage, Cathy took a deep breath. The show was over apart from an encore in which she was to sing *Gypsy*. The cheers from the audience said it all; the show was a fitting tribute to a sadly missed superstar and had been a roaring success. The band trouped back onto the stage with Cathy close behind. She approached the microphone, and the crowd went silent. She gave a short speech in which she thanked everyone for coming and told the audience that Ed still lived through Eddie, and that Kevin was a worthy successor as the lead vocalist.

She mentioned her dress and said that she'd worn it the first time she'd met Ed. 'He must have liked it,' she said, 'because after a lot of problems, heartaches, and God knows what else, we finally got married and had two beautiful children. One sadly is no longer with us and has gone to join her father in heaven. I can't say any more because I'm all choked up and I've got to sing… so take it away, Romany.'

As he struck up the opening bars of *Gypsy*, Cathy shouted, 'This one's for you Ed, I love you.'

There was a huge cheer as Ed's image appeared on the screen behind the band. Cathy began singing and put everything into the song. Gazing out into the auditorium, she thought she could see Ed standing at the back. She focused on the image and saw nothing but him. Stevie Nicks' lyrics rang out, holding the audience spellbound as they listened, and watched the film of Ed's life being played out before them. Towards the end of the song, Romany put in extra lead and she was able to dance until its finish.

The song was over and the film ended in a shot of Cathy, Ed, and the children in a close-up. Cathy was still focused on the image at the back of the auditorium; it was Ed and he was applauding vigorously. The cheers and applause rang out from the audience as the curtain went down, and when it rose again, every member that had taken part was on stage. The kids clustered around Cathy who held Eddie in her arms. He repeatedly pointed and waved to the spot where she had seen Ed. She walked to the microphone and said, 'thank you so much for your support. I'm sure that Ed has been watching; he must have loved it. Thank you to all of the acts that have performed tonight. Ed touched them all in one way or another.' There was a huge cheer as Cathy acknowledged the acts standing behind her. 'What a beautiful gesture,' she said, 'and thanks to the kids who brought their own special brand of skiffle music. Let's not forget old Vic as well for making this possible.'

Vic strode out and bowed. He scratched his head. 'I'm lost for words,' he said. 'All I can say is, thank you all.'

'Good,' shouted Romany, 'at least we won't have to suffer a speech.'

There were roars of laughter, and then Cathy addressed Eddie. 'What was it you wanted to say?' she asked.

Eddie laughed and clapped his hands. 'Thank you for coming to my daddy's show,' he said, nestling into Cathy's shoulder.

The curtain came down for the final time, and Cathy lowered

Eddie to the stage, watching as Kevin was besieged by the press, photographers, girls, and all the usual hangers-on. They followed him to his dressing room, and Vic, as usual, had organised a party at his house to celebrate. She made her way to Kevin and said, 'I'm not going to the party. I'm going home with Fawn and Eddie. I really don't feel very well. You were great tonight, really great.'

Kevin was concerned and held her to him. He knew she was going into hospital for surgery on her gall bladder and imagined that she'd probably over done it with the concert and its gruelling schedule. 'I'm not going if you're not,' he protested.

'You have to, you're the star attraction.'

A smiley photographer tapped Cathy on her shoulder. 'Cathy, darling, I never did get that interview, did I?'

'She's tired,' interjected Kevin. 'She hasn't had a good year, and hasn't recovered from losing her husband yet.'

'It's okay,' said Cathy. 'You can have your interview and photos and then I'm off home to bed. It's been a long day for Eddie too.' She settled herself into an armchair, and the pleased photographer got out his notebook. He asked about Ed and Eddie, music, and a million other things. Her head was spinning and she couldn't answer some of the questions as she was simply too tired, but those she could, she answered to the best of her ability. Her pains were coming back as well, but she gritted her teeth and continued with the interview. Fawn entered the room with Eddie, Michael, and Steven, and the photographer put down his notebook and began taking photos. He took several: Cathy with Kevin; Cathy with her three children; and several group photos to finish. The session over, she hugged Michael and Steven, telling them how proud she was of them, and how they would always be welcome at her home. 'Just remember,' she said. 'I love you; I always have, and always will.'

She was interrupted by Tony entering the room and telling the boys to get a move on. Vic had ordered a mini cab for them and was paying for it himself. He desperately wanted her under contract again, and under him at the office the following day, so a mini cab fare was a small price to pay.

Cathy bid her boys a final farewell and swallowed hard, knowing that the next time they would see her would be at her funeral, or in hospital for the remainder of her days. She got to her feet and left the room with Fawn, Kevin, and Eddie. The photographer, meanwhile, was delighted. He'd got some great shots and they'd be on the front pages tomorrow. 'Hey Kevin, I haven't finished with you yet,' he cried.

Kevin held a very sleepy Eddie in his arms. 'Back in a mo,' he said. 'I'm just seeing Cathy to the car.'

Outside, Cathy's trusty chauffeur was waiting. Fawn got into the car, and Kevin handed Eddie to her. The child snuggled up to her and promptly fell asleep. He turned Cathy to face him. 'Marry me,' he said.

Cathy could feel the tears beginning to fill her eyes. 'I can't,' she said, 'but I do love you, Kevin. Anyway, this is no time to discuss marriage, your public awaits.'

'I don't want to go.'

'You have to. Tell you what, if I have a nap and wake up feeling better, I'll join you at Vic's party, I promise.'

'Kevin?' Vic's voice pierced the air. Cathy clung to him in a loving embrace, knowing that this was to be their final cuddle, and then he left with Vic.

Romany ambled over as Cathy got into the car and, pressing a key into her hand, said, 'Great show, babe. Ed would have been proud of you.' He grinned and went back inside the building.

Mr Shores put the radio on, and *Afternoon Delight* burst forth. Cathy smiled, recalling how many times she'd sampled afternoon delight with Ed. It had almost been a ritual, as every afternoon at about three o'clock they used to head to bed, simply to delight in each other.

'What a pretty song,' she said, closing her eyes. Mr Shores agreed, saying that he didn't like much modern day music, but he quite liked the track that was playing. Fawn winked at her. She knew what Cathy was thinking.

Reaching home, Cathy dismissed Mr Shores telling him that he could retire for the night. She bid him goodnight and put Eddie to bed while Fawn made some coffee downstairs. He stirred as she tucked him in and, opening one eye, asked, 'was I good?'

'You were perfect,' replied Cathy, 'you were a star. Daddy would have been proud of you.'

'Daddy was there; I saw him,' said the sleepy child, rubbing his eyes.

'Did you darling? Well I'll let you into a secret, I saw him too.'

He sighed. 'Love you, Mummy.'

Cathy kissed him on his forehead. 'Love you too.'

She lay down beside him and felt a kiss on her cheek, and she knew that once more Ed was with her. After a few minutes, she saw that Eddie had fallen asleep and headed downstairs to join Fawn. She went to the oak dresser, removed two letters and, handing them to Fawn, said, 'I've written down my instructions for my funeral, and I know I can trust you to carry them out. I want my ashes scattered at Bacton with Ed's and Amara's because we were really happy there, and I want this done on 14th February, on St Valentine's Day.'

She grimaced and doubled up in pain again. Fawn put her arms around her as she started to cry from the pain. Fawn noticed that Cathy's ankles were badly swollen, so much so that the skin appeared to be shiny and changing colour but she put this down to the cancer moving on. Cathy looked dreadful. Whereas before she'd looked pallid, her face now had a yellowish hue, and the whites of her eyes had taken on the same appearance. Her liver and kidneys were obviously starting to fail, and Fawn wanted to call for an ambulance, but she knew her sister-in-law would refuse to go to the hospital. She could see Ed in the doorway and he was beckoning. As the pain subsided, Cathy sobbed into Fawn's shoulder. 'I'm scared,' she cried. 'I need Ed.'

Fawn looked over at the doorway again and saw Ed move towards both of them, still beckoning. 'Cathy, let's get you to bed, unless you want me to call for an ambulance'.

She shook her head. 'No, if I go into hospital I'll be given morphine and chemo. I want to die on my own clock, so I'll just have to up the pain killers. I can't last much longer; my body's going through Armageddon. It's only the concert that's kept me going this long.'

Fawn helped her to her feet. She guessed that the cancer had returned because of the shocks she had had over the last year. First Ed's death, then Amara's, followed by Seth's revelation about Miriam. That was enough to resurrect anything, and of course Cathy hadn't been attending hospital for check-ups owing to the fact that she was grieving. Together they ascended the stairs and, once inside her bedroom, Cathy's legs gave way and Fawn had to help her onto the bed. By the bedside were sleeping pills and pain killers. Fawn could see Ed reflected in the mirror. He was very clear now. 'I'll bring you some water, Cathy,' said Fawn, 'then you can take your pills.'

Cathy closed her eyes and Fawn saw him move toward the bed. She wiped the tears from her eyes and returned minutes later with a glass and a jug of water. Placing it on the bedside cabinet, she settled herself in an armchair and watched over Cathy. She didn't intend to sleep, but the day had taken its toll and had exhausted her.

Minutes later, Cathy awoke. She looked over to Fawn and saw that she had fallen into a deep sleep. She could feel arms around her again and looked up to see Ed. 'Come to me, baby,' he whispered.

A pain ripped through her body; a pain much worse than normal. Her body felt as if it was being ripped asunder. She felt she couldn't take any more. She had no choice; the pain killers were no longer working. Reaching for her sleeping pills, she unscrewed the top of the bottle and swallowed a handful. After washing them down with a glass of water, she lay back down and waited for them to work.

Closing her eyes, she drifted for what seemed an eternity, and visions began to flash before her eyes. She was three years old in her dancing class, clad in a short tunic with white ankle socks and pink ballet shoes. 'Point your toes,' barked her instructor. The vision switched to her at seventeen in a ballet company dancing 'Giselle'. She saw her mother in the audience, looking a picture of health, which changed to her in hospital, a victim of cancer on her death bed.

Tony loomed large and it was her wedding day, then Sandy was in her arms. Ed was getting clearer now and she saw her first meeting with him. The first kiss followed by a slap, Rusty's caravan, the field, *Itchycoo Park* blaring from Ed's radio as they made love for the first time, the waterfall and picnic followed by her hippy wedding. Steven appeared, followed by her second pregnancy, and Tony's anger because of it. Then there was a toothy grin from Michael. She felt sad. She had wanted to talk to her sons before they'd left, but Tony had spirited them away before she could. Steven was going to be a great musician, and Michael had his heart set on being a leading photographer. She smiled as she recalled the way he had attended to the board on stage, constantly changing the dates from the forties to the eighties. They were lovely children and she never regretted having them, even though Tony had wanted her to have an abortion in both cases. She consoled herself that at least Ed had tried to guide them whenever possible, and had bent over backwards for them when they'd spent Christmas together.

She was getting sleepy now; saw herself in the dance contest and her surprise at winning it. Faye crossed her line of vision, what a beautiful person she was but she was just like a little girl. She waved at Cathy and giggled; then she was gone as quickly as she had appeared. Mrs Beaumont's wig floated in the swimming pool, and then Ed was making love to her whilst on the phone to Faye. America was very muddled, and then Sandy flashed across her vision smiling. Her divorce from Tony, and Sandy's death, made her weep, and then a very happy Kevin went down on one knee and kissed her hand on their first meeting. Soon they were singing together, and then she saw her wedding to Ed. He was beside her now; it was as if he'd never gone.

Eddie laughed and she saw his cherubic face. 'My baby,' she wept. Ed held her and pointed to the corner of the room. Cathy could make out the shape of a young girl holding a small child. The light of the moon shone on them both and Cathy recognised them instantly. 'Sandy,' cried Cathy, 'Amara. My beautiful girls.' She looked up at Ed and then back to the corner, but the girls were gone. Ed held her tighter and smiled. 'You're mine now, forever. Come to me, baby.'

Cathy was panicking. Something heavy was pushing her down. She was scared and tried to rise but couldn't. Her mind was in overdrive. She was dying. 'I'm scared,' she cried. 'Help me.'

Over and over, Ed repeated, 'you're mine.' They were fused as one, on the cusp of life and death, and Ed pinned her down. 'Kiss me, my angel,' he said.

Cathy knew this was the kiss of death, and averted her face. 'Don't be scared, darling, it's easy,' he murmured. She clung to him, terrified, as his lips came down on her and she was locked in the embrace of death. 'Come to me baby... no more pain... no more heartache. Hold me tighter, baby, tighter.' Cathy clung to him until she sank lower and lower into unconsciousness.

Fawn awoke a short while later. She could hear giggling outside, and went to the window. Staring out to the garden, she saw Ed and Cathy in the moonlight. She turned quickly and, seeing the still figure on the bed, offered up a prayer. 'Thank God,' she sighed, and closed Cathy's eyes. 'Together at last.'

Chapter Twenty-One

Romany excused himself early at the party and sped off towards home with some pills that Vic had assured him were truly amazing. He freshened up and waited for Cathy, wondering what was keeping her. He poured himself a drink and reclined on his sofa, picturing the night's events ahead. A sudden chill struck him, and his dogs began to snarl as a voice called his name. Looking over at his bar, he saw Ed laughing at him, but he dismissed it; it had to be the pills. Looking out to his garden, he spotted Cathy and then she vanished. Romany opened the door impatiently and walked outside with his dogs following him, their hackles raised. They charged off to the bottom of his long garden, and once again he saw her, this time running from the dogs. She was screaming, 'Romany, help me.' Then once more she vanished.

He went back inside thinking he didn't like these pills at all. He sat back down on the sofa, but suddenly Ed loomed over him, then faded just as quickly as he'd appeared. The lights went out and doors and windows blew open. 'Fuck Vic and his pills,' he said nervously to himself. 'I know he said they were good, but I didn't want to go to hell.'

As Ed's laughter rang out, the lights came back on and the stereo began to play. Romany ran around the house closing every door and window before the phone rang, making him jump, and when he answered it Ed's laughter greeted him. Scared, he replaced the receiver as the chandelier above his head fell crashing to the floor, missing him by inches. The television hurled itself across the room and shattered, sending debris everywhere.

This was a trip that Romany didn't need, and he headed upstairs to his bedroom to sleep it off, only to find his oyster-coloured satin sheets were covered in blood. He heard a multitude of crashes coming from downstairs and, rushing back down, found his cocktail bar demolished with broken bottles lying everywhere. His new display cabinet was destroyed and the stereo continued to play Ed's first major hit single. Disorientated, he tried to pull the wall plug out and discovered to his horror that it wasn't even connected.

Suddenly, Cathy's voice called from upstairs, and the lights in the house began to flash, as at a disco. She was begging him to come to her, and once more he climbed the stairs, heading for the room where the voice appeared to be coming from. When he arrived, she wasn't there and she began to lure him from room to room, appearing, and then vanishing. He felt as if his sanity was in doubt, and he decided to get a glass of water as there was nothing stronger left, but as he turned on the tap, blood poured forth instead. 'Fuck these pills,' he cried again, landing on the floor as someone pushed him over.

He tried every tap in the house and they all emitted blood until then he heard a voice calling softly to him from his bedroom. 'I'm here,' it breathed, over and over again. Exhausted, he approached the room and saw Cathy lying on his bed with her arms open. The sheets weren't bloodstained any more; the whole thing had to have been a bad trip. He must have been hallucinating; she looked real enough now. He rushed to embrace her, but grasped nothing. Gazing around him in a daze, he saw her framed in the doorway, but then she vanished once more. He heard someone go downstairs, and he wept tears of frustration.

'Stop it, Cathy, for Christ's sake, stop it,' he shouted. Walking to the landing, he looked down and saw her beckoning to him at the bottom of the stairs. His head was fit to burst, and he started down the stairs until he heard someone behind him. Looking over his shoulder, his eyes met Ed's who gazed at him with a merciless expression on his face. Romany felt a push and found himself hurtling down the stairs. 'No!' he screamed. 'No!' He hit his head on the bottom stair and, mustering what little strength he had left, looked up to see Ed laughing at him before darkness enveloped him.

Kevin had enjoyed the party more than he thought he would. Vic had introduced him to all the right people, who were in fact all the wrong people, and several girls had given him their phone numbers, even though he wasn't interested. He was in mid conversation with a redhead when he began to feel strange. His vision became impaired and all of a sudden he passed out. Vic, in his wisdom, had doctored his drink, having become pissed off with listening to Kevin saying that he wanted to leave. He was having none of it and had stooped to his usual level of devious, selfish behaviour. The concert had been a great success, so there was no way Kevin was leaving early.

When Kevin awoke, he found himself in the arms of the redhead who was now topless on the sofa. Shocked, he sat up and pushed the girl away, who protested before slumping across him. He wriggled out from under her and was relieved to find himself fully clothed. Brushing himself down, he went in search of Vic and found him conversing with Gerry. 'I want to get back to Cathy,' he said.

Gerry frowned. 'Cathy's here. I saw her in the garden.'

Kevin was overjoyed; obviously Cathy was feeling better and had decided to join him. He scoured the garden, but could see no sign of her and, disappointed, returned to Vic. 'Couldn't find her,' he said, dejectedly.

'Well, she must be here if Gerry's seen her,' he replied. 'Try upstairs and, if she's not there, we'll play Frankie Valli, singing *Oh What a Night*; that'll flush her out. It was Ed and Cathy's all-time favourite; they said it was their song.' He puffed on his cigar and turned his attention back to Rosaleen. He was trying to make sense of her. He'd offered her all kind of deals but she'd flatly turned him down and not even showed at the party.

Several couples had decided to go outside to dance, as the house was very stuffy and stank of booze and pot. It was a chilly night, but it wasn't cooling the ardour of a couple over by the summer house. They were lost in each other, and disappeared inside it.

Al Simpkins staggered over. 'Saw Cathy a minute ago,' he slurred. 'She was with an Ed look-a-like. There's quite a lot of them here tonight; they make a fortune pretending to be him. You should try it Kevin. You look more like him than anyone else I know.'

Kevin sighed. Maybe Cathy had turned up earlier, seen him in the arms of the redhead and found herself another companion for the night. He was pissed off, realising that Vic must have laced his drink with something as he'd never passed out before. A young girl was asking for a dance and he politely accepted. She gushed all over him and asked if he wanted to take her home, but he declined saying that he had a girlfriend already, and wasn't the cheating kind. 'Makes a change,' said the girl, 'but we could be discreet; no one needs to know.'

Kevin shook his head and gazed at his young partner. 'I would know, and I won't cheat on my girlfriend. I'm afraid that, delectable as you are, the answer is no.'

Vic sidled over. 'Any sign?' he asked. 'Al said he saw her too.'

Kevin shook his head. 'Okay,' said Vic, eyeing up the young girl. 'I'll get the DJ to play some *Saturday Night Fever*, and then we'll play some Frankie Valli stuff.' He wandered over to the DJ and spoke to him before returning to whisk the young girl away, with a wink at Kevin.

As soon as *Saturday Night Fever* began, there was a surge onto the dance floor and Kevin looked around him. But try as he may, he simply couldn't find Cathy. Finally, as Frankie Valli's *Oh What a Night* came on, he spotted her dancing with an Ed look-a-like. The couple were dancing on the veranda of the summer house. Vic had the music on full blast, and Kevin watched from a distance, feeling jealousy engulf him as the couple moved as one. She looked as if she was enjoying herself, and he didn't want to cut in until the song was over, just in case she'd seen him with the redhead. He had some grovelling to do if that were the case.

As the song ended, the couple embraced, and Kevin had had enough. Everyone else was back inside the house apart from Cathy and her partner. As he walked towards them, they walked further into the garden, hand in hand, before stopping under Vic's tree and embracing once more. There seemed to be a strange, luminous glow surrounding them, but he put it down to Vic's garden lights. 'Cathy,' cried Kevin, and his heart missed a beat as the couple turned to face him. They smiled, and the male swept her up into his arms as they melted into the scenery. Suddenly Kevin realised what he was witnessing. It wasn't an Ed look-a-like, it was the real thing, and he held his beloved Cathy. 'No!' screamed Kevin. 'Give her back to me, you fiend.' But the couple were gone as if they'd never been there.

Kevin raced back to the house and threw himself into Vic's arms, spilling his whiskey all over him. 'He's taken her,' he cried.

'Who?' yelled a startled Vic, attempting to wipe himself down with a couple of tissues that he had in his pocket.

'It wasn't a look-a-like, it was the real thing, and he took her,' sobbed Kevin.

'Kevin, Ed's dead.'

'So is Cathy. She's with him.'

Vic's brain felt as if it was about to explode. Surely Kevin wasn't loony too? After listening to him raving for another thirty minutes, Vic called a mini cab and allowed him to leave, telling him that he was seeing things and that when he arrived home, he'd find Cathy waiting for him.

Arriving home, he raced upstairs and found exactly what he'd expected. He held the deceased Cathy to him crying. 'Why darling, why?' he sobbed to himself.

He felt for a pulse, heartbeat, any sign of life, and found nothing. Defeated, he went downstairs and awoke the staff. Ada Shores broke down in tears. 'That poor little mite. No father and now no mother; whatever will become of him?' she sobbed.

Ruby stuck her head around the door. 'I heard Mrs Gold singing. She was with her husband. It was beautiful, just like that Emily Bronte book.'

Ada Shores gave the girl a hefty clout around her ear. 'Go back to bed,' she snapped. 'Your head is full of silly nonsense.'

Ruby fled, holding her ear. 'I did see them; I'm not lying,' she cried, 'and it was very romantic.'

Kevin returned upstairs. He walked across to her bed again and kissed Cathy; she was icy cold. Fawn appeared in the doorway and handed him a letter. 'For you,' she said, sadly. Kevin felt the room spin before he passed out.

When Romany awoke, it was daylight. He didn't know why he was at the bottom of the stairs but, as he surveyed the wreckage everywhere, his memory came flooding back to him. In anger, he rang Cathy, and when Ada answered the phone, he demanded to speak to Mrs Gold. Romany was furious when Ada told him that it was impossible, stressing that his home was wrecked and that he was going to involve the police.

'You'll look stupid if you do. There's no way that Mrs Gold was involved. Anyway, you were probably on one of your silly trips and did it yourself.'

Kevin took the receiver from the trembling housekeeper. 'I demand to speak to Cathy,' screeched Romany down the phone.

Calmly, Kevin said, 'according to her doctor, Cathy died in the early hours of the morning, so I'm afraid that you'll never be able to speak to her again. Goodbye.' He replaced the receiver and read Cathy's letter for about the tenth time. It said that Fawn had been given instructions for the funeral and the scattering of her and Ed's ashes.

'I will return at midnight on the fourteenth of February to visit you at Bacton. I could never bring myself to tell you that I was dying. When I went into hospital earlier in the year, it was with suspected gallstones, and I simply expected to have my gall bladder removed as soon as I had the concert behind me. However, they did many tests and scans and discovered that my cancer had returned. The day that you took me to hospital for my results I was told that my condition was inoperable and that my only hope was to have chemotherapy to prolong my life by a few months. I would have accepted if the treatment would have saved me, but I chose not to lose my hair, throw up constantly, and let my son watch me slip away. There was no cure, only hospitalisation and pain killing treatments. I was going to die whatever I did. When you took me to the solicitors, I made my will, and you have been well provided for.

I hope that you will keep your promise to me and raise Eddie, he adores you. I have provided for my sons but they won't receive anything until they are eighteen, when I hope that they will take up residence with you and their half brother. I'm going to Ed, he needs me and I really do want to be with him. You know that he visits me; we are one soul. Ed was always the one for me and neither of us has been in a situation that has made us think otherwise. I still love you Kevin and I always will, but I had to go.

The concert was wonderful and so were you, so I feel that I am leaving on a high where I am at least still functioning by myself. Sometimes the pain has been unbearable, but I console myself knowing that the last time people saw me I looked okay, even if I didn't feel it. If I'd told you about this before, you would have talked me into having chemo so that you could keep me with you longer and hope for a miracle cure.

I love you and would have married you had I not been dealt this cruel blow. You brought so much love and tenderness into my life. Please listen to and learn 'Autumn Stone' by the Small Faces, and then you will know the depth of my feelings for you. It's our song.

I'm sorry for what I've done, but I made the choice to go rather than live out my days with no quality of life to speak of. Please forgive me and don't you forget; I will visit you at midnight, February fourteenth. God bless.

Your ever loving Cathy

Vic Lee arrived later that day, having just visited Romany's home. Kevin paced up and down the room. 'I don't want to live now I know how Cathy felt when Ed died.'

Vic lit up a cigar. It was his sixth this morning which he put down to stress. 'It was suicide. She wanted to die, and what an exit... the press haven't got wind of this yet. The morning papers have the two of you on the front page and there'll be no prizes for guessing what tomorrow's headlines will be. People will be talking about the concert for weeks, but as for Cathy, well, she was always good at making entrances, but her exit was classic. She was a pro to the last; real Romeo and Juliet stuff, and that's the story I'll feed to the press. Fantastic. She always said that Ed visited her, and it was as if she was building herself up for this; completing the concert and then committing suicide.'

'Shut up Vic; we were going to get married.'

'Then why did she kill herself? Sounds as if she wasn't as keen as you.'

'Because she had terminal cancer and couldn't take the pain any more. She bore the pain alone, Vic, and Ed did visit her; I saw him several times. He was at your party too.'

'Kevin, you're overwrought.'

'My mind wasn't playing tricks on me. Al and Gerry saw her at your party, and the doctor confirmed that she was already dead at that time.'

'Then they were mistaken. Maybe Rosaleen turned up; she's a dead ringer for Cathy. Speaking of which, could you sweet talk her for me? I want her under contract, and you look like Ed's younger brother. It would be as if Ed and Cathy were reincarnated, and the fans would love it.'

'Are you mad or just inhuman?'

'Life goes on, does anyone know about the cancer?'

'I think her sister-in-law does.'

'Best kept quiet. I prefer the Romeo story.'

'What?'

'Forget the cancer; you said you'd seen Ed since his death. I can see the headlines now: "Love conquers all beyond the grave. Ed and his gypsy reunited at last as Cathy takes own life".'

'You're sick.'

'Not as sick as you, and even Romany's gone loony. He swears that Ed and Cathy haunted him last night and destroyed his house. He even thinks that Ed pushed him down the stairs. Probably a combination of gas explosion and drugs.'

'And how is the evil bastard?'

'A gibbering wreck, but he's been sedated.' Their conversation ended as Eddie ran into the room. He threw his arms around

Kevin, and Vic patted his head. 'Hallo, Superstar,' said Vic. 'I loved your skiffle last night.' Eddie beamed a sunny smile and then dashed out into the garden. Vic had had enough. He needed to ring the press and to prepare himself with some answers to the questions that they would fire at him. 'Let me know if you need anything, Kevin,' he said, walking to the front door.

'I need Cathy, but she's gone, so there's nothing I need from you. Eddie's my sole responsibility now, except when I'm touring and then Fawn will take over. I can work as hard as Ed, and I'll be bigger.'

Vic shrugged his shoulders. Only time would tell. His mind focused on Rosaleen; he'd seen her before but couldn't recall where. Then it hit him; it had been at this very house one Christmas when the air had rung with the sound of children's laughter and he'd been persuaded to dress up as Father Christmas. Rosaleen had looked after Cathy's children so that she could carry on with her gigs. He looked around the room. There was no laughter now, no Ed or Cathy, and the place seemed very sombre. The oppression was getting to him, so opening the front door he left. He was aware that his cheeks were wet and realised that he was crying.

'Pull yourself together,' he said out loud, and then, opening his car door, he got in and drove away.

Kevin had decided to drive down to tell Tony and the boys about Cathy's demise. It was important that they knew the truth, and realised that Cathy's suicide was due to the cancer, and that she hadn't left them by choice. If Vic got his 'Romeo and Juliet' story printed it could devastate the boys. He had to warn them of Vic's story so that they knew it was all lies. He would break the news as gently as possible, but knew that there would be tears. He'd noted Vic's fast departure and that he was crying. Maybe Vic had a heart after all. Wandering out into the garden with his guitar, he saw Eddie sitting on a bench where he had often sat with his mother. Kevin joined him and handed him his guitar. The child took it and began strumming and singing. 'Very good,' said Kevin and clapped his hands as Eddie finished his song.

Eddie handed the guitar back to Kevin. 'You play, you were good last night and so was Mummy. She's with Daddy now. Daddy doesn't have to be lonely any more. Will you be my daddy, Kevin?' His little eyes clouded over and he got onto Kevin's lap. 'Will I die too?'

He began to sob, and Kevin held the child to him. 'What a question for a little boy to ask. Daddy had a car accident, and Mummy was very ill. You'll live to be a hundred.'

Eddie clambered down from Kevin's lap and picked up a stick. Leaning on it, he did an impression of an old man and screwed up his face. 'Like this?'

Kevin laughed and tickled the child. 'That was very good. In fact you'll probably live to be two hundred. Now, what shall I play for you?'

Eddie climbed back onto the bench and settled beside Kevin, requesting *Rhythm Sticks* as the song to play.

Kevin tried a couple of verses and then turned to Eddie. 'How was that?' he asked.

'Rubbish,' cried Eddie, clapping his hands with glee.

'Let's go and see Wacky; he might live to be two hundred as well.' Kevin put his guitar down and lifted Eddie up. Giving him a piggy back he shouted, 'hi ho, Silver,' and ran towards the stable block as Eddie urged him to go faster. Kevin laughed, but felt as if his heart would break.

Seth knew exactly when Cathy had died; he'd been in bed and elbowed Megan. 'The bitch is dead,' he cried sitting bolt upright. 'Two down, one to go.' He threw the bed clothes off and let out a whoop of joy. Then he unlocked the back door and threw off all his clothes. He'd had a bonfire earlier and it was still burning. He threw some logs on it and started dancing around it like a whirling dervish. Megan got out of bed and decided to make some coffee.

Seth was very happy about something. She stared out of the back door and into the garden. In the darkness, she could see a stark naked Seth dancing like a lunatic. It was a cold night so Megan closed the door. It looked as if he'd finally lost the plot now. She was past sleep and settled into an armchair. What did he say? Two down and one to go? It was then that the penny dropped; was Cathy dead? Would Seth harm an innocent child? She was horrified. She'd watched as Seth had driven Eden crazy, helped with the bonding ceremony, believing that it was all fake and spectacle. A child was another matter, what sick plan did he have for this poor little innocent? Had Seth developed powers over the years that she knew nothing of? The whole thing was turning nasty. She'd had enough. She was going to leave. Her thoughts were interrupted by Seth who rushed into the room, cackling hysterically. 'Eden must be delighted,' he said. 'We'll travel to Surrey tomorrow to offer our condolences, or you will, and then you can offer to take the child out for the day.'

'We don't know if Cathy's dead; this is all in your head.'

'I saw Ed remove her from this mortal coil. She is dead.'

'You are mad.'

'All we have to do is remove that spawn of the devil from the crazy, corrupt lifestyle, and get him into my car.'

'Kidnap and blackmail, I suppose.'

'No you stupid bitch, I'm going to give him to Eden. His family will be complete then.'

'He's just a child.'

'So was my sister, and Eden murdered her.'

'He was a child and it was a tragic accident.'

Seth stopped cackling. 'You weren't there.' His mood had now changed, and he sat down on a sofa with sobs wracking his body. 'My sister had gone for a walk and taken her kaleidoscope with her. Somehow, Eden had got past his mother and had followed Miriam. The adults had the picnic hamper packed and everyone was ready to leave so I went looking for her. When I found her,

Eden was with her. Miriam spotted me and waved, and then she began to walk back to the house. I could hear Eden screaming, "mine", over and over again, and he started kicking her because she wouldn't hand over the toy. I ran towards them as he started throwing loose rocks at her. Several of them struck her but as I drew closer, Eden's mother rushed past me, obviously worried that either child was going over the cliff edge.

She was horrified as her precious son pelted Miriam with stones and rocks. Miriam was backing away now, getting closer and closer to the cliff edge; she was crying and lifting up her arms to shield her face from the stones. Eden's mother grabbed him and hauled him back towards the house, but he sank his teeth into her hand, forcing her to let go of him. I still wasn't close enough to intervene even though I was running as fast as I could. Eden rushed back to Miriam who, sensing the danger, threw the kaleidoscope to him. He ignored it, kicking and shoving her, screaming, "mine, mine". His mother wasn't fast enough and the final shove sent Miriam over the edge. Eden nearly went over himself but his mother grabbed him just in time.

'She screamed, "oh Eden, what have you done!" I blacked out and the power of speech eluded me for ages. When my speech returned weeks later, I told my parents what had happened but they thought that I'd been hallucinating as I'd struck my head on a rock when I'd fallen. So the golden-haired angel got away with it. Isn't that murder, Megan?'

Megan was shocked. This was the first time that he'd opened up completely about the incident; no wonder he hated his cousin. 'Come back to bed,' she said.

Seth dried his eyes and stood up. 'Not yet, I'm celebrating. I am the God of Hellfire.' Then he resumed his maniacal laughter and ran back into the garden. Yawning, Megan got to her feet to close the back door that Seth had left open and went back to bed. She'd go with Seth, but once inside the house she would tell Fawn of Seth's plan and get him arrested. She was not going to allow an innocent child to die. Seth was twisted and dangerous, but demonic? No way. Closing her eyes, she saw two orbs hovering around the room, but as the fire was still burning in the grate, dismissed them as dust particles reflected in the fire.

'Lack of sleep,' Megan said to herself out loud and shut her eyes once more.

She awoke when Seth finally came to bed, and had to listen as he said, 'tomorrow completes everything; we'll drive to the exact place where Miriam died and push the little bastard over the edge.' Megan protested that the child was innocent, and Seth's response was to kick her out of bed and tell her to sleep on the floor like a dog. Leaving the room, she spotted the orbs again; they were taking shape and moving towards Seth. She wondered if she was going insane too. Curling up in an easy chair, she fell asleep.

The following morning she slept in. There was no sign of Seth so she made herself a cup of herbal tea and had a bath. As she relaxed in the lavender bubbles, she wondered why Seth wasn't up. It was very unusual for him to sleep in.

Half an hour later she picked up the daily paper and read the news. Cathy and Kevin were front page owing to the concert, but there was no news of Cathy's death. Obviously Seth could have been wrong, but she recalled that it had been the early hours of the morning when Seth had informed her of Cathy's death, so maybe the press didn't know about it yet. The front door opened and in strode Seth's happy band of followers, laden with suitcases and gifts. They were surprised to see no sign of Seth, and Megan still in her dressing gown. 'He had a late night,' Megan told them.

Brian, Seth's right hand man laughed. 'Enjoy the peace then, Megan,' he said and went upstairs to unpack. Megan made some tea and glanced at the grandfather clock as it chimed three thirty. If she woke Seth, he would be angry, and if she didn't wake him he'd still be angry. Brian offered to do the deed and walked to the bedroom. Minutes later he returned ashen faced. 'Megan, come with me.' Bewildered, Megan followed him into the bedroom and surveyed her common law husband. He lay on his back with his eyes wild and staring, his features were contorted and his jaw gaped. Megan staggered and fell into Brian's arms as the shock engulfed her.

He was dead; her nightmare was over. There would be no more beatings every time she ran away. No more would she have to indulge in practices that she hated. She was free, and Eddie was safe. She looked at Brian and collapsed, sobbing.

Brian helped her to the living room and gave the others the news. Still stunned, Megan informed Brian and the rest of them that she was going to vacate the cottage, and that they would have to find alternative accommodation. They weren't happy about it, but as they paid no rent they could hardly argue. Two of them left later that day, but Brian had a hidden agenda and told Megan that he would love to step into Seth's shoes, as he'd always found her desirable. Megan laughed as she looked at herself in the mirror. 'Don't take the piss, I've got eyes. Seth has taken my looks away from me over the years and worn me down. I'll never let another man near me again. Wherever I go, you will not be coming with me. It's my time now, and for the first time in my life, I'm putting myself first and living my life, my way. So forget it.' Rejected, Brian moved out that night.

Two days later, Kevin returned from his gig. It had been a strange one. Romany was so sedated that he didn't appear to know what he was doing most of the time. Kevin hated him, but had to give him credit for performing at all. Wearily, Kevin climbed the stairs and looked in on Eddie. The boy was staring out of the window. 'Looking at the stars?' asked Kevin.

Eddie shook his head. 'Look, Mummy and Daddy.' Kevin looked out and saw Ed and Cathy bathed in the moonlight. He gasped as the couple stared back at him and then, in a blink of an eye, they were gone. Eddie turned to Kevin and hugged him. 'Love you Daddy-Kevin.'

'Love you too, Eddie,' replied Kevin, and carried the sleepy child back to his bed.

After leaving the room, he went into Cathy's room and gazed at the huge poster above the bed. The gypsy girl who had not only stolen Ed's heart, but his too. He sat on the bed weeping, knowing that already she was living her new life with her beloved husband. He'd given a short speech at the concert that night but had been unable to complete it properly; his voice failing him as he spoke of Cathy's fight against the cancer that had killed her. Vic finished it off for him but had found himself getting choked up as well, and left the stage as red roses were thrown.

On 14th February, Kevin was going to scatter Ed's, Cathy's, and Amara's ashes at Bacton, as she'd asked. This would be his final gesture to her, apart from learning *Autumn Stone*. He'd listened to the song and was soothed by the lyrics, knowing that Cathy had said that it was their song. She had loved him, but had never shown it until the end, probably because of the cancer. Outside, the wind blew. The funeral was next week, and he wondered how he would get through it. Getting to his feet, he walked from the room and went into his own. Picking up his guitar he began to play *Autumn Stone*, and he thought he heard someone say goodbye. Kevin sighed and felt a kiss on his cheek. He looked up to see Cathy standing by the window. He got to his feet and reached for her but she was gone. He walked to the window and saw her run to Ed who was waiting under the oak tree. Kevin opened the window. 'Goodbye,' he cried, as Ed swept Cathy into his arms. And then they were gone again.

From the next room, he heard Eddie say, 'Bye Mummy and Daddy, I love you.' Then as an afterthought, he added, 'love you, Kevin.'

Forcing back the tears, Kevin replied, 'Love you Eddie, goodnight son.'

Conclusion

14th February 1983

Fawn couldn't sleep and stared out of her caravan window. There was a full moon. Ed's, Cathy's, and Amara's ashes had been scattered earlier that day, exactly as Cathy had asked. Fawn was very concerned about Kevin. He'd driven down from Surrey that day with Eddie, and appeared to be bearing up well, but Fawn knew that this was just a front for Eddie's benefit. At the funeral, he'd collapsed across Cathy's coffin and had to be pulled from it. At one stage, Fawn thought that he was in danger of being incinerated as he clung to the coffin crying, 'no, no, no!' as the curtains began to close around the coffin. Rusty had to restrain him, using brute force to avoid a double cremation.

Kevin and Eddie had come to Bacton for the week. It was very cold owing to the time of year. Fawn shivered, the night was still, the sea calm, but she was aware of paranormal activity. She lit the gas fire and pulled her faded pink dressing gown around her. Staring out of the window again, she looked over to her left where Sky's caravan stood. Sky had stayed for the funeral and then headed back to her beloved Ibiza, leaving her caravan conveniently empty for Kevin and Eddie. From Fawn's bedroom, Rusty could be heard snoring loudly. Kevin was obviously awake, as his light was on. He was awaiting Cathy's promised manifestation. Fawn put the kettle on and yawned. Picking up her crystal ball, she gazed into it and saw many visions, but after a while her eyes grew heavy and she replaced the ball onto its cradle and covered it with a black cloth. The clock said eleven thirty, so she began to dress herself and prepare for the night's events. At eleven forty-five, she left her caravan and headed over to Kevin with a flask of tea. She knew that Cathy would need her help to allow herself time with Kevin. Fawn tapped on the caravan door, and a very excited Kevin opened it. He had his guitar around his neck and had obviously been practising *Autumn Stone* as the record was on the turntable.

'I just can't get it right; that Steve Marriot has such a fantastic voice. No wonder Ed and Cathy loved him. I don't recall much about the band apart from *Itchycoo Park*, *Tin Soldier*, and *All or Nothing*. I was ignorant of their other material. It's great. I'm recording *Autumn Stone* as a tribute to Cathy, if I can ever get it right.'

Fawn opened a cupboard and removed two cups; she placed them on the table, and then poured out two cups of tea from her flask. 'Steve Marriot is unique, but so were the rest of the band. Kenny was a wizard on drums, Ian a maestro on the keyboard, and Ronnie Lane wrote some of the most beautiful songs ever. You have to put your own personal seal on *Autumn Stone* if you're going to record it. You're unique too.' Kevin eyed the clock on the wall, and Fawn smiled. 'Relax Kevin, it's not time yet; concentrate on your song.'

A cup of tea later, Kevin resumed practising, and Fawn listened intently. Something was happening. She could see a small bright orb darting around the caravan walls. Her eyes grew heavy, and she felt herself begin to drift. Kevin was frustrated. He so wanted this song to be special. Fawn settled herself beside him as her energy began to deplete, and the orb began to take shape. Kevin crossed to the record player and placed the needle on the record. 'Let's hear from the expert,' he said.

'Your version is beautiful,' said Fawn in a distant voice.

'Beautiful, truly beautiful,' said a familiar voice behind him.

Kevin turned to find Cathy on one knee, taking his hand in hers; she kissed it. It was just like their first meeting, but in reverse. Kevin gazed over at Fawn. She was slumped across the sofa as if she were unconscious. Raising Cathy to her feet, Kevin held her at arms' length and then held her close as they danced to *Autumn Stone*.

Tears of joy ran down Kevin's face, he couldn't believe what was happening. 'I love you so much, Cathy,' he sobbed. 'I really miss you.'

Cathy stared at him, quite content to be held in his embrace. 'I love you, too,' she murmured. The warmth exuding from her body was amazing. Kevin had thought he'd be able to walk right through her as she was a spirit but her body was a solid mass owing to Fawn's energy. The embrace lasted to the end of the record and then the warmth grew cooler as Cathy's features became patchy, like an oil painting. Her face became even more grainy as the coolness became cold. 'I'll always love you. Just call my name and I'll be with you.' Her voice became a whisper and her body became an orb once more.

Fawn stretched and woke up. She looked at Kevin and noted the amazement etched on his face. Eddie had got up and was framed in the doorway. He was clapping his hands with delight. 'Saw Mummy dancing with Kevin. Can we go to the beach tomorrow? You won't die, will you, Kevin?'

'Yes to the beach, and no to the dying; you're stuck with me,' Kevin replied.

'And Wacky and Patch?'

'Of course, we mustn't forget them.'

Eddie rubbed his eyes. 'I'm going back to bed now.' Kevin followed him to his bedroom and tucked him in his bed. The child snuggled under the bedclothes and drifted into a contented slumber. Kevin couldn't understand how the child had accepted Cathy's presence. It didn't seem natural. He walked back to the living area and sat on the sofa as Fawn poured out another cup of tea.

'It's crazy, what just happened,' said Kevin.

'No, it's love,' replied Fawn. 'Cathy wanted you to see that she was okay. She's fine with Eden and her two girls. No more pain, no more stress, and no more bad dreams.'

'Bad dreams?'

'Their life was tied up around dreams. They met, fell in love, and commenced their dream. Eden broke it by dabbling with Seth and getting drawn into his mind games, and then Cathy left and the dream became a nightmare. Eden tracked her down in 1973, and the dream resumed. In America it splintered due to drugs and Eden's insecurity. Then, after detoxing and two suicide attempts, followed by spells in mental institutions, he got his act together and married her. The dream was on once more but then he developed paranoia and embarked on a course of infidelity, causing Cathy's world to collapse. She stuck by him and they tried to break free of Vic's clutches. Every time they thought they were out, Vic found a way to stall them. At the time of Eden's death, they had bought their mobile home and were ready to embark on their new life. His death destroyed Cathy. She couldn't live without him, or he without her. So, through all of their time together, they drifted in and out of a broken dream.'

'But I loved her with every fibre of my being.'

'She loved you too, and that's why she's left you her most precious possession, Eddie, her son. She knew that you would raise him well.'

'I will, and maybe in the future, her other two sons will move in with Eddie and me. Cathy would like that, but I wish that she'd told me about her cancer.'

'She didn't wish to burden you; she died with dignity, not gasping her last breath on a hospital bed. It was only a matter of time before the cancer killed her, probably only weeks. At least you can recall her last days and the concert. She was warm, vibrant, and gave a moving tribute to her beloved husband.'

Kevin's eyes were getting tired; he finished his tea, stretched, and yawned. 'Thanks Fawn, for everything. I've got to get some shuteye; my boss wants the beach tomorrow. At least that's something I can do for Cathy; give Eddie my love and do my best for him. He'll always come first. It's the first day of the rest of my life tomorrow, so I have to be strong.' He hugged Fawn and let her out of the caravan before heading to bed.

In his dreams, he saw Cathy and awoke, calling her name. A kiss on his lips and a whispered, 'I love you' comforted him. Turning his face to the light he got another glimpse of her. She looked so beautiful.

'Cathy, I love you too, darling, but go to Ed, he's waiting for you. I'm letting you go. I'm here for Eddie, Steven, and Michael; just visit me when you can.'

A kiss on his cheek and a whispered 'thank you' made his tears begin to flow once more as the apparition disappeared. Fawn had been right. Ed and Cathy had been through hell trying to live this dream but now they could resume it. He was being selfish trying to try to hang onto Cathy when she wanted to be with Ed. He gazed around the room. He was sleeping in the very bed where they'd made love many times, but he had to let go. It wasn't going to be easy, but it was essential.

His thoughts turned to song writing and, getting out of bed, he found his writing pad and scribbled down some lyrics. He was going to call this song, *Drifting In A Broken Dream*, and dedicate it to Ed and Cathy.